THE SAVAGE TALES OF SILAS FLINT

THE SAVAGE TALES OF SILAS FLINT

KEVIN G. BECKMAN

KGB Books

First Edition September 2022

Published by KGB Books, in the United States of America

ISBN 979-8-218-06810-3

THE SAVAGE TALES OF SILAS FLINT

KEVIN G. BECKMAN

THE COLD ROAD

1

Witch Hunter Captain Silas Flint gazed out the window of the moving train. The full moon filled the sky. The grassy meadows, open plains, and charming hamlets once again gave way to Salem's sprawling cityscape. It had been one month since he and his assistant, Supernumerary Ricardo Navarro, had departed from the Cascadian Empire's capitol after successfully rooting out the traitor Jennifer Edwards from Fort Ingalls, the Witch Hunter Chapter House within the city. Shortly after they returned to Fort Marsing in the east, Flint's younger brother Charles had announced the birth of his so-called Empire of Medea, punctuating his declaration with the detonation of an American nuclear weapon somewhere in the Dead Lands far to the east. Flint shook his head. Charles had used his dark magic to project images of himself and the mushroom cloud in the sky, like some ancient moving picture projector. He'd addressed himself to the continent of North America and North America had heard.

Accompanying him to Salem were Navarro, Witch Hunter General John Abernathy, and the reformed witch Zelda Fletcher (*Reformed according to the letter of the law if not the spirit,* Flint thought.) Navarro and Fletcher had left for the dining car several hours ago and Flint expected they would both be deep in their cups by now. He checked his pocket watch. 9:15 p.m. There was a knock at the door to Flint's train compartment.

"Enter," he said.

The door slid open, and Abernathy stepped inside. He

was dressed similarly to Flint – black long coat, tall, wide brimmed hat – with only the gold epaulettes on his shoulders marking his rank. He was a trim man in his late fifties. His grey hair had begun its turn to white; if Flint recalled correctly, Abernathy would turn sixty next year. Age hadn't slowed him yet. He'd fought by Flint's side during the Jordan case several months earlier when Fletcher had turned herself in to the Witch Hunters, partly to escape her demon possessed former lover who had destroyed her hometown of New Rome.

Flint had just started to rise from his seat when Abernathy waved him off. "As you were," he said. Flint sat down and Abernathy joined him at the small table. He took off his hat, ran a hand through his hair. Blew out a breath.

"Are you alright sir?" Flint asked.

Abernathy nodded. "Yes, I'm fine, thank you."

Flint said nothing.

Abernathy laughed. "Don't think you can stare me down, young man."

"I am sure I do not know what you are talking about sir."

"I used that trick a lot in my younger years."

Flint smiled.

Abernathy shook his head. "And in this case, you're right. I have a lot on my mind."

"I suspect everyone does sir."

"I'm tempted to join Mr. Navarro and Miss Fletcher and have enough libations to forget. For tonight at least."

"I take it you refer to our impending meeting with His Majesty."

"Yes, among other things."

"Have you met him before sir?"

"I have," Abernathy said. "Eleven years ago, when I was appointed to lead Fort Marsing. He attended the ceremony at the Cathedral. We spoke briefly afterward. The man is... formidable."

"I confess that I feel trepidation as well, sir," Flint said. He knew that his familial relation to Charles would become public knowledge after the latter's dramatic entrance onto the international scene, but he hadn't expected that Peter II, Emperor of Cascadia, would personally request his presence at the Imperial Palace. Abernathy had been summoned as well, along with all the other Witch Hunter Generals within the Empire.

"I wouldn't worry too much," Abernathy said. "I'm sure that His Majesty is simply looking for any insights you have into Charles's nature."

"He may dislike what I have to say."

"My advice? Say it anyway. What I saw when I met him, everything I've heard from General Hickock since then... he has a talent for seeing through any prevarication."

Flint smiled. "I look forward to seeing General Hickock again." Witch Hunter General Jeremiah Hickock oversaw Fort Ingalls. The man was a giant with a rich country drawl, long hair and beard, in stark contrast to the more reserved, courtly Abernathy.

"As do I," Abernathy said. "We only see each other at the Order's annual conclave. I imagine that we'll..."

There was a knock at the door.

"Enter," Flint said.

Navarro opened the door and stepped inside, followed by Fletcher. Flint could see that they'd both had much to drink, but neither appeared incapacitated yet.

"Boss, sir," Navarro said, nodding to Flint and Abernathy in turn.

"Hey fellas," Fletcher said, waving. Flint rolled his eyes. She'd been at Fort Marsing for months. There'd been talk of her joining the Order as a Supernumerary. She still had much to learn about respect for her elders and the chain of command. "We almost there?"

Flint nodded. "Yes. We should be arriving momentarily." The train was slowing. Fletcher went to the window and peered out into the neon jungle of Salem's nightscape.

"Amazing," she said. "Fucking amazing."

"I take it this is your first time to Salem?" Abernathy asked, looking bemused.

"Yeah... yeah it is," she replied, her attention still focused outside. "Never thought I'd ever get the chance to visit here."

"Too bad it's on business," Navarro said.

She looked to Flint. "Our meeting's not until 10 tomorrow morning. Do you think we could... you know, go sight seeing before then? Or afterward maybe?"

Flint raised an eyebrow. "Assuming you are not too badly hung over, I think that can be arranged."

"Don't make any promises yet Zelda," Navarro said. "I hear General Hickock mixes the best cocktails."

Abernathy grinned. "I can confirm. I may join you."

"Hmph," Flint said. The train's brakes squealed as it

pulled into the station. The others left for their quarters to grab their travel cases. Flint wasn't especially pleased to return to Salem so soon, but man proposes, and God disposes as the old saying went. He rose from his seat, pulled his long coat tight, adjusted his hat. He went to the bed and put on his gun belt. Flint expected that he would have to surrender his pistols and sword before being escorted into His Majesty's presence. Leaving his weapons out of reach always made him feel anxious, but protocol must be observed.

The train shuddered to a halt, its whistle giving a final blast. His weapons and uniform secure, he grabbed his travel case and stepped out into the hallway, where other passengers had begun to disembark. As usual, they gave Flint a wide berth, though not so wide as in the east where Witch Hunters were fewer in number compared to the west. Navarro had once suggested that the citizenry kept their distance more due to Flint's demeanor than his office. Either reason suited him.

He stepped down from the train car and onto the platform. He scanned the crowd and located his companions, moving to join them. No sooner had he arrived when a familiar giant of a figure dressed in black pushed his way across the platform. At 6'6" tall and nearly 300 pounds, it took him little effort.

"How do friends?" Witch Hunter General Jeremiah Hickock said with a wide grin splitting his bearded face. Abernathy smiled and stepped forward for a handshake, his smaller hand disappearing in Hickock's meaty grip.

"Hello Jeremiah," he said. "It's been too long."

"That it has John, that it has. We ought to get together more often than once a year." Disengaging from Abernathy, Hickock spread his arms wide and put his hands on Flint's and Navarro's shoulders. "And if it ain't my two favorite guest stars! How you boys been? It's been, what... five, ten minutes?"

Navarro laughed. "Feels like it, sir."

Flint nodded, smiled. "It is good to see you again, General."

Hickock shifted his gaze to Fletcher. "And this here must be the witch from New Rome."

Fletcher grinned. "Former witch. Zelda Fletcher. It's an honor to meet you sir. I heard about what happened here last month."

"Whole damn Empire's heard of it now," Hickock said. "'The Night of Chaos' is what the reporters are calling it. Come on. Let's walk and talk." He led Flint and his companions off the platform and into the brick hallways of the station. Before Flint and Navarro had put down the traitor Edwards, she had opened a magical gateway within Fort Ingalls which had unleashed legions of demons on Salem. For good measure, the witch had raised the city's dead, forcing the Salem Police Department and the Imperial Army to engage in a protracted battle with the zombie hordes. The train station appeared unscathed. The hallways still stank of cigarette smoke, alcohol, and urine. Flint expected the rest of Salem had fared worse.

"Been a little hectic since you boys left," Hickock continued. "Still a lot of reconstruction going on. The

Minister of Justice resigned to, ah, 'spend more time with family.'"

"I bet," Navarro said. Jennifer Edwards was the daughter of the now former Minister of Justice Benjamin Edwards. The Order, the police, and the media had all been approached by imperial functionaries and warned away from publicly speaking her name. Flint supposed it didn't matter anymore with Minister Edwards out of the government, but one could never tell whose reputation needed protecting, whose connections needed maintaining.

"I understand that His Majesty personally led the 42nd Division into the streets," Abernathy said.

"Sure did," Hickock nodded. "I told him it was Captain Flint and Mr. Navarro who sealed the portal and cut the zombies' strings. He was fixin' to give you boys a special commendation, but then, well... next thing you know, Charles fucking Flint drops a God damned nuke back east."

Fletcher blinked. "Whoa... you guys can talk like that?"

"Huh?... Oh." Hickock laughed. "Pardon my language. I don't think John's ever said so much as a 'damn.'"

Abernathy chuckled. "I was known to let loose on occasion in my younger years."

"Anyway, that's where you come in, Captain," Hickock said.

"General Abernathy speculated that His Majesty wishes me to share any insights I have into Charles."

"That's about the size of it," Hickock said. The group exited the station. The first thing Flint noticed was the surrounding buildings were still covered in burn marks, riddled with bullet holes, and stained with blood. Hickock led them to a black automobile parked at the curb. The price of gasoline made automobiles a luxury for much of the Empire, but here in Salem they were a common sight. Fletcher stopped and gawked at the car.

"Shotgun," Hickock said. "I reckon it'd be an awfully tight squeeze with the five of us in the back..." He noticed Fletcher's hesitation. "Something wrong, Miss Fletcher?"

"No, no," she said. "It's just... this will be my first time riding in an automobile."

Hickock chuckled and patted the roof. "She ain't much to look at, but she's been with the Order almost as long as I have. I sometimes forget y'all don't have as many of them back east."

Flint opened the door for Fletcher and she gently stepped inside, followed by Abernathy and Navarro. Flint climbed in after them. He noted that Abernathy and Navarro took the seats across from where Fletcher sat, forcing Flint to sit next to her. Hickock got into the passenger seat next to the driver, who was a Supernumerary like Navarro. "Take us home, Linus," Hickock said.

"Yes sir," Linus replied. He shifted gears and the automobile pulled away from the curb and into Salem traffic. Hickock turned in his seat, leaning over the headrests of Abernathy and Navarro's seats.

"We can talk more about it at the Fort," he said, "But basically we're all going to be meeting with both his Majesty and the Committee."

Flint took this in silence. The Continuing Committee on Paranormal Activity and Magical Anomalies was made up of select members of the Cascadian Parliament. They seldom held public hearings so he was grateful that he wouldn't have to witness grandstanding for the media.

"I expect the armed services and the CIS will want their piece of the pie too," Abernathy said, referring to the Cascadia Intelligence Service.

"Oh yeah, them too," Hickock said. He looked to Flint, Fletcher, and Navarro. "Captain, you and Navarro are there to give them the skinny on Charles. Miss Fletcher, they'll be wanting you to give any insights you can share as a... reformed witch."

Fletcher swallowed. "I'll share whatever I can."

Flint reflected that he, Navarro, and Fletcher had all come a long way. He'd never expected to come face to face with the Emperor in his life, and doubted they had either. "We shall do our duty, sir," he said. Navarro nodded.

"That's all God expects of anyone," Hickock said. "Now, once we get back to Ingalls, we'll get you four settled in your quarters, and then you're all invited to the dining hall for a little get together I've organized for you and our other guests."

"How are the others, by the way?" Abernathy asked.

"Fine, fine," Hickock said. "Seth arrived at 3, Malachi about an hour ago." Witch Hunter General Seth Brandt oversaw the northwestern quarter of Cascadia out of Fort Rochester near the city of Olympia, while General Malachi Davis was stationed at Fort Plummer near Spokane in the northeast.

"I, uh, heard you make some pretty good cocktails," Fletcher said.

Hickock laughed. "I enjoy a little mixology. There's this

drink I invented folks call Witch Bane. Never thought I'd get to serve one to a former witch!"

2

Charles Flint stood facing the computer monitor with his hands behind his back. At his side was Lilian Turner, a survivor of the twenty-first century's Occult War. In the room with them were four of the colleagues Charles had made over the years as he set his master plan into motion. Over the past few weeks, they'd made their way to the American nuclear missile bunker where he and Turner had established their base of operations. Charles supposed the bunker would do for now, but he hoped to build a fortress befitting an emperor atop this relic of the old world.

"What's the plan Flint?" asked Emil Parlow. He was a lean and hungry looking figure. Charles, remembering his Shakespeare, made a mental note to keep a close eye on him. Parlow and his student Samantha Quinn had proven useful during the Hermiston operation last year, but Quinn had fallen to Charles's brother Silas. Charles suspected that Parlow and Quinn had been something more than simply teacher and student because the former was so eager to avenge the latter.

Charles held up a hand for silence, his gaze focused on the computer screen. "Rob," he said, addressing the computer. He still couldn't believe the Americans named their machines. The screen chimed in response. "Focus on Denver."

The computer chimed again, and the screen zoomed in on Denver, the capitol of the United Mountain States. There they were. Charles estimated there were at least four divisions of the UMS Army assembled on the outskirts of the city, around forty thousand men. He knew that President Hugh Fitzroy could call up another two divisions if necessary, and that he would leave at least one in reserve to defend Denver. No matter. Charles had no intention of marching against Fitzroy's capitol, but he knew they would be marching against his soon enough. Speaking of which, he supposed that he would need to think of a name for the capitol of his new empire.

"Amazing device," murmured Constance Deville, peering at the computer screen. She was a blonde woman with high cheekbones and cold eyes. "I understand that it speaks?"

"I am Rob," came the computer's disembodied voice from the walls. "I can understand and answer questions that I am at liberty to answer."

"Er... Rob," Deville said. "How is it that you are alive? I know of no magic that can..."

"That's enough for now," Charles interrupted. "We have more pressing matters to attend to."

"I'll say," replied Arnold Schreck. He was a former Colonel in the Cascadian Imperial Army until Charles had helped him discover his talent for magic. He squinted at the image on the screen. "It looks like Fitzroy is going to hit us with everything and everyone he's got. And what do we have?"

"We have magic, we have this machine, we have those

magnificent missiles, and the will to win... what more do we need?" laughed Ingrid Barnett. She smiled at Charles. "Not to mention our fearless leader of course."

Charles grinned and dipped his head in acknowledgment. Turner rolled her eyes. "Take it from me," she said. "We're going to need more."

Barnett cocked her head. "I suppose you've done this sort of thing before?"

Turner smiled. "I have actually. I learned from Simon Magus himself."

The other four's eyes widened; their jaws dropped.

"A story for another time," Charles said before they could start shouting questions. "Suffice it to say we have enough for now, but we are going to need more. More witches and wizards, more funds, more troops, and more time for our nation to become self-sustaining. That's where you five come in. Arnold?"

"Sir?"

"If you were in the enemy's shoes, how would you go about suppressing a rebellious section of the country?"

Schreck stroked his chin. "Um... Computer? Rob?"

The monitor chimed.

"Can you zoom out?"

The computer beeped. The view of Denver shrank until they had a view of the entire UMS.

"Zoom in on the border between Langston and Grissom."

The computer buzzed. "There are no known counties by those names within this part of the United States."

"What...?"

"It's a twenty-first century era machine," Turner said.

"Oh. Right. Er... the border between Montana and Wyoming... right here," Schreck said, tapping the screen with his finger.

The screen focused on a railroad track that through a narrow mountain pass. "There," he said, pointing. "The fastest route from here to Denver is the Simmons Line. This pass is a choke point."

Deville crossed her arms. "Ambush?"

"If it comes to it," Charles said.

"Another missile?" Parlow asked.

"I'd recommend against it," Turner said. "If we're going to rule this territory, we shouldn't poison the land if we can avoid it."

"Why not destroy Denver?" Deville asked.

"Because that would turn the entire continent against us," Charles replied. "For now, we're going to stay on the strategic defensive. This region is sparsely populated, with weak ties to Denver. The next few weeks are crucial. We're going to prove to the world that the UMS is unable to take back this land by force. If we keep the war contained, it's unlikely that any other nation will be willing to stick their neck out for Fitzroy."

"Unlikely," said Schreck, "But not impossible."

"The Witch Hunters won't stand for this, for us having a nation of our own," said Parlow.

Charles made a dismissive gesture. "The Witch Hunters are lapdogs of Emperor Peter. If he won't go to war, then neither will they."

"I hear all of their Generals are meeting in Salem," Parlow said.

"Oooh! Now there's a juicy target," Barnett giggled.

Turner scowled. "I'd bet money that Silas will be there too."

Charles blinked. Yes, Silas would undoubtedly be summoned to the imperial capitol. He knew that Silas preferred to keep their fraternal relationship a secret. He snickered. No chance of that happening anymore. The entire continent now knew the name Charles Flint. They'd ask Silas to provide a psychological profile of him. No matter. They'd grown up together, but Silas never really knew him or what he was capable of.

"Yes, I suppose he will be," he said out loud.

"So what are going to do about it?" Parlow growled.

"Nothing."

"What do you mean nothing?!"

Charles glared at him. Parlow raised his hands in a placating gesture. "Forgive me," he said.

Nodding, Charles said, "One war at a time. Once we've secured our position here against the UMS, then we'll talk about Cascadia and the Witch Hunters. Now, as to the matter at hand, I have assignments for each of you." Pointing at each of them in turn, he said, "Arnold. I'm putting you in charge of organizing our ground defense. I don't expect you'll find many live volunteers at this stage, so feel free to raise as many dead as you can handle." Schreck nodded.

"Constance. I've taken the liberty of marking some promising locales on your map. You've always been interested in old world technology. See what you can scavenge."

"Yes sir."

"Ingrid. There's a city to the northeast of here. I'd like you to be our ambassador to the locals. Emphasize that nothing will change as far as their day-to-day lives, their work, are concerned. The only difference is their taxes are coming here instead of Denver now."

She giggled. "And if they refuse your rule?"

He smiled. "I have total confidence in your powers of persuasion. Emil."

"Sir."

"For now, you'll stay here with Lilian and I." He patted a book that rested on the computer console, bound in cured human flesh. It was the accursed tome *In Realis Magicae*, written by Abdul Hakim Nazari, a disciple of Simon Magus himself. "There are some spells in here that we'll need, and I could use an extra pair of hands."

Parlow frowned but nodded.

"You have your assignments. Go."

Schreck, Barnett, and Deville raised their right fists and yelled in unison, "Gloria Medea!"

Charles raised an eyebrow.

"We felt we needed some kind of salute or battle cry or something," Barnett laughed.

"Go on, get out of here," Turner said, shaking her head, stifling a smile.

After the three had departed, Turner put a hand on Charles's shoulder. "I still can't believe we're actually doing this."

"Sometimes I can hardly believe it myself. But this is what I've been working toward my entire life."

Parlow crossed his arms. "So, what are these spells you spoke of?"

"Insurance," Charles said. "As Arnold mentioned earlier, it's unlikely but not impossible that the other slugs on this continent might decide to be heroes and come to President Fitzroy's aid. The spell I'm thinking of will give us all the time in the world to build up our strength and strike when and where we choose."

"So why not do that now?"

"Because my dear Emil, we need to demonstrate to the world that the Empire of Medea cannot be conquered by force of arms first."

"I still say we should take out the Witch Hunter Generals while they're all gathered in one spot."

"And my answer is still no. I know you're eager to avenge your student, but we can't afford a preemptive strike against Cascadia. Not yet. Be patient my friend. I promise you that we will humble the Emperor in due time."

"Come on you two," Turner said. "It's been a long time since I've had a chance to look at that book. If we're going to do what I think Charles is planning, we'll need to build up our strength."

"You go on ahead," Parlow said. "I'd like to ask this computer a few questions."

***

After Flint and Turner had left him, Parlow dug into his coat pocket and took out what looked like a sapphire. He put it on the floor and spoke the incantations. A column of light arose from the jewel, reaching up to the ceiling. Within the column stood a man, the most perfectly ordinary man Parlow had ever laid eyes on. Parlow was hard pressed to think of ways to describe him: average height, average build, nothing at all distinguishing about him – which is what made him such an effective killer.

"Hello Emil," the man said.

"Hello Roger," Parlow replied. "How's Salem?"

"Target rich."

Parlow laughed.

"Is it a go?" Roger asked.

"Charles says no."

"He's not the one who's paying my fee."

"True." Parlow thought for a few moments. Charles was right. They really couldn't afford all-out war with Cascadia now. But he could at least avenge dear Samantha. "Are you familiar with Silas Flint?"

Roger nodded. "I expect the whole Empire is now."

"Kill him."

"Only him? Seems like a wasted opportunity."

"I agree. But orders are orders. Feel free to kill anyone who tries to stop you. Maybe you'll get lucky and the Emperor will try to defend him."

3

Silas Flint surveyed the scene. He and his companions

were in the grand ballroom of Fort Ingalls. The electric lamps were crafted to look like ancient gas lanterns. A live band of Supernumeraries provided the music. They made a valiant effort to keep the songs upbeat, but the mood among the gathered Witch Hunters and their assistants remained somber. Generals Abernathy, Hickock, Brandt, and Davis conferred to one side, away from the crowd, a veritable ocean of black hats and coats. Flint himself stayed near the bar, nursing a glass of red wine over the past hour. Even Navarro and Fletcher were more subdued than usual.

"Captain Flint?"

He looked to his left and saw a familiar face. The last time Flint had seen Witch Hunter Captain Bartholomew Kennedy, the man had been spattered from head to toe in the blood of ghouls. Now his uniform was immaculate as he extended his hand, which Flint shook.

"Ah, Captain Kennedy," he said. "You appear none the worse for wear after our adventure in the tunnels last month."

"Likewise. And please, call me Bart."

"Very well. Please, do address me as Silas."

Kennedy clinked his glass of whiskey against Flint's wine glass. "Can I interest you in a cocktail Silas?"

"Later, perhaps," Flint said, taking another sip of wine. "How has Fort Ingalls fared since Mr. Navarro and I took our leave?"

"Fine, fine. Other than the giant hole in the courtyard, the damage was superficial. As for us... well, we've tried to carry on as usual, but Charles is on everyone's minds.

More specifically, however many nuclear weapons he may still possess."

Flint nodded. "I would not worry overmuch about those. He is a diabolical fiend, but he is not completely insane. He seeks to rule, to dominate. He cannot do that if he incinerates the continent in nuclear fire."

Kennedy was silent for a moment. Flint knew the man had to be teeming with questions.

"Look, Silas... I know you're going to testify before His Majesty and the committee tomorrow but..."

"I will answer what I can."

After a brief pause he said, "I had a lot of questions, but now that I've had time to think, I suppose they all boil down to one: do you think there will be war?"

"Undoubtedly. Charles will not be content with whatever rump state he carves from the United Mountain States. He speaks of wanting to be left alone, but I assure you that he does so only to buy time. Time to build up whatever forces he can before he begins to expand his so-called empire. If circumstances permitted, I would urge His Majesty to declare war, post-haste."

Kennedy sighed. "Circumstances don't permit."

"Indeed not. I do not believe Charles will make a pre-emptive nuclear strike, but he will take his chances if his back is pressed to the wall."

"I hate to say it, but it's ingenious in its twisted way," Kennedy said. "He couldn't win a conventional war with the UMS, let alone Cascadia, if we were to take the fight to him now. But with those damned nuclear weapons?"

He shrugged. "I'd hate to be in the Emperor's shoes right now."

Flint nodded. "More's the pity for President Fitzroy. Even if nuclear weapons were not a part of the equation, that region of the United Mountain States is rife with difficult terrain. I too am loathe to admit it, but Charles chose an excellent locale to wage a defensive war."

Flint caught movement in the corner of his vision. Abernathy was waving him over. He could see Navarro and Fletcher making their way through the crowds toward the Generals. "Please excuse me," he said to Kennedy, who nodded in acknowledgment. Flint finished his wine with one gulp and left the bar to join his companions. The smell of cigar smoke wafted past Flint's nostrils. That had to be General Brandt; from what Flint had heard of the man, the only time he didn't smoke was at Mass. At least he had good taste in tobacco. Flint seldom partook himself, but now he felt a craving.

"Captain," Abernathy said when Flint reached the group. "I don't believe you've ever been formally introduced?"

"I have not, sir."

"May I present General Seth Brandt of Fort Rochester, and General Malachi Davis of Fort Plummer."

"Captain," Brandt said, giving Flint's hand a firm shake. As he'd expected, Brandt was surrounded by a thick haze produced by the cigar which hung from the corner of his mouth. Like Abernathy, Brandt was a trim man with thinning grey hair, his face leathery with deep creases and wrinkles, no doubt exacerbated by his lifetime of smoking.

"A pleasure, Captain," said Davis, giving Flint another handshake. He was a black man who shared Hickock's hulking stature. Flint could see that Davis shaved his head, his mouth framed by an iron grey goatee.

"It's an honor to meet you both, sirs," Flint said. He indicated his companions. "And may I present my assistant, Supernumerary Ricardo Navarro, and our associate Zelda Fletcher." Another round of handshakes.

"I heard that you're a former witch, Miss Fletcher," Davis said.

"Yeah," she replied. "I'm trying to give it up, but there are some things I can do that are going to be with me the rest of my life."

"Such as?" Brandt asked.

"Oh, you know... I can overhear people's thoughts. Read minds if I really focus. Present company excluded of course."

"More importantly, Miss Fletcher believes she can lead us to Charles," Abernathy said.

Brandt raised an eyebrow.

"How?" Davis asked. "In his declaration, he said that his little empire is in the old Montana territory. Can you read him from so far away?"

"No," she said. "What happened is, what everyone saw in the sky? I think that was for the public. While he was speaking, I felt this... I don't know, tug? It was like I was being pulled to the east. I'd bet money that everyone who can use magic felt the same thing. It's like he was broadcasting his location to us like... uh..."

"A lighthouse?" Navarro prompted.

"Yeah... yeah, that's a good comparison," she said. "I doubt I could point it out on a map, but yeah... if we went east, I could lead you straight to him."

The Generals all exchanged glances. Flint knew what they had to be thinking.

"I will personally vouch for Miss Fletcher's commitment to our cause," Abernathy said.

"Me too," Navarro said. "She saved our asses twice."

The corner of Flint's mouth quirked up. "Yes. I too can testify to Miss Fletcher's character. She still has much to learn, but her contributions over the last few months have been invaluable."

Hickock looked to Brandt and Davis. They looked at each other.

"Good enough for me," Brandt said.

"I'll take your word for it, John," Davis said.

"Now that that's out of the way," Hickock said, "I wanted to sound out all of you on what we're going to say tomorrow."

"We supposed to get our stories straight or something?" Navarro asked.

"No, no, nothing like that. Y'all feel free to give your honest opinions. Whatever you do, don't hold back if the Emperor asks you something. I'm especially interested in what you folks from back east are thinking. If Flint the Lesser is in old Montana, that makes you on the front lines now."

Flint frowned. "If it were my decision to make sir, I would move for war. Strike Charles now and strangle his blasphemous 'empire' in the cradle."

"Silas and I found one of Charles's little jewels in New Rome a few months back," Navarro said. "He left us a message. From what I saw of him then, and everything that's going on now? We're going to be fighting him someday, may as well get it over with."

"For what it's worth, I'm with them," Fletcher said. "He's going to go batshit crazy if he goes too deep into magic."

Abernathy and Davis looked at each other. Abernathy said, "We are, of course, faithful servants of the Church and the Empire. I know a bit more about Captain Flint's background then the rest of you, perhaps. I don't wish for war, but I'm afraid we'll get one, one way or another."

"I say nip it in the bud," Davis added.

Now Hickock and Brandt looked to each other. "I'm inclined to agree," Brandt said. "There's a big problem though."

"Those damn nukes," Hickock said. "I ain't afraid of a fair fight. But if we go out lookin' for one, I'm afraid the west is full of tempting targets for that son of a bitch. Uh... sorry, Captain. No offense."

"None taken."

"Well, that went about how I figured it would," Hickock continued. "But like Silas said earlier, it's not our decision to make. Just so we're all on the same page, if the Committee or His Majesty directly asks about it, y'all okay with me saying we recommend war?"

After a brief pause, everyone nodded.

"Alright then." Flint reflected that the four generals were technically equal in rank, but Hickock, as the Witch

Hunter General of the imperial capitol and the one who dealt with the Emperor the most frequently, was considered the first among equals and their unofficial spokesman.

"God willing, we'll all get through this together," Hickock went on. "That's all I had for y'all. Enjoy the get together if you can. And Miss Fletcher?"

"Uh... yes... sir?"

"If you'd be so kind as to accompany me to the bar, I do believe I promised to mix you a Witch Bane."

"This I got to see," Navarro said.

"If you don't mind, I believe I will join you," Abernathy said, smiling.

Davis laughed. "I always had you figured for a teetotaler, John."

"Even I like to partake from time to time. Captain? General Brandt?"

"I shall abstain for the present."

"I think I'll finish this smoke and call it an early night," Brandt said. "Oh! Where are my manners? Cigars, anyone?"

"After reconsideration, I believe I shall join the rest of you at the bar," Flint said.

Brandt grinned. He reached into one of his long coat's inner pockets and withdrew a cigar, offering it to Flint. "Another time perhaps."

"Thank you," Flint said, putting the cigar into one of his own coat's inner pockets. The haze of smoke around General Brandt was beginning to make Flint's eyes water.

He estimated that he would need a few days of fresh air before he ventured to light up.

4

Roger Klemm weaved his way through the ballroom of Fort Ingalls, a platter loaded with martinis balanced on his hand, a towel draped over his arm. The Supernumerary whose place Klemm had taken was taking a magically enhanced nap in the barracks. The Fort had increased security since the Night of Chaos incident last month. If any of the Witch Hunters present decided to draw their sword, it would no doubt shine brighter in Klemm's presence. Then he imagined there would be a lot of hard questions for... what was his name? Geoffrey Harold, that was it. Klemm killed people for money, but he didn't think of himself as a mere assassin. No, he was an actor. His magic allowed him to shapeshift into any person he chose. Not just their outward appearance; he copied his subjects down to the blood, the teeth, the fingerprints. It allowed him to perform his kills up close and personal, his victims' last thoughts being that a friend or a loved one had murdered them. Then he would revert to his true form and slip away, leaving that friend or loved one to take the fall. What could they possibly say in their defense when there might be witnesses at the scene or their fingerprints on the murder weapon?

Before he could shapeshift into another person though, he needed something of theirs: a fingerprint, a hair, a drop of blood, some saliva, anything would work but it had to be theirs if the spell was going to work. That was one of the reasons he had taken the risk of infiltrating Fort Ingalls tonight. By taking that waiter's place, he would have access to hundreds of new shapes to assume once he got his hands on some used glasses and utensils. His boss, Emil Parlow, had told him to target Silas Flint, and only Silas Flint. Klemm still thought it was a wasted opportunity to decapitate all four Witch Hunter Chapter Houses at once. But he was a professional and he would obey his client's wishes.

"Can I interest any of you in a drink?" he asked a small gathering of Witch Hunters in his path.

"Oh, yes. Thank you, Mr. Harold," said a female Templar who took a martini off Klemm's platter. Shit. She knew the real Harold. It was an inevitable danger with Klemm's M.O., but he was confident he could bluff his way through it.

"Of course, ma'am," Klemm said in Harold's voice.

Another Witch Hunter, a man, took a glass. He gave Klemm a pat on the shoulder. "Thanks for volunteering for tonight, Geoffrey," he said.

"No trouble at all, sir. It's a lot easier than what we normally do, am I right?"

The Witch Hunters laughed. "Amen to that," the male Witch Hunter said. "Don't forget to get yourself some dinner and a few drinks tonight."

"Yes sir," Klemm said, smiling. "Excuse me." He resumed his rounds. If he stuck to generalities and platitudes in someone else's form, he could usually maintain his cover. The longer he wore his magical disguises, the more likely it became someone would ask something only his patsy would know, especially in a tight knit community like the Knights Templar of the Order of Saint Benedict. He'd have to hurry if he was to get what he needed.

There. By the bar. Klemm grew up in Salem and easily recognized the hulking figure of General Hickock. And what was this? Two other men in the trademark long coats of the Templars, with gold epaulettes on their shoulders. He suppressed a smile at this stroke of luck. It was a pity the fourth one wasn't present, but if he could only pick up some of their used glassware... being able to morph into Witch Hunter Generals would definitely come in handy in the future. There was a Supernumerary with them as well, a Mexican by the look of him. By his side was none other than Captain Silas Flint. Klemm weaved through the crowd.

The closer he got, the more Klemm saw the resemblance between Silas and Charles. The whole continent, if not the whole world, saw Charles Flint's projection in the sky last month. Charles cut a rough looking figure with his longer hair, the dark circles beneath his eyes, the stubble that was not quite a beard yet. The elder Flint – Klemm believed Silas was the older brother anyway – was more polished with a face that appeared carved from marble. Silas was nursing a glass of red wine. Klemm briefly considered slipping some poison into the drink but dismissed the idea. Too many Witch Hunters around. One didn't last as long in the trade as Roger Klemm had by taking unnecessary risks. He'd get his hands on used glassware from the Mexican or one of the Generals, take their shape, get close to Silas, and stick a shiv in his heart. Klemm knew the basic spells to conjure fire or lightning in his hands; every magician could do those tricks on their first day studying the craft. But the flashy stuff drew attention. Not to mention those damned swords that Templars carried, blades that could absorb magic. An ordinary knife or a gun though? Witch Hunters were as vulnerable as anyone else. He approached the two Generals who were leaning on the bar.

"May I take your glasses, gentlemen?" Klemm asked.

"Yes, thank you," said one, putting it on Klemm's platter. He was a white man, late fifties to early sixties. "I believe General Hickock will be providing the drinks in a minute."

"Thank you," said the other, a giant of a black man with a goatee. "I'm sorry, you are...?"

"Supernumerary Geoffrey Harold sir," Klemm answered.

"Got nominated for waiting tonight, eh?" the black man asked.

"I volunteered sir. It's a nice break in the action, especially after the Night of Chaos."

"I'm sure. Thank you, Mr. Harold."

Klemm inched his way toward Silas and the Mexican. Hickock was fussing around with bottles of liquor behind the bar. Klemm ignored him. Hickock was too well known a figure in Salem to be useful as a disguise, with too many idiosyncrasies for Klemm to bother learning. Reaching his target, he tapped the Mexican on the shoulder.

"Hey," Klemm said, "I can take that glass for you."

"Oh, sure, thanks," the Mexican said, handing it over. "Ricardo Navarro, by the way."

"Geoffrey Harold." They shook hands. "Is that your partner there?"

"Yup, sure is."

Klemm got closer. Flint's back was to him as he scanned the crowd. He tapped him on the shoulder.

"Yes?" Flint asked, turning. Klemm resisted the urge to raise his eyebrows. Even before tonight he'd crossed paths with hundreds of Templars. Their trade was hunting his kind, but most of them were just ordinary human beings with interests, hobbies, hopes and dreams like anyone else. Up close, Flint looked like he lived for little else besides the hunt. They were on opposite sides, but Klemm recognized a fellow killer when he saw one.

"Would you like a refill sir?" he asked. "Or I can take that glass for you...?"

Flint finished the wine with one gulp and put the glass on Klemm's platter. "A refill will not be necessary, thank you."

"Very good sir."

Excellent, Klemm thought. Now he would take the used glasses somewhere private, use the appropriate spells to absorb the essence of their users, and he'd have an impressive array of new disguises. Once that was done, he'd need to find a way to get close to Silas again. The Mexican, Navarro... taking his shape would be the best bet. No one would question a Supernumerary staying close to his partner. He'd take Silas's form first, send Navarro off on some errand, then shapeshift into the Mexican and shank the Witch Hunter, leaving Navarro to take the fall. Flint dead, a fat paycheck, and his assistant goes to the gallows. Klemm loved it when a plan came together.

"Hey! Miss Fletcher!" Hickock shouted. He waved someone over. "I got your drink ready!"

Klemm looked to his left. A woman was making her way to the bar. *Easy on the eyes,* he thought. She looked to be in her early twenties, long black hair tied back in a ponytail. She wasn't in a Templar or Supernumerary uniform though. What was her story?

They locked eyes. Klemm was about to smile and nod when he felt a sharp pain in his skull. What the hell was... no. She raised an eyebrow. Then she squinted at him. Klemm couldn't believe it: this woman, whoever she was... she had the talent. She was a witch. And she could sense his power. Time to go.

"Hey..." he heard her say. Klemm picked up his pace, hurrying, but not so quickly as to draw attention. The job had just gotten more complicated.

***

"Is everything alright, Miss Fletcher?" Flint asked. The woman looked like she had seen a ghost. She stopped before him; her gaze focused somewhere over his shoulder. He turned, saw nothing but his fellow Templars and Supernumeraries conversing and sharing drinks. "You appear troubled."

"That guy... do you know who he is?" she asked.

"To whom do you refer?"

"He's a Supernumerary... looks like he's a waiter to-night. He took your wine glass."

"I am unfamiliar with him. Is there a problem?

"I don't know... I thought I felt something from him for a second, but then it was gone."

"Something...?"

"Yeah... it's... I don't know how to describe it. It's like his thoughts weren't his. Like it was someone else wearing a suit. Or a disguise."

Flint scanned the crowd, but the Supernumerary waiter was gone. "Hmm..." he said. "Perhaps General Hickock would know."

"We can ask him over drinks!"

5

Emil Parlow lay in his bed, hands behind his head, staring at the ceiling. This American underground facility Charles and Lilian had discovered was no doubt spartan by twenty-first century standards, but here in the twenty-sixth century? He wondered if the Emperor of Cascadia himself lived in such luxury. Electrical lights in every room, an enormous dining room and kitchen equipped with half a dozen refrigerators, some of which contained magically preserved selections from the twenty-first century (Lilian couldn't get enough of a soda called Dr. Pepper.) And that... computer, Rob. Charles and Lilian both swore that it (he?) wasn't alive, but it was able to speak, to answer questions and obey commands. Parlow thought it was a pity that the computer had no historical knowledge of the world more recent than 2075, the year Lilian and her then colleagues had frozen it in time, but still... he sometimes wondered if science would have surpassed the power of magic had its development not been disrupted by the coming of Simon Magus. Parlow wasn't an expert in the history of science, but by his estimate the wealthiest cities – like Salem – had technology roughly analogous to the early twentieth century. The rest of the continent's technology ranged from the nineteenth century to the Middle Ages. He snorted. Those savages in La Floride no doubt lived in grass huts.

Samantha though... she couldn't get enough of technology. He sighed. Samantha Quinn had been his best student. An endless appetite for knowledge about magic, science, technology... she would have been overjoyed to see this bunker built by the old United States. He had admired that hunger she had. He'd eventually grown to love it, and her. If things had gone differently, he would have asked her to marry him. But then came Silas Flint.

Parlow and Quinn had a neat little operation going in Hermiston, near the Columbia River in eastern Cascadia. The Snake River Trading Company sent shipments throughout the Empire with its fleet of river barges. Magic was officially illegal in Cascadia, the Witch Hunters tasked with policing all paranormal activity. Businessmen and bureaucrats tended to be a bit more flexible, willing to look the other way with a well placed bribe here, or a threatening display of fireworks there. Parlow had focused on stealing and smuggling items that he could quickly turn around for a tidy profit. Occasionally he discovered a book or an enchanted object that proved useful in his studies of magic. Quinn had been more interested in whatever old world technology, or books on the subject, that she could find. It galled him that her hobby – a perfectly innocent hobby shared by magicians and mundane citizens alike – is what led to their downfall.

That damned college kid... he had to be a hero. He drew a gun on Samantha, and she struck him down with a lightning bolt to the face. What was she supposed to do, let him shoot her? If he'd only surrendered that silly artifact when Samantha demanded it from him, they might both still be alive. But the boy's parents were well connected. They raised a fuss – really, Samantha did them a favor, putting the stupid brat out of his misery – and Knight Templar Captain Silas Flint was dispatched to Hermiston along with his little Mexican sidekick. They discovered Parlow's operation during their investigation of the boy's death. He and Quinn made a last stand together. She died. He survived. Every day he woke up, he felt the stinging shame of having survived when the woman he loved hadn't.

He still agreed with what Charles had said earlier. The time wasn't right for total war with Cascadia. It was by far the largest and richest nation in the western half of North America. He believed in Charles's vision of a nation where the magically gifted could practice their craft openly. Parlow wasn't sure what Charles's plans were for the non-magic users who resided in this part of the United Mountain States, but that would come in due time, he was sure. But with Silas Flint in Salem, with Roger so close by... no, Parlow would not allow this opportunity to pass him by. He had no idea if Charles wanted to take care of Silas himself. It would make sense if he did. If Silas were to be murdered in the next few days, seemingly by someone close to him... well, what Charles didn't know wouldn't hurt him.

Parlow smiled. His relationship with Roger Klemm was strictly professional, but he thought they could have been fast friends despite their differences. Klemm had no interest in magic for its own sake; he only cared about magic insofar as it helped him work his bloody trade. The man knew practically nothing of magical theory, but Parlow had never met a better practitioner of shapeshifting. Most magicians could alter their appearance to look like someone else, but Klemm... he could make himself into an exact duplicate down to the fingerprints. How can anyone catch an assassin whose disguises are flawless? Klemm's rates would be extortionate coming from a mundane killer, but his talent was worth the price.

Parlow noticed a glow in his peripheral vision. He'd left his sapphire on the desk in his room, and it was pulsing with a soft blue light. He furrowed his brow. Could that be Klemm? Had he accomplished his mission already? Only one way to find out. He swung his legs off the bed and went to the desk. He waved his fingers and muttered the spell to open communications. The familiar column of light rose to the ceiling. Inside was a man's face Parlow didn't recognize.

"Is that you Mr. Klemm?" he asked.

"Yes," the assassin replied. "Just a minute." He closed his eyes, took a deep breath. The face appeared to liquefy for a second before reforming into Klemm's true form. Parlow thought that even if Klemm didn't have the talent for magic, he'd be a formidable assassin. His true appearance was more that of a mild-mannered bureaucrat than a professional killer.

"That was quick," Parlow said. Normally, once Klemm accepted a contract, he didn't speak to his client again until the job was done.

"Job's not done. There's been a complication," Klemm said.

Parlow raised an eyebrow. "So deal with it."

"I don't kill anyone I'm not paid to kill."

He sighed, knowing this would cost him. "Who's the problem then?"

"There's a witch here."

"Meaning?"

"Meaning she's apparently working with the Witch Hunters."

"What?!" Parlow caught himself before his voice rose to a shout. "I'm sorry... how do you know she's working with them?"

"I could sense her power, and she could sense mine. I got out of there before she could point me out. But she was laughing and carrying on and having drinks with all of them. I don't know how or why but... it looks like she's on their side."

Parlow growled in frustration. This did indeed complicate things. Klemm could pass for anyone he chose among the sheep, but magicians could sense his shapeshifting spells even if they couldn't guess his real identity. What's more… his eyes widened.

"Yeah," Klemm said. "I figured you'd guess the next part."

"If a witch has gone over to the Templars…"

"She could lead them right to your little nation-building project out there."

Parlow's mind raced. A witch who had gone over to the lambs… why on earth would any magician do that? Did Charles know about this? He cursed himself. If he asked the younger Flint about this person, then that would lead to questions about how Parlow learned of her, and to knowledge of his paying Klemm to operate in Salem against Flint's express orders.

Klemm could surely find an opportunity to terminate Silas when the witch wasn't around. Get him alone somewhere. On the other hand… if she really was working for the Witch Hunters, there was the remote possibility that she could one day lead them here. And there was the principle of the thing to consider. Charles Flint had proclaimed a new nation. In a sense, everyone who could use magic was a citizen of that nation, whether they resided within its borders or not. A witch joining up with the Templars, serving the lambs… it was treason most foul.

"You still with me Emil?" Klemm asked.

Parlow shook himself. He looked to Klemm. "How much will it cost me to have you put her down as well?"

Klemm raised an eyebrow. "Never killed a fellow magician before. That could be… interesting. I'll tell you what:

you're one of my best clients. My usual fee for each kill, but with a twenty percent discount for taking out both."

"It's a deal."

Klemm nodded. "Good enough. I'll contact you again when the job's done." The column of light disappeared.

Parlow went back to bed. He didn't expect he would get much sleep tonight, despite Lilian's recommendation that they all build up their strength. He wasn't sure what Charles was having them work on at the moment; something to do with the flow of time. When this was over, he'd love to get his hands on that copy of *In Realis Magicae* that Charles had acquired somewhere. Then he'd ask the computer what it knew about...

He bolted upright. The computer. He looked around the room. "Computer...?" he whispered.

The walls chimed.

"Computer... were you able to hear all of that?"

"I see and hear everything that occurs within the perimeter of this facility," Rob's voice said.

"Can Charles and Lilian hear our conversation?"

"No. They can only hear our conversation if you request it."

He relaxed a bit. "Could you... keep my conversation with Roger to yourself?"

"I will do so Mr. Parlow. However, I must inform you that Lilian Turner is the current system administrator. If she gives me a direct order to reveal the contents of your conversation with Mr. Klemm, I must comply."

"That's fine. I'll just have to make sure she and Charles never learn the truth."

"As you say, Mr. Parlow."

"As long as I'm going to be awake anyway... Computer, I had some questions about what you remember of the Occult War."

6

Silas Flint was seated at a long table facing a semicircle of desks atop a raised dais at the head of the room. In the center of the semicircle, three steps led up to an ornate throne. On the walls were portraits of notable Emperors in Cascadia's history, including Michael Flagg, the founder and first Emperor of Cascadia. Above the throne was a portrait of Peter II, the reigning Emperor, in the olive drab tunic of an Imperial Army officer. Guards were posted at the rear of the chamber where Flint and his party had entered, and at the head of the room past where the dais ended.

Flint had surrendered his sword and pistols upon entering the Imperial Palace. He felt naked, but custom must be observed. To his left were Generals Hickock, Brandt, and Davis, and on his right were General Abernathy, Fletcher, and Navarro. The men had donned the dress uniforms of the Order: the Templars with steel chest plates, a pauldron on the right shoulder, scarlet trim on their heavy long coats, silver buckles on their hats; Navarro in a field grey tunic with matching trousers, black boots, and peaked cap with a Saint Benedict medal in the center, lined with gold trim. Fletcher was not a sworn member, but Flint had loaned her the money to purchase a dress for the occasion.

She appeared none the worse for wear after several of Hickock's drinks the previous night, but her eyes flicked around the chamber. He sympathized.

An imperial functionary entered the room. "All rise."

Flint and his party all rose from their seats. From the door at the head of the room entered thirteen men and women in tailored suits and immaculate dresses. They silently filed up onto the dais, taking their places behind their desks, staying on their feet. Flint recognized a few of them from newspaper stories he'd read over the years: Warwick Grissom, the Count of Astoria; Anita Velasquez, Countess of Ashland; the others were strangers. When the last woman stopped behind her seat, the functionary called out, "Oyez, oyez, oyez, the Emperor approaches."

Everyone knelt on their left knee. Flint cast his eyes downward. The door at the rear of the room swung open. He heard the tapping of boots on the tiled floor, echoing throughout the room. The sound moved past the table and Flint looked up. Emperor Peter II strode toward the dais, ascended the steps. He was a man of late middle age, a fringe of grey stubble encircling his bald head, a thick grey beard reaching down to his broad chest. He wore the same olive drab military tunic from his official portrait, a purple cord encircling right shoulder, but otherwise devoid of medals or rank insignia. Reaching the throne, he turned to face the room, scanning the assembled members of Parliament and the guests they had summoned to testify. Flint averted his eyes before the Emperor could see him looking up. His Majesty sat down in his throne.

"Be seated," he said. The room echoed with the sound

of scraping chairs, rustling coats, coughs, sniffs. Flint rested his hands on the table, interlocking his fingers. He kept his focus straight ahead, but in his peripheral vision he could see that Navarro and Fletcher looked ill at ease. Flint knew that Navarro hated wearing the Supernumerary dress uniform, but at least he didn't have to don the heavy cuirass of the Templars.

Grissom, seated on the Emperor's right at the foot of the stairs, picked up a gavel and gave it a rap. "This meeting of the Continuing Committee on Paranormal Activity and Magical Anomalies is called to order," he said. "Our first order of business will be the opening prayer. Would one of our distinguished guests be willing to do the honors?"

"I will," Abernathy said. Making the sign of the cross, he began, "In the name of the Father, and of the Son, and of the Holy Spirit."

"Amen," everyone answered.

"Most Holy and Blessed Trinity," Abernathy went on. "We ask your blessing upon today's proceedings. Please grant us the grace to see the way forward in these difficult times. Grant that we, your humble servants, may act in accordance with thy holy will. O Blessed Mary, Ever Virgin..."

"Pray for us."

"Saint Joseph, terror of demons."

"Pray for us."

"Saint Benedict, patron against witchcraft."

"Pray for us."

"In the name of the Father, and of the Son, and of the Holy Spirit."

"Amen."

"Thank you," Grissom said. He looked to his left. Sometime during the prayer, another woman had entered the chamber. Two guards set up a table, stool, and typewriter for her. She sat down, cracked her knuckles, and gave Grissom a nod.

"Before we proceed, I would ask you all to please state your full names for the record," he said. He nodded toward Davis. "We'll start with you sir."

"Templar General Malachi Raphael Davis."

"Templar General Seth Felix Brandt."

"Templar General Jeremiah Christopher Hickock."

"Templar Captain Silas Albert Flint."

"Templar General John Polycarp Abernathy."

"Zelda Naomi Fletcher."

"Supernumerary Ricardo Diego Francisco Juan Pablo Nepomuceno María de los Remedios Cipriano de la Santísima Trinidad Navarro y Castro."

The parliamentary reporter stopped typing, looked up.

"If there are no objections, Ricardo Navarro will do," Grissom said, the corner of his mouth quirked up. Navarro nodded. "Would you all please rise?"

After Flint and his companions stood up, they were approached by an imperial soldier who was serving as the Sergeant at Arms. Facing the Committee's guests, he said, "Please raise your right hands." After they had all done so, he continued, "Before Almighty God and all of the angels and saints, and in the presence of His Majesty, Emperor Peter II, do you swear to tell the truth, the whole truth, and nothing but the truth, so help you God?"

"We do," their voices echoed.

"Be seated," Grissom said, whom Flint assumed had to be the chairman of the Committee. "Ladies and gentlemen, your Majesty, we gather today to address the so-called declaration of independence made by one Charles Flint four weeks ago. I'm sure that we all have questions, ones that I pray our Templar friends have answers for. I would like to begin today's proceedings with a question for General Hickock."

"Yes sir?" Hickock said.

"The so-called Night of Chaos last month... was the perpetrator in league with Charles Flint?"

Flint exchanged glances with Abernathy and Navarro. They knew the truth of the matter along with Hickock. The late Jennifer Edwards had been a student of Charles and used her position within Fort Ingalls to ambush and murder her fellow Templars. Hickock paused and thought for a moment before answering.

"I would say yes. The late and unlamented Commander Edwards..."

"Strike that name from the record," a woman on the committee interrupted. Flint didn't recognize her, but she was undoubtedly a friend of the ex-Minister of Justice Benjamin Edwards.

Grissom said, "I really don't think it matters anymore Barbara. Everyone in this room knows who the traitor was." The woman, Barbara, frowned but didn't reply. "Please, continue General."

"As I was sayin', the late and unlamented Jennifer

Edwards was turned by Charles Flint himself several years ago."

"We can confirm," Abernathy said. All eyes shifted to him. "Captain Flint, Mr. Navarro, Miss Fletcher, and I were in communication with Charles Flint shortly before his announcement."

Grissom blinked. Another man on the committee whom Flint didn't recognize spoke up: "I'm sorry... you were in communication with Charles Flint? How? Why?"

"I may be able to explain," Flint said. "Mr. Navarro and I were sent to Salem last month, at the request of General Hickock, as part of a covert operation to discover the identity of the traitor within the ranks of Fort Ingalls. During that mission, we recovered a sapphire which serves as a sort of magical communication device. Our associate Miss Fletcher activated it upon our return to Fort Marsing. My brother possessed the sapphire's twin. We... exchanged words."

Countess Velasquez raised an eyebrow. "And how, exactly, was Miss Fletcher able to activate it?"

Fletcher cleared her throat. "I'm a former witch."

The Committee members stirred, whispers were exchanged, notes scribbled. Flint saw the Emperor lean forward, his chin resting on his interlocked fingers.

"This is..." Grissom said.

"You dare bring a heretic and a witch to the Imperial Palace itself?!" barked another woman on the Committee. The Committee members raised their voices, some calling for calm, others demanding that Fletcher be arrested on the spot. The Emperor brought his fist down on his throne's armrest.

"Enough!" he bellowed. The room instantly fell silent. He inclined his head toward Abernathy. "Speak."

"Miss Fletcher turned herself in to Fort Marsing several months ago," Abernathy said. "She has proven her repentance to my satisfaction, and I unreservedly vouch for her character."

"As do I," Flint said.

"Same here," Navarro said.

The Emperor cocked his head. "Young man," he said, addressing Navarro.

He swallowed before answering, "Uh, yes, sir, Your Majesty, sir?"

"Are you related to Mr. Angelo Navarro?"

"Yes. Sir. Your Majesty. I'm his only son."

The Emperor nodded. "Please give him my regards when next you speak with him and express my gratitude for accepting the contract for the new Templar Chapter House. You may continue Mr. Grissom."

Grissom straightened his tie, cleared his throat. "Yes, well... to continue my previous line of questioning, you say that Edwards was a student of Charles. Did he order her attack on Salem?"

Flint closed his eyes. He thought that Cascadia should declare a preemptive war against his brother, but he wouldn't lie to advance the cause. "I do not believe so."

"Oh?" A man on the Committee leaned forward. "Why do you say that Captain?"

"I apologize sir. I do not..."

"Martín Sanchez, Captain."

"Thank you, Mr. Sanchez. Mr. Navarro and I confronted Commander Edwards. Before we slew her, she spoke of seeking revenge for the execution of her mother for witchcraft."

"Would it be accurate to say that she was settling a personal grudge against your Order?"

Flint pursed his lips. "Yes," he said. "She nursed her resentment against us throughout her life even as she served with us. My brother found her an eager convert."

"Gentlemen," a woman on the Committee said. "Forgive me for what will no doubt sound like a foolish question but: What is the purpose of the Knights Templar of the Order of Saint Benedict?"

"To seek and destroy supernatural threats to the safety of God's children," Brandt spoke up.

"To exhort practitioners of the dark arts to renounce their heresy," Davis said.

"To kick monsters' asses," Hickock said. The Committee chuckled, and Flint saw the corners of the Emperor's mouth turn up.

"And if those same practitioners of the dark arts refuse to reform their lives?" the woman asked.

"If they persist, they inevitably go mad," Abernathy said. "Then we often have no choice but to stop them. Permanently."

"But some do repent," Sanchez said.

"Indeed," Flint replied. "Miss Fletcher's presence here is the proof."

"What I'm wondering is..." the woman said.

"I beg your pardon, Miss...?" Flint asked.

"Senator. Senator Hillary Gordon. What I'm wondering is this: what if your brother is telling the truth?"

The chamber stirred, and all eyes focused on Gordon.

"I do not follow you."

"Consider: the late Commander Edwards unleashed Hell upon Salem to settle her private grudge against your Order. You said yourselves that you don't think she was following Charles's orders. Please don't misunderstand what I'm about to say. We all appreciate everything your Order has done for the Empire since its foundation. But what if Charles Flint's so-called empire is the final solution?"

"What do you mean?" Hickock asked.

"What I mean is this: if witches and wizards have a nation of their own, then won't they leave us alone? Here they practice in secret until their experiments and ambitions come to your attention. But if they all pull up stakes and head out to this Empire of Medea..."

"Then we won't have as many 'incidents' like the Night of Chaos," finished another man on the Committee.

Flint's nostrils flared. He'd been afraid of this. And the devil of the matter was that he sympathized. It would indeed make the Witch Hunter vocation less hectic if a significant number of magicians left their native countries and flocked to Charles's redoubt. But Flint knew it would not that be easy.

7

Roger Klemm ascended the staircase, briefcase in hand.

He could have taken the elevator, but he preferred to walk as much as he could. He was currently wearing the form of Miles Whitmore, an attorney at the law firm of Oates and Chamberlain which happened to be a few blocks from the imperial palace. Inside the briefcase were the parts to a rifle of Klemm's own design. Klemm had strode into the firm's cafeteria in his true form claiming to be there for a job interview and had managed to snag one of Whitmore's used coffee cups. The fingerprints and saliva had done the trick. Klemm didn't know Whitmore from Adam, but the lawyer had introduced himself, shaken his hand, wished him luck with the interview. Klemm disliked lawyers as a rule, but this one had seemed decent enough. Too bad he might go down for what Klemm was about to do. Wrong time, wrong place amigo.

Klemm smiled. He thought that rifles were for amateurs: they made noise, they left shell casings, they were often difficult to conceal. A true professional got close. Unfortunately, the witch's powers meant that his normal M.O. was off the table for now. She'd sniff him out before he got within knife or pistol range. But a long-distance rifle shot? It would be the last thing she'd never see. He'd seen both Flint and the witch enter the imperial palace earlier this morning alongside Flint's sidekick and four Witch Hunter Generals. They were no doubt in the hot seat over Charles Flint's nation building project. Klemm would get to the top floor, take his shot, and get out of there. He'd probably have to leave the rifle behind, but it would have Whitmore's fingerprints all over it.

Klemm, like everyone else in North America, had

witnessed Charles's proclamation of his new empire. Sounded good in theory if he could defend himself against all comers. Those bombs of his... nuclear, he believed the term was. They certainly made a compelling argument for him to be left alone. Son of a bitch might pull it off. Klemm liked the idea of not having to worry about the Witch Hunters anymore, but what on earth would he do with himself? He'd been an assassin since he left home as a boy. No, the demand for his skills, the money, it was right here in Cascadia. He'd stay put. If this new nation of magicians succeeded, they could use someone with his talents here in the imperial capitol. If they failed, well, life would go on as it had before. The market for professional assassinations was recession-proof, as they say. Maybe if the Empire of Medea was still around in his old age, it could be a nice place to retire.

Klemm reached the top of the stairs. He opened the door on the landing and stepped out onto the roof. The sun was dimmed by the haze of smog that perpetually enveloped Salem. He much preferred the electrical lights, abundant automobiles, and target rich environment of the big city to the small towns of the countryside that still relied on gas lanterns and horse drawn carriages, but he had to admit the latter had much better air quality. Shutting the door behind him, he cast a spell that would hold the door in place even if they used dynamite. He didn't want any interruptions. Klemm would kill to defend himself, but he avoided killing nontargets whenever possible. It was sloppy, unprofessional, and made it more likely he'd get caught.

He whistled a tune as he opened the briefcase, removed the pieces, and assembled the rifle. The internal magazine could hold five rounds, but he only brought one bullet. Klemm never missed when he was on a job. He whispered another spell and the rooftop shimmered around him. It was unlikely anyone would spot him at this height, but just in case someone happened to look out the window of an adjoining skyscraper, the rooftop would appear empty, just as it should be. Klemm didn't know and didn't care how the magical camouflage worked, only that it did. Let scholars like Parlow worry about the theory of it. Klemm had meant it when he'd called him one of his best clients, but he thought the normally stoic Parlow was allowing his emotions to get the better of him this time. Klemm knew that Silas Flint had killed Parlow's student Samantha Quinn, and that his feelings for her were more than just that of a teacher for a favorite pupil. Assassinations that were only about revenge seldom made the client feel any better after it was done. They were often the start of a cycle of vengeance that would leave many more dead. But a job was a job. So long as his clients paid up, his was not to reason why, his was but to kill or die.

He balanced the rifle atop the ledge of the rooftop and peered through the scope. Yes, this spot would do nicely. He had a perfect view of the front gates of the imperial palace. Klemm reflected that the Cascadian Empire was nearly 400 years old, and in all that time no Emperor had ever been assassinated. He thought maybe two or three members of Parliament had been killed in bar brawls, but otherwise the legislature was similarly murder-free. He'd take any job if the money was good enough, but he was secretly relieved no one had ever hired him for a political hit; he did have to live in Salem after all. The tightened security after a political hit would make it harder for him to earn money.

All visitors to the imperial palace entered and exited through the front gates. Now it was just a matter of waiting for his quarry to emerge. Once he took out the witch, it would be simple to get close enough to Flint and shank him.

"Why don't you take them both out?"

Klemm conjured a ball of fire in his hand, spun, and hurled it in the direction of the voice in less than two seconds. He saw a young Hispanic man, black hair slicked back, a grin on his face. The stranger raised his hand and the fireball dissipated in midair before it could reach him. The dispassionate corner of Klemm's mind noted that the stranger had to be a wizard, but the rest was in survival mode. He reached into his suit jacket, drew his pistol, and aimed it at the stranger in one swift motion.

"That's none of your concern, friend," Klemm said. "Why don't you just run along and forget you ever saw me?"

The stranger cocked his head. "That's not your face," he said.

"You're smarter than you look."

"Do you really think your gun would be any more effective against me than your spell?"

Klemm gave the stranger a grim smile. "It will be if I

empty it into your head." The smile vanished. "Walk away. Now. Last warning."

A chuckle. "No, I don't think I will. I came to watch a master at work."

"You don't know anything about me."

"I know that you're not really Miles Whitmore. I know that you're Roger Klemm, the middle child of Ronald and Eloise Klemm, assassin for hire, and one of the greatest living practitioners of shapeshifting in the world."

Klemm raised an eyebrow. "Okay, so you read my mind or did your homework or whatever. I don't do partners, and I don't do audiences. Beat it."

"And miss watching you kill my poor lost Zelda? I wouldn't miss it for the world. But to return to my earlier question: why not take out both Zelda and Silas Flint while you're up here?"

Okay, now this guy was starting to piss him off. "What's it to you?"

"Let's just say it's personal."

Klemm snorted. "Get in line."

"Hmm, yes. Your client wants to avenge his lost love, cut down by Captain Flint. And Zelda must go because she could sniff you out through your disguises. My interest is deeper than that. Those two killed me several months ago."

Oh, for Christ's sake. He lowered his gun. "So you're undead? Great. Just great." He holstered the weapon. "You're out in the sun, so you're not a vampire. You can speak in complete sentences, so you're not a zombie. Ghost?"

"In a manner of speaking."

"The fuck is that supposed to mean? You're a ghost or you're not."

The stranger laughed. "Death is only the beginning."

"Whatever. I've got a job to do, so either go away or shut up."

"Ah yes, forgive me. It's been too long since I've been able to converse with a human being. You needn't worry, you know. They won't be coming out for a good long while."

Klemm said nothing. He returned to his post, shouldered the rifle, resting the barrel on the rooftop ledge, and peered through the scope at the gates to the imperial palace.

"Oh, where are my manners?" One second the stranger was twenty feet away, the next he was at Klemm's side. "I haven't introduced myself."

"Don't care."

"My name is Francisco Cortez. Zelda and I used to be... together."

"Don't care."

"I discovered a certain tome months ago: *In Realis Magicae*. It was written by..."

Klemm looked up. "I can see why she killed you."

What happened next almost made Klemm want to recite the prayers of his childhood. Cortez's eyes blazed red. A nimbus of black fire burned around him. Shadowy tentacles emerged from his body, writhing in the sunlight. It lasted only a second, but for the first time in his life, Klemm understood what it meant to put the fear of God into someone.

"That was rude," Cortez said. "You don't need to answer if you don't want to. Just listen."

Klemm nodded. Whoever or whatever this kid was, he'd clearly done time in Hell.

"As I was saying," Cortez went on, "I found a copy of *In Realis Magicae.* It was written by Abdul Hakim Nazari, a handpicked disciple of Simon Magus himself. As the title might suggest, it contained priceless wisdom about the true nature of magic. I learned that my lifelong pursuit of wealth was ultimately meaningless."

Klemm blinked. "Good for you."

Cortez chuckled. "Yes, I can see that its message would fall on deaf ears, with you. Believe me, the irony isn't lost on me that I died so soon after accepting that truth. Who knows? Maybe if I'd never found that book, Zelda and I would still be together, picking pockets, cracking safes, robbing trains, and Silas Flint would have never crossed our paths."

"No offense, but is there a reason you're telling me all this besides being lonely?"

"You're going to fail."

"Excuse me?" Klemm looked up at Cortez, who only smiled in reply. "Let me tell you something kid: when I accept a job, I finish it. I don't fail. Ever."

"You still haven't answered my question: why not take them both out when they emerge from the palace?"

"Not that it's any of your business, but Flint is wearing his dress uniform which includes steel plate body armor."

"Surely a man of your skill could make a headshot at this distance."

Klemm snorted. "It's possible, but unnecessarily risky. He'll be surrounded by people. As soon as I pull the trigger, it's going to be pandemonium down there. I'm being paid to take him out along with your ex-girlfriend. She can see through my disguises. She's not wearing armor. I kill her here, Flint loses the one person who can tell him I'm not what I seem, I get him alone somewhere and finish the job. Simple. Safe. Effective."

Cortez nodded. "You make a good case."

"I'm glad you think so."

"You're still going to fail though."

"Look kid, or whatever you are, if you don't have anything constructive to contribute to the conversation, then with all due respect, fuck off."

Cortez laughed. "Would you like to know why you're going to fail?"

"Doesn't matter. I won't."

"I have to admit, I admire the pride you take in your work. If Silas Flint and Zelda Fletcher were ordinary people, they wouldn't stand a chance against you. But you can't see what I see. The other side has taken an interest in them both."

Klemm's brow furrowed. "The other...?" After a moment, the penny dropped, and he barked a laugh. "What, are you saying God is looking out for them? He's going to strike me down or send an avenging angel to come get me?"

"Nothing so crude. That's not how they work."

"God hasn't protected anyone else I've killed. I'll take my chances."

"I can offer you..."

"Not interested."

"But you haven't heard..."

"Don't need to. Not interested."

Cortez chuckled. "Suit yourself Roger. I'll be watching. If you change your mind, call out to me and I will hear."

"Francisco Cortez, got it," Klemm said, dismissing him with a wave.

"Not that name. Ichthil."

"Ick...what?" He looked up but the young man had vanished.

Asshole, he thought. Okay, so the kid had power. From that little display earlier, he was clearly possessed or something. Klemm knew that many magicians offered themselves up for possession to make casting easier. Magic took its toll on the human body, but demons could take it for them. Not Klemm though. No, demons were grifters, con artists. They came to you with offers that sounded too good to be true, and they were. They always found a way to get you in the end, no matter how Jesuitical you were in the negotiations. This was just a job like any other. He didn't need help from the other side. If God Himself tried to interfere? He'd cross that bridge when he got to it. No way some punk kid who got a raw deal from Hell was going to shake his confidence, break his concentration. He resumed his position, keeping an eye on the palace gates through the scope.

After a few moments he looked up again. Damn that kid. He was getting a bad feeling about this mission after all. No matter. He'd accepted the job and he would see it through to the end, one way or another. Klemm expected that he'd go to Hell someday, but he wouldn't do it for taking a sucker's deal.

8

"I must vigorously disagree," Silas Flint said.

Senator Gordon looked to Grissom, who said, "Please, Captain, explain."

"With all due respect to the Committee, no one in this room knows Charles as I do. He is a diabolical fiend whose lust for magical power knows no bounds and respects no persons. You are all no doubt thinking of his professed desire that his so-called empire be left in peace. That he desires to establish trade and diplomatic relations with the nations of North America. I tell you plainly that it is all a ruse."

The Committee members all leaned forward. Even the Emperor looked to be giving Flint his full attention. He hoped that he wouldn't start sweating.

"From our childhood, Charles has consistently dis-played a fascination with the dark arts. By its nature, magic twists the mind and corrupts the soul. It instills in all who practice it the will to dominate. My late parents and I became aware of his proclivities when he was young. We, along with our parish priest, tried our utmost to dissuade him from choosing the dark path. He professed to renounce his evil ways with much weeping, but we learned, to our sorrow, that he lied to us. Our parents paid the price for his devilry."

"Are you saying...?" Gordon asked.

Flint closed his eyes and took a deep breath. "His magic mutated them into twisted abominations. When I refused his offer to join him, he ordered his creations to kill me. I defended myself. Before the end, they regained enough of their humanity to ask me to end their misery."

The Committee murmured among themselves. The Emperor's eyes were closed, his fingers steepled.

"I think I speak for everyone here when I say that you have our condolences, Captain," Grissom said.

Flint nodded in acknowledgment. "Charles has recently acquired an ancient tome, one written by a wizard who learned his craft from Simon Magus himself. I can assure the Committee members, and you, Your Majesty, that if he speaks of peace, he does so only to buy himself time."

"Time for what?" Sanchez asked.

"To build up his strength, to gather like minded magicians to his side, to plumb the depths of sorcery in order to attain his true goal: domination of this continent. And then the world."

"What course of action do you propose, Captain?" Senator Gordon asked.

Flint's nostrils flared. "If it were my decision to make, Senator, I would declare war on his new nation. Immediately."

"Hear hear," Hickok said, rapping his knuckles on the table, the others quickly following his example.

After a few moments, Senator Gordon spoke up. "Thank you for your input, Captain, everyone. But as you pointed out, it is not your decision to make."

Flint scowled but said nothing.

"You said that magic twists and corrupts. But is it not possible to change? To reject it? Your associate Miss Fletcher is proof of that, is she not?"

"May I say something?" Navarro spoke up. Grissom nodded to him. "Zelda's proven that she wants to change her ways. Me, Silas, General Abernathy, she helped us put down a demon-possessed wizard outside of Jordan a few months ago. And after that she helped us exorcise a witch's ghost from an old American military base out in the UMS. I've seen Charles before. He left a message for us in the ruins of New Rome. I don't know him as well as Silas, but everything I saw tells me he's going to come for us sooner or later."

"I know where he is," Fletcher blurted.

"I'm sorry?" Grissom asked.

"Oh, uh, sorry. I don't know how this parliamentary stuff and rules of order or whatever work but..."

"You were saying?" Gordon interrupted.

Fletcher cleared her throat. "When Charles projected his image in the sky? At the same time, I felt a tug in the back of my mind. I think every magic user could feel it. He's calling every witch and wizard on the continent to go join him out there. I could lead anyone straight to him."

The Committee members all turned around in their seats to look up at the Emperor. He said nothing. They turned their faces back to their guests.

"Supposing that we went to war with the Empire of Medea, whether tomorrow or years from now, there's still one major problem," Sanchez said. "Charles Flint is in possession of nuclear weapons."

"Can any of you explain how that is even possible?" Countess Velasquez asked. "History isn't my strong suit, but it's my understanding that the newest models would still be over four hundred years old, and the Americans weren't known for building things that last."

"Yeah, I can explain," Fletcher said. "I don't know exactly how it works, but there's magic that can slow down or even stop the flow of time around the caster. That ghost witch Rico mentioned, back in the twenty-first century she used the souls of everyone who was stationed at that military base to keep her own soul tethered to this world, and keep the base artificially preserved by suspending time inside it. Or really slowing it down, one of those."

"So it's possible some other magicians from back then may have done the same to nuclear bombs..." Grissom said.

"However they did it, Charles has them and knows how to use them," Gordon said. "Does anyone here know how we could defend ourselves from such an attack?"

The room was silent. Flint didn't have an answer and he doubted anyone else did either.

"He said that so long as we don't attack him, he won't attack us," another woman on the Committee said.

"And if we were to make a preemptive strike against him, the western half of the Empire is filled with populous targets for those nuclear weapons: Olympia. Astoria. Salem," Gordon said. Murmurs arose among the Committee members.

"So... what?" Sanchez asked. "We allow a power mad wizard to dictate our foreign policy?"

"I didn't say that..."

"Sure sounds like it."

The Committee broke down into recrimination and accusation. Flint looked to his left. Hickock nodded toward the Committee and shrugged. The Emperor rapped his knuckles on the arm of his throne and the noise died down.

"Captain Flint," he said.

"Yes, Your Majesty?"

"Do you believe that your brother desires war?"

"Yes sir. There is no doubt in my mind."

"When?"

"That I do not know sir. I expect that his attention is currently focused on the government of the United Mountain States. If he can secure his territory, then it is only a matter of time before we are at war."

"Do you believe he would use nuclear weapons against us?"

"No sir."

"Explain."

"He seeks to control, to rule. He believes that magicians are superior to those who have no talent for magic. He wants to lead the world into what he believes would be a new golden age, with himself at its head. Nuclear weapons would kill millions and poison the land for generations. He wants us to believe he will use them. But a preemptive strike? No. I do not believe he would. He has no interest in ruling the dead."

The Emperor drummed his fingers on his armrest. He nodded to Grissom.

"General Abernathy, General Davis," Grissom said. "Your garrisons are stationed near the border with the UMS. Have either of you detected an increase in supernatural activity? More foot traffic passing by your Chapter Houses?"

"No sir," Abernathy replied. "Fort Marsing generally has at least 90 percent of its active duty Templars and Supernumeraries investigating cases, but that's normal for us."

"Same here," Davis said.

"General Hickock, General Brandt?"

"Other than last month's incident, no sir," Hickock said.

"We've heard rumors of active cults around Olympia. Otherwise, no," Brandt said. Flint noted that he appeared fidgety, no doubt pining for a nicotine fix.

"If it came to war, are the Templars prepared to assist the Imperial Army?" Sanchez asked.

"If it comes to it, we'll lead the march into Medea ourselves," Hickock said. The other generals nodded.

"And what if the government should choose to recognize this Empire of Medea?" Gordon asked.

After a moment's hesitation, Hickock replied, "I believe I speak for all of us when I say that we are servants of God and the Empire, and that we'll abide by whatever His Majesty and Parliament decide."

"For what it's worth, I'm in agreement with Captain Flint," Davis said.

"Same," Brandt said. "Present company excepted, but

I've never known a magician to walk away when more power is on the table."

"I concur," Abernathy said. "Captain Flint and Mr. Navarro are a credit to the Order, and their words are not to be taken lightly."

Flint, Navarro, and Fletcher said nothing.

The Committee members conferred in whispers. Flint saw several taking notes. He too would abide by whatever the Emperor and Parliament decided, but he prayed that they would join the United Mountain States in declaring war upon Charles. War would come, and the longer they put it off, the longer and bloodier that war would be.

"Thank you all," Grissom said. "You've given us much to consider. With His Majesty's permission, I move for a one hour recess."

"Second," said a woman on the Committee. Grissom looked up and the Emperor nodded.

"When we return, we will be joined by the Joint Chiefs of Staff and the head of the Cascadia Intelligence Service. I'm afraid that only those with top secret clearance may attend for this session. Captain Flint, Mr. Navarro, Miss Fletcher, you three are excused for the rest of today. Please remain in Salem until the Generals are dismissed. We may require further testimony from you." He rapped his gavel on his desk. "Committee adjourned for one hour."

Everyone in the room rose from their seats and bowed at the waist as the Emperor took his leave. His boots tapped on the tiled floor. He stopped at the table where Flint and his party had been seated.

"Captain Flint, Mr. Navarro, Miss Fletcher, I would like

to speak to you in private this evening. Be back at 7 p.m." With that, he resumed his march and left the Committee meeting room. Flint exhaled a breath he hadn't realized he'd been holding.

"Not bad Captain, not bad at all," Hickock said, slapping Flint on the back, causing him to stumble.

"Holy shit, I can't believe it, the Emperor spoke to me, he spoke to me personally, I never thought I'd..."

"Calm yourself, Mr. Navarro," Flint said. "I suspect that we will all have the opportunity to speak with him at great length this evening."

"Oh... oh yeah... damn."

"How are you faring, Miss Fletcher?"

She looked shaken. "I... Goddamn, I never thought..."

Flint gave her a sharp look.

"Oh, uh, sorry. But God... bless it. The fucking Emperor wants a private meeting with us? I was just thinking, if only mom and dad could see me now."

Brandt reached into one of his long coat's pockets and withdrew a cigar and lighter. "Don't worry too much about it. You did good earlier. Just be truthful, even if you think it'll piss him off. It'll only piss him off more if you hold back or lie to him." He lit up, took a drag, gave a contented sigh as he exhaled a ring of smoke.

"It would appear that you three are free for the rest of today," Abernathy said.

"Should we hang around here?" Navarro asked.

"I don't think that will be necessary. If you think our couriers are talented, the Emperor's put them to shame.

Trust me, they'll find you when it's time to head back here tonight," Abernathy chuckled.

"May I ask the nature of your meeting with the Joint Chiefs and Intelligence Service?" Flint said.

"Mainly it'll deal with Army and Navy strength, deployments, CIS agents in place, Templar numbers, stuff like that," Davis said. "To be honest, I envy you three getting a break for the rest of today."

"I presume that the military and intelligence services will wish to speak with us as well."

"Oh yeah," Hickock said. "Don't worry, you'll get your turn. Hell, y'all might be granted top secret clearance by the time they're done with you."

Fletcher and Navarro looked at each other, smiled.

"So we'll be, like, secret agents?" Fletcher asked.

"Do I get a tuxedo?" Navarro said.

Abernathy smiled. "Not unless you want to work for His Majesty's government. In any case, you all have some time to kill. Why not see more of Salem? You and Silas didn't have the opportunity the last time you were here. I'm sure Miss Fletcher would enjoy a tour."

She glanced at Flint before nodding. "Yes. Yes, I would."

"We shall not be visiting any local taverns before our meeting with His Majesty, Miss Fletcher," Flint said.

She crossed her arms. "I don't know what you're talking about Captain Flint."

"Hmph."

"Now that you mention it," Navarro said. "I could use some grub."

Flint dug into a trouser pocket and took out his pocket

watch. 12:30 p.m. "Perhaps we can pay a visit to the imperial kitchens."

"Oh, hell no," Fletcher said. "This is the capitol of the Empire! We can do better than the cafeteria!"

Flint raised an eyebrow. "Oh? I take it that you will be treating us to a fine dining experience?"

"I'm the poor repentant witch, remember? You're Mr. Money."

The Generals laughed. Hickock handed Flint a small leather pouch that jingled.

"My treat, for all that you and Ricardo did for us last month. Go on now, take 'em some place nice. Tell 'em I sent you, you'll get a table right quick," he said.

Flint nodded. "Er... thank you. Sir."

"Don't suppose we could go back to Ingalls and change?" Fletcher asked, looking down at her formal dress. "It's beautiful, but not really my style."

Flint sympathized. His steel chest plate and shoulder pauldron were heavy. He knew Navarro disliked his own dress uniform, but the look on his assistant's face said he'd rather eat first.

"We will have to don our formal wear again for our meeting with His Majesty. Let us find our lunch first. Then perhaps we can return to Ingalls for a change of garb before touring the city."

"Suits me," Navarro said.

Fletcher sighed. "Fine. I sure could go for a burger. Hope I don't get anything on this dress."

Flint snorted. "In one breath you yearn to experience

the finest cuisine that Salem has to offer, and in the next you ask for a common hamburger."

"Yeah, well... don't they have gourmet burgers somewhere, or something?"

Navarro laughed. "Now you're talking my language."

"Hmph."

9

Roger Klemm felt a tingle up his spine. That could only mean one thing: it was almost time for the kill. He didn't know if it was related to his talent for magic, or just the product of long experience in his bloody trade, but he always sensed when it was about to happen. The witch – Zelda, that kid had called her – must be on her way out of the palace. He had considered Cortez's words. If Flint was there, he might be able to score a head shot. But he hadn't survived this long by taking unnecessary risks. One shot, center mass? He could do that blindfolded. He'd take out Zelda, then find an opportunity to ice Flint. He snorted. Maybe at Zelda's funeral.

He brought his eye to the scope. Two royal guardsmen flanked the heavy palace gates. Foot traffic flowed in both directions on the sidewalk: bureaucrats, lawyers, beat cops, imperial soldiers, blue collar working stiffs, vagrants, men and women from all walks of life. It was ironic; even when he was mingling with the rabble in one of his magical disguises, he may as well have been as far away from them as he was now. He was, in fact, the middle child of his family, as Cortez had said. His parents loved him, but they simply didn't notice him as much as they did his older brother Sam or his baby sister Dana. No one noticed him when he wore his true face, and that's the way he liked it. It's what made him so good at infiltration and assassinations.

The tingling grew stronger, and Klemm slowed his breathing. He emptied his mind. The pedestrians slowed down in his mind's eye. The time grew near. Any minute now.

He frowned. There it was again: that bad feeling. He couldn't explain it. He'd never felt this way before, not even before his first contract kill. That had been the normal performance anxiety that everyone felt when beginning a new career. This time... Klemm had the peculiar feeling that this could be his last mission.

"It could be."

Klemm jumped, and then chided himself. Cortez. He had materialized out of thin air behind Klemm's right shoulder.

"Really not a good time, kid," Klemm said, keeping his eye on the scope.

"Of course. I understand. As I said earlier, I just came to watch a master at work. I can't help but think that you could be so much better. You could be the best that ever lived if you would only..."

"No means no. I don't know what you're offering. Don't care. Don't need it."

A chuckle. "Very well Roger. Oh, by the way, another question occurred to me since last we spoke. You're wearing the form of Miles Whitmore. You've camouflaged yourself up here so no one can see you. Your rifle though… does your camouflage spell hide the muzzle flash? Muffle the sound of the gunshot?"

Klemm sighed. "No."

"Seems like you're taking an unnecessary risk. I thought you avoided those?"

"It's not a risk if Whitmore takes the fall. It's his fingerprints that are going to be on this weapon once I ditch it."

"Ah, of course, of course. It seems you've thought of everything."

"Always do."

"I'm sure. Well, carry on then. I'll be quiet now."

About damn time, Klemm thought. He felt a shift in the air, and then it was gone. He sensed Cortez had vanished again. All the better. The tingling was reaching a crescendo. Almost there.

***

"Come on, hurry up!" Fletcher called over her shoulder. Navarro was keeping up without any problems. She had to admit, he cleaned up nicely. Those Supernumerary dress uniforms were sharp, even on Navarro's heavier set frame. Flint, on the other hand, was taking his sweet time. She knew that Silas was wearing heavy steel plate underneath that scarlet trimmed long coat, but time was a wasting, and she was eager to have lunch, get changed, and see as much of Salem as she could before tonight.

She could hear Flint mutter something under his breath, despite the tapping of his boots on the floor.

Fletcher smiled. She'd been a prostitute, a thief, a witch, and... what was she now? She was with the Templars, but she wasn't a sworn member of the Order. She doubted even they knew what her future with them entailed. In any case, she'd thought she'd met all the different kinds of men the world had to offer, but she'd never met a human being like Silas Flint before.

"How you holding up Zelda?" Navarro asked, falling in to step beside her.

"I'm starving, to be honest."

"No shit, me too. I meant with... you know, everything."

She thought a moment. "I don't know. Like happy and scared shitless at the same time."

"Why scared?"

She laughed. "Uh, because the Emperor himself wants to see us later?"

Navarro shook his head. "What you said earlier? I thought the same thing, if only mom could see me now."

"It's like, for the first time in my life, I actually feel kind of happy. I feel like I'm doing something good. I guess... well, I'm just afraid I'll screw it up somehow."

"Eh, I think everybody feels like that once in a while."

"Even Silas?"

Navarro looked over his shoulder. Flint was taking his time to scan portraits on the wall, peer inside open doors, nod to royal guardsmen he passed. He'd no doubt want to collect his weapons on his way out.

"Well... he's never said so, not to me anyway, but I'm sure he does too. Especially nowadays. Speaking of the boss..."

They walked a few more paces in silence. Navarro cocked his head. She raised an eyebrow.

"Speaking of the boss…?" Fletcher asked.

"Oh, come on," he laughed.

"I don't know what you're talking about."

"Of course you don't."

"What? I think of him as a good friend. He saved my ass from jail. And a giant tentacle monster. And a ghost witch. He's crazy brave, but he's a stubborn asshole, a stuck-up weirdo, he's…"

"Uh huh," Navarro said, grinning.

"Ugh, whatever," Fletcher said, picking up her pace. She hoped she wasn't blushing. At least they were near the end of the hallway. She could see the great double doors up ahead. Those would take them out into the front court-yard, and from there the gargantuan gates that would open onto the streets of Salem. She had been disappointed at first when Flint had forbidden any alcohol before their big meeting, but now she felt it was for the best. She didn't want to blurt out anything she shouldn't say in front of the Emperor… or in front of Silas.

The royal guardsmen flanking the entrance nodded to her as she passed them. *I can get used to this,* she thought. She wondered if her biological parents were still alive, and what they'd think if they knew their daughter was strutting around the imperial palace. *Without shackles even!*

She stepped out into the courtyard. It was brimming with soldiers, men in tailored suits, women in sensible dresses, all the human machinery necessary to keep an empire humming along. Her rehabilitation program officially forbade the use of magic. Silas was right earlier; it was addictive. Every time she used it, she felt giddy, eager to delve ever deeper, to see how great her power could grow. She'd almost lost control a few months ago during their expedition to that old American military base. And yet Flint, Navarro, even Abernathy had looked the other way when she used her magic against their common enemies. Maybe she could work something out with the Order: promise to only use magic against monsters, other witches, that sort of thing. Looking at all these bureaucrats and politicians scurrying around in the courtyard made her doubt that she'd ever be truly happy in some mundane office job. The Knights Templar of the Order of Saint Benedict though... it had only been a few months since she'd turned herself over to them, and she'd seen more adventure and excitement than she had in years. And she was doing good work to boot. Maybe she could bring it up with Flint and Navarro over lunch.

She looked over her shoulder. Flint had finished his rounds inside the palace and increased his pace to catch up with her. The corner of her mouth turned up. Silas Flint... out of all the Witch Hunters at Fort Marsing, General Abernathy had sent him to bail her out of the Jordan city jail. Navarro had picked up on it, damn him, but she wasn't quite sure about her feelings toward Silas. He was handsome, and they'd been through some harrowing experiences together, but if she was being honest with herself, he still intimidated her a bit. He'd told her several times over the last few months that if she went too far with her use of magic and lost her mind, he'd summarily execute her. She wasn't sure if he was joking or not; even Navarro was seldom sure if his boss was speaking in jest, and he'd been with him for five years. In any case, she decided not to test him on that point. *Shit,* she thought. *Am I here because I really want to change my ways? Or am I sticking around for him?*

"Are you in a hurry Miss Fletcher?" Flint asked.

"What? Oh... well, yeah, kind of. I need some food." She grinned at Navarro. "Food I say! My body cries out for sustenance," she said in her best imitation of the dour Witch Hunter.

"You've got a real talent for the High Speech, Zelda," Navarro said, laughing.

"If that will be all," Flint said, "A guardsman was gracious enough to recommend a nearby restaurant that serves what you two are looking for."

"What about you boss? What you in the mood for?" Navarro asked.

"You gonna condescend to eat poor people chow like the rest of us?" Fletcher asked with a smile.

Flint raised an eyebrow. "Miss Fletcher, Mr. Navarro and I often subsist on Templar field rations: jerky, hard bread, and water. Believe or not as you wish, but I am not above partaking in a well made hamburger."

"Really? Would you share a beer with us too? Uh, not right now of course, but..."

"Beer is never my first choice, but if it is offered by my host, I would not decline."

"Damn Zelda, you might get him to loosen up some day after all," Navarro said.

She took a deep breath. "Hey, Silas…"

"Yes?"

"You going to let me walk unescorted?"

Flint rolled his eyes and extended his arm. Fletcher looped her arm around his. *Yeah,* she thought, *Yeah, this feels right.*

***

There. Emerging from the gate was Zelda Fletcher, Silas Flint, and Ricardo Navarro. Fletcher was in a light blue, ankle length dress, her black hair hanging loosely about her shoulders. It really was too bad she had to die, Klemm thought. But he'd accepted the contract and die she would. She was walking arm in arm with Flint, still in his Templar dress uniform, heavy steel armor on his torso and a pauldron on his right shoulder, his long black coat trimmed with scarlet, a silver buckle on his black hat. Navarro was behind them on Flint's right.

He slowed his breathing. Breathe in. Breathe out. Klemm assumed that Fletcher knew some basic healing spells. If she could maintain her focus, she could recover in seconds from anything less than a head shot, or a shot through her heart. One shot, one kill. It wasn't just the sniper's motto this time. Now Klemm felt as though his life depended on it.

Take her out, then change shapes to get close to Flint to take him out as well. Easy payday. Nothing could go wrong. Breathe in, breathe out. Almost there. Fletcher's torso was centered in the crosshairs. Breathe in.

Bang, you're dead.

He breathed out and pulled the trigger.

***

"We must proceed north along Flagg Boulevard," Flint said.

Fletcher looked up at him. "Uh…"

"We will make a right turn at the palace gates."

"Well why didn't you say that to begin with?"

He sighed. Fletcher smirked. If there was one thing she was certain about, it was that teasing him was a lot of fun. Over the last few months, she'd learned that Templars were trained in the High Speech, which, as far as she could tell, meant using four words whenever one would do. Most of the Templars spoke like normal people when they weren't on the job, but she had never heard Flint speak in the common tongue. Navarro had told her that Flint slipped occasionally when he was under great duress, but he'd kept his cool in Jordan and out at Mountain Home Air Force Base. That was one of the reasons she found him so compelling. She had magic powers, and she'd been scared shitless when facing the demon Ichthil and the undead witch Nevaeh Carey. All Flint had was his sword, his pistols, and one hell of a powerful religious faith.

Zelda.

What the fuck?! She knew that voice. Francisco. He'd been possessed by Ichthil in their hometown of New Rome and leveled the place before she had put him down with the help of the Templars. His demonic form had been blown to bits by Templar grenades. She remembered his voice whispering in her mind that death was only the beginning... was this real? Did she hear him just now?

Yes, you did Zelda. I told you, didn't I?

She saw something in her peripheral vision. It couldn't be. That slicked black hair. That wicked grin. She turned just as there was a crack in the distance. Then all she could feel was fire.

***

"Zelda!" Flint cried. He'd seen a muzzle flash and heard a gunshot. A second later, Fletcher collapsed in his arms, her dress a bloody ruin, her breathing a ragged wheeze. All around him, civilians screamed and either dove to the ground or ran for cover. Police officers drew their pistols, imperial soldiers raised their rifles. Navarro came to Flint's side, his face white, and together they lowered Fletcher to the ground.

"The muzzle flash came from that building!" Flint bellowed, pointing at the skyscraper. "Lock it down! You there, guardsmen! Secure the palace! Protect the Emperor!"

***

"Son of a *bitch!*" Klemm snarled. He had her, goddamn it, he *had* her! The perfect kill shot, and she turned. She *turned!* He threw down his rifle in disgust. He'd missed her heart. There was a chance she'd bleed out before she could heal herself, but something told him that wasn't going to happen. It was perfect. Everything was going perfectly, and then she turned. Why? How?

He peeked over the edge of the roof. Police officers and imperial soldiers were making a beeline toward the building. Someone had seen the muzzle flash, but he was confident he was still hidden by his camouflage spell. He ground his teeth. Time to get out of here.

"I thought you never missed?"

Electricity crackled on Klemm's fingertips. On top of everything else, the little shit was back, materializing behind him. "Fuck off," Klemm growled.

Cortez smiled. "Don't get mad at me. You're the professional. Although, to be fair, I did visit my dear Zelda a second ago."

Klemm's eyes widened. He slowly turned to face Cortez, his mouth hanging open. "You what?"

The younger man laughed. "I couldn't let her die without saying goodbye first, could I?"

Klemm advanced on Cortez, drawing his pistol from his waistband. "You spoiled my shot... you miserable, goddamned, piece of..."

Cortez held up a hand, and Klemm bumped into an invisible wall. He backed up, fired his pistol, the bullets disintegrating before they could reach Cortez.

"Why?!" Klemm screamed. "Tell me why, you bastard!"

"Because we need each other Roger," Cortez answered. "You need to kill Silas Flint and Zelda Fletcher. I have a burning desire for revenge, far more important than your need for filthy lucre."

"What do you need me for?" Klemm asked. "If you're so powerful, why haven't you taken them out yourself?"

"Because there are rules," Cortez said, frowning. "I'm bound by them, but the living are not."

"What could... oh. Now I get it." Klemm laughed, despite the circumstances. "You're not a ghost. You're a demon."

"Guilty as charged," Cortez said. "I am one with Ichthil. And we need a willing host in this world to come into the fullness of our power."

"And what? You think I'd let you take me, after you fucked up my shot? You hit your head on the way down into Hell?" He turned his back on Cortez. "I wasn't interested before, and I'm even less interested now. I'll find another way to finish the job." He advanced toward the edge of the rooftop. Magical energy washed over him, and he felt his body shrink and contort, his face elongate, feathers sprouting all over him. Where once Roger Klemm had stood, there was now a bald eagle. With a screech, Klemm took flight, his eagle eyes giving him a much sharper view than his human eyes ever could. He didn't enjoy taking nonhuman forms, but when all else failed, it always made for the perfect escape plan.

Roger glided through the air, rising higher on the current. This was a setback, but the mission wasn't over. Even if Fletcher healed herself, there would be another...

He crashed into another invisible wall. He screamed in pain, the sound emerging from his beak as an eagle's cry.

I'm afraid I can't let you leave Roger.

Cortez. Somehow the rat bastard had created a magical

barrier around the building. Demonic laughter echoed in Klemm's mind.

That's right Roger. Ordinary humans can pass through it. Those of you with the talent cannot. But look on the bright side. If you can't get out, Zelda can't come in.

What do you want?!

I want you to let me in Roger. You're going to have to if you hope to get out of this alive. Now I suggest you get back to the rooftop. People are going to notice a bald eagle flying around in circles.

With a snarl, Klemm circled around and alighted upon the rooftop, shifting back into his human form. Cortez stood there, hands behind his back, a crooked smile on his face. Klemm advanced on him, and the young man made no move to stand aside or back way. Klemm leaned in until they were nose to nose.

"I don't need you," Klemm said, biting off each word. "Flint and his little sidekick will come in here. I'll kill them both. Then I will walk out of here and find a way to kill your little Zelda."

Cortez smiled. "We'll see, Roger. We'll see."

10

Flint cradled Fletcher in his arms. Her face had gone a paler shade of white. Her teeth were stained red with blood. Navarro got down on his knees, tore open his uniform tunic, ripped off a piece of the white t-shirt underneath. He pressed it into the bullet hole in in Fletcher's side. Her eyelids drooped.

"Come on Zelda... stay awake! Stay with us!" Navarro cried. Looking up at the crowd that was gathering around them, he shouted, "One of you get a doctor! Now!"

Flint jostled her and her eyes shot open.

"God... damn..." she grunted.

"Miss Fletcher... Zelda..." Flint said. "Can you heal yourself?"

She gritted her teeth and hissed.

"It's going to be alright, Zelda," Flint said.

She looked at him with her mouth agape. "You... you said..."

"Miss Fletcher. I am afraid that I cannot allow you to die. You have my permission to use one of your healing spells."

Her face relaxed and she gave a chuckle. "I heard you... Silas... you... talked... like a... normal guy."

"If you are unable to heal yourself, then we have no choice but to await a doctor."

"Fuck... that..."

Flint could feel warmth spreading through his hands, through the heavy leather gauntlets of his dress uniform. Fletcher's eyes rolled back in her head. Navarro removed the strip of fabric he'd used to staunch the blood. Flint saw a soft light come through the bullet hole in her side. She ground her teeth and moaned in pain. The flesh around her wound rippled and churned. The slug emerged from her body, flattened by the impact, and clinked as it hit the pavement. The wound sealed itself shut. Fletcher opened her eyes. She was streaming with sweat and began panting, as though she had just run a marathon.

"That... was a close one," she said, sounding exhausted. She looked up into Flint's icy blue eyes, seemed to notice for the first time that she was in his arms, her head held up off the pavement. She held his gaze for a moment before looking away. Flint wasn't sure if the redness in her cheeks meant she was blushing or if it was a result of her exertion. He cleared his throat and let her go, rising to his feet. He extended a hand. She took it and he pulled her up off the ground.

"I trust that you are none the worse for wear," he said.

"Yeah, yeah, I'm fine now," Fletcher replied. She lifted her arm, saw the hole in her dress. "Oh... sorry Silas."

"Think nothing of it," Flint said. All was silent around him. He saw that the crowd of civilians, police officers, and imperial soldiers that had gathered round them were all staring, mouths agape. Navarro cleared his throat.

"She's on our side," he said.

They all began chattering at once.

"She's a witch!"

"She's with them?!"

"Unnatural, you ask me..."

"Does the Emperor know?"

"Wait until I..."

"Hear me!" Flint barked, and everyone fell silent. "Miss Fletcher is a ward of the Knights Templar of the Order of Saint Benedict. She has proven an invaluable ally in our conflict with the forces of darkness. You will not touch her, or you will answer to the Order, and to me."

The crowd was silent, but Flint saw a few nodding

heads. He drew his sword from his hip and pointed it at the skyscraper where he had seen the muzzle flash.

"The gunshot came from yonder building. There is an assassin in our midst! We must bring the vile criminal to ground! Come, follow me!" With that, he strode forth, sword at his side, not bothering to see if anyone followed. A few moments later, he heard footsteps hurrying after him. Navarro and Fletcher came to his side.

"How many are joining us?" Flint asked.

"About a dozen cops, maybe a platoon of royal guardsmen," Navarro answered.

"I suggest you return to the palace and acquire your weapons, Mr. Navarro. I suspect we will need them."

"On it boss." He turned on his heel and sprinted back the way they had come.

"Miss Fletcher," Flint said, "You have just been shot. It is not necessary that you..."

"Don't even start," she interrupted. "No way I'm letting some asshole get away with shooting me. Not without getting some payback."

"I sympathize. However, do not take this as an opportunity to freely exercise your powers. I would prefer to capture our would-be assassin alive. It is unlikely that he is working alone. I will make him confess the architect of this vile scheme."

They pressed on in silence. Navarro jogged to catch up, his bold action rifle slung across his back, tomahawk and pistol on his belt. Flint looked over his shoulder. As his assistant had said earlier, he saw uniformed police officers and imperial soldiers, along with a few civilians carrying revolvers. Sirens wailed in the distance. Tires screeched and he saw armored troop carriers stop outside the gates of the imperial palace, disgorging more soldiers, armed with automatic rifles (*modeled on old world AK-47s, he thought*) who took up positions covering every avenue of approach.

"These guys don't fuck around, eh boss?" Navarro asked.

"No, Mr. Navarro, they certainly do not."

Fletcher rolled her eyes. "Would it kill you to talk like a normal person? I know you can do it."

"I am sure I do not know what you are talking about."

She laughed. "Don't play dumb with me, when you thought I was dying you... oof!" She reared back, rubbing her nose.

"What's wrong?" Navarro asked. "You okay?"

"Yeah," she replied. "Felt like I ran into a wall or something."

Flint stopped. He looked to Fletcher. He looked to his front. They were one block away from the office building where he'd seen the muzzle flash. The impromptu posse of police officers and soldiers stopped as well.

"What's up?" a cop called out.

"All of you, please proceed. Post guards outside the doors. Our shooter is inside. Do not allow anyone to leave until you have fully canvassed the building," Flint said. "Move!"

The cops and soldiers filed past him. Templars had no legal authority to command the civil police or the Imperial Army but they generally deferred to the Witch

Hunters nonetheless. There was no evidence to suggest that they were dealing with a supernatural threat yet. Flint's instincts told him that sorcery was afoot, and he believed the others could sense it too. He backtracked to where Fletcher and Navarro waited.

"Miss Fletcher," Flint said. "Lead the way, if you please."

"Me? Well, alright." She started walking. "If you say so, I'm happy to be the one in charge for on... ah! Damn it!" She backed away again. Flint saw it this time: a strange ripple in the air, like she had thrown a stone into a pond. "The fuck?!" A trickle of blood ran out of her nose, which she wiped off with her arm. The corner of Flint's mouth turned up in the beginning of a smile.

"Mr. Navarro," he said, waving his assistant forward.

Navarro's eyes shifted left, right, up, down. Flint could hear his sharp intake of breath as he strode forward. His assistant looked like he expected to hit a brick wall, but he passed the spot where Fletcher had stopped without incident.

"The hell is this?" he muttered.

Flint joined Navarro. "Miss Fletcher," he called. "You have my permission to cast a spell. Please send a ball of fire, a bolt of lightning, any magical projection you can muster in our direction."

"Say what now?" she asked.

"Humor me."

Shrugging, Fletcher held out her hand, palm up. Arcs of electricity danced over her arm, her wrist, her fingertips. She clenched a fist, building up energy. She wound up as though pitching a baseball, and a bolt of lightning leaped from the palm of her hand, arcing up, over her companions' heads. Before it could pass over Flint and Navarro, it was stopped by an invisible force. The lightning dissipated in midair.

"O...kay," Fletcher said. "I haven't seen that one before."

"No witches allowed, I guess," Navarro said.

"So it would seem. Our assassin apparently does not wish to see Miss Fletcher in person."

"Guys... there's something you need to know," Fletcher said. "Earlier, when I got shot? Just before it happened, I felt a presence: Francisco. I thought I saw him too."

"Francisco, as in your old boyfriend, the googly eyed tentacle monster we blew up?" Navarro asked.

"To be fair, he only became a googly eyed tentacle monster after we broke up."

"Cortez," Flint growled. "Even in death he seeks to work his devilry."

"Well, I'm not sure about that," Fletcher said. "It didn't feel like he was there to kill me."

"Yeah," Navarro said. "The way the bullet went in... if you hadn't turned just then, I think it would have gone right through your heart. Lights out. Was he there to save you or something?"

"I didn't get that feeling either. And why would he want to save me? I'm the one who got him killed."

"In any case," Flint said, "It would appear that you can go no further for now. Return to the palace and inform the Generals of what has transpired. Mr. Navarro and I shall hunt down this assassin and bring him to justice. If Mr. Cortez has returned from the grave, then we shall put him back in the ground where he belongs. Come along Mr. Navarro."

"Be careful!" Fletcher called after them.

They proceeded to the entrance of the office building. The plaque on the wall beside the front door named it the Mansfield Building, established 2409. Another plaque listed the current occupants of the building: research, marketing, and law firms whose names meant nothing to Flint. The door was flanked by two uniformed police officers.

"Captain Flint!" one of them said, extending a hand.

"Do I know you sir?" Flint asked, giving him a firm handshake.

"We've never met, but we know what you and Mr. Navarro did last month."

Flint nodded. "What is the situation?"

The other officer replied, "Got a few hundred very scared suits in there. The others are canvassing the place right now."

"Very good." Flint and Navarro went through the revolving door and entered the lobby. It was dominated by a marble fountain in the shape of an angel, the water pouring from a bowl it held above its head.

"Nice," Navarro said. "Like something out of Revelation, pouring forth God's wrath."

Flint looked to his partner and raised an eyebrow.

"Or, you know, something like that," his assistant muttered.

"Mr. Navarro, I could not have put it better myself. Let us see what Salem's finest have managed to find."

11

Roger Klemm, wearing his true form, rushed down the stairwell toward the ground floor alongside dozens of other lawyers, bureaucrats, and assorted businesspeople, the unlucky ones who couldn't fit onto an elevator. The air was rank with fear and sweat. He would have laughed aloud if he were alone; he was just as frightened as everyone else, but for a different reason. That damn Cortez had locked him in. These normals would all eventually be cleared by the cops and be free to go. But Klemm was stuck here as long as the kid, demon, whatever the hell he was decided to maintain that magical barrier.

He saw two cops on a landing below, attempting to direct traffic. He chided himself for losing his cool. Miles Whitmore, the real one, was probably still in the building. His fingerprints were on the rifle. He just had to give the cops their killer. He reached the landing, approached one of the cops.

"Excuse me," he said.

"Please proceed to the lobby sir, we'll get to you as soon as possible, get everyone home," the cop replied, distracted by the flow of humanity.

"Officer, I work on the top floor," Klemm said. "I saw a lawyer, Miles Whitmore, on his way up with a briefcase. A few minutes after I saw him pass by, I heard the gunshot. You should send someone up to the roof or search his office. I bet you'd find a rifle."

The cop faced him. He looked Klemm up and down.

He nodded. "Thank you for the tip. Please proceed to the lobby."

Klemm went on his way, smiling when he was far enough away from the cop. That was one problem taken care of. They'd find the rifle where he left it, Whitmore's fingerprints all over it. The lawyer would take the fall, and he'd be cleared. Now he only had to worry about the Witch Hunter. That son of a bitch Cortez no doubt sealed the building because Flint would be on his way here.

Does that upset you, Roger? I thought it was your job to kill Silas.

Klemm frowned. *It is,* he thought. *But it's my job to do. I don't need your help, and I sure as hell don't need you locking me in here.* He continued making his way down the stairwell alongside everyone else who worked in the building.

Think of it as an incentive, Cortez's voice echoed in his mind. *If you can kill Silas Flint here, now, then I'll remove the barrier and you'll be free to go. I don't think you can do it though. Not without my help.*

Let's just agree to disagree.

What would be the point of possession anyway? Klemm never drew on enough magical power at one time to cause any permanent damage. Changing his form made him momentarily dizzy. His hands burned a bit after conjuring lightning or fire. Nothing he couldn't handle.

We could do so much more than that Roger, Cortez whispered. *We can bear the physical cost of casting magic, yes. But with your talent? We could help you take on new forms, the forms of beings that are not of this world. Why restrict yourself to taking on the forms of other humans, or ordinary beasts?*

"It's kept me alive so far," Klemm muttered aloud.

"What's that?" asked a man who was a few steps ahead of him on the stairwell. "You say something?"

"Just talking to myself," Klemm said, smiling. "Hell of a day, huh?"

"I'll say," the other man said. "The Night of Chaos last month, wizards forming their own nations, now a sniper takes a shot at the imperial palace? Feels like the end of the world."

"I hope not."

"Yeah, same here. I'm Mike, by the way. Mike Gresham."

"Roger Klemm."

Gresham snapped his fingers. "Now I remember you!"

Klemm held his gaze. "You do?"

"Yeah, you came in this morning for a job interview, right?"

Klemm's shoulders relaxed a bit. "Oh, yeah, that was me."

"Well, trust me, this is definitely not a normal day for us."

"Yeah. It's not a normal day for me either."

They proceeded in silence for another few floors. On the fourth floor landing, two imperial soldiers stood guard, directing traffic out of the stairwell and into the fourth floor offices.

"Is there a problem sir?" Klemm asked one of them.

"Lobby and lower floors are getting a little crowded," the soldier replied. "Find a place to hunker down in one of those offices. God willing, we'll find the son of a bitch soon and get all of you out of here." He waved Klemm and

Gresham through. They entered a hallway that appeared like every other hallway in the building, lined with doors that led to offices, law firms, and who knows what else. Men and women loitered in the halls, whispering about the day's events, gossiping about who the assassin might be, who was up for promotion, who was dating who... Klemm shook his head. He knew at an early age that he wasn't cut out for some humdrum office job like his parents had tried to push on him.

Pathetic, aren't they? Cortez said. *So many souls that are born, live, and die in the same city, never realizing their true potential.*

Klemm sighed. *Let me guess, I'm one of them, right? Not living up to my true potential.*

A laugh. *You said it, not me.*

He weaved his way through the crowded hallway, looking for an empty office, bathroom, closet, anything. He had an idea, but he'd need a place to change first. There. Ahead on his left was a door. The plaque on the wall beside it read FRANKLIN BAILEY, ATTORNEY AT LAW. He opened the door and stepped inside. In the center of the room was a desk, occupied by an older man with iron grey hair. The office was lined with bookshelves and filing cabinets. The old man, presumably Bailey, looked up from the papers he was reading.

"Can I help you?" he asked.

"Yes," Klemm said, advancing toward Bailey. "You look like you could use a good nap."

"What on earth are you..."

Klemm pointed at him and whispered a spell. Before

Bailey could finish his question, his eyes drooped. He yawned, rested his head on his desk, and was soon snoring. Smiling, Klemm approached the old man and plucked a hair from his immaculate coif. He rubbed it between his thumb and index finger, getting a feel for Bailey.

Ah... I think I see what you're doing, Cortez whispered. *Don't you think a young woman would be better though?*

No.

Why not?

I don't like taking women's forms, Klemm replied. Some shapeshifters went mad that way, the sick perverts. He closed his eyes, let the magic wash over him, wrinkling his skin, his brown hair shifting to grey. The spell changed his body. His clothes would require a little illusion magic, but that was no great trick. He and Bailey were of similar build. A simple palette swap on his suit... done. He was now an exact duplicate of Franklin Bailey, attorney at law. He left the office, the real Bailey still snoozing away on his desk. In the hallway, he kept his back to the door, whispered another spell, and it locked behind him. Bailey would be out for hours, and who would think to check on him when he was out here for all to see? He went back down the hall the way he had come.

"Hey Frank," said a young woman in a tailored pantsuit, leaning on the wall beneath portraits of long dead former occupants of the offices. "How you holding up?"

"Just trying to stay busy," Klemm replied. "I'm going a little stir crazy to be honest. How much longer will they be down there?"

The woman blinked. "What's got into you?"

"What do you mean?" Shit. Was he overplaying the part? Did he get Bailey's personality wrong?

"You've only been in your office a few minutes. You just said ten minutes ago that we have to be patient and wait for the cops to sort it out."

"Ah... yes, well, I'm not getting any younger. Time stands still for no one, and we have important work to do for our clients."

She smirked. "You do probate. I don't think anyone's in a hurry."

"My client is waiting on a big inheritance!" Klemm called over his shoulder as he moved on. Even though interacting with people in someone else's form could be dangerous, he had to admit that he enjoyed the bewildered looks on their faces when someone they knew had a sudden personality change. The woman had implied that Bailey was a more patient type. Wouldn't he be surprised when he woke up to questions about his transformation into a hard charging go getter?

Klemm exited the hallway onto the stairwell landing. He approached the soldier that he'd spoken to earlier, tapped him on the shoulder.

"Yes sir?" the soldier asked.

"Young man, I need to speak to the Witch Hunter right away," Klemm said.

The soldier started to say something, stopped. "Sir... how did you know that there's a Templar downstairs?"

"The rumor mill never stops... Corporal," he said, glancing at the chevrons on his sleeve. "I have reason to believe there is sorcery at work here."

"Sorcery...?"

"Yes. And if there's a magician around, he needs to know right away."

The soldier thought for a moment. Finally, he nodded and said, "Follow me sir."

The Corporal led Klemm down the stairs toward the lobby, passed by several uniformed police officers and plain clothes crime scene analysts, no doubt on their way to the roof. Klemm smiled. If nothing else, it would buy him time once they collared the real Whitmore. Time enough to shank Flint. Once that was taken care of, he could finish off Fletcher, collect his fee, and take a nice long vacation. This mission was proving to be a bigger challenge than he'd expected. Maybe he'd head south when it was over. There were rumors that the casinos of old Las Vegas were still operational, and he'd have money to burn.

12

Silas Flint stared at the crowded lobby, his arms crossed. The myriad lawyers, bureaucrats, and other workers who made their living in the Mansfield Building milled about, the murmur of hundreds of conversations filling the room. Navarro approached and joined him at his side.

"What do we know, Mr. Navarro?" Flint asked.

"Not much," his assistant replied. "Cops say this is the happening place to be for all the young strivers looking to make their career. They all want to become a partner at one of these fancy law firms, or they use a job here as an in for a cushy gig with the imperial bureaucracy. Which means there's a lot of traffic through here every day, lots of strangers looking for a job."

Flint sighed. "So no one noticed anyone or anything particularly suspicious."

"Nope. Our shooter is just another guy with a briefcase, just another fish in the sea."

A police officer made his way through the crowd toward the Witch Hunter, a miniature radio on his shoulder. Arriving, he tipped his hat. Flint nodded in acknowledgement.

"How can I assist, Officer?" he asked.

"We might have something, Captain. We got a tip from somebody up near the top floor. Says he saw a guy who works here, Miles Whitmore, headed up to the roof with a briefcase. Heard the gunshot a few minutes later."

Flint and Navarro looked each other.

"You got him?" Navarro asked.

The cop nodded. "We found Whitmore near the top floor, and he's being questioned now. We sent some CSI's up there and..." The radio on his shoulder buzzed. "Excuse me." He turned his back to take the call.

"Can't be this easy," Navarro said.

"I concur," Flint replied. "It is unlikely the assassin would be someone who is well known among the community."

"So what would this guy Whitmore be doing, going up on the roof? And if he wasn't the shooter, why would that witness lie about it?"

"We have too many questions and not enough answers."

"I think we got at least one answer," the cop said. "Just heard from the guys up on the roof. We got a rifle. And they've found some prints on it. We're going to check them against Whitmore's now. If they're a match, we got our guy."

"Officer," Flint said. "Are you at liberty to share what your compatriots have learned from Mr. Whitmore's interrogation?"

The cop's brow furrowed. "Uh..."

"Can you tell us what your buddies have learned from the suit?" Navarro asked.

"Oh, yeah, for you guys, definitely."

"I suggest that you question his coworkers as well. I suspect that Mr. Whitmore will be able to account for his whereabouts at the time of the shooting. I believe his coworkers will confirm his story."

The cop raised an eyebrow. "You think our witness got it wrong?"

"Perhaps."

The cop turned his back to speak on the radio again.

"What are you thinking sir?" Navarro asked.

"It is only a theory thus far. I will need more evidence before I can be..."

"Excuse me, Captain?"

Flint looked up. A young soldier stood before him, alongside an older man in a grey suit, his iron grey hair immaculately coifed. "Yes, Corporal, what is it?"

"This is Mr. Franklin Bailey, a lawyer who works on the fourth floor. He said he had some information for you."

"Thank you, Corporal." The soldier nodded and excused himself.

"What do you got for us sir?" Navarro asked.

"Thank God you're here Captain," Bailey said, extending his hand. Flint shook it. "I have reason to believe there's a magician in the building."

"Oh?" Flint asked. "Have you seen or heard anything out of the ordinary?"

"Oh yes sir. I work in probate up on the fourth floor, but my son in law works up near the top floor, criminal law. Anyway, he told me that he heard strange chanting coming from one of the offices. Latin and such. He opened the door and saw a pentagram on the floor! Painted in blood!"

"Did he now?"

"Oh yes sir. I can show you."

Flint pursed his lips, glanced at Navarro. "I see. Well, I should say that this demands further investigation. Come, Mr. Navarro."

Bailey's face twisted into an expression Flint couldn't quite read. Frustration? It was gone as soon as it appeared. "Yes, yes, we should go."

"Lead the way, if you please."

Flint waited for Bailey to advance a few steps before he followed. Navarro was close at his side when he whispered to him, "Something wrong sir?"

"This is all too tidy," Flint whispered back. "Consider: a witness claims to have seen Miles Whitmore, a well-known figure within this establishment, ascending to the rooftop. Second, the police find the assassin's weapon, almost as if it were left there purposely. Third, Mr. Bailey claims to have heard a secondhand account of witchcraft taking place within the same building where our assassin just made an attempt on Miss Fletcher's life."

"You think someone's trying to frame Whitmore?"

"Presently, I have only my instincts to confirm it."

"Well, they've never steered us wrong before."

"There is something else," Flint said. "At the reception last night... Miss Fletcher felt that there was something off about one of the Supernumeraries."

"'Off?'"

"She said that his thoughts did not seem like his own."

Navarro was silent for a few moments. Flint saw now that Bailey was leading them toward an elevator. The police officers and soldiers in the lobby shooed the crowd away, clearing a path for the three men.

"I can think of a few reasons why she'd get that feeling from someone," Navarro said. "None of them good."

"Indeed."

Bailey pushed the UP button next to the elevator door. Flint studied Bailey more closely. No visible tattoos, no scars... he looked like a well to do upper middle-class lawyer. There was no reason to suspect him of anything untoward. But there was something off about him somehow. Flint's Templar sword, blessed by the Holy Father himself, always glowed in the presence of magic. The invisible barrier surrounding the Mansfield Building triggered its usual reaction which made him fear that it would be less reliable inside. If there was a magician present, he may have no way of knowing it until it was too late.

The elevator dinged and the doors slid open. Bailey stepped inside. After a moment's hesitation, Flint and Navarro followed him. Bailey pressed the button for the thirty-eighth floor. The three men faced the door as it slowly closed. Flint heard a clank followed by a soft hum as the elevator began its ascent.

Navarro nudged him with his elbow. Glancing at his assistant from the corner of his eye, Flint saw him nod his head toward Bailey's right hip. He squinted. It was faint, but he saw the outline of a pistol tucked into the older man's waistband, printed by his suit jacket. He furrowed his brow. There were no laws against civilians concealing firearms on their person, but it was odd that a probate lawyer of his age would feel the need to bring one to work.

"Mr. Bailey," Flint said.

"Yes?"

"Do you usually bring a pistol to your office?"

"What?" He glanced down at his right hip. "Oh, this... well, you know, after the, ah, Night of Chaos last month, one can never be too careful."

"What model is that?" Navarro asked.

Bailey hesitated a second before answering, "It's a Petersen 9."

"No shit? You were in the Army?"

"Yes... yes, I was," Bailey said.

"What was your specialty?" Navarro asked.

Another hesitation. "Artillery." A chuckle. "I always did like the big guns. Kind of messed up my hearing though."

Flint kept his face neutral while his mind raced. The Petersen 9 was the standard issue sidearm of the Imperial

Army. It was unusual but not unheard of for officers being allowed to keep their pistols after putting in at least twenty years of service. But something didn't seem right. He had met many imperial soldiers throughout his career. Bailey did not have any of the telltale signs of twenty years or more in the Army, especially if he'd served in the field artillery. He claimed that his service had diminished his hearing, but so far he hadn't displayed any signs of hearing loss. "Indeed?" Flint asked. "My father served with the 109th Artillery Regiment in his youth."

"Oh yes!" Bailey said. "The 109th. Outstanding unit. I didn't serve with them, but they had a reputation in my day. They loved to blow things up, even by Army standards."

"There is no such regiment."

Bailey chuckled. "What are you talking about? Of course there..."

"No. There isn't," Navarro said.

Flint's hand moved toward the pistol holstered on his right hip. Out of the corner of his eye, he saw Navarro's fingers inch toward his own sidearm. Then something happened which he had never expected. Bailey's face twisted into an angry snarl. His limbs bulged in his clothes, tearing the suit, black fur sprouting everywhere. His eyes turned yellow. His incisors lengthened into fangs. Where once there had stood an aging city lawyer, there was now a hulking gorilla. The beast roared, spraying the elevator with spittle.

"Kill this abomination!" Flint bellowed.

13

Flint drew his pistol, but before he could aim, the gorilla punched him in the sternum. The heavy steel breastplate of Flint's dress uniform absorbed much of the impact, but he was slammed against the elevator wall, dropping the gun. Navarro cleared his holster and fired. The gorilla howled in pain as the bullet tore into its back, but it swung its fist around. Navarro ducked, the blow smashing into the elevator doors, leaving a massive dent. His ears ringing, Flint drew his sword. He realized he would need to adjust his technique in the tight quarters of the elevator. The gorilla hopped in place and beat its fists on the elevator floor, causing it to shake. Navarro stumbled and the beast sprang, ramming its shoulder into his stomach. They crashed against the wall, and Flint heard his assistant wheeze as the wind was knocked from him.

"Ricardo!" Flint cried. He rushed forward, sword aimed at the beast's heart. Before the blade could find its mark, it arched its back until it made a handstand. It used one of its feet to slap the sword aside, the other to crack Flint across the jaw. He grunted, spun with the impact. Navarro had slumped to the floor but he retained his grip on his pistol. He fired again, and Flint's eardrums screamed. He tasted blood in his mouth. With a snarl, the gorilla advanced on him. The angle was wrong to bring his sword around, so Flint rammed the pommel into the monster's nose. Blood gushed forth, staining Flint's leather gauntlets. The gorilla grunted and shook its head.

Navarro jumped onto its back, pistol and tomahawk in

his hands, and wrapped his arms around its throat. The monster roared and whipped its body back and forth to shake him off.

"Now boss!" Navarro shouted.

Flint readied his sword. His ears were ringing, his head ached, his ribs cried out in pain. He had to go for its heart, while taking care not to ram the blade all the way through and into Navarro. Normally Supernumeraries wore leather body armor in the field, but his assistant's dress uniform was just a simple tunic.

"Your judgment is at hand, monster!" Flint snarled.

Just as he prepared to lunge, the gorilla reached up and over its head, grabbing hold of Navarro's collar. It flung him off its body, and Navarro crashed into Flint, both men collapsing to the floor. Flint lost his grip on his sword.

The gorilla roared in triumph and raised both fists above its head, preparing to deliver the deathblows. Flint drew his secondary pistol from the holster on his left hip. He fired in the gorilla's direction, the bullets making a slapping noise against the monster's chest. Navarro rolled over, grabbed his own pistol, and joined Flint, the two men emptying their magazines into the beast. It howled in pain and stumbled backward.

Flint growled and climbed to his feet. The weight of his steel armor was taking its toll. Navarro handed Flint his sword, which was shining bright in the presence of the shapeshifter's dark magic. Flint spat a mouthful of blood onto the floor. Before he could ready his sword to deliver a killing blow, the gorilla leapt, punching through a panel on the ceiling, and out of the elevator car, its pained cries echoing in the darkness.

Flint leaned against the elevator wall, breathing hard. He sheathed his sword and holstered his pistols. With a grunt, Navarro climbed to his feet and recovered his weapons.

"Jesus Christ…" he said. Flint gave him a sharp look despite the pain. "Oh, uh, sorry sir. But that was… that guy is…" He stopped, took several deep breaths.

"Yes…" Flint said. "Mr. Bailey… or whoever he is… he is… a shapeshifter."

"So that means… he could be anyone… or anything… God damn, that hurts," Navarro said, rubbing his back. His bolt action rifle was still slung across his back; Flint expected it had rammed into his assistant's spine during the battle.

"I am loathe to admit it, but I would not be averse to receiving one of Miss Fletcher's healing spells at the moment," Flint said.

The elevator shook. They heard a screeching sound as it shuddered to a halt. They glanced up, down, toward the elevator door.

"End of the line?" Navarro asked.

"If that were the case, then the doors should have opened…"

A loud bang. The floor shook beneath them.

"Open the doors! Quickly!" Flint cried. Together, they rushed to the elevator doors. Flint took one, Navarro the other, and together they pried them open. The elevator hadn't quite reached the next floor, but there was just enough room for them to crawl up and out.

The elevator shook again. Navarro made a stirrup with his hands. Flint put one boot down and his assistant gave him a boost. Flint pulled himself through the opening and onto the carpeted floor of a hallway. He rolled over and lowered his hand. Navarro gripped it, Flint dug in his toes into the floor, and gave a yank, pulling Navarro through just as the elevator cable snapped. They heard screeching metal as the car plunged down, down through the shaft, before crashing onto the ground floor.

The two men rolled onto their backs, breathing hard. After a few moments, Flint sat up, stifling a groan. He ached all over, but duty called. Navarro sat up with a grunt.

"I fucking hate shapeshifters," he said.

"I share your feelings Mr. Navarro," Flint replied. They helped each other to their feet. Navarro unslung his rifle, holding it at the low ready.

"Hey boss," he said. "You bring any extra ammo with you?"

"I am afraid not. I confess that it did not occur to me that we would need any today."

"Yeah, same here. My gun's empty, but I still got five shots in the rifle."

Flint pursed his lips. Templar pistols were all loaded with silver tipped bullets, designed specifically for supernatural threats. They could no doubt borrow more ammunition from the police or the soldiers, but their ordinary bullets may not prove as effective against the shapeshifting magician. On the other hand...

"We may have an advantage," he said. "The magical barrier which surrounds this building prevented Miss Fletcher's passage. If she cannot come in..."

"Maybe this asshole can't get out," Navarro finished. "But if he can't get out, then wouldn't that mean someone besides him put up the barrier?"

"Yes. Most curious."

"Even if he can't get out though, how are we going to find him? He could be anywhere in the building. Or anyone. There's still hundreds of civvies, cops, and soldiers here."

"That is true. But I believe I know of a way to bring him into the open again."

14

Roger Klemm, human once again, took refuge in a luxurious office on the top floor. He slumped against the wall and slid down onto the floor. One of the problems with taking nonhuman forms was that his thinking grew clouded. In his gorilla form, his mind had been consumed by a red haze, his only thought being to kill his target. It wasn't until he'd already been shot several times that he realized he was in trouble. He'd managed to escape from the elevator car and sever the cable, but he had a gut feeling that Flint and Navarro were still alive. He knew enough basic healing spells to save his own life, but those silver tipped Templar bullets were much worse than the ordinary ammunition carried by cops and soldiers. His body had expelled the slugs, and he had stopped the bleeding, closed the wounds, but he still felt painful burning sensations everywhere he'd been shot. And he was exhausted, utterly spent. That was another problem with taking the form of a raging beast: it burned up his stamina. His stomach growled as though he hadn't eaten in days.

He rested his head against the wall and took several deep breaths. The top floors of the Mansfield Building were deserted, all of its inhabitants' directed downstairs by law enforcement. CSI's might still be on the roof, inspecting his rifle. Unfortunately, his fight with the Witch Hunter and his assistant had probably blown up that plan. They knew there was a shapeshifter in the building now, which meant Whitmore would be in the clear.

"It looks like you're in quite the pickle, Roger."

He closed his eyes and sighed. And then there was this asshole.

"Yeah, I suppose I am," he said.

Cortez snickered. Klemm looked up and saw the young man before him, hands behind his back, that smartass grin on his face.

"Don't get me wrong," Cortez said. "That was a good move, transforming into the beast. Good old brute force can break a Templar's defenses more easily than magic."

"That was the idea," Klemm said. "For all the good it did me."

"More than you may think. Flint and Navarro are fairly battered and bruised. And they're low on ammunition."

With a groan, Klemm rose to his feet. He willed the

pain to stop, but the spell didn't work as smoothly as it used to. He'd never been shot by a Templar before. That silver burned like hell, disrupted his concentration.

"Hmm, yes," Cortez said. "I remember that feeling. Lead bullets are easy to come back from. But those silver tipped Templar bullets... terrible. You never will quite feel the same."

A thought occurred to Klemm and his heart sank. "That barrier... it's still up, isn't it?"

Cortez nodded.

"God damn it," Klemm growled. "What the hell is wrong with you? I can't leave, but those two can come and go as they please. They can go get more ammo or have more brought to them."

"Yes, I suppose they could."

"Why?! Why are you doing this to me?!"

"You know why."

Klemm barked a laugh. "You can't just possess me. You need me to accept it willingly."

Cortez nodded.

"But I'm not giving you what you want, so you're backing me into a corner, forcing me to accept you into me."

"I'm not forcing you to do anything. You're free to continue alone, carry out your mission all by yourself. You're the one who keeps saying you don't need my help, that you'll kill Flint and Navarro through your own skill. So do it. Get it done, and I'll keep my word and remove the barrier. Of course, there's another option that would convince me to release you from here."

Klemm scowled but said nothing.

"As a gesture of good will, I'll even clean your suit for you," Cortez said. He waved his hand, and the bloodstains on Klemm's suit vanished, the torn fabric knitting shut as though he'd never been shot.

Klemm snorted. "Spells for tailoring were never my strong suit," he said.

"Understandable. It's been years since the last time you were shot, am I right?"

Klemm said nothing. He checked his pistol: seven rounds in the magazine, one in the chamber, plus two additional magazines with fifteen rounds each in his jacket pockets.

"I'm not your enemy Roger."

"Could have fooled me." He went to the door of the office, nudged it open, took a quick glance to his left, right. No one was in the hallway, but there might be cops or CSIs in the offices, or on their way down from the roof.

"They know there's a shapeshifter in the building," Cortez said, "But they still haven't seen your true face."

Klemm snorted. "It's about goddamn time you started being constructive."

"If I were you, I'd take the shape of one of the police officers or soldiers. Maybe then they won't be so suspicious of you carrying an Imperial Army sidearm."

Klemm frowned and chided himself. That was a stupid error on his part. He'd assassinated a two-star general a few years back and kept the target's sidearm as both a souvenir and to confuse law enforcement whenever he was forced to leave shell casings behind. Why had he told

Navarro the truth about the weapon's make? It hadn't occurred to him to lie.

"That's how they get you, you know," Cortez said.

"What are you talking about?"

"Earlier you asked if God Himself would strike you down. That's not how He works. It's the little things. You stuck your gun in your waistband in a way that made it visible through your jacket. They noticed it and asked you what model you carried. You told the truth about it because you didn't think it would matter. Then Flint tested you by naming a fictional regiment, and you took the bait."

Klemm closed his eyes, felt the familiar magic wash over him like a warm bath, his features twisted and re-molded themselves. He now wore the appearance of the soldier who had led him to Flint and Navarro downstairs. Another bit of illusion magic, and his suit was transformed into an Imperial Army uniform, leather holster on his right hip for his Army-issued pistol.

"What's your point?" he asked.

"My point is this: do you think it would have made a difference if you'd concealed your pistol more carefully? Or if you were more knowledgeable about active duty Army units? Something else would have given you away."

Klemm stared at Cortez, blinked.

"This disguise you're wearing now, for example. Do you even know this soldier's name?"

"You just told me to..."

"It's a stopgap measure at best."

Klemm spread his arms. "So, what? That's it? God won't

let me win here? Then why don't I just turn myself in to them? If there's no way for me to complete the mission, then maybe I should try to make a deal."

"That's one solution. Making a deal with them might keep you from being burned at the stake. With all the blood on your hands though, you'd probably still spend the rest of your life in a prison cell with no windows. But there is another solution, a better one."

Klemm crept down the hallway, toward the stairwell. Cortez, hands still behind his back, levitated one foot off the floor and floated after him.

"What's the point? I mean if God Himself is interfering with my work here, what difference would your help make?"

Cortez's face lit up with a warm smile. Still levitating, he darted in front of Klemm, who reared back in surprise. Cortez grabbed his hand, gave it a warm shake. "Am I finally getting through to you?" he asked. It was all Klemm could do not to laugh aloud. Cortez might be possessed by a demon, or one with it, whatever he'd said, but he looked like a twenty-something puppy right now.

"I'm not agreeing to anything yet," Klemm said, withdrawing his hand. "I'm just curious. I haven't cracked a Bible in twenty years, but I'm pretty sure your side can't stop God any more than us mere mortals can."

"I'm glad you asked my dear Roger. You're right. We can't wage war on God directly. That was Simon Magus's great mistake which led to his downfall. He brought humanity the gift of magic so that you would no longer be pawns in God's design. We can break free of His shackles."

"But wouldn't He stop us or…"

"I told you, He doesn't work like that. He's subtle, He manipulates, He arranges things so that humans think they have free will, that they're choosing their own path, but they're only following the path laid out for them, like a locomotive on its track."

Klemm frowned. He thought he heard footsteps on the floor above him. "This is all interesting, but I need a plan if I'm going to get out of here in one piece."

"You have the gift of magic Roger. But you've only ever splashed about in the shallow end. Join with me, and I will show you how deep it can go. You'll have the power to escape this place, to kill Silas and Zelda."

"And then what?"

"And then whatever you want. You can collect your fee from Emil. I think you might lose interest in wealth for its own sake, but you'll be free to continue your line of work if you choose. That's what we can offer you Roger: the freedom to choose your own path, forge your own destiny. You can't complete this mission alone. Without us, your destiny is either execution or prison. Join us, and you can go anywhere, do anything. You'll walk the cold road as a lion among sheep."

Klemm said nothing. He glanced up at the ceiling again. He heard footsteps descending the stairwell at the end of the hall. He ducked inside another office, Cortez following, phasing through the door as though it weren't there.

"What happens to me though?"

Cortez cocked his head. "What do you mean?"

"I mean... you're Francisco Cortez, right? But you said you're one with whatshisname, Ick.."

"Ichthil."

"Right."

"It's true, Ichthil and I are one. His knowledge, his power, his being, they are mine to command. And they can be yours too. And you will still be Roger Klemm. Only... better."

Klemm closed his eyes, took a deep breath.

"I'll think about it."

15

Silas Flint and Ricardo Navarro entered an office on the third floor. Seated at the desk was a disheveled man in a rumpled suit. Flanking him were two familiar faces. Detective Elijah Earle stepped forward, followed by his partner, Detective Jay Marsten.

"Well well," Earle said, a smile on his face. "Didn't think we'd be seeing you two again so soon." He and Marsten exchanged handshakes with Flint and Navarro.

"Changed your mind about the big city after all?" Marsten asked.

Flint gave a small smile. He and Navarro had made the detectives' acquaintance during the Fort Ingalls case last month. "It is good to see you again, Detectives," he said.

"Do you guys get all the weird cases now?" Navarro asked.

Marsten rolled his eyes. "You could say that. Since

you boys came by last month, we're like Salem PD's own Templars, only without the fancy silver bullets."

"Doesn't seem anything weird about this case though," Earle said. He pointed at the disheveled man with his thumb. "Seems open and shut to me."

"What is the situation?" Flint asked.

"This is Miles Whitmore, a lawyer who works near the top floor," Earle said. "According to one of our unis, he was seen heading up to the roof carrying a briefcase. We sent some CSIs up there to take a look, and they find a scoped rifle along with one shell casing. They found prints on the rifle, so we brought in Mr. Whitmore here for questioning. We took his prints a few minutes ago and sure enough, they're a match for what we found on the rifle."

"I'm telling you, it wasn't me!" Whitmore shouted. "You've got this all wrong, I've never fired a gun in my life!"

Marsten held up his hand. "Easy friend, we're not finished yet."

"Let me guess," Navarro said. "You've got other witnesses that say he wasn't anywhere near the roof."

"Yeah," Earle said, furrowing his brow. "How'd you know that?"

"Don't tell me," Marsten said, sighing. "More magic shit."

"I am afraid so, Detective," Flint said. Turning his attention to Whitmore, he asked, "Mr. Whitmore, it is my understanding that these offices receive many job applicants every day."

"Yes, yes, that's right."

"I know it may be difficult, but you must try to remember: did you encounter any strangers during your duties this morning?"

Whitmore closed his eyes and said nothing for a few moments. His face lit up. "Now that you mention it, yes, I did see a new face during lunch today, in the cafeteria. Said his name was Roger Klemm, that he was there for a job interview."

"At any point, did you make physical contact with him?"

"Yeah, we shook hands."

"Thank you, Mr. Whitmore. Detectives, I recommend that you release him."

They raised their eyebrows. "You want to explain what's happening, Captain?" Earle asked.

"He's not our guy," Navarro said. "Our guy's a shapeshifter."

"The fuck?" Marsten asked.

"Mr. Navarro is correct, Detective. We had a brief but violent encounter with our perpetrator several minutes ago."

"We heard there was some kind of accident with an elevator," Marsten said.

"No accident," Navarro replied. "Asshole turned into a gorilla, beat us up, smashed the car, probably broke the cable."

Marsten ran his hand over his forehead, through his thinning hair. "Christ, why can't we ever have normal killers?" Flint gave him a sharp look. "Oh, uh, sorry."

Earle crossed his arms. "So, you're telling me this perp can look like anyone? Turn into animals even?"

"Yes," Flint said. "A shapeshifter must first make physical contact with the original, so to speak, or something that belongs to them, before he can assume their form. I suspect that this Mr. Klemm shook hands with Mr. Whitmore to acquire his shape for his repertoire."

"Yeah, and he's really good at it if he can match a target down to the fingerprints," Navarro said. "Normally these guys only try to fool your eyes but seems like our guy can fool even your CSIs."

Earle blew out a breath, shook his head. "I'm remembering something you said to me last month, sometimes the laws of science don't apply."

"Yes," Flint said. "Fortunately, we Templars have experience dealing with this wretch's vile kind."

"Um," Whitmore said. "Am I free to go?"

The detectives looked at him, at each other.

"Yeah," Earle said. "Go on, you're free to go. Thank you for your cooperation. And... sorry for the mix-up."

The lawyer scurried out of the office.

"Guess we're back to square one," Marsten said.

"Not necessarily," Flint said. "There are other factors at work here."

"What do you mean?"

"You guys know who got shot earlier?" Navarro asked.

"Yeah," Earle said. "We heard it was a young woman you two were with. That she took a bullet in the side, but she's up and walking around like it was nothing."

"That was our ward, Miss Zelda Fletcher," Flint said. "A

repentant witch who healed herself through her magical talents."

"A Witch Hunter hanging out with a witch?" Marsten said. "Sounds like the plot of a bad romance novel." Navarro stifled a laugh.

Flint cleared this throat. "Be that as it may, Miss Fletcher was unable to join our investigation. According to her, there is some sort of invisible barrier surrounding this building which prevented her entry."

"There's the police and army perimeter," Earle said. "Our guys haven't run into any problems."

"Zelda thinks it's a barrier that only keeps out magic users," Navarro said.

"Does this Klemm character not want her coming in?" Marsten asked.

"I am certain that he does not," Flint said. "Shapeshifters are often unable deceive their fellow magicians. Miss Fletcher has the talent for peering into others' minds. Mr. Klemm may be able to physically imitate his subjects down to the blood, but he cannot disguise his thoughts."

"So we can't use our best shot at ferreting this guy out," Earle said.

"Silas and I had an idea though," Navarro said. "If she can't get in, then maybe Klemm can't get out."

"Why would he lock himself in?" Marsten asked.

"He would not, if he is responsible for this barrier. We suspect that he is not, however. Such a spell would require immense power, power that I am not certain he is capable of mustering."

"Okay," Earle said. "Let's assume for the sake of

argument that he can't leave this place. That still leaves a whole lot of people in the building, and he could look like anyone. Or anything."

"And that's a pretty big assumption," Marsten added. "If he can turn into animals, maybe he goes to the roof, turns into a pigeon or something and flies the coop." He shook his head. "I can't believe I just said that."

"Yes..." Flint said. "I suggest that you post guards at every point with access to the roof." He thought for a moment. He drew his sword from his hip.

"What are you... whoa," Earle said. The blade emitted a soft white glow.

"I've heard stories about Templar swords," Marsten muttered. "They glow when there's magic around, right?"

"Yes," Flint said. "As I expected, it is reacting to the presence of the barrier outside."

"It was shining a whole lot brighter when we were close to Klemm in the elevator though," Navarro said.

"And that has given me an idea for drawing our suspect into the open. Detectives, if you would be so kind, please send word to the Imperial Palace of what has transpired here and request that Generals Abernathy, Hickock, Davis, and Brandt join us. Further, please request reinforcements from Fort Ingalls. Once they arrive, we will begin evacuating the building."

"I get it," Earle said.

"Get some more people here with more of those swords," Marsten said.

"Precisely. Mr. Klemm may be able to disguise himself

in the eyes of men, but he cannot hide from the light of God."

The detectives looked at each other.

"Yeah, I'm definitely not cut out for your job, Captain," Marsten chuckled.

"We'll get on it," Earle said.

"Hey, while you're at it, let them know me and Silas need more ammo, yeah?" Navarro said.

The detectives nodded and left the office to make their calls. Navarro stuck his hands in his trouser pockets.

"Don't suppose we could go get changed, could we boss?"

Flint shook his head. "Be grateful you do not have to wear this steel plate, Mr. Navarro."

"Saved you back there though, didn't it?"

"Indeed. I expect that I have the bruises to show for it."

"Maybe Zelda could take a look at that, get you fixed up again."

Flint grunted. "I should not like to rely overmuch on her occult talents, even if they are used to heal."

Navarro chuckled. "She's right about you, you know."

"Oh?"

"You can be really stubborn sometimes."

"If I know Miss Fletcher, you are no doubt omitting more colorful adjectives."

Navarro laughed.

16

Roger Klemm, still wearing the form of an imperial

soldier, stood at attention on the 25th floor stairwell landing. Uniformed police officers passed him with nods or waves as they ascended the stairs. He flagged one of them down.

"What's going on?" Klemm asked.

"Templar's orders," the cop replied. "He wants guards on all the upper floors and on the roof. Said the suspect might try to escape that way. How he would get off the roof I have no idea, but nobody's getting past us."

The cop excused himself. Klemm gave a rueful smile. If they only knew that he'd already tried and failed to escape from the roof. He sensed a now familiar presence materialize behind him. "And it could have worked too, no thanks to you," he said.

Klemm couldn't see him, but he knew Cortez wore that smartass grin again. "If you're so confident that you can complete your mission, why would you need to escape?"

He turned face Cortez. There was something different about him now. The kid's eyes had a more reddish hue, surrounded by dark circles.

"What's wrong with you?" Klemm asked.

Cortez scowled. "Flint… he's so close, and yet I can't touch him. Not yet."

Klemm said nothing, tried to think.

"He's bringing in reinforcements, you know," Cortez said. "More Templars, more swords that can detect you."

Klemm growled. "So take down your little barrier. Let me get out of here, regroup, form another plan."

A laugh. "Sorry Roger. You're committed now. It's do or die. Literally."

"God damn you," Klemm muttered.

"He already did."

Klemm got an idea. He looked up and down the stairwell, making sure he was alone. He opened the door on the landing and reentered the hallway. There had to be a janitor's closet somewhere.

"I wonder what you're up to?" Cortez asked, levitating behind him.

Ignoring him, Klemm opened a door and found what he was seeking. A standard janitor's closet stocked with toilet paper, garbage bags, and cleaning equipment. He grabbed a broom and whispered a spell. The broom shimmered in his hand and took on the appearance of a sword in a scabbard.

"Hmm," Cortez said.

Klemm thought back to a job he'd done five years ago. Silas Flint wasn't the first Witch Hunter he'd been contracted to kill. His body molded, rippled, reshaped itself into the form of Knight Templar Malcom Ridgeway. The original Ridgeway had been stationed at Fort Rochester up north. It had been long enough since Klemm had shanked him, and he was far enough away from Olympia that he was confident no one here would recognize the dead man. Another bit of illusion magic, and his suit jacket lengthened into a black Templar long coat. He fastened the illusory scabbard through a belt loop on his trousers.

"Aren't you forgetting something?" Cortez asked.

Shit. He was right. He needed a hat. He grabbed a cardboard box, dumped out the garbage bags inside, and remolded it into the Witch Hunters' trademark black hat.

"Impressive," Cortez said, nodding. "I hope for your sake that nobody recognizes this as a disguise."

"Shut up," Klemm said. Now it was just a matter of blending in with the other Witch Hunters when they arrived. Flint would no doubt want them to gather somewhere so he could deliver instructions, maybe a rousing speech about how they were a light in the darkness or some such heroic nonsense. They'd break to go scour the building, he'd approach Flint as though to say it was an honor to meet him or something and deliver the killing strike.

"That's a good plan Roger, a very good plan indeed," Cortez said.

"Would you stop that?"

"Stop what?"

"Stop reading my thoughts."

"I apologize, but I really can't help it." He chuckled, shook his head. "Poor Zelda. It nearly drove her mad when I taught her the trick all those years ago, but she learned how to tune out the noise."

"Whatever. But I kill Flint and you drop the barrier, right?"

"That is what I said, yes."

"Remind me to ask Emil for more money when this is over."

"Whatever you say, Roger."

Klemm returned to the stairwell and made his way down. He passed a few cops and soldiers along the way, but aside from the occasional curious glance, they took no notice of him. The other three Templar Chapter Houses were out in the boonies, self-contained communities, but Fort Ingalls wasn't far from here. Nothing unusual about Witch Hunters being out and about in the city, particularly if word got out that there was a shapeshifter in the building.

He stopped on the third floor landing and entered the hallway. It was still packed with civilians, milling about, some fearful, others grumbling, wondering when they would be free to go. The murmuring around him fell silent when they noticed his Templar uniform.

"Master Templar!"

"Sir Templar!"

"Witch Hunter!"

"What's going on?"

"Did you get the shooter?"

"When can we leave?"

"I've got a lot of work to do..."

Klemm raised his hands for silence and the shouts died away. "I thank thee all for thy patience," he called out. He knew the High Speech was formal, but in the back of his mind he wondered if he was overdoing it. "I wish to assure thee that reinforcements are on their way. Together with my brothers and sisters in arms, we shall bring this wicked fiend to justice."

"Is the shooter a magician?" someone shouted.

"I'm afraid so," Klemm called back.

The whispers, murmurs, broke out again. He saw worried faces, smelled the fear. The Night of Chaos was still fresh in these people's minds.

"I shall remain with you all until my fellow Templars

arrive. Fear not, for God is with us." He made his way through the hallway, looking for an office where he could take refuge. The people parted for him, some bowing their heads, others offering pats on the shoulder, unwittingly giving him more disguises to add to his collection. He finally found an empty office, gave a final wave to the people outside, and shut himself in.

"That must be a pleasant change," Cortez said, materializing behind the desk. "The awe struck looks, the affection of the people..."

Klemm snorted. "It's a change alright," he said. Hardly anyone took notice of him when he wore his true face. "By the way, can ordinary people see you or hear you?"

"Not unless I want them to."

"Then keep your mouth shut. I don't want anyone outside to wonder if I'm talking to myself."

As you wish, Cortez said, his voice echoing in Klemm's mind. *I'll be quiet now, but I'll still be around. Remember, if you change your mind about accepting my help, just call out to me, and I will hear you.*

Klemm reverted to his true form, sat down at the desk, putting his feet up. This mission wasn't turning out the way he'd hoped, but he'd get the job done. He always did.

17

Generals Abernathy, Hickock, Davis, and Brandt were silent. After their arrival at the Mansfield Building, Flint and Navarro had summarized the events of the afternoon.

"You gentlemen look a little worse for wear," Davis said.

"You need some medical attention?" Brandt asked, after exhaling a plume of cigar smoke.

Abernathy chuckled. "Don't bother, Seth. These two won't quit until the job's done. Or they're dead."

"I kind of got that impression of them last month," Hickock said with a grin.

"In any case, sirs," Flint said, "Mr. Navarro and I are confident that our shapeshifter is still in this building."

"Zelda still stuck outside?" Navarro asked.

"Yes," Abernathy replied. "She used some rather colorful language to express her displeasure, including some terms I think even General Hickock is unfamiliar with. She said to tell you that she's sorry she can't join us."

"One thing I don't get," Hickok said. "If our shooter didn't put up this anti-magic barrier, then who did? And why?"

Flint remembered something Fletcher had said earlier. "I have a theory. Miss Fletcher claims that she saw the spirit of her former lover, Francisco Cortez, shortly before she was struck down by the assassin."

Abernathy's eyebrows went up. "The same Francisco Cortez we put down outside of Jordan?"

"Yup," Navarro nodded.

"'We?' You been going out into the field without us, John?" Brandt asked with a smile.

Abernathy chuckled. "I do like to escape from Fort Marsing from time to time."

"Amen to that," Hickock said. "The Night of Chaos was the most action I've seen in years."

"You two get to have all of the fun," Davis laughed.

"Assuming Cortez has returned from Hell," Abernathy said, "Could he be in league with our shapeshifter?"

"It is a possibility," Flint said. "But why he would choose to lock Mr. Klemm inside the building and Miss Fletcher outside, I do not know."

"Whatever the reason," Hickock said, "We'll put Klemm to the stake and Cortez back in the fiery pit where he belongs. I got a couple squads of Templars and Supernumeraries from Fort Ingalls on their way. Oh, and something for you two." He reached into his long coat's inner pockets, withdrew four pistol magazines in his giant hand, tossed them to Flint and Navarro, who caught them and reloaded their sidearms.

"Thank you, General," Flint said.

The meeting adjourned and the six men left the conference room on the Mansfield Building's ground floor. Flint took a spot near the fountain in the lobby, arms folded, waiting for reinforcements to arrive. The space was still packed with civilians who gave Flint a respectable berth. After a few minutes, Navarro joined him.

"Remember the last time we had to deal with one of these shapeshifters?"

Flint snorted. "How could one forget? You believed that everything and everyone you saw was a potential shapeshifter for a week afterward."

"Hey, you can never be too careful around these shitbirds."

"I concur. This Mr. Klemm seems to be more skilled at his craft than most, but he is not perfect. We must maintain our vigilance. It is the seemingly minor details that always give them away, such as the concealed pistol that you noticed. Which reminds me, I have not had the opportunity to praise you for your keen eye, Mr. Navarro. Well done."

"Just doing my job boss... but thanks." He was quiet for a few moments. "Something else I've been thinking..."

"Yes?"

"Why would he have shot Zelda? I mean, no offense sir, but I can think of a lot more people who'd want you dead than her. So why'd he take the shot against her and not you?"

Flint thought before replying. "The only possibility that comes to mind is that we have met our assassin before."

"What do you... oh, shit. You said earlier she thought there was something off about one of the guys at the reception last night."

"Yes. She said that his thoughts did not seem like his own, that he was working as a member of the wait staff."

Navarro's eyes widened. "If he was at Fort Ingalls... then that means he touched a lot of stuff, a lot of people. He could take any of our shapes."

"Yes... even you or myself."

"God damn..." Navarro muttered. "And now there's a bunch of people from Ingalls on their way here now."

"Mr. Klemm is undoubtedly aware that Miss Fletcher is able to see through his disguises. Whether he is the architect of the barrier or no, we shall have to rely on General Hickock's knowledge of his people, and on our holy blades to light the way."

"If she can sniff him out, then maybe he needs her out of the way to get to another target."

"Indeed. It is for that reason that I hope we are able to capture this heretic alive."

"With all due respect sir…"

"I believe it was Detective Marsten who once said that when someone prefaces their statement with, 'With all due respect,' it means that an insult is coming."

Navarro laughed. "I'm just saying we don't have the best track record at bringing in magicians alive. Even by Templar standards."

Flint gave an icy smile. "Mr. Klemm went to the trouble of infiltrating both Fort Ingalls and a building within sight of the Imperial Palace which tells me that he is no fanatic bent on a suicide mission. I believe that if we capture him alive, he will cooperate with us if given the proper incentives."

"Yeah. I guess the hard part will be finding him."

Fifteen minutes later, Flint saw the first group of Templars from Fort Ingalls arrive, filing into the building alongside their Supernumerary assistants. Envy was a sin, but he felt the sting of jealousy that they were in their field uniforms instead his own steel plate. Navarro looked as though he shared Flint's feelings, seeing his fellow Supernumeraries in their denim jeans and leather body armor. The Generals directed traffic toward the conference room. Once everyone had assembled, Flint and Navarro followed, making their way to the front. The Generals soon joined them, Hickock in the lead. He turned to face the room.

"Listen up!" Hickock bellowed, and all conversation

fell silent. "I'm sure y'all have heard by now that we got a shooter. He tried to kill one of our guests earlier today. We got reason to believe he's still in the building... and that he's a wizard. A shapeshifter."

The room broke out in murmurs. Hickock waited for them to die down before continuing: "Captain Flint and Mr. Navarro here had a scuffle with him earlier. I'm gonna turn things over to them now. Captain?"

"Thank you, sir," Flint said. He looked out at the crowd, recognizing some of the faces from the Night of Chaos last month. They nodded back. Other faces were unfamiliar to him, but they all gave him their rapt attention.

"The shapeshifter's name is Roger Klemm. He came here this morning under the pretense of a job interview. We believe he took the form of Miles Whitmore, a lawyer who works in the building. Mr. Whitmore's fingerprints were found on the rifle that was used to fire on Miss Fletcher earlier this afternoon. Multiple eyewitnesses put Whitmore away from the rooftop at the time of the shooting. Soon afterward, a lawyer named Franklin Bailey claimed knowledge of witchcraft practiced within this building. It was when Mr. Navarro and I entered an elevator with him, that he revealed his true nature. We repelled his attack, but he managed to escape."

The room was silent.

"We have reason to believe that Mr. Klemm is trapped within this building. But he can appear as anyone. As any beast. Further..." He took a deep breath. "Mr. Navarro and I have reason to believe that Mr. Klemm infiltrated Fort Ingalls last night."

A collective gasp rose from his audience. Hickock's eyes widened, the other Generals shifting uncomfortably.

"According to Miss Fletcher, there is an invisible barrier that surrounds this building that prevents the entry of any who possess the talent for the dark arts. Everyone in this room passed through that barrier, and it is for that reason I am confident that you are all trustworthy. However, Mr. Klemm may have acquired some of our shapes during his mission last night. I suggest that we pair off. Do not get separated from your partner. He may attempt to imitate one of us."

Everyone exchanged glances with each other.

"When you get your partner," Navarro said, "Maybe think of a password only you two know or think of a question only the real you would know the answer to."

"Our first task will be to evacuate this building of all civilians," Flint said. "I would ask for volunteers from my brother and sister Templars. Stand guard by the front doors with your swords drawn. The magical barrier that surrounds this place causes interference with their blessed properties, but they will shine bright in the presence of that son of Satan, of that I can assure you. Inspect everyone who leaves this building. Once the civilians are evacuated, we will begin our search for Mr. Klemm in earnest."

He fell silent. Hickock glanced at him, Flint nodded. "Alright," Hickock said, "You heard the man. Let's move."

Murmuring amongst themselves, the Templars and Supernumeraries left the conference room. Through the open doors, Flint saw a Knight and Lady Templar take posts on either side of the building's front door.

Hickock slapped Flint on the back, making him stumble. "Good plan, Captain," he said. "I'm wondering though... you think you could have let us know sooner you think our guy was in my Fort last night?"

"I apologize, sir," Flint said. "It did not occur to Mr. Navarro and I until a few minutes ago."

"Water under the bridge now," Brandt said, lighting up another cigar.

"Excuse me, Captain Flint?"

He looked and saw a young Templar standing before him, brown eyes shimmering with... admiration? He couldn't be sure.

"May I help you, Sir...?"

"Hey," Brandt said. He worked the cigar around to the other side of his mouth. "What's your name, young man?"

The Templar hesitated for a second before responding, "Marcus Brisby, sir."

"Brisby... huh," Brandt said.

"Is there a problem, General?" Brisby asked.

"You look a lot like... well, never mind."

"How can I assist, Mr. Brisby?" Flint asked.

"Oh, I just wanted to meet you sir. I saw you last month during the Night of Chaos. You and Mr. Navarro were amazing. I guess... well, I just wanted to shake your hand and say thank you. You're a real inspiration and I hope I can be as good a Witch Hunter as you some day."

Flint kept his face neutral. It happened occasionally, younger Templars being starstruck in his presence. In

Flint's mind, he was simply performing his duty and noth-ing more.

"I thank you for your kind words, Mr. Brisby, and I…"

"Wait a second," Hickock said. "You said your name's Brisby? And you were here last month?"

"Yes sir."

"I'm an old man and my memory ain't what it used to be, but I'm pretty sure I've never heard your name or seen your face before. How long you been at Ingalls?"

"Never," Brandt spoke up. "I recognize you now. Malcom Ridgeway. Except Ridgeway died five years ago. His throat was slit."

The room was silent for a moment.

"Seize hi…" Flint started to shout, but before he could finish, Ridgeway's hand liquified and reshaped into a thin blade, which he whipped toward Flint's face.

18

Flint arched his back, leaning away from the blade, but he felt an icy burn as it swept across his chin, followed by a warm dampness. A second later, Navarro tackled the shapeshifter to the ground.

"Motherfu… ah!"

Klemm grabbed hold of Navarro's tunic. Arcs of electricity danced over Navarro's body, but he held on. The Generals drew their swords in unison, the blades shining brightly in Klemm's presence.

"Roger Klemm!" Davis shouted. "You are surrounded! In the name of God, stand down!"

Klemm's body shifted beneath Navarro, and the Supernumerary was flung away, colliding with Flint, and they collapsed in a heap on the floor. Klemm had changed again, this time into a hulking grizzly bear. The beast's roar echoed in the conference room, its spittle spraying the floor.

"Ah shit," Hickock muttered. He drew the .44 magnum revolver on his hip, but before he could aim, the bear swiped with its claws, scoring deep gouges in the breastplate of Hickock's dress uniform, and the General was slammed against the wall. Abernathy and Brandt fired their pistols into the bear's shaggy hide, but it roared in defiance and charged the two generals. Davis leapt onto the animal's back, driving his sword between its shoulder blades. The bear shrieked in agony, vigorously shaking its body. Davis held on, his face a rictus snarl of anger. Abernathy went to Hickock's side while Brandt emptied his pistol's magazine into the bear's head. The flesh sizzled, but Klemm's healing powers kept him going, his body expelling the slugs and closing the wounds almost as quickly as his assailants could deliver them.

Flint rose to his feet, wiping the blood off his chin with his sleeve. He could hear screaming outside as civilians stampeded for the exit. The doors to the conference room slammed open, a squad of Templars and Supernumeraries rushing in, weapons drawn. The bear twisted its body and flung Davis aside.

"Open fire! Send this devil back to the abyss!" Flint yelled.

Klemm shifted again. His body rippled and shrank. The

bear had become a bat. The squealing, flapping creature made a beeline for General Brandt.

"Ah! Damn it!" he grunted, swatting at the bat as it scratched at his face, leaving bloody claw marks on his cheek.

"You little..." Navarro growled, striding toward the General, a murderous look on his face.

"Sir...?" one of the Templars asked, his pistol aimed in the bat's direction as it flapped between Brandt and Navarro.

"Hold!" Hickock yelled, rising to his feet with Abernathy's help. The bat glowed, shimmered, changed shape again. Now Klemm had morphed into a hummingbird. The tiny creature buzzed around the conference room before darting past the squad of Templars and Supernumeraries and out the door.

"Do not let it out of your sight! Take it down!" Abernathy shouted, pointing with his sword.

"Yes sir!" cried a Templar. "On me!" The squad charged after Klemm.

"Is everyone alright?" Davis asked.

"Bastard ruined my armor," Hickock grumbled, rubbing his hand over the deep claw marks on his chest plate. "Other than that, I'll probably be black and blue for a while."

Flint dabbed at his chin, his leather gauntlet coming away bloody. "I am largely unharmed."

"Same here," Brandt said, hand over his bloody cheek.

"Just got my battery recharged a little," Navarro said.

"Has he been to the zoo? How the hell does he know all those animal shapes?"

"Captain," Davis said.

"Yes sir?"

"Klemm seems to be focused on you. He could have gone for any one of us, but he chose to strike out against you."

"Yes..." Flint said. "Curious."

Abernathy stroked his chin. "You said that Miss Fletcher was able to detect Klemm, despite his disguises."

"Yes sir."

"So Klemm tried to take her out," Brandt said.

"If she'd died, then we might never have found out our boy's a shapeshifter," Hickock said.

"Holy shit," Navarro said.

All eyes turned to him.

"It's you," he said, looking at Flint. "It's you sir. You're his other target."

Flint blinked, thought. Yes, it made sense. He thought back to the previous night, the reception at Fort Ingalls. He remembered now, a Supernumerary serving as a waiter had taken his wine glass from him and quickly departed. It was shortly afterward that Fletcher had approached and said something seemed off about the waiter. That had to have been Klemm, no doubt beating a hasty retreat before Fletcher could get a better read on him.

"It is a distinct possibility," Flint said.

"Have you ever had any run ins with Klemm before today?" Davis asked.

"Not to my knowledge, sir. I suspect that Mr. Klemm

is a hired assassin. It is my hope that we can capture the vermin alive and learn who is puppet master controlling his strings."

Hickock grinned. "You get all the interesting missions, eh Captain?"

"You don't know the half of it," Abernathy said, chuckling.

Brandt reached into his inner coat pocket, took out another cigar, struck a match to light it. "Hate to say it," he said, blowing out a ring of smoke, "But it's not likely our boys and girls can catch him when he's a damn hummingbird."

"He won't be able to sustain that form for long," Davis said. "He's wounded, for one. I'm no zoologist, but I'm guessing his metabolism sped up to match his new shape. He's probably starving by now."

Abernathy crossed his arms, paced. "Yes... he'll need to find a spot to heal himself. That will drain his stamina further." He looked at Hickock. "We may not have the manpower to occupy every room in this building yet..."

"But we can stake out the cafeteria, the front door, the roof, and all the stairway landings at least," Hickock finished, stroking his beard.

Flint felt Navarro nudge him with his elbow. "I know it sounds weird, what with everything going on, but this is kind of fun to watch, sir," Navarro whispered as the Generals continued their discussion.

The corner of Flint's mouth turned up. "One does not attain the rank of Templar General without surviving a long and interesting career," he whispered back.

"Captain," Abernathy said.

"Sir?"

"You said that you believe Klemm is a hired assassin."

"Yes sir. Consider: he successfully infiltrated Fort Ingalls but chose not to take advantage of the many opportunities for sabotage that were surely available to him. Second, as General Davis pointed out, he could have assassinated any one of you, but when his moment came, he chose to lash out at me. I believe that Mr. Navarro is correct: I am one of his targets. It is quite possible that he meant to assassinate me last night but cried off when he realized that Miss Fletcher could detect him."

"And now Miss Fletcher is locked out by this barrier, whatever it is," Hickock said.

"And Klemm is locked in," Abernathy said.

"We hope," Davis said.

Brandt exhaled a plume of cigar smoke. "For now, I say we proceed as though he isn't trapped here. Stick with Captain Flint and Mr. Navarro's plan. Check every living thing in this building at swordpoint if we have to, seal off the roof, go floor by floor."

The others all nodded. "One more question for you, Captain," Abernathy said.

"Yes sir?"

"Do you think your brother could have hired Klemm?"

All eyes turned to Flint. He shook his head. "I do not believe so sir." He sighed. "Though I confess it is only a feeling."

Hickock frowned. "We'll get a hold of him and beat the truth out of him."

"Amen to that," Navarro said, driving his fist into his palm. "It's been a while since I did a good interrogation, and this asshole's got it coming."

Flint dug into his trouser pocket, checked his pocket watch. 3:16 p.m. He feared that he would miss his appointment with the Emperor that evening, but he was sure His Majesty would understand.

"That gives me an idea," Navarro said, looking over Flint's shoulder.

"Oh?" He snapped the watch shut.

"Klemm might be able to look like you, but he doesn't have your watch."

"I don't expect he can talk like you either, Captain," Hickock said, grinning.

"Generals," Flint said. "You should..."

"Nope," Brandt said, shaking his head.

"We need all the warm bodies we can muster," Davis said.

"We'll pair off and join the search," Abernathy said.

"You and Ricardo go on ahead," Hickock said.

Flint nodded, adjusted his hat, pulled his coat tighter around him. He drew his sword. The blade emitted a soft white glow. The barrier was still up.

"Come along, Mr. Navarro. We shall see Mr. Klemm in shackles before dusk."

19

Roger Klemm zoomed through the stairwell, ascending ever higher. He had expelled the slugs from his body before taking the form of a hummingbird, but the wounds still hurt like hell. His body felt like it was on fire. And his stomach growled. He needed to find shelter, somewhere he could take human form again. Heal his wounds, hopefully find some food... Christ, he was starving.

He stopped on the 17th floor and shifted to his true form, tumbling onto the landing. He groaned in pain as he rolled over on his back, gasping for breath. He'd known hunger, back when he'd run away from home as a boy, but nothing like this. Klemm had never needed to shapeshift so many times in one day before. It always drained him, and he regained his strength with a celebratory meal after every successful job. Now though... he felt like he hadn't eaten or drank in days.

"The walls are closing in, Roger."

Klemm didn't have the strength to even groan. He glanced to his right and there was Cortez again, looking like the cat who had caught the canary. Klemm opened his mouth to tell him to shut up, but only a dry croak emerged.

"Magic is wondrous and can satisfy appetites both subtle and gross... but it has a price."

Klemm ground his teeth, tried to summon his healing magic. His back was killing him where that black bastard had stabbed him earlier.

"Look at you now. Poor Roger. At this rate you'll starve or die of dehydration before the Witch Hunters find you."

Klemm faced a hard choice. He could heal his body, but he wasn't sure if he'd have the strength to take the form of a beast again. Not until he could find some food and water, replenish his stamina. Cortez was right, damn him. He could sense the magic eating away at his body.

"We're not all bad, you know. I'm not your enemy. Here. Take it."

Klemm looked up. Cortez offered him a tankard of water, a slice of bread. They stared at each other for a few moments. Cortez nodded. Klemm took them. He devoured the bread slice in three bites, chugged the water. He coughed, sputtered, finished chugging, tossed the tankard aside. He breathed deeply. It wasn't much, but Cortez's gift would keep him going a little longer. Speaking of which...

"So what's your fee?" Klemm asked. "Your kind doesn't do gifts."

Cortez smiled. "Consider that a free sample. You've never drawn upon the power to any great extent. Not before today. You'll need to if you hope to escape in one piece, but I'm not sure that your body can take it. Let me help you. Join with me, and you'll no longer need to worry about the limits of your body, your human frailties."

Klemm's shoulders slumped. He took another few deep breaths. Cortez stood still, hands behind his back, smiling.

"Tell you what," Klemm said, looking up. "I've got one more trick up my sleeve."

Cortez nodded.

"If you so much as give me a dirty look, if you try to interfere again... then I'll turn myself in and take my chances with the Witch Hunters. Maybe go see a priest, get you exorcised."

"I have to admit, my masters are rather enjoying the

show. We agree to leave you alone for this one last trick of yours. Suppose you fail though... what then?"

"I won't."

"We'll see. Our offer to you still stands. Until you're dead of course."

Klemm smiled. "You'll see. I'll finish the job, get paid, and be eating, drinking, and making merry by dusk." He walked away from Cortez, opened the stairwell door, and entered the 17th floor. It was deserted. There had to be something, anything... they couldn't all go to the ground floor for chow. He opened doors one by one. An office here, a janitor's closet there... finally. He found a room with scattered tables, chairs, and a refrigerator. Klemm smiled. That was another thing he loved about living in Salem: refrigerators were luxuries in much of the Empire, but commonplace here in the imperial capitol. He strode toward the machine, opened the door, his smile growing wider. Jackpot. He grabbed the first brown paper bag he laid eyes on, WADE written on it in black ink.

Thanks for the chow, Wade, Klemm thought. A roast beef sandwich, an apple, a bottle of soda. He devoured the food, chugged the soda, belched. That hit the spot. He'd need the energy for what he was about to do.

Those damn swords. They glowed in the presence of magic. The Templars claimed it was because they were all blessed by the pope in Rome. Klemm thought they were a bunch of hypocrites who had magic of their own. They had that Zelda woman on their side after all, didn't they? However those blades worked, they'd eventually find him. But if they glowed everywhere...

Klemm closed his eyes, extended his arms, palms out. He reached out with his mind, tried to picture the building's innards. Good old Salem; most reliable power grid in the Empire. He pictured the closest power station. The building would no doubt have a generator too, so that would have to go as well. He focused on the electrical wiring, the cables, the lights. He pictured them going out in his mind. Sweat beaded on his forehead. He'd used his power to turn out the lights before, but never on this scale.

There. The electrical lights overhead flickered and died. He smiled. He'd done it. The Mansfield Building's electricity was out. If it wasn't for that damn barrier, he probably could have taken out the entire block's power. No matter, this would do. Now that the electricity was out, he'd shed some magical light on the situation.

Every magician knew how to stick balls of witchfire on the walls. A harmless spell, meant to provide light, and nothing more. The fire didn't even burn if you stuck your hand in it. But this harmless spell would save Klemm's life and give him the means to finish the job.

The fire materialized on the palms of his hands. His every nerve burned. He growled in pain, urged the fire to spread. He thought of every floor, every room... almost there. Klemm screamed as the fire exploded outward from his body. He collapsed, drenched in sweat, his skin tingling. He laughed. He'd done it. A ball of fire hovered in the room, casting his surroundings in a blue glow. He could see it in his mind's eye. Every hallway, every room was illuminated by his witchfire. And that meant the

Templars' swords would glow brightly around everything and everyone.

He crawled to the refrigerator. There had been other sack lunches in there. Klemm just needed to regain enough strength for a little more shapeshifting. Enough to finally kill that stubborn son of a bitch Flint and get the hell out of here. He devoured another sandwich.

Sorry to disappoint you kid, he thought, *But I don't think I'll need to make a deal today.* His body shimmered, remolded. He'd gotten two out of the four Witch Hunter Generals at Ingalls the other night. After the fight in the conference room earlier, he'd acquired a third. Roger Klemm took the shape of Witch Hunter General Seth Brandt.

20

Flint and Navarro crossed the lobby. Many of the civilians had fled in terror at the sound of the Generals' gunfire earlier. The hardy souls who remained had formed two lines, filing out of the building two at a time. Templars stood on either side of the door; their swords raised as civilians passed beneath them. Flint noted that the blades' glow was dull. Klemm hadn't attempted to escape through the front door yet. There was nothing for it now but the grim slog of inspecting every floor, every room. The corner of his mouth quirked up. Pulp novels often portrayed the lives of Witch Hunters as nonstop action, but the truth was much of it was hours of careful investigative work for every minute of action.

"Got any ideas sir?" Navarro asked.

"I do," Flint said. "I am Mr. Klemm's intended target. We are presently assuming that he cannot leave this building. Even if he can, I believe that..."

He felt the hairs on the back of his neck stand up, a peculiar tingling in his spine. His experience had taught him that it could only mean witchcraft was afoot. Before Flint could voice a warning, the lights in the lobby flickered and died. The civilians looked up, bewildered at the loss of power. A moment later, a whooshing sound filled the room. Balls of witchfire materialized on the walls, and the confused murmuring of the workers rose to panicked chattering.

"Calm yourselves!" Flint bellowed. All eyes focused on him as he strode toward a ball of blue fire on the wall. He removed a gauntlet, passed his hand through the flames unharmed, his face neutral.

"This foul sorcery is offensive in the eyes of God," Flint said, "But as you can see, it cannot harm us." The murmurs died down. The civilians still looked nervous, but they resumed their advance toward the front door.

"What do you suppose that's all about... shit."

"Is there a problem, Mr. Navarro?"

"Look."

Flint saw it now. The Templars standing guard by the doors. Their swords shone brightly now, almost as bright as Flint's sword had in his battle with Klemm earlier. He frowned.

"Clever bastard," Navarro muttered.

"Indeed. This will complicate the hunt, but the Holy Spirit guides us. We shall not fail."

"What were you about to say earlier sir?"

"Even if Klemm is able to leave this building, I believe he will make another attempt on my life, here."

"Whole place is packed with cops and soldiers though, and more Templars are on their way."

"That is true, however we must consider this latest act of devilry. He would not have summoned these foul witch-fire lights if he meant to give up his mission so easily. No, he is interfering with our blades' abilities because he intends to kill me before he leaves this place, whether he is imprisoned here or no."

Navarro nodded. "Makes sense. One thing still doesn't add up though. Who put up that anti-magic barrier outside?"

Flint pursed his lips. "I do not have an explanation yet, but I am becoming more certain that it was not Mr. Klemm. We caught him unawares in the elevator and he was forced to attack then. He chose to attack again earlier despite your presence and the presence of the Generals. That speaks to desperation, something one would not expect from a professional assassin."

"Maybe he's got a schedule to keep. He's got to kill you by a certain time, or he loses out on payday or something."

"That is a possibility. Or perhaps some third party has trapped him here until he completes his mission. In any case, we shall hunt him down and Mr. Klemm will face God's justice. Let us go."

Flint drew his sword which shone brightly in the gloom. Navarro unslung his rifle. Together, the Witch

Hunter and his assistant made for the stairwell to begin their long ascent.

***

Roger Klemm strode through the hallway in the form of General Brandt. He'd need a few extra accessories to complete the disguise, but those should be easy enough to acquire. He just needed to find some Witch Hunters. As he approached the stairwell, he heard two men's voices echoing, laughing. He squared his shoulders and opened the door. Before him were two men in rumpled suits. They stopped their conversation to look at him. One of them, a black man, said, "You doing alright, uh... General?"

"Yep," Klemm said. "Doing fine, all things considered. General Seth Brandt." He extended his hand. The black man shook it.

"Detective Elijah Earle," he replied. "This here's my partner, Detective Jay Marsten." Marsten, a white man with thinning hair, shook Klemm's hand as well.

"Brandt... you're from up north, right?" Marsten asked.

"Yep. Fort Rochester, near Olympia."

"You lost your hat," Earle observed.

Klemm ran a hand over his head. "Yeah. Shapeshifting son of a bitch jumped us downstairs. Guess I lost it in all the commotion."

"I don't know how you guys do it," Marsten said, shaking his head.

"You get used to it," Klemm replied. "What's the situation?"

The two detectives looked at each other. Earle said, "We got word from downstairs. It's going to be floor by floor, room by room. Us cops and the Army guys are going to work our way down from the upper floors, the Templars are going to start from the ground and work their way up."

"Speaking of which," Marsten said, "What are you doing up here by yourself, General? I heard that we're supposed to stick together."

"We are," Klemm said. "I partnered up with one of the Supernumeraries. He has a sister who works here. Thought she might still be hiding out up here. I warned him not to go alone, but he gets in the elevator and off he goes."

"Find him yet?" Earle asked.

"No. I'm starting to worry, frankly. I'm afraid our wizard might have got him."

"Need any help?" Marsten said.

"Yeah. Keep an eye out for him, would you? He's about six feet, 180 pounds, brown hair, brown eyes. Name's Geoffrey Harold. I'm going to head back down. God willing, we'll cross each other along the way."

The two detectives looked at each other again. "Yeah... sure," Earle said.

"God be with you both," Klemm said, nodding. He felt the two detectives staring after him as he descended the stairs. No matter. Even if they suspected that he wasn't who he appeared to be, they had no way of proving it, and two greying detectives weren't about to shoot down a Witch Hunter General on a hunch. Klemm smiled. The job had turned out more complicated than he'd expected, but he felt like he was finally back on his game. The next part of his plan would be crucial. Normally he avoided killing nontargets, but this time it was him or them.

He continued his descent, passing a few more cops and soldiers. Klemm wondered if he'd run into Flint along the way. He heard more voices. There. Two Witch Hunters were coming up the stairs, their black hats and black long coats unmistakable. He'd need their equipment.

"Ah, good," he said. They looked up at him as he came down the stairs. They came to attention.

"General Brandt," one of them, a man, said.

"Sir, what are you doing up here?" said the other, a woman. "And what happened to your hat?"

"Change of plans," Klemm said. "I think I found our guy. I need you two to come with me."

The Templars looked at each other. "Sir," the man said. "Why are you here by yourself? I thought we were supposed to stay in pairs."

"Oh, for God's sake," Klemm muttered. His hands elongated into sharp metal points, and he rammed them into their faces. Their blood gushing forth, the Templars gurgled, twitched, and were still. He withdrew his blades, and they reformed into his hands. Working quickly, Klemm ditched his Petersen 9 – damn, he'd miss that gun – and took the male Templar's sword and two pistols with their holsters. He snorted. Templar guns were puny little things. He checked one of the magazines. Eight rounds, plus one in the chamber? He supposed he shouldn't throw stones;

he seldom got into extended gunfights either. Finally, he donned the male Templar's hat. Perfect.

Flint and Navarro would be working their way up the building. Klemm figured the Generals would join the search, so it wouldn't appear too suspicious if he ran into them wearing Brandt's form, but he was prepared to take on the appearance of another Templar at a moment's notice. Now it was a matter of patience and waiting for the right opportunity.

21

Flint heard a commotion on the stairs above him. A scream, followed by cursing.

"Hurry," he said to Navarro, and they began a head-long sprint up the stairs. Flint could hear his assistant wheezing behind him. He smiled. Navarro was an excellent fighter, but cardio was never his strong suit. They reached the landing where the noise had originated.

"Aw son of a bitch," Navarro said between deep gulping breaths.

A crowd of Flint's fellow Templars had formed. Before them were the bodies of two Templars, a man and a woman. The backs of their heads were bloody ruins, skull fragments and brain matter spattered on the wall. Flint closed his eyes and sighed, offering a quick mental prayer for the repose of their souls.

"What happened?" he asked.

A Lady Templar and her assistant stepped forward. "We

were the ones to find them, Captain. This was Sir Stephen Lagrange, and Lady Mary Hill."

Flint knelt for a closer look. He observed that Lagrange's hat was missing, along with his sword and pistols. He frowned and rose to his feet.

"Klemm is responsible for these heinous murders," Flint growled. "I suspect that he is currently disguised as a Templar. Listen, all of you. It is imperative that you do not let your partner out of your sight. Mr. Klemm can copy his subjects down to the blood, but he does not know us. He does not think like us. If you have not already done so, decide on questions to ask one another, the answers to which only your real companion would know."

The Templars and Supernumeraries nodded, their faces set in grim determination. Klemm had now killed two of Ingalls' own Templars, which made the hunt personal. Navarro nudged Flint as the others dispersed to resume the search.

"That reminds me boss. What should we ask each other?"

Flint thought for a few moments. "I shall ask you the name of your biological mother."

"Okay," Navarro said. "And for you?"

Flint pursed his lips. "Ask me how my parents died."

Navarro took a deep breath. "You sure?"

"Yes. I have only shared the truth with those I trust implicitly."

"Right. Okay. Where to now sir?"

"I believe our brothers and sisters have this floor, and

the one above it covered. Let us go up two floors and resume our search there."

He adjusted his hat, pulled his long coat tighter around him, and continued climbing the stairwell. Klemm's witch-fire cast everything in an eerie blue hue with long shadows. He hoped that they could capture their prey before nightfall. Magical light was harmless, but it made his skin crawl.

He heard Navarro taking deep breaths behind him. "Couldn't we take the elevator sir? There's got to be more than just the one."

"The electricity has been cut off. Even if Mr. Klemm operates one through his occult powers, we have posted guards beside every elevator door on the lower floors. The police and imperial soldiers are stationed on the upper floors. Surely you do not wish to stand guard duty?"

"Yeah... guess not... I just... remind me to go on a diet after this is over."

"I assuredly will Mr. Navarro, though I have never had success on that subject before."

***

Roger Klemm waited inside an office on the ninth floor. He could hear the footsteps of two people down the hallway. They opened each door, cleared the room, and moved on to the next. Klemm didn't think he had enough left in the tank to risk another animal transformation; he'd stick to human forms for now. He had other tricks up his sleeve though. If he was going to blend in with the Witch Hunter ranks, he'd need to find a partner.

He inched the doorway open. Getting down into the prone position, he peeked around the corner. People tended to keep their focus at eye level and often missed ground level movement. He saw one Witch Hunter and one Supernumerary about ten doors down. Not Flint and Navarro, damn it. Oh well. He'd find them soon enough. Klemm focused his mind. It wasn't often that he needed to use magic other than shapeshifting, but he was confident he had it in him. He pointed to his left, toward the Witch Hunter and his assistant. The sound of a gunshot echoed at the end of the hallway.

"What?!" the Witch Hunter cried. Before the man could move, Klemm pointed to his right, and another gunshot echoed at the opposite end of the hall.

"Sir..." the Supernumerary said.

Klemm used his illusion magic to alter and project his voice: "Your judgment is at hand, assassin! Have at you!"

For a second, the two hesitated. Then the Templar made his decision. "Check the stairs, see if they need help. I'll take this end."

"Yes sir!" The Supernumerary, carrying a shotgun, sprinted toward the stairs. The Templar advanced toward Klemm. He smiled and shifted his appearance to that of General Brandt again. He staggered out of the office as though he were hurt and exhausted. Which wasn't far from the truth now that he thought about it.

"General!" the Templar cried. He rushed to Klemm's side. "Are you alright sir? Are you hurt?"

"I'm fine, I'm fine," Klemm said, but allowed the Witch Hunter to put a hand on his shoulder. "I saw him. I saw our man again. I'm afraid..." His breath hitched in his throat.

"Sir?"

"I was partnered with a Supernumerary from Ingalls. He... didn't make it. Bastard turned into some kind of monster, pulled the poor man up into the ceiling."

The Templar's face went ashen. He made the sign of the cross and Klemm saw him whisper a quick prayer.

"We will make him pay, General, that I promise you," the Witch Hunter said.

Klemm nodded. "Yes, we will. I'm sorry, you are...?"

"Sir Ronald Meriwether, General." They shook hands.

"That's a good name, Ronald. That was my father's name."

"I wish we could have been formally introduced under better circumstances, sir."

"As do I, Mr. Meriwether, as do I. If you don't mind, I'll join you and your assistant. We shouldn't be wandering around alone in this place."

"Of course, sir. We should go find Mr. Suarez. We heard gunfire back toward the stairs as well."

The two men found the Supernumerary, Suarez, in the stairwell, looking confused. Klemm suppressed a smile.

"General!" Suarez said, snapping to attention.

"General Brandt, may I present my assistant, Supernumerary Ramon Suarez."

"A pleasure," Klemm said, shaking Suarez's hand. "What's the situation here?"

"It's a hell of a thing, sir. Both me and Sir Meriwether

heard gunshots from this direction... but there's nothing here. I haven't found any shell casings."

"No doubt our target is attempting to trick us," Klemm said. "He's trying to separate us."

"Shit," Suarez said.

"No harm done this time, but from now on, we stick together," Klemm said.

"Yes sir," said Meriwether.

"Let us continue the search."

***

Flint heard a single gunshot several floors up. "Hurry!" he cried, and charged up the stairwell, sword and pistol at the ready. Navarro panted but kept up. Flint could hear voices up ahead. After ascending another two floors, they arrived at the landing to find a Templar, his Supernumerary assistant, and General Brandt. Flint's chest burned but he kept his face neutral, his breathing under control.

"General," Flint said, clicking his heels, bowing his head.

"Captain Flint," Brandt replied.

"Mr. Navarro and I heard gunfire."

"Shapeshifting bastard got my partner," Brandt said. "We lost him, unfortunately, but everything is under control for now."

Flint glanced at the other Templar. The man nodded and said, "Bernardo and I found the General just a few minutes ago." He extended his hand, and Flint shook it. "Sir Ronald Meriwether. May I present my assistant, Supernumerary Bernardo Suarez."

After the introductions had been made, Flint said, "General... did you take the elevator?"

Brandt nodded. "Yeah... the one that's still working anyway, just before the power went out."

"You alright sir?" Navarro asked.

"Yes, yes, I'm alright, thank you."

"Sir, for the record, I object to you and the other Generals taking part in this operation," Flint said.

Brandt nodded. "Duly noted."

"You should not be alone sir. I respectfully suggest that you..."

"I'll join you and Mr. Navarro," Brandt said, cutting him off. "Sir Meriwether, Mr. Suarez, you go on ahead. I'd like a word with these two."

Meriwether and Suarez looked at each other. "Of course, sir. Come Bernardo, let's give them some privacy."

After they had left, Flint said, "Is there a problem sir?"

"No problem, Captain. I wanted you and Mr. Navarro to see where Mr. Harold and I were ambushed. I think our killer may have left behind some important clues, and I wanted your opinion."

Flint nodded. "Of course, sir. Lead the way."

As Brandt led them down the hallway, Flint's mind raced. There was something off about the General. He hadn't seen Brandt step into an elevator, but he supposed it was possible he missed him during the commotion downstairs. He was in his dress uniform, but the buckle on his hat appeared to be ordinary steel rather than the customary silver. Flint had been introduced to Brandt less than 24 hours ago, so he couldn't claim to know him well. Even so, he sensed there wasn't something quite right about him, but he couldn't put his finger on it.

"By the way Captain," Brandt said. "We haven't had the chance to speak much since your arrival last night. But I heard about what you and Mr. Navarro did in Salem last month. Very impressive."

"Thank you, sir." Flint was sure of it now. There was something off about him.

"Excuse me sir," Navarro said, "But you said you were partnered with Harold?"

"That's right."

Navarro glanced at Flint, and replied, "I met him the other night. Seemed like a good guy."

"I agree, Mr. Navarro," Brandt said. "He was."

Flint didn't recall ever meeting a Mr. Harold and wasn't sure why Navarro had given him that look. Perhaps he too sensed that something was off about the General but didn't know the man well enough to figure out what was wrong. He exhaled in frustration. Flint hated shapeshifters. They sowed suspicion and distrust through their very existence.

He paused for a second, sniffed. That was it. He resumed his pace.

"General," Flint said. "I am afraid I left my cigar in my other clothes. Might I trouble you for another?"

Brandt hesitated before answering, "Don't have any on me, Captain. Sorry."

Navarro sniffed too. "Funny... I've never seen you without one sir."

"I'm trying to cut down."

"Even so," Flint said, "It is most curious that I cannot smell cigar smoke."

Brandt stopped. Sighed. "Fuck," he whispered.

The three drew their pistols simultaneously.

22

The next few moments passed in slow motion for Klemm. Flint was on his right, Navarro on his left. Even as he drew his pistol with his right hand, he summoned lightning with his left. He didn't have the time or the necessary concentration to conjure a lethal blast, but that was fine, he just needed the Supernumerary out of commission for a minute or two.

He could hear his heart pounding in his ears. Flint was wearing steel plate body armor which meant Klemm had to score a headshot to finally put his target down. Klemm's illusion magic made it appear that he too had body armor, but in truth he was still wearing a plain suit. He could see Flint's finger start to squeeze the trigger of his pistol. Klemm squeezed his pistol's trigger at the same time. He saw the muzzle flash, heard the bang. He felt strangely at peace, despite his plan going awry, again. Thanks to his healing magic, he could come back from anything short of decapitation. These two bozos couldn't.

He felt Flint's silver tipped bullet smack into his stomach. Klemm's legs crumpled beneath him, but he saw two things: his lightning bolt struck Navarro, the Mexican slamming against the wall, dropping his pistol. Klemm felt fire in his belly. He saw Flint wince... but the lanky Witch Hunter stayed on his feet.

Shit, Klemm thought.

***

Flint felt heat on his left cheek and sensed a hot dampness. The bullet had grazed him. His ears ringing, Flint advanced on the fallen Brandt – who appeared to melt and shift before his eyes, reforming into an average looking man who winced in pain. Out of the corner of his eye, he saw Navarro stirring. He appeared shaken but alive. Flint focused on Klemm. He had to end it now, before the wizard could heal from his wounds.

"Roger Klemm!" Flint shouted. He drew his sword, which now shone brightly in the darkness. "Roger Klemm, I abjure thee, in the name of God! It is over!" He saw the bloody wound in Klemm's stomach glow, the flesh healing itself. Flint fired another two rounds into Klemm's left and right shoulders. The wizard screamed in pain and fell onto his back, writhing in agony. He reached for his fallen pistol, but Flint rushed forward and kicked it away. Navarro, his senses recovered, picked up his own pistol and kept the shapeshifter covered.

"Sir..." he said, glancing at Flint's left cheek.

"It shall have to wait," Flint replied. The wound burned and he would need stitches, but duty first. He aimed the point of his sword at Klemm's throat, the wizard glaring up at him murderous rage. "Roger Klemm, I charge you with the murders of Sir Stephen Lagrange and Lady Mary Hill, and the attempted murders of Zelda Fletcher, and myself."

Klemm raised a hand to conjure another spell, but Navarro kicked him in the ribs. The wizard gasped and coughed.

"Don't even think about it, shithead," Navarro growled.

Flint gave Klemm an icy smile. "Your healing powers have their limits Mr. Klemm. If you test us, you will learn what those limits are."

With Navarro covering the shapeshifter, Flint holstered his pistol and touched a hand to his left cheek. The gauntlet came away bloody. He expected he would carry a scar for the rest of his life if he didn't have it sewn up soon. No matter. It wouldn't be the first. He heard the pounding of boots behind him. The others must have heard the gunfire. They would put Klemm to the question and learn the truth of who hired him.

***

Klemm's mind raced. He raised his hands in a gesture of submission. That goddamn Mexican... he seldom allowed his emotions to get the better of him, but kicking him when he was down? He'd make that little bastard pay if it was the last thing he did.

He looked up at Flint. The left side of his face was a crimson mask, blood pouring freely from the deep crease in his cheek. He almost had him. Almost. If he'd only been a little quicker on the draw, if only he hadn't gotten shot, he could have drilled the Witch Hunter right between the eyes.

"'Almost' isn't good enough in your trade, Roger."

He looked past Flint and Navarro, saw Cortez standing behind them, that ever-present smile on his face.

"Go away..." Klemm growled.

"Fat chance," Navarro replied.

"Wasn't... talking to you... asshole..." Klemm ground his teeth. Flint was right, damn him. His healing powers did have their limits. He'd healed the gut shot, but Klemm knew he was nearly spent. And with the Witch Hunter holding him at sword point, he couldn't incinerate him with magic; the blade would absorb his spell before it even left his hands.

"Tick tock, tick tock," Cortez said, laughing.

"Don't just stand there, you piece of shit, *help me!*" Klemm shouted.

Flint's face remained an inscrutable mask, but Navarro's brow furrowed.

"So who are you talking to, huh?" he asked.

"Are you asking me for something, Roger?" said Cortez.

"Only God can help you now, Mr. Klemm," Flint said. "If you renounce the dark powers, confess your sins, do penance, and give us the name of your employer, you may yet find mercy when you appear before the Judgment Seat."

"Don't believe him," Cortez said. He floated toward Klemm, phasing through Flint and Navarro as though they weren't there. "There's no mercy for you in this world or the next. You'll hang for your crimes, after they're done torturing you."

Klemm could hear running footsteps from both upstairs and downstairs. The cops, the soldiers, the Templars... they were all closing in on him. Closing in to rob him of his freedom and eventually his life.

"It doesn't have to end like that Roger," Cortez said, leaning in until they were almost nose to nose. "We both know you're done if you refuse my help. You're spent. Even if you were at full strength, you don't have it in you to take on everyone in this building. And they're all converging on you now."

Klemm said nothing.

"How about it?" Navarro asked. "Who hired you? Who wants Silas dead? And Zelda?"

Klemm's eyes flitted between Flint, Navarro, and Cortez.

"Yes," he whispered.

"I beg your pardon?" Flint said.

"What was that, Roger?" Cortez asked.

"I need your help," Klemm replied.

Flint grunted. "I daresay you need help beyond my power to provide Mr. Klemm, but if you speak truly, this is a good first step and..."

"You're making the right decision, Roger," Cortez said, talking over Flint. "Together, we can make the world howl in despair."

"What happens now?" Klemm asked. He could see them now, the other Templars along with a few cops and soldiers, jogging toward them.

"Now you shall be remanded to Fort Ingalls, where you will be put to the question..." Flint said.

"Now? Now you're going to feel a little weird," Cortez said with a smile. The boy's body shimmered and disintegrated into a black mist that entered Klemm's nostrils, his mouth.

***

Flint felt the hairs on the back of neck stand up. Klemm had either gone mad, talking to someone who wasn't there... or he was talking to someone who was there but that he and Navarro couldn't see. Something wasn't right. He glanced at Navarro from the corner of his eye. The man looked as ill at ease as Flint felt.

"Sir... something's wrong," Navarro said.

Flint returned his focus to Klemm, and it took all of his self-control not to gasp aloud. Klemm's body shuddered, arcs of magical energy danced over him.

"Captain Flint!" One of the Templars rushing toward his position called out to him. Klemm's eyes were shut.

"Rise, Mr. Klemm," Flint said. "You have a reservation in the Ingalls dungeons."

Klemm still shook, but Flint saw now that it was suppressed laughter.

"What's so funny?" Navarro said, nudging the assassin with his toe.

Klemm opened his eyes, which now glowed red. The shadow he cast was no longer human but that of a writhing mass of tentacles.

"What's funny," Klemm said, "Is that I refused this gift for so long."

23

Flint fired his pistol, the bullet smacking into Klemm's forehead. His head snapped backward, blood and skull fragments spattering the hallway floor. But Klemm lowered his head, a manic grin on his face, his teeth elongated and needle-like. Navarro aimed and fired his rifle, the bullet hitting Klemm center mass, an expanding circle of black ichor staining the man's suit even as the round exploded out of his back. The assassin laughed, cold and cruel.

"If only you knew how long we've waited for this, Flint," Klemm hissed.

"On me!" Flint cried. "Smite this monster's heathen soul!"

Templars and Supernumeraries rushed to their side. Forming ranks, they opened fire on Klemm with pistols and rifles. He raised his hand, and a wall of translucent light formed in the hallway, separating the assassin from Flint and the others. The bullets disintegrated on contact, the wall of light rippling like a pool of water. Flint's ears rang, but he waved his hand in front of his face, signaling everyone to cease fire.

The bullet holes in Klemm's forehead and chest knitted themselves shut. The man kept his eyes on Flint, and the Witch Hunter suppressed a shudder. Klemm was clearly possessed, and there was no telling how the demon inside him would manipulate his shapeshifting abilities.

"The dark powers will not avail you, foul heretic!" Flint shouted.

"We've learned a few tricks since last we met, Captain," Klemm said, laughing.

"If we have met before, then I assure you this will be the last time!"

"Yes, Silas. Yes, it will be."

Klemm's body rippled. Four limbs sprouted from his torso as his skin darkened, hardened, became glistening chitin. A tail burst from his lower back, lengthening, sharpening into a vicious stinger. His fingers melded; his hands stretched until they were pincers. Klemm was gone, and in his place was a scorpion the size of an automobile.

The arachnid scuttled forward. Flint heard moans and screams of terror behind him. The scorpion reached for him with one of its pincers, but he dodged to his right, bringing his sword down in an overhead slice. The blade glanced off the scorpion's chitin, but the short hairs on its claw sizzled and burned. Navarro fired, worked the bolt, fired again. The high powered silver tipped rifle rounds pierced the scorpion's armor, thick yellow blood oozing from the holes.

The other Supernumeraries fired their rifles into the colossal scorpion. Flint and the other Witch Hunters added fire to the assault, but Flint could see their pistol rounds weren't strong enough to pierce the monster's armor. Glancing behind him, he saw a few police officers and soldiers making a run for it. He couldn't blame them;

their ordinary lead bullets would likely be of little use against the demon. Among those who remained, he saw Detectives Earle and Marsten firing their service pistols. Flint prayed they would survive the battle to come.

"Aim for the eyes! Aim for the eyes!" Navarro bellowed.

The Supernumeraries directed their fire into the scorpion's face. The monster screeched in pain, but it lunged with its stinger. It slammed into Flint's chest plate and he was knocked off his feet, colliding with other Templars who all fell like bowling pins.

"Reload!" Navarro shouted. A Supernumerary tossed him a five round stripper clip, which he inserted into his rifle, slammed the bolt home, aimed, and fired into the scorpion's dripping maw.

The arachnid appeared to melt. Flint was helped to his feet by two other Templars. His dress uniform had saved his life again, but the chest plate was dented and sizzling. He hoped the scorpion's venom wouldn't burn all the way through to his skin.

The scorpion was gone. In its place was a pool of bubbling black slime. Navarro and the other Supernumeraries kept it covered with their rifles, waiting for the next attack. Flint advanced to the front, sword and pistol at the ready. Navarro glanced at him from the corner of his eye.

"You should get out of here sir," he said. "He's after you."

"Precisely, Mr. Navarro, and that is why I will not leave." Standing at Navarro's side, keeping the pool of slime covered with his pistol, he shouted, "Roger Klemm! Show yourself! You wish to kill me? I am here!"

A gust of foul wind blew through the hallway, and Flint heard soldiers and police officers coughing and gagging. The poor souls weren't used to the devil's tricks, Flint thought.

"Roger's not alone, Captain," said a deep voice that echoed from everywhere and nowhere.

"It matters not if Mr. Klemm has all the legions of Hell at his back," Flint said. "Neither he nor you are a match for the grace and the might of our Lord!"

A blood curdling roar echoed in the hallway. From the pool of slime emerged a mass of writhing tentacles.

"Open fire!" Before Flint could finish yelling the order, the hallway erupted in another hail of gunfire. A corner of Flint's mind wondered if his hearing would ever recover. One of the tentacles whipped out toward Flint, but he brought his sword up in time, slicing it off. Despite the chaos around him, Flint felt as though he'd done this before.

Another tentacle whipped forward, wrapping around Navarro's waist. He dropped his rifle, drew his sidearm and the tomahawk on his belt. He hacked away as Flint rushed to his aid. His sword shone bright as he sliced clean through the unclean beast. Navarro dropped to the floor.

"Christ," he spat, as he shrugged the remains of the tentacle off his body. The pool of slime congealed, reformed into a familiar sight, one Flint had hoped he'd never see again. A hideous, gibbering monstrosity, a black slug-like being with masses of tentacles, burning red eyes scattered over its body, with a gnashing beak at the front. He, Navarro, General Abernathy, and Zelda Fletcher had encountered it before outside the city of Jordan, fresh from its leveling Fletcher's hometown of New Rome.

Flint and Navarro withdrew, joining the firing line of Templars and Supernumeraries. No orders were needed or given. They poured gunfire into the creature as fast as they could pull triggers. It took no need of the silver tipped bullets, its wounds closing almost as quickly as they were opened. Tentacles shot forward, one coming right for Flint. He parried it in time, his sword cutting it in two down the middle. Another tentacle wrapped around a Supernumerary and pulled him into the monster's hungry beak before the man even had time to scream. He disappeared in a cloud of bloody mist and a sickening crunch. Flint's fellow Templars holstered their pistols and drew their swords, the blessed steel illuminating the hallway brighter than the electric lights ever could.

The tentacles came faster, and in greater numbers. It seemed as though for every one a Templar sliced off, two more took its place. More men and women were snagged and pulled screaming into the monster's insatiable maw. The last of the police officers and soldiers broke and ran.

"Boss," Navarro said. He hacked away at another tentacle with his tomahawk, while firing his sidearm with his offhand.

"Fall back!" Flint cried.

The Templars and Supernumeraries quickened their pace, walking backwards, firing at the beast, cutting it when its tentacles got too close. A bead of sweat ran down the side of Flint's face. He thought back to his first encounter with this demon outside of Jordan. It was only with Zelda Fletcher's assistance and some well-placed explosives that he and his companions had defeated this monster then. And right now, he had neither.

24

Zelda Fletcher paced up and down the sidewalk. It galled her that she was unable to join the Templars inside that skyscraper. She'd circled the entire block, but no matter what angle she tried, that invisible barrier was there like a brick wall. She'd even tried opening a manhole cover, thinking it might not extend underground, but it was still there, and she'd stained her dress and shoes for nothing. She snorted at the memory. Her dress was already stained with her blood. What was a little raw sewage?

She hadn't tried any more magic. Silas had warned off the crowd earlier, but now that he was gone, she figured it was best not to tempt fate by trying another spell. The cops had cordoned off the block, but Abernathy had had a word with them before entering the building, and she had been permitted to stay inside the yellow tape.

"Hey!" She waved at a nearby cop. "Excuse me? Hello? Officer?" The young police officer ambled over to her.

"Can I help you, Miss...?"

"Zelda Fletcher. I think General Abernathy told you guys about me?"

The cop nodded. "Yes, I remember."

"Can you tell me what's going on in there?" She waved at the Mansfield Building.

The cop pursed his lips. "I wish I could say."

"Oh, come on. I'm a guest of the Order, I think you can..."

"It's not that," the cop said, shaking his head. "I mean I honestly don't know. They locked the building down a few hours ago. Last I heard, they're going room to room looking for the shooter."

"And?" Fletcher asked.

"And that's it. It's been radio silence for a while now."

Fletcher swore under her breath. Who the hell was responsible for that damn barrier? Someone wanted to keep her away from the hunt, but why? It must have had to do with her telepathic powers. The corner of her mouth turned up. People who didn't know her well made her out to be a perfect mind reader who could peer into the depths of men's souls and know their darkest secrets. In truth, she found it a pain in the ass more than anything. She could overhear people's surface level thoughts, but she had to work at it to go deeper than that. If she did, her target would notice. And most people weren't worth reading anyway. She'd learned early on how to tune out the noise. Otherwise, she was certain that she'd have gone mad.

Her mind went to Francisco. He was the one who helped her realize she was a witch. It was he who had identified her mind reading powers, and he who had taught her how to tune out the constant white noise. Did she really see him earlier? She had helped the Templars blow up his demonic body months ago. She remembered hearing him whisper in her mind that death was only the beginning.

She'd brushed it off as a pre-death one liner, empty bravado before he'd died. But what if he was right?

She paced back and forth. The more she thought about it, the more convinced she grew that he'd saved her life earlier. If she hadn't seen him, if she hadn't turned before the sniper pulled the trigger, the bullet might have gone right through her heart. She could heal herself, yes, but not if death was instantaneous. But why would Francisco have saved her? If anything, he'd want her dead. If that was really him she'd seen earlier, that is. She shuddered. Magic was all fun and games when you were tossing fireballs and lightning bolts or influencing some poor sap's mind to make him hand over his wallet. But messing around with life and death, souls and demons... she'd never wanted any part of that aspect of the craft. That's what made her turn on Francisco, what felt like a lifetime ago.

She was worried about Abernathy, Rico, and Silas. It was ironic. When she was using her powers to enrich herself at the expense of the wealthy, Francisco had told her that if the Witch Hunters ever captured them, they'd be tortured to death. She'd taken a risk turning herself in to them in the Jordan city jail all those months ago. But she'd feared Francisco more than she'd feared the Templars. And all things considered, they'd really grown on her. She helped them hunt down members of her former gang. And in return, they'd given her room and board, plus a rehabilitation program to wean her off using magic. They said using magic was unnatural and opened her up to demonic influence. She believed them, and she made a good faith effort to turn away... but it was difficult. Silas was right. Magic was addicting.

Silas... she liked Rico. She'd grown to think of Abernathy as the grandfather she'd never known. But she realized Silas was the reason why she stuck around Fort Marsing when she could have slipped out at any time. She didn't think she had a chance in hell of Silas ever looking at her as a woman. Stubborn asshole lived for his job and nothing else. But she liked him. He was the most intriguing man she'd ever met, and even if he never made a move on her, she'd stick around for his sake. Especially if his lunatic brother was bent on dropping nukes or building some crazy country bent on world conquest.

She had confidence that he could track down the shooter and either bring him in or deal out a little frontier justice. But nonetheless it pissed her off that she couldn't be there to help run him down. Nobody shot Zelda Fletcher and got away with it. If only she could...

Hello Zelda.

She blinked, looked around.

You remember me, don't you?

Francisco, she thought.

I'm touched. I haven't forgotten you.

What do you want?

You, of course.

She snorted. *I've moved on. You should too.*

The dead are remarkably single-minded, Zelda. Ever since you killed me last spring, all I've thought about is revenge.

Good luck with that, she thought. *I'm not a saint, but even I know there are rules. You can't touch me now.*

Oh, that's where you're wrong. I'm back.

She felt it now. Her mouth dropped. Francisco was nearby. Not as a ghost, but in the flesh.

How?! she thought.

Laughter echoed in her mind. *You'll find out. I've removed the barrier. Feel free to come in if you dare. If not, that's fine. I'll be coming for you as soon as I kill your new boyfriend.*

What the fuck are you... She gasped. Silas.

Yes, Francisco said. *And don't think you'll kill me again like you did last time. I've learned from my mistakes.*

His voice fell silent. She looked around. Everything appeared normal on the outside, but she could sense something had changed inside the Mansfield Building. She strode toward the spot she'd probed earlier, the place where the barrier began. She tentatively stuck out a hand. It passed over the invisible boundary that had stopped her earlier. She took a step forward. Nothing.

She picked up the hem of her dress off the ground and jogged toward the Mansfield Building.

Hang on Silas, she thought. *I'll help you send this bastard back where he belongs.*

25

Silas Flint brought his sword down in an overhead slash, cleaving through the ebony tentacle. It plopped on the floor, twitching and writhing. Beside him, Navarro aimed and fired his rifle. One of the beast's eyes exploded in a shower of ichor, spattering Flint's battered chest plate. Other Supernumeraries, armed with automatic rifles, emptied their magazines into the demon's body. The streams of bullets stitched holes in its hide, spraying the hallway with its corrupted blood. Moments after they appeared, the bullet holes melted, twisted, and sealed themselves shut.

"Fall back to the stairwell!" Flint called. He had no idea if he was the ranking Templar present, but the other Witch Hunters and Supernumeraries continued their withdrawal. The gelatinous demon continued its advance, its razor-sharp beak snapping, but the unrelenting stream of gunfire, plus the Templar blades, slowed it down enough that they were able to continue their retreat without any further casualties.

"Silas!"

Flint glanced over his shoulder. General Abernathy stood in the doorway leading to the stairwell. He ushered Templars and Supernumeraries past him, into the stairwell, down to the lobby.

"General!" Flint shouted. "You must withdraw sir!"

"Absolutely not!" Abernathy yelled back. "All of you, move! Hurry!" The General had his sword in one hand. In his other hand, Flint saw an olive drab sphere with a metal lever: a grenade.

"Mr. Navarro, covering fire!"

Navarro fired from the hip, worked the bolt, fired again. Each shot made another of the demon's eyes explode. It screeched in pain and anger. Navarro fired one last shot directly into its open mouth. The foul stench of burning, corrupted flesh assailed Flint's nostrils. He cut through another tentacle that reached toward his assistant.

"Here I am, monster!" Flint bellowed. "Come and receive a foretaste of the judgment that awaits you!"

The monster roared, its spittle soaking the hallway. Abernathy pulled the pin of his grenade. He raised his thumb from the lever, the stainless steel metal flying away from the sphere. He underhand tossed the grenade directly into the demon's open beak, the sphere disappearing down its gullet. Flint, Navarro, and the other remaining Witch Hunters and Supernumeraries turned and sprinted toward the doorway. Once Flint passed, Abernathy followed, slamming the door behind him, bracing it with his shoulder.

There was a loud boom which shook the entire floor. Flint could hear something wet slapping against the door. The stink of burnt flesh threatened to make him gag, but he maintained control. Abernathy locked eyes with him.

"Unless I'm very much mistaken," Abernathy said, "I think we've seen this abomination before."

"Yes sir," Flint said. "That is the demon we confronted outside of Jordan."

"What about Klemm?"

"That *is* Klemm," Navarro spat.

Abernathy raised an eyebrow. "Captain?"

"I am afraid so," Flint said. "We had him, sir. We were preparing to arrest Mr. Klemm, but he assumed the form of that hideous monstrosity."

Abernathy took a deep breath. He opened the door, peeked around the corner, and shut it again in the space of three seconds. "It's reforming."

Flint pursed his lips. "I suspect that we will need more explosives if we are to slay this beast once and for all."

Abernathy shifted his gaze toward the other Templars and Supernumeraries gathered on the landing and the stairwell. "All of you, get as many grenades as you can carry, and get word to Fort Ingalls to send even more. Notify the police and the Army as well. Move!" They nodded, saluted, and took off down the stairs at a sprint.

"Silas," Navarro said. "I was thinking. Klemm wanted to take you out. If there's still any part of him in that thing, he might still focus on you."

Flint nodded. "It is a possibility."

"If that is the same monster we fought outside of Jordan," Abernathy said, "I suspect it will want us three. And Miss Fletcher."

"We ought to keep it contained in this building," Flint said. "We will destroy this entire structure if that is what it takes."

"If he's still got his shapeshifting power, then maybe we should stay up here," Navarro said. "Keep shooting and don't let up until we get some more firepower. Pin him down."

Abernathy chanced another peek through the doorway. His shoulders slumped and he sighed. "I think we might be too late for that, Mr. Navarro. It's gone."

Flint approached the door and looked around the corner. The hallway stank of cordite and burnt flesh. The walls were stained black with ichor and gunpowder residue. But there was no trace of the demon, the googly eyed tentacle monster as Navarro had named it months ago.

"So what now?" Navarro asked.

Flint scowled. "If Klemm has indeed retained any of his humanity, I concur with you, General: he will make another attempt on my life. If not... then I fear he is little more than a rabid animal and will seek to kill and devour as many souls as it can lay its filthy hands on."

"Then we shall slay it again, and save God's children from its evil grasp," Abernathy said. "Let's meet up with the others."

26

Roger Klemm reformed into his normal self. He had taken refuge in another empty office on the floor above where he'd fought the Templars. He felt like his entire body was electrified. He'd never felt such power before. It was like his mind had expanded tenfold. He knew the shapes of other creatures now, beasts that were not of this world. He could do anything at all. Klemm stifled the urge to laugh aloud.

Why so secretive, Roger? Cortez's voice echoed in his mind. *There are no secrets between us anymore. All that we have is yours. Everything is yours for the taking if you have the will.*

Klemm chuckled but stopped himself before it devolved into manic cackling. "I still have a job to do," he said aloud.

Of course, Roger, Cortez whispered. *And we are happy to help you. Silas Flint and Zelda Fletcher have a debt to pay, and we mean to collect.*

"Right. And I mean to collect my fee." He took a deep breath. Klemm had never taken the form of a demon before, and that thing, whatever it was he became, had devoured several Templars and Supernumeraries. It was an odd feeling. He didn't feel like he had eaten.

We are one with Ichthil, but he remains separate from us in some ways, Cortez said. *You've received a small taste of the power he can offer you. If you want more, he needs more blood. More souls.*

"Plenty more where those came from," Klemm said.

What will you do now?

"I mean to kill Silas Flint and his little girlfriend too."

Excellent.

Klemm gathered his thoughts. He still didn't fully trust Cortez and his demonic buddies. He had more power, yes, but he doubted it made him invincible. He wouldn't rush headlong into combat with the entire Ingalls garrison.

You could, you know. You could lay waste to the entire city. You can do anything you want.

Klemm shook his head. "Yeah, well, I still plan to live here after this is all over, so no thanks on that part."

Of course. By the way, I've removed the barrier. You can leave if you wish, but you should know that I've invited Zelda to join us.

Shit, Klemm thought. *She can detect...*

No. She can't.

He furrowed his brow. *Huh? Why not?*

You're the best at what you do, Roger. You can change your body to be a perfect copy of someone else. But you never could guard your true thoughts.

Klemm snorted. *Never needed to before.*

But now you can. We can shield your mind from Zelda's probing. You can walk freely among the lambs, and not even she can detect you anymore.

Klemm smiled.

***

Flint, Navarro, and Abernathy trudged downstairs toward the lobby. It appeared the remaining civilians in the building had all been escorted out – or fled in terror from the gunfire of their battle with Klemm. Flint was grateful that they were out of harm's way, but this meant that Klemm would most likely attempt to blend in with the Templars again.

When they reached the ground floor, Generals Hickock, Davis, and Brandt stepped forward. "You gentlemen alright?" Hickock asked.

Abernathy nodded. "Yes, for now." He summarized their encounter with Klemm, and Flint filled in the gaps.

"He impersonated me, huh?" Brandt asked, puffing on a cigar. "Maybe he's not as smart as we think he is."

The smell of tobacco smoke cheered Flint's heart. That was definitely the real Brandt.

Davis frowned, crossed his arms. "If he's able to take the forms of demons now, then our shooter must have made a deal with the devil's minions."

"Yes," Flint replied. "As General Abernathy said, we have encountered his demonic form before."

"Remind me how y'all beat him last time?" Hickock asked.

"With Zelda's magic, and a few grenades," Navarro answered.

"Speaking of which," Abernathy said, pointing.

Flint and the others directed their gaze to the front door. Zelda Fletcher marched toward them, her high heels clacking on the tiled floor. Her dress was still spattered with her blood and sported a ragged hole where the bullet had penetrated, but otherwise she appeared none the worse for wear.

"Hey! Hey guys!" she called out. Fletcher hurried to meet them. Closer, Flint could see her hair was a mess, her makeup running, but he was pleased to see her. If she was there, then that could only mean...

"I take it that the barrier has been removed," Flint said.

"Yeah," she replied. "And you'll never guess who took it down."

"Cortez," Flint sighed.

"Shit," Navarro said. "If the barrier's gone, then he's free to leave."

"Miss Fletcher," Abernathy said. "Can you sense Klemm's presence? Or Cortez's?"

She closed her eyes, and Flint saw them flutter beneath her eyelids. After a few moments, she looked at Flint and the others, shaking her head. "No... I can't. Just before I came in, Francisco spoke to me in my mind. After he finished, it's like his presence vanished without a trace."

"If you can't sense him..." Hickock said.

Brandt blew a ring of smoke. "...He's definitely got an upgrade."

Flint stroked his chin. "I think I begin to understand now," he said.

"What do you mean, sir?" Navarro asked.

"Let us assume that Cortez is the one who erected the barrier, trapping Klemm inside the building, and locking Miss Fletcher outside. Our encounter with Klemm in the hallway would seem to confirm that he has been possessed or is otherwise receiving help from the powers below. Perhaps Cortez manipulated Klemm into accepting possession."

Abernathy nodded. "It makes sense. Assuming it's Cortez who's possessed Klemm, he would definitely be out for revenge against us."

"Klemm wants to kill Silas and Zelda for business, Cortez wants to kill them for pleasure," Navarro said. He looked to Flint, then Fletcher, a small grin on his face. "You two make friends everywhere, huh?"

Hickock blew out a breath. "So, what now? If he can get out now, how do we know he's not in the wind?"

"And how would we find him if he is?" Davis said.

Flint gave a wintry smile. "I do not believe that shall be a problem, sirs. As Mr. Navarro pointed out, both Klemm and Cortez wish me and Miss Fletcher dead, each for reasons of their own. Even if he is now free to come and go as he pleases, I do not believe he will be leaving soon."

"So stick to our old plan?" Brandt asked.

"Yes... but I have an idea of how we can make our search a little easier," Abernathy said.

"What are you thinking, John?" Hickock said.

"If Mr. Klemm is indeed possessed, then that means he's acquired the weaknesses of the powers below. Jeremiah, we should check to see if the telephones are still working. If not, send a courier to ask Cardinal Benítez to come pay us a visit."

Flint nodded. "An excellent idea sir. General Hickock, you should also send word to your armorer that we shall need more explosives."

"Already on it, Captain."

Fletcher raised a hand. "Francisco made it sound like it he's really got it in for us. Maybe Silas and I could bait him somehow?"

"Did you have something in mind, Miss Fletcher?" Flint asked.

She smiled. "As a matter of fact, I do."

Flint checked his pocket watch. 5:46 p.m. Yes, he thought, he would definitely miss his appointment with the Emperor.

27

Roger Klemm morphed into form of General Malachi Davis. He wanted to laugh aloud. Normally when he changed his shape, it took something out of him, like he'd just run up a flight of stairs. Now though? He felt nothing at all, like he could do this all day. Before, he could only take the shape of a person or an animal (he was one of the Salem Zoo's most generous patrons) that he had made physical contact with, or something that belonged

to them. Now he felt like he could take the shape of anything he could imagine.

*Don't get carried away, Roger, Cortez whispered. Some of
the old rules still apply.*

*Speaking of the old rules, let's get something straight, Klemm
replied. I still have a job to do, and I still intend to collect
my pay.*

*Whatever you say. You don't need to sneak around anymore
though.*

*That's how they got you though, isn't it? You took on too
many of them at once.*

Klemm felt a wave of anger wash over him. It wasn't
from him though; it came from Cortez or Ichthil, or whoever he was speaking to.

*Yes, Cortez said. But I don't intend to repeat that mis-
take. I've got a little surprise prepared if they think to try that
trick again.*

"I appreciate the upgrade," Klemm said out loud, "But
I'm sticking to my usual methods." He left the office
where'd holed up and stepped out into the hallway.
Klemm had to admit the Templars had a good plan, staying in pairs. But that was a double-edged sword for them;
if they found him in the form of General Davis walking
about alone, they'd hesitate long enough for him to bluff
his way out or kill them. And now he was confident that
he could take on the whole building if it came to it.

He could sense that he was free to leave if he chose.
Cortez kept his word on that part at least. He also sensed
that Zelda Fletcher was present now. He had a hunch this
would be his best opportunity to take out both of his

targets. If they decided that he was gone, he'd have to go through it all over again: trailing them, remaining out of sight, waiting for another chance to strike. And if he was being honest, enough things had gone wrong for one day. No, he was eager to get the job finished now and get out of there for good.

Still plan on visiting old Las Vegas? Cortez asked.

"Yeah, as a matter of fact."

Sin City, they used to call it.

"Sounds right up your alley."

It had its uses. Let me offer you a friendly piece of advice though: if you choose to visit, beware of Doctor Kato.

"Who?"

He rules most of the old Nevada, and magicians who fall into his clutches meet a bad end.

"What, is he a Witch Hunter?"

No.

"And what do you care? You're already dead, and he can't touch demons, right?"

He has his ways, and we would prefer not to wind up as one of his test subjects.

That caught Klemm off guard. He couldn't sense any of Cortez's memories or Ichthil's thoughts, but he got the impression they felt contempt toward the Templars. Probably because they devoted themselves to God. But now, when they spoke about this Doctor Kato, he could sense they felt... not fear, exactly, but they weren't fans of his idea to party hard in Vegas after a job well done. No matter. It was still his body. He was in control. He'd do whatever he damn well pleased. Now, it was time to focus on the hunt and get this shit done, once and for all.

***

Flint and Navarro got down on their left knees. His Eminence Santiago Cardinal Benítez, Cardinal Archbishop of the Archdiocese of Salem, entered the lobby, his scarlet trimmed cassock brushing the tiled floor as he strode to meet them. The cardinal held out his hand, and Flint kissed the ring on his finger.

"Your Eminence," Flint said. Navarro kissed the ring as well.

"Captain Flint," Benítez said. "Please, rise. It's an honor to meet you."

"The honor is mine, sir," Flint replied.

"General Hickock tells me that Salem has you two to thank for ending the Night of Chaos last month."

"Just doing our job sir," Navarro said.

"And the people of God thank you for it," Benítez said. "I understand you require my assistance."

"Yes sir," Flint said. "An assassin has made several attempts on my life, and the life of our associate, Zelda Fletcher."

Fletcher, standing off at a discreet distance, nodded a greeting to the Cardinal, who nodded in return.

"We have reason to believe that our assassin is now possessed," Flint said.

"On top of that, our guy is a shapeshifter," Navarro

added. "He can turn into animals or make himself look like anyone."

"I see," Benítez replied. "How can I help?"

"Miss Fletcher and I have formed a plan to draw him out into the open. Mr. Klemm may be unaware that his demonically fueled power comes with certain limitations."

Benítez's eyes lit up. "Ah... I believe I see where you are going with this." He stroked his chin. "I may need to bring in additional clergy. I'm not certain I can do this alone."

"Whatever you deem best, sir," Flint said.

Benítez excused himself and joined the Templar Generals who had gathered at the other end of the lobby. As he passed by the other Templars and Supernumeraries, they bowed their heads, some genuflecting. Fletcher joined Flint and Navarro.

"Um..." she said. "If he consecrates this building, is that... you know... going to affect me?"

"No," Flint said.

"Not unless you've been making deals with demons behind our back," Navarro said with a grin.

Fletcher chuckled. "No, no, never."

"Does he make you nervous?" Navarro asked.

"Who, the Cardinal?" She thought a moment. "Kind of. I don't know. I mean you guys are one thing, but he's, like, a real priest. I guess I was worried he'd want to smite me, or burn me, or tell me to get out. I'm a witch after all. And I'm not Catholic, either."

"I believe His Eminence is aware of your status as a guest of the Order," Flint said. "And so long as you make a sincere effort to reform your life, the Church will never turn you away."

"Good to know," she said, smiling. "So once he does his thing, you ready for our part?"

"I believe so," Flint said. "You are certain it will work? Cortez is a damned soul in league with the powers below. He is no longer the man you once knew."

"You can't hear him in your head like I can," she replied. "He's changed some, yeah, but I think there's still enough of him left that he'll come after us when we need him to."

"I don't like getting separated from you though," Navarro said. "It's kind of my job to watch your back, you know?"

"Fear not, Mr. Navarro," Flint said. "I expect that if Miss Fletcher's plan is successful, we shall be reunited soon enough."

***

Klemm, still in the form of General Davis, stalked the hallways upstairs. This was incredible. His magical talent had helped him sense the presence of others before, but looking back on it, it felt like he'd been looking at them through a wall of mud. Now he could see and hear them clearly. There were too many voices in the lobby below to make out specific conversations, but now the presence of the Templars, the cops, the soldiers... it was like they were shining beacons in the gloom. Speaking of which, he could see a squad of soldiers in one of the functioning elevator cars, rising to meet him. In all the excitement earlier, he'd forgotten about his spell to interfere with the building's electricity. It must have dissipated when he lost his concentration.

He took a deep breath, prepared to bluff his way though it if they questioned him, or fight it out. The car moved past his floor and continued its ascent. He exhaled. What were they up to? No matter. He wasn't as worried about ordinary cops and soldiers. The Witch Hunters, always the damn Witch Hunters. Puny little apes, thinking they could oppose the plans of Hell itself, hunting and killing those with the power to shape their own destinies, to command the elements, to transcend death itself. He should kill them all, here and now.

Klemm shook his head. What had come over him? He didn't like Templars, but he avoided them when he could. He'd never felt that kind of murderous hatred for them before. What could... Cortez.

Can you blame me though, he whispered in Klemm's mind.

"I sympathize, but I need to keep a clear head," he replied out loud. Now, where would Flint and Fletcher be? Probably down in the lobby, curse his luck. Maybe he could draw them away somehow. Kill them one at a time, but he felt like he could take on both at the same time if it came to it.

A bright light flared from below, forcing Klemm to look away. Whatever it was, it burned. He felt pain all over his body. Nothing he couldn't handle, but he'd never felt anything like it before. He growled low in his throat.

"What... is that?"

A priest has entered the building, Cortez said.

"Why does it burn?"

That is Santiago Benítez. Be cautious. Most priests are worthless, but this one... he has caused my masters trouble in the past.

"But why would that affect..."

Why do you think, idiot? You've pledged yourself to our side.

Klemm scowled but said nothing. He guessed he'd never be able to set foot in a church for the rest of his life. Not that he had since he was a kid, but still... wait.

"Why would they ask the Cardinal to come here?"

No doubt they think to separate us. It matters not. Come, let us find our quarry. My revenge is long overdue.

Not to mention my fee, Klemm thought.

28

Silas Flint and Zelda Fletcher stepped into the elevator. Flint pressed the button for the tenth floor and the doors silently shut. There was a clank, followed by the hum of the car ascending through the shaft.

"So..." Fletcher said.

Flint said nothing.

"You... ah... you doing okay?" she asked.

"I am fine, thank you. Are you alright?" Flint replied.

"Oh yeah, yeah. Doing just fine."

The car continued to rise and they both fell silent. Fletcher kneaded her hands, smoothed her dress. She took a breath, exhaled. Flint stood still as a statue.

"Hey," she said. "About earlier..."

Flint said nothing.

"I asked you once, but you never really gave me a straight answer."

Flint was silent.

"How come you always use the High Speech? We both know you spoke in the Common Tongue right after I got shot, when you were... uh... you know... holding me."

Flint glanced at her from the corner of his eye, returned his focus to the elevator door. "It is a long story, Miss Fletcher, one I do not have the time to regale you with presently."

"Okay, okay, fair enough. But... ah... will you regale me with it? You know, some day?"

"Perhaps. For now, let us focus on the task at hand. The others will need the elevator."

"Looking forward to it."

The elevator shuddered to halt. There was a ding as the doors slid open. Flint drew his sword with his right hand, one of his pistols with his left. As he expected, the blade shone brightly in the darkened hallway, partly due to being so close to Fletcher. He aimed his pistol to his left, then to his right, as he stepped out. Fletcher followed him. He noticed that she had not brought a pistol of her own.

"Miss Fletcher," he said.

"Oh, come on. I'm only going to use magic against the bad guy."

"You and I have been over this, and I trust that Lady MacFarlane has gone over it with you during your stay with us at Marsing. Magic is inherently corrupting, whatever your target or your intentions may be."

"Yeah, I know, I know. But it's the quickest way to get Francisco and Klemm out here."

"And for that reason, I will look the other way this time. But I exhort you, again, in the name of God, to renounce your powers once and for all."

She grinned. "So I guess there's no point in asking if you'd like me to heal that cut on your cheek."

"Not unless you plan on doing so with a thread and needle."

She shook her head and chuckled. Flint knew she was, in fact, weaning herself from her use of magic, and how much of a struggle it was for her. It pained him that, in days to come, she may need to use her powers when it came time for a reckoning with his brother, Charles. Magic twisted even the noblest intentions. He had encountered magicians who claimed to use their powers for good before. And sometimes they did, for a while at least. But they always descended into evil and madness if they persisted too long. He had told Fletcher on numerous occasions that if her power drove her mad, he wouldn't hesitate to put her down. He hoped it would never come to that. Despite her heathen ways, she had grown on him over the last few months.

Flint took a glance back at the elevator. Klemm had shut the power down earlier that afternoon, but whatever he had done, everything appeared to be in working order again. He saw the bulbs above the elevator door light up and go out as the car made its rounds. Cardinal Benítez had summoned some of his most trusted clergy to assist with his part of the plan. He expected there would be no mistaking it when they had finished their task.

"So what now?" Fletcher asked.

Flint scowled. "Now, I suggest that you do what we came here to do."

"Okay. It's gonna be okay Silas."

"I shall cover you."

The corner of her mouth turned up. Then she closed her eyes in concentration. She raised her hands and moved them as if sculpting a pot from clay. Flint saw sparks appear, then fire trailing from her fingertips. His sword glowed even brighter. He found this business distasteful, but he prayed that the Lord would forgive them for trafficking in the dark powers this time.

Fletcher smiled. As the fireball took shape, Flint saw her smile stretch into a manic grin. Her shoulders shook with barely suppressed laughter.

"Miss Fletcher. More control, if you please."

She shook her head, set her face in a grim stare as she focused on gathering her power. Flint had no talent for magic, so he couldn't claim firsthand knowledge of the temptations Fletcher was surely feeling. Why some people were still born with the curse of magic centuries after the twenty-first century Occult War was something of a mystery; Flint had no idea why his brother Charles could use magic while the rest of the family could not.

No matter. Fletcher looked like she was nearly finished. With an animal cry of triumph, she raised her hands. The fireball levitated above her palms.

"Hey Francisco," she shouted. "You want us? Come and get us!"

Flint held his sword and pistol at the ready. He was confident that the Holy Spirit would lead them to victory, but he felt doubt gnaw at his heart. He could take Klemm, but he wasn't as sure that he and Fletcher could take the tentacle monster alone. He prayed that the Cardinal and his priests finished their part in time.

***

Santiago Cardinal Benítez faced his men, four Benedictine priest monks from the Cathedral in Salem. Benítez offered a quick mental prayer to the Holy Spirit to guide him in what was to come. He was happy in his vocation, but he often wondered if he could be doing more in the never-ending battle against the forces of heresy and witchcraft. His own confessor had assured him that he was following God's will for his life. Besides, witch hunting was a young man's vocation (despite General Hickock participating in the action last month.)

"Gentlemen," Benítez said. "The Knights Templar of the Order of Saint Benedict have asked for our assistance on their latest case. I'm sure you're all aware of the shooting that took place here earlier today."

The monks nodded.

"The Templars have discovered that the shooter is a magician. And that he is now possessed by a demon from the bowels of Hell."

They made the sign of the cross and whispered a prayer of protection.

"It is an offense to God, a sin that cries out to heaven for vengeance, that a demon would befoul the capitol of the Empire. Salem... no, all of Cascadia, is proof of God's love for us, of His guiding us and inspiring mankind to rebuild after the coming of Simon Magus nearly five hundred years ago."

The monks set their mouths in thin lines, and they nodded their assent.

"They believe the monster is still within this place, the Mansfield Building. He may be able to hide from the eyes of man, but he will not be able to hide from the light of God. Let us pray."

He turned his back on the monks, got down on his knees. He heard their habits brush against the tiled floor as they joined him on their knees.

"In the name of the Father, and of the Son, and of the Holy Spirit," he said, making the sign of the cross.

"Amen," the monks answered in unison.

"Saint Joseph, terror of demons," Benítez said. "Hear our prayer..."

***

Klemm felt it: someone was using magic somewhere below him. He felt the rage building up within him. Cortez was gnashing like a wild beast in his mind.

You bitch, you fucking traitor, I'll kill you, you stupid little...

"Hey," Klemm said out loud. "Calm down. We need to approach this..."

They're alone.

"All the more reason to..." He was cut off by an excruciating headache. He dug his knuckles into his temples, ground his teeth. "What are you doing?" Klemm spat.

We're going. Now.

The pain diminished enough for Klemm to regain his composure. "If they're by themselves," he said, "Then that means they've probably got a trap waiting for us."

Do you doubt the power we have given you?

"No, but I..."

THEN GET MOVING.

Klemm felt another spike of pain in his head. "Alright, alright! Give me a moment to think." He grumbled, adjusted his uniform. He was still in the form of General Davis. That was one option; he didn't think Flint or Fletcher knew the real Davis well enough to tell immediately if he was the fake or not. On the other hand, Flint would be the most suspicious of a Templar walking the hallways alone.

As much as I've enjoyed watching you work, Roger, I think the time is over for such artifices, don't you? Cortez said.

Klemm snorted. "So, what? Just brute force it?"

Why not? They know you're in the building. They know you're a shapeshifter. They'll never believe you if they catch you by yourself, no matter how perfect your disguises.

He frowned. "Coming at them head on isn't exactly my style."

True, but you've never had help from the powers below before.

"Fine then. Show me what else I can do with these new powers."

***

Flint kept his gaze focused toward the stairwell, Fletcher covering the other half of the hallway. He held his sword at the ready in his right hand, one of his pistols in his left. He backed up a few steps, collided into Fletcher who was apparently also backing up.

"Oh, uh, sorry," she muttered.

"Hmph." Flint didn't like being separated from Navarro any more than his assistant did. In their five years together, they'd grown used to each other's fighting styles, knowing how the other moved, and to stay out of their way. This was the first time that he and Fletcher had been alone together. He hoped that the others had taken their places.

He heard the elevator hum. He glanced at the lights, saw they were going in ascending order now. "Can you sense anything?" he asked.

"No," she said, shaking her head. "If he's still here, I can't read him. You think he's gone?"

"It is possible, but unlikely. If I recall correctly, you have never been able to read me either."

"Yeah... someday you'll have to teach me how you manage that trick."

"There are no tricks involved, Miss Fletcher. Only discipline."

The elevator lights began their descent. He tightened his grip on his weapons.

"Hey Silas?"

"What is it?"

"You think I could ever... you know, formally join the Order?"

The corner of Flint's mouth turned up. "I suppose that stranger things have happened. Perhaps we can discuss it with General Abernathy during the locomotive trip back to Fort Marsing."

The elevator stopped on their floor. There was a ding as the doors slid open. Before them stood a familiar face. He was of medium height and medium build, with sandy brown hair parted on the side, brown eyes. He now wore a tailored suit that had seen better days, with dark armpit stains and numerous tears and frayed threads.

Flint kept the man covered with his gun. Fletcher's fingers arced with electricity. "Can we help you?" she asked.

"Yeah, actually," he replied. "I don't normally do it like this, but I've got a partner who's dying to meet you."

"Roger Klemm," Flint said.

Klemm nodded. He closed his eyes and his head slumped forward as though he had dozed off on his feet.

"Roger Klemm, I charge you with witchcraft, with the attempted murder of..."

"I heard you the first time," Klemm mumbled.

"I'll summarize then," Fletcher said. "You're the piece of shit who shot me earlier today, and now you're gonna pay. Start talking and maybe we can cut you a deal."

"A deal...?" Klemm whispered. "What could you possibly offer me?"

"Give us the name of your employer," Flint said. "Tell us who hired you, and you may yet avoid the gallows, Mr. Klemm."

Klemm kept his head down, but his shoulders began to shake. After a moment, Flint could hear his laughter.

"That's awfully generous of you, Witch Hunter," Klemm said. "It's a much better offer than you gave my other half. There's just one problem though."

Flint raised an eyebrow. The electricity dancing on Fletcher's fingertips increased in intensity.

Klemm looked up. His pupils glowed red, and streaks of black flowed through the whites of his eyes. "Of what use is your mercy to one who is already dead?"

29

Black tentacles erupted from Klemm's chest. Two shot forward and wrapped around Flint's and Fletcher's throats before they could react, lifting them off the floor. Flint's vision was clouded with a red haze. He couldn't breathe but he managed to raise his gun and fire at Klemm. A bolt of lightning shot from Fletcher's index finger. Flint's eyes widened but he couldn't call out a warning. The bolt struck Klemm in the chest. As he'd feared, the electricity coursed through Klemm's body, through the tentacles, and into Flint and Fletcher. For a moment it felt as though every nerve was on fire, but the tentacle's grip loosened, and they fell to the ground with Flint losing his own grip on his weapons. Every part of him ached, but he drew his secondary pistol and fired at Klemm, who shielded his face from the barrage of gunfire.

"Sorry!" Fletcher called out. Ignoring her, he holstered his secondary, and picked up his sword and other pistol.

"Destroy this son of Satan!" Flint shouted. That was the code phrase to begin the attack, but he imagined the gunfire was signal enough.

Klemm's face liquified, reshaped itself, and now he appeared as a young Hispanic man with slicked back hair and a manic grin on his face.

"Francisco?!" Fletcher said.

"Yes," he hissed. "This one was kind enough to give us his body and..."

Fletcher conjured a fireball and hurled it at Klemm. He raised his hand and it exploded against an invisible barrier, Flint shielding his face from the sparks with his long coat sleeve. Klemm laughed. "Oh, come on Zelda," he said. "Even in life, I was always better at..."

The door to the stairwell at the end of the hall slammed open. "Surprise, motherfucker!" Navarro shouted. He aimed and fired his rifle. Klemm turned just in time to catch the bullet in his forehead. The back of his skull exploded in a shower of ichor and brain matter. His legs crumpled beneath him, he collapsed on the floor and lay still.

Navarro came running. Close on his heels were other Templars, Supernumeraries, police officers, and soldiers. They all held their weapons at the ready, keeping Klemm covered. Navarro came to Flint's side. "You okay sir?" he asked.

"I am fine, thank you," Flint replied.

"How about you Zelda?"

"Yeah, I'm alright." She shuddered. "Can't believe I ever dated this piece of shit..." Her face lit up and she turned to Flint. "Oh, and uh... sorry. Again. For what happened earlier."

Navarro raised an eyebrow.

Flint straightened his long coat, adjusted his hat. "I suppose that scientists will find it edifying to learn that electricity generated by witchcraft is just as conductive as that generated by natural means."

"Hey, Captain Flint." He looked to his right and saw that Detectives Earle and Marsten were among Navarro's squad. "I'm no expert on assholes like this," Earle said, nodding toward Klemm, "But I'm pretty sure there's no coming back from a 7.62 round to the head."

"Be on your guard, Detective, everyone," Flint said. "We cannot yet be cer..."

Klemm's body liquefied, reformed. Standing in its place was a seven-foot tall, skeletally thin humanoid creature in a black suit. Its head was a perfect sphere, the skin whiter than snow. It had no ears, no nose, only two black pearls for eyes, and a mouth that took up the entire lower half of its face, filled with dozens of needle-like teeth. The tails of its suit jacket lengthened and split into more tentacles. Flint and the Templars present hacked off those that reached for them, but the police and soldiers weren't so fortunate. A young Private, a tentacle wrapped around his waist, fired his entire rifle magazine into the creature, but it seemed to absorb the bullets with no ill effect. The soldier screamed in terror, his cries cut off when the creature bit down, crunching through the bones of his spine and tearing the soldier's head off, swallowing it whole.

"Oh shit, oh shit, oh shit..." Marsten yelled. The monster had him, its tentacle wrapped around his waist. His partner Earle leapt and stomped his feet down upon the inky black appendage, firing his pistol point blank into it, but it regenerated as quickly as the detective fired.

Flint and the Templars sliced off tentacles as quickly as they could. Fletcher conjured another fireball and hurled it toward Klemm. The acrid stench of burnt flesh filled the hallway. Navarro and the Supernumeraries continued firing, their silver tipped rifle rounds having a greater effect than the lead bullets of the police and soldiers.

Flint made his way through the melee to the two detectives and brought his sword down in an overhead slash, cleaving through the tentacle wrapped around Marsten's waist and creating a deep gash in the tiled floor.

"Jesus Christ," Marsten said, pushing the tentacle off from his waist. His suit was stained and torn where its suckers had latched onto him.

The creature roared. It was not the roar of any earthly beast, but of something from the bowels of Hell. Flint winced. It hurt his ears even more than all the gunfire. The police and the soldiers seemed to wilt before him. Some dropped their weapons to cover their ears. Others began sobbing.

"Stand your ground!" Flint cried. "We cannot allow

him to escape yet!" He prayed that Cardinal Benítez and his priests were nearly finished.

***

Cardinal Benítez poured out the last few grains from the pouch, meeting one of the Benedictine monks in the center. Together, he and the priest monks had encircled the entire Mansfield Building with blessed salt. A bead of sweat ran down the side of his face. He didn't think the Lord would hold it against him if he fumbled the words, but he wanted to get everything right for the sake of everyone still inside, waging war against one of the devil's own.

He knelt on the sidewalk and the others joined him. Civilians had crowded around the edge of the police cordon. Many of them knelt with Benítez and the monks.

"Let us pray," he said. "In the name of the Father, and of the Son, and of the Holy Spirit."

"Amen," the monks replied.

"Heavenly Father," Benítez began. "We beseech Thee, in the name of Thy Son Jesus Christ, to bless and consecrate this building. Extend Thy hand and banish the child of Hell within. Come to the aid of Thy children now, as You and the entire Host of Heaven came to the aid of this world when the darkness of Simon Magus threatened to consume us all. Saint Benedict, patron against witchcraft."

"Pray for us," the monks answered, along with the kneeling civilians who could hear Benítez.

"Saint Joseph, terror of demons."

"Pray for us."

"O Blessed Virgin Mary, Queen of Heaven."

"Pray for us."

"O God, come to my assistance."

"O Lord, make haste to help me."

"In the name of Thy Son, Jesus Christ, we beg Thee, O Lord, banish the serpent from our midst, and send the Holy Spirit to guide Thy Templars."

"Amen."

"In the name of the Father, and of the Son, and of the Holy Spirit."

"Amen."

Benítez stayed on his knees, offered his own private, mental prayers for the sake of everyone inside. *Stay strong,* he prayed. *Stand faithful and true, and with God's help, we shall vanquish this demon and roll back the tide of darkness.*

***

The creature lashed out with its hand, the claws on its fingers tearing open a police offer's abdomen. She fell to her knees, staring in shock as her intestines poured out. A tentacle wrapped around Flint's sword hand. He cried out as he felt it squeezing. He'd be forced to drop his sword soon.

Navarro snarled in rage as he brought his tomahawk down, slicing clean through the loathsome appendage. Fletcher dodged and weaved through the melee, almost too quickly for Flint's eyes to follow, no doubt the result of another spell to increase her speed. He decided this was another instance where he could look the other way at her use of magic. She focused her magical fire into tighter beams, like blowtorches, as she burned through tentacles, coming to the aid of as many as she could.

"Fuck!" a Supernumerary shouted. Klemm had yanked the woman's rifle out of her grasp. She drew her side-arm and emptied the magazine into Klemm's throat. The silver hissed and bubbled as it burned through his corrupted flesh, but the wounds healed, albeit more slowly than before. Klemm pointed at her with his index finger. The claw extended, punched through the woman's throat, and withdrew again in a few seconds. She clutched at her throat as her life's blood poured out over her fingers.

"We're gonna need more firepower boss," Navarro shouted.

Flint nodded, kept slashing, trying to make his way to Klemm through the forest of tentacles, wary of the monster's fangs and claws.

"Miss Fletcher!" he yelled.

She looked over her shoulder at him.

"Concentrate your fire on its body!"

She nodded. One second she was a few feet from Flint, the next she was almost nose to nose – if this form had a nose, that is – with Klemm.

"What..." the creature growled.

Fletcher raised the palm of her hand and a magical blowtorch flame ignited, scorching the soulless black pearls that were the creature's eyes. Klemm screeched in pain and fury, the wall of tentacles flickering as he lost concentration.

"I will eat your heart, and then your soul, you little bitch…" Klemm growled. Or perhaps Cortez. Flint wasn't sure which personality was in control now.

"No means no," Fletcher said, a wicked grin on her face. She summoned more fire just as Klemm tried to run her through with his claws. They struck at the same time. Fletcher screamed as the claws pierced her shoulder and went out through her back. Klemm howled in agony as the flames burned off the left half of his face.

"Zelda!" Flint and Navarro cried in unison. She staggered but remained upright.

"I can heal myself!" she bellowed. "Stay on him!"

"I'm out of ammo," a Supernumerary called, dropping his rifle.

"Templars!" Flint shouted. "On me! Cut him down! Cut him down!"

The Witch Hunters charged, swords ablaze with holy light.

"Lord Jesus, guide my blade!"

"Begone, foul demon!"

"Go back to the fiery pit!"

"We are the instruments of God's justice!" Flint snarled as he advanced. "Prepare yourself for the darkness that awaits you and your master, Klemm!"

Klemm spun and faced them. The creature opened its mouth so wide that Flint thought its head might split in two. It spewed forth a stream of green vomit. It splashed against Flint's chest plate, already cracked and burned from his earlier encounters with Klemm, the metal sizzling and burning once again. He heard Templars shriek in unimaginable pain behind him. With horror, Flint realized they were in their field uniforms, which did not include chest plates. He heard several of them drop to the floor even as he continued his advance.

With a cry of rage, Flint sprinted the last few feet and rammed his sword into Klemm's chest. The blade emerged from his back, and the stench of burnt flesh grew even fouler as the blessed steel burned inside Klemm.

The creature wrapped one hand around the blade. Its flesh burned even as black blood dripped onto the floor. Klemm laughed, the sound like grinding metal.

"It's going to take more than one little sword to stop me, Captain," the creature rasped. "Perhaps I'll bring your head to Emil."

The monster opened its mouth again. Flint prepared to let go of the sword and back away, but then the creature stopped. It looked all around.

"What..." it began. Then it howled. It shrieked and writhed. "It burns! It burns, it burns, it burns, it burns..." Its cries broke down into babbling, gibbering madness. The monster liquified, tried to take a new shape, but something was interfering. It roiled, and shifted, but couldn't take solid form. Its screams caused an icy ball to form in Flint's stomach. His sword clattered to the floor.

The gelatinous mass pushed past Flint and the others and crashed through a window, out into the darkening cityscape.

"Zelda, tend to the wounded," Flint said. "The rest of you, follow me! We shall bury this fiend once and for all!"

30

Pain. It was all Roger Klemm felt, all he knew, all he could see. As he tumbled from the window and the street rushed up to meet him, he tried to take shape, any shape, but the pain was too much.

What happened? Klemm thought.

Those filthy, worthless, little priests, Cortez answered. *They consecrated these grounds.*

What does that mean?

It means we need to get out of here. Now.

Easier said than done, Klemm thought. He'd been beaten up before. He'd been stabbed, shot, bludgeoned, but his healing spells always fixed him right up. But this... this was beyond anything he'd experienced before. This burned worse than any fire, magical or natural, he'd ever felt.

He smacked into the pavement. If he'd been in human form, the fall would have killed him. In his gelatinous, shapeless form, it was just a bump. The ground burned beneath him, but not nearly so bad as the inside of the Mansfield building. He concentrated, willed himself to human form. Just as he finished coalescing into his true form, it occurred to him that he should morph into something that could fly, just to get away from here more quickly. Oh well. If there were cops around, he could take them out and get going.

He pushed himself up into the barrel of a gun. Witch Hunters and Supernumeraries had the building surrounded. He didn't recognize the Witch Hunter who had his pistol pointed in his face, but nearby were the four Witch Hunter Generals, who also kept him covered with their pistols.

"Last chance, son," Hickock said. "You can surrender and start talkin'..."

"Or we can send you directly to Hell," Abernathy said.

"Make your choice, kid," Brandt said, blowing out a puff of cigar smoke.

"Because either way works for us," Davis said.

***

Flint and Navarro sprinted down the stairs, the others on their heels. Flint hoped that Detectives Earle and Marsten had made it. His steel chest plate was flaking, peeling. A chunk fell out and clattered to the floor. His cheek still stung, and his ears were ringing with a high pitched whine as background noise. He heard Navarro say something, but the sound was muffled, like the man was underwater.

"I beg your pardon?" Flint shouted.

"I said, you still want to take this shitbird alive, sir?!" Navarro yelled back.

"If at all possible," Flint said. He was in excellent cardiovascular condition if he did say so himself, but the long day and the weight of his dress uniform were wearing on him. It was a pity his uniform was coming apart, but he was grateful for the reduction in weight. "But I fear that may no longer be an option."

They emerged from the stairwell and sprinted across the lobby, to the front door. Bursting out into street, he saw that the sun was nearly below the horizon, casting the city in an orange glow. He could hear the distant honking of automobiles, but it appeared that his colleagues had cleared the block. Before him he saw a wall of Templars and Supernumeraries, the Generals among them. Kneeling on the pavement was Roger Klemm, once again in his true form.

Flint advanced on the fallen assassin. His breathing was elevated, and he tried to calm himself. Behind him, he could hear Navarro take deep gulps of air.

"Roger Klemm," Flint called out. "You know the charges against you. This is your last chance. Surrender. It is over!"

Klemm hunched over, rocked back and forth. He was outside the Mansfield Building now, but its consecration was still affecting him. Flint hoped that being inside hallowed ground had driven the demon from him, but one could never let down one's guard against the children of Hell.

"Over...?" Klemm said.

"You heard the man," Hickock said, cocking the hammer of his revolver.

"Over," Klemm said again. He looked up. "It's like I once told Zelda."

Flint and Navarro looked at each other.

"Death is only the beginning," Klemm said.

The ground quaked beneath them and Flint, Navarro, everyone, lost their footing. Klemm liquified, expanded, grew. Flint looked up from the ground and saw the gelatinous, slug-like demon that he had faced outside the city of Jordan months ago.

"Open fire!" the Generals called, almost in unison.

The street erupted with the thunder of pistol and rifle fire. Flint and several of the other Templars - including Captain Kennedy from Fort Ingalls - charged toward the beast, swords at the ready. They hacked and slashed and spun and cut, the demon's tentacles falling to the ground, writhing, and twisting. Flint swore he would not meet this monster a third time.

***

Zelda Fletcher cast another healing spell, and the cop's wounds knit themselves shut. She shuddered. They were nasty looking, bloody from where the tentacle had wrapped around the man's waist.

"Jesus Christ," he said, patting himself.

"You're... you're a witch?" another man asked.

"Yes. No. It's complicated," Fletcher said, throwing up her hands.

The detective extended his hand. "Detective Jay Marsten." She shook it.

"Elijah Earle," the other man said, giving her another handshake.

"Zelda Fletcher," she said.

"Hey..." Marsten said. "Are you the girl who got shot earlier today?"

"The one and only," she said.

"Captain Flint told us a little bit about you," Earle said. "Are you two... uh..."

"No."

"Oh. Okay. Didn't mean to pry, just curious."

I'm curious about us too, she thought.

"Did we get the bastard?" Marsten asked.

"I hope so. I..."

The building shook around them. The cops and soldiers looked around, on the verge of panic.

"Ah shit, not this again," Earle muttered.

Fletcher rushed to the broken window. Looking down into the street, she saw something that had haunted her nightmares for the last few months. Francisco. Or rather his master, the demon Ichthil. It looked like the entire Fort Ingalls garrison had turned out for what she hoped would be the final battle.

"I've gotta get down there," she said.

"Elevators are working," Earle said. "If you hurry you could..."

"No time!" Fletcher called and jumped out the window.

***

"Die, monster! Die, once and for all!" Flint shouted. The demon was pinned down by gunfire, and he rushed to its side with the other Templars. They systematically hacked and slashed their way into its gelatinous hide. From the demon's beak came a high pitched, ululating cry of pain that made Flint's head hurt.

"Your judgment is at hand!" Flint bellowed. The demon reached out with a tentacle and grabbed a Supernumerary. The man screamed and fired his sidearm into the appendage, staining the street with its black ichor.

"Look!" someone shouted. Flint looked up and saw

Zelda Fletcher levitating through the broken window from which Klemm had escaped, lowering herself to street level. His mind flashed back to their first encounter with the beast. She had levitated herself and Flint onto its back, where he had cut a bloody hole into its body and dropped two grenades. Perhaps they could...

The beast roared and the entire block shook. Looking up, Flint saw its back bubbling, roiling, taking a new shape. It hardened into a black tortoise shell covered in pointed spines. Demonic laughter echoed from everywhere and nowhere.

"It won't be that easy this time little Witch Hunters," a voice boomed. The demon shook.

"Take cover!" Fletcher screamed. "Take cover now!"

Flint dove to the ground, covering his head with his hands. He heard an explosion, followed by the screams of the wounded and dying. Chancing a look, he saw that the demon had expelled the spines from its shell. It looked like dozens of Templars and Supernumeraries were down. He climbed to his feet.

"Sir!" Navarro yelled. Flint started to turn.

"Stay right there, sir." Navarro put one hand on Flint's shoulder. He felt a tug on his back. Navarro came around and showed him one of the spines. "Maybe you should start wearing that steel plate all the time, huh boss?"

Flint nodded his thanks. He was exhausted. Fletcher lighted upon the ground next to more wounded and began to work her craft.

"I guess he remembers the last time," Navarro said, waving at the demon's shell.

Flint took a moment to catch his breath. This was a setback to be sure, but he was confident that they would prevail. They would have to get more creative about...

"You hear that sir?" Navarro asked.

"I am afraid my hearing may be permanently damaged after today, Mr. Navarro," Flint replied. He wasn't sure what he was supposed to hear over the sound of gunfire, screams, and demonic roars. Wait. He caught it now. It sounded like grinding metal.

"What in the world?" he said.

The sound grew louder. Templars and Supernumeraries in the rear heard it too and looked. Flint's mouth fell open.

"Holy shit," Navarro said.

Rolling into view was a single tank. Flint knew that the Cascadian Army had tanks, but he had never seen one outside of his history books before. It was an ugly machine, all sharp angles and rivets. Cascadia generally had little use for American aesthetics when designing their machines, favoring function over form. The tank's turret swiveled into place, its main cannon targeted at the demon's gnashing beak. Flint's eyes widened.

"Run!" he shouted. He, Navarro, and other Templars scattered in every direction. The cannon thundered. The demon's beak exploded but the creature did not stop moving. The hatch on top of the tank's turret opened. Flint's mouth fell open again.

Emperor Peter II climbed out. Another member of the tank crew handed him what looked like a long tube. Flint couldn't make it out at this distance. Then he saw that one end was pointed. The Emperor jumped down onto the street and took a knee.

"RPG!" someone shouted.

The rocket fired from the tube, exploding inside the hole made by the tank round earlier. The Emperor threw down the empty weapon. Another member of the tank crew popped out of the hatch, and he tossed his monarch a war hammer, who caught it with his right hand. One end tapered to a vicious spike.

"You piece of shit!" Peter shouted, advancing on the demon. "You dare defile my city? You dare to attack my people?! This is our land! Ours! Your kind has no place here!"

The Emperor sprinted toward the monster. "I'll send you back to Hell myself!" he roared.

He was almost upon it when the Templars regained their senses.

"Protect the Emperor!" Hickock shouted.

"Follow me!" Abernathy yelled.

The Generals, the Templars, Supernumeraries, and Flint and Navarro all rushed toward the fallen demon. It's tentacles continued to move, but it was slowing down. They lacked the strength they had earlier. Now it was nothing but the grim business of hacking, smashing, and burning the creature into submission, sending it back down into Hell where it belonged.

31

Klemm's mind reeled. The ground burned beneath him.

The fucking Emperor himself had just blown a hole in his body. A part of him wanted to laugh. If he got out of this alive, that would make for a great story to tell at the bar. He could feel the slash of every Templar blade, the sting of every bullet.

What now? he thought.

Now we... Cortez's words were cut off by a cry of pain. Klemm hurt, but whatever it was the priests had done, the effects were more intense with Cortez. It made it hard for Klemm to think. He tried to change his form into something, anything, but Cortez's screams were clouding his mind.

Shut up! Klemm snarled. He had to get away from this consecrated ground, reform his body, find a way to escape. He reached out with his mind. This current form had eyes all over its body, threatening to overwhelm his perception. He felt his frustration mount. The Templars had him surrounded.

Is this the end? he thought. *Am I going to die?*

Fear not, Cortez grunted. *If you die here, then you will descend into Hell. Not as a common damned soul, but you shall be a prince of the underworld in repayment for you pledging yourself to us in this...*

Thanks, but I'm not ready to die just yet, Klemm replied. There had to be a way. There was always a way.

He screamed in pain, and his demonic form roared. He scanned himself, looking for the source of this new... holy shit. There he was, Emperor Peter II himself, making wide sweeps with that damned war hammer. Klemm would have felt honored that the Emperor took notice of him, if the old man wasn't trying to kill him.

There. A gap had opened in the Templar lines as they rushed forward to hack him to pieces. He'd never attempted a trick like this before. He wasn't sure if he could pull it off, but it was literally do or die now.

He gathered his strength and projected a tentacle from Ichthil's body. Templars and Supernumeraries dodged, rolling out of the way, but he made contact with a Witch Hunter, wrapping it around her body. She cried out, and her brothers and sisters rushed to her aid. Klemm only had one shot at this. He focused his consciousness on the appendage. At the same time, he prepared to cast the greatest illusion spell of his life.

What are you doing? Cortez asked.

Trying to get us the fuck out of here. In his mind's eye, he could see another Witch Hunter rushing to help the woman Klemm had his grip on. He roared in defiance, hoping against hope he could pull this off. There. The tentacle wrapped around the female Templar morphed into a black serpent, with Klemm in control. He'd done it: he changed his shape while leaving a piece of himself behind in the form of the demon Ichthil. He was in two places at once. Not for long though.

Klemm, in the form of the serpent, unwrapped himself from the female Witch Hunter. He slithered away from the battle.

Not bad Roger, not bad at all.

I should thank you, Klemm thought. *I'm not sure I could have done that without your upgrade.* Even so, he felt exhausted. He would need to regain his strength before he could have another go at his targets.

***

Flint spun and slashed. The demon was slowing down even further. Demons were pure spirit so he knew they could not kill this creature for good. But when they possessed a person or otherwise manifested physically, their bodies could be destroyed, sending them back to Hell. That was the best they could hope for this day, and he meant to keep going until this one was burnt to cinders.

"Captain Flint! Captain Flint!"

He looked over his shoulder, saw a Lady Templar running toward him. He returned his focus to the titanic demon before him and noticed that it was laying still. Had they done it? Was it over?

"Captain Flint," she said, reaching him, taking deep breaths.

"What is it, Lady...?"

"Joan Gaines," she said.

"Is there a problem, Lady Gaines?"

"I... I was there during your speech in the lobby. You're in charge of this case, right?"

Flint wasn't sure who was in charge at the moment, but he replied, "Yes."

"I think a piece of this monstrosity is trying to get away."

He turned and looked at her now. Behind him he could

hear the Emperor's battle cries of rage, the Templars and Supernumeraries joining him.

"What do you mean?"

"One of its tentacles grabbed me earlier. Before anyone could cut me free, it morphed into a great serpent and slithered away."

He grabbed her by the shoulders. "Where?"

She pointed toward a gap in the Templar perimeter. "It went that way. Some of the others are after it now. I thought you would like to..."

"Thank you," Flint said. He stepped away from the melee, looked around. Spying his assistant, he shouted, "Mr. Navarro!"

Navarro turned. He was knee deep inside the demon's carcass, his dress uniform black with its blood. Flint doubted his own uniform looked any better. Navarro jogged out to meet Flint. Reaching him, his face split with a savage grin, he said, "I think we got him beat, sir. Again." The creature's tentacles lay limp upon the pavement, with only the occasional twitch.

"There may yet be work to be done," Flint said. He related what Lady Gaines had told him. Navarro's grin slowly transformed into a scowl. When Flint was finished, his assistant shouted in anger, kicking a severed piece of the demon's hide.

"God... damn him!" Navarro yelled.

"I know precisely how you feel, Ricardo. Come. We cannot allow him to escape."

"I am *not* going through that shit again," Navarro said, and took off running toward the spot where their quarry was last seen. Flint's eyebrows went up, but a moment later he took off after his assistant.

***

Klemm slithered through an alley. He still hurt all over, but the pain was diminishing the further he got from the Mansfield building. This form wouldn't do though. He'd need to change into something that could fly, or at least run. But the goddamn Templars would no doubt commandeer some automobiles if word got out that a cheetah was running through the city streets. Flight it was.

Cortez, he thought, *You still with me?*

I am here.

I need some more juice.

Nothing.

Cortez?

That may be a problem.

What the fuck? Klemm concentrated, drew on his personal reserves of magic, shifted into human form, taking the shape of his target, Silas Flint. He looked down, patted the simulated dress uniform. He knew the Witch Hunter's chest plate was damaged, and he had that graze wound on his left cheek. The details on the ruined armor might not be perfect, but he doubted anyone would notice the differences as long as it looked cracked and burned.

"Talk to me Cortez," Klemm said out loud.

Our time spent within hallowed ground has weakened our bond.

"Which means what?"

Which means I need time to rebuild my strength, just as you do.

"Fuck!" Klemm screamed, kicking a garbage can. "Why the fuck didn't you tell me details like that before?"

Cortez laughed. *Would you have refused my offer if you'd known? When Flint had you at the point of his sword?*

"So what now?"

Fear not. Our bond is weakened, not broken. I can restore some of your personal reserves of power. In the mean time, I'm sure you will think of something. You always do.

"Can you still hide me from your ex-girlfriend?"

Yes.

Okay, that was something. As far as the Templars knew, he was still in the shape of the demon Ichthil. With Cortez shielding him from Fletcher's mental powers, he could slip in disguised as Flint and shank the bitch. Then he could change to someone or something else, get Flint, and get the hell out of there. He could still get it done. When he accepted a job, he did not fail, ever, and he wouldn't fail this time.

***

Zelda Fletcher put her hands on the wounded Witch Hunter's chest. She felt the familiar warmth flow through her, out of her fingertips, and into her patient. The man's bloody wounds closed, his bones knit. He opened his eyes, looked at Fletcher in astonishment.

"What sorcery is..."

"You're welcome," she said, stepping away, looking for

anyone else who needed her attention. She knew she was running low on power. Her hands burned and she felt like she hadn't eaten in days. She smiled. All of this began when she, Silas, and Rico had decided to grab a burger for lunch. God, it felt like days ago, but it was only hours. The sun had almost set. She'd seen the Emperor arrive in his tank and join the fight. What was it the Generals had told her after their meeting – always be truthful with him, even if you think it will piss him off? Looking at the man swinging that war hammer, bellowing profanities, knee deep in demonic gore, she made a mental note to never do anything to piss him off.

She looked around for Silas and Rico. She prayed they were still alive. If anything happened to them... well, she was too far down this path to turn away from the Templars now, but a small part of her would surely die with them. Rico was her best friend among the Supernumerary ranks. And Silas...

There they are. They were running toward a gap in the Templar lines, through which she could see an alleyway. What was that about? Was something going on? Francisco hadn't spoken to her in a while, and she still couldn't sense him. The googly eyed tentacle monster looked like it was almost done. If her friends needed her help, then by God she would provide it.

She willed herself off the ground, and flew across the battlefield, toward the spot where Silas and Rico were running.

"Miss Fletcher!"

She looked to her left and saw General Abernathy, his sword and his uniform stained black with demonic ichor.

"Mind the magic, please," Abernathy said, the corner of his mouth quirked up.

"Ugh, fine," she said, and lighted upon the ground. She picked up the hem of her bloody dress, and started running.

32

Flint and Navarro arrived at the entrance to the alleyway. A half dozen Templars and their Supernumerary assistants were waiting for them.

"What is the situation?" Flint asked the first one he saw.

"The snake, or the demon, or whatever he is was last seen entering this alley."

"Anyone in these buildings?" Navarro asked.

"No, the police evacuated the entire block earlier this afternoon and they have it cordoned off down the street. If he tries to escape on foot, they'll get him."

"Very good," Flint said. "Hear me! Our quarry is Roger Klemm, a shapeshifter possessed by the spirit of Francisco Cortez, a wizard who sold his soul to the powers below. He is an assassin by trade, so be on your guard. We cannot allow him to escape. Take him alive if you can, but do not hesitate to put him down if you must."

"Yes sir!"

"Yes Captain!"

Flint cracked his neck. He ached all over, and his cheek still pained him, but those would have to wait. He would turn 34 next year. The prime of a man's life, but he felt much older.

"You alright boss?" Navarro asked.

"Yes, for now," Flint replied. "I weary of this heathen's blasphemous devilry. His apprehension is long overdue. Let us be on our way."

Before Navarro could answer, a familiar voice rang out: "Hey! Hey guys! Wait for me!" He saw Fletcher running toward them from across the Mansfield Building Plaza. She looked haggard, dark circles under her eyes, smoke rising from her blistered fingertips.

"Been hitting the juice a little too hard?" Navarro asked.

"Just... trying to... heal as many as I can," she said. She put her hands on her knees and doubled over, gasping for breath. "Goddamn... I haven't used magic that much... in years."

"Miss Fletcher, you ought not use your power anymore today," Flint said.

"So don't... get hurt... anymore... today..."

"Easier said than done," Navarro said, looking at the alleyway.

She recovered her breath and stood up. "I'm coming with you. I need to see Francisco dead. Again. And get some payback on that asshole, Klemm."

"'Vengeance is mine, sayeth the Lord,'" Flint quoted.

"Yeah, yeah," Fletcher said, waving him off.

"Can you sense him?" Navarro asked.

She shook her head. "Still can't."

Flint scowled. "Then we shall have to hunt him down the way God intended."

***

Klemm watched from the second floor of the apartment building adjacent to the alleyway. The building was empty, no doubt evacuated by the cops or the Army earlier today. Lots of places to set up an ambush. He still wore the form of Silas Flint. It looked like the real Flint, Navarro, and Fletcher were going to stick together. He wasn't sure if he could take them all on solo, and he lacked confidence that Cortez would recover in time to provide more of those promised superpowers. No problem. He'd pulled off tougher hits. He just needed to get the trio separated somehow. Time to get back to basics.

Cortez had restored his strength at least. He waited, sensing the other Templars splitting off with their assistants, forming teams of two. He'd have to do something about those swords of theirs, again. Maybe light up the place with witchfire. But if he did that, he may as well put a neon sign out front with his name on it. On the other hand, they knew he was either in this building or the one across the way. If he did nothing, it would only buy him a few extra minutes. Those...

He grunted in pain. That headache was back.

"Cortez," he growled.

Don't even think of trying to escape.

"It hadn't occurred to me but..."

This is the best chance you have to take them both out.

"I'm open to suggestions. You back to full power yet?"

Not quite. But as it happens, I do have an idea to get them separated.

***

Zelda Fletcher scanned the alleyway. It ran between two buildings, neither as tall as the Mansfield Building, both looking like apartment complexes. Behind her she could hear Silas giving last minute instructions to the other Templars and Supernumeraries. Rico borrowed some more rifle rounds and another pistol magazine.

It occurred to her that if she couldn't sense Klemm or Francisco, then she might not be of much help. Silas didn't want her using any more magic. In truth, she wasn't sure if she could anyway. Her stomach rumbled. She felt like she'd sleep for a week after this was all over. Who was she if she wasn't a witch? She had no experience in tracking people; she'd never needed to before when she could sense their presence. The others had formal training in hunting magicians, interrogation, marksmanship, swordplay, and all the rest that came with being a professional Witch Hunter.

She might not have any experience with the more traditional methods of a manhunt, but she'd be damned if she sat on the sidelines while Francisco was still out there. She thought back to how they'd parted ways back in New Rome. He'd been boasting about how allying himself with the powers of Hell had magnified his powers tenfold when she stabbed him. She'd fled the scene. She'd heard his transformation into that tentacle monster thing, heard the ensuing battle between him and the cops even as she ran for her life. He'd followed her to the city of Jordan where she'd turned herself in to the local sheriff's office and been picked up by Silas and Ricardo. Together they'd blown Francisco to bits, but now he was back. No, she had to see this through to the end, put her old life behind her once and for all.

"Hey Silas?" she said.

The grim Witch Hunter turned to face her. "Yes, Miss Fletcher?"

"Could I... could I borrow one of your guns?"

He reached behind his back, drew the pistol he kept holstered on his rear left hip, handed the gun to her butt first.

"Stay close," he said. "We three shall take the north building."

She nodded. Flint shifted his gaze to two other Templars and their Supernumerary partners.

"All of you, on me," Flint said. "We shall split into three teams. Do not lose sight of your partner. Let us go."

Flint led the way, Navarro close on his heels, and Fletcher fell into step behind them. They entered another lobby, but on a smaller scale than the one in the Mansfield building. Couches, chairs, and tables lined the room. One wall was taken up with mailboxes. The other had a bank of elevators and the stairwell. Fletcher swore that if she never saw another staircase in her life, it would be too soon.

"How you want to split up sir?" Navarro asked.

"The three of us shall start on the ground floor," Flint replied. "Captain Forrest, I should like you and Miss…"

Zelda.

She perked up, tuning out Flint. Francisco.

Yes, Zelda, it's me. I see you're still hanging around those losers.

Fuck you, she thought.

Francisco snickered. For a moment, he sounded like his old self. *I see you haven't changed much.*

I've changed a lot.

Yes… refusing to use your talent, except to aid these cretins. So much wasted potential.

She scoffed. Out of the corner of her eye, she saw Navarro give her a questioning look. *Who are you to talk about potential?* she thought. *You went over to the dark side, and now you're dead.*

Then why are you talking to someone who is dead?

Whatever. We'll find you and put you down for good this time.

Death is…

I heard you the first time, asshole.

I'll even make it easy for you, for old time's sake. Roger and I are on the sixth floor. Come find us, and I will show you just how powerful I have become, how powerful you could be.

She waited a few moments. Navarro tapped her on the shoulder.

"What's going on? You sense something?"

"You could say that." She turned to face the others. "Francisco was just whispering in my head. He said that he and Klemm are holed up on the sixth floor."

One of the other Templars raised an eyebrow. "It must be a trap," she said.

"Yes," Flint said. "Undoubtedly."

"Should we all go up there in one group?" the lady Templar's assistant asked.

"It could be a diversion. We all go together while he slips out on another floor," said the male Templar, Captain Forrest.

Flint thought for a few moments. "Our quarry is focused on Miss Fletcher and myself. He is no doubt trying to separate us. Let us proceed to the sixth floor."

"Okay," Fletcher said. "Elevator?"

Flint and Navarro looked at each other. "Ah... if it's all the same to you guys, we'd prefer to take the stairs," Navarro said.

"No, no more stairs," Fletcher said, shaking her head. "If he tries to mess around with the cable or something, I can levitate the car."

Flint scowled but nodded.

33

Flint's party assembled inside one of the elevator cars and he pushed the button for the sixth floor. He didn't like relying on Fletcher's magic to save them if Klemm attempted to sever the elevator cable again, but it was undoubtedly quicker than taking the stairs. And if he was being honest with himself, he was relieved to get a small break. He touched his cheek again. The blood had dried at least.

All was silent except for the hum of the elevator. His mind drifted back to the meeting with the Committee and the Emperor that morning. If this assassin was hired by Charles or one of his confederates, it would no doubt sway their opinions on whether to extend diplomatic relations to his upstart break-away state. He dug out his pocket watch, flipped it open. 9:05 p.m. He wondered when or if the Emperor would reschedule their appointment.

The elevator dinged and the doors slid open. Flint nodded to Navarro, who nodded back. They drew their sidearms, and went out the left side of the door, the other Templars and Supernumeraries taking the right, with Fletcher bringing up the rear. Flint was pleased to see her two handed grip on the pistol he had loaned her. God willing, she would soon make a final break with her magical powers and live a full life as an ordinary child of God.

Flint scanned the hallway, saw, and heard nothing. He looked over his shoulder. Captain Forrest was looking back at him, shaking his head. Nothing on their side either. Flint used hand signals to direct the other four to proceed down their side of the hallway. He drew his sword. As he expected, it shone bright, much brighter than Fletcher's presence alone would cause.

Together, Flint, Navarro, and Fletcher proceeded to their left. All was silent save for the creaking of their steps upon the floor. Flint had found it curious at first that Klemm didn't take the opportunity to escape the city, but the pride of magicians was often their downfall. Accepting demonic possession only magnified their overconfidence.

It appeared that they would have to search every apartment in the building.

"What the...?!" Fletcher cried.

They spun around and saw a column of shadow had enveloped her. They could barely make out her form inside. She aimed her pistol up, down, to the sides.

"Zelda!" Navarro yelled.

Flint charged, prepared to tackle her away from whatever trap the fiend had laid for her, but by the time he reached her, the column had vanished, taking Fletcher with it.

***

Fletcher felt weightless, like she was levitating. All was darkness and shadow. She raised her pistol, lowered it again. If the others were still out there, she didn't want to risk hitting them. And besides, what was there to shoot at?

"Silas!" she screamed. "Rico! Where are you?!"

She still couldn't sense Francisco, but he had to be behind this. Was this it? Was she going to die, alone, in the darkness? She felt despair weigh on her heart, but as soon as it appeared, the darkness vanished. She was back in the hallway. She looked around. The others were nowhere to be seen. She was alone.

Keeping a two handed grip on Silas's pistol, she crept forward. Looking at one of the apartment doors, she saw a brass number: 1105. She cursed herself for not paying closer attention to the doors when she was with the others. 1105... did that mean she was on the eleventh floor? Why?

She thought about calling out, hesitated. Wouldn't that lead Francisco right to her? She reconsidered. If he was responsible for bringing her here, then he no doubt knew where she was already.

"Silas!" she called. "Rico! Hello?"

Nothing. Shit.

Maybe she could take the elevator back down to the sixth floor. Why would Francisco have brought her up here? Some kind of trap? Silas would know. She needed to find them before...

She heard footsteps at the end of the hallway. The stairs.

"Hello?" she called.

The door slammed open. It was Silas. His blue eyes blazed beneath the brim of his Templar hat, a red line and dried blood on his left cheek. He'd have a nasty scar if he didn't get it sewn up soon or allow her to heal it for him. It occurred to her that she hadn't had the chance to ask about how his steel plate armor had gotten so damaged. Stubborn son of a bitch was too close-mouthed for his own good.

"Miss Fletcher!" Silas called out. He holstered his pistol, sheathed his sword, and ran to her. Fletcher's eyes widened. Before she could react any further, he was upon her, wrapped her in a bear hug. "Praise God that you are unharmed."

Her mouth fell open as a fierce red blush arose in her cheeks. She gently patted him on his broad shoulders.

"Yeah... yeah, I'm fine," she said. This was... wow.

"I was worried," he said, releasing her.

"Yeah, I, ah, I can see that," she said, looking to the side.

"What happened?" he asked.

"I don't know," she said. "We were on the sixth floor, I was following you guys, when suddenly I'm surrounded by darkness. I couldn't see you or hear you. Thought I was a goner there for a second, but then here I was. Uh... where is here, anyway?"

"The eleventh floor," Flint said. "After you disappeared, we split up to search for you. Navarro's on the tenth floor. Come on, we should let him know you're okay."

"Yeah, yeah, definitely," Fletcher said. "Lead the way."

Flint nodded. "I apologize for my display earlier."

"Oh... don't be sorry. I just, ah... well, you know. You've never..."

He smiled. "Maybe we can talk about that later."

She kept her face neutral, but she was certain that she was bright red now.

"Let's get out of here and find Klemm," he said, and started walking toward the stairwell. Fletcher, too stunned to think clearly, fell into step behind him. She still couldn't sense anything from Silas. Even when he let the mask slip, he kept that iron discipline, shielding his thoughts from her. Could he...? No. He couldn't. He was a Witch Hunter, more zealous than most, and she was a witch. There's no way he would ever... wait.

"What did you say?" she asked.

"When?" he said, looking over his shoulder.

"Who's on the tenth floor?"

"Navarro."

"Yeah, but what else did you say?"

He stopped, turned to face her. "I'm sorry?"

"There, you did it again."

"I am confused."

"You spoke in the Common Tongue."

"Zelda, the High Speech is only for certain circumstances..."

She raised her pistol and fired twice into his chest. Flint's eyes widened. The bullets punched bloody holes in what appeared to be solid steel plate. And the blood was black. Flint's face became a rictus snarl of animal rage.

"You're dead, you fucking traitor," he said, but in a voice not his own. It was Klemm's voice, overlaid with Francisco's.

***

They heard two gunshots above them. Flint and Navarro looked at each other.

"Make haste!" Flint bellowed. "Our quarry is at hand! Find him and make him pay for his outrages!" They all sprinted toward the stairwell. Flint prayed that Fletcher was the shooter. He didn't know what he would do if it was Klemm who had shot her down. His pistols each had eight rounds plus one in the chamber. Both Fletcher and Klemm could heal themselves as long as they were conscious.

"Shit... more stairs," Navarro panted.

Flint didn't know which floor the gunfire had come

from. He hoped that there would be more noise to come. Noise meant Fletcher was still alive.

***

Fletcher fired again, but Silas – or Klemm rather – extended his hand, and the pistol was yanked from Fletcher's grip, sailing over Klemm's shoulder and down the hallway.

"You can do better than a Templar peashooter, Zelda," he said. His body liquified, reshaped into Francisco, looking the same as when she'd last seen him in human form months ago. "Come on doll," he said, a manic grin on his face. "You've been letting yourself go, hanging out with the Witch Hunters."

"You piece of *shit!*" she screamed and charged her former lover. That caught him off guard, long enough for her to cast a spell. She'd never tried it before now, but it was exactly what this bastard deserved. She felt a surge of energy through her muscles, and prayed the spell worked as advertised, otherwise she'd be in big trouble. She slugged him in the jaw, and she was rewarded with the crack of bones and shattering teeth. She'd read about the spell years ago, something about giving the caster the strength of ten men. And now Francisco was about to get the beating of his life.

His head whipped around. His dislocated jaw set itself into place again. She ducked behind him and leapt onto his back, driving her fists down onto his skull, his neck, his collar bone. Every time she heard the crunching of bone, and every time it regenerated before she could strike her next blow.

Francisco laughed in triumph. His head rotated 180 degrees and she found herself staring into his blood red eyes, his maniacal smile with too many teeth that were too sharp.

"That's my girl!" he bellowed. His body liquified and she fell to the floor. Before she could rise, he had reformed his human body, looking down at her with both scorn and lust. She shuddered with disgust. "But you rejected us! You'll never know true power! Die now!"

Before she could raise her hands, he grabbed on to her throat. Her air was completely cut off; it was a miracle her neck wasn't crushed in that vice grip. With one hand, he picked her up off the ground, raised her over his head. He jumped, twisting his body around until he was on top of her. And then he choke slammed her through the floor. And the next floor. And the next.

***

Flint heard several crashes in quick succession, each one louder than the next. They stopped on the floor directly above them. "Hurry!" he shouted. His party continued their mad dash up the stairs. He could hear Navarro's wheezing through the blood pounding in his ears. One way or another, it would end soon. They reached the ninth floor. Without slowing down, he raised his leg and heel kicked the door open with a bang.

Over the next two seconds, he saw a hole in the

hallway's ceiling, Fletcher laying still upon the floor, and a Hispanic man standing over her, his body crackling with arcane energy. Flint aimed and fired his pistol. The bullet caught the man in the back. He grunted as black blood sprayed from his chest. He began to turn around, but Navarro unslung his rifle, aimed, and fired. The high powered rifle round smacked into the man's head and he dropped to the floor. His body liquified, began taking a new shape.

"Annihilate this monster! Show no mercy!" Flint bellowed. He charged, not waiting for the others to join him. Klemm was struggling to take solid form again, but Flint was on him before he could finish his transformation.

"Your judgment is at hand!" Flint shouted. He stabbed his sword straight down into the gelatinous mass that was Klemm. A shriek of pain echoed in the hallway. The other Templars rushed to Flint's side and added their sword blows to the melee. Navarro and the other Supernumeraries rushed in, the former with his tomahawk in hand, the other two with Bowie knives. They stomped, they stabbed, they cut and sliced. The hallway was spattered with bits and pieces of Klemm's liquid form.

"You shall pay for your crimes!" Flint bellowed. "You have befouled our world long enough, demon! Prepare to return to your masters below!" He felt the rage rise further. A corner of his mind noted that Fletcher still hadn't moved. Oh yes, Klemm would pay.

Flint detected movement. A piece of black slime was inching away from them. He flicked his sword to remove the ooze that had stained it and stalked after the moving puddle. It sped up, and he increased his pace. The black ooze morphed and shaped itself into human form. Roger Klemm, seated on the floor, pushed himself away from Flint, his hands raised. Klemm's suit was soaked in blood, his face a red mask, his breathing ragged.

"I surrender," he gasped, coughing up blood. "I surrender!"

The others joined him, the Templars keeping him covered with both sword and pistol. Flint kept his guard up. It could be another ruse.

"No job is worth this," he said, blood trickling from the corner of his mouth as he gave them a weak smile.

"Roger Klemm," Flint growled. "This is your last chance."

"Yeah, yeah, I understand," Klemm wheezed.

"You got a lot to answer for, shitheel," Navarro said.

"I tell you the name of my client... and you don't burn me. Deal?"

Flint scowled. He wanted to kill him and be done with it. But that was his lust for vengeance talking. Roger Klemm deserved to die for all that he had done today, and no doubt had dozens of other crimes to answer for. But he was a hired gun. His employer would be a much better prize.

"Yes," Flint spat. "If you have information for us, then you shall die in prison rather than at the stake."

"I guess that's the best I can hope for," Klemm laughed, before breaking down into another bloody coughing fit.

"Give us a name," Navarro said.

"Yeah... yeah..." Klemm said. "His name is... *Ichthil.*"

His hands lengthened into blades which shot out toward Flint and his party. They all opened fire simultaneously. Flint saw Navarro spin and fall to the floor, felt his blood spatter his face. Klemm's body jostled and shook as dozens of silver tipped rounds tore him apart. The slide of Flint's pistol locked open when he fired his last round. Tossing it aside, he stalked forward, made a wide sweep, and Klemm's head flew from his shoulders, bouncing off the wall, and rolling away. His body slumped over and was still at last.

34

"Ricardo!" Flint cried. He rushed to his fallen assistant's side, while two of the others checked on Fletcher. Navarro was on his back, his uniform a bloody ruin, but his chest continued to rise and fall. Flint saw a ragged hole in his side. Captain Forrest threw off his long coat, tore off a strip of his white dress shirt, and pressed it to Navarro's wound. He hissed in pain.

"Ricardo?" Flint asked.

"Really wish you'd let me change my clothes earlier boss," Navarro whispered.

Flint smiled. Navarro's customary leather body armor would indeed have been a better choice, but the enemy didn't always cooperate with their plans. Flint patted him on the shoulder and looked up at the two women tending to Fletcher, who was groaning in pain. She rolled over onto her stomach, and Flint could see her body glowing with a regenerative spell. He decided to overlook it this time. Breathing hard, Fletcher rose to her feet, staggering. The Lady Templar and her assistant steadied her.

"Goddamn," Fletcher muttered. "Don't think I'll ever try that one again... Rico!" She stumbled forward. Flint rose to catch her. She felt lighter. The bags under her eyes had grown more prominent, and he could smell her skin burning.

"I don't... I'm not sure if..." she said.

"It's alright, Zelda," Flint said.

She looked up at him. Even her face looked thinner. Her overuse of magic was eating away at her body. She stared at him for a moment, looked over his shoulder, no doubt seeing Klemm's body. She returned her gaze to Flint.

"It's really you," she whispered.

"Yes."

She broke from Flint's grasp, shuffled to Navarro. Falling to her knees, she looked at his wound and drew in a breath.

"I think I have enough left in me to fix it, a little," she said. "You might have a scar, Rico... sorry."

"That's okay," Navarro whispered. "It'll make for a good story to tell the ladies."

Fletcher chuckled. She held out her smoking hand which began to glow. Flint saw Navarro's stab wound slowly mend. Fletcher gritted her teeth. Another few seconds and she cried out. The glow vanished. Navarro winced, touched a hand to his side. The flesh was red where Klemm's blade had sliced him, and Flint reckoned that Fletcher was correct about a scar being left behind, but the bleeding was stopped.

Her shoulders slumped and she fell forward.

"Zelda!" Flint cried. He rushed to her side. He took off a gauntlet, pressed two fingers to her neck. Her pulse was steady. Then she began to snore.

Flint scoffed, but he was relieved. Navarro sat up with a groan, rubbing his side.

"How do you feel, Mr. Navarro?"

"I could really go for that cheeseburger."

***

Emil Parlow sat at his desk inside his quarters in Charles Flint's underground bunker. Flint had dismissed him and Lilian Turner for the day after hours of poring over *In Realis Magicae*. Parlow had to admit he was impressed at the scale of Flint's ambition. Turner had been born in the twenty-first century and had arrived in the year 2533 the old-fashioned way: aging. She was reluctant to share the secret of her unnaturally long life and youthful appearance, but Charles believed he had discovered a neat trick. Traveling forwards and backwards in time appeared impossible, but the book's author, Nazari, spoke of another way, of going sideways in time.

He hadn't heard from Roger all day. He knew that the man's methods often required time to learn his target's patterns, their friends and loved ones' patterns. Still, he was impatient to get this business finished. The sooner Flint and Fletcher were dead, the less likely it was Charles would deduce that Parlow had gone behind his back against his express orders. But were they really his express orders? He had forbidden a strike on Salem it-self, or against the Witch Hunter Generals. Parlow didn't recall him saying anything about not targeting his older brother Silas.

A chime sounded. He looked around.

"Emil." It was Charles's voice. "Would you join us in the observation room?"

Parlow looked at the clock on the wall. It was a little after ten p.m. Not late, but what would Flint want at this hour? He pushed himself away from the desk and left his room. The hallway was lit by those special lights the old world used... fluorescent, that was the word. He supposed they would burn out some day. They'd have to rely on witchfire then. It might make the place the place feel more like home. After a few turns, Parlow stepped into the observation room with its banks of panels, knobs, dials, and the viewscreen that took up most of its wall. Charles and Lilian were there, staring intently at the screen. The computer, Rob, was focused on a bird's eye view of what looked like Salem.

Shit, Parlow thought.

"Ah," Charles said, noticing him. "Thank you for join-ing us, Emil. Lilian and I were doing some research when Rob brought something interesting to our attention."

"Oh?" Parlow said, keeping his face neutral.

"Yes, quite," Turner said. "Rob, zoom in on the Impe-rial Palace."

The computer buzzed. "There are no..."

"The Oregon state capitol building."

The screen dropped toward the palace, giving Parlow a sense of vertigo.

"Magnify," Turner said. "Move west a bit."

The screen adjusted to their left. Parlow saw it now. It looked like the Templars, the cops, and the Imperial Army had cordoned off a city block near the palace. They surrounded a great black mass in the plaza of one of the taller skyscrapers.

"What am I looking at?" Parlow asked, squinting at the screen.

"Rob, replay what you showed us earlier. Zoom in as close as you can," Charles said.

The computer zoomed in further, and the figures on the screen began to move. He saw streams of gunfire strike the black mass, which was lashing out with what looked like tentacles. His mouth fell open. He'd heard stories about moving pictures, but he'd never seen it with his own eyes before. As the computer continued to play, he saw the creature fire projectiles of some sort – Rob couldn't get in close enough to show further detail, and many Templars fell like bowling pins.

"The best part is coming soon," Turner said.

A vehicle, much larger than an automobile, rolled down the street toward the melee. It fired and the black monster exploded. A few seconds later, a lone figure emerged from the vehicle. Another streak of fire, another explosion. Then the Templars swarmed the creature, whatever it was.

"That's enough," Charles said. The playback froze. "What do you make of that, Emil?"

Parlow furrowed his brow. That couldn't possibly have anything to do with Klemm. The assassin worked alone. As far as Parlow knew, he could only assume the forms of earthly things. Whatever that thing on the screen was, it was not of this world. "I have no idea..." he said.

"As it happens, I have a fairly good idea," Charles replied. "This isn't the first time I've seen that demon."

"Oh?" Parlow said.

"Indeed. The former owner of my book delved too deeply into magic he wasn't quite ready for. As I understand it, he became one with the demon Ichthil, whom I'm told resembles a great black slug with tentacles and a nasty beak. He leveled the city of New Rome before my brother and his little friends destroyed him outside the city of Jordan," Charles said.

"Imagine that," Parlow said.

"Hmm, yes," Charles said. "It's a pity so many people had to die, but I might not have gotten my copy if they hadn't. Blood and souls make the world go round, as Nazari said. Or something to that effect."

An awkward silence passed between them. When it became too much to bear, Parlow asked, "Was there anything else, sir?"

"Yes," Turner spoke up. "You wouldn't happen to know anything about Ichthil manifesting only a few blocks from the Imperial Palace, would you?"

"No... why would I?"

"Yesterday morning you were keen on the idea of a first strike against Salem," she said.

"Well, yes, I was. I won't deny it. But Charles forbade it, I accepted his decision, and that was the end of it."

"Now that you mention it Lilian," Charles said, circling to Parlow's left, "I also recall that Mr. Parlow asked to stay behind for a bit. He had a few questions for Rob, he said." Turner went to Parlow's right.

He felt an icy ball form in his stomach but said, "Yes. I wanted to ask him some historical questions about the Occult War. That's all."

"Did you?" Turner said. "You could have asked me. I lived through it. And unlike the computer, I remember everything after the war as well."

Parlow laughed, his eyes darting to either side of him. "Oh, well, you know, you two were busy and I didn't want to bother you with my idle curiosity."

"It wouldn't have been a bother at all, Emil," Charles said. "We're making history here. It's good to be curious about the history of our magician ancestors. Since you brought it up, I'm curious about what you learned yesterday."

"Me too," Turner said, a predatory expression on her face. "Computer, replay all interactions you had with Emil Parlow yesterday."

Oh no.

"I understand Miss Turner," Rob's monotone voice said from everywhere and nowhere. The computer, damn that stupid machine, replayed his conversations with Klemm, ordering him to kill Silas Flint, and then adding Zelda Fletcher to the contract. It started to play the historical question and answer session that took place once he'd concluded his business with the assassin, but Turner raised a hand.

"That's enough, Rob," she said.

Charles shook his head. "Emil, Emil, Emil…"

Parlow felt panic rise in his gorge. "You said we wouldn't make a first strike against the city, and I didn't."

"Then what do you call that?!" Charles screamed, waving at the view screen.

"I don't know anything about that!" Parlow yelled back. "That wasn't me!"

"No, it was just your hired gun," Charles said.

"Roger Klemm… I've heard of him," Turner said. "Supposed to be a genius at shapeshifting spells."

"One would think a professional assassin would be more subtle," Charles said, the corner of his mouth turning up.

"He is!" Parlow said. Charles glared at him in silence. "You never said anything about not targeting Silas."

Charles sighed. "Again, one would think an intelligent listener could have picked up on the implication, but I see that you're an idiot who needs things spelled out for you."

Parlow balled his fists. "Now listen here you little…" His words were cut off by an invisible vice grip around his throat that slammed him against the wall, holding him up off the floor. Parlow gagged and clawed at his neck, tried to summon a spell, something, anything, but the grip was relentless.

"No, you listen," Charles growled. "I don't know what you think we're doing here, but I am trying to build a nation for our brother and sister magicians. A legitimate nation, recognized on the international stage!" His voice rose to a shout and he clenched his fingers, the invisible grip tightening around Parlow's throat. His eyes rolled back in his head. The grip loosened a bit, but only enough for Parlow to scream as he felt a stream of magical electricity course through his body. His teeth chattered, his limbs twitched, his body smoked. It stopped, and his head slumped forward.

"Don't leave us yet, Emil," Charles said, a smile on his face. "I need you to hear the rest of what I have to say."

Parlow looked up.

"That's it," Charles said. "I appreciate terrorizing the lambs as much as the next wizard, but there is a time and a place for it. The United Mountain States government is going to hit us with everything they have in the weeks to come, and we're going to need all the help that we can get. That includes the ordinary people who reside within our borders. I told you that presently we can only afford one war at a time. I sympathize with your desire to kill Silas, but not at the expense of what I'm trying to accomplish here. And if you can't understand simple orders, then you're more useful to me in death than in life."

Parlow was spun around in the invisible grip and slammed against the wall again, his back to Charles and Lilian. He felt a pinch on his back and then all went dark.

***

Charles tore Emil Parlow's spinal column from out of his back, a sphere of magical energy catching the blood before it ruined the floor. He smiled. That spell to increase one's physical strength was really something.

"Did you get all of that, Rob?" he asked.

The computer chimed. "I have audio and visual records of your conversation with Mr. Parlow."

Charles laughed. "Computer, there are times I envy how dispassionate you are."

Turner approached him. "I don't. Bravo, by the way. You did the right thing."

"Yes," Charles said, looking at the spinal column in his hands. "I was beginning to wonder where we'd find a supply of ingredients for your elixir." Turner's life extension formula needed human cerebrospinal fluid as a key ingredient. It was how she, a woman born in the year 2030, had lived to the year 2533 and not aged a day.

"This one will do nicely," she said. "And as a bonus, when it comes from a magician, it's even more powerful. I figure the prisons can always supply us with more."

"And we permanently remove drains on society," Charles snickered. "Come, let's go get some prepared. You taught me the recipe, but I still need to see how it all comes together. And to taste it."

"That's the bad news: it tastes like pickle juice."

Charles shuddered. "I suppose eternal life has its price. We should find some whiskey to wash it down."

35

Silas Flint, Ricardo Navarro, and Zelda Fletcher sat on a bench inside a hallway of the Imperial Palace. It had been three days since they'd slain Roger Klemm. A demon manifesting so close to the royal family's home had led to many hard questions from the Cascadia Intelligence Service, the heads the armed services, the Cascadia Bureau of Investigation, and other agencies none of them had ever heard of before. At least they'd been granted a day to rest and recover from their exertions. And now they were back for their long delayed appointment with His Majesty, Emperor Peter II.

Flint and Navarro had each been fitted for new dress uniforms, as the ones they had worn that day were ruined beyond repair. Fletcher was in a new dress, and she appeared much healthier after gorging herself on food and drink and sleeping for the rest of that day. Human beings were never meant to use magic, Flint thought, which is why it ate away at their bodies, and why many magicians offered themselves up to the powers below, to diminish the physical toll magic took on them.

"I'm surprised we're not going to be in, like, the throne room or something," Fletcher said, looking around. To their left was a wooden door bearing the royal family's crest, flanked by two royal guardsmen.

"I believe His Majesty maintains a personal office for meetings he does not wish to be a part of the public record," Flint said.

Navarro rubbed his side. As Fletcher has predicted, there was a scar on his flank. Flint's bullet wound had been tended to with thread and needle, but he expected he'd bear a lifelong scar as well. "You think His Majesty's going to tear us a new one?" he asked.

Flint sighed. "I do not know. I hope not." General Hickock had assured them they had nothing to worry about, but Flint wouldn't blame the man a bit for being angry. This was the second time in as many months that the forces of darkness had defiled the imperial capitol itself, something the Knights Templar of the Order of Saint Benedict were sworn to prevent. "Remember what the Generals told us."

"Always tell him the truth..." Fletcher said.

"Even if you think it's going to piss him off," Navarro finished. "I really don't want to piss him off."

"Yeah, no shit," Fletcher said. "I mean when I was a kid, I always thought that Emperors and counts and nobles and all the rest were just rich people who ordered poor people around but..."

"His Majesty had a distinguished military service record before he ascended the throne," Flint said.

The guards came to attention. The wooden door opened, and a young woman poked her head out. "His Majesty will see you now," she said.

As they rose from their seat, Flint dug out his pocket watch. 3 p.m. Whatever else one thought about the Emperor, the man was punctual. They stepped into what looked like another waiting room. Couches lined one wall, occupied with businessmen, imperial functionaries, and others looking for a special boon with His Majesty. The woman led them behind her desk to another door. She opened it and motioned for them to go through.

They lined up before the Emperor's desk and knelt on their left knees. Emperor Peter's back was to them, his hands behind his back, as he stared out a window that took in much of Salem's cityscape. He still wore a plain, olive drab military tunic, with a black leather belt and purple cord around his right shoulder. The woman shut the door behind them. The Emperor turned around.

"Please rise," he said. Once they had done so, he sat down at his desk, motioned at three chairs in front of it. "Have a seat."

Flint took the center chair. He could sense that Navarro and Fletcher were nervous. He offered a quick mental prayer for the guidance of the Holy Spirit.

The Emperor took a deep breath. Now that he could see the man up close, Flint thought he looked much older than his 55 years. Peter smiled.

"Better late than never, eh Captain?"

Flint smiled back. "Of course, Your Majesty."

"I understand that you three are the ones who put down the wizard."

Flint pursed his lips. "We slew Mr. Klemm, yes."

The Emperor grinned. "And here I thought my tank and my RPG finished the job."

"Uh, not to take away from what you did, sir, uh, I mean Your Majesty," Navarro said.

"Yeah, that was, uh... well, pardon my language, but pretty badass. Your Majesty. Sir," Fletcher stammered.

The Emperor chuckled. "'Sir,' will do."

"Yes sir," the three responded in unison.

He favored them with another grin. He drummed his fingers on the desk. "Captain Flint."

"Yes sir?"

"I asked you a few days ago if you believed your brother wanted war."

"I remember sir."

"Was this Klemm an agent of your brother?"

He thought for a few moments, then shook his head. "I do not believe so sir."

"Oh?"

"Hiring assassins is not his style. Charles always did prefer more personal confrontations."

"That... monster... he was a hired gun?"

"Yes sir," Navarro replied. "And he was targeting Silas and Zelda."

The Emperor raised an eyebrow. "Indeed? I think this may be the first time in Cascadian history that an assassin was this close to the Imperial Palace but didn't intend to kill an Emperor." He drummed his fingers again. "But if he was an assassin, why would he draw attention to himself in such a dramatic fashion?"

"Well, the thing is, sir, Klemm wasn't working alone," Fletcher said. "He was possessed by the spirit of Francisco Cortez."

"Should I know that name?" Peter asked.

"Mr. Cortez was responsible for the destruction of New Rome this past April," Flint said.

The Emperor closed his eyes, sighed, made the sign of the cross. "May God have mercy on those poor souls," he said. Opening them again, a distant look came over him. "I considered becoming a Witch Hunter in my youth, you know. But my father talked me out of it. As his first-born son, I was expected to succeed him. And it's been my honor and privilege to reign since his passing. I'm fulfilling my God-given vocation. But it's times like these I wish I could take a more active role against the forces of the night."

The trio said nothing.

"If you're right about your brother, I may get my wish," Peter sighed.

"May I presume to ask what the government will do sir?" Flint asked.

The Emperor focused on him. "Understand, Captain Flint, that it's not entirely my decision to make. My instincts tell me that you are correct. One day we will be at war with this so-called Empire of Medea. But I fear the mood in Parliament is leaning toward a wait and see position."

Flint sighed. "I see."

"So we're not doing anything sir?" Navarro asked.

"No," the Emperor said. "I'm ordering an expansion of the armed services. That Templar Chapter House that your father is working on? I've also ordered construction to begin with all possible speed and diverted additional funding and materiel. God willing, it should be consecrated by next spring."

"I am pleased to hear it sir," Flint said.

"And you, Miss Fletcher," Peter said.

She swallowed. "Yes sir?"

He smiled. "Some members of the Committee are still outraged that I would deign to speak to a known witch, but on behalf of the Empire, I wish to extend our thanks for your assistance in our battle with Mr. Klemm."

She nodded. "Uh... you're welcome. Sir."

"You said that you could probably pinpoint Charles's location."

"Yes sir, I think I can."

"We may need use of your talent in the future."

"I'll be ready sir."

"Captain Flint, how would you feel if I asked you to transfer to Salem?"

Flint was stunned. He opened his mouth, closed it again. Recalling Hickock's words, he said, "I would feel most displeased sir."

"Oh? May I ask why?"

Flint reflected that His Majesty didn't need to ask 'May I' of anyone and he took it as a compliment. "I am uncomfortable being such a short distance from my place of birth. It has many bad memories. Were it my decision to make, I would never set foot within Mount Angel again. It... it feels like my greatest failure, sir."

The Emperor nodded. "I understand, Captain. I won't order you. But should you ever change your mind, both General Hickock and I would be honored to have you serve in Salem."

"Thank you sir."

"And the more I think on it, Fort Marsing will be on the front lines when or if we go to war. I am sure you would prefer to be closer to the action."

"Yes sir."

The Emperor rose from his seat, the trio following. "You three have given us much to consider. Thank you all for being here. I've instructed the Committee to leave you in peace for now, and you should be returning to

Marsing soon once General Abernathy has completed his testimony. I just need two more things from you."

Flint and the others came to attention almost by instinct. "Yes sir?"

"Captain Flint, Mr. Navarro, I meant to offer you both a special commendation for your service here last month before international events interfered. You've done Salem another service, and both you and Miss Fletcher deserve recognition. Please be in the Great Hall in thirty minutes."

They nodded. "Yes sir."

"And…" he opened his desk, tossed Flint a jingling sack of coins. "Please enjoy yourselves tonight. Inside you will also find a note from me that should get you in to any establishment you choose and skip the line."

Flint put the pouch inside his long coat pocket. "Thank you, sir."

"You are dismissed."

They genuflected before the Emperor and excused themselves from his office. Once they got out into the hall, Fletcher grabbed Flint's arm.

"Holy shit! The Emperor is treating us!" she yelled.

"Where you want to go boss?" Flint said, grinning.

"I shall choose this time," Flint said. "And I have had my fill of hamburgers, thank you."

EPILOGUE

Doctor Nobusuke Kato stood inside the telegraph office, hands behind his back. His clockwork guardsman stood by the chattering machine, waiting for the tape to finish printing, waiting with the patience only a machine could have. The automaton was humanoid, its gears visible through its armpits, two lightbulbs serving as its eyes. The telegraph stopped clicking. The robot tore off the tape.

"The latest news," it said in an echoing voice.

Kato read the message. The telegraph office was on the Las Vegas Strip. He often reflected that the city, once a den of iniquity, was now a masterpiece of clockwork perfection. His automatons served as security and as casino staff. Kato found gambling distasteful, but even he had to admit it was an excellent source of cash. And with unfeeling machines dealing cards and counting chips, there was no room for human error, no possibility of fraud or theft. Tourists grumbled about how cold the experience was, but he had no time for human weakness.

"Fascinating," Kato said. According to his agents in Salem, there was another supernatural incident, this one involving a demon of considerable size and power. And the demon had been slain by Witch Hunter Captain Silas Flint. Was he any relation to Charles Flint, the wizard who had appeared in the sky last month, proclaiming the birth of a new nation?

"What will you do, father?" the robot asked.

Kato stroked his chin. A nation of magicians. When he'd first heard the idea, he'd thought that it would interfere with his plans. He needed as many magicians as he could get his hands on, and it simply wouldn't do if they all went north. The more he thought on it, he realized that Charles Flint's new nation could fit in nicely with his own ambitions. He just needed to approach it properly.

He snorted. It wasn't often that he needed to engage in international diplomacy. Other nations had nothing he wanted, and they could seldom afford anything he had to offer. This Empire of Medea though...

"I believe it's time we extend recognition to Flint," Kato said.

"Which one, father?"

Kato smiled. He never laughed – humor was simply noticing an incongruity – but he sometimes found his servants' literal-mindedness amusing. "Charles," he said. "I think we may be able to form an arrangement that will be mutually beneficial."

THE WARLOCK'S CROWN

Greater love hath no man than this, that a man lay down his life for his friends.

- John 15:13

Arturo Vasquez: The Great Necromancer. A demon in human form, a man with appetites so gross and depraved that it is said Hell itself would not take him. A torturer of bodies, a devourer of souls, a scholar, a rebel, a monster. Incalculable is the scale of his evil, unimaginable the scope of his crimes against God and nature, uncounted the number of his barbarities. If ever there was a compelling argument for atheism, it was he, for how could a good God allow one such as Arturo Vasquez to be born?

- The Witch Hunter's Guide to North America, 11th edition, pub. January 31, 2512

1

W itch Hunter Captain Silas Flint pushed his way through the forest. This place had once been a national park during the time of the old United States, but now it was just another primeval piece of wilderness reclaimed by nature over the centuries. The leafy canopy obscured what little daylight could pierce the roiling thunderclouds overhead, and all would have been darkness were it not for his blessed sword lighting the way. The screams, roars, gunfire, and magical blasts were becoming fainter behind him, diminishing to a dull roar. He prayed that his friends were alright. General Abernathy had ordered Flint to disengage from the battle and pursue his brother, Charles Flint, Emperor of Medea. Flint had no talent for magic, but he could nonetheless sense that Charles was nearby. Waiting for him.

Flint cut through branches, underbrush, and tall grass. Whatever trail had existed when this place was a recreational park had long since vanished. He felt Charles's presence beckoning. Flint's dress shirt was stained with the blood of dozens of magicians and the black ichor of demons and undead. His long black coat weighed heavy on him. Before he had departed the fight, his assistant, Supernumerary Ricardo Navarro, had given him extra magazines for the two pistols holstered on his belt. General Abernathy had given him additional pouches of blessed, exorcised salt. Zelda Fletcher, the repentant former witch, his... what was she now? For some reason, Flint couldn't recall the nature of their relationship. But she had given him a dagger, the blade forged from pure silver. It seemed familiar somehow. Had he used it before? He couldn't remember. As he pressed forward, he took his pocket watch from his waistcoat pocket, flipped it open. Odd. He couldn't read the time. It was as though the numbers and the hands were in a fog. Even the picture of his family inside the lid – taken when he and Charles were just entering adolescence, when his parents were young and healthy and fully human – was blurred.

He heard a soft roar before him. That could only the ocean. He was nearly there. Charles was waiting. He sliced another branch. Adrenaline and, he prayed, the guidance of the Holy Spirit kept him pushing on. Flint was drenched in sweat. This part of Cascadia had a temperate climate, but the day's hard fighting was taking its toll on him. And now he would no doubt be going into battle once again. The final battle of his life, perhaps. Flint realized he still retained hope that Charles would repent, renounce the dark powers, that they could be reconciled and be family again. Yes, he hoped for all these years. He had retained that hope even in the aftermath of Charles mutating their parents into twisted abominations, even when Flint had been forced to defend himself, even after they regained enough of themselves to cry off and beg him to put them out of their misery. He felt his eyes water, but he girded his spirit for battle.

There. Light up ahead. The forest thinned and he saw dim sunlight through the wall of trees. A crack of thunder boomed overhead. He unholstered one of his pistols. Years of training and casework had made Flint an expert at both swordplay and gunfighting. He wondered if God had arranged it all in preparation for this moment. He took a deep breath and stepped out of the forest, emerging from the tree line onto the rocky ground.

Before him the ocean extended to the horizon. A rocky outcropping extended out over the water. The sky was thick with clouds, and Flint sensed the storm was about to break. Lightning lit up the horizon, followed a second later by a deafening crash of thunder. He sensed movement on his left. Of course they would be here. The Weird Sisters. Three young women with identical faces, one with snow white hair, one with hair like darkest midnight, the third's a fiery red. In front of him, standing at the edge of the cape was his brother, Charles Flint. Beside him was a square of concrete blocks containing a flagpole. Flint saw a plaque at its base – some kind of old world monument? – but couldn't make out the writing. Atop the pole was a torn, tattered American flag, whipped by the cold wind.

Charles's back was to him, his hands clasped behind him. He wore black boots and a long coat like Flint's. "Ave, Frater," Charles said, still looking out over the ocean.

"Charles," Flint replied. "In the name of God, I..."

"Oh, give it a rest, Silas," Charles said. "You should know better than to use the High Speech with me. Just once, before the end of all things, can we not talk like brothers again?"

Flint kept his brother covered with his pistol, tightened his grip on his sword, which shone brightly in the gloom. "What's more to say?" Flint asked. "After everything that's happened, I'd hoped you would repent. Surrender. There's still time to…"

"No, there isn't," Charles said. He chuckled. "I'll say this about you brother: once you've put your mind to something, you never give up. Well, neither do I. I've come too far to surrender now."

"Charles, for God's sake, why? What do you hope to accomplish here, now? Even if we fight, even if you kill me, you know the Order and the Empire will hunt you to the ends of the earth."

"Because I'm right!" Charles snapped. "You know I'm right, Silas. Magic isn't going away, ever, no matter how long your pitiful Order hunts us, kills us. We magicians are the next step in human evolution. The Empire is mired in the past. The nations of this continent, they're repeating the same mistakes that got them annihilated in the Occult War. If anything, I should be asking you and your kind to surrender."

"My kind?" Flint said. "You mean human beings who live as God intended?"

"And look where that's gotten you," Charles laughed. "We have the power, brother. Simon Magus brought us magic for the betterment of humanity, so we would no longer be slaves to an absentee God."

Flint scowled. "Mind your blasphemy, heretic."

Charles sighed. "I thought you could be a real human being for a second, but now I see the fearless Witch Hunter again. Believe it or not Silas, even though you've been a pain in my side, I have to admit I'm impressed at how you've managed to make it this far."

Flint pursed his lips. "You will not yield?"

"Never."

"Then you leave me no choice."

"Nor do you. For what it's worth, I never wanted it to come to this either. But only one of us is walking away from this place."

Charles spread his arms, his hands burning with witch-fire. Flint gripped his sword and pistol. Another crack of thunder. Rain began to fall, first a drizzle, and seconds later a downpour.

"Die now!" Charles yelled.

"For the Empire!" Flint shouted. The two brothers, light and dark, charged toward one another. Here, at the edge of the world, they would decide the fate of...

***

Flint snorted, woke, bolted upright. He was drenched in sweat, his eyes wide, darting everywhere. He was in bed, inside his living quarters at Fort Marsing. Moonlight shone through his window, bathing the room in a pale glow. He ran a hand over his close cropped hair. He fumbled, sweeping his hand across his nightstand, looking for the electric lamp switch, and his pocket watch. Finding both, he clicked on the light and flipped the watch open.

1:42 a.m. Breathing hard, he swung his legs out of bed, his bare feet touching the stone floors. A dream. It had been a dream. Curious. Flint never remembered his dreams, but this one was still clear in his mind. Charles... and someone else. Three someones.

He looked up and started again. He could make out three silhouettes in the darkness beyond the glow of his lamp. He reached under his pillow and drew one of his pistols, cocking the hammer as he brought it to bear on the intruders.

"Identify yourselves!" Flint shouted. "I swear that I shall..."

"Please excuse us Silas," said a female voice.

"We know it was rude to enter without knocking," said a second.

"But then again, would you have let us in if we had?" said a third.

Flint sighed, decocked his pistol, but held on to it. "You again," he said.

Mallory, Monica, and Madeline Proctor stepped out of the darkness and into the moonlight. They appeared as they had in his dream, as they always did: young women in their mid-twenties with identical faces, in shimmering white, ankle length dresses, Mallory with snow white hair, Monica with hair of midnight black, Madeline with fiery red.

Flint realized he was wearing only a pair of shorts. He wrapped a blanket around his body. The sisters giggled. "Is there any particular reason you three have invaded my living quarters?" Flint said.

"Hmm, that is an improvement," Mallory said.

"Could it be he is growing to trust us?" Monica said.

"I would not bet money on it," Madeline said.

"I will concede that you have proven yourselves useful on several cases," Flint said. The three witches had appeared to him and Navarro outside the city of Oglethorpe months ago, providing them with a silver dagger (had that been in his dream?) that Flint had ended up needing for the case. They had appeared again during their time in the imperial capitol of Salem and provided clues that helped them track down a Templar who had secretly gone over to the dark side, using her position to murder other Witch Hunters. "Your presence within these hallowed walls is an affront. If you have nothing of vital import to relate, then I must insist that you depart, post-haste. I have no interest in being social with you, and I…"

"Did you have a bad dream, Silas?" Mallory asked.

"You have never paid attention to dreams before," Monica said.

"Perhaps you should start," Madeline said.

Flint raised an eyebrow. "What would you know of it?"

"We told Ricardo once that we had been shown a great vision."

"A vision of two brothers, light and dark."

"At the edge of the world, beneath weeping skies and an old world flag."

Flint blinked. He opened his mouth, shut it again. After another few moments, he said, "You caused that dream?"

"Yes," they replied in unison.

"Why?"

The three sisters exchanged looks. Then they shrugged.

"Perhaps it is nothing," Mallory said.

"It was only a dream after all," Monica said.

"Or perhaps a prophecy," Madeline said.

Flint sighed, rubbed the bridge of his nose. "If that will be all..."

"Not quite."

"There is one more thing."

"Do you remember when we first met?"

"How could one forget?" Flint said. They'd appeared out of nowhere in the middle of a dense forest alongside Dry Creek, on the road to Oglethorpe in the south. Flint recalled chiding himself for allowing three witches to catch both him and his assistant unawares in such a dramatic fashion.

"You'll be visiting Oglethorpe again, soon," Mallory said.

"You should ask Matthew for advice," Monica said.

"We are your elders, but you don't listen to us. You should listen to him," Madeline said.

Flint looked down. The city of Oglethorpe was named for retired Witch Hunter General Matthew Oglethorpe, General Abernathy's predecessor as the commander of Fort Marsing. The General's advice had proven invaluable in tracking down the werewolf that had been plaguing his city this past May.

"Why will we be...?" Looking up, he saw that the sisters were gone. "Hmph," he snorted. Flint supposed he should try to get some rest, but he didn't think he'd be getting any more sleep this night.

***

Hundreds of miles to the northeast, Charles Flint woke with a start, sitting upright in bed, his hands ablaze with sorcerous fire. He'd been on a rocky outcropping, beside an American flag that had seen better days. The skies were pregnant with rain, lightning, and thunder... and Silas was there. They had exchanged words, they'd charged one another. There were others too. Three women. He tried to remember what they looked like, but the image wouldn't come.

He looked around. His room was that of the former commanding officer of this facility, an underground American nuclear missile bunker that he and his colleague Lilian Turner had unearthed a few months ago. There were no windows, and all was black.

"Computer, lights," Charles said. The room was lit up by the fluorescent lights overhead. He looked around. Everything appeared in order. The bunker was controlled by an old world computer that had introduced itself as Rob. Lilian assured him that Rob was just a machine, a relic of the old United States that wasn't truly alive, but sometimes he wondered.

"Rob... what time is it?" he asked.

The walls chimed. "The time is currently 0142 hours," Rob said in that monotone voice.

Almost two in the morning. Charles rubbed his face. His beard was coming in nicely. Wizards were often portrayed in popular culture as having wild, unkempt beards.

Charles had never let his grow out before, but he was beginning to like it. He'd keep it under control though. An emperor had to maintain certain grooming standards.

What was that – a dream? A vision? He snorted. Silas always said dreams were nonsense, the product of over-active imaginations. Charles kept a more open mind. Sometimes they were nonsense. Sometimes they were a portent. He'd woken up before the dream showed him the outcome of his fight with Silas. That was one thing of which he was certain: one day he and his older brother would share a final confrontation, and that only one of them would walk away. Who were those three women though? His instincts told him they had an important part to play in the events to come, but the more he focused on it, the more difficult it was to remember them. No matter. All would be revealed in the fullness of time.

Charles supposed he should try to get some rest, but he had a feeling that sleep wouldn't come again this night. May as well get some work done.

"Rob," he said, "How goes the UMS Army's progress?" Five weeks ago, he had projected a titanic image of himself in the sky, one that reached to every corner of North America. He had proclaimed the birth of his new nation, his Empire of Medea. That he was carving his new empire out of the old Montana country, a province of the United Mountain States, was of no concern to him, but UMS President Hugh Fitzroy was understandably outraged.

"Sensors indicate five divisions are presently in formation around Denver," Rob replied.

Charles snorted. Fitzroy had blustered and threatened,

but so far, his army hadn't departed from Denver yet. Charles wasn't privy to the meetings between the UMS President and his generals, but he imagined there was much squabbling about logistics, troop deployments, how many divisions would stay to guard Denver. Charles smiled. He had a trump card that no one else on the continent had: this bunker held an arsenal of operational nuclear missiles. Whenever those slugs got around to making their way north, they'd find a nasty surprise waiting for them.

He considered waking Lilian Turner, telling her of his dream, decided against it. Turner was a remarkable woman. She was born Lilith Harkmoore in the year 2030, had seen the coming of Simon Magus with her own eyes, been gifted the power of sorcery from the Great Magician himself... and with his help she had devised an elixir of life, one that stopped the human aging process. Now, in the year 2533, she didn't look a day over her biological age of 29.

Whether it was just a dream, or a prophecy didn't matter. When the time came, Charles was confident that he would be the survivor of his last meeting with Silas.

2

Professor Valentina Morales looked through her binoculars. She saw seven towers stretching toward the sky from a moldering stone castle. Morales shuddered. Even at this distance, the structure felt wrong somehow. Mathematics wasn't her field of expertise, but even she could see that the angles were off somehow. It hurt her head to look at it for too long, but she'd have to get used to it if her team was going to make heads or tails of it.

She felt an icy chill run up her spine despite the late summer heat. Another reason why the castle was wrong was that it shouldn't exist at all. It had been the home of the necromancer Arturo Vasquez. He had terrorized eastern Cascadia for years before he was slain by the celebrated Witch Hunter Matthew Oglethorpe forty years ago. By all accounts, Oglethorpe had overseen the destruction of Castle Vasquez – nicknamed "la casa del diablo" by the locals. He'd razed it down to its foundation, leaving not one stone standing upon another. Legend had it that the castle reappeared, intact, the next morning. The then Emperor had ordered the Army to smash it to bits, and they'd unloaded a division's worth of artillery on the structure... and there it was again, the very next day. The Emperor had offered a bounty to anyone who could successfully destroy the castle for good, but to no avail. It had been subjected to every form of combustion known to man, and it always rose again. Eventually the Witch Hunters and the Empire had given up and settled for quarantining the area.

Not that a quarantine was strictly necessary. She and her team had left the city of Danville hours earlier, following the Owyhee River until it branched off into Skull Creek. She snorted. It had been called that long before the coming of the necromancer, before the twenty-first century Occult War even, but it figured he would build his home on the banks of Skull Creek Reservoir. She scanned the landscape around the castle, saw nothing but dry, cracked dirt. Nothing lived there, not even a blade of grass. Nothing could live there, she expected. The water looked dark, but she couldn't tell if it was black or blood red.

Don Riffey came to her side. A former soldier in His Majesty's Imperial Army, the University had hired him and several of his buddies to act as security for the expedition. "Still sure about this?" he asked.

"No," Morales responded, "But we don't have much of a choice."

Several weeks after that crazy wizard Charles Flint appeared in the sky, announcing the birth of his so-called Empire, the Emperor himself had contacted the University of Redmond's Paranormal Research Department. He hadn't ordered it, exactly, but he had asked if they would be so kind as to forward all archived materials pertaining to Vasquez's reign of terror almost half a century ago. Flint's territory was within the United Mountain States, but Vasquez had attempted something similar back then, seeking to break away from Cascadia to form his own little kingdom of the dead. Emperor Peter no doubt wished to know more about how his predecessors handled the crisis.

The head of the Department, Professor Zachariah Meyer, had complied with the Emperor's request, of course. It then occurred to him that the most recent expedition to Castle Vasquez was over thirty years ago, and Professor Morales, as the newest tenured member of the Department, was the lucky girl who drew the short straw.

Riffey shuddered. "That place doesn't feel right."

"I couldn't agree more," Morales said. "The last time

the University sent an expedition out here, the place was deserted, but in their notes, they describe lots of... unexplainable phenomenon."

"If it's deserted, then why do we need to be out here?" Riffey asked. "I mean what's changed?"

"You mean besides a wizard armed with nuclear weapons?" Morales spoke in jest, but the more she thought about it, the more she thought this trip was about politics and nothing more. Professor Meyer was fulfilling his patriotic duty in obeying the Emperor's request. He probably thought that ordering a new expedition to this cursed place would show initiative, and the University's willingness to cooperate in any way they could with the government's plans for dealing with Medea. Who knows? They might get lucky and discover something new. If nothing else, it would provide grist for Morales's books. *Publish or perish* had been the rule of academics for nearly a thousand years.

"Hey," Riffey said, nudging her.

"What?"

"Let me see your binoculars."

She handed them to the security guard who held them to his eyes, scanning Castle Vasquez.

"You see something?" she asked.

He handed the binoculars to her. "Take a look."

She brought them to her eyes. "What am I..." There. She saw it now. One of the windows on the highest tower. A shadow was moving back and forth. Like a human being pacing around inside. It couldn't be a person though. No one in their right mind would take up residence in a place like Castle Vasquez. The shadow stopped in the center of the window. She couldn't make out any details, but she wondered if it was looking at her.

She lowered the binoculars. Swallowed.

"It's your call, doc," Riffey said.

She shivered again. They had a priest with them, Father Colm McConaughey, one of the University chaplains. She wished that the Order could have sent a Witch Hunter to stand guard over them, but they didn't do private security. They'd probably call them mad for even considering exploring Castle Vasquez again. They might be right.

"I... uh..." she said.

"I get paid either way," Riffey said. "You want to pull out of here, no judgment from me."

She swallowed. Christ, why did it have to be her? She wondered if this was some elaborate hazing ritual that all new professors had to endure. Well, in any case, she was no fighter, but she wasn't a coward either.

"We'll proceed. If anything... unusual is going on here, then we can pull out."

"You're the boss," Riffey said. He excused himself and went back to the riverbank where her team was breaking for lunch and watering their horses. She had about a dozen graduate students with her, Riffey and five of his men, plus Father McConaughey. Twenty people. Whoever or whatever she saw moving in the tower... surely they wouldn't cause trouble with that many people present. She hoped.

Everyone packed up their garbage and prepared their horses to resume their journey. Despite the forbidding locale, Morales enjoyed visiting the east whenever she could. It was ironic; back when the United States still existed, the west was considered the wild frontier. Since the Occult War ended, the frontier was in the opposite direction. Gas lanterns and horse drawn carriages were more common in the east than electricity and automobiles. The population was less dense, the imperial government's presence was thinner, and it was altogether more dangerous than the west. But the air was cleaner, and nature more beautiful.

At least their journey had been beautiful so far. Rolling hills, grassy plains, and dense forests dominated the east. Oglethorpe and Danville were charming little cities. But as her group drew closer to their destination, there was an abrupt change in the landscape. One second their horses were moving quietly over green grass, the next their hooves clopped on hard blackened dirt. They passed a grove of dead trees, their bare branches reaching toward the sky like damned souls trying to escape the fiery pit. It was August, the dog days of summer, but she believed the chill would be with her until they departed this haunted place.

"Hey professor!"

Morales, her reverie broken, saw that Carlos Ramirez, one of her graduate students, was riding alongside her now. She nodded to him. "Mr. Ramirez," she said. Morales was pretty sure he had a crush on her. He wasn't bad looking, but besides being his doctoral adviser, she was ten years his senior. Nothing would or could come of it.

Ramirez looked around at the empty landscape. "Kind of spooky, huh?" he asked.

"That, Mr. Ramirez, is an understatement," she replied.

"It's weird. Why would Vasquez make his castle indestructible?"

"We're not sure, exactly. After he died, the Witch Hunters burned all his books and notes. Almost everything we know about him comes from interviews with surviving eyewitnesses, and of course, General Oglethorpe."

Ramirez sighed.

"Is there a problem, Carlos?"

"I don't know... I understand why they did it, burning all his stuff. I guess I was just thinking about how we lost so much potential research material."

"Careful," she chuckled. "If a Templar heard you talking that way, he might want to bring you in for questioning." She continued, "And yes, I understand why they did it too. This is just rumor, you understand, but apparently Vasquez put a curse on his grimoires. Anyone who studies them too closely goes mad."

"Even so," he said, looking around. The castle loomed ahead. "I think this trip has already given me an idea for my thesis."

"Oh?"

"Yeah. The use of magic in regeneration. Healing wounds for one, and uh... I guess it works on inanimate objects too," he said, waving at the castle.

Morales said nothing. Ramirez would learn soon enough that the Knights Templar of the Order of Saint Benedict kept a tight rein on what academics were permitted to talk and write about regarding magic. Personally, she didn't see what the problem was. Most people didn't have the talent for magic, and those that did either learned their craft from another magician or had access to books the academic world had no knowledge of. Still, she believed in the value of her department and her work. Like it or not, magic was a part of their world now, and humanity deserved to know the truth of it as best they could understand it. Maybe the coming of Charles Flint and his new nation of magicians would open up new research opportunities. Or maybe the Order would restrict them even more. Time would tell.

The group was silent save for the jangling of their saddlebags, the clopping of the horses' hooves. There was no breeze, no birdsong, no insects, nothing. This was consistent with what the first expedition had encountered, but Morales still found it uncanny. Father McConaughey came to her side.

"Almost there," he said.

"Yes," she replied. They had come to the shores of Skull Creek Reservoir. She wondered if what she had seen earlier through her binoculars had been a trick of the light. The reservoir was as quiet and still as everything else, looking more like a pane of glass than a body of water. She had a hunch that nothing lived in the water either, neither fish nor plants, and that she could see clear through to the bottom if she took a boat out onto it. They might have to set up their permanent base camp further away from the castle, where there was still living grass for the horses.

After another few minutes, they arrived at the outer keep of Castle Vasquez. A low wall surrounded the castle proper, with what looked like guard huts stationed at regular intervals. Why a necromancer as powerful as Vasquez would have needed guards, she didn't know. Probably staffed by zombies or vampires or some other loathsome creatures. Looking up, she saw that one of the seven towers was floating, connected to the rest of the castle only by a single staircase.

Morales and McConaughey dismounted. The priest shielded his eyes against the early afternoon sun. "Well," he said, "Everything looks calm. But I'm sure you feel the same sense of unease that I do."

She nodded.

"General Oglethorpe had several priests perform exorcisms on this structure," McConaughey went on. "I can do it again, just to be safe."

"Yes... yes, I think that would be best, Father."

The other members of her party dismounted. Riffey and his men checked their weapons: pistols, rifles, shotguns. Normally, universities only hired armed security for expeditions aimed at digging up old world artifacts, most of which commanded a premium on the black market. Morales remembered hearing about an archaeology professor who'd discovered an old American Air Force Base over in the United Mountain States, and they'd seen some hard fighting. This time, she'd asked for guards and Professor Meyer had approved it with no questions asked. The horses whinnied, tapped the hard ground. Yes, they'd have to set up basecamp further away. Oh well, the daily walk would do them all some good.

Father McConaughey was dressed in the solid black of a diocesan priest, despite the summer heat. He went to his horse's saddlebags, dug out a purple stole, a book of prayers, holy water, and a pouch of blessed salt. Just as he put the stole around his shoulders, a sharp whistle sounded from the closest guard hut.

"Hey everybody!"

Riffey and his men kept their weapons at the low ready. The male voice sounded cheerful enough, but one could never tell, especially in a place like this. Out of the hut stepped a young man, who looked to be in his early twenties, thin, dressed in a plain black t-shirt, blue jeans, and a red baseball cap. Whoever this kid was, Morales thought, he had a sunny enough disposition for such a cursed place.

"Hi," she called out. "Can we help you?"

"I was about to ask you the same thing," the young man replied, smiling.

"What on earth are you doing out here?" McConaughey asked.

"Me? Oh, I sort of take care of this place."

"What?" Morales asked.

"Yeah! It's a great job. Gives me plenty of time to do homework. I like the peace and quiet too," he said. His hands were in his pants pockets.

"You're alone?" Riffey asked, joining the group. "And unarmed?"

"There's nothing out here, really," the kid said, shrugging.

"Then why does it need a caretaker?" Morales asked, raising an eyebrow.

"Oh, you know. Once in a while people come by, wanting to take a look at the big bad Castle Vasquez. If they're just tourists or looky-loos, I can give them a tour. If they're looking to cause trouble, then I can call in the Army or the Templars." He never stopped smiling. "Hey, Father, what's with the purple stole? Somebody need to confess?"

"I, er... I am about to perform an exorcism on this accursed site," McConaughey replied.

"Oh, I don't think that will be necessary," the kid said. "I've been here a long time, and nothing unusual is going on." He snapped his fingers. "I can show you guys. Give you a brief tour."

"Uh..." Morales said. Of all the things she'd expected, this was not on the list. The kid seemed normal. She didn't get any bad feelings around him, and she felt that she was a good judge of character. "What did you say your name was?" she asked.

The kid smiled wider. "Call me Robin."

3

Silas Flint stepped up to the firing line. Fort Marsing's marksmanship range was a short distance south of the main gate, consisting of manmade berms dug from the hilly landscape. It had been a long, hot summer and today promised to be no different. He'd left his long coat and hat inside his quarters, wearing only his white dress shirt, black waistcoat, and black trousers for today's excursion. He kept his hair short, but a few days earlier he'd found his first grey hair. He knew he'd have to retire some day or – more likely – die on the job. Until then, he meant to keep his skills sharp.

"Shooters ready," called out Gunnery Sergeant Manuel Mendoza, Fort Marsing's weaponsmith and shooting instructor. Several other Templars had joined Flint at the portion of the range devoted to pistol marksmanship. Witch Hunters seldom engaged in extended gunfights; they mostly drew their pistol for summary executions of troublesome magicians. But one could never be sure these days.

Mendoza blew his whistle. Steel plates flipped up from behind the berm twenty-five yards away. Flint saw someone had painted a crude caricature of a witch, complete with pointy hat and snaggle teeth, on his plate. Keeping two hands on his pistol, he aimed, squeezed the trigger eight times, and heard eight pings. The other Templars took their shots.

"Cease fire," Mendoza shouted, waving his hand in front of his face. "Cease fire on the firing range!" Flint and the others set their pistols down on the tables next to each lane. "Check your targets!"

They all marched out onto the range to inspect their shot groupings. Flint scowled when he saw his. Seven shots to the witch's forehead, one down and to the left, below her right eye. A flyer. He would have to practice more.

"Not bad at all Captain," Mendoza said, looking around Flint's shoulder.

"It is acceptable," Flint replied, "But it could be better."

Mendoza chuckled. "Only God gets it perfect the first time."

Flint took out his pocket watch from his waistcoat. 11:14 a.m. He estimated the temperature to be in the mid-80s. Yes, it would be a hot one today. He heard a distant crack, followed by cheers. Some of the Supernumeraries had organized a baseball game. His assistant, Supernumerary Ricardo Navarro, was no doubt earning many of those cheers. The corner of Flint's mouth turned up. Navarro could be a glutton and a drunkard, but he was an outstanding baseball player. There had been talk of organizing games between each of the four Templar Chapter Houses throughout the Empire, and Navarro would definitely be on Marsing's team.

Knight Templar Reginald Withers approached Flint from one of the other lanes. "Sir Withers," Flint said, nodding.

"Captain Flint," Withers replied, nodding in return. "How are you faring since your return?"

Withers was no doubt referring to the small scar on Flint's left cheek, a souvenir from his trip to Salem a week and a half ago. He'd been grazed by a bullet from the assassin Roger Klemm. After he put down Klemm, Flint had seen a doctor who'd disinfected and sewn up the wound, but he expected there would always be a noticeable scar. Klemm had been a magician as well, and there was no telling what kind of devilish spells he'd put on his weapons. "I am doing well, thank you," Flint replied. "And yourself?"

"Fine, fine," Withers replied. "Just waiting for Charles to drop the hammer on the UMS Army."

"Yes," Flint murmured. The last he'd heard, the President of the United Mountain States, Hugh Fitzroy, was still marshalling his forces around Denver in preparation for their march north into the old Montana territory, to put down Charles's attempt to break away and form his own blasphemous nation of magicians. The UMS was a poorer nation than Cascadia, less mechanized. They had locomotives, but their automobiles, to say nothing of tanks, were thin on the ground.

"It's driving me crazy," Withers said. "Feels like a phony war."

Flint offered a grim smile. "That is not the first time that phrase has been applied to the early stages of a war," he said. His smile fell. "And when that war began in earnest, it changed the face of the planet."

"I know we're supposed to carry out our duties for now... but that's always in the back of my mind," Withers said.

"I understand your apprehension, Reginald," Flint replied. "But all that we can do for now is trust in the guidance of the Holy Spirit to see us through these dark times."

Mendoza blew his whistle again and the shooters returned to the firing line. Flint was just about to reload his pistol when a young man approached him. He was dressed in leather body armor and blue jeans. Around his shoulder was a brown leather satchel.

"Ah, Mr. Breckenridge," Flint said.

Supernumerary Samuel Breckenridge offered Flint a salute. "Good morning, sir," he said. Breckenridge was one of Fort Marsing's many couriers tasked with delivering orders and personal mail to all who resided within its walls. "I've got a letter for you." He reached into his satchel and withdrew a plain white envelope, held it out.

"Oh?" Flint said, taking the envelope. "My new orders I presume?"

"I don't think so sir. It bears a postmark from Oglethorpe. Which reminds me, there's another letter from Oglethorpe in here for Ricardo."

"You shall find him..."

"Oh, I know sir," Breckenridge said. He grinned. "Sir Archer said he's out on the baseball field."

Flint snorted. Sir Andrew Archer ran the courier office. Flint had never met the man face to face, but he had an almost preternatural talent for knowing where every inhabitant of Fort Marsing was at any given time. Breckenridge excused himself with another jaunty salute and set off to find Navarro. Flint tore open the envelope and read the letter inside.

August 9, 2533

Dear Silas,

I pray that my letter finds you alive and well. I've heard through the grapevine that your recent trips to Salem have been rather harrowing experiences, but my heart tells me that you have emerged victorious. I wish that I was writing under better circumstances, but I fear that the tide of darkness is encroaching upon us once again. Two days ago, a priest came to Danville, naked, covered in blood, and gibbering as though completely mad. The doctor there could find nothing physically wrong with him, but his mind is shattered, his spirit broken. He was escorted to Oglethorpe, where we have specialists in psychological disorders. Before he was taken to the madhouse, he asked to speak with me. He confirmed my greatest fear. His name is Father Colm McConaughey was part of an archaeological expedition from the University of Redmond. Recent developments on the international scene have sparked interest in the old castle of Arturo Vasquez. I'm sure I don't need to explain its significance to a student of history such as yourself.

No one knows the details of what happened there except Father McConaughey. According to the University, his group numbered twenty souls. The rest are unaccounted for, and I fear the worst. If you are not currently investigating a case, would you be so kind as to pay my family a visit? I would very much like to see you again, and I believe I can be of assistance if the necromancer's fiends are still haunting the area. Ricardo is invited as well. I believe Julia has written her own letter to him.

Yours in Christ,
Matthew Oglethorpe, KTOSB, Gen., Ret.

"Shooters ready," Mendoza called out, but Flint barely heard him. He reloaded his pistol, holstered it, and walked away from his lane. Mendoza gave him a quizzical look but said nothing. Flint's mind returned to his encounter with the Sisters several nights ago. They had told him that he would be visiting the city of Oglethorpe soon, and that he should ask the General for advice.

Worse, the General's letter had mentioned Castle Vasquez. Every Templar knew of Oglethorpe's epic struggle against Arturo Vasquez, the greatest threat to Cascadia within the last century (*Perhaps Charles will prove more terrible still,* Flint thought.) Everyone also knew of the wizard's seemingly indestructible castle. Neither the Order nor the Empire could permanently level the structure, but other than its unnatural durability, no magical activity had been reported in the area in thirty years, not since the last academic expedition. Flint snorted. He was a firm believer in the value of studying history, but some things were better off buried and forgotten. What was it this new expedition hoped to find? If they were curious about the last time a magician tried to secede from an established nation, they could have asked Oglethorpe; he lived it. Their curiosity may have cost them their lives and their souls. They may have awakened a sleeping monster.

Flint strode toward Marsing's main gate. Robert Carrow, retired Witch Hunter and current stable master, nodded to Flint as he rubbed down one of the horses. Flint expected that he and Navarro would be needing two of them soon.

***

Witch Hunter General John Abernathy sighed, took off his reading glasses, and rubbed the bridge of his nose. It had only been a little under two weeks since he'd returned to Fort Marsing from Salem, but it felt like a lifetime ago. After a thorough grilling from the Emperor himself and the Continuing Committee on Paranormal Activity and Magical Anomalies, he began to wonder if he'd made a mistake accepting promotion to General and appointment to lead Fort Marsing all those years ago. He dismissed the thought. He was following God's will as best he understood it, and that was that. And then there was that unpleasantness with the assassin, Roger Klemm. He shuddered. Shapeshifters were the worst.

Abernathy was alone in his office. Most of his workdays were taken up with correspondence, assigning Templars to investigate reported supernatural activity throughout the southeastern quadrant of Cascadia. The Emperor had announced the construction of a new Templar Chapter House in the West, near the ancient city of Bend. *It can't come too soon,* Abernathy thought. Every Chapter House usually had close to ninety percent of its garrison out in the field, but in the last few days, the tempo had increased even more. Another Chapter House would hopefully lighten the workload a bit. Evil never rested, but human beings had to.

Back to it then. He reached for another letter from his inbox when he felt a presence inside his office. There had been no knock at his door, and they had not opened. Keeping his focus on the letter, he reached underneath his desk where he kept one of his pistols from his days as an active field investigator.

"That will not be necessary, John," said a female voice.

"We mean you no harm," said another.

"It is good to finally speak to you in person," said a third.

Looking up he saw three women, middle aged, one with white hair, another with black, the third with red. They wore the white blouses, black trousers, long coats, and capotains of Lady Templars. All of them were beautiful. Especially the redhead, who reminded him of his late wife, Teresa. He shook his head, his mental guard going up. Abernathy had a good idea of who they were.

"The Weird Sisters," he said.

They cocked their heads in unison.

"There's that name again," the white haired woman said – Mallory, if he recalled Flint's case reports correctly.

"Silas calls us that and we do not know why," the black haired one – Monica – said.

"We are sisters, but we are not weird," said the redhead, Madeline.

"I take it Shakespeare isn't popular with your kind," Abernathy said, raising an eyebrow. They only smiled in response. "What brings you here?"

"This one is simple."

"Silas will be here soon."

"You should let him go."

"Let him go?" Abernathy asked. He looked to the side, thinking. "What on earth does that..." Shifting his gaze forward again, he saw the women were gone. He snorted.

Abernathy had only read about the Proctor Sisters in Flint's case reports, but now he understood what the dour Witch Hunter had meant when he described them as 'maddeningly cryptic.' They'd said to let him go. Where? Why?

There was a knock at his office door.

"Enter," he called.

The oaken double doors swung open, and none other than Silas Flint stepped inside, a folded paper in his hand. Abernathy kept his face neutral, but he felt the hairs on the back of his neck stand up. Neither he nor Flint understood why the Sisters were assisting him, but they were two for two so far. He hoped they'd maintain their record.

***

"Captain Flint," Abernathy said, rising from his desk. "Please, come in."

Flint went forth to meet his commanding officer. They shook hands, and Abernathy indicated one of the chairs in front of his desk. "Have a seat." After Flint had sat down, the General eased back into his own chair. "What brings you here, Silas?"

"Sir," Flint said. "I have just received a letter from General Oglethorpe." He handed it to Abernathy, who put on his reading glasses and scanned the document. When he finished, he put it down on his desk. Took a deep breath.

"Castle Vasquez," he muttered.

"Indeed," Flint replied. "You were new to the Order then, were you not?"

"Yes," Abernathy nodded. "That was back in 93. I was still a Supernumerary, barely out of training. General Oglethorpe was a Captain at the time. He and his assistant ventured into the castle while the rest of us held off Vasquez's army of the dead." A distant look came over him. "That... was a costly victory."

"General Oglethorpe slew that foul heretic," Flint said. "But you were unable to destroy the castle."

"No," Abernathy replied. "I was there during one of the attempts. I saw it, Silas. We planted enough explosives to level a mountain. The castle crumbled. And the next morning, there it was again, as though nothing had happened."

Flint nodded.

"There's nothing inside Castle Vasquez," Abernathy went on. "At least there wasn't the last time the Order was there. And we haven't received any reports of unusual activity coming from there... until now, anyway."

"Curious that the University would send another expedition there if there is nothing new to be found," Flint murmured.

"Hmm... perhaps it's an academic looking to write another book. In any case, it sounds like they found more than they bargained for."

"Indeed sir," Flint said. "And it is for that reason that I request..."

Abernathy's mouth fell open.

"Sir? Is something amiss?"

The General shook his head. "Yes. Yes, Silas, you have

my authorization to visit Oglethorpe. The city and the General."

"That is not all sir," Flint said. He paused. "Several nights ago..."

"Were you visited by the Sisters?" Abernathy asked.

"Why... yes sir, I was."

"They were here just before you came in."

Flint raised an eyebrow. "Were they?"

"Yes. I was reflecting on their... indirect way of speaking that you've written on before when you knocked. They said to let you go."

Flint's nostrils flared. "To Oglethorpe, I presume."

"That's how I'm choosing to interpret it."

"I still do not appreciate being a pawn in whatever tangled webs they weave," Flint said. "But in this case, I believe it would be best to follow their directive."

"I agree," Abernathy said. "You and Mr. Navarro should gather your things, depart as soon as possible."

4

Ricardo Navarro stepped up to home plate, gave his baseball bat a few practice swings. Behind him was Supernumerary Pablo Ruiz as catcher, and retired Supernumerary Alfred Carruthers as umpire.

"You're going down, Rico," Ruiz said, smiling behind his catcher's mask. He punched his mitt. "Right over the plate."

Instead of replying, Navarro pointed his bat to the

outfield. The other Supernumeraries and Templars sitting in the makeshift bleachers and folding chairs cheered.

"Oh, you're gonna be like that huh?" Ruiz said, laughing. "A round of drinks says you're out."

"You're on," Navarro replied with a grin.

Carruthers shook his head. "We gonna play or what?" he asked. He'd been at Fort Marsing for decades, had trained General Abernathy when he'd joined the Order, and then served alongside him as his assistant after he'd become a Templar. Now he ran the cantina that served the Supernumerary barracks within the Fort's walls. Carruthers looked to his right, and said, "Hold up."

Navarro looked and saw Sam Breckenridge approaching the field. Looked like somebody was about to get some new orders. Navarro prayed that it wouldn't be him. It felt like he and Silas had only returned from Salem yesterday, though it had been nearly two weeks. Navarro still had a scar on his right hip where the assassin Roger Klemm had stabbed him.

Shit, Navarro thought. Breckenridge was headed directly for home plate. He supposed he shouldn't complain though. It was the nature of the vocation.

"I reckon we can call time for a bit," Carruthers said. He took off his baseball cap and waved to the other players.

"Saved by the courier," Ruiz said, chuckling.

Breckenridge approached Navarro, nodding to the other players and a few of the spectators. "Hey Rico," he said.

"Hey Sam," Navarro replied. "I'm guessing me and Silas got a job?"

"Not that I know of. I just got a letter for you. Post-marked in Oglethorpe."

Julia. It had to be her. Navarro had met a lot of women in his travels with Silas. The nature of their vocations made forming lasting relationships difficult. But Julia Oglethorpe, daughter of the retired Templar General Matthew Oglethorpe, was the one he thought of the most. They'd met during the werewolf case in the city of Oglethorpe several months ago. She'd written him three times since then, but he was on the road so often, he had trouble keeping up.

Breckenridge handed him the envelope. Tearing it open and removing the letter, Navarro began to read:

August 9, 2533

Dear Rico,

I pray that this letter finds you well. Dad said that you and Silas had two close calls in Salem over the last month. I'm sure you were both as magnificent as ever. Dad is writing to Silas right now. He's afraid something terrible has happened at the old castle of Arturo Vasquez. I'm worried about him, to be honest. He doesn't like to talk about that case, not with me or George or even mom. But now he's really upset. I think hearing about the castle again has brought up a lot of bad memories.

I was just writing to see how you're doing. And I'd really like to see you again, but I know your vocation keeps you on the road a lot. If I'm right, and dad needs an active duty Templar to come check things out, I hope you and Silas get the job. You're always welcome here.

Yours in Christ,
Julia Oglethorpe

"What's up?" Ruiz asked, peering over Navarro's shoulder. Carruthers joined them as well.

"Got a job?" Carruthers said.

"Maybe," Navarro said. "General Oglethorpe thinks something's going on at Castle Vasquez."

Carruthers spat. "God damn," he muttered.

"Shit," Ruiz said.

"Yeah," Navarro replied. "You were there too, weren't you, Alf?"

"Sure was," Carruthers replied. "John and I both were. Poor kid was pretty new to the Order back then, and we all get saddled with taking on a whole damn army of the dead. Lot of people distinguished themselves that day. A lot of us died too."

"What could be going on there?" Ruiz asked. "I heard the place has been deserted for forty years."

"Dunno," Carruthers replied. "Place is empty last I heard, but we couldn't tear it down, no matter what we tried. We gave up after a while."

"Sounds like the General's daughter is pretty taken with you," Ruiz said.

"Yeah," Navarro replied. "Yeah."

"Offer you some advice?" Carruthers asked.

"Of course."

"If you two tie the knot, have her move in here."

"Alf, come on, we don't know each other that well."

"Yet," Ruiz said, smiling.

"Take it from me," Carruthers said. "If you get married while you're active duty, damn magicians love to go after our families." His face hardened. Navarro didn't know all the details – Carruthers was notoriously laconic – but he knew the man had seen much loss in his life.

"Look," Ruiz said, nudging Navarro. He looked up and saw his boss, Captain Silas Flint, making his way toward the baseball field. Flint was in his full uniform, black long coat and tall black hat conspicuous in the summer sun. His two pistols were on his belt along with his Templar sword.

"Hey." Ruiz extended his hand, and Navarro shook it. "God be with you, Rico." He grinned. "I'll get a round of drinks out of you yet."

Navarro smiled back. "Not today." He called over his shoulder. "Hey! Ed!"

Supernumerary Edward Braddock jogged toward home plate from the booth that served as the team's dugout. Reaching the group, he said, "Hey... got a case?"

"Looks that way," Navarro said, inclining his head toward Flint. "Take over for me, would you?"

Braddock smiled. "Yes sir."

Carruthers clapped Navarro on the back. "You two take care of yourselves out there. Don't fuck around. If you end up going into the castle, it might try to play tricks on you. You focus on the job and kick the shit out of anything that tries to stop you."

Navarro laughed. "You give the best pep talks."

"Follow my advice, you might live long enough to give 'em yourself."

Navarro excused himself and went out to meet Flint before he reached the field. As he passed the crowd of spectators, he caught movement in the corner of his eye. Looking to the bleachers, he saw three gorgeous Hispanic women, all dressed in the field uniforms of the Supernumerary: leather body armor and blue jeans. He kept walking as he observed. The one in the middle held a piece of cardboard. Written on it in black block letters was, DON'T FORGET YOUR RADIO.

***

Silas Flint strode toward the baseball field and saw Navarro coming to meet him. Flint was sorry that he had to interrupt his assistant's recreation. Baseball was a far healthier alternative to some of Navarro's other activities. But servants of the Lord must always be ready to leave at a moment's notice. He saw Navarro look to the bleachers, tracking them as he continued to walk. Flint noticed that he also held a folded sheet of paper. Mr. Breckenridge must have made his delivery. Good. Perhaps his assistant already had an idea of where they were headed.

They met a few feet away from the bleachers. It looked like the game was set to resume. Flint heard the gravelly voice of Alfred Carruthers shouting for the players to take their places and to play ball.

"Good morning, Mr. Navarro," Flint said.

"Morning sir," Navarro replied. "Let me guess: Castle Vasquez?"

Flint raised an eyebrow. "Indeed. I presume that your letter spoke of it as well."

"Yeah. Mine's from Julia, she said the General was writing to you."

"Yes. General Oglethorpe fears that a great evil is stirring within the bowels of that hellish domicile. He has requested that we pay a visit to him and his family."

"Figured."

"General Abernathy has given us leave to pursue this case. I propose that we leave for Oglethorpe today, post-haste."

"Sure thing, boss," Navarro said. "I'll go get changed, get my gear, and we can head out."

"Very good."

Together the two men made their way back to Fort Marsing's gates. Navarro's words had reminded Flint of the first time they met the Oglethorpe family. The daughter, Julia, was most taken with Navarro. His assistant often flirted with beautiful women they encountered on their travels, and Flint typically paid it no mind. That time though...

"Have you maintained your correspondence with Miss Oglethorpe?" Flint asked.

Navarro shrugged. "I've tried. But you know, it's not always easy to find the time to write back."

Flint nodded. "I shall repeat my advice to you from earlier this year: if you choose to pursue her, be on your best behavior, for her father is more fearsome than most."

"Uh huh," Navarro chuckled. "Speaking of which, how about you and Zelda?"

Flint blinked. "I do not know what you are talking about." Zelda Fletcher had left Fort Marsing yesterday morning with Lady Templar Diana McFarlane on a case where Fletcher's experience as a witch was expected to be useful.

"Oh, come on boss," Navarro said. "Everybody knows that she..."

"I will say no more."

"Okay, okay."

"Gather your things. We depart as soon as you are ready."

Flint stopped at the gate while Navarro continued to the Supernumerary wing of the fortress. He approached the stables where the stable master, Robert Carrow, stepped out from his shack.

"Good morning, Captain," he said.

"Good morning to you, Mr. Carrow."

"Going out on a case?"

"Indeed. Mr. Navarro and I shall be visiting the city of Oglethorpe once again and we should like to make use of one of your carriages if you please."

"Lovely city," Carrow said. "Would you mind terribly if I drove? I'd like the chance to see Matthew again as well."

"We would be honored to share your company, Mr. Carrow. As it happens, we may need to draw upon your experience."

"Oh?"

"Yes. The General fears that there are dark deeds taking place within the walls of Castle Vasquez once again."

Carrow's face went pale, and he made the sign of the cross. "God help us," he whispered.

Flint and Carrow prepared a carriage for the journey to Oglethorpe. The stable master put together a team of horses, while Flint packed as much ammunition and field rations into the storage compartment as he and Navarro would be able to carry. A few minutes later, Navarro appeared. He had changed into his field uniform: leather body armor and blue jeans. Two bandoliers of ammunition crisscrossed his chest, his bolt action rifle slung across his back. On his belt were his pistol and tomahawk.

"I'm ready when you are, sir," he said.

"Excellent," Flint said. "Mr. Carrow and I are nearly finished with our preparations."

"Hey boss, there's one more thing. I didn't get the chance to mention it earlier."

"What is it?"

"I saw them again. Those weird sisters."

Flint paused. "Did you? What did they have to say this time?"

"They told me to bring my radio," he said, patting a leather pouch on his belt. Several months ago, Flint and Navarro had visited an abandoned, intact American Air Force Base far to the east. The archaeological team had let Navarro take a miniature radio of twenty-first century manufacture as a souvenir. The Proctor Sisters had communicated with them through the radio during their first trip to Salem earlier that summer.

"They visited my quarters several nights ago," Flint said. "And they appeared to General Abernathy in his office this morning."

"Shit," Navarro said. "I can tell already this is going to be a tough case."

5

"Your judgment is at hand, witch! Stand down, and God may yet have mercy on your heathen soul!" Lady Diana McFarlane shouted. By way of response, a bolt of sorcerous lightning shot from the second story roof of the abandoned house where their quarry had taken refuge. McFarlane held her sword aloft, and it absorbed the magical blast. No matter how many times Zelda Fletcher saw it happen – and she'd seen it happen a lot over the last few months – it still amazed her. When she was still a practicing witch herself, she'd heard stories about Witch Hunters' blades, blessed by the pope in Rome, which could absorb any magic cast their way. It made her rethink her own relationship with the Almighty.

"The dark powers shall not avail you!" McFarlane yelled. "This is your last chance, witch! Surrender now or face summary execution by my hand!"

The house was silent. McFarlane and Fletcher had taken refuge behind the rusted hulk of a derelict automobile that looked like it had been sitting there since the twenty-first century Occult War. Yesterday morning, McFarlane had been ordered north to the city of Parma where Fort Marsing had received reports of supernatural activity. Fletcher, as McFarlane's unofficial assistant, had accompanied her.

"What do you think, Miss Fletcher?" McFarlane asked.

"Looks like the bitch wants to do it the hard way," she replied.

"I agree. On the count of three, we step out and advance. Stay behind me." Before McFarlane could begin her count, Fletcher noticed movement from one of the windows.

"Wait," she said. "Look at that."

The house's inhabitant had tied a white pillowcase to a curtain rod and was waving it through the open window.

"Hmph," McFarlane said. "Perhaps she's smarter than she looks. Keep your guard up though." Together, the two women rose to their feet and stepped out from behind the ruined automobile. They advanced on the house, McFarlane taking point, her sword at the ready. Fletcher could raise a shield of magical energy to protect them from any sneak attacks if the witch thought to try anything, but her rehabilitation program was aimed at weaning her off the use of magic. After that experience with the shapeshifting assassin Roger Klemm in Salem, Fletcher didn't need any more convincing; her overuse of magic during that case had almost wrecked her body.

"Susan Glade!" McFarlane called. "Step outside with your hands on your head!"

A few moments later, Glade exited the house, fingers interlocked on top of her head. She was of late middle age, her brunette hair streaked with grey. Glade had worked as a pharmacist, the perfect cover for her alchemical experiments. Something must have gone wrong because the townsfolk became aware of her true nature when the walls of her office began bleeding.

Glade locked eyes with Fletcher, cocked her head. "You..." she said. "You're one of us."

"Was," Fletcher replied.

"How... why would you ever..." Glade started.

"Miss Fletcher is living proof that redemption is possible," McFarlane said. "Zelda, if you would do the honors."

She nodded. Fletcher wasn't formally sworn to the Order, but she wore the uniform of a Supernumerary. Inside a pouch on her belt was a pair of shackles, forged from the same blessed steel as Templar swords. "Nice and easy now," she murmured. Glade gave her a dirty look but allowed herself to be handcuffed. Magicians needed the use of their hands for spellcasting, and the shackles were meant to prevent them from using their dark powers. Fletcher snorted.

"Is there a problem, Miss Fletcher?" McFarlane asked.

"I was just wondering... do Silas and Rico ever bring someone in alive?"

McFarlane grinned. "Besides you, you mean?" She thought for a few moments. "It's rare. A great number of their collars die before being taken into custody. Even by the Order's standards."

Glade scowled. "Must be my lucky day," she said. "What happens now?"

"Now we return to Fort Marsing where you will be put to the question," McFarlane said. "I warn you, Mrs. Glade: if you have consorted with demons or murdered innocent souls in your unholy experiments, you will..."

"No!" Glade shook her head. "No, I never did anything like that! I just…"

"The Inquisitors will determine that," McFarlane said. "However, if you spoke truly, then there is hope for both your life and your soul."

"I'm proof of that, again," Fletcher said. "Come on, let's go." The house where Glade had taken refuge was outside the city proper, and they set off toward Parma. Fletcher felt good. She'd grown up on the street, used her magical talents to commit petty crimes to get by, but after she'd turned herself in to the Witch Hunters – to Silas Flint and Ricardo Navarro in particular – they'd given her a place to stay and the opportunity to repay her debts to society.

She liked Diana well enough, but so far her most exciting cases had always been alongside Flint and Navarro. The Order tended to pair up Templars and Supernumeraries by gender. McFarlane was the unofficial leader of Marsing's Lady Templars, she needed a new assistant, and that was that. Fletcher wondered if she'd be permitted to formally join the Order someday. They'd probably need to be satisfied that she was off magic for good first.

"Zelda."

Fletcher looked up. She squinted. Someone was approaching them on horseback. "Who could that be?" she wondered.

"I can't make them out at this distance," McFarlane said. Turning to Glade, she asked, "Friend of yours?"

"Don't look at me," the witch muttered.

They continued trudging toward the city. As the rider got closer, Fletcher relaxed. It was a woman in

Supernumerary uniform, a brown leather satchel hanging from her shoulder, her horse's saddlebags no doubt packed with other correspondence.

"Good afternoon, ladies!" the rider cried.

McFarlane smiled. "Good afternoon, Erica," she said. "I don't believe you two have been introduced yet. Zelda Fletcher, may I present Erica Rowling, courier extraordinaire. Miss Rowling, Zelda Fletcher."

Rowling dismounted, approached Fletcher to shake her hand. "It's nice to finally met you in person!" she said. "I've heard a lot about you! All you've done with Lady McFarlane and Captain Flint and how you have a crush on..."

"Shut up," Fletcher said through gritted teeth, hoping she wasn't blushing too hard.

"Oh! Sorry," Rowling said. "I mean, I don't want to embarrass you or anything, but everyone knows that..."

"Did you have something for us, Miss Rowling?" McFarlane asked.

"Oh! Yes, I do," Rowling said. "One second." She dug through the satchel around her shoulder. "Here you go!" McFarlane took the proffered envelope, Fletcher coming to her side to read over her shoulder.

August 9, 2533

Lady McFarlane,

If my calculations are correct, you are still within Parma city limits with a prisoner in tow. General Abernathy directs you to turn over your prisoner to Miss Rowling's custody. You and Miss

Fletcher will proceed to the Cascadia Express station southwest of Fort Marsing and take the first available train to Redmond. General Abernathy would like you to meet with Professor Zachariah Meyer of the University of Redmond's Paranormal Research Department. Ask him about the reasons for ordering a recent expedition to Castle Vasquez. Determine his motivation and deal with him accordingly.

I remain yr. mst. obt. srvt.
Andrew Archer, KTOSB

Fletcher raised an eyebrow. "College town huh?"

"It would appear so," McFarlane said. "Miss Rowling. Zelda and I need to head to the train station. We can all ride back to Marsing together. From there, General Abernathy said for you to take Mrs. Glade into custody and escort her to the Inquisitors."

Rowling saluted. "Yes ma'am! I'll do my best!"

"And as for you, Mrs. Glade?"

The witch gave McFarlane a sour look.

"I'd be on my best behavior if I were you. Miss Rowling is more fearsome than she looks, and she would love for you to give her an excuse."

Glade looked at Rowling, who giggled. "Uh... yeah, sure," Glade said.

"Let us be on our way then." Rowling took point, followed by Glade. Fletcher nudged McFarlane as they followed them.

"Is that true?" she whispered. "What you said about Erica?"

"She's gentle as a kitten. Most of the time."

***

Flint checked his pocket watch. 2:25 p.m. He expected they would arrive in Oglethorpe in time for dinner. He hoped they wouldn't be interrupted by the case, as they had been last time. Carrow was seated in the carriage's boot, while Flint and Navarro relaxed inside. Paved roads were less common in the east than in the western half of the Empire, but Carrow proved an excellent coachman, keeping the jostling to a minimum despite the rough terrain.

"What time you got, sir?" Navarro asked. He had his rifle across his lap and idly wiped on it with a cleaning rag.

"It is nearly 2:30," Flint said.

"You think the Sisters are gonna play it like last time?" During their first trip to Salem that year, the Proctors spoke to them through the radio at the top and bottom of every hour as though they were radio newscasters. Flint found it an irritating pretense since they had demonstrated their ability to appear anywhere they chose, but if that was how they wished to be, there was nothing he could do about it.

"I know of one way to find out," Flint replied.

Navarro opened a pouch on his belt and withdrew the radio. Flint knew that police officers and soldiers carried small radios that allowed them to communicate with each other over short distances, but the tiny device Navarro had could apparently pick up radio stations from the furthest corners of the Empire. Flint estimated that western Cascadia's technological progress had recovered to that of the early twentieth century, but they hadn't quite mastered everything yet.

Navarro thumbed the power button and the radio sputtered to life. He rolled the tuning wheel, the red needle moving toward 1530 AM, the Sisters' preferred station. Navarro turned up the volume to compensate for the sounds of the moving carriage. It sounded like the tail end of a jazz piece that Flint didn't recognize. The song ended, followed by a three note chime.

"This is Mallory Proctor," came a familiar female voice from the radio.

"Joining her is special correspondent, Monica Proctor."

"With Madeline Proctor to cover sports."

"And now for your news at the bottom of the hour," they said together.

Flint sighed. Navarro said nothing.

"I am afraid we cannot provide as much assistance this time," Mallory said.

"We can tell you this, however," Monica said.

"Castle Vasquez is not as empty as you think," said Madeline.

The two men looked at each other. "Can you provide any clues as to what awaits us?" Flint asked.

"Don't suppose you got any more presents for us?" Navarro said.

"Matthew should be able to provide you with the tools you need."

"An old enemy awaits you within the castle."

"And a new enemy seeks that which lies hidden inside."

"Hey," Navarro said. "You girls are pretty powerful magicians yourselves. How come you can't help us out much this time?"

There was a pause.

"If we venture too close to Castle Vasquez..."

"We may be caught in its snares..."

"And that would be disastrous for everyone."

"What on earth do you..." Flint started.

"The Proctor Sisters, signing off," they said in unison. A different chime sounded, and another jazz piece began. Navarro turned the radio off.

"What do you make of that sir?" he asked.

"If we are headed to a place where the Weird Sisters fear to tread, then we should visit one of Oglethorpe's parishes and make our confessions before proceeding."

6

Charles Flint and Lilian Turner dined in silence inside the bunker's mess hall. Late in the twenty-first century, Turner and her then colleagues had cast a spell to magically preserve the facility, including its stores of supplies. She had told Charles that these so called "MREs" weren't the best in old world cuisine, but they filled the belly, and that was enough. He took it in stride. In due time, he would be indulging in feasts fit for the Emperor of all Magicians. Turner took a drink from her can of Dr. Pepper.

"What will you do when we run out of that stuff?" Charles asked.

She sighed. "I suppose I'll have to go back to sarsa-parilla."

"That stuff will rot your teeth."

She raised an eyebrow. Charles laughed.

"That was my parents talking. They discouraged Silas and I from drinking soda. I suppose I never developed the taste for it."

"As long as it's just us and the computer here," she said, "You never did tell me the whole story of what happened with your family."

He shrugged. "Not much to tell really. My parents and Silas were all devoted Catholics. When I told them that I had the talent for magic, they were appalled, naturally. They hauled me off to our parish priest who gave me the usual blather about how magic is offensive in the eyes of God, that it opens one up to demonic influence, and so on. I'm sure you've heard it all."

She snorted. "They haven't changed much in almost five hundred years."

"I told them what they wanted to hear, that I was very sorry and wouldn't do it again. But I kept at it. I met some others who had the talent and they taught me much. But I was young and inexperienced. I began to think that we should rule the world, use our talents for the betterment of mankind."

Turner nodded.

"I experimented with a spell that was admittedly be-yond my ability back then. I thought to control the minds of my parents. If they refused to see the benefits of magic, I would make them see. Unfortunately, in the process of twisting their minds, I twisted their bodies as well. Silas... didn't appreciate that."

She smirked. "You have a gift for understatement."

"I like to think so. Looking back on it, I know where I went wrong, both with the spell that changed my parents, and with my philosophy: if we try to rule through force alone, they will fight back."

"Like now, for instance?"

Charles laughed. "Touché. Computer?"

The walls chimed.

"How goes the UMS Army's progress?"

"Sensors indicate no large scale movement around Denver," the computer said.

Turner frowned. "What on earth are they waiting for?"

"Oh, I imagine there's a lot of squabbling about the risk of our nuclear arsenal. And they're right to be afraid. I'll be contacting President Fitzroy soon."

"The purpose being?"

"To urge him to stand down and let us have this territory."

Turner scoffed. "You seriously think he'd allow us to have most of Montana without a fight?"

"That's the beauty of it," Charles said, chuckling. "If he stands down, he'll be chased out of office in disgrace as a coward. If he sends his Army north, we will destroy them one way or another, and he'll be chased out of office in disgrace as an incompetent. And we deprive his successor of an Army to boot."

She nodded. "Sounds good, in theory. But as my

father used to say, no plan survives first contact with the enemy."

"Even so, I like our odds." A blue glow shone inside his coat pocket. "Speaking of which…"

Charles withdrew a sapphire and placed it on the dining table. He whispered an incantation. A column of light rose from the jewel, and the translucent figure of a man materialized inside. He was heavy set, his thinning hair combed across his scalp in a vain attempt to hide his baldness.

"Good afternoon, Professor," Charles said.

"Master Flint," the man replied, dipping his head.

"How goes the adventure down south?"

The professor looked down and sighed. "There may be a problem."

"There always is," Turner said, rolling her eyes.

"What sort of problem?"

"The expedition is lost," the professor said. "They went into Castle Vasquez a few days ago and…"

"What?!" Turner cried. "Did you say Castle Vasquez?!"

The professor cocked his head.

"She's with me," Charles said. "You were saying?"

Clearing his throat, the professor continued: "It seems the entire team was lost save for one, the chaplain. They found him outside Danville, naked, drenched in blood."

"And you've been unable to contact our boy?" Charles asked.

"No. If he's still alive, he's not responding."

Charles drummed his fingers on the table. Turner fidgeted, bit her lip. He had a good idea of what she wanted to say. Of all the magicians in his circle, he'd known her the shortest time, but he'd grown to trust her more than most. Perhaps he should have shared this latest project with her. Oh well. Time enough for that later.

"There's something else, sir," the professor said.

"Go on."

"The priest has been taken to the madhouse in Oglethorpe."

Charles sighed. "And that means General Oglethorpe will hear about it."

"And he'll contact Fort Marsing," Turner said.

"What would you have me do, sir?" the professor asked.

"Maintain your cover for now," Charles replied. "Offer condolences to the families if the others turn up dead. I appreciate your efforts, but I'll take over from here. Looks like I'll have to send someone else to claim our prize."

"Very good, sir. Out."

The man vanished, the column of light withdrew into the sapphire, and Charles pocketed it. He sighed and rubbed his temples. It was too bad about the professor's protégé, but one couldn't make a nation without breaking a few skulls.

"Charles..." Turner said.

"Now Lilian," he replied. "Don't take it personally. I wasn't sure this project would bear fruit in the first place, but Professor..."

"It's not that." Her face was pale.

"Are you alright?" He took her hand. "I haven't seen you this shaken since I pulled you from the void between worlds."

"You can't send anyone to Castle Vasquez."

He blinked. "I beg your pardon?"

"You're not old enough to remember Arturo Vasquez." She shuddered. "I've tried hard to forget."

"I recall reading newspaper articles about his reign, and a few biographies..."

She barked a laugh. "None of them can do him justice."

Charles chided himself for not bringing Turner in sooner. With this wondrous American technology all around him, with all the planning he had done and still needed to do for his Empire of Medea, it hadn't occurred to him to ask her for more details about Vasquez. "Tell me more," he said.

She took a deep breath. "I've killed a lot of people over the last five hundred years. Vasquez had me beat by an order of magnitude in less than one lifetime. I've never killed anyone without good reason. He did it both for his experiments and just for fun." Turner shook her head. "I have never met another wizard who took such delight in torture, in inflicting pain just for the sake of it."

"But he's dead now," Charles said.

"I wonder," Turner replied. "He was the greatest necromancer this world has seen since the Occult War. Matthew Oglethorpe supposedly killed him, cut off his head, burned the body."

"I should think that would be the end of it."

"Normally it would be, for a lesser magician. But Vasquez... I find it hard to believe he'd be put down that easily. His castle, for example."

Charles nodded. Yes, every witch and wizard knew of

the seemingly indestructible Castle Vasquez. And of the prize inside.

"I know what you're after," Turner said. "You think to find the Warlock's Crown."

"Yes."

"Why?"

"Two reasons," Charles said. "It's said to confer tremendous magical power on the one who wears it. I heard that Vasquez succeeded in creating an object that can act as a channel for magic, and we're going to need all the magic we can gather to fully realize our plans. And second... an emperor needs his crown. If I were to get my hands on it, it would further legitimize my rule. It would be a potent symbol of our people taking their place on the international stage."

She shook her head. "The Witch Hunters went through every inch of Castle Vasquez that they could access, burned everything they could find."

"'That they could access,' are the key words there."

"Other magicians have tried to find it and had no luck."

"True, but things have changed in the last few months. My sources tell me there has been... activity near Castle Vasquez, the first in forty years. I think that my display this past June may have awakened something."

"Or someone," she said, shivering. "This is a bad idea."

"I hardly think..."

"The castle is alive, Charles. Vasquez imbued it with a portion of his dark power. Demons walk its halls, and I don't mean that metaphorically. I've heard that they can take physical form at will inside the castle."

He raised an eyebrow. "Can they? In that case, I may need to call in a specialist to handle this for me."

She crossed her arms. "Supposing this 'specialist' can find the Crown, supposing it even exists anymore, what's to stop them from taking it for themselves?"

Charles smiled. "One thing all of the books mention is that Vasquez placed a curse on his most prized possessions. Those who don't know the trick to unlocking them will be driven mad."

"And you know this trick?"

"I do, actually, thanks to my book," he said, referring to *In Realis Magicae*, written by one of Simon Magus's lieutenants, Abdul Hakim Nazari. "Nazari knew ways to defuse enchantments that I'm sure even you haven't heard of."

She said nothing for a few moments. "I still think this is a bad idea."

"You may be right. The Crown may have been destroyed, or it's beyond our reach somehow. If so, then we lose nothing. But think of what we have to gain if it's still hidden away somewhere."

Turner sighed. "I know better than to argue once your mind is made up. Who's this specialist of yours?"

"Her name is Destiny. Appropriate, don't you think?"

7

The carriage slowed to a halt. Flint checked his pocket watch. 6:52 p.m. Navarro opened the carriage door and stepped out, slinging his rifle, and stretching. Flint followed suit. The days would be getting shorter soon, but for now the setting sun cast everything in a warm orange glow. Carrow had stopped just outside the walls of Oglethorpe by one of the city's stables. Boys rushed forward to take care of the horses and carriage. Carrow cracked his back, rolled his neck a few times.

"How fare you, Mr. Carrow?" Flint asked.

"I'll be alright," Carrow said, his smile deepening the wrinkles and creases in his face. "It's been a while since I went for such a long ride is all."

"What time is it, boss?" Navarro asked.

"It is nearly seven o'clock."

"Right around the General's dinner time. Think he's expecting us?"

"I hope we're not imposing," Carrow said.

"I do not believe it will be a problem," Flint said. "But we should make haste, nonetheless."

The three men strode toward the city gates. A guard seated inside a booth by the great doors looked up from his paperback book. He did a double take and rushed out to meet them.

"Captain Flint?" he asked.

"Indeed, sir," Flint replied.

The guard extended his hand, which Flint shook.

"It's an honor to have you back sir!" the guard said. Then his face fell. "Oh... is there more trouble in the city? I haven't heard any..."

"There is no witchcraft here that we are aware of," Flint interrupted. "We simply wish to make a social call upon General Oglethorpe and his family."

Looking relived, the guard said, "Of course, sir. You

and your assistant are always welcome here. Give me one second." He went back inside his hut. A moment later, a buzzer sounded, and the great gates swung open.

"I could get used to this," Navarro said, grinning.

"I'm a little old to be fist fighting werewolves," Carrow chuckled.

"We did not engage in fisticuffs with the beast, in point of fact," Flint said.

"You stabbed it through the eye with a silver dagger. Close enough," Navarro replied.

"In any case, let us be on our way."

The three men strolled into the city. Oglethorpe was much how Flint remembered it: cobblestone streets with horse and carriage traffic, the occasional automobile honking at pedestrians. General Oglethorpe was the first to settle the area after his retirement from active duty, but his fame had drawn hundreds of civilians who sought a new life or hoped to catch a glimpse of the celebrated Witch Hunter. Over the course of a few years, the General found himself surrounded first by a town and then a major city numbering in the thousands. Then, much to the General's bemusement, his neighbors insisted on naming the city for its most famous citizen. Oglethorpe had no interest in politics, and no official position within the city's government, but his words carried much weight.

"Lovely city," Carrow murmured. Many of the shops along the street were closing up for the day, but a few restaurants and taverns were packed. The strains of music punctuated the scene, along with the smells of sizzling meat and cigarette smoke.

"Looks like everything's back to normal," Navarro said. Flint thought the casual observer would have never guessed that a werewolf had rampaged through the city streets only three months ago.

Flint led his companions down the street and made a left toward an isolated neighborhood. Along the way, pedestrians and drunken tavern-goers cheered and waved at them. Navarro waved back, but Flint kept his focus on the task at hand. There it was. They approached a two story house built in the old Gothic style, creepers of ivy curling up the sides, with an immaculate lawn. A wheelchair ramp was beside the steps leading up to the front door.

"Did the General really walk again when you faced the werewolf?" Carrow asked as they proceeded down the walkway toward the steps.

"Sure did," Navarro said. "One of the most badass things I've ever seen."

"God be praised," Carrow said.

Flint knocked on the door. A few moments later, a middle-aged woman opened it. Her greying hair was tied back in a pony tail and she wore an ankle length dress. Her face lit up, the wrinkles around her eyes crinkling with her smile.

"Captain Flint!" she cried.

Flint clicked his heels and bowed his head. "Mrs. Oglethorpe. I pray that we are not intruding."

"Of course not! Come in, come in!" She looked over her shoulder. "Matthew! George! Julia! Look who's come to pay us a visit!"

She beckoned for her guests to enter. Flint heard her

greet Navarro and Carrow. He looked around the parlor. It hadn't changed a bit. To his right was the living room. One of the walls was devoted to photographs taken throughout Oglethorpe's career, including a picture of him amidst the ruins of Castle Vasquez. Straight ahead lay the kitchen and dining room, and it smelled like dinner would be ready soon.

George and Julia Oglethorpe came down the stairs. They were in their early twenties, if Flint recalled correctly. The son definitely favored his father's looks.

"Captain Flint!" George said. Flint extended his hand. George took it and pulled the Witch Hunter into an embrace. Flint stiffened for a moment, then relaxed, and patted the young man on the back.

"It is good to see you again, young man. I trust that you are staying out of trouble?" he said.

"Trying to anyway," George said with a sheepish smile.

"Captain Flint," Julia said. She wore a dress like her mother's and made a small curtsy.

"Good evening, Miss Oglethorpe."

She laughed. "Please, call me Julia."

"I will, Julia. I believe you will find Mr. Navarro in the parlor."

She blushed. "Oh, um... thanks. Excuse me."

When she had gone, Flint asked, "How is your father, George?"

The young man's face darkened. "He's... doing alright. After you and Rico left, he was the most energetic I've seen him since I was a kid. Over the last few days though... well, you'll see for yourself."

"Silas Flint, as I live and breathe!" came a booming voice from down the hallway. Flint shifted his gaze and saw retired Witch Hunter General Matthew Oglethorpe. The old man was in his wheelchair, and he rolled himself forward to greet his guests. A plaid blanket lay across his lap. A wispy fringe of white hair encircled his otherwise bald head. The veins in his bony hands were visible as he wheeled himself down the hall. His body was weak, but his mind, Flint remembered, was as strong as ever. Reaching his guest, the General offered Flint a firm handshake.

"It's good to see you again, Silas," the General said, smiling.

"The honor is mine, sir," Flint said, bowing his head.

"Formal as ever, I see," Oglethorpe chuckled. "I'm officially retired of course, but I order you to address me as Matthew tonight."

The corner of Flint's mouth turned up. "I am ever obedient to my superiors, Matthew. I hope that we are not intruding."

"Not at all, not at all," Oglethorpe said. "I had a feeling you and Mr. Navarro would be coming to visit us soon. Jane has been preparing extra helpings every night, just in case."

"We have another guest with us as well."

"Oh?"

Carrow stepped forward. "Hello Matthew."

Oglethorpe's face lit up. "Robert? My God, what a surprise!"

Carrow came to Oglethorpe and the two old men embraced, patting each other on the back. "Silas and Ricardo told me a little about their case here a few months ago," Carrow said.

Oglethorpe pursed his lips. "Yes... terrible business that. The local political scene is still reeling a bit from the aftermath." He shook his head. "But none of that right now. Please, all of you, join us for dinner this evening."

"It would be our pleasure sir... er, I mean, Matthew."

***

Dinner was a convivial affair. The Witch Hunters swapped stories of their strangest cases. Whenever the table roared with laughter, Flint managed his wintry smile. George and Julia updated their guests on the goings on in their professional lives; George was apprenticed to a local lawyer and hoped to pass the bar exam one day, while Julia worked for one of the textile mills. Flint noted that she and Navarro exchanged furtive glances more than once. Flint nursed his glass of red wine. The grandfather clock in the living room chimed 9 p.m.

"Well," Jane said. "I think it's time we wind it down. George, Julia? Would you two help me clear the table? I think your father needs to discuss some things with our guests."

"Sure mom," George said.

"Gentlemen," Oglethorpe said. "If you would join me in my study?" He pushed himself away from the table. Carrow rose and went to wheel Oglethorpe to their destination. Flint and Navarro rose as well.

"Talk later?" Julia said to Navarro.

"Yeah, definitely," he replied, squeezing her shoulder.

They followed Carrow and Oglethorpe down the hallway and through a door on their left. The room was dominated by an oaken desk cluttered with books and papers. One wall was taken up entirely with packed bookshelves, the other with more photographs taken throughout Oglethorpe's career. One depicted Oglethorpe when he must have been newly sworn in as a Templar; by his side was an older man in the field uniform of a Supernumerary, whom Flint took to be Oglethorpe's then assistant.

The General noticed Flint looking at the photograph. "Malcolm Keyser," he said. "He was my first assistant, right after I passed the trials. I learned a lot from that man. I might not be here today if it weren't for him."

Navarro peered at the photograph around Flint's shoulder. "You mind me asking what happened to him, sir?" he said.

"He passed on about thirty years ago," Oglethorpe said. "He died surrounded by his family. We should all be so blessed." Turning his attention to Carrow, he asked, "What about you Robert? How's Melissa?"

Carrow's face fell. "She passed away a few years ago," he said.

"My condolences, old friend."

Carrow nodded. "We had a good life together."

"Speaking of which," Oglethorpe said. "Mr. Navarro."

Navarro swallowed. "Yes sir?"

"My Julia thinks rather highly of you."

"Oh, uh, well... I, uh, think highly of her too, sir."

Flint kept his face neutral but felt amused at Navarro's discomfiture.

"Believe me," Oglethorpe said, "I understand that this vocation makes marriage and family life difficult. I would ask that you never hurt her. Do I make myself clear?"

"Yes sir," Navarro nodded.

"Good." Oglethorpe sighed. "Now... I'm afraid we have business to discuss. Er... I'm afraid I don't have enough chairs for everyone."

"That is quite alright, sir," Flint answered. "Mr. Navarro and I can stand." After Carrow had taken the one chair in front of Oglethorpe's desk, the General sighed again.

"Is it true?" Carrow asked. "I heard that there's activity near Castle Vasquez."

"I'm afraid so," Oglethorpe replied.

"Please tell us everything that has happened, Matthew," Flint said.

8

One mile outside the city of Danville, a ring of fire appeared on the grassy plain. The interior of the ring turned black as pitch, a portal to the world between worlds. Out of the portal strode Destiny Lee. She was an Asian woman in her late twenties, dressed in black and wearing a heavy backpack, her hands engulfed in witchfire as she whispered a spell, closing the portal behind her. In just a few seconds, she had journeyed from Charles Flint's bunker in the northern United Mountain States to southeastern Cascadia, a trip that would have taken days by train, months on foot. On the other hand, she reflected, traveling the old fashioned way was much more scenic than the inky void of magical portals.

Charles Flint had contacted her earlier in the day, asking her to investigate Castle Vasquez, specifically for the Warlock's Crown. Lee had heard of it of course, but she had always figured it for a myth. But Charles Flint had saved her from a literal pitchfork wielding mob years ago. She owed him her life. If he wanted her to go on a scavenger hunt, it was the least she could do.

Lee had never visited Castle Vasquez before, and so couldn't teleport there directly, but her memory of Danville and its environs got her close enough. She'd spend the night in the city and set out in the morning. Lee began walking. The city's lights were visible in the distance. Best to approach it on foot. No sense in spooking the locals dropping in via portal. The last thing she needed was attention from the Witch Hunters.

After a twenty minute stroll through the wilderness, Lee came to the wall surrounding the city. One of the guards manning the gate stepped out to greet her.

"Evening," he said.

"Good evening," she said, putting on her brightest smile.

The guard smiled back. "What brings you all the way out here, this time of night?"

"I was on my way to the United Mountain States. Was thinking of joining up, taking the fight to that crazy wizard, Charles Flint. Just need a place to stay for tonight."

The guard's brow furrowed. "You're walking to the UMS? Without a gun?"

She waved her hand past his face. "Don't worry about it."

His jaw fell slack for a moment. He shook himself and said, "Well, guess I shouldn't worry about it. None of my business."

She smirked. "I don't suppose you could recommend a hotel?"

"Oh, yeah. There's a hostel about two blocks north of the gate when you go inside. Can't miss it. It's the Travel Inn."

"Much obliged, friend!"

The guard waved to his companion inside their shack. A moment later, the gates swung open.

"Enjoy your stay in Danville ma'am."

"I will, thank you."

She passed through the gate and into the city. Lee estimated the time was close to 10 p.m. The streets were quiet, save for the occasional cop on horseback or a drunken reveler stumbling home. She shook her head. Idiots. She couldn't wait for Charles to make his new empire self-sufficient. Then Lee wouldn't have to pretend to be one of them anymore, one of the ordinary rabble.

The Travel Inn was where the guard said it would be. She signed in under her deceased mother's name and flipped a silver coin to the old woman sitting at the front desk. Lee entered her room. It wasn't the best hotel room she'd ever stayed in, but it wasn't the worst either. They had electricity at least. She flung her backpack down on the bed, opened it, and removed some of its contents: a change of clothes, magically reinforced glass vials with alchemical reagents, and three books, one a basic spell grimoire, a book on recent Cascadian history, and the last on demonology.

She opened her history book to the last chapter. The war against Vasquez occupied an odd place in Cascadian history. The Witch Hunters weren't officially a branch of the imperial government, but they worked together so closely as to make little difference. The then Emperor had, of course, sent the Imperial Army to put down Vasquez's attempt to break away from Cascadia, but the soldiers weren't used to fighting the undead and had either died in droves or fled in abject terror. It was the Witch Hunters who bore the brunt of the fighting. The most intriguing part to Lee was that both the Templars and every scholarly tome on the subject all agreed that Witch Hunter Captain Matthew Oglethorpe and his assistant Supernumerary Jonah Byers fought their way through the castle together. Byers died along the way, but Oglethorpe managed to slay Vasquez alone.

The necromancer was gone – supposedly – but his castle remained. Like all magicians, Lee knew healing spells that would bring her back from injuries that would kill one of the lambs. But Vasquez had apparently devised a spell that could regenerate his castle despite the many attempts to destroy it over the last forty years. Why he would do such a thing was a mystery, to magicians and lambs alike. The most popular rumor had it that Vasquez enchanted his castle to protect the Warlock's Crown which remained hidden away somewhere inside, beyond the reach of ordinary mortals.

She clapped the book shut. Lee was many things, but she was not ordinary. Charles had told her of his communication with the professor: a university expedition to the castle had gone missing save for one priest who was now hopelessly mad. One member of the party had been a magician, but neither the professor nor Charles could get in contact with him. She shook her head. Young wizards and witches often overestimated their power over the demons of Hell. She'd studied the subject for years, knew their tricks, and how to keep them under control. A colleague had once joked that it was easy to outsmart demons because they always lie, even when they have nothing to gain from it. That was an oversimplification, she thought, but not too far off the mark.

Lee yawned. She'd leave for Castle Vasquez before dawn. If the Crown existed, she'd find it and bring it to her savior, her Emperor, Charles. If it didn't exist, well, not many witches could boast surviving the dangers of Castle Vasquez.

***

Professor Valentina Morales flattened herself against the wall. She believed she lost her pursuer for the moment, but the creature had proven that it could smell them. She had to get out of there. She had to contact the Witch Hunters. They could track down any surviving members of her team. She was a college professor for God's sake, not cut out for dealing with... those things.

The torches on the wall flickered. Her breath fogged as the temperature dropped. Dear God, they were close by. As if to punctuate her fear, she heard one of the girls screaming, her voice echoing from everywhere and nowhere.

"Mmm," came Robin's voice. "That's the stuff."

Morales whimpered.

"Don't leave us so soon Valentina," Robin's disembodied voice said. "Arturo would love to meet you."

She peeked around the corner, saw nothing but a hallway lined with doors. Had she already been this way? She could have sworn that she...

Robin laughed. "Castle Vasquez is alive my dear. It doesn't want you to leave either. You'll grow to like it here, give or take a few centuries."

Morales sprinted toward the nearest door, ducked inside. Torches and candles flickered to life. She was in some kind of study: a desk, bookshelves, a grandfather clock. She furrowed her brow. The bookshelves were all loaded with leather bound tomes. At least she hoped they were leather. According to all of the reports, the contents of Castle Vasquez were all destroyed, burned over forty years ago.

"As you can see, we're doing a little remodeling," Robin's voice echoed. "A little blood, a few souls, and this place will be good as new."

She slumped against the door, slid down to the floor, buried her face in her arms.

"Are you giving up Valentina? Too bad. As it happens though, you may earn a brief reprieve if you were to help us find one of your students."

She looked up.

"He's not what you think he is," Robin said. "Your boy is a wizard."

"My…" she said.

"Unfortunately, that means he knows how to hide himself from our gaze. We sense that he has a soft spot for you though."

Morales looked around the room. There was no trace of Robin, whoever or whatever he was. No… there. The flickering candles on the desk cast a shadow on the wall, humanoid in shape, with two great curling horns on the sides of its head.

"Good eye, Professor," Robin chuckled. Two red eyes appeared where the shadow's face would be. And then a third, larger eye opened on its forehead.

Morales was too tired, too shocked to scream. She'd seen and heard too much already. She hid her face in her hands and curled up on the floor, crying.

"Don't worry," Robin said. "Personally, I'd love to get my claws into that silky skin of yours. But Arturo made a convincing case that you'll be more useful to us alive. For now. Who knows? I'm not making any promises, but if you were to play your cards right, you might even get out of here alive. Think of the book you could write about your experiences here."

Morales said nothing. She cried, and shivered, and prayed that she would wake up, that it was all a terrible nightmare. A few moments later, she felt something nudge her. She gasped and scrabbled onto her hindquarters. Standing before her was Robin, appearing as a young man again, in his jeans, t-shirt, and red baseball cap.

"See? We're not all bad," he said, smiling. "Now do get up. You're going to help us find Carlos Ramirez."

9

Flint leaned against one of General Oglethorpe's book-cases, his arms crossed. Navarro rested his arm on the opposite wall. Carrow sat before the General's desk, look-ing uncomfortable. Flint sympathized; Carrow had been on active duty forty years ago and had seen hard combat outside the walls of Castle Vasquez.

"As I wrote in my letter to you, Silas," Oglethorpe said, "A few days ago a Father Colm McConaughey was found wandering around outside the Danville city limits, naked, and covered in blood."

"And they couldn't find a scratch on him," Navarro said, Flint having briefed him on the contents of Oglethorpe's letter during their carriage ride.

"Right," Oglethorpe replied. "Nothing physically wrong with him that their doctors could find, but the poor fellow was gibbering like a lunatic."

"God help him," Carrow whispered, making the sign of the cross.

"Do you happen to know the words he was saying?" Flint asked. Sometimes there were clues to be found in what appeared to be nonsensical.

"He kept mumbling, 'It's alive,' over and over again. I believe I know what he was referring to: Castle Vasquez."

Flint blinked. "I do not understand, sir... Matthew."

"I mean Castle Vasquez is itself a creature of darkness," Oglethorpe said, shuddering. "Forgive me. It's been a long time since I've spoken about it to anyone. Not even my family."

"Take your time, sir," Navarro said.

After a few moments, Oglethorpe continued: "Vasquez was deeply immersed in the powers below. I don't understand all the details, but he imbued the castle with magic born from Hell itself. It wavers between this world and the next. It changes its layout around you. I remember Jonah and I would go down a hallway, only for a brick wall to manifest behind us a second later, forcing us down that path." A faraway look came over the General's face.

"Nonetheless, you and your assistant prevailed," Flint said.

Oglethorpe sighed. "Jonah didn't make it. He sacrificed himself so I could keep going to Vasquez's inner sanctum."

"I'm sorry, sir," Navarro said.

The General acknowledged him with a nod. "Suffice it to say, I did battle with the necromancer and emerged victorious, by the grace of God. Just before his head died, he vowed that he would return. After we burned the body, we destroyed the castle with some well placed explosives. I believe you were admiring the photograph of me standing before the ruins the last time you were here, and earlier this evening."

Flint nodded.

"The morning after that picture was taken, we awoke to find Castle Vasquez restored, as though we'd never been there."

"Yes," Carrow said. "I was there too. We set more charges, destroyed it again. I saw it come tumbling down with my own eyes. For good measure, we waded through the ruins with sledgehammers, made sure there was not one stone standing upon another. The next morning, it was back. Again."

"Why would he have done that though?" Navarro asked. "What's the point in making an indestructible castle if you don't live long enough to enjoy it?"

"I have a fairly good idea," Oglethorpe said. "Vasquez was so powerful partly due to the Warlock's Crown."

Flint started. "You mean to say that accursed thing is real?"

"It is," Oglethorpe said. "Vasquez wore it when we fought."

"What's it do?" Navarro asked.

"Magic is unnatural," Oglethorpe said. "Human beings were never meant to wield such power. As I'm sure you two are aware, it takes a physical toll on a magician's body."

Flint nodded. He'd seen Zelda Fletcher waste away before his eyes when she'd used too much magic during the Klemm incident last month.

"It's long been the dream of witches and wizards to create an object that can handle the dark powers they draw upon..."

"Like a magic wand?" Navarro asked, grinning.

Oglethorpe smirked. "Yes, but magic tears right through ordinary wood or metal. This is just my personal theory, but I believe that by its nature, magic craves the spirit." He frowned then. "Vasquez spent most of his adult life murdering the innocent, capturing their souls, for the singular purpose of crafting his crown. I believe those souls are trapped within it somehow, that it is they who bear the cost of magic instead of he who wears the crown."

Flint's nostrils flared. "You said that Vasquez wore it during your battle. What became of it after you slew him?"

"Before I struck the final blow, his last act was to cast it into one of those magical portals." Oglethorpe shook his head. "Of all the things he could have done, he chose to do that. Forty years later, and I'm still wondering if he had something planned in the event of his death. Something to do with the crown."

"So the crown was never recovered," Flint said.

"No. It's only been forty years, but it's become something of a legend. We went through every inch of Castle Vasquez, burned everything we could find, but no trace of the crown. A team from the University of Redmond went out there thirty years ago. I have the book the professor in charge wrote about it somewhere in here."

"What'd they find?" Navarro asked.

"They found it empty. Some of them reported unexplained phenomena – icy chills, voices, shadows... nothing we haven't seen before, but it frightened them terribly. But other than that, they found nothing of note. Both the Order and the Empire declared the area around the castle and Skull Creek Reservoir to be quarantined. But after thirty years of no activity, we let down our guard."

"And now something's happened," Carrow said.

"Yes," Flint said. "I said to General Abernathy that it was most curious the University would choose to send out another expedition, in light of... recent events."

"Your brother," Oglethorpe said. "When I saw his projection in the sky, I feared that he would be another Arturo Vasquez, on a much grander scale. I don't know whether to be relieved or frustrated that I am no longer on active duty."

"It's possible they sent another team just out of curiosity," Navarro said. "Vasquez tried to break away from Cascadia, Charles is trying to break away from the UMS. Trying to gain new insights from the past or something."

"It is possible," Flint said, "But foolish, nonetheless." He paused to think. "Matthew. You said in your letter that Father McConaughey recovered his lucidity enough to speak with you."

"Yes," Oglethorpe nodded. "He confirmed what Ricardo was just saying. Professor Meyer of the Supernatural Research Department ordered the new expedition."

"Hmm..." Flint said. "I expect that we shall be dispatching Templars to question the professor's reasoning. In any event, would it be possible to arrange an interview with Father McConaughey? I would learn more of what transpired if practicable."

"I can speak with the chief psychiatrist," Oglethorpe said. "I can't guarantee he'll have any new insights to share. He was teetering on the edge the entire time we spoke."

"And then there's all those college kids," Navarro said.

"Yes," Flint murmured. He stroked his chin. "Mr. Navarro, I believe Castle Vasquez merits investigation. If the archaeological team lives, it is our duty to bring them to safety."

"And if they don't?" Navarro asked.

"Then at the very least, they are owed a Christian burial."

"I agree," Oglethorpe said. "I don't know who or what may have gotten their hands on them, and twisted Father McConaughey, but if the powers of darkness are stirring within Castle Vasquez, they must be put down."

Carrow raised his hand. "I just thought of something," he said. All eyes turned to him. "Forgive me Silas, but my thoughts were dwelling on your brother. He fancies himself an emperor. What if he or one of his confederates is responsible for what happened to the archaeological team?"

Flint closed his eyes. "Because he seeks the crown."

"Yes," Carrow said.

"It is possible," Flint said. "Charles and I share a love of history. He would definitely have knowledge of Vasquez's reign of terror, and of the stories surrounding the crown."

"Well, no offense sir," Navarro said, "But it'd be kind of a relief if it was just your brother or one of his sidekicks."

"Oh?"

"Yeah. I'd much rather deal with them than Arturo Vasquez."

"Believe me," Oglethorpe said, "You would."

10

Destiny Lee pushed her horse to a gallop. There wasn't any hurry to her mission, but it wasn't often that she got to ride, and she intended to make the most of it. The sun was just coming over the horizon, promising another hot summer day. Out here in the east there weren't roads as such; more like well worn trails, though she spied the occasional patch of asphalt from the pre-Occult War days. Beside the trail was the Owyhee River. She estimated she still had an hour's ride before it branched off into Skull Creek. From there, she'd follow it to Skull Creek Reservoir, where Castle Vasquez awaited. She smirked. Vasquez had to have chosen that locale on purpose.

As she rode, she went over her plan. She'd read *Castle of Horror*, written by Professor Alec Rogan, the man who led the University of Redmond's expedition to Castle Vasquez thirty years ago. According to Rogan, there was a 'dead zone' extending for a one mile diameter around the castle. No plants or animals, only dry, cracked dirt. That was unusual, she thought. The castle must be positively infested with ghosts and demons to have such an influence on the surrounding landscape. The first thing she'd do is set up camp at the edge of the dead zone. She preferred not to enter the castle until it was necessary. Before she did that, she'd need to conjure up a guide.

Lee thought back to her first meeting with Charles. She'd grown up in a village named Seabeck in the far northwest of Cascadia. She'd known that she had the talent for magic at an early age. The first time she cast a spell – a simple fireball – her parents had thrown her out. It had been difficult, but after years of practicing and refining her craft, she returned to Seabeck to wreak vengeance on the people who had spurned her.

She frowned. Ah, the arrogance of youth. She overestimated her power and underestimated the town's social ties. They banded together to fight back. They nearly had her when Charles appeared from out of nowhere. He laid waste to the mob with fire and lightning, and they'd fled in terror. He explained his plans to her and she was his from that moment on. A nation of their own, a home of their own, where they could be themselves... she realized then that that was what she had wanted all along. And if Charles meant to build it, she would assist in any way she could. He deserved a crown, and if the Warlock's Crown existed, then by the powers below, she would bring it to him.

There. Skull Creek. She urged her horse south. Castle Vasquez awaited.

***

Silas Flint and Ricardo Navarro sat in the waiting room of St. Dymphna's Sanitarium for The Mentally Unbalanced. Carrow had wheeled Oglethorpe into the hospital director's office. Flint studied the Bible that had been on the waiting room table, while Navarro flipped through Flint's copy of *The Witch Hunter's Guide to North America.*

"Amazing... fucking amazing," Navarro muttered.

"Hmm?" Flint grunted.

"Oh, uh, sorry sir," Navarro replied. "I was just reading about Castle Vasquez. Can't believe the General and his assistant went in there alone back when it was... you know, occupied."

"General Oglethorpe is a remarkable man," Flint said. "It is unlikely that we shall see his kind again in our lifetimes."

"Oh, I don't know about that sir."

Flint said nothing, resumed reading the Gospel. The account of Christ commanding the demons to enter the herd of swine seemed appropriate, given their destination.

After another few minutes, Carrow pushed Oglethorpe into the waiting room. Accompanying them was a bespectacled woman in a white lab coat. Flint and Navarro put down their books and rose to meet them.

"Captain Flint, Mr. Navarro," Oglethorpe said, "May I present Dr. Ashley Arrington, chief psychiatrist of St. Dymphna's."

"A pleasure, Doctor," Flint said, clicking his heels and bowing his head.

"Captain, sir," she said, nodding to them both. "For the record, I think it's a bad idea to agitate Father Colm any more than he already is. However, General Oglethorpe tells me that you two plan on investigating the place where... where he became unbalanced."

"That is correct, Doctor," Flint replied. "We have reason to believe that his madness..."

"We don't use that word here," Arrington said.

"That his... illness was caused by the powers below."

She closed her eyes and took a deep breath. "Okay. You two may see him. But I will be right outside, and I will terminate the interview if it causes him distress. Understood?"

"You're the doc, doc," Navarro said.

Arrington beckoned for them to follow, with Carrow and Oglethorpe choosing to remain behind. As the doctor led them down the hallway, Flint noted it was lined with doors, each having a small window that allowed passers by to check on the patients. The facility appeared to be well kept, sharing the faint scent of ammonia that all hospitals seemed to have. Arrington took a left when the hallway forked. Flint followed her, but from the corner of his eye, he detected movement down the opposite hallway. Turning, he saw the Proctor sisters in nurses' uniforms.

"What the devil..." he started.

"Hmm?" Arrington said, turning to face him.

"You see something boss?" Navarro asked.

Flint advanced several paces back the way they had come, peered down the hallway. The Sisters were gone. "No," he said. "Please, lead the way, Doctor."

After another few turns, they stopped outside another door. Flint peered through the small glass window and saw an old man in a hospital gown, sitting on the edge of his bed, his face buried in his hands. Arrington knocked, and then opened the door, stepping inside with Flint and Navarro on her heels.

"Father?" she asked.

Father Colm McConaughey did not look up or stir at all.

"Father, you have visitors. Silas and Ricardo."

Again, McConaughey did not stir.

"They'd like to ask you some questions, Father."

Still nothing.

Arrington looked to Flint and Navarro, shook her head. "I'll be outside," she said. She exited McConaughey's room, shutting the door behind her. Flint took the opportunity to look at the priest's quarters. The staff must have judged him to not be a suicide risk for his bed was neatly made. The room boasted a desk with a Bible and a priestly breviary. Two rolling chairs were present as well, which Flint and Navarro took for themselves.

Seated before the broken priest, Flint said, "Father McConaughey."

The priest said nothing.

"Father McConaughey, I am Captain Silas Flint, Knight Templar of the Order of Saint Benedict. This is my assistant, Supernumerary Ricardo Navarro."

"Good morning, Father," Navarro said.

McConaughey looked up. "Witch Hunter?" he whispered. "Like Matthew?"

"Yes, Father, that is correct," Flint said.

"It's alive," McConaughey said. "It's alive. I wasn't good enough. I wasn't good enough. It's alive. I'm a coward. I failed them. I failed God. I..."

"It is alright, Father," Flint said, raising his hand in a placating gesture. "Are you able or willing to tell us what transpired at Castle Vasquez?"

"Castle Vasquez..." McConaughey said.

"Yeah. You were there. With the college. You were part of a team," Navarro said.

"College... yes... that's me. I'm a priest. I'm a chaplain. For Redmond. I... oh God." He shook all over and began to weep. Flint didn't know what to do but wait for the priest to regain his composure.

"My faith was weak," McConaughey said. "And now they're dead. They're dead, I'm sure of it. Robin. Robin. Robin. That boy, that demon boy..."

Flint felt a tingle up his spine. "What did you say?! Robin?" He looked at Navarro, who nodded. They'd both heard that name before.

"Yes, Robin, Robin with his red hat and..."

"Thank you, Father, you have been most helpful," Flint said, rising to his feet. He patted the priest on the shoulder. "I shall keep you in my prayers, Father McConaughey. Do not despair. Saint Peter himself wavered when our Blessed Lord needed him the most. He remembered himself, and so shall you. Come, Mr. Navarro."

The two men left the priest, who had curled his knees into his chest and was rocking back and forth. They found Arrington waiting for them in the hallway.

"What happened?" she asked.

"Father McConaughey confirmed our suspicions," Flint said. They made their way back to the lobby where Oglethorpe and Carrow were waiting for them.

"How is he?" Oglethorpe asked.

"Was he able to tell you anything?" Carrow said.

"Yes, more than he realized perhaps," Flint replied.

"General, let us retire to your house. I would not discuss this here."

11

The four men assembled inside Oglethorpe's study. Flint summarized their meeting with the broken priest. The General stroked his chin.

"Robin..." he said.

"Yes," Flint replied. "Robin Redcap, a demon from the abyss."

"Me and Silas have run into him twice this year," Navarro said. "Up in Canyon Cove, and at an old American military base in the UMS."

"Oh dear," Oglethorpe said. "This may be worse than I thought. There is an additional aspect to Castle Vasquez I haven't mentioned yet: demons can physically manifest within its walls, at will."

"Oh... shit," Navarro said.

"I couldn't have put it better myself," the General said. That far away look came over his face again. "That was how Jonah fell: single handedly holding off a horde of demons while I went on ahead."

"If Robin Redcap is present within the castle, then I fear the worst for the archaeological team," Flint said. "Nonetheless, we cannot abandon them to their fates."

Navarro nodded. "I'm with you sir."

"Mr. Carrow, if you would be so kind as to lend us your carriage once more?"

"Of course," Carrow nodded. "I'm with you as well."

"There is one more thing I feel that you should know, Matthew," Flint said.

"What is it?"

Flint took his pocket watch from his waistcoat and flipped it open. 8:55 a.m. "It may be quicker to show you, sir. Mr. Navarro, your radio if you please." His assistant handed him the radio. Flint flipped on the power. Jazz music filled Oglethorpe's office.

"What is this?" Carrow asked.

"I think we still have another few minutes," Navarro replied.

The song ended. The familiar three note chime sounded.

"This is..." Mallory's voice began.

"Yes, yes," Flint interrupted. "Now is not the time for your silly pretense."

There was a pause.

"How rude," the Sisters said in unison.

"What?!" Oglethorpe cried. "They... they can hear you?"

There was a knock at the office door. Before anyone could answer, the door opened and in strolled Mallory, Monica, and Madeline Proctor.

Oglethorpe and Carrow looked at each other, looked to Flint and Navarro.

"You were at the hospital earlier," Flint said.

The Sisters nodded.

"Good morning Matthew, good morning Robert," Mallory said.

"It is good to meet you both in person," Monica said.

"We rather like being news reporters though," Madeline said.

Oglethorpe shook his head. "I'm sorry, but who are you? And how did you get in here?"

"They are witches," Flint said, scowling. "May I present the Proctors. The Weird Sisters."

"Proctor?" Oglethorpe cocked his head. "I've heard that name before."

"It does not matter," Mallory said.

"Silas and Ricardo should leave soon," Monica said.

"A witch draws near to Castle Vasquez," Madeline said.

"Silas and I met these girls on our way here a few months ago," Navarro said. "They gave us the silver dagger Silas used to kill the werewolf."

"Yes," Flint said. "They also were of some help during our first trip to Salem this year."

The Sisters giggled. "'Some help,' he says," they said together.

"First Zelda, now these three," Carrow said. "The Order may start to wonder about Fort Marsing."

"Have you ladies anything else useful to add to our conversation?" Flint asked.

"Yes, but it is for Matthew," Mallory said.

"You still have what Jonah gave you," Monica said.

"You should let Silas and Ricardo borrow it," Mallory said.

There was a flash of light. When it dissipated, the Sisters were gone. In their places were three cats, one white, one black, one orange. They meowed and rushed out of the office.

All was silent for a few moments. Navarro spoke up:

"Hey, out of curiosity, General, Robert... what did they look like to you?"

"What?" Oglethorpe asked. "Er... they were three women, early fifties I'd say, grey hair..."

"Hm?" Carrow said. "I saw three blonde women. Early forties maybe."

"Huh. That's interesting. Whenever I see them, I see three Mexican girls," Navarro said.

"In any event," Flint broke in, "They have proven useful in the past, and so I tolerate their presence. For now. And if what they said is correct, then Mr. Navarro and I should be departing soon."

"Proctor..." Oglethorpe said. "I've heard that name before, I'm sure of it, but I can't remember where right now. And how on earth would they know about..." He trailed off.

"Problem sir?" Navarro asked.

"I..." He sighed. "They knew about Jonah."

Flint said nothing.

"Before we parted ways," Oglethorpe went on, "Jonah gave me something for when I tracked down Vasquez." He opened a drawer in his desk and withdrew a small box. He flipped open the lid to reveal a Saint Benedict medallion. Flint instantly recognized the cross with the Latin inscriptions and abbreviations encircling it. On the other side would be a depiction of Saint Benedict, the patron saint against witchcraft and patron of the Order.

"I'm not sure why they'd want you to take this," Oglethorpe continued. "Other than its sentimental value to me, it's no different from any other Saint Benedict medal.

But... if they've helped you in the past... then perhaps it is best that you take it for now." He offered it to Flint.

Taking it, Flint said, "Thank you sir. I swear before Almighty God and all of the angels and saints, that I shall return it to you when this case is finished." He adjusted his hat, straightened his long coat. "Come along, Mr. Navarro. You and I have an appointment at Castle Vasquez. Mr. Carrow, if you would be so kind as to prepare our carriage for the journey?"

"Right away," Carrow said, rising from his seat. After giving Oglethorpe another hug, he excused himself and left for the stables outside the city walls.

Navarro went to Oglethorpe's wheelchair and began pushing the General outside into the hallway. "It really is a shame we only meet whenever the forces of darkness are troubling the land," Oglethorpe said.

"I agree, sir," Flint replied.

"On the other hand, we'd be out of a job if they never did," Navarro said, chuckling.

"Hm. That's true," Oglethorpe said. "I was a Witch Hunter for so long, I don't even recall if I ever dreamed of being something else."

"Nor do I, sir," Flint said.

They reached the living room, where Jane, Julia, and George Oglethorpe awaited them.

"Will you be on your way, Captain?" Jane asked.

"Yes, Mrs. Oglethorpe. Mr. Navarro and I shall be departing presently."

"God be with you out there," George said, shaking both of their hands.

"Good luck, Captain," Julia said, offering a curtsy. "Rico..." She embraced him and kissed him on the cheek. "Come back alive."

He hugged her back. "Definitely."

"May Almighty God bless you both," Oglethorpe said.

"Thank you, sir," Flint said. "Come Mr. Navarro. Let us send that unholy monster back to the fiery pit."

***

Carlos Ramirez ran up the stone staircase. He'd lost them for now; those cloaking spells the professor had taught him worked against both human and demon alike it seemed. Now he just needed to find a way out of this hellish nightmare. The staircase went on and on. He panted, his face streaming with sweat. Something was wrong. By his estimate he'd run up seven flights worth of stairs, but Castle Vasquez wasn't that tall.

There. He saw the staircase end, but there was no landing. It went all the way up to the ceiling where a trap door awaited. Seeing no alternatives, he reached the end, praying that the trap door wasn't barred. He pushed it open, clambered through, and slammed it behind him. All was dark and musty, as though no human being had set foot in there for centuries, even though the castle was less than fifty years old.

Ramirez couldn't see his hand in front of his face. There was nothing for it but to risk a witchfire spell. He whispered the incantation, hoping it wouldn't give his location away. A ball of blue fire appeared above the palm of his hand, and he cast it into the darkness. It stuck on the closest wall. What he saw filled him with despair.

He was in the basement again. He'd been down there last night during his mad flight from the monsters that had torn apart some members of the team or spirited the others away. He'd run upstairs for what felt like an hour, but somehow, he was down in the basement again.

A fiendish laugh echoed in his ears. "I can't see you," said a man's voice, "But I can sense your power."

Ramirez said nothing, looked for a place to hide, more out of instinct than any expectation that it would help him.

"Come to me, little wizard," the voice said. "The blood, the flesh, the souls of the lambs are adequate, but you on the other hand..." Ramirez heard what sounded like the smacking of lips. "My fellow magicians make for the best sport." More laughter.

He wanted nothing more than to curl up into a ball and cry. This isn't what he signed up for when Charles Flint had recruited him and the professor months ago. Ramirez wanted to settle down in a place where he could practice his craft openly, not hide who he really was from everyone he cared about, including Professor Morales... Valentina. He hoped that she was alright. The last he'd seen her, she'd managed to get away from that Robin kid. Or did Robin allow her to escape? He feared that he would never know.

"Hey Carlos," said another voice. Robin. "We know why you're really here. You think to find Arturo's crown."

Ramirez said nothing.

"He's not willing to give it up. You know how necromancers can be," Robin laughed.

Ramirez sensed something. Another magician was nearby, outside the castle perhaps.

"What have we here?" said the first voice.

"Oh... it looks like Charles has sent someone to rescue our boy," Robin replied. Ramirez felt hope soar in his heart.

"More likely, they think to take my crown," said the first voice.

"All the better," said Robin. "Perhaps we can get through to Charles that way."

12

Destiny Lee stood at the edge of the dead zone surrounding Castle Vasquez. It was as though someone had salted the earth around it; if she took another step, she'd have one foot on blackened soil, the other on green grass. One didn't need to be a magician to know this was an evil place. Even though General Oglethorpe would have her burned at the stake, she couldn't help feeling a grudging admiration for the man. To enter that place with only a sword and pistols, and win? She was grateful that so few Witch Hunters were of his caliber.

She shrugged out of her backpack and set it down on the grass. She took out one of her magically reinforced glass vials. Inside was a mixture of salt and powder ground from human skulls. She twisted the cap off and began pouring it in a circle on the ground. That done, she took out her book of demonology. She'd done this part hundreds of times over the years, but it still made her nervous. Getting the pronunciation of a single word wrong could cost her life. She began to read, chanting in a language that wasn't meant for human tongues. Ancient grimoires from before the Occult War claimed it was the language spoken by the angels before Lucifer's fall. Lee didn't know about that, but whatever it was called, it worked.

A puff of black smoke materialized within the circle. The puff grew to a cloud, and then a column of noxious fumes that stank of rotten eggs. A pair of burning red eyes opened within the smoke, and she heard a low growl.

"What do you want, little witch?" asked a voice that sounded like crushed gravel.

"Tell me your name," Lee replied.

"No."

Lee raised her hands. Sorcerous lightning shot from her fingertips, entered the circle, and arced over the form inside. She saw that it was hulking and ape-like, with two horns that curled back from the top of its head. The demon grunted. Lee kept up the assault for another few seconds, then lowered her hands.

"Your name," she repeated.

"No."

"You might be thinking that didn't hurt very much. That was just a small taste of what I can do. I can turn up the pain if you like."

The demon laughed. "Break this circle and I can turn up the pain as well."

Lee waved her hands, pulling in as much magical

power as he could muster. A ball of lightning materialized between her palms. She molded it, shaped it, gave it more power. When she was ready, she held out both hands again. A larger, stronger bolt of lightning struck the demon. This time it howled in agony. The hairs on the back of her neck stood up. She maintained her fire, the demon twisting and writhing within the circle.

"Stop... stop!" it cried.

She continued her magical assault. Between the demon's cries, she yelled, "Your name!" She saw the demon's silhouette fall to one knee. It raised a hand, the fingers tipped with claws the same length as Lee's forearms. She lowered her hands, and the electricity stopped.

"My name is Astaroth," the demon growled.

"Astaroth... hmm..." Lee thought for a few moments. Then she blasted the demon with everything she had. Its scream caused the entire area to shake. Her eardrums would have been ruptured if not for the demon being enclosed in the circle, dampening the effect. "You aimed too high, monster," she said with a wicked smile. "I wonder what the real Astaroth would think of a lesser creature like you masquerading as the Great Duke of Hell? I could send you directly to him, you know."

"No!" the demon cried and fell silent. Just as Lee prepared to renew her attack, it muttered, "My name is Bifrons."

Lee smiled. "Bifrons, raise your right hand." She saw its shadowy form raise its right hand. Excellent. "Bifrons, I command you to rematerialize on the dead soil. Take the form of a man."

The smoke vanished. Shifting her gaze toward the castle, she saw the air ripple. A burst of flame appeared before her, molding itself into the shape of a human being. The flames burnt out, leaving behind a man in a tailored black suit. The man's head was lumpy and misshapen, the nose flattened, the eyes sunken, strands of thinning hair combed over its scalp.

"What do you want of me?" Bifrons asked. He was missing many teeth, and the ones that were present were jagged stumps within black gums.

"I would like you to be my guide through Castle Vasquez," Lee said. "I know that the great necromancer imbued it with his power, so much so that your kind can roam its halls freely. You will tell your friends to leave us alone. You will help me avoid whatever tricks or traps Vasquez left behind."

Bifrons smiled at her. "Why? What is it you think to find in there?"

"The Warlock's Crown."

The demon laughed. "Then you are a fool. Vasquez has hidden it in a place that is beyond even the gaze of Hell."

"We'll see. Now move."

***

Carlos Ramirez faced a hallway whose end extended beyond his sight. It was lined with doors on either side, old fashioned wooden doors with staves and iron rings for handles. If circumstances were different, he might have appreciated the medieval architecture. Instead, he was growing increasingly frustrated at the maze-like interior of Castle Vasquez. No matter which direction he took, or which stairs he climbed or descended, or which doors he opened, he'd wind up some place that he'd been before. It was like the castle was rearranging itself, forcing him to go in circles. He heard another scream, a man this time. It sounded like one of Don Riffey's boys. Poor bastard. Ramirez wasn't squeamish about killing for a good cause, but whoever or whatever had taken the others clearly did it just for pleasure. He couldn't decide which would be worse: getting captured by demons or by the spirit of Arturo Vasquez.

Ramirez sprinted down the hallway. He was exhausted and keeping up his cloaking spell only drained him further. He had to find something to eat or drink soon before he passed out, which would mean certain death. He laughed; otherwise, he would cry. This place had been abandoned for forty years, save for whatever demons or ghosts haunted the area. There wouldn't be any food or water. There was no way out. No way out. No way…

"Carlos?"

He stopped, his jaw dropping. That was Professor Morales's voice. It couldn't be though. It had to be another demonic trick. She was nowhere in sight, but he heard her as though she were only a few feet away.

"Carlos, it's me," her voice echoed. "Are you there?"

Ramirez said nothing.

"I know that you're… a magician. A wizard," she said. "I hope you're able to hear me somehow."

Ramirez kept quiet.

"These things... Robin... they want you for some reason. They told me that if you reveal yourself, let them take you... they'd let me go."

Still he said nothing.

"I can't ask you to sacrifice yourself for me," she said. "I just wanted you to know that I'm so very sorry for dragging you and the others into this."

He closed his eyes and sighed. To hell with it.

"I can hear you, Valentina," he whispered.

She gasped. "How..."

"Magic," he said, with a tight grin. "I don't know where you are, but I can hear you and speak to you."

"Carlos," she said. "Robin is..."

"A demon, yes, I figured as much. What do they want with me?"

"I'm not sure. I can hear Robin's voice and someone else's voice too, a man. It's the man who wants you."

Ramirez felt a ball of ice form in his gut. "Valentina, listen to me," he said. "Don't believe them. Demons always lie. They won't let you leave this place, even if I turn myself over to them."

She said nothing for a few moments. "What do we do then?" Her voice sounded on the verge of breaking.

"Look around you," Ramirez said. "Can you describe where you are?"

Silence for a few moments. "It's a dining room," she said. "There's a long banquet table with place settings, goblets... there are skeletons sitting in all of the chairs."

"Are they moving?"

"What?!"

"Valentina... are they moving?"

A pause. "N... no. No."

That was something at least. "Okay. Listen to me. Stay where you are. I'll come find you."

A nervous laugh. "I have no idea how I got here. I don't think I could leave if I wanted to."

"I know that feeling, believe me. Just stay calm, Professor. I'll get us out of here." *I hope,* he thought to himself. He'd been wandering for hours and hadn't seen anything like a dining room anywhere yet. Normally a banquet hall would be on the ground floor, but who the hell knew in a place like this? And then there was Valentina. He felt mostly certain that was really her that he'd spoken to, but it was possible – likely even – that it was another demonic trick. But he felt that he had to try. Even if it turned out to be a trap, it was as good a place as any to go. Now he just had to...

He caught something in the corner of his eye: an open doorway that led to another stairwell. Had that been there a minute ago? Ramirez was sure that it wasn't. Next to the door was a wooden sign with a skeletal hand painted on, pointing at the doorway. Above it were the words BANQUET HALL.

"You've got to be shitting me," he muttered.

***

Silas Flint flipped open his pocket watch. 1:25 p.m. They'd made excellent time, and he estimated that they would be arriving at the outskirts of Danville within the hour. From there it would be another two hour journey to Skull Creek Reservoir where Castle Vasquez awaited them.

The road had been smooth so far, but Flint expected the terrain to get rougher the further to the southeast they went. Navarro sat across from Flint, idly wiping at his rifle with his cleaning rag. He looked up.

"Something wrong, boss?" he asked.

Flint shook his head. "Nothing at all, Mr. Navarro. I was simply pondering our next step. And..." He reached inside his long coat, took out the Saint Benedict medal that Oglethorpe had given him. "I was curious why the Sisters would want us to have this."

"Can I see it?"

Flint handed it to his assistant. Navarro gazed at one side, and then the other. He held it closer to his face, squinted.

"Do you see something amiss?" Flint asked.

"Looks like blood." He handed the medal back to Flint, who took a closer look. Yes, there was a dark red stain in the lower right quadrant of the engraved cross.

"I wonder..." Flint muttered. He looked to Navarro again and said, "I believe it is time for the news."

Navarro took the radio from the pouch on his belt, turned it on. They caught the last few notes of a jazz tune Flint didn't recognize. The three note chime sounded. Then silence. The carriage was quiet except for the muffled snorting of the horses and the pounding of their hooves. Flint and Navarro looked at each other, at the radio, at each other again.

"Uh... you guys there?" Navarro asked.

Another few moments of silence.

Flint scowled. "Hmph. So much for their..."

"Are you going to interrupt us again?" the Sisters said in unison.

Flint blinked. "No..."

"This is Mallory Proctor."

"Joining her is special correspondent, Monica Proctor."

"And with the weather, Madeline Proctor."

"And now for the news," they said together.

Flint sighed and rubbed the bridge of his nose. He thought he saw the corner of Navarro's mouth quirk up.

"How can we help, Silas?"

"You are almost to your destination."

"This is going to be a difficult case."

"Is it?" Flint asked. "The Holy Spirit guides us. We shall not fail."

"We hope so."

"Hey," Navarro said. "As long as you're there... how come you help us on some cases and not on others?"

"We've told you before that we are only permitted to give you indirect assistance."

"And before you ask, we are not going to tell you who permits and forbids."

"We can tell you that they have confidence in you, but you need to be pointed in the right direction from time to time."

"That is our job," they said together.

"If that is the case," Flint said, "Have you any further suggestions, or information, or gifts for us?"

"Only one piece of advice," Mallory said.

"When you arrive at Castle Vasquez..." Monica said.

"You should send Robert back to Danville," Madeline said.

Flint and Navarro looked at each other. "Whatever for?" Flint asked.

"He will know," they said.

"I got another question," Navarro said. "Why do you look different to everyone? I mean, to me you look like three Mexican girls, to General Oglethorpe you looked like older ladies. What gives?"

They giggled.

"We have found that men are more likely to listen when we appeal to their eyes."

"It is a trick that has served us well for centuries."

"It doesn't always work though. Silas sees us as we really are."

"And we are not sure why," they finished together. "The Proctor Sisters, signing off." The three note chime played.

"This is Nick Sanderson for 1530 AM, Cascadia's number one station for classical North America. Our next song is..." Navarro turned the radio off. Flint recalled hearing that the DJ Nick Sanderson had died some time ago and that 1530 AM was officially defunct, but there he was again.

"You see them as they really are..." Navarro said.

"Yes," Flint replied. "To me they appear to be in their early twenties, with white, black, and red hair."

"Wonder what that means."

"It matters not. We must be prepared for the horrors of Castle Vasquez."

***

Zelda Fletcher looked out the window of her train compartment. The locomotive's whistle sounded, and its brakes squealed as it pulled into the Redmond station. She found it funny; since she'd turned herself in to the Knight Templars of the Order of Saint Benedict a few months ago, she'd been on more train and automobile rides than she had in the previous twenty-four years of her life combined. Her hometown of New Rome had neither automobiles nor a train station. Her ex-boyfriend Francisco Cortez had taught her to use her magical talents, promising her great power. Now New Rome was destroyed, Francisco was in Hell, and Fletcher felt like she was seeing more of the world now than she ever could have as a practicing witch.

There was a knock on her compartment door. A moment later the door slid open, and Lady Diana McFarlane stepped inside. "How are you doing Zelda?" she asked.

"I'm alright," Fletcher replied.

McFarlane sat down in the booth across from Fletcher. "May I ask you a personal question?" McFarlane asked.

"Do it."

"Do you want to be my assistant?"

Fletcher blinked. "Uh..."

McFarlane grinned. "It's okay to say no. You develop a thick skin in this vocation."

"Why do you ask?"

"Silas."

Fletcher felt her cheeks burning. "What about him?"

"You like him."

"That's..."

"None of my business?" McFarlane smiled. "You're right, it isn't. But for right now, the Order, in its infinite wisdom, has paired you with me. If you don't like it, then we can talk to General Abernathy and get you reassigned, perhaps. But until that happens, I need to know that your head is in the right place."

Fletcher felt irritation rise in her gorge and was about to make a biting remark but thought better of it. "Yes. Yes, I'm with you Diana. Sorry. I don't mean to be distant or distracted or whatever."

McFarlane patted her on the shoulder. "Think nothing of it. May I offer you some advice though?"

"Sure."

McFarlane pursed her lips, looked to the side. "I've known Silas longer than you have. The heart wants what it wants but... well, he's..."

"Intense?" Fletcher asked, grinning.

McFarlane laughed. "That's putting it mildly." She grew serious again. "I've never met anyone as devoted to the vocation as him, not even General Abernathy. You could tell him to his face that you want his babies and he'd probably say that he can't, not while there are magicians terrorizing God's people."

"Jesus Christ, I don't..."

McFarlane gave her a sharp look.

"Uh, sorry," Fletcher said. "I mean I haven't thought

that far ahead but…" She thought for a moment. "He, uh… does like women… right?"

"Yes," McFarlane said, chuckling. "Of that there is no doubt, trust me."

"Oh yeah?" Fletcher asked, raising an eyebrow. "And how would you know, hmm?"

Now McFarlane blushed, cleared her throat. "Well, let's just say there's a reason why the Order generally pairs us off by gender."

"Uh huh," Fletcher said, smiling. "To answer your question, yes, I do want to be your assistant. I was just thinking… leaving aside whatever I feel for Silas, seems like he gets the real hard cases."

"Heh, yes, there is something to that. 'The Ruin of Witches' they call him now. But believe it or not, even he gets his share of boring cases."

"Like this one?" Fletcher asked. The train came to a halt, with one final blast of its whistle.

"Interviewing a college professor doesn't sound too exciting, does it?" McFarlane asked. "You never know though. Sometimes it's the cases that sound simple enough that turn out to be the most complicated." She rose from her seat. "Now. Let's grab our things and go see this Professor Meyer."

13

The setting sun cast the countryside in an orange glow. Flint and Navarro disembarked from the carriage, and Carrow climbed down from the boot to stand at their side. He had stopped at the edge of what appeared to be a circle of dead soil surrounding Castle Vasquez. Flint had seen photographs of it, but they failed to do it justice. A low wall enclosed the castle proper. Even at this distance, Flint could see dead vines climbing the moldering brick. He counted seven towers, one of which was floating in midair, tethered to the rest of the structure by a single staircase that extended beyond another tower, unsupported by anything but the dark power which he sensed all around him. Beside him, Carrow closed his eyes and took a deep shuddering breath.

"Mr. Carrow," Flint said.

"Yes?"

He wasn't sure how to proceed. May as well be honest about it. "Along our way, Mr. Navarro and I communicated with the Weird Sisters again."

Carrow looked at him, said nothing.

"They said to tell you that you ought to go back to Danville," Navarro said.

Carrow was silent for a few moments. "I don't like leaving you two alone out here. If you need to get away quickly..."

"Fear not," Flint said. "God is with us."

The stable master cocked his head. "God is with us... you just gave me an idea. Perhaps it is best I return to Danville for now."

"What you got in mind?" Navarro asked.

"Vasquez was never possessed to the best of our knowledge," Carrow said, "But the man was so fiendish, so depraved... so closely aligned with the powers of Hell, he could be repelled by the light of faith. I imagine that if his spirit haunts this castle, he would be even more vulnerable now." He pursed his lips. "Danville has two parishes and a convent of Carmelite nuns. It's been forty years, but I'm sure whoever's there now knows the history of this place. We could use their help."

Flint nodded. "Very good, Mr. Carrow. Their prayers will be of much avail. If the Fathers would be so bold as to come here, we may need make use of their faculties for exorcism. Mr. Navarro and I shall begin our search for the archaeological team."

"Or their bodies," Navarro muttered, making the sign of the cross.

"Do you really mean to enter the castle tonight?" Carrow asked.

"Indeed," Flint said. "Mr. Navarro, unpack the luggage compartment if you please. Our flashlights are inside. Although…" He drew his sword from the scabbard on his left hip. As he expected, the blade emitted a soft white glow which signified the presence of magic all around them. He sheathed it. "I suspect my blessed steel would suffice to light the way."

"What's the story behind that?" Navarro asked, pointing at the floating tower. "My papa taught me a little about architecture, but I'm pretty sure that shouldn't be possible."

"I don't know why he did it," Carrow said, "But that tower holds Vasquez's inner sanctum, so to speak. It's where Matthew fought him."

"We shall make our way to the fiend's lair in due time," Flint said.

"May the Holy Spirit guide you," Carrow said. He climbed up onto the carriage. The horses needed little prompting to take off at a canter; they'd grown progressively more uneasy the closer they got to the castle. The two men watched the carriage disappear over a hill.

Flint patted down his long coat, extra pistol magazines clacking against one another. If what Oglethorpe had said was true – that demons could physically manifest at will within the castle – he wasn't sure how much good his guns would do, but better to have and not need extra ammunition than need and not have. Navarro reached inside the t-shirt underneath his leather body armor, dug out a crucifix he wore around his neck, kissed it, and let it hang outside his armor. He unslung the bolt action rifle from his back.

"Are you prepared?" Flint asked.

"As I'll ever be."

"Then let us be on our way." Flint drew his sword and one of his pistols. They advanced toward the edge of the circle and felt the temperature drop. With his next step, Flint crossed from a grassy plain to what looked and felt like a blasted desert. The dead soil crunched beneath his boots. Navarro was right behind him, rifle held at the low ready, scanning for threats. Flint saw his breath fog.

"How you want to do this sir?" Navarro asked.

"We shall enter through the front door, of course," Flint replied. "I always favor the direct approach."

The castle loomed before them. A barred gate was in

the center of the surrounding wall, a small hut beside it. As they approached the structure, the light grew dimmer. Flint looked up. The setting sun hadn't touched the horizon yet, but it was now a milky white, like the moon. Navarro followed Flint's gaze.

"Shit," he said. "I can look right at it."

"I would suggest that you refrain," Flint replied. He pointed at the hut. "I expect there will be some sort of mechanism inside that can operate the portcullis. We should..." He caught movement inside the window of the guard post. He aimed his pistol, Navarro his rifle. Together, they crept forward, keeping the hut's doorway covered. When they were only a few feet away from the entrance, someone stepped out of the hut.

He was dressed in torn blue jeans, white shirt, and ratty duster. The lower half of his face was covered by a red scarf, his head by what looked like a cowboy hat right out Flint's history books. The flesh around the man's eyes – which were a burning yellow - was wrinkled and tinged with purple, as though he was holding his breath.

"Welcome strangers," the man rasped. "Welcome to Castle Vasquez."

Flint thumbed the hammer of his pistol with a click. "Identify yourself," he growled. "Be you living or dead?"

The man chuckled, a sound like crunching gravel. "Both and neither."

Navarro raised his rifle a bit. "Any good reason why we shouldn't put you back in the ground?"

"You're welcome to try. I'd pray for you to succeed. But I don't think you would," the man said. "As for my identity... my name is Marcus. Or was. I think. It's been a long time."

"What is it that you want?" Flint asked.

"The master of this castle... Arturo Vasquez... he's the one keeping us here. Any magician can raise the dead, but him... he can raise us where we remember who we are. Where we know what we're doing even as he..."

Navarro nudged Flint, nodded toward Marcus. Flint saw it now. The creature before them appeared as a man, but its shadow was that of a hulking ape-like creature, with two wings on its back and two great curling horns on its head.

"Please strangers," Marcus said. "Free us from our..."

Flint aimed and shot him in the forehead. Marcus's words were cut off, his head snapped back, a shower of black ichor spraying the wall, and the apparition crumpled to the ground. Flint and Navarro advanced, their weapons aimed at the body.

Marcus raised his hand and a stream of hellfire rushed toward the two men. Flint raised his sword, the blessed steel dissipating the flames before they could engulf them. Snarling, Marcus's body contorted and reformed itself into a hulking gargoyle like creature, its simian features twisted by rage and hate. Navarro fired his rifle, worked the bolt, fired again, taking the beast in the head and the chest. Its face a bloody ruin, the monster roared in defiance. Flint darted forward, bringing his sword around in a sweeping cut that sent the demon's head flying from its shoulders. Black blood spattered over Flint. He used his sleeve to wipe the drops from his face, his lip curled in disgust. Before the demon's body could finish falling forward, it vanished in a puff of smoke.

A man's laughter echoed around them. "I know that blade," the man's disembodied voice said. "I've felt its sting before. But you're not Matthew."

"I am Silas Flint!" He pointed his sword at the gate. "Whoever you are, the dark powers are of no avail against the power of God!"

The man snickered. Navarro scanned in every direction, looking for the source of the voice. It went on: "Flint... are you... ah, yes. I see the resemblance now. This is too good to be true. Brothers of light and darkness. It's poetry! I'll say this for your God, He can have a mordant sense of humor."

"Tell us where you are, shitbird," Navarro growled. "Me and Silas will laugh it up when you're dead."

"You missed your chance, boy," the voice responded. "Matthew killed me before you were born."

Flint inhaled sharply, his nostrils flaring. His fear was confirmed. "Vasquez..." he whispered.

"You've heard of me! I'm touched," Vasquez replied.

"You no longer belong in this world!" Flint bellowed. "You are an impotent shade, a shadow of the monster you once were! Be you living or dead, the children of God will send you to Hell where you belong!"

"Impotent, am I?" Vasquez said. Flint couldn't see him, but he sensed that he'd touched a nerve. "It's true that I'm not as strong as I was in life... but that will not be a problem for much longer, thanks to my visitors."

"Where are the others?" Navarro said. "What have you done with the university team?"

"University? Is that who they are? They came here to study my home like some ancient American ruins?" Vasquez laughed. "And now we are studying them. It's been too long since I've had living test subjects."

Flint felt hope stir in his heart. There was a chance the team members still lived, but they would have to hurry. God only knew what diabolical experiments the necromancer's shade would perform upon them. "We have come to liberate your captives," Flint growled. "And you will not stop us, Vasquez."

"It isn't me you need to worry about," Vasquez said. "It's my friends from below. Some of them are very eager to meet you in the flesh."

"If all you've got are big apes like these," Navarro said, kicking Marcus's demonic body, "Then we'll take our chances."

"We'll see boy, we'll see. But first, you must get inside."

The sky was cloudless, but they heard a thunderclap. A wall of blue flame burst forth from the ground in front of the gate. Flint shielded his eyes. The unholy fire's heat made beads of sweat appear on his forehead. Navarro joined him at his side, wiping sweat from his brow.

"Guess the front door's out," he said.

"We must search the grounds for another entrance," Flint replied.

"He's herding us."

"No doubt. We must rely upon the light of faith and the strength of our arms. Come."

***

Destiny Lee looked out the window in an upstairs hallway. She'd felt a surge of magical power, sensing that it was outside. The sun was setting, but the dark magic of this place dimmed its glow, making it more like moonlight. She saw wavering shadows and heard the crackling of flames. Someone had summoned a wall of fire to block the main gate. Bifrons joined her.

"Something wrong, Mistress Lee?" he asked, his semi-human face split by a nasty grin.

"Who is responsible for that?" she said, pointing at the fire's shadows.

"Vasquez, I think."

"Why?"

Bifrons laughed. "Oh, come on. You must sense them too."

Lee sighed. She had but didn't want to believe it. A Witch Hunter had arrived, no doubt with an assistant in tow. They couldn't possibly know about her mission to find the Crown. Searching for the lost archaeological team perhaps? She hadn't seen any trace of them yet, nor the wizard who'd been hiding in plain sight among them. No matter.

"Bifrons," she said. "I want you to..."

"You don't need to order me," he interrupted. "We're happy to do it for fun."

"Good." With those two out of the way, she could

continue the search uninterrupted. Not that it had borne fruit yet. She snorted in frustration.

"I told you," Bifrons said. "Wherever Vasquez has hidden the Crown, even we can't see it. Release me, and I'm willing to overlook your assault on me earlier. We'll allow you to go in peace."

Lee smiled. "Nice try," she said. "But I know better than to take the word of your kind."

Bifrons shrugged. "Then we will walk in circles until you give up. My kind have all the time in the world."

She frowned. Bifrons had helped her avoid the pitfalls that Vasquez had laid generations ago. She had to admit that she was impressed by the necromancer's ingenuity, a mixture of illusion magic and simple booby traps she hadn't seen before. But still there was no sign of the Crown. Perhaps it was time for a more direct approach.

"Take me to him," she said. "Take me to Vasquez."

Bifrons cocked his misshapen head. "Vasquez is dead."

She pointed at the demon, a small bolt of electricity leaping from her fingertip, enveloping her guide, who grunted in pain. "Don't get smart with me, demon," she hissed. "You know what I mean."

Bifrons chuckled. "Your wish is my command. Follow me."

***

Carlos Ramirez heard music up ahead. He'd gone down the stairwell which had appeared earlier, and it led to another seemingly endless hallway lined with torches which burned with blue witchfire. As he advanced, he recognized the instrument: a harpsichord, he believed it was called. Ramirez's stomach growled. He'd been maintaining his magical cloak about his person for what felt like hours, and he felt himself weakening. He'd need to find some food soon to replenish his stamina. Otherwise, he'd be forced to drop his cloak and take his chances with anyone – or anything – roaming the halls with whatever magical fire or lightning he could still conjure.

The hallway was lined with more doors. He stretched out with his senses. Valentina was close. She was at the end of the hallway which stretched beyond his sight. He quickened his pace. As he passed the wooden doors, he heard noises: spattering liquid, whispers he couldn't make out, peals of laughter. He shuddered. The professor and Charles always went on about how the ordinary masses who couldn't use magic were the enemy, that they'd kill him if they knew his true nature. He believed them, but he'd spent months with his class. Even grown to like some of them. Ramirez was willing to sacrifice their lives if that's what it took to ensure Medea's future, but leaving them in the hands of Vasquez or his demonic horde? Nobody deserved that.

The music grew louder. Ramirez didn't recognize it, but the melody weighed upon him. What was the point of his mission? Even if the Crown existed, what hope did he have of finding it? What hope was there that Valentina was alive? He stopped, leaned against the wall. He felt tears well up. Life, dreams, hope... all temporary, flickering lights in the endless void. Only death was eternal. Only...

He shook himself. What had come over him? That train of thought wasn't like him at all. It had to be the castle. It was trying to break him. He had to find Professor Morales, save her if he could. If she was dead, he'd get the hell out of there. The Professor and Charles weren't even sure if the Crown could be recovered. It had been worth a shot, but if he had to return to them empty-handed, so be it.

Ramirez pushed on. Valentina's presence grew stronger. He jumped at a distant boom. Was that a gunshot? A child's laughter echoed behind one of the doors he passed. Ramirez stopped. The hallway ended at two double doors. Standing on either side were two skeletons. Green fires burned in their eye sockets. Their bony hands held spears. Ramirez dropped his magical cloak. The skeletons did not react. He summoned fire to his fingertips, prepared to blast them to bits. The skeletons stood aside and opened the doors for him. Ramirez beheld a grand banquet hall. The ceiling was dominated by an enormous chandelier, ablaze with candles lit by blue witchfire. Ramirez squinted; the chandelier was made of human bones. A blood red carpet extended from the doorway to the far side of the hall. In the center was an oak dining table with a dozen chairs on either side, a skeleton seated in each one.

More surprising was that the table was set for a feast. Ramirez smelled roast suckling pig and crab bisque, saw plates of fresh fruit and goblets of wine. His mouth watered and he swallowed. There was no sign of Valentina. The back of his mind urged caution, but his appetite overcame him. Ramirez rushed forward. The harpsicord music continued, but he took no notice of it. Arriving at the table, he found a platter with a roasted turkey surrounded by covered dishes. Removing the metal covers, he saw mashed potatoes, gravy, stuffing, green beans, and other delights. He reached out with his senses, detected no enchantments or illusions. It was normal food.

He tore off one of the turkey's legs, dunked it in the gravy, and took a bite. He closed his eyes, savoring it. Delicious. The harpsicord music changed... before, it urged him to despair. Now it swelled in what sounded like triumph. He could feel his strength returning as he continued to devour the turkey leg. Ramirez wanted to laugh. He felt like he could take on the entire Cascadian Army single handed. He'd find Valentina and...

Something was wrong. He felt sluggish. His arms felt like they weighed a ton. His muscles bulged as he tried to take a step back, but his feet felt like they were encased in cement. The music stopped.

"Carlos..." Valentina's voice echoed. "I'm sorry. They made me do it. I didn't want this. I'm sorry."

Ramirez's body seized up, frozen in place. He couldn't move. Couldn't blink. He could still breathe but was otherwise immobile. He'd managed to take a step back before his body stopped responding to his commands and was off balance. Panic rose in his gorge as he tipped over. Instead of landing in a heap, he remained locked in place, like a statue. He heard footsteps approach.

"Well, well, well..." said a man's voice. "I've been waiting for you, young man."

Ramirez couldn't blink but he could still move his eyes.

They darted everywhere, searching for the speaker, but he remained out of sight.

"That was rude, by the way," the man said. "You didn't even introduce yourself to my guests before you gorged yourself on their food." He laughed. "They partook of my table and found themselves much like you are now: paralyzed, helpless. They could do nothing but watch as I had their families brought here and butchered."

Ramirez couldn't even whimper in fear.

"I've got something better planned for you," the voice said. "Your friends provided many of the parts I need, but there was still one piece missing, one piece that only a fellow magician could provide."

Ramirez felt bony fingers caress his scalp. He wanted to struggle, to blast this... thing, to bits with his magic, but his body still would not move. The magic would not respond to his summons.

"I've studied thousands of bodies, thousands of brains, to learn the secret," the voice whispered. "I admit I still don't know how it works. I don't know how Simon Magus could make magicians of anyone who accepted his blessing. But I know that our brains are different from the lambs. And if I'm going to return to the fullness of my power..."

The speaker loomed over Ramirez. He saw its face and felt like his eyes would bulge out of his skull. The scream of terror that welled inside him would not come out, but his mind reeled, his thoughts dissolved in unthinking panic.

"I'm afraid I'm going to need yours."

14

Silas Flint and Ricardo Navarro crept around the castle's outer wall. Navarro held his rifle at the low ready while Flint led the way, the glow of his blessed sword lighting their path. Flint scanned the landscape, looking for another gate or something that hinted at a hidden door. A cunning creature like Vasquez no doubt had secret tunnels and passages everywhere, for all the good they had done him in life.

He heard a sound of crumbling brick, a trickle of dust sprinkling his black coat.

"Look out!" Navarro cried. He brought up his rifle and fired. Flint heard a screech above him, a chilling mixture of human and animal. Looking up, he saw a desiccated corpse with black wings. Its leathery flesh was stretched tight over its bones, green fires burning in its eye sockets. Two long blades extended from the points of its elbows. Flint aimed and fired his pistol twice, the silver tipped bullets smacking into the creature's chest. It howled again, the two men wincing at the noise, but keeping their weapons at the ready.

The abomination dove toward them. Flint and Navarro rolled out of the way just as it landed where they'd been standing. Rising to his feet, Flint advanced on the corpse, firing his pistol. He saw dust pour from the bullet holes. The corpse flared its wings and hissed. Just as Flint got within arms-length, Navarro leapt onto the creature's back, tomahawk and pistol in hand. The creature screamed and shook like a dog, but Navarro held on. Wrapping one arm around its throat, Navarro began bashing its head with his tomahawk. Clouds of grave dust billowed from its cranium, making him wretch and lose his grip. As soon as his assistant was away, Flint brought his sword down in an overhead swing. It cut through the monster's shoulder and down to its belly. With a sigh, the corpse crumpled to the ground. Not taking any chances, Flint brought his sword down again, severing its ruined head from its body.

Panting, Navarro climbed to his feet. He holstered his pistol and tomahawk, picked up his rifle.

"Well done, Mr. Navarro," Flint said.

"Thanks boss," Navarro said. He looked down at the monstrosity's body. "Zombies are bad enough, but flying zombies?" He shuddered. "Vasquez is one sick fuck."

"I could not have put it better myself," Flint replied. "We must..." He stopped. His eyes narrowed. He took a knee beside the monster's body.

"You find something?" Navarro asked.

The creature was naked save for a ragged pair of denim jeans, its legs in tatters. Flint carefully patted it down. He rolled it over onto its stomach. In its right hip pocket, there was a wallet. He fished it out and rose to his feet. Navarro joined him at his side as he opened it. Flint sighed.

"Shit," Navarro said.

There was an identification card inside, embossed with the seal of the University of Redmond next to a photograph of its owner. The monster had once been a man named Dale Oaks, born 2508. He'd had brown hair, brown eyes, and a friendly smile. Flint felt rage boiling within.

"This is unholy beyond words!" he snarled.

Navarro made the sign of the cross. "Sorry Dale," he whispered.

Flint tucked the ID card into one of his pockets. "We must find a way inside."

"Sir... what if..."

"Even if they have all been twisted into these... mockeries of life," Flint interrupted, "We have a duty to put them out of their misery. If even one still lives, we must rescue them from this circle of Hell."

"Right... right," Navarro said, nodding. "How we gonna get in though?"

"There must be a way," Flint said. "For now, let us continue our inspection of the grounds. I expect that we shall..."

There was a crack, then an explosion of soil and dust. The two men looked out at the dead zone and saw a rotting hand breaking through the ground. Another crack, another hand. Then another. And another. The air was rent with dozens of groans. Rotting corpses and skeletons dug themselves from the earth. The stench of decay made their eyes water but Flint and Navarro raised their guns, took a step back. The dead zone surrounding the castle was becoming an ocean of the dead. Green fires burned in all their eye sockets, making the gloom nearly as bright as day.

"Sir..." Navarro said, looking to Flint.

"Run!"

They took off at a sprint. In those few seconds, Flint could see that there were more bodies than he and Navarro had bullets. The cracking of dry soil and the groans of the dead followed them as they ran, the tide of undead growing ever larger. Flint knew that, as a rule, zombies could only manage a stumbling shuffle, but if Vasquez could make them fly, he could no doubt make them run as well.

Onward they ran. The outer castle was aglow with the light cast by the green fires in the eyes of the dead. Vasquez's laughter thundered in their ears.

"Run little rabbits! Run!" he shouted.

Flint could hear Navarro panting. They had to get out of there. He dared not look over his shoulder, but he knew the hungry dead numbered in the hundreds, if not thousands by now.

He saw three silhouettes ahead, waving their arms. If they were more undead, then he and Navarro would have no choice but to make their last stand. He began mentally reciting the Act of Contrition, in preparation for his likely death. He only prayed that he didn't end up as a puppet of Vasquez.

"Silas!" Navarro cried. "Look!"

As they drew nearer, he could see them now: the Weird Sisters. They beckoned the two men toward them. Flint pushed himself to run faster, Navarro close on his heels. The groans of the undead pursuing them were now peppered with growls and the gnashing of their broken teeth.

Closer now. He could see some sort of stream pouring forth from a section of the castle's wall that jutted out. One of the Sisters gestured, and a heavy iron grate swung open. Another pointed at the opening. Flint and Navarro made one final sprint and dove inside, falling to the floor in a heap. They heard the grate slam shut behind them followed by the thudding of bodies. Breathing hard, they helped each other up and looked behind them. The zombies snarled, barked, strained to reach through openings in the grate, but it held fast. Flint and Navarro looked at each other, looked out of the grate again.

"I guess you saw them too?" Navarro said, raising his voice over the din of the undead.

"Indeed," Flint nodded.

"Hope they're alright."

"No doubt they escaped through some sorcerous means."

"Yeah..." Navarro said. "What is this stuff on the... ugh!"

Flint looked down. From a distance, the stream had looked like water and he had assumed that they were in some sort of cavernous sewer. By the light of his sword and the fires of the zombies, he saw that the stream was blood. His white shirt was stained crimson. He felt momentary panic as he patted his waistcoat, but his pocket watch was secure. He flipped it open. The second hand was still ticking along, but it was moving backwards.

"Something wrong, boss?" Navarro asked.

"No," Flint replied, snapping his watch shut. "Let us press on."

"Twenty silver says we meet some ugly sewer monster down here."

"I do not gamble Mr. Navarro."

"You just don't like losing."

Flint peered down the tunnel. On either side was a

walkway above the central canal where they stood, blood sloshing over the tops of their boots.

"There is that. And I believe I would lose this particular wager, yes."

***

Destiny Lee followed the demon Bifrons to a set of double doors flanked by two skeletons, armed with spears tipped with obsidian blades, green fires burning in their eye sockets. Raising the dead was a simple trick that most magicians knew, but she sensed something different about these two. When she raised a dead body, it was little more than a mindless automaton. These though... she sensed an animal cunning in them. Almost like they were intelligent.

The skeletons pointed their spears at her. Bifrons waved them off. "Our guest wishes to speak with your master."

The skeletons cocked their heads, as though listening to a distant voice. They backed off, resuming their posts, spears held at port arms. The doors swung open. Bifrons gestured for her to pass. "I can go no further," he said.

"What?" she asked.

"Vasquez does not allow my kind to visit him in his lair, save by invitation."

Lee swallowed. "Very well. Wait here."

The demon smiled. "Your wish is my command."

Lee stepped through the doorway. She felt a cool breeze wash over her mixed with the stench of decay. There were no torches. She whispered a spell, conjured a ball of witchfire to light her way, but its blue glow was swallowed by the darkness; she couldn't even see the walls. She saw another doorway ahead. It opened onto a balcony which overlooked the castle's inner courtyard, the outer wall, and the surrounding dead zone. Her eyes widened; the castle was surrounded by an army of the dead, stretching as far as she could see. The landscape was aglow with the light of the fires in their eyes.

Looking around, she saw an opening in the balcony for a staircase. The stairs went up, unsupported by anything except the dark magic she sensed all around her. Looking up, she saw that they led to the floating tower she'd seen outside. Its windows were illuminated by that same green glow.

She swallowed again. Lee was confident in her magic and fighting skills, but she knew her limitations. She was no match for Charles, and she sensed that whatever was up there was beyond even him. She took her first step onto the staircase, and felt a chill overcome her despite the late summer heat.

Lee ascended. She focused her gaze on the top of the staircase, which ended at another balcony and door. There were no railings, and she feared vertigo if she looked down. The cold grew stronger the higher she climbed. She felt an invisible weight pressing on her chest. What was she doing here? She was no match for Vasquez. If his crown still existed, she'd never lay eyes on it. She should get out of here, now. It would be simple enough: open a portal and escape to Charles's bunker. Tell him the crown was lost forever. But why even bother with that much?

His vanity project was doomed to fail. The only thing in the cosmos that was eternal was death...

She shook her head. What had come over her? It had to be this place. Vasquez, or maybe the castle itself, was trying to break her. Lee ground her teeth and hurried up the last few steps. The landing was dominated by a great doorway, the top carved in the shape of a human skull. She took a deep breath and entered.

15

Silas Flint and Ricardo Navarro climbed onto the brick walkway above the canal, each holding a flashlight and pistol. The tunnel was silent save for the sloshing of blood below. Flint's instincts warned him of danger everywhere, and he moved as quickly as stealth would allow. Then again, the denizens of this nightmare could no doubt sense them whatever precautions they took.

"Boss," Navarro whispered.

"Yes?"

"What do you think is going on with the Sisters?"

Flint said nothing. The Proctors had said they could only render them indirect assistance. They had sounded genuinely worried about approaching Castle Vasquez themselves. And yet they had just shown them their escape route and even opened the grate for them.

"It is a mystery, to be sure," he replied. "And it is doubtful they would provide us with a direct answer, in any case."

The two men fell silent as they moved. Flint knew

they had to be beneath the castle but was otherwise in the dark, literally and figuratively. He shone his flashlight down into the canal. The blood was flowing back the way they came. Perhaps if they continued straight, they could find its source, and with it a way up into the castle proper. He scowled as he pondered what could produce such a steady flow of blood in such a volume.

Behind him, Navarro scanned for threats in every direction. Ahead, they saw a tunnel branch off to their right.

"What you thinking?" Navarro asked.

"For now, we shall follow the... current and trace it to its source," Flint said.

As they passed the tunnel entrance, they heard skittering from inside. They stopped, shone their flashlights down the tunnel, but the darkness swallowed their meager glow. Navarro swallowed.

"Steady, Ricardo," Flint said. "This is not the first time you and I have had to spelunk the underground depths of some fiend's lair."

"Yeah," Navarro said, "But we never went up against anyone like Vasquez before."

"General Oglethorpe defeated the villain, alone, when Vasquez was at the peak of his power. He is but a shadow of his former self. Be he shade or undead, he will be no match for the two of us, for God is on our side."

Navarro's mouth fell open. He started to say something, stopped, and then chuckled.

"Does something amuse you?" Flint asked as they left the tunnel behind them. He felt the air grow colder, but the stench of blood and decay still rankled his nostrils.

"I been with you five years boss, and I still don't know how you do it sometimes."

"Whatever do you mean?"

"I mean the other Supernumeraries at the Fort wonder if you're even human. Shit, even the other Witch Hunters think you're... I don't know, hardcore?"

Flint snorted. "I assure you that I am all too human. For example, presently I feel..."

They heard something stir up ahead. The blood rippled like someone had thrown a stone into a pond. The two men stopped, keeping the end of the tunnel covered, bracing their pistols on their flashlights. Flint risked looking at his partner, using body language to indicate something – or someone – lay ahead. Navarro nodded. He holstered his pistol, hooked the flashlight on his belt, and unslung his rifle. Flint hated to lose half of their light, but they may need additional firepower for whatever lay ahead. They resumed their creeping pace. Flint heard dripping all around him. Something spattered onto his nose. He wasn't surprised to wipe his face and see blood come away.

Something churned in the blood which roiled and bubbled up ahead. The walkway curved to their right. They emerged into a circular chamber with a great pool of blood. Flint felt the hairs on the back of his neck stand up. Whatever it was they heard earlier, it was in here. Navarro raised his rifle, keeping it trained on the center of the pool. Flint scanned the chamber. He spied a door in the center of the walkway on the opposite side. They'd have to walk around the pool to reach it. Flint glanced at Navarro and nodded toward the door. Navarro nodded back in acknowledgement.

The two companions crept forward, hugging the wall. Flint's flashlight cast long shadows along the moldering brick. Out of the corner of his eye, he noticed carvings along the wall, runes from a language he did not recognize. When they reached the halfway point, he saw a carving that depicted some sort of creature. Squinting at it, Flint thought it resembled a giant hound with the wings of a bird. A sense of déjà vu overcame him. He'd seen that creature before, somewhere.

The chamber shook. Flint and Navarro steadied themselves against the wall. Like the walkway they'd traversed to arrive here, there were no guard rails surrounding the pool of blood. Flint heard bubbling, like a pot of water brought to a rolling boil. His eyes widened when he saw that it was coming from the blood pool. Together, he and Navarro aimed their weapons at the center while continuing their walk to the door. If some monster from the abyss was hiding in the pool, Flint resolved to put it down before they made their escape.

A gargling roar filled the chamber. Before either man could say anything, something burst from the pool of blood, spattering them. Navarro recoiled in disgust while Flint focused on the creature which emerged from the murk.

A great hound hovered before them, its fur black as ink, its slavering jaws too wide with too many needle sharp teeth, with burning red eyes and two feathery black wings on its back. The epiphany struck Flint like a clap of thunder. This was the monster depicted in the wall carving, a demon he now remembered from his studies as a novice Witch Hunter. Bracing his pistol on his left wrist, Flint fired. Navarro fired his rifle, worked the bolt, fired again, almost as quickly as Flint could pull the trigger of his own gun.

The demon shook itself like a wet dog, showering the chamber with more sticky blood. The smell of copper was overwhelming. It took no notice of the bullets that pierced its shaggy hide. It focused its burning gaze on the two men. Navarro aimed and fired, the rifle round piercing one of its red eyes. It screeched, a peculiar mix of a dog's howl and an eagle's cry. It shook its head, pawing at the ruined eye socket.

"Hurry!" Flint cried.

They sprinted the remaining distance to the door in the center of the far wall. Instead of a knob, there was a rusted iron ring. Flint yanked on it. There was some give, but the door would not open. Locked.

"Shit," Navarro muttered. The demon roared behind them. In one swift motion, Navarro spun around, aimed, fired again, this time catching the beast in the throat. Its demonic cries shifted to a dry wheeze.

Flint rammed the door with his shoulder. He was rewarded with the sound of dry wood cracking, but it still did not open.

"Together!" he cried. Flint and Navarro raised their knees and kicked simultaneously. The walkway wasn't wide enough for the additional leverage a walking start would provide. He hoped this would be enough. The door flexed backward, but still didn't open.

"Look out!" Navarro shouted. On instinct, Flint dove and rolled to one side. A second later, the flying demon smashed into the wall where he'd been standing. He heard the door give way in a shower of dust and splinters. That was one problem solved, but now the demon was in their path, with Flint on one side and Navarro on the other. Worse still, Flint had dropped his flashlight in the tumble. The demon faced him, its remaining eye illuminating the gloom.

Flint drew his sword. The blessed steel lit up the chamber, and the demon winced, hesitated.

"Go back to the abyss!" Flint bellowed, taking a step forward. The hellhound growled. He got an idea. He holstered his pistol and reached into one of his long coat's inner pockets, withdrawing a crucifix. The cross emitted a white glow, like that of his sword. He saw a similar glow behind the creature. Navarro was obviously following his lead, taking out his own.

"It is not we who command you, monster! It is Christ Himself who compels you! In the name of God, begone!"

The monster whimpered like an ordinary dog. It cringed and withdrew into itself, but did not budge from its spot blocking the door. Flint pursed his lips. If they had to fight this demon from hell, so be it. The white light from his sword and crucifix grew brighter.

"Why do you torment us before the time?" the demon spoke, its voice sounding like two beasts speaking in unison.

"Return to the fiery pit with your master!" Flint shouted. "Every knee shall bend at the name of Jesus!"

As Flint continued his advance, he saw the glow from Navarro's crucifix grow brighter. The corner of Flint's mouth turned up. Navarro was a glutton, a drunkard, and no model of Christian piety, but the man had strong faith. He was within striking range now. Flint wasn't sure if his sword would be any more effective at driving off the demon than their guns; if this was truly a demon in the flesh, then they could never truly destroy it.

Quick as a viper, Flint slashed with his sword. A trail of fire followed in its wake as the demon's corrupted flesh split open. It screamed in that mix of dog and eagle again, and dove from the walkway into the pool of blood. Navarro aimed his rifle at the spot where it had submerged, but Flint raised a hand.

"I believe that we have driven it off, for now," he said.

Navarro sidestepped toward the now open doorway, keeping the pool covered. "Haven't seen one like that before," he said.

"I have seen its likeness depicted in the old manuals," Flint replied. "I believe that was the demon Glasya-Labolas. He revels in manslaughter and bloodshed."

"I'll say," Navarro said, curling his lip at the pool of blood. "Wait... shit. I remember General Oglethorpe saying that they could take physical form at will here."

"Indeed. We can destroy their unclean bodies, but demons are spirits, beyond our power to permanently slay. The best that we can hope for is to drive them off for a time."

"How you doing on ammo, boss?"

Flint dug inside his long coat pockets which clattered with the number of extra magazines. "I am well supplied," he said.

"You lose your flashlight?"

"Yes," Flint nodded. "However, from this point forward, I believe that my sword shall be more effective at lighting the way."

"Sure hope some of those kids are alright."

Flint sighed. A sense of foreboding overcame him. His instincts told him that they would be lucky to find even one survivor of the archaeological team. But they had come this far. They owed it to them, and it was their duty, to try.

"As do I, Mr. Navarro, as do I. Now, let us see where this path takes us."

***

Destiny Lee groped her way through the corridor. All was darkness and her help was to keep one hand on the icy brick wall. She'd attempted another witchfire spell, the blue flame was snuffed out as soon as it left her palm. Despite the chill, her forehead was beaded with sweat. She hadn't felt real fear since that night in her hometown, when the torch bearing mob had her cornered. That time Charles had come to her rescue. She didn't think he'd be there this time.

Lee tried to think. Every time she attempted to gather her thoughts, some noise from the darkness would startle her: dripping, skittering, clacking, or worst of all, a child's laughter. What had she been thinking? If the crown existed, she doubted that Vasquez's shade would want to hand it over. That was one of the defining characteristics of the dead: they were set in their ways for eternity.

When she took her next step forward, two balls of green fire ignited on the floor, on either side of the hallway. "Shit!" she yelped. Lee took deep breaths. She didn't know whether to laugh or cry. Vasquez had power great and terrible, but at what cost to himself? She was about to find out.

Lee pressed on. The green fire illuminated the path, at least. Every few steps, another pair of fireballs would ignite. The churches all said that humanity was never meant to wield magic, that it was unnatural and offensive to God. She'd always dismissed it as sour grapes from those who didn't have the talent. But this place... if God existed, if anything was offensive to Him, it would be here.

Her breath fogged. The hallway seemed to curve. She'd already walked further than the tower's dimensions should have allowed. Either it was another illusion spell, or Vasquez was strong enough to bend the laws of time and space. Every few steps, more green fire appeared. She heard something now. Was that chanting? She strained to listen. Lee couldn't make out the words, but she was certain it wasn't English. She went forward. The chill grew stronger, the chanting louder. No, she thought, it's definitely not English. It wasn't Latin either, which was the preferred language for the oldest and most powerful grimoires. What could...

"We call it Xiraeyk," came a male voice from behind her. She spun, her hands aglow with sorcerous lightning.

"Who the…" she said.

Before her stood a young man who looked to be in his early twenties, in a white t-shirt, blue jeans, black boots, and a red cap. No. This wasn't a young man. This was a devil in disguise.

The young man snickered. "Very good young lady. I was right about you."

Lee squared her shoulders. Vasquez scared the shit out of her, but she knew how to handle demons. "I take it you're the familiar."

The young man smiled, nodded. "Indeed. Robin Redcap is my name."

Lee raised an eyebrow.

Robin laughed. "If you think knowing my name will give you power over me, then go ahead. Try. See what happens."

Lee scowled. "What do you want, demon?"

"My friend Arturo Vasquez asked me to entertain you for a few minutes. He's… ah… not quite dressed yet."

"Dressed? What does a dead man need with…"

Her question was cut off by a distant scream. She shivered. That scream was filled with pain and despair the likes of which she'd never heard before, not even when Charles laid waste to her home town.

"You'll see what I mean in a short while," Robin said with a smile that didn't reach his eyes.

"Robin Redcap…" Lee muttered. "I've been studying

demons most of my life. I don't recall running across that name before."

"I never had much reason to enter this world before, not until Simon Magus returned to bring you creatures the gift of magic. Since then, I've only responded to the summons of a select few. One of whom is Lilith Harkmoore. You've met her, haven't you? She goes by Lilian Turner now."

Lee's nostrils flared. Yes, she had met Turner when she visited Charles at his bunker before this mission began. According to Charles, she was over five hundred years old, had seen the twenty-first century Occult War – and Simon Magus himself – with her own eyes.

"But Arturo... ah..." Robin closed his eyes and shuddered with pleasure. It made Lee's stomach churn. "Arturo is only the second human whom I've worked for as a familiar in the last thousand years or so. Which reminds me, I should check on Lord William some time. Although... I doubt that Hermitage Castle is as durable as Castle Vasquez."

Those names meant nothing to Lee. She looked over her shoulder. The chanting continued. A gust of icy wind blew through the corridor, making her shiver. Robin stood still, smiling.

"That was a mean trick you played on poor Bifrons, by the way," Robin said, clucking his tongue.

Lee shrugged. "If he wasn't strong enough to resist me, he gets what he deserves."

"Spoken like a true disciple of Hell. Have you considered forsaking Charles's so-called empire, and joining with us?

After all..." Robin grinned, showing off fangs. "Your kind always end up joining us, one way or another."

Lee frowned. "Vasquez hasn't."

"Vasquez is in a league of his own, child. Beyond Charles Flint, and certainly beyond you."

Thanks to the Crown, she thought.

"Yes... the Warlock's Crown," Robin nodded. Lee chided herself; of course he would be able to read her thoughts.

"Bifrons told me that Vasquez hid it in a place that was hidden even from Hell's gaze," she said out loud.

Robin nodded again.

"How is that possible?" Lee asked. "Aren't you pure spirit? What could be outside of your vision?"

"That may be something you should ask Arturo yourself."

Lee thought for a moment. In for a penny, in for a pound. "Would he consider giving it up?"

"Why would he want to do that?"

"Why wouldn't he? He's dead. He doesn't have a body anymore. Why would he need something that protects its wearer from the physical costs of magic?"

Robin threw back his head and laughed. Wiping his eyes, he said, "You're half-right."

She furrowed her brow.

Robin cocked his head. "Ah. Arturo will see you now. I will offer you this advice: he was and is a man of appetites so gross and depraved, that he has earned the favor of Hell. For the moment, his appetites are... appeased. He's willing to hear you out. But tread carefully. Even if you state your case well, he may decide to bisect you for his amusement."

Robin was enveloped by a ball of green fire which vanished a second later, taking the demon with it, leaving only a faint whiff of brimstone. Lee blinked, swallowed. She turned and faced the corridor again. The chanting had quieted but was still there. She went forward. Along her way she passed an oil painting. It was a portrait of a man, with mocha skin, black hair slicked back over his skull, a neatly trimmed black goatee surrounding his mouth. He wore black armor with a blood red cape held in place by two clasps in the shape of human skulls. His face looked chiseled from marble. Lee thought he would have looked handsome were it not for his expression of disdain. That had to be Vasquez as he appeared in life.

She kept walking until the hallway ended at a door. She took a deep breath. The green witchfire had continued to appear every few steps, casting the hallway in its unnatural light. She stepped forward through the door, gasped in terror, frantically caught herself on the doorframe. There was an emptiness past the door, an inky void with white spots of light. It was as though it opened into the night sky itself, into... what did the science books call it... outer space?

A man's laughter came from the void, such that it made Lee shudder.

"It's quite all right, Destiny," said the male voice. "I've been expecting you. You may enter. You will not be harmed. At least not by the void."

She hesitated.

"A demonstration, perhaps?" the voice asked. She heard something hit the floor. It rolled toward her. It sounded hollow, like an empty coconut. It rolled to the edge of the doorway and into the light. A sharp intake of breath. It was the head of Carlos Ramirez. His face was frozen in a rictus of pain and terror. The top of his skull was gone. His brain had been scooped out. Lee had seen much death and destruction in her short life, but this...

"Come forth, little witch. Come to me. We have things to discuss, you and I."

16

Lady Diana McFarlane and Zelda Fletcher stepped down from the carriage and onto the street. Redmond was a college town, and they'd seen numerous taverns along the way with drunken revelers on the patios, enveloped in noxious clouds of tobacco smoke. After a brief stop at the University – the faculty and students had gone home for the day – they'd acquired Professor Meyer's home address and were now ready to make a house call.

Fletcher looked down the street. Another tavern was at the end of the block. It was faint, but the music from inside made it all the way to where they were standing. She licked her lips and McFarlane smirked.

"Feeling thirsty?" she asked.

Fletcher laughed. "Now that you mention it, I could use a drink, yeah."

"I know precisely how you feel. But work before pleasure."

Before them stood the Professor's house. It was a plain, grey, two story affair, with an immaculate lawn and a knee high white picket fence separating the yard from the sidewalk. A light flickered from one of the upstairs windows. Probably an office or a personal library, Fletcher thought.

"So... uh... how do we do this?" she asked.

"We have no evidence incriminating Professor Meyer in anything untoward," McFarlane replied. "For now, we'll take the diplomatic approach. But..." She pursed her lips. Fletcher looked at her.

"But?"

"I'm not sure," McFarlane said. "My instincts tell me to question this one carefully. Do you sense anything?"

Fletcher closed her eyes, reached out with her mind. Her brow furrowed. She could not sense anyone in the house. What was that saying? The lights are on but nobody's home.

She opened her eyes and said, "I got nothing."

McFarlane looked up. Following her gaze, Fletcher saw the curtains in the upstairs window part a little. A silhouette peeked out, and the curtains closed.

"Zelda?"

"Weird," she said. "I don't get anything from whoever that is. If that's the Professor, he's a lot better disciplined than most. The only other people I can't get a bead on are you guys. Templars."

"Curious..." McFarlane said to herself. "Well, let's go meet this well disciplined Professor of ours."

The two women opened the gate, strode up the pathway to Meyer's front door. McFarlane rapped on the door. "Professor Zachariah Meyer," she called.

No response.

"Maybe he saw your hat and got nervous," Fletcher said.

This time McFarlane used her fist to pound on the door. "Professor Zachariah Meyer! I am a Lady Templar of the Order of Saint Benedict! I command you to open this door at once!"

Still nothing.

McFarlane pounded on the door again. "I know that someone is in there! Open the door, I say!"

Nothing.

"Time for plan B?" Fletcher asked.

McFarlane took a step back, preparing to kick the door in, when they heard a series of clicks and clacks from the other side. The door opened a crack, held in place by a chain. A middle aged man peered through the opening. Fletcher could see he was balding, with reading glasses perched on his nose.

"What is the meaning of this? Have you any idea what time it is?" the man – presumably Professor Meyer – asked.

"Didn't you hear us?" Fletcher asked.

"I am quite engrossed in my research," Meyer snapped. "I'll have you know that..."

"Yes, Professor, I'm sure that it's vital to the survival of the Empire," McFarlane interrupted. "My assistant and I would like to question you about..."

"My office hours are three to five p.m. on Tuesdays and

Thursdays," Meyer said. "Your silly questions can wait until then. Good night to you." He shut the door. They heard the locks and deadbolts engage. The two women looked at each other.

"So much for the diplomatic approach," Fletcher chuckled. "How you want to play it now?"

McFarlane frowned. "Miss Fletcher, I do not believe I have the strength to force open this door. You are authorized to clear the way."

Fletcher grinned. She had to give McFarlane credit: in the short time they'd been together, she'd proven open minded about Fletcher's magical powers, and didn't grumble about it nearly as much as Silas. Fletcher willed the power to manifest on the palms of her hands. Fire? No, it wouldn't do to burn the man's house down, even if he was an asshole. Lightning? It might cause a power surge and fry everything on the block. Ice it was.

Fletcher drew in the ambient moisture in the air, willed it to sub-zero temperature. A ball of ice formed between her hands as she gestured, like molding a jar from clay. She moved her hands apart and the ice stretched, elongated to form sharp points on either end. Fletcher levitated the spike above her head, thrust her arm like she was hurling a javelin, and the giant icicle zipped forward, smashing into the front door.

The icicle shattered into a thousand shards. The air rippled around the door and Fletcher felt an invisible force push back against her mind.

"Zelda...?" McFarlane asked.

"Magic…" Fletcher replied. "This guy's got a magic barrier!"

"Stand aside," McFarlane growled. She drew her sword, and sure enough, it was shining bright in the evening gloom. At once, the magical barrier surrounding Meyer's house appeared. It whined and buzzed as McFarlane brought the blade down upon it. Bolts of energy crackled all around them as the sword absorbed the dark magic. It pushed McFarlane back. She ground her teeth and dug in her heels. Fletcher could only watch; her own magic would only be dissipated by McFarlane's sword.

With a sound like shattering glass, the shield disappeared in an explosion of sparks. McFarlane pointed her sword at the door. Nodding, Fletcher decided to forego the elements, and yanked the door from its frame with pure psychokinetic force.

"Zachariah Meyer!" McFarlane cried. "In the name of God, I command thee to come forth and account for your actions!"

There was no response – Fletcher doubted that even McFarlane expected one – and the two women crept through the shattered doorframe. Now that the shield was gone, Fletcher could sense magic all around them. Whoever this guy was, he was deep in it. The power was emanating from upstairs.

"Let's go," Fletcher said, taking the lead, McFarlane close on her heels. She often wondered if she'd have been of any use to the Order if she didn't have the talent for magic. It might have been a long time before anyone suspected Professor Meyer of witchcraft if she hadn't discovered the magical shield protecting his property. Oh well. Like Silas said, some things you just have to leave up to God.

They charged up the stairs. At the top was a hallway with doors on either side. One door to their left was ajar, flickering yellow light from within spilling out into the otherwise dark household. A second later, the lamplight shifted to the telltale blue of witchfire. They heard Meyer whispering but couldn't make out the words. McFarlane brushed past her, sword and pistol at the ready. Fletcher drew her own sidearm and followed. She smirked. Sometimes a good old-fashioned bullet was more effective at stopping a magician than spellcraft.

McFarlane and Fletcher reached the doorway. They saw Meyer levitating above the floor, streams of fire encircling his arms. The room was both an office and library as Fletcher had surmised. Meyer took no notice of them, appearing entranced by whatever spell he was preparing. Fletcher's mouth fell open. Looking to McFarlane, she saw that her partner had come to a similar realization: Meyer was preparing to torch the room and all the books and papers in it.

Together, the two women fired their pistols. One bullet caught Meyer in the chest, the other in his stomach. The wizard fell to the floor with a groan. Blood pooled beneath him, but after a few moments, the pool stopped expanding. With a snarl, he raised the palm of his hand. A stream of fire burst forth. McFarlane parried with her sword, the fire drawn to it, burning out before it could touch the two women. Meyer's eyes darted toward a bookshelf.

"Zachariah Meyer, you cannot hope to stand against the children of God!" McFarlane shouted. "Stand down and... oof!"

"What the... ow!" Fletcher cried. A heavy leather bound book had flown from the shelf and smacked into the side of her head. She heard McFarlane grunt in pain again, and assumed the same thing was happening to her. Soon the library was filled with flying books, flapping like bats. Every time they tried to raise their pistols, a book slammed into their wrists, spoiling their aim. Through the maelstrom, Fletcher thought she saw Meyer wearing a manic grin.

"Zelda!" McFarlane shouted. "Stop him!"

Shielding her eyes, Fletcher saw that Meyer had levitated himself off the floor, the bloody bullet holes in his torso knitting shut before her eyes. Once he was fully healed, he'd no doubt try that fire spell again. Fletcher turned her gaze toward the heavy wooden chair before Meyer's desk. She grasped it in her mind and willed it to fly toward the wizard. The chair obeyed and crashed into Meyer's side.

"Argh!" he cried. "Damn you, you bitch!"

The books stopped in midair, which gave McFarlane the chance she needed. Striding forth, she reversed her grip on her pistol and smacked the butt across Meyer's jaw. Blood sprayed from his mouth as he fell to the floor again. A second later, the books all crashed to the floor as well.

"Zachariah Meyer!" McFarlane snarled, holding the tip of her sword at his throat. "I charge you with witchcraft! In the name of the Knights Templar of the Order of Saint Benedict, I place you under arrest! You will be remanded to the custody of the Inquisition where you will be put to the question!"

Meyer raised his hands in what appeared to be surrender. His mouth moved but neither woman could hear the words.

"If you think to strike us with your foul sorcery, you will find that this blade is imbued with the power of the Almighty. Your wicked powers cannot harm us," McFarlane said. "Surrender, and it will go easier for you. Or you will die here. The choice is yours, wizard."

Meyer continued to mouth words that neither woman could hear. Fletcher leaned in closer to him. McFarlane was right. If he tried to zap them, the sword would absorb the blast. What was he...? Her eyes widened. She recognized the spell he was reciting. It was beyond her ability, but she realized what was about to happen.

"Diana..." she said.

Meyer smiled, his teeth stained with blood. A ring of fire appeared, encircling the fallen wizard. The space within the ring turned black, and Meyer fell out of sight.

"What in God's name..." McFarlane started.

"It's a portal!" Fletcher said.

The fiery ring flickered.

"Can you keep it open?" McFarlane asked.

Fletcher reached out. It was fighting her, attempting to close.

"I... not for long," Fletcher said, through gritted teeth. Sweat broke out on her forehead.

"That heretic will not escape us so easily," McFarlane growled. She holstered her pistol. Before Fletcher could react, McFarlane wrapped an arm around her waist, and together they leapt into the portal after their quarry.

***

Silas Flint and Ricardo Navarro climbed what felt like an endless staircase. The door which the demon Glasya-Labolas had guarded revealed a short hallway which ended at the foot of some brick stairs. The two men silently began their ascent. The higher they rose, the more Flint sensed the wall to their left receding from them. His sword illuminated moldy bricks to their right, which they used as a guide, but to their left was a seemingly endless chasm.

Navarro reached down and picked up a piece of brick that had broken off from the stairs long ago. Winding up, he hurled it away from the staircase and into the darkness. They waited for five seconds. Ten. Twenty. They did not hear the brick hit the floor below nor the wall beyond. If the wall was still there.

"Papa would not approve of this architecture," Navarro said with a nervous laugh.

"God Himself would not approve," Flint replied. He ached all over. Their flight from the undead outside, their battle with the demon dog, these interminable stairs... Flint recalled his conversation with Navarro earlier. Yes, he was all too human, and he felt it in his bones right now. But their sacred duty required that they see this rescue mission through, whether they could save any of the college students or not.

He could hear Navarro wheezing behind him. Flint

sympathized; if he were alone, he might be doing the same. But part of his vocation was setting an example to others, and he drove through his fatigue.

"How much further does this damn thing go?" Navarro asked.

"I suspect we may be caught in some illusion," Flint said. "It is not possible for the stairs to go on this long, and..."

They heard a wet smack in the distance which echoed throughout the cavernous chamber. The two men looked at each other, out into the void, at each other again.

"I see why your talents are so valued among Fort Marsing's baseball teams," Flint said.

Navarro snorted. "I'm good sir, but I'm not that good."

They heard a deep rumbling in the darkness. The stairway shook, and they steadied themselves on the wall. They heard pebbles and dust raining down.

"Sir..." Navarro said.

Flint spared a glance at his assistant and saw the man frozen in panic, staring out into the void. A giant red eye had appeared. It was easily twice the size of a railroad car. And its malevolent gaze was focused on them.

"Oh dear," Flint said.

A roar filled the chamber. Flint and Navarro fell to their knees, hands over their ears. Flint couldn't think; the only thought in his head was to block out that noise before his ear drums ruptured. He looked up and saw an enormous scaly fist bearing down on him.

Navarro leapt to his feet, grabbed Flint by the collar of his long coat, and yanked him out of the way just in time. The fist smashed through the wall below them. The bricks exploded into the darkness. There was nothing on the other side.

Regaining his senses, Flint rose and shouted, "Run!"

The two companions sprinted up the stairs. They ran and ran, but that colossal eye stayed with them. It was as though they were running in place. The scaly fist swung down behind them, smashing the stairs. Retreat was no longer possible. They could only go up.

That ear splitting roar assaulted their ears again, and again they fell to their knees. Flint ground his teeth, tried to stifle the cry of pain that threatened to erupt from his throat. He retained the presence of mind to see the fist come down on the stairs above them. They gave way, the bricks tumbling down into the darkness and out of sight.

Navarro looked up, saw their predicament. They now stood atop a lonely column, alone in the dark with whatever grotesque titan that was hidden by shadow. He nodded to Flint, who nodded back.

His ears still ringing, Flint drew one of his pistols. "Come forth, ye abomination!" Flint shouted. His own words sounded distant and tinny to him.

"We're not going down without a fight!" Navarro snarled.

All was silent. They looked all around them but saw no sign of whatever monster was hiding from them. Flint made a slow turn around their island, holding his sword aloft. It shone brightly, but it wasn't enough to pierce the darkness.

Then they heard it. Quiet at first, it grew louder. A

chuckle, the tone so low that they felt it rumble in their chests.

"Die," came an unearthly voice from all around them. Flint cocked the hammer on his pistol, Navarro topped off the rounds in his rifle.

Into thy hands, O Lord, I commend my spirit, Flint thought.

The red eye appeared. It grew larger until it nearly filled their field of vision. Flint could make out black scales surrounding it. He aimed his pistol at its pupil.

A bright light shone down from above. The eye closed and its owner reared back, grunting in pain.

"This way!" they heard a female voice.

"What the..." Navarro said.

Flint looked up and it took all of his self-control not to let his mouth fall agape. A panel of light had appeared in midair above them. Reaching down from the other side were none other than the Proctors. Gone was their customary detachment. For the first time since he had met them, they looked terrified.

"Move, Ricardo! Move!" Flint shouted. They sprinted up the remaining few stairs that were left before they ended at the void.

"Jump!" the Sisters yelled in unison.

Out of the corner of his eye, Flint saw that scaly fist again, headed toward the column on which they stood. Together, Flint and Navarro jumped. Mallory Procter grabbed Flint by the wrist, Monica took Navarro's. The witches yanked them up through the panel just as they heard the smashing of bricks below them. Flint and Navarro flew and crashed to the floor. They heard a crack of thunder. Looking up, they saw that the panel was gone. They were lying on polished marble.

Navarro got up first, helped Flint to his feet. They were in what looked like a foyer. On one end of the room was a pair of sturdy wooden doors. Twin staircases, lined with blood red carpet, rose to the mezzanine above them, where Flint could see more doors. The room was lit with torches burning with green fire.

"Well," Navarro said, "I guess that's one way to get past the front door."

Flint spied the Sisters standing a few feet away. They huddled together, their eyes darting to every corner of the foyer. Yes, something definitely had them frightened. Or someone.

"I... thank you, for your assistance," Flint said.

"Yeah, seriously," Navarro said. "But... I thought you girls said you couldn't help us directly."

Mallory cleared her throat, stood up straight. After a beat, her sisters followed suit.

"Yes... well..." she said.

"Circumstances have..." Monica said.

"Things are... different, this time," Madeline said.

"You mean you're actually gonna get your hands dirty?" Navarro said.

"I..."

"We..."

"You see..."

Flint couldn't help but smirk. "You seldom provide us with simple answers. Again, Mr. Navarro and I are grateful to you for saving our lives. I..." He sighed, rolled his eyes.

"I can scarce believe my own words, but I would welcome any further assistance you wish to provide. If you are unable or unwilling, then well enough. You have given us the opportunity to continue our mission. I pray that my assistant and I are able to repay you in kind at some later date."

The Proctors said nothing. Flint squinted. Was that color he saw in their normally porcelain cheeks?

"You are welcome, Silas," Mallory said.

"We are testing the limits of our roles in these events," Monica said.

"We are not sure if we will face judgment," Madeline said.

"As long as you're here," Navarro said, "Do you know if any of the college kids are still alive?"

The Sisters nodded.

"Some still live."

"Vasquez and his cohorts focus their attention elsewhere for the moment."

"That is one reason why we have risked appearing now."

"Can you point us in the right direction?" Navarro asked.

Together, the sisters pointed to their right, down the hallway that extended beneath the staircase.

Flint nodded. "Thank you." He checked both of his pistols. He knew they were both fully loaded, but the ritual helped to calm his mind. "Mr. Navarro, let us proceed. Never have I so eagerly wished to close a case."

Together, they made their way past the stairs, underneath the balcony, and down the hallway. He assumed that the Proctors would vanish back to where they came, but he was startled when he heard them call out behind them, "Please stay alive Silas, Ricardo."

The two men stopped, looked behind them. They were gone.

"You know," Navarro said, "I got a bad feeling sir."

"Oh?"

"Shit's got to be serious if they're getting involved like this."

Flint snorted. "I concur. I never would have expected them to directly intervene, and yet I daresay we owe our lives to them."

"If I didn't know better sir, I'd call it a miracle."

"Let us not get carried away, Mr. Navarro."

17

Destiny Lee strode forth into Vasquez's inner sanctum. As the necromancer had promised, her feet hit what felt like a stone floor despite it appearing as though she had stepped into the night sky. Pinpoints of light surrounded her like stars and the chamber was freezing. Her breath fogged as she went forward, her boots tapping on stone that she couldn't see. Her mind told her it had to be an illusion spell, but it didn't help her sense of vertigo.

"That's far enough," came Vasquez's voice.

She stopped and looked around. Nothing but what appeared to the blackness of the night sky.

"Beautiful, isn't it?" Vasquez asked. "Centuries ago,

before the Occult War, humanity dreamed of journeying the depths of space beyond this planet. They thought to find other worlds, other life. But I know the truth." She heard him shudder. "There is nothing. In all the universe, our world is the only one with life. There is only the cold. Only the silence. Only the void. It is eternal. As is death."

Lee swallowed. Despite the chill, she could feel a bead of sweat trace down her back. The pinpoints of light vanished, plunging the chamber into absolute darkness.

"Man's dream of exploring the stars died with the Occult War. But now there are new depths to plunge. A different kind of darkness to embrace."

Lee said nothing.

"You'll find out some day," Vasquez said. "I sense that you wish to see. I will grant you this kindness, although you may not think it a kindness."

A dim light rose, illuminating the room. Lee managed to keep her composure, but her eyes widened. A sharp intake of breath.

The floor of the room was dominated by a great mosaic: a circular painting of a black armored figure – Vasquez? – overseeing a burning field, corpses impaled on stakes, devils feasting on human entrails, skeletons wielding spears and torches attacking a village. On either side, she saw dozens of shadows, all with burning red eyes, some purring, some growling, some giggling. She heard their saliva drip on the floor with a sizzle and a stink of sulfur.

Before her, beyond the edge of the mosaic, three stone steps led up to an altar. Upon it was a headless body, its chest cut down the middle, its ribcage split open. She assumed it was poor Carlos. On the other side of the altar, another series of steps led up to a black throne. A figure sat in the throne, but she couldn't make out its features which were obscured by shadow. It stirred and two balls of green fire appeared where its eyes should be.

"Welcome, Destiny," the figure – Vasquez – said. The fires moved, and she realized he must be looking down at the altar. "Was this one a friend of yours?"

"N... no. No," she said. Lee struggled to control herself. It had been a long time since she'd feared for her life. She sensed that more than just her life was at stake. "He... he was an agent of my Emperor, just as I am, but we never met."

Vasquez tittered. "Emperor Charles, isn't?"

"Yes. Sir. Yes sir." She glanced at the horde of demons on her right. She knew she could handle two or three at a time at most, but this... mob. She'd never imagined any magician capable of commanding so many at once.

"My companions and I saw his image appear in the sky, heard him proclaim the birth of his empire of magicians."

"May I ask what you thought, sir?"

Vasquez chuckled. "I admit that you have impressed me with your composure, Destiny. You hide your terror well."

Lee said nothing.

"Robin Redcap has told me something of your Charles and his companion Lilith. Did you know that she was born before the Occult War?"

She nodded.

"Which tells me that she lived when I walked the earth

as a mortal man, and yet she did not come to my aid during my war with the Templars."

"I don't know anything about that, sir. I've only met her in passing."

"No matter. Few magicians have the stomach to follow me this far down the path. And that leads into why you are here. You seek my crown."

Lee swallowed. "Yes sir."

"Why?"

Before Lee could answer, Vasquez barked a laugh. The demons inside his hall laughed with him. Despite her fear, she felt a flash of anger at their derision.

"Poor Destiny," Vasquez said. "You thought to find it hidden away in some secret vault that everyone else missed. You never expected to find me instead."

She hesitated for a few moments before replying, "No sir. I didn't. I don't think anyone would have."

Vasquez chuckled. "In truth, my return is a surprise even to me. By my calculations, I had another fifty or sixty years to wait." He growled. "My spirit was too weak when I last had visitors. I could do nothing but watch as those ignorant children meandered through my hallways, thinking they could even begin to capture the magnitude of my achievements.

"But then," he went on, "I saw your Charles appear in the sky. He's playing with old magic, not seen since Simon Magus himself walked the earth. Tell me, where did one so young acquire such power?"

Lee cleared her throat. "Some time ago, he recovered a copy of *In Realis Magicae*."

"Did he now? I wonder... I once owned a copy myself, you see. The Templars burned all my possessions after I died, but I have found that that book has a life of its own." He laughed. "If it's my copy that he's using... oh, the delicious irony. In any case, by that time I had recovered enough of my strength to fully manifest in spirit. And then this boy," he said, waving a bony hand toward the altar, "...and his little friends came to my doorstep. What's more, he was a fellow magician! He provided that last ingredient for me to return ahead of schedule."

Vasquez rose from the throne. He levitated, floating down to the floor a few feet away from Lee, but she still couldn't make out his features, hidden as they were by shadow.

"It's not everything that I hoped it would be," he said. "I suppose that's what I get for rushing the regeneration process. In another few decades, I'd have regained my handsome features, which I believe you were admiring earlier."

Lee cleared her throat, looked down.

"There is a problem, however," Vasquez said.

"What's that sir?"

"A Witch Hunter and his little assistant have once again violated the sanctity of my home."

Lee nodded. "Yes. I sensed them earlier."

Vasquez fell silent. It was difficult to see him, but Lee thought that he was shaking.

"The Templars," he spat. "It was they who ruined my great project. It was they who interrupted my ascension."

Lee didn't know what he referred to but thought it best to keep quiet for now.

"If it weren't for them, I would be a god. A god of death." He hissed. "I have waited long enough. I will not allow them to set me back again. I..." He stopped. Cocked his head. "What..."

"Is there a problem sir?"

"I sense... others... they... no... no!"

An unseen force blew Lee off her feet. She rolled with the impact on the floor, but still had the wind knocked from her. In the commotion, she heard the demons surrounding them whimper. Some vanished at Vasquez's outburst, others were knocked to the ground as she was. The light in the room grew brighter, the magical darkness vanishing. She looked around and wished that she hadn't.

Hanging from the ceiling were a series of giant chains. They ended in serrated hooks. Hanging on each one was a bloody corpse, no doubt members of the archaeological team, each one in varying state of desecration. Runes in a language she didn't recognize were carved on the stone walls. Her eyes fell on Vasquez, and she groaned in despair.

"What's wrong, Destiny?" he snarled. "Don't you like this face?"

Lee thought of herself as a strong and independent woman. She feared no man and had risen to her position through her determination and iron will. But Vasquez, this hideous monstrosity that he'd become... she wanted to curl up in the fetal position and sob like a girl.

"Get up," Vasquez growled. "You want my crown? Join with me now, and I will consider your request."

Lee took a deep breath. Remembered who she was. She climbed to her feet. She could do this. She believed in herself. But God... that creature...

"I'll... I'll assist you in any way that I can. Sir," she said, averting her eyes from Vasquez. "What... what would have you have me do?"

"You have a talent for working with our friends below," Vasquez said. "Deal with the Witch Hunter."

She nodded. "And you sir?"

He growled like a lion. "If they think to interfere... I'll make them regret taking their side... I'll make those three regret the day they were born," he said, more to himself than to her. The green fires in his eye sockets focused on her. "Go."

Lee sprinted from him as fast as her legs would carry her.

***

Diana McFarlane and Zelda Fletcher tumbled through the void, cold winds buffeting them from every direction. McFarlane hung onto her sword which shone brightly, a single candle in an endless tide of darkness. Fletcher had never been inside a magical portal before. She'd heard of them, of course; a magician could use them to instantly travel anywhere they had visited before even if it lay thousands of miles away. But she'd always thought it was like stepping through a doorway. Fletcher had never anticipated that there was... an in-between place.

Fletcher imagined herself in her mind's eye, willed herself to be still. It slowed her momentum enough for her to gain her bearings. She flew toward McFarlane who was still in freefall. Fletcher wrapped her arms around McFarlane's waist. The Witch Hunter looked like she was about to vomit but maintained her composure. She silently pointed with her sword.

It was difficult to see anything, but Fletcher saw it now: Meyer was a short distance away, flying through the darkness. Fletcher, with McFarlane in tow, flew after him.

Meyer glanced over his shoulder and his eyes widened. He picked up speed and increased the distance between them. Fletcher pushed herself harder, but McFarlane's weight still slowed them down. She saw a circle of light appear before Meyer. Fletcher ground her teeth. The bastard was about to escape to God knew where.

Meyer disappeared through the hole. Fletcher strained to get a magical grasp on the portal. It flickered in the dark. Her head felt like it was about to burst. The glow of McFarlane's sword grew brighter still. Fletcher glanced down, and she gasped. There were creatures here. Below them the... ground?... was writhing with movement. She heard McFarlane groan. Looking to her left, her vision was filled with a colossal eye.

Fletcher didn't believe she had it in her, but she added a burst of speed to their headlong flight, and they passed through the portal. She heard it shut behind them with a zipping sound. Then they hit what felt like cobblestone.

The two women rolled with the impact, Fletcher hearing McFarlane's sword clatter to the ground. There was something else... gasps, screams, panicked murmuring.

Groaning, she looked up. They were in a city street, but she didn't recognize the place. A crowd had gathered around them, pointing and gawking.

McFarlane, looking green around the gills, picked up her hat from where it had fallen and put it back on. She staggered. Fletcher climbed to her feet and rushed to her partner's aid, but McFarlane held up her hand, waving her off. She pulled her long coat tighter, adjusted her blouse, and faced the crowd.

"I am Lady Diana McFarlane of the Knights Templar of the Order of Saint Benedict," she said, raising her voice so all could hear her. "My assistant and I are in pursuit of a known heretic who attempted to escape through that... blasphemous wound in God's creation. Did any of you see a man emerge from that hole before us?"

"Yeah!" cried a few voices near the front of the crowd.

"That man is a wizard and a traitor!" McFarlane shouted. "He may try to escape this city on foot. Notify your police!"

"Which way was he headed?" Fletcher asked.

"East on ninth street!" a man yelled back, pointing.

"Come on," McFarlane said. The crowd dispersed, some running, some wandering back to what looked like taverns. Fletcher smirked. Wherever they were, these people were no strangers to magical happenings. Speaking of which...

"Where the hell are we?" she asked.

"Danville, I believe," McFarlane said. "I recognize the... ugh..."

She staggered again and rushed into an alleyway. Fletcher followed, and saw her partner doubled over, vomiting onto the street. She went to McFarlane's side, put a hand on her back.

"Hey... you okay?"

McFarlane coughed, wiped her mouth with the back of her sleeve. "Yes. I'll be alright now," she said. "That trip through the portal... dear God. Do magicians have to go through there every time?"

"I think so," Fletcher nodded. "I don't know how to open one myself, but I've heard stories about them. I wasn't expecting whatever that place was."

"You seem to be alright," McFarlane said, standing up straight.

"Maybe it's harder on... uh... you non-magical types. That was amazing, by the way. What you did."

McFarlane laughed. "Looks like this case is turning out to be exciting after all, eh?"

Fletcher laughed with her. "Come on, we better get after him."

They left the alleyway and returned to the street. As they headed east, McFarlane said, "What's to stop him from opening another portal?"

Fletcher thought a moment. "The only thing I can think of is it might have taken a lot out of him. Might need time to build up his strength for it again. If we're close, I'll sense it if he tries."

"Then we must run him to ground before he can make the attempt."

"He couldn't have gotten too far. He didn't have much of a head start." She looked around. "You said this place is Danville?"

"Yes. It's not much to look at, but it's close to..." She stopped. "Castle Vasquez."

"You think he's going to hide out there or something?"

"I don't know," McFarlane replied. "From what I've heard, the castle is abandoned save for whatever spirits or demons might be haunting the area. Let's go find this bastard and ask him."

They resumed their hunt. McFarlane had a few more dizzy spells but otherwise appeared recovered from experiencing the terror of the void. Fletcher felt exhilarated. This was turning out to be almost as dangerous – and fun – as one of her adventures with Silas. Maybe when this was all over, she could ask General Abernathy about being formally sworn to the Order. Right now she felt like – what was it the academics called it? An adjunct member.

A block away they heard the beat of galloping horses. Glancing to her right, Fletcher saw uniformed police officers on horseback plunging headlong down the street, in the same direction she and McFarlane were headed.

"They may have located our quarry," McFarlane said. "Hurry!"

The two women sprinted down the sidewalk. Fletcher hated running but decided against levitating herself; no reason to spook the locals more than they already had been. Ahead, she saw the wall that surrounded the city, along with its great gate. A crowd had gathered outside. As they ran closer, Fletcher saw two men dressed in black, talking to another much older man, wearing a long sleeved shirt and a flat cap. The older man looked familiar but she couldn't quite make him out yet.

They finally reached the group. With the men were women whose ages ran from early twenties to what looked like late eighties, all wearing brown religious habits. Fletcher made a note to become more familiar with the Church's myriad religious orders before asking to be sworn to the Templars. McFarlane wasn't breathing hard, but Fletcher put her hands on her knees and took deep breaths.

"Diana?" the old man asked.

"Robert!"

That was it. Fletcher recognized him now: Robert Carrow, Fort Marsing's stable master.

"What on earth are you two doing here?" Carrow asked.

"I'll explain later," McFarlane said. "Miss Fletcher and I are in pursuit of a wizard. Have any of you seen a man running by here? He is of middle age, grey hair, balding..."

"Yes," Carrow replied. "He stole a horse from the stable. The last we saw, he was headed southeast."

"Could he be on his way to Castle Vasquez?" Fletcher asked.

Carrow's face went pale. "Silas... Ricardo..." he whispered.

"What?!" Fletcher cried. "What about them?!"

"They're at Castle Vasquez right now. They're looking for an archaeological team that went missing inside. The

Fathers, the Sisters, and I were on our way there to lend them our prayers and to exorcise that accursed place."

McFarlane and Fletcher looked at each other.

"Do your carriages have room for two more, Mr. Carrow?" McFarlane asked.

He nodded.

"You there, Officer!" McFarlane waved down a cop on horseback. He urged his mount forward. When he reached the group, he nodded in greeting.

"How can I help, ma'am?" he asked.

"Does this city have a telegraph office?"

"Yes ma'am."

"I need you to wire Fort Marsing for me."

***

Professor Zachariah Meyer urged his mount to a gallop as his mind was consumed with curses and recriminations. *Damn those Templar whores*, he thought. Worse, the younger one was a witch. Why on earth would she be assisting a Witch Hunter? That magical barrier he'd erected around his home was meant to ward off the prying eyes of his fellow magicians; he never anticipated that the Witch Hunters would have one working for them. As soon as Meyer had sensed her power, he fled to his office. He'd spent years accumulating his collection of grimoires, histories, and most importantly, tomes on Vasquez and the Warlock's Crown. It pained him but he knew he'd have to burn them all before they fell into Templar hands. If they discovered his notes on the subject, his correspondences with Carlos Ramirez, Charles Flint, and others in the Cascadian government...

Ramirez. Meyer sighed. The boy had shown promise, both as an academic and as a magician. That he wasn't responding to Meyer's magical calls could only mean one of two things: he was in dire straits, or he was dead. But what could account for those developments? The castle was abandoned. The Templars reported that demons could physically manifest within its walls, but they had apparently declined to do so after the fall of Vasquez. If they were responsible for the archaeological team's demise, why now?

Meyer's horse plunged headlong through the night, its hooves a staccato beat on the cobblestone road, the moon lighting their path. Meyer knew the road would give way to a worn dirt trail before long. He whispered a spell, replenishing the horse's stamina, draining his own reserves a bit more. It was a risk; he didn't have the strength to open another portal so soon. But even if those Templar bitches took the time to telegraph Fort Marsing from Danville before pursuing him, they wouldn't be able to send another Witch Hunter to his Redmond home in time to secure his library before he returned. He smiled. Maybe he wouldn't have to burn everything after all. His cover was blown in any case. It was too bad, Meyer thought. Academia suited him. Oh well. The Empire of Medea would need its own university, where magic could be freely taught and practiced. And who better than him to serve as its first dean?

Charles had said that he was going to send someone

else to search for the Crown. A plan formed in Meyer's mind. He'd join up with this person. If they'd already found the Crown, then they could escape together, secure Meyer's library, and head out to Medea. If not, then Meyer would join the search. Before sending the team to their fate, he'd shared the clue with Ramirez. Meyer wasn't sure if it would come to anything. Professor Rogan had interviewed the Witch Hunter who slew Vasquez, Matthew Oglethorpe, for his seminal work *Castle of Horror*. According to Oglethorpe, the necromancer used the last of his strength to open a portal and hurl his crown inside. Then Vasquez said something that had puzzled scholars and magicians alike ever since: *Now it's with my heart.*

Meyer furrowed his brow. He had been a child when Vasquez fell and had been entranced by his story even before he learned that he had the talent for magic. He'd spent half a lifetime studying that chapter of Cascadian history, read every first hand account, every monograph on the war, every biography of Vasquez, but no one could decipher the man's words. He couldn't have meant it literally, as his body had been burned to ash. What could...

He shook his head. Now wasn't the best time for speculating. He had to get to Castle Vasquez, link up with Charles's lieutenant, and together they would recover the prize for their master. He pushed the horse harder.

18

Silas Flint and Ricardo Navarro crept down the hallway. On either side of them, sconces on the walls held torches that burned with green fire. Flint led the way, sword in one hand and pistol in the other. Navarro followed closely, rifle at the low ready, scanning the hallway for threats. Their path was lined with doors. The two men tried the first few, but all were locked. Flint leaned in toward one, pressing his ear against it, and heard a seemingly endless chorus of despairing wails on the other side. He'd nodded to Navarro, who kicked the door in. It opened into a burning red sky which stank of sulfur, filled with dark clouds that crackled with green lightning. Looking down from the edge of the doorway, he could not see the ground. The wails and cries were deafening but he could make out the silhouettes of humanoid forms twisting in the winds among the clouds. Flint yanked the door shut, and it locked again with a thunderclap, followed by laughter which was deep enough in timbre to be felt in their chests.

"Was that...?" Navarro asked.

"An illusion and nothing more," Flint replied.

"I don't know sir... looked pretty real to me."

The Witch Hunter was silent for a moment before saying, "Even if our eyes did not deceive us... I daresay that whatever poor souls are lost in there are beyond our help."

Navarro swallowed, looked around. The hallway stretched ever onward. Wherever it ended, it was beyond their sight. "How we going to find them?" he whispered.

Flint closed his eyes and sighed. He had no idea. Whatever sorcery had created that endless stairwell beneath the castle must have had them ensnared again. This case was hopeless. Even if the Sisters were right and some of the archaeological team survived, there was no way to find them. There was no way out of this corner of Hell. No way out. No way out. No...

Flint grunted. He took off his hat and rubbed a hand over his close cropped hair. Navarro looked him up and down.

"You okay? You look like you're coming down with something, boss," he said.

Flint put his hat back on. He checked his pocket watch. The hands were spinning too quickly, in opposite directions. His gaze fell on the picture of his family inside the lid. The corner of his mouth turned up. It felt like a window into another world. It occurred to him that this was the last time he and Charles had appeared in a photograph together. He thought of it as the last time his family was together, happy and intact, although they wouldn't break apart for another few years. The image of his parents smiling for the camera, of Charles appearing shy and withdrawn, of himself with a wide toothy grin – had he smiled like that even once since then? He couldn't recall. But seeing them always strengthened his will when it threatened to waver.

"I..." Flint said. He took a deep breath. "The atmosphere of this hellish nightmare weighs heavily upon me. I felt tempted to despair."

Navarro nodded. "I hear you, sir. Ever since we got here, I've been... I don't know, wondering what the point of it all is."

Flint raised an eyebrow. "And now?"

Navarro patted his rifle, his face set in grim determination. "Whatever happens, I'm with you to the end. We made oaths to God when we joined up, and I'm seeing it through."

The green torchlight flickered, dimmed, then rose again.

"Very good, Mr. Navarro. Even if they choose not to manifest, this fiendish redoubt is infested with the powers below. There is no doubt they will attempt to prey upon our vigor and weaken our resolve. We must hold fast to our faith above all else."

"Yeah. At this point, I'm thinking prayer might be the only chance we have of finding any..."

They heard a woman scream from somewhere further down the path, her shrill cry echoing throughout the stone halls. The worst of it, Flint thought, was they had no way of being certain that the screams they heard came from human throats, or if they were demonic imitations meant to lure them into traps, until it was too late.

Before either man could say anything, they heard a series of booms, followed by another scream, this one more animal-like. They looked at each other.

"That was..." Flint said.

"Gunfire!" Navarro finished.

"Move!"

They took off at a sprint. They heard another boom, another bestial shout. *Come Holy Spirit, fill the hearts of Thy faithful, and kindle in them the fires of courage,* Flint recited in his mind. Many ancient prayers of the Church had been altered since the Occult War, and he thought that he and

Navarro would need all of the divine assistance they could get to see them through.

Around them the walls shimmered like a reflection on the water. Flint kept up the mental prayer: *Saint Michael the Archangel, defend us in battle. Be our protection against the wickedness and snares of the devil...* Behind him, he heard Navarro murmuring even as he huffed to keep up the pace. He only caught some of the words: "Saint Benedict, pray for us."

Another boom, to their left. The two men stopped before a door, identical to the dozens of doors they'd passed already, but whatever they had heard earlier was coming from this one. Flint aimed a kick at the iron ring that served as a handle and the door crashed open. Tightening his grip on his sword and pistol, he led the way inside.

It led to a stairwell that descended down into the depths of the castle, but that wasn't the first thing they noticed. The walls and the floor were alive, writhing with cockroaches, spiders, centipedes, scorpions, maggots, and other loathsome things. Every step resulted in a wet crunch beneath their boots.

"Shit," Navarro spat. "I fucking hate spiders. I really do."

Flint sympathized but said nothing as he led his assistant down the stairs. He worried that they would be too late. He winced at the yellow slime that squirted from every step, the chittering, the squishing.

"Gah!" Navarro cried, one hand scrabbling at his collar where his body armor met his t-shirt. Flint felt the tickle of a centipede crawling up his pant leg. He bent forward at the waist and smacked the insect with the butt of his pistol, and he felt it explode in a spray of pus. Flint shivered and looked forward to a long shower after their mission was over.

Down the stairs they went, following the sound of occasional gunfire. As they proceeded, Flint thought the booms were growing louder. He could make them out more clearly now: someone was firing a shotgun. Then he heard an inhuman voice echoing below.

"You're only making this harder on yourself," it hissed. "You're the extras. Arturo was going to give you a quick death, but we will make you beg…"

Boom. Flint and Navarro reached the bottom of the stairwell. They were in another hallway, illuminated by burning green torches. On either side of them were what looked like prison cells. The walls were stained with old blood, the coppery stench burning in their nostrils. They heard a growl, as from a great cat, ahead of them, down the corridor and out of sight. They hurried, the voice growing louder.

"My children grow hungry," it said. "Do they not deserve crumbs from their master's table?"

They heard a man gag in revulsion. The corridor forked. As they ran, Flint caught glimpses of skeletons within the prison cells. Some of them moved. The voice was coming from the right. They turned the corner and stopped in their tracks.

The path was a dead end. Backed against the wall they saw young people, covered in blood and filth, but they were alive, if scared out of their wits. With them were two older men, both armed with shotguns and pistols, and one older woman who was sitting on the floor, her back against the wall. Flint counted eleven altogether. Standing before the group was a nightmarish figure. It had the body of a man wearing black armor. Its head though was that of a great lion. Its mane was in tangled knots with braids, gold rings, and other gaudy baubles tied in. Flint pointed his sword at the demon.

"Sabnock!" he shouted.

The demon turned. Its leonine muzzle was spattered with blood. It held a sword in its right hand, the blade dripping with some writhing mass. Squinting, Flint saw that worms were falling from it.

"Who dares speak my name?" the demon rumbled. It advanced toward Flint and Navarro. The green torchlight flickered as a breeze washed over them. Flint thought he heard moans of despair accompany the foul wind.

"I am Captain Silas Flint!" he replied. "You shall not harm these innocent souls, ye infernal monster! The power of God is upon you!"

"Innocent," Sabnock laughed, cold and cruel. "Be gone, little man lest you share their fate."

Navarro shouldered his rifle and fired. The bullet smacked into Sabnock's forehead. Behind him, the college students screamed and wretched as its corrupted blood spattered over them. The boom of a shotgun echoed in the enclosed space, sparks flying from the demon's armor. It roared more in fury than in pain, spraying Flint and Navarro with steaming spittle and worms. Flint fired his pistol at the demon's head as he advanced toward it. Sabnock screamed in rage, brought its sword down in a great overhead smash. Flint holstered his gun and gripped his sword with both hands in time to parry the blow. Sparks flew, the metal whined as his blessed steel contacted the blade forged in hell. The demon bore down with all its unnatural strength. Flint's knees threatened to buckle. He gritted his teeth.

Before his legs gave out, Navarro charged past him. He'd slung his rifle, now carrying his sidearm and his crucifix. He leapt, kicking out with both legs, pushing the demon away from Flint. Navarro hit the ground, sprang to his feet. Before the demon could regain its balance, Navarro ran to it again and pressed the crucifix onto its cheek. A hissing sound rose, the demon's flesh burning beneath the cross. It screeched like a cat. It blindly lashed out, its fist striking Navarro in the ribs. He flew across the chamber and smacked into the wall. Flint saw his assistant stir on the floor even as he advanced on Sabnock. He drew his pistol again, firing into the demon's face until the slide locked open on empty. The demon yowled and scratched at its face; the silver tipped rounds burning inside it. With a roar of defiance, Flint brought his own sword around, slashing across the demon's feline face. Its lower jaw fell to the floor, a flood of black ichor and worms spewing from the wound in its face. Dropping his empty pistol, Flint whipped out his own crucifix from his coat's inner pocket and pressed it against Sabnock's face.

"I know your name, Sabnock!" Flint screamed. "In the name of God, I command you to leave this place! It is not I, but Christ who compels you! Return to Pandemonium in failure! You shall not have these souls so long as we draw breath!"

The demon twisted and writhed. Its arms locked up at unnatural angles. Its figure turned black and dissolved, like ashes blowing away in the wind. As soon as it was gone, Flint rushed to Navarro's side.

"Ricardo," he said. "Are you unharmed?"

"No," his assistant coughed. Flint helped him to his feet. Navarro rubbed his side and winced. "But I'm good to go."

Flint blew out a breath he hadn't realized he'd been holding. Turning, he got a good look at the prisoners for the first time. Eight young people, three boys, five girls. They were bruised and bloodied all over. Worse, some had visible cuts and within them he could see more worms and maggots. The two older men looked to be in shock, their eyes wild and darting. The older woman had not stirred from her place on the floor. Flint holstered his pistol, sheathed his sword, and raised his empty hands. Navarro did the same.

"I am Knight Templar Captain Silas Flint," he said. "This is my assistant, Supernumerary Ricardo Navarro. We mean you no harm. We have come to liberate you from the forces of darkness."

"Knight... Templar..." one of the older men breathed. "You... you're a... Witch Hunter?"

"Yes," Flint nodded.

"How... no... it's a trick... you're one of them... it's a trick!" the other man shrieked. He started to raise his shotgun. Flint's hand rested on the butt of his pistol.

"No!" one of the girls cried. "Barry... didn't you see? They had crosses! He has one of those swords!"

The man – Barry – looked at her, looked at Flint and Navarro. He dropped his shotgun, fell to his knees, and began to cry. "Thank God... thank God..." he murmured.

The other man lowered his shotgun and shuffled his way toward Flint and Navarro. As he stepped into the light, Flint saw that he was missing an eye. Like the others, he was a mess of bruises and cuts, every open wound infested with writhing worms.

"Are you... really... real?" he whispered.

"Yes," Flint nodded. "May I ask who you are sir?"

"Don... Don Riffey..." he replied. "I am... I was... head of the... security team."

"You and Barry been fighting these monsters all by yourselves?" Navarro asked.

"Yes..." Riffey replied. "For all the good its done... the other students... they... they took them and..." Riffey fell to his knees and began to sob. "Oh God... God forgive me..."

"Do not despair Mr. Riffey," Flint said, putting a hand on Riffey's shoulder. "You and your companion have performed above and beyond the call of duty."

Flint and Navarro left Riffey to his tears as they went to inspect the other prisoners. As he'd feared, Flint saw that all were in shock, and some were in no condition to walk out of there. They gazed at him in a mix of adoration, gratitude, and mind-numbing fear. He went to the woman sitting on the floor. Her face was still hidden in her arms. Dropping to one knee, Flint asked, "Madam, may I ask who you are? Are you able to speak?"

The woman didn't reply.

"That's Professor Morales," one of the boys said, coming to Flint's side.

"What happened to her?" Navarro asked as he tended to the worst of the students' wounds. He carried a few basic first aid supplies in pouches on his belt, but Flint knew there wasn't nearly enough to help everyone here.

"We don't know," the boy replied, the side of his face caked with dried blood and scabs. "We got separated from her early on. Then that kid Robin dropped her off here and she's been sitting there ever since. Won't look up."

"Robin Redcap," Flint growled.

"What?" the boy said.

"He's another demon, one we've had run ins with before," Navarro said.

"That... that monster you fought, just now," said one of the girls. "How did you...?"

"Sabnock," Flint said, as he rose to his feet. "I recognized him from my studies. Knowledge of their true names are essential to banishing the demons of Hell, but they cannot be truly slain. All that we can do is send them away for a time."

"I guess... I guess that leads to my next question..." Barry said, wiping snot from his nose. "How the hell are we going to get out of here?"

Flint pursed his lips and looked to Navarro, who gave him a similarly pained look. Even after they left the dungeons, Castle Vasquez was still surrounded by an ocean of undead.

"We... uh... we're still working on that part," Navarro said.

"Oh Jesus, oh God..." one of the girls said, her voice breaking. "We're going to die here. I know it. We're going to fucking die..."

"Enough," Flint snapped. "All of you have survived thus far through the grace of God. He shall not abandon us now."

"Where was God when those... things took the others?" a boy snarled at Flint.

He closed his eyes and sighed. "I am deeply sorry for the loss of your friends. But now is not the time for re-crimination. Now... who among you is unable to walk?"

The others parted, and Flint saw two youths, a boy and a girl, sitting on the floor, away from Morales. Their legs were a bloody mess, infested with worms. Gangrene would set in soon if it hadn't already. Without immediate medical care, those two would die soon. He knelt beside them, brushed as much of the vermin away as he could. He put his hands on their foreheads. Burning with fever.

"How long have you all been here?" Navarro asked.

Riffey ran a hand over his head. "Christ... I don't know. What's the date today?"

"August 11th," Flint said. Or was it the 12th now?

"Jesus," Barry said. "It's been a week... a goddamn week in..."

Flint chose to ignore the blasphemy this time. "Mr. Navarro, I believe that I misplaced one of my pistols. Would you be so kind as to fetch it for me?"

Navarro nodded, and went to where Flint had dropped

it, giving the Witch Hunter time to think. He looked to Barry. "I am sorry, Mister...?"

"Giles. Barry Giles."

"Mr. Giles, how is it that you and Mr. Riffey retained your weapons?"

"Me and Don... we've been on the move most of this time. A bunch of... shit, a bunch of walking skeletons took the kids. We stayed hidden, been looking for them all this time... a goddamn week... feels like it's only been a few hours."

"Yes," Flint murmured. He took out his pocket watch and flipped it open. The hands were spinning backwards like the propellor of an ancient flying machine.

"We finally found them down here," Riffey said. "Then that... lion thing cornered us."

Navarro brought Flint his empty pistol. He slammed a fresh magazine inside, racked the slide, and holstered the weapon. "Our first step is to escape from this dungeon," he said.

"How you two doing on ammo?" Navarro asked.

"Pretty low," Riffey said. The two security men wore bandoliers and Flint could see they were mostly empty.

"Do you have the strength to carry the wounded?" Flint asked, indicating the two students with the ruined legs.

Giles sighed but nodded.

"I believe that Mr. Navarro and I can lead the way to the front parlor. At least you will be away from this squalor."

"Then we can get out of here?" asked a girl.

"That, uh, might not be the best idea right now,"

Navarro said. "The last we saw, there was an army of the dead waiting outside."

A collective gasp arose, followed by cries, wails, prayers, and curses.

Flint rose a hand for silence. "We shall cross that bridge when we come to it. Mr. Riffey, Mr. Giles, please assist the wounded. The rest of you, follow me."

The students looked around, in a state of near panic, but they followed. Morales stayed where she was. Flint approached, got down on one knee, gently shook her shoulder.

"Professor Morales?"

No response.

"Professor Morales, I implore you. We must depart from this accursed place."

She looked up. Flint stifled a gasp.

Her eyes were missing. Her empty sockets were caked with dried blood.

"Leave me," she said. "I deserve this."

"No, Professor, you do not. I must insist. I will carry you if need be."

He draped her arm around his shoulders and lifted her to her feet. One of her students came forward and took her by the hand.

"It's okay Professor," she said. "I'll guide you."

Flint nodded to the girl and took his place at the head of the procession. He drew his sword and one of his pistols. Together, Flint, Navarro, and the survivors of the archaeological team made their way through the dungeons back to the staircase. Flint whispered every prayer he knew as they moved.

***

Zelda Fletcher gazed out the window of the carriage. McFarlane was up in the boot with Carrow. Riding inside with her was one of the parish priests from Danville, a Father Chester Dowling. McFarlane and Carrow had given her a brief history lesson on Vasquez's reign of terror. Dowling wasn't old enough to remember those times, but his grim expression spoke to his knowledge of the tales. He made eye contact with Fletcher.

"Are you really a witch?" he asked.

"Former witch," Fletcher said, suppressing a sigh.

Dowling nodded. "God be praised for granting you the grace of repentance," he said.

Fletcher said nothing. Her classes at Fort Marsing taught that it was God Himself who prompted her to repent of her former life, using her magical talents to exploit others for her personal gain. She wasn't sure about that; truth be told, she'd felt disgusted by her former lover Francisco who had begun to murder innocent people to fuel his power. He'd wound up possessed by a demon, and both she and Silas had killed him. Twice. She didn't want to end up like that and had thrown herself on the mercy of the Templars. She'd expected to be imprisoned or executed, but they'd taken her in and helped her build a new life. She'd always have the talent for magic; there was nothing anyone could do about that. The least she could do is use her powers for good, even if it made the Templars uneasy. Was the hand of God behind all this? She didn't know. She supposed it was one of those things you just took on faith.

She heard Dowling gasp. He made the sign of the cross and began reciting prayers. She looked out the window again. The landscape was illuminated by the full moon. She looked up.

"Jesus!" she cried.

The moon had changed. It now appeared to be a giant human skull. She felt like its eye sockets were looking right at her. Now that she thought about it, there was something odd about the moonlight: it was tinted green.

She returned to her seat. Dowling looked at her.

"You are welcome to pray with me," he said.

Fletcher swallowed. The poor guy couldn't sense what she felt. This was the most powerful, most... evil magic she'd felt in her life, even more than what had taken up residence in Francisco's damned soul.

"Yeah... yeah, I think I will," she said. They'd need all the divine intervention they could get.

19

Destiny Lee ran down the floating staircase, ran through the double doors at the bottom, through the hallway, and back to the corridor where she'd parted company with the demon Bifrons. The two skeletal guardsmen remained at their posts. The demon was where she'd left him. She put her hands on her knees, panting, her heart thundering.

She was willing to do almost anything for Charles, to help him realize his dream, indeed, the dream of all magicians, to have a safe haven of their own. But work with that, that... thing, Vasquez? Dear God, what was she doing?

Bifrons laughed. "You got more than you bargained for, witch."

Lee wanted to blast the demon back to Hell, but it was right. She knew that Vasquez had no intention of giving her the crown if she did his bidding. He'd probably add her soul to his collection if she stuck around too long. To get the crown, she'd have to figure it out on her own. Something Vasquez had said...

"He spoke of a great project, of his 'ascension.' What did he mean by that?" she asked.

Bifrons frowned. "The Weakling became one of you, long ago. He made himself into one of you filthy creatures of mud and slime."

Lee raised an eyebrow.

"Vasquez sought something similar. Just as the Enemy became one of you, he seeks to become like us. We are pure spirit, though we can take flesh within the walls of this castle."

"So... what, he wants to be a demon?" Lee asked.

"You're not thinking big enough," came a voice beside her.

Lee spun, the power coming to her fingertips. Robin Redcap stood before her, still wearing the guise of a young human man.

"We possess great power," Redcap said, "But Arturo

wants more. You heard him. He's somewhat enamored of the void. He wishes to become death."

Lee barked a laugh. "That's not possible. Death is..."

"It comes to all living things, does it not?" Bifrons asked.

"To what end though?" she said.

Redcap smiled. "Life is pain. You creatures live out your meaningless existence for a time, and then you die, hoping that He will reward you for being good dogs. I can assure you that the great majority of your kind end up below, with us."

"Vasquez wants to put an end to all earthly suffering, to wipe away every tear, to bring peace and order to a place that shouldn't even exist, to creatures who shouldn't exist," Bifrons said.

"The peace of the grave," Lee muttered.

"Yes," the two demons said together.

"Well, I plan on living," Lee said. "If he wants to become the new Grim Reaper, he's welcome to try. I'm just here for the crown."

"Hmm, yes, the crown," Redcap said. "It's a pity that we don't know where it is."

Lee folded her arms. "I don't believe you."

"Very smart," Redcap laughed. "But Bifrons is in your thrall. He spoke truly. We cannot see it."

"Maybe so," Lee said. "But a lie of omission is still a lie. There's something you two aren't telling me." She stopped, thought for a moment. "And why would you want me to have it? You're Vasquez's familiar."

"Indeed I am," Redcap said. "But my first loyalty is not

to him. My masters below are aware of Charles's plans. We know what is coming for him even as we speak." He laughed. "He made many enemies with his little announcement, enemies he hasn't even begun to suspect."

Lee said nothing.

"The good news for you is that we have decided that Charles Flint can use the crown more effectively than Arturo. You said it yourself earlier; he is dead, or more precisely, in a limbo between life and death. He has no further use for it though he may not realize it. He hides it out of spite."

Lee snorted. She looked at the two demons. "You may not be able to see it... but you must have some idea of where it could be."

They made a show of stroking their chins. "Vasquez hates it so much," Bifrons said.

"Hates what?"

"You disgusting things are made in His image and likeness," Redcap said, looking up toward the ceiling, before spitting on the floor.

"Vasquez has tried to erase that part of himself," Bifrons said. "But he cannot. The Enemy will not allow it."

"So he cut it out like a tumor," Redcap said.

"I'm not following you," Lee said.

"Vasquez used his power to remove as much of his humanity as he could," Redcap said. "He could not destroy it, so he removed it instead."

"And that's it? That's where he hid the crown?"

"It is as good a place to start as any," Bifrons said, shrugging.

"He cut out that part of himself," Lee muttered. What the hell could that mean? An idea formed in her mind. She thought back to Professor Rogan's interview with the Witch Hunter, Oglethorpe, for his book. According to Oglethorpe, Vasquez had said something when he ditched the crown. What was it though? She growled in frustration.

Redcap and Bifrons looked up.

"What is it?" Lee said.

"I think a friend of yours is approaching," Bifrons said.

"And he's bringing company," Redcap said.

"A friend of mine...?"

"Yes..." Redcap said. "Another magician. He smells like an educated man."

The only person Lee could think of was that college professor who'd organized the University's expedition. Charles had told her about him before she set out for Danville, a deep cover operative who'd been in place for years. If he was on his way here, either Charles had guessed that she'd need help, or something had gone wrong.

"And the company?" she asked.

The demons growled.

"I smell the stink of the Enemy about them," Bifrons said.

"Priests... nuns... two Templars..." Redcap said, sniffing. "And... hmm. Oh my."

"What is it?" Lee said.

"Their pet witch is with them."

Something had gone wrong then. Professor Meyer was no doubt fleeing for his life. Why here though? No matter.

If he was on his way, perhaps his specialized knowledge on Vasquez and the crown would be useful.

"Bifrons," she said. "That Witch Hunter you and I sensed earlier... where is he now?"

"He is leading Vasquez's latest toys out of the dungeons. He sent poor Sabnock away."

"I know him," Redcap giggled. "It's my old friends Silas Flint and Ricardo Navarro."

Lee started. She knew that Charles's older brother was a Witch Hunter, but out of all the Templars at Fort Marsing, Abernathy sent him? She would have laughed in other circumstances.

"Something's wrong," Redcap said, scowling. "I smell... I smell..." His face darkened. He bared his teeth, which elongated into fangs. The demon dropped his human disguise. His nose and ears lengthened into points, his skin stretched and wrinkled and blackened. Two curling horns extended from the back of his skull. And a third eye opened in the center of his forehead.

"What is it?" Lee asked.

"They're getting involved..." Redcap muttered. "This complicates things. But if they're intervening directly..."

"Then we can get our hands on them," Bifrons said.

"What the hell are you two talking about?" Lee said, exasperated.

"Nothing that concerns you," Redcap said. "Bifrons, why don't you escort your mistress outside to meet up with her educated friend before Vasquez's army devours him?"

***

Silas Flint and Ricardo Navarro led their party up the stairs. The students cried and whimpered and recoiled in disgust at the infestation of insects and other vile creatures, but they each made it through. They returned to the red carpeted hallway that connected to the front parlor. Flint's stomach rumbled and his throat burned with thirst, but he pushed himself onward. Looking over his shoulder, he saw the survivors looking everywhere in panic. He sighed. They'd no doubt be mentally scarred for the rest of their lives. But, he swore, they would live. So long as they lived, there was hope. He stopped and waited for Giles and Riffey to catch up, then resumed, keeping in step with them.

"Gentlemen," Flint said. "May I ask how you subsisted during your time alone?"

"Huh?" Giles said.

"What'd you guys do for food and water?" Navarro spoke up.

Riffey shuddered. "We had some MREs. Once those ran out... well, this place is full of bugs."

Flint pursed his lips. He was trained in basic survival but hoped they could escape before it came to that. "And the rest of you?" he asked.

One of the boys answered, "They'd give us bread and water. I think they wanted to keep us alive for..." He trailed off, his eyes watering.

"I understand, Mister...?" Flint said.

"Jason Rowan. They... they took the others... I..."

"That is quite alright, Mr. Rowan, I believe that I can surmise the rest."

They all heard rhythmic clacking ahead. Flint raised a fist, and everyone came to a stop. Navarro looked at him, held up four fingers. Flint nodded. He turned to Giles and Riffey, motioned for them to shield the students and the Professor. The two security men looked near their breaking points, but they nodded.

The clacking grew louder. Flint could see them now: four human skeletons marched toward them with military-like precision, armed with spears.

"Mr. Navarro, strike them down, if you please," he said.

His assistant raised his rifle. Four booms in quick succession, each one followed by a skull exploding into shards, the body disintegrating into a pile of bones. It was over before the students even had time to scream. Navarro drew four bullets from the bandoliers crisscrossing his chest and topped off his weapon. Flint faced their group.

"You see?" he called. "The enemy can be put down. If we maintain our vigilance, then we shall escape from this horror. The exit lies this way. Follow me."

When he turned around, he saw a brick wall that hadn't been there before. The path ahead was blocked. The corridor now branched off to their right. He blinked.

"How the hell did that get there?" Navarro whispered.

"General Oglethorpe told us that the castle itself is a creature of darkness," Flint said. "I, for one, do not intend to dance to its tune." He strode past Navarro, holstering his pistol, and taking out his crucifix. Together, the white light emanating from his sword and cross caused the brick wall to flicker and waver. "Your illusions are no match for the light of Christ!" Flint shouted. *"Ex umbris ad lucem! Begone!"*

Flint kicked at the wall which exploded in a shower of grave dust and crumbling brick. The path lay open. He looked behind him at the group whose mouths were all agape, save Navarro who only grinned. "This way," Flint said.

The survivors quickened their pace, Flint waving them down the corridor. He could see the fear in their faces, but now there was also hope. Navarro came to his side.

"Got any ideas on what to do about the ones outside?" he asked.

Flint sighed. "Only one, and I confess that it does not appeal to me."

They fell into step behind the students. The girl was still leading the mutilated Professor by the hand. Morales barely looked up. Flint's heart went out to her. She could learn to function without her sight, but psychologically and spiritually, she may never recover. He offered a prayer to the Holy Spirit to guide Morales – indeed, all of them – to deliverance.

"Vasquez summoned those zombies out there," Navarro said. He winced. "So if we take him out..."

"Theoretically, they would crumble or return to the grave from whence they came," Flint said.

"Theoretically? That's how it's always worked before," Navarro said.

"Yes. However... my instincts tell me that this case is different. We have never faced a necromancer of Vasquez's equal. Moreover, when General Oglethorpe did battle with the fiend, Vasquez was a mortal man. His return from the grave may have... strengthened his power."

Navarro shrugged. "You never know. Maybe he's weaker than he was back then."

Flint snorted. "I would not have expected you to become the optimist in our partnership."

"Hey... I got an idea, sir."

"By all means."

"You think maybe the Sisters could help out some more?"

Flint thought for a few moments. "I suppose that it is worth a try."

The party arrived in the front parlor, but Flint saw that it had changed. A fountain had appeared in the center of the floor. It depicted a man on his knees, hands on his head, the stone mouth carved in a rictus scream. From the mouth came a never-ending stream of blood that bubbled in the fountain's pool. Suits of black armor holding spears stood at port arms at the foot of each staircase leading to the mezzanine floor above.

"Hold up," Navarro called. The students and security men came to a halt. They clung to each other, eyes wild, looking everywhere for threats. Flint approached the great double doors that opened into the courtyard. He inched it open, peeked through, shut it again. It was as he feared: the army of undead waited outside, the green fires in their eye sockets so numerous as to be painful to behold.

"What's going on? What's out there?" Riffey said.

"You do not want to know," Flint muttered.

"We're going to die here, aren't we?" one of the girls said.

"Not while I draw breath," Flint replied. He had an idea. Reaching into one of his long coat's inner pockets, he withdrew a pouch of blessed, exorcised salt. He looked around the parlor. Beside the front door, two other doors were to their left and right. The hallway was in front of them. And there were the two staircases. He might need to use all of it, but the salt would slow down any on-coming foes.

Flint poured out a thin half circle of salt before the front doors. Black steam rose from the floor, but the salt was in place. He repeated the process before every point of ingress that he could see. It nearly depleted his supply, but the parlor was as secure as he could make it.

"Mr. Navarro, your radio, if you please."

His assistant tossed him the handheld. Flint thumbed the power switch. Harpsichord music filled the parlor.

"What the hell is that?" Giles asked.

Flint furrowed his brow. He looked at the dial. It was turned to 1530 AM, the Sisters' preferred station. The jazz music they favored wasn't there. Just this... he didn't know the melody, but it weighed upon him. It made him want to sit down on the floor and await death. Familiar laughter echoed from the radio.

"You three made a mistake coming here," said the voice of Arturo Vasquez.

What followed sounded like a series of explosions and the hum of electricity.

"Damn you to Hell!" Vasquez snarled.

More explosions, the roar of a burning fire, shattering glass.

"Die now!" Vasquez shouted.

"Silas!" The Proctor Sisters cried out together.

20

Flint looked up at Navarro. His assistant's face went pale, but otherwise he concealed the same dismay that Flint felt in his stomach. The Proctors irritated him to no end; he felt soiled somehow whenever he had to deal with them. But they had saved their lives earlier that night, to say nothing of the assistance they'd provided in the Oglethorpe and Salem cases. If they were in trouble...

"What the hell is that all about?" Riffey asked.

"You got one of them two-way radios?" Giles chimed in.

"Friends of yours?"

"Sounds like they're in trouble..."

"We're going to die, we're going to die..."

The students broke down into panicked wails and moans.

"Silence!" Flint barked. After a few moments, the students calmed down. All eyes were on him. "Ladies, gentlemen," Flint said. "I cannot lie to you. Our situation is grim. This castle is infested with demons within, and a mob of restless dead without."

The students cringed and whimpered. Riffey and Giles appeared stoic, but Flint could see them swallow.

"So what do we do?" Rowan said.

Flint sighed. This would be the hard part. What he said

now would make or break them. "The architect of your suffering is none other than the vile necromancer Arturo Vasquez himself. I know not how, but he has returned from the miserable death that he deserved."

Another round of panicked murmuring. Flint looked to Professor Morales. Her shoulders slumped. Tears formed at the corners of her empty eye sockets.

"This is all my fault," she whispered. "I wasn't strong enough... I should have said no... oh God, it's all my fault."

"No, Professor," Flint said. "Vasquez alone is responsible for all that has transpired here. And it is he who must answer for it."

"What are you saying?" Giles asked.

Flint looked at Navarro, who nodded back. Squaring his shoulders, Flint replied, "There is only one avenue of escape, one way that any of us will survive this nightmare: we must slay the heretic Vasquez once again."

"Holy shit..." Riffey said.

"How?!" one of the girls cried out. "What can we do? We don't have guns or swords or anything..."

"They do," said a boy. "They're going to leave us behind. They're going to leave us alone."

"No..."

"You can't!"

"Oh God..."

"Hey!" Navarro shouted. All the voices fell silent. He went on: "Either we take out Vasquez now, or we just wait here to die. Me and Silas had to outrun a fucking army of zombies outside to get in here. We don't have enough ammo to take them all out."

"So what the fuck are we supposed to do?" Rowan shouted.

Before Flint could answer, there was a bang on the front doors which bent with the force of the impact. His eyes widened. The undead in the courtyard must have heard them or smelled them. The students cried out in terror. Riffey and Giles rushed to the suits of armor at the foot of both staircases. They yanked the spears from the displays, rushed to the front doors, and shoved them through the iron rings which served as door handles. Another crash. The doors bent again, but the spears held. Flint pursed his lips. It would buy them a few extra minutes, but the dead never tired, never flagged. It was only a matter of time before they broke in.

Riffey and Giles clutched their shotguns as they shrank back. They stood in front of the huddling students, but Flint and Navarro could both see that the security men were near their breaking point. Navarro looked to Flint.

"Sir..." Navarro said.

Flint closed his eyes and took a deep breath.

"Silas... I... I think..."

Flint sighed. He knew what his assistant was about to say.

"If taking out Vasquez is our only way out of here..." Navarro said.

"Yes," Flint replied.

"These guys..."

"I know."

The doors banged again. The green torchlight flickered. Flint wasn't sure, but he swore that he could hear laughter above them. Looking up, he saw nothing, but he knew that they were being watched. He sighed. There was only one thing for it. He wasn't sure if it was the oppressive air within the castle, or if, for the first time in his career, fear was making him hesitate.

"Mr. Navarro…" he began.

His assistant looked at him with a mixture of awe and anxiety. "Sir…"

Another bang. The wooden doors groaned. The students shrank back. Flint studied their bruises, their festering wounds. They had their whole lives ahead of them. Earning diplomas, choosing a vocation, marriage, children… it was for people like them that he fought. Flint occasionally felt a yearning to marry and start a family of his own so that the Flint name would carry on, especially now that his brother would undoubtedly blacken it in the history books. The corner of his mouth turned up. He'd never given it serious thought before, but it occurred to him that whether he survived or not, what he was about to do would earn him a place in the history of the Templars until the Second Coming.

The doors banged.

"Mr. Navarro, Mr. Riffey, Mr. Giles," he said. "You have a responsibility to protect these students. I exhort you, in the name of God, to gird your loins like men. What you do here will echo in eternity. Stand fast, and your rewards will be great in Heaven."

"We're all gonna be okay, sir," Navarro replied. "I'll stay with them until the end."

Riffey and Giles looked taken aback.

"What... what are you doing...?" Riffey whispered.

"You're leaving?" Giles said.

"Hear me!" Flint said, raising his voice so the students could all hear him. They focused their attention on him, taking no more notice of the bangs on the front doors or the skittering, clicking, and laughter coming from the halls above them.

Flint paced back and forth, making eye contact with all the students in the front row. "I know that you are tired. I know that you are afraid. You have all suffered beyond the limits of human endurance. Many of your friends have been taken from you. I know that some of you feel tempted to despair." He drove his fist into his palm. "Do not surrender! The enemy can take your life, but only you can give him your soul!"

The students were silent.

"God has not abandoned us," Flint went on. "He sent us His Only Begotten Son who died for us, and in so doing, destroyed death! The greatest battle has already been won. The undead outside, the demons inside, they know this! In their pride, they think to overthrow the order of God, to challenge the Divine Will! All the powers of Vasquez, all the powers of Hell may rage, they may unleash the full might of their fury upon us." His shoulders slumped. "Simon Magus, slain by St. Peter and the power of God in ancient times, returned to this world and brought with him the scourge of magic. He nearly destroyed our ancestors. But..." He drew his sword, holding it aloft, pointing at the ceiling. The blade shone bright. The students stared at it in awe, some shielding their eyes.

"Simon Magus is dead, and we are still here!" Flint bellowed. "This I swear to all of you now, before Almighty God and all of the angels and saints: Arturo Vasquez shall torment this world no longer! It is he who has brought Hell to this place. And it is I, with the guidance of the Holy Spirit, through the intercession of the saints, and the help of our Lord, who shall send that monster back to the lake of fire!"

The students said nothing, but they gazed at Flint, mouths agape.

"You say that you do not have swords, that you do not have guns," Flint said. "All of you have the most powerful weapons of all. Pray for Mr. Navarro, for Mr. Riffey, for Mr. Giles. Pray for me. I go now to hunt down Vasquez and send him back to the fires of Hell. My assistant and your guards will protect you from any of the powers below that dare to show their vile faces. We will escape from this place. Trust in God and do not lose hope."

Before Flint could turn away to set off, the students who were able to walk rushed forward. They patted him on the back, hugged him, shook his hand.

"We're with you!"

"We'll pray for you!"

"Come back alive..."

Some of the students held back. Flint sensed that they were skeptical, but he would have to entrust them to the Lord. He disengaged from the crowd, to where Navarro, Riffey, and Giles waited for him.

"Shit, you might make a believer out of me after all, Captain," Giles said.

"I'll go at 'em with a knife if I have to," Riffey said, his expression grim.

Navarro shook Flint's hand. "That's why you're the boss, boss. Don't think I could ever give a speech like that."

Flint gave him a wintry smile. "The Lord provides the graces we need to fulfill our vocations."

"You know sir, I just thought of something."

"Oh?"

"Yeah... remember what General Oglethorpe told us?"

"That had occurred to me as well." Flint closed his eyes. "I fear that I am not Matthew's equal."

"You got this, sir."

Flint nodded to Navarro. His sword and pistol at the ready, he jogged up the stairs onto the mezzanine. As he proceeded down the hallway, he could hear his assistant calling out orders: "Okay. Riffey, you take that side. Giles, you cover that side. I'll take the middle. You see anything that isn't human, blow its fucking head off."

Flint shook his head. Navarro may not have had his talent for inspiring others, but the man knew how to fight. What worried Flint was the other part of the General's story. Navarro no doubt remembered it as well: Oglethorpe's Supernumerary assistant had died so that his partner could press on and slay Vasquez. After offering a quick mental prayer for Navarro's safety, Flint began the search for a way up to the floating tower where the necromancer awaited.

***

Zachariah Meyer looked up. The moon bore the image of a grinning human skull, its light a sickly green. *Impossible,* he thought. It had to be an illusion. The last time something like this had happened was... his eyes widened. *Vasquez.* Had the Great Necromancer returned from the grave? His heart thundered in his chest, almost drowning out the horse's galloping hooves. A dome of green light appeared on the horizon. Within it, Meyer could see the towers and spires of Castle Vasquez. He swallowed. For all his scholarly work on the subject, he'd never had the opportunity to visit before. It was a pity he had to come here alone. Charles had no doubt sent some unthinking brute to search for the crown. They'd need all the help they could get.

Onward, Meyer rode into the night. Skull Creek was on his right. Looking down, he saw the water had turned black and bubbling. The grass and the trees thinned around him. *Odd,* he thought. The dead zone surrounding the castle only extended for one mile, and he knew he wasn't that close yet. If Vasquez was back, perhaps the corruption was spreading. Meyer shivered. The necromancer was the greatest magical threat that Cascadia had faced in its four-hundred-year history. Much of Vasquez's writings had been burned by the Templars, and what scholars knew of his plans had come from oral histories from his enemies. He'd sought to break away from Cascadia; that much was not in dispute. But his long term goal? There was no hard evidence, but Meyer had an idea. The man had virtually worshiped the void, loved death in all its dark splendor. No matter.

After another few minutes hard riding, Meyer crossed over from the grassy plains and groves of forest into the dead zone. His horse reared and he struggled to hold on. The beast was no doubt finished with its journey, no matter what he did. Meyer dismounted, slapped the animal on its rump, and it took off in the opposite direction for all it was worth. The air was thick with magic, so much as to overwhelm his extrasensory perception. Meyer's head swam. He felt a great weight on his chest and he struggled for breath. He'd never felt tempted to suicide in his life, but it all fell on him at once. What was the point of going on?

He sensed them before he heard them. A shuffling, scraping sound. Banishing all despair from his mind, Meyer raised his hands, streaks of fire dancing around his fingertips. Vasquez may have been a more powerful necromancer than most, but even his undead were no match for the flames. There. The first one stumbled into sight. It had been a woman in life. The flesh was parchment thin and stretched tight over her jutting bones. Green fires burned in her eye sockets. Looking over her shoulder, Meyer saw an ocean of green fire behind her. He gasped. There had to be thousands of them out there, in the darkness.

Meyer held out his hand. A stream of fire enveloped the dead woman. It didn't scream or snarl. The only sound was the whoosh and crackling of the flames. He thought he heard a soft moan from the creature before it fell to its knees and then onto its face.

He backed up a step and collided with something. He turned. "Shit!"

Behind him was a wall of undead. Where the hell had they come from?! He spun around, and now there were more in front of him. He was surrounded.

Meyer swallowed. He still didn't have the juice to open another portal, but maybe he could levitate himself above the mob... wait. He heard a steady crunching sound, like a metronome. The undead before him parted. An armored figure strode through the crowd. Its armor was black as the night. Like the zombies around him, its flesh was stretched tight over its skull. A halo of green fire surrounded its bald head. In its sockets were two bloody eyeballs. It grinned, revealing a mouthful of black teeth.

"Zachariah Meyer," the apparition said in a rumbling voice. "My master, the great Arturo Vasquez, bids thee welcome."

Meyer maintained the magical fire on his fingertips. "And you are?"

"I am Anton. I serve my master as his ambassador."

"What do you want?"

"We know why you are here, Zachariah Meyer. You think to steal my master's crown and gift it to your child Emperor."

Meyer said nothing.

"Vasquez will never give it to you. You will never find it."

Meyer kept quiet.

"Leave now, and my master will grant you your life. Persist, and you will serve him in death."

Before Meyer could say anything, motion caught his eye. Looking up, he saw a winged figure soaring through the sky, another figure seated on its back. They were moving fast. As one, the undead looked up and shrieked. Meyer winced, covered his ears.

In that moment, he felt unnaturally powerful arms wrap around him and then he was airborne. He gasped in fright. Anton stared after him and he shuddered. He looked up and saw he was held by a misshapen man, his head lumpy, his eyes askew, his teeth rotten. On his back were two leathery bat wings... and one Asian woman, her long raven hair flowing behind her from the wind.

"What...?" he said.

"You must be Professor Meyer," the woman said. "I'm Destiny Lee, the one Charles sent. This is my thrall, Bifrons."

The man-demon thing grunted.

"You and I have a crown to find," Lee said, smiling.

***

"Mr. Navarro..." a girl said.

"Yeah?"

She pointed down the ground floor hallway. Navarro saw two torches flicker out at the end. Then the next pair blew out. Then another.

"All of you, move!" Navarro said. The students, some carrying their wounded friends, another leading Professor Morales by the hand, rushed to one side. Another pair of torches went out. Navarro couldn't see anything, but he had a good idea of what was coming. He took a knee, shouldered his rifle, fired. He heard a bestial grunt.

A ragged hole appeared in midair, dripping black ichor onto the floor. Navarro fired four more times in rapid succession, working the bolt quicker than the students' eyes could follow. He withdrew five more rounds from the bandoliers across his chest, reloaded. Taking a guess, he raised his point of aim and fired again. That got it, whatever it was. A hulking shadow, flickering in and out of sight, waved one arm, held a clawed hand to the spot where its face would be. Navarro threw down his rifle, drew his sidearm and his crucifix from his belt. The cross glowed in his hand as he aimed and fired his pistol, the rounds smacking into the creature's head.

"You won't touch them!" Navarro bellowed, as he continued his advance. The demon took a step back. Navarro kept coming, kept firing. The slide of his pistol locked open on empty. He was prepared to drop the gun and draw his tomahawk, when the translucent demon dissolved into black smoke and flew away.

"That's right! That's right!" Navarro shouted. "That's what you get!" He picked up his empty pistol, loaded another magazine, racked the slide. He strode back to the parlor where the students and security men waited. "You see?" he called. "They can take physical bodies here, but they can't take..."

"Navarro!" Riffey shouted. "Drop!"

Navarro dove to the floor, rolled forward into the parlor. He felt a breeze and sensed something heavy had swung at the spot where his head at been a moment ago. Turning, he saw a demon – the one he had just been shooting at? – advancing toward him. This one had the body of a man and the head of a crocodile. He backed up, firing his pistol all the while. He crossed the threshold of the hallway back into the parlor. The demon roared, took a step forward, and then screeched as its foot contacted the blessed salt Flint had poured on the ground earlier. It vanished.

"You okay?" Giles said.

"Yeah..." Navarro said. He holstered his pistol, picked up his rifle. *Come on, Silas,* he thought. *O Blessed Virgin Mary, Our Lady of Guadalupe, pray for us...*

***

The carriage stopped, jolting Fletcher and Dowling in their seats. She could hear the horses whinnying... no, almost wailing in panic.

"What..." she said.

Next, she heard Carrow and McFarlane jump down from their perch.

"I take it we've arrived," Dowling said.

Fletcher opened the door and stepped out. The night was nearly bright as day with green light. She felt a sharp buzzing in her skull. This was even worse than that haunted American military installation that she'd visited with Silas and Rico a few months ago. She looked up and gasped, nearly falling onto her backside.

Carrow and McFarlane stood before her. And in front of them was an army of the dead. Corpses, skeletons, zombies of every age, sex, race looked out at them, green fires burning in their eyes. Some held swords, others spears, and a few had what looked like rusting rifles, thick with grave dust and grime. They stood still, but she could hear groans, growls, and hisses everywhere.

"Oh... shit..." she breathed. The horses were in a panic, their eyes rolling up in their heads. She couldn't blame them. McFarlane and Carrow said nothing.

The army of the dead parted, stepping aside to form a path. She could hear clanking, a steady pace growing louder. From out of the crowd appeared a zombie encased in black armor. Its bloody eyeballs spun in their sockets independently of each other before focusing on the two Templars.

"You children and your false God have no place here," the zombie spoke in a rumbling voice.

McFarlane crossed her arms. "Then why don't you make us leave?"

Fletcher rushed to her side, whispered in her ear: "What the fuck are you doing?"

The zombie grinned, its desiccated lips stretching too far over its blackened teeth. The undead closest to it wheezed and barked. Christ... were they laughing?

"Many of your ranks joined us that day," the talking zombie replied. "You will join them soon enough, for my master, the Great Arturo Vasquez, has returned."

"Lies!" Carrow shouted. "Your master is dead!"

The zombie laughed again, a sound that made Fletcher's skin crawl. "The master of life and death is not so easily slain. When he comes into the fullness of his power, the world will howl in despair. My master offers you a proposition: join us now, and your deaths will be swift. Refuse, and you will become his new toys. Especially your pet witch."

"Fuck off, asshole," Fletcher spat.

"My name is Anton," the zombie replied. "It matters not to me which you choose. The result will be the same. Perhaps we will raise your Templar friend to come for you."

Fletcher felt her heart drop. *Silas...*

21

Silas Flint jogged through the second floor. Beneath his feet was a blood red carpet with two gold stripes on either side. The stone blocks that formed the walls and ceiling were carved to resemble skulls or screaming human faces. If his calculations were correct, he expected to meet the west wall of the castle soon. Assuming it didn't change around him or trap him in an endless loop again. He was familiar with many of the scholarly tomes on the war against Vasquez. He struggled to remember the sketches and descriptions of the floor plans. The lives of Navarro and the archaeological team depended on it.

He heard a buzz and crackle. Flint assumed a fighting stance, sword and pistol at the ready. A moment later, he realized that he still had Navarro's radio on his person, stuffed into his trouser pocket.

"Silas," came a female whisper.

Flint, keeping his eyes forward to scan for threats, holstered his pistol and dug out the radio.

"I am here," he whispered back. He moved as he spoke, his sword lighting the way.

"It is Madeline."

Flint blinked. Madeline was the redhead if he recalled correctly. But something felt off.

"Where are your sisters?" he asked. There had to be a staircase somewhere.

A pause. "They fight with Vasquez."

"Where are you?"

"In the necromancer's inner sanctum."

Flint tried a door. Locked. "I am currently on the second floor, moving west. Can you direct me where to go?"

"I..." Madeline broke down into a sob.

"Miss Proctor?" Flint asked.

After a few moments, she replied: "I... it is difficult for us to be separated from one another."

"Can you tell me where to go?"

"The castle seeks to trap you in an infinite loop," she replied. "The door will be on your right. You must..."

An explosion crackled through the radio. Madeline gasped and all fell silent.

"Miss Proctor?" Flint asked. "Miss Proctor, are you there?"

A buzz and more crackling. "These traitors cannot help you any further, Witch Hunter," came a male voice.

"Vasquez," Flint growled.

The necromancer laughed. "You pathetic little ape. You have no idea why they come to you, do you?"

Flint said nothing and kept moving. He thumbed the power switch off. Proctor had said the correct door would be on his right. But they all looked identical. How would he know which one to choose?

He'd switched the radio off, but Vasquez's tinny voice continued to speak from it: "These three have much to answer for. Oh yes. They think that you're the key to them getting a second chance. And so they've soiled themselves, taking orders from the enemy."

The glow of Flint's sword grew brighter. Maybe that was how he would know.

"There are no second chances, there is no forgiveness, no hope," Vasquez spat. "They made their choices, and I'm going to make them pay. I haven't decided yet whether to devour their souls myself, or to leave them to their judgment. I suppose it would have the same result in the end," he said, laughing.

My Lord and my God, Flint prayed. *Guide my sword. I am the most unworthy of your servants. I cannot save my friends without You. Guide my sword to the exit. I implore Thee to come to our aid.*

Flint kept moving. He thought that he was walking straight ahead, but after a few moments, his shoulder collided with the wall. Did the castle move? Did he move? He wasn't sure. But the tip of his sword rested on a door.

Thank you, my Lord, Flint thought. He pulled on the iron ring. Locked. He heard gunfire back the way he had come. He had to hurry. Flint retreated to the other side of the hallway. He got a running start, aimed a kick at the door's lock, and it smashed open. It revealed a stone staircase going up.

The radio crackled again. "My familiar tells me that he

has had encounters with you before," Vasquez said. "He's so eager to meet you in the fullness of his power."

The wall beside the staircase rippled and shimmered. A creature stepped away from it, its skin mimicking the pattern of the stones. Its body shifted, the skin turning black. It grew, both in height and bulk, soon towering over Flint. A pair of wings erupted from its back. Two great curled horns extended from its skull. Its face was vaguely humanoid, with two beady red eyes, a great hooked nose, and a mouth that stretched too far, revealing dripping fangs. Flint scowled. He had seen its shadow before. As if on cue, a third, larger eye opened in the center of its forehead.

"Robin Redcap," Flint said.

The demon gave him a mocking bow. "Captain Flint. It's good to see you again, old friend."

"As I recall," Flint replied, "I shot you down like a rabid dog in Canyon Cove earlier this year."

Redcap growled. "That time I was in possession of a weak human vessel. Now you face me in the flesh."

"The outcome shall be the same, monster!" Flint shouted.

"I'm going to relish tearing your soul apart," Redcap giggled. His eyes burned with hellfire. "Let's go."

Before Flint could aim his pistol, Redcap's shoulder rammed into him. Flint flew back through the doorway, across the hall, and smacked against the wall, knocking the wind from him. He lost his grip on his sword and pistol. Dazed, Flint heard Redcap's thundering footsteps approaching. He drew his second pistol and fired in the demon's direction. Redcap moved faster than Flint's eyes could follow. As soon as he pulled the trigger, the demon had already dodged, and Flint heard the slugs chipping away at the wall. Redcap reached for him with an enormous scaly hand. Flint rolled out of the way toward his sword. He grabbed it on the way back onto his feet.

"I'm having fun," Redcap said. "Are you?"

Flint holstered his pistol and drew his crucifix from his coat pocket.

"Ah, bringing out the big guns, are we?" Redcap purred.

The sword and the cross shone bright. Flint took a step forward, but Redcap stood his ground. Flint advanced another step. He'd caught his breath and his confidence grew. Redcap winced and shielded his face.

"It is not Silas Flint whom you face, hell spawn," Flint said. "Now the light of Christ is upon you!"

Redcap took a step back.

"Even I have to admit," the demon said, "You're stronger than most who have braved these halls. But you're not strong enough!"

With a snarl, Redcap drove his fist through the wall to his right, smashing the brick, punching through to the room beyond. Flint kept his focus on the demon, but from the corner of his eye, he saw what lay inside: rotting corpses, skeletons, all wearing the long coats and capotains of Witch Hunters.

Redcap smiled, his fangs dripping, the saliva burning the red carpet. "You'll make a fine addition to Arturo's collection. Perhaps I'll bring Charles your sword and pistols as souvenirs."

The corpses stirred and groaned. Green fires ignited in

their eye sockets and their bones cracked as they turned their heads to look at Flint.

The Witch Hunter scowled but continued his advance on Redcap. "If you are so powerful in your physical form, then why summon these wretches to fight for you, coward?"

The demon bowed toward the undead Templars. "You misunderstand, boy. I love to kill before an audience."

A second later, Redcap was flying, soaring toward Flint who raised his sword from pure reflex. The demon attempted to avoid the blade by flying higher, but his bulk and the low ceiling caused the sword to scrape along his chest. Redcap screeched in pain, black ichor raining down on Flint as the demon landed in a crouch behind him. Flint spun around to face his foe.

Redcap remained in a crouch as he traced a clawed finger along the gash on his chest. He licked the corrupted blood from his claw with a forked tongue.

"It's been a long time since I tasted my own blood," Redcap said, grinning. "Sour."

"I shall paint the walls with your foul entrails, demon!" Flint shouted.

"Come on then," Redcap replied, rising to his feet.

Flint heard shuffling behind him. Turning, he saw the undead Witch Hunters advancing on him, arms outstretched, eager to devour his flesh. He stuffed the crucifix back in his pocket, drew his pistol, and fired. The bullet smacked into the forehead of the zombie closest to him, and it fell to the floor with a grunt, the fires in its eyes dying. Before he could aim another shot, he felt a crushing grip around his waist. Flint screamed; Redcap had him in his grasp, and the demon's hand felt like it was red hot. The demon shook Flint like a rag doll until he dropped his sword and pistol.

Redcap turned Flint around. The Witch Hunter's feet dangled above the floor. He was almost nose to nose with the demon. Redcap's three eyes gazed at him, and in them Flint could see a billion souls writing in agony, burning in fires that could never be quenched.

"I changed my mind," Redcap growled. "I think I'll just eat you."

The demon's mouth opened wide, far wider than it should have. Its breath was a carrion stink that made Flint's eyes water. It's forked tongue flicked against his cheek. He struggled but Redcap's grip was as unyielding as a vise.

Mom, dad, Flint thought. *I'm sorry. I failed you again. My Lord and My God, hear my prayer: please protect Ricardo and the others. St. Joseph, pray for me. St. Benedict, pray for me. O Blessed Virgin Mary, pray for us sinners who have recourse to thee...* He closed his eyes.

"Eh?!" Redcap grunted.

Flint felt a peculiar warmth spreading throughout his chest, and a white light pierced his eyelids. Redcap dropped him and Flint fell to all fours, gasping for breath. The light was emanating from inside his long coat.

"What have you done?!" Redcap screeched. "This isn't fair!"

Flint peeked inside and saw that the light was coming

from the Saint Benedict medal that General Oglethorpe had given him the other day.

Gunshots boomed in the hallway. The zombified Templars fell to the ground. Flint looked up. More gunfire, the bullets smacking into Redcap who twisted and writhed with each hit. He turned to get a look at the shooter, but the light was blinding. All he could see was the silhouette of a man with shoulder length hair.

"Impossible!" Redcap roared. "You're not supposed to be here! You can't be here!"

"Come on, son," Flint heard the man say. "You're not alone."

Flint rose to his feet, picked up his sword and pistol, and added his gunfire to that from his unknown benefactor. Redcap shrieked in agony, more from the light than the pistol and rifle rounds. Flint got to within arm's length of the demon. Redcap cringed, shielding his face. He dropped his arms and gave Flint a look of pure unearthly hatred.

"You can't kill me," Redcap hissed. "And where you're going, not even heaven can help you."

"Give Vasquez my regards, if you can," Flint snarled. He stabbed his sword into the giant eye in the center of Redcap's forehead. It exploded in a shower of gore that spattered over Flint's sleeve and chest. The demon grunted, its two smaller eyes rolling up in its head. Its body dissolved into a swarm of flies that buzzed around Flint, flew through the doorway he'd kicked open earlier, and up the staircase. They were gone.

Flint wiped the loathsome ichor from his person as best he could. The white light dimmed enough for him to see his savior: he was an older man, his shoulder length hair iron grey, with white stubble on his chin. He wore the leather body armor, denim jeans, and black boots of a Supernumerary. A bolt action rifle was slung across his back. Flint's mouth fell open.

"You are..." he whispered.

The man nodded. "Heaven isn't deaf to your prayers, young man."

"My assistant..."

"Don't worry about him. You need to stop Vasquez."

Flint was too stunned to reply. The man clapped him on the shoulder.

"You remind me of one of my old partners," he said, smiling. "Now get moving. The others need your help too."

Flint shook himself. He picked up his other pistol, holstered it. He nodded to his savior. "Your name is a hallowed one in the history of the Order," he said.

The man smiled. "All glory and honor to the name of the Lord."

Flint smiled back. He offered a quick mental prayer of thanksgiving and set out for the staircase. Before he passed through the doorway, the man spoke up again.

"Tell Matthew that I said hello, and that I'm very proud of him."

22

"Get out of the way!" Navarro snarled, pushing a college boy to the floor. He fired his pistol, taking the zombie in the head. He kept firing at the oncoming horde until his pistol locked open on empty. Behind him, he could hear Riffey and Giles firing their shotguns. Sweat ran down Navarro's face. The two security men were nearly out of ammunition and would have to switch to their pistols soon.

From the moment that Navarro had banished the demon in the hallway, the restless dead had come swarming from the other hallways. He dropped the empty magazine, inserted a fresh one, racked the slide. The archaeological team huddled around the fountain of blood in the center of the room. Navarro holstered his pistol, unslung his rifle, and took another shot. The powerful rifle round went through three zombies who fell to the floor with a grunt. He gave a grim smile. They did have one advantage: the hallways were too narrow for the tide of undead, and the bodies were piling up. At this rate, the fresh ones wouldn't be able to push their way past the rotting, makeshift barricades.

"I'm out!" Riffey shouted. He dropped his shotgun to the floor, drew the pistol on his belt.

Shit, Navarro thought. The two security men had different models of pistols than Navarro's own, so they couldn't even share magazines. "Make 'em count!" Navarro bellowed. Riffey picked off a few more zombies with aimed headshots. *Not bad at all*, he thought. If they survived all this, maybe he would ask Riffey and Giles if they'd ever considered joining the Order.

"Mr. Navarro?" He felt a tug on his pant leg.

"What?" He looked down and saw the sightless Professor Morales sitting on the floor.

"Are we going to make it?" she asked.

By way of answer, he aimed and fired four times in rapid succession, more zombies hitting the floor, adding to the pile of corpses in the west hallway.

"Keep praying," he shouted as he reloaded.

Giles fired his shotgun, and a zombie's head exploded in gore. He dropped the weapon and drew his sidearm, dropping two more.

"You guys are pretty good at this!" Navarro bellowed over the gunfire, the groans, the splatters.

"Hard to miss when they're this close!" Giles shouted back.

Sweat dripped into Navarro's eyes. He smiled. He'd need a bath and a change of clothes before he saw Julia again. Julia. Flint often criticized what he called Navarro's womanizing. Navarro didn't mean to, but the nature of their vocations meant they traveled a lot. He knew fornication was a sin, but, well, that's what confession was for, right? He didn't want to do that with Julia though. Well, he did. Very much so. But she was different. He remembered his promise to General Oglethorpe. Whether they ever married or not, he swore that he'd do right by Julia Oglethorpe.

"Riffey! Duck!" Navarro bellowed. The security man dove to the floor. Navarro dropped his rifle, drew his tomahawk, and hurled it with all his might. It spun end over end across the room, the blade embedding itself in the forehead of a zombie that was nearly on top of Riffey. It fell flat onto its back. Navarro sprinted across the room, dove, rolled, yanked the tomahawk out of the zombie's head, and drew his pistol.

"You're going down!" Navarro screamed. He swung the blade, fired his pistol into the mob. Riffey added his own gunfire to the fray as the two men backed away. Giles picked up Navarro's rifle and fired five shots, dropping the undead each time. He tossed the empty weapon to Riffey, who handed it to Navarro. He holstered his sidearms and reloaded it.

"That's a fine weapon," Giles said.

"If you two need a job once this is over," Navarro said, "You can join up with us and get one just like it."

The banter distracted Navarro from thinking about their grim situation: they were slaughtering their on-coming foes, but they were simply too many. Navarro had thought to establish a perimeter around the students and the professor, and they'd held out for longer than he'd expected. But with Giles and Riffey out of shotgun shells and rapidly running out of pistol ammunition, it was only a matter of time. Navarro felt his heart drop. *Guess I won't get to do right by Julia after all,* he thought. *Thank you Lord, for giving me the opportunity to serve the Church and protect your people. I'm not good at praying but... please don't let us end up like these... things.*

A white light shone from the mezzanine above them, bright enough to make everyone wince. Professor Morales looked directly at it.

"I... I... I can see," she stammered.

"What?" Navarro said. The zombies stopped, their rotting faces staring up above them. The light dimmed enough for the others to get a good look. An older man stood upon the balcony, with shoulder length grey hair, the uniform of a Supernumerary, and a bolt action rifle like Navarro's in his hands. He looked down at the cowering students, at Navarro and the security men. He smiled.

"Just like old times," the man said.

***

Bifrons landed upon one of Castle Vasquez's outer walkways along its surrounding wall. Destiny Lee climbed down off his back as the demon released Professor Meyer from his grasp. The older man huffed and straightened his suit jacket. From here, Lee could see the inner courtyard and the dead zone outside. If anything, the legions of undead had grown more numerous, the fires in their eyes making the night nearly as bright as day, casting everything in a sickly green.

Meyer looked around, awestruck. "Castle Vasquez... I've always wanted to visit. To actually see it..."

"We don't have time for a tour," Lee said. "We need to find that crown and get the hell out of here."

"What? Oh, yes, of course... Bah. I should have come here with the archaeological team instead of sending Carlos."

"Believe me, you shouldn't have," Lee said. She shuddered. "Killing is one thing, but what he did to them..."

"What who did?" Meyer asked, raising an eyebrow.

"Vasquez. He's back."

"What?!" Meyer rushed forward, grabbed Lee by the

lapels of her black denim blouse. "That thing was telling the truth? Vasquez has returned already?!"

Lee brushed his hands away. "Yes. I saw him myself. If I never see that... thing again, it'll be too soon."

Bifrons snickered.

"Incredible..." Meyer whispered. He wandered over to the parapet and placed his hands upon it, gazing out at the army of the dead filling the landscape. "I don't know all the details, but in life, Vasquez spoke of a way to return from death once every hundred years. It's only been forty... how on earth could he have...?"

"Something to do with the archaeological team, and your boy, Carlos," Lee said. "I saw what was left of them in Vasquez's chambers. He... I think he used parts from each of them to build himself a new body."

Meyer snapped his fingers. "Of course! His spirit wouldn't have been strong enough when the first team came here thirty years ago. And he'd have needed a magician to provide the spark for his new body to handle magic... oh."

"What?"

"Oh dear," Meyer said. "That would mean... it's me. I'm responsible for his early return. I unwittingly sent him what he needed."

Bifrons grinned, exposing his rotted teeth. "I sense that this does not please you. If it's any consolation, you're not solely responsible. Charles Flint used a spell from Vasquez's copy of *In Realis Magicae* to declare the birth of his new empire, and that made his blackened soul take notice of this world earlier than expected. Even so, you have the gratitude of my masters below. They expect Vasquez to send us many more souls."

"Do you have any idea where he could have hidden the crown?" Lee asked Meyer, ignoring the demon.

He stroked his chin. "I was pondering that very question when I ran into Vasquez's emissary, just before you showed up." He looked to Bifrons, pointed at him with his thumb. "I take it they've been no help?"

"No. They claim they can't see it."

"Hmm... fascinating."

They heard a series of booms somewhere below them. Gunfire.

"What?" Meyer said.

"I imagine that will be Silas Flint and his sidekick," Lee said. "Last I heard, they'd found some survivors."

"They... they did? Really?"

Bifrons shrugged. "Vasquez chose to let some of them live. Some of them wish that he hadn't."

"Professor?" Lee prompted.

"Oh! Right. After Vasquez cast his crown into a portal, he said to Oglethorpe, 'Now it's with my heart.'"

That was it, Lee thought. "Bifrons and Redcap told me that Vasquez cut out a piece of himself. Something about how he hated that humans are made in the image of God. Do you have any idea what that could mean?"

Meyer furrowed his brow. Below them, the undead began chanting the necromancer's name. He glanced down at them from the parapet.

"Amazing... even his foot soldiers have the power of speech..."

"Goddammit Professor!" Lee snapped. She wanted to get out of here and never look back.

"With his heart... image of God..." Meyer muttered.

Lee's mind raced. Like most citizens of Cascadia, she'd been born and raised Catholic. An idea formed in her mind. "Professor... where was Vasquez born?"

"Up north, in Canyon Cove. Why?"

"Was he ever baptized?"

"If he was, there are no records of it. His father's unknown, his mother was a prostitute who gave him up for adoption, he spent most of his childhood in a Church orphanage..."

"So no family," Lee sighed. She wanted to punch the wall. This was hopeless.

"No family," Meyer agreed. "You may be on to something though..."

"How?"

"Back when I was an undergraduate, I remember reading interviews with the other orphans, with the staff. They said there was only one thing that Vasquez ever loved... it's the only thing I can think of."

Lee looked to Bifrons, who favored her with another nasty grin. "Does it look like love has any place here?" he laughed.

"So maybe he would have hidden it somewhere in Canyon Cove?" Lee asked.

"It's a long shot, but it's our best lead."

"Does the orphanage still stand?"

"No, it burned down years ago. I think they built an office on top of it or something."

Shit, Lee thought. "So what was this one thing he loved?"

"His dog."

"What?!" Lee blurted. "A... dog? A fucking dog? Is that supposed to be a joke?"

"No joke," Meyer said, spreading his hands. "The other children all agreed that his dog Chuy was the only friend he ever had."

Lee wanted to laugh at the absurdity of it. Vasquez had been born a normal human being, but it was impossible to imagine that repulsive creature she'd seen ever having been a child, let alone caring about a dumb animal. Still, it would give her an excuse to finally get out of here. She was confident of her hold over Bifrons, but if Vasquez grew any more powerful, he might decide to sic his army or more of his demonic allies against her than she could handle. Who knows? Maybe Silas Flint would put him down, like Oglethorpe did decades ago. Then they could search for the crown at their leisure. If he failed... well, then she imagined that the whole world would have bigger things to worry about.

"I think it's time we made a field trip to Canyon Cove," Lee said.

"I don't think I have the juice to open a portal yet," Meyer said.

"Don't worry about it, I got it."

"I cannot accompany you in this form," Bifrons said. "Beyond the boundaries of Vasquez's power, I will become pure spirit once again."

Lee looked the demon up and down. It had served her

well during her time in this cursed place, but she knew better than to let it off its leash when she needed to focus her mind on opening a portal.

"Bifrons," she said. "I give you my final command: go to Hell."

"No!" the demon shrieked as it vanished in a ball of fire and the stench of brimstone.

Lee drew upon the power. Her hands were engulfed in blue flames. She recited the incantations, raising her voice over the groans and chanting below. A ring of fire appeared on the walkway. The interior of the ring turned black. She and Professor Meyer stepped through, and the portal closed behind them with a zipping noise.

***

Zelda Fletcher swallowed, the anxiety in her chest making it difficult to breathe. Anton, that black armored zombie thing paced back and forth at the edge of the dead zone. Whatever evil power was animating him and that endless ocean of undead behind him apparently did not allow them to step outside of the perimeter. But she noticed something as she looked at the ground: the grass was withering, dying, so slowly she might not have noticed if she hadn't been so eager to avoid making eye contact with Vasquez's emissary.

A few paces away, Father Dowling and the other Danville parish priest, Father Max Chandler, had donned their purple stoles and were reciting prayers from their books of exorcism. The nuns – she'd since learned that they were

Carmelites, were kneeling and praying their beads. Lady McFarlane stood like a statue, her hands resting on the pommel of her shining sword which she had planted in the earth. Fletcher could see her mouth moving, no doubt adding her own prayers to the mix.

Fletcher felt frustrated. There had to be something more they could do. She believed in God, but she wasn't sure He would pay attention to the prayers of someone like her: a magician, a witch, a sinner. She wanted to blast her way to Castle Vasquez and come to Silas and Rico's rescue. She wanted... she noticed that McFarlane was looking at her.

"Zelda," she said. "Sometimes this is the only thing we can do."

Anton laughed. "Do you really think that your God will lift a finger to help you? By my master's black hand, the dead shall rise. His power grows as all light dies."

"Now he's writing poetry," Fletcher said, rolling her eyes. McFarlane snorted.

"Jest while you can, child. Soon you will know only the cold embrace of death..." Anton stepped over the edge of the dead zone. His foot erupted in flames as soon as it touched the grass. The zombie grunted but prepared to take another step.

"Back!" Chandler shouted. He thrust with a vial of holy water in his left hand. A few drops splashed onto Anton, who roared in pain and backed away into the dead zone. He opened his mouth, revealing a tongue that looked like a black slug. It licked over the dry parchment skin where his lips should have been.

"I'll eat you first," Anton growled.

"Eat this," McFarlane said. In one quick motion, she drew one of her pistols, aimed, and fired. The bullet struck Anton in the cheek below his left eye. Dust blew out from the back of his head. He remained on his feet.

"The last moments of your lives will be pain and terror," Anton said. "And then you will never feel anything again."

Fletcher went to McFarlane's side. "Maybe we should go back to Danville, telegraph for some reinforcements from Marsing?" She knew that the Witch Hunter had already sent a message to dispatch another Templar to Professor Meyer's house in Redmond to secure whatever contraband he had hidden away.

McFarlane sighed. "It'd take hours for them to arrive."

"Doesn't look like those guys are going anywhere," Fletcher said, waving her arm at the undead horde.

"Yet."

Fletcher ground her teeth in frustration. If only she'd learned how to open portals when she had the chance! If only there was... wait. She grabbed McFarlane's arm.

"What's wrong?" she asked.

"I can go back," Fletcher said. "Let me take one of the horses, I can go back to Danville, telegraph Marsing."

"Zelda, it's a two hour ride at least..."

"Not for me," she smiled.

"Huh?"

"I can't open portals, but I know a spell that can make the horse a lot faster. A lot."

McFarlane looked at the zombies, at Fletcher. She frowned.

"Are you sure?"

"Diana... I'm sorry. I don't have faith like yours. I can't just sit here and do nothing."

"We're not doing nothing."

"That's not what I meant! I just..." Her shoulders slumped. "God doesn't listen to people like me."

"Hey." McFarlane put a hand on her shoulder. "He does. He does." She closed her eyes, sighed. "Very well. Ride safe."

"Take care of yourself," Fletcher said, pulling her partner into a hug. They patted each other's backs. Breaking away, Fletcher went to Carrow, who was kneeling in prayer. "Robert, I need to borrow one of the horses."

Carrow rose to his feet, and silently disconnected one of the horses from the carriage reins. He opened the carriage's baggage compartment, took out a saddle and reins, prepared the beast for travel. Fletcher climbed on to it, whispered a spell. The horse's ears perked up. She nicked the reins, and the animal took off at blinding speed, leaving flaming hoof marks in its wake. Her eyes watered from the wind.

Hang on Silas, she thought. *God, if you're listening, please keep him and Rico safe.*

23

Silas Flint ran up the stairwell, sword and pistol in hand. The radio in his pants pocket buzzed and crackled.

Occasionally, he heard what sounded like an explosion or a surge of lightning.

"Die traitors!" Vasquez shrieked.

He heard three women cry out, either in pain or surprise.

Flint pushed on. He didn't know which way to go, and it sounded like the Sisters were occupied at the moment. However, the more he ran, he noticed that his sword was being subtly pulled. Just as he was about to pass one of the innumerable, identical doors in the third floor hallway, the blade tapped one of them. Not slowing down, Flint aimed a kick at the lock, smashing it open.

"Dear God..." Flint whispered.

The room he'd discovered was an open pit with a narrow brick arch spanning its length. Peering over the edge, he saw a bed of barbed spikes, many with moldering skeletons impaled on them. Across the pit, he saw another door.

Flint shook his head. He still felt off balance after Redcap had shaken him, but the others were depending on him. He took a deep breath. Keeping his focus on the door across the pit, he took off at a sprint. The bridge was barely wide enough for one man to cross it. It gently arched as it went. Flint put one foot in front of the other, ignoring his light headedness. He was halfway there already. Focus on the goal and tune out the distractions; it had served him well over his fifteen year career. Just a little further.

The chamber shook and the bridge beneath his feet lurched.

"Ugh," Flint grunted. He teetered on the edge, lost his

balance, and fell. He caught himself on the edge, resting his weight on his forearms, managing to hold on to his weapons. Below him he heard screams and laughter. He glanced down, and his eyes widened. The skeletons impaled on the spikes below were moving. They pulled themselves off from their spikes and began climbing over each other. They quickly formed a tower, standing on each other's shoulders. One of them reached for his ankles.

Flint heaved himself onto the walkway, careful not to roll over the other side. He scrabbled to his feet and fired his pistol down into the pit. The bullets shattered the skull of the nearest skeleton and the sternums of the ones below it. The tower fell with a clatter.

He scanned the chamber for more threats. Not seeing any, he resumed his headlong sprint, making it to the other side. The doorway led to another staircase, and he took the steps two at a time, moving ever upward. His lungs burned in his chest, sweat soaked his hat and clothes, but Flint pushed himself forward.

The stairs led him to another hallway. Along the walls, between the burning green torches, were paintings. Flint kept jogging but he caught details as he passed them. One depicted Hell's capitol city of Pandemonium. His eyes detected movement. He stopped for a moment, and saw the figures depicted in the painting were moving: the flames flickered, tiny demons paced the city's walls, damned souls filed inside its massive gates.

He squinted. One of the miniature demons was looking at him. A moment later, a massive, clawed hand reached out from the painting, reaching for Flint. He brought up his sword and parried with a slash, cutting a thick black line across the hand's palm. He heard an animal shriek, and the hand withdrew inside the painting.

"Silas!"

The Sisters had cried out from the radio in his pocket.

"Hurry!"

Flint resumed his sprint. Ahead of him, several of the doors opened. Rotting corpses strode forth, armed with barbed spears, green fires burning in their eyes, maggots crawling in and out of their mouths.

"Vasquez, Vasquez, Vasquez..." the chanted. They marched toward Flint with perfect military precision.

"You shall not stop me!" Flint bellowed. He aimed, fired his pistol. The round struck the first one in the face, breaking off its lower jaw. The corpse kept advancing, a gaping black hole where its mouth had been, swarms of maggots spewing forth. Flint fired again, taking it in the forehead. It fell to the ground in a heap.

Flint roared and charged his foes. Two of them stabbed with their spears, but he dodged, brought his sword around, slicing off the top of one of their rotting heads. Its scalp flew away from its head, its brain matter spattering its comrades.

Flint spun to avoid another stab, but the barbs along the spear head sliced through his long coat, barely missing his skin. He was among them now, firing at point blank range, painting the hallway with brains, ichor, and the loathsome crawling things that feasted on their innards.

"Fall back and await your turn at judgment, unclean

ones!" Flint screamed. His pistol locked open. He dropped the magazine, reloaded, and kept firing.

The doors kept opening and the undead kept coming. Flint was tiring but he kept moving, a ballet of destruction. As he slaughtered his way forward, the rational part of his mind recognized the classic magician tactic: Templar swords could absorb magic, but Templars themselves could be worn down through combat. He prayed for strength and courage.

"Argh!" Flint screamed. The tip of a spear scraped a bloody line across his thigh. "Damn you!" he shouted, as he fired into the corpse's forehead. Flint could see it was only a flesh wound, but God only knew what sort of unholy infection would follow if he didn't end this soon.

"Vasquez!" Flint bellowed. "The judgment of God is upon you! These miserable wretches are no match for a Knight Templar!"

"Die, die, die," the corpses chanted as they continued their advance.

Flint dodged, slashed, shot, and pushed his way through them. The hallway was narrow and hindered his movement, but it hindered theirs as well, and that gave him an advantage. These bone walkers were smarter and more skilled than other undead that Flint had fought, but they were still limited creatures. Their single-minded focus on Flint created gaps in their lines as they struggled to force their way past each other to get to him.

"Unh," Flint grunted as another spear grazed his arm, drawing blood. He had to get out of here, fast. He holstered his pistol and drew his crucifix. The cross shone bright, dimming the green torches. The corpses hesitated, and that gave Flint his opening.

Staying close to the wall, he sprinted down the hallway. His breathing grew ragged. He left a bloody trail behind him. He needed to tend to his wounds, but he had to escape first. The hallway gently curved. Flint prayed that he wouldn't be caught in another infinite loop. The corpses disappeared around the corner, but he could still hear them shuffling, groaning, chanting Vasquez's name.

Flint reached the end of the hallway where there were two great double doors, flanked by skeletons holding spears at port arms. As he got closer, the skeletons came to life, pointing their spears at him. Flint drew his pistol and fired twice. Their skulls shattered, the bodies collapsing into piles of old bones. Flint opened the doors only to find complete blackness. Not even his sword could light the way, but he ran onward.

He saw a light ahead; another door. He stepped through it and onto a balcony overlooking the castle's courtyard and the surrounding countryside. Flint pursed his lips, his nostrils flared. Everything was ablaze with green light. Vasquez's army was so numerous, he found it a wonder that the castle didn't collapse beneath their weight. They all looked up at him.

"Vasquez, Vasquez, Vasquez!" Tens of thousands of voices chanting the necromancer's name. Flint felt the vibrations in his chest. The balcony led to the floating staircase that he and Navarro had seen outside. It led up to a single tower, tethered to the rest of the castle like a satellite. Flint glanced at his wounds; the blood had begun to congeal at least. Taking a deep breath, Flint ran for the staircase. Like the bridge over the pit of spikes, there were no rails. The tails of his long coat flapped behind him as he ran. Flint kept his eyes on the tower, making sure not to look down lest he be struck by vertigo.

After what felt like hours, Flint reached the top. The stairway ended at another balcony. An open doorway stood before him, the top carved to look like a human skull.

Guide me, O Lord, he thought. Flint took a deep breath and plunged into the darkness.

***

"Uh…" Riffey said, looking up at the old man on the mezzanine with his one good eye. "I take it he's one of yours?"

Navarro said nothing, mouth agape.

The old man leapt over the banister and landed on his feet in the center of the parlor. The white light enveloped everyone. Navarro winced. Riffey, Giles, Morales, and the students all gasped. Navarro saw the worms that had infested many of their wounds shrivel up and blow away as black dust. They blinked, patted themselves.

The man came to Navarro, put a hand on his shoulder.

"Come on son," he said. "We got monsters to kill."

Navarro grinned. "That's what we do."

The old man smiled back. "And nobody does it better."

Navarro looked all around him. It was hard to tell with their faces so badly rotted, but he could have sworn the undead were cringing, backing away. He wasn't certain who their benefactor was, but he had a pretty good idea.

"Hey," he said.

The old man looked at him.

"How is it... up there?"

"You'll find out."

"Not any time soon, I hope."

The old man barked a laugh. Then he raised his rifle and fired. His target didn't explode in a shower of gore, but rather dissolved in a stream of white flame, its dust blowing away.

"You got guns like that if we join up?" Giles asked.

"Let's go!" the old man bellowed.

Navarro raised his rifle and started firing into the mob.

***

Zelda Fletcher saw the walls of Danville approaching, and not a moment too soon. Her horse was spent, its sides and its mouth foamy. She felt bad for the creature; it didn't know it was magically enhanced for speed, didn't realize it was blown. Hopefully it would recover, but there was no time to worry about it now. She pulled back on the reins, and it came to a stop just outside the stables. Boys came running, staring at it with awe. The trail of fiery hoofprints it left in its wake still burned bright.

"What the fuck?!" one of them said.

"Telegraph office!" Fletcher shouted. "I need to get to the telegraph office!"

"This way," an older man said. He led her through the

city gates, pointed down the street. "Two blocks down this street, take a right, and you're there."

"Thanks!" Fletcher started running. She worried about McFarlane, Carrow, the priests and nuns, and Silas and Rico. McFarlane was right; it would take hours for reinforcements from Marsing to arrive. But they needed to know what was happening. They needed to know that the Great Necromancer had returned. She just hoped there was still someone manning the Danville office at this hour.

Thank God, she thought. There were lights on and somebody was home. She shouldered the door open. An old man in shirtsleeves, tie, and a visored hat looked up at her from his desk behind a counter.

"Where's the fire, Miss?" he asked.

"Castle Vasquez," Fletcher wheezed.

"What?!" he cried, rising from his seat.

"I need to wire Fort Marsing. Get some more Templars out there."

"Right away. Follow me."

He led Fletcher to another desk that had the telegraph machine. The old man sat down and put his hand the machine, ready to take her dictation.

"This is Zelda Fletcher," she said, and the old man began tapping. "Vasquez has returned." The old man looked up at her with horror, but he kept translating. "Silas Flint and Ricardo Navarro are inside the castle. Lady McFarlane and I are on the outskirts. Army of undead present. Send reinforcements immediately." After a pause, she said, "That's all."

The old man leaned forward on the desk, face in his hands. "Not again... not again..." he mumbled.

Fletcher patted his shoulder. "Not if we can help it."

She excused herself, left the office, and ran back to the stables outside the walls. "I need another horse!" she called.

After a few minutes, one of the stable boys brought her another animal, saddled up and ready to go. "Okay, that'll be..." he said.

"Fort Marsing will reimburse you," Fletcher said, elbowing him aside and climbing up onto the horse. She whispered a spell, and she felt a surge of energy enter the beast. The horse whinnied, reared up, its front legs kicking in the night sky. Fletcher smiled. This one seemed to like its unnatural enhancement.

"Ya!" she cried, and the horse surged forward, leaving another trail of flaming hoofprints behind it.

24

Silas Flint made his way through the tower. His boots crunched with every step. By the light of his sword, he could see the floor was strewn with human bones. A carrion wind blew through the hallway, making his coat flap around him. He heard buzzing and saw flies, no doubt drawn to the blood on his arm and leg. Swatting at the vermin, Flint pressed on. There were no torches in this place, but balls of green fire burned on either side of the hallway. His breath fogged; were it not for his heavy coat, he would be shivering. The path gently curved. Along the way he encountered an oil painting of Vasquez as he appeared in life, as he looked when Oglethorpe confronted him forty years ago. Flint felt its eyes follow him as he passed.

He heard a woman scream further down the hallway.

"The Proctors..." he said to himself. He started running. The hallway curved, the bones scattered as he sprinted, the green fire flickered as he passed.

Saint Michael the Archangel, defend us in battle, Flint prayed. He arrived at another set of double doors. He stopped to catch his breath. He was exhausted, his wounds ached, his heart thundered in his chest. Flint pulled on one of the iron rings on the doors. Locked. He heard sizzling from the other side and smelled burned flesh.

Flint rammed his shoulder into the doors and they fell open into the void. Flint gasped, his arms pinwheeling. All he could see was the emptiness of space, stars as pinpricks of light. He lost his balance and fell. The wind was knocked from him as he landed upon the stone floor. He climbed to his feet, looked all around him. There was nothing but the void. His sword shone bright, but it could not illuminate the room enough for him to see.

"Vasquez!" Flint snarled.

Nothing.

"Arturo Vasquez!" Flint called. "Matthew Oglethorpe delivered justice upon you! I come bringing your second judgment! Face me, coward!"

The illusory stars vanished and the room was plunged into darkness. Flint held his sword aloft, its glow burning white, but he couldn't see beyond its radius. His breath fogged even as his forehead was beaded with sweat. He moved forward, his boots tapping on the floor, the sound echoing.

"Matthew…"

It was Vasquez's voice, dead ahead.

"Matthew and I fought when I was a mortal man," Vasquez growled. "My power has doubled since then, Witch Hunter."

"Your pride will be your downfall again, heretic!" Flint shouted.

Vasquez chuckled. "Your guardian angels won't be able to save you this time, boy."

Two balls of green fire burst into existence before Flint. Then two more. And two more. They kept going until they formed a circle in the center of the room. Within the circle of fireballs, Flint saw a mosaic floor painting of Vasquez overseeing a field of slaughter. The darkness lifted. Around him, Flint saw a series of chains hanging from the ceiling. At the end of each one was a human body impaled on a barbed hook. Some were missing arms, others their entire lower halves below the waist. All had their chests cut open. Beyond the circle was an obsidian altar, upon which lay a headless body, desecrated like the others.

From the alter a series of stone steps led up to a black throne. Beside the staircase, Flint saw Mallory Proctor, her wrists bound by seething black energy. To his right was Monica Proctor, similarly bound. To his left was Madeline, who looked as though she'd been beaten to a pulp.

Above them all stood Vasquez. Flint narrowed his eyes.

He'd seen enough horrors in his fifteen year career to last a lifetime, but this one may have topped them all.

Vasquez wore an ornate robe decorated with sewn depictions of human skulls and demonic faces. His arms were covered in stitches, the skin a patchwork of grafts torn from human bodies. Green light shone through the gaps. His face was a similar patchwork of samples taken from others, like a chess board stretched thin over a grinning skull. Two bloody eyeballs with brown irises sat in his sockets, more green light shining behind them. His hair, black in life, was now half brown and half blonde.

"This body can barely contain my power," Vasquez hissed. "But it will be more than enough to tear your soul apart, you Templar scum." He giggled and waved his arms at the Sisters. "These three shall bear witness as I carve out your heart. Before the end, all of you will know that God has forsaken you, and death conquers all." The fires behind his eyes glowed brighter. "Let's go."

Vasquez held out his hands, palms facing Flint. A skull appeared, engulfed in green fire. It jetted toward Flint, screaming like a damned soul. Flint dove and rolled out of the way, the skull smashing into the floor where he stood, shattering the stone in a shower of chips and dust. Rolling to his feet, Flint aimed his pistol and emptied the magazine in Vasquez's direction. The necromancer vanished. A second later, he reappeared almost on top of Flint. Vasquez raised his hand, and a stream of green fire burst forth from his palm. Flint raised his sword. The blessed steel absorbed the magic, but the sheer force of it pushed him backwards. Vasquez vanished again. Flint felt the hairs on the back of his neck stand up. He sidestepped just in time to avoid a javelin of ice that flew past where his head had been. He felt the breeze as it passed and shattered against the wall.

Flint dropped his empty pistol and drew his second. He fired at Vasquez just as the necromancer conjured another screaming skull. Flint was a second too late rolling out of the way, and he felt the heat of the explosion, which left him covered in dust.

Before he could get up, Vasquez grabbed the collar of Flint's long coat and flung him across the chamber. Flint grunted as he slammed into the wall, barely maintaining his grip on his weapons. He looked up and saw Vasquez levitating toward him. Flint then saw that he had landed near Monica Proctor. The witch took no notice of him. She was in a trance, or magically sedated, perhaps. An idea occurred to Flint. He rose to his feet and touched his sword to the black lightning which bound the witch's wrists. The blade vibrated in his grip; an explosion of black sparks showered against his chest. Monica fell to her knees, gasping for breath.

"No!" Vasquez shrieked. He raised his hands, and now a stream of flaming skulls shot toward them, their screams echoing.

Monica grabbed Flint's wrist and everything seemed to stop. The skulls were frozen in midair.

"What in the world...?" Flint said.

"You cannot escape me that easily!" Vasquez shouted. More streams of green fire spewed forth. Monica raised her hands. It looked to Flint as though some sort of magical barrier was forming around them, but the spell sputtered on her fingertips. Flint felt it pass into his sword, the hilt vibrating in his grip.

"Oh dear," she said. She pulled Flint to one side, there was a crack as of thunder, and everything was in motion again, the flaming skulls crashing into the wall where they had been standing a moment ago.

"What are you doing?" Flint cried.

Vasquez laughed. "They know how to step sideways in time. As do I."

Monica pointed at Vasquez, a bolt of lightning firing from her fingertip. It exploded into sparks as it struck a barrier that formed around the necromancer.

"I am Hell's champion!" Vasquez shouted. "All of you will be burned by the fire that is never quenched, devoured by the worm that never dies!"

The necromancer conjured a boulder of ice and sent it hurtling toward Flint. Monica summoned a fireball which knocked it off course, smashing into the alter, sending the desecrated body flying.

"Free the others!" she shouted at Flint.

He nodded and sprinted toward Madeline. He heard Vasquez snarl something in a language he didn't recognize. A wall of bones erupted from the floor, extending to the ceiling, cutting him off from the red headed Proctor sister. Flint turned his face away just before he crashed into the wall, but the impact jarred him. Skeletal hands reached out from within the wall and wrapped him in a crushing embrace. He groaned as the breath was squeezed from him. His arms were pinned. His grip on his weapons loosened.

An unseen force rammed into the wall and Flint felt the vibrations in his bones. From the corner of his eye, he saw Monica gesturing. Another invisible blow. Flint twisted and struggled. A third strike, and then Vasquez was upon her. They vanished. Flint screamed as he turned his body and finally fell to the floor. Monica and Vasquez reappeared, the witch sporting a bloody cut on her cheek. Flint holstered his pistol and, using a two handed grip on his sword, began hacking away at the wall of bones. They splintered, shattered, sprayed him with dust.

"Silas!" Monica shouted.

He spun and brought up his sword just in time to parry a strike from Vasquez who now wielded a giant scythe. The necromancer, levitating above the floor, was a whirlwind of strikes, spinning, parrying, and lashing out at Flint who was hard pressed to deflect the blows. Flint backed up just in time to avoid a slice that would have disemboweled him, but instead cut a thin red line across his abdomen, soaking his shirt and waistcoat in blood.

"Why do you fight, boy?" Vasquez said as he advanced on Flint. "Death comes for us all. Death is our constant companion." He made an overhead sweeping cut. Flint ducked, stabbed with his sword, only for Vasquez to deflect the blow. "You fight, you struggle, you suffer for an indifferent God who cares nothing for your pain, your sorrow."

Monica conjured ball lightning. It shot toward Vasquez but was dissipated when it struck the magical barrier surrounding the necromancer. Without even looking at her, he gestured with one hand. A javelin of human bone, sharpened to a razor point, flew from the wall toward the witch, who vanished before it could strike her.

"I will bring the gift of death to the world," Vasquez said with a smile that exposed teeth sharpened to points in blackened and bloody gums, green light shining through the gaps. "I will become death!" Another sweeping cut which Flint barely managed to dodge. "When the world is dead, there will be no more pain, no more sorrow, no more temptation, no more struggle. Only one will: mine."

"Your madness ends here, Vasquez!" Flint darted forward, surprising the necromancer. He stabbed with his sword. Vasquez twisted out of the way, but Flint grazed his side, tearing his robe and the patchwork skin beneath. A green mist escaped from the wound, following Flint's blade, absorbed by the blessed steel.

"Damn you!" the necromancer shrieked. He levitated away, out of Flint's reach. Instead of pursuing, Flint focused on the wall of bone. He got a running start, shouting at the top of his lungs, leapt, and brought his blade down upon it. It exploded in a shower of grave dust and bone fragments, revealing Madeline Proctor who still appeared comatose.

Flint could hear Vasquez and Monica hurling spells at each other behind him. He rushed to Madeline's side, touched his sword to the black magic binding her. The sword glowed as it absorbed the spell, and she collapsed onto all fours.

"Miss Proctor," Flint said, shaking her. No response. "Madeline!"

"Argh!" Monica screamed. Flint looked up and saw that a giant skeletal hand had broken through the floor and had the witch in its grasp.

Madeline's eyes flew open and Flint was startled to see them gleaming with red light.

"YOU WILL NOT HARM MY SISTER!" Madeline screamed, causing the entire chamber to rumble. A nimbus of blue fire ignited around her body, and Flint scrabbled out of the way as she shot forth like a comet toward the necromancer.

Green fire appeared around Vasquez, and with his own roar he rocketed toward Madeline. Flint got to his feet and ran toward the altar. Mallory was still trapped, and he sensed that the other two would need her help.

He heard groans and the rattling of chains all around him; the bodies of the college students were stirring. Flint watched in horror as they pulled themselves off their hooks. Those who had no legs hovered in midair. Green fires burned in their eyes.

"Silas!" Monica cried from where she was still trapped in the skeletal fist. "On your right!"

Flint looked and saw the empty pistol he had discarded earlier vibrate, levitate off the floor, and then it flew toward him. An unseen force yanked a fresh magazine from inside his long coat. He watched his pistol reload itself and it flew into his empty holster. Despite the chaos around him, Flint thought, *A neat trick, that.*

"Vasquez! Vasquez! Vasquez!" the undead students chanted.

"I failed you," Flint called out. "I could not save you. But so help me God, I shall end your suffering!"

He thrust his sword into the gaping chest cavity of a zombie that was almost upon him. The undead student writhed, twisted, and was still. Before he could yank out the blade, another one, legless, flying, soared toward him, its arms outstretched, its teeth gnashing. He brought up his pistol and fired, the silver tipped bullet piercing its brain, and the desecrated corpse fell to the ground with a sickening splat.

The headless body laying upon the altar sat up. Green fire erupted from its neck and formed into the shape of a burning skull. It raised its hand and sorcerous lightning shot forth. Flint pulled his sword out just in time to absorb the blast. From behind he was tackled to the floor by one of the shambling corpses. He could hear its gnashing teeth, smell its carrion breath. Flint rolled over on top of the unholy monster, pressed his pistol beneath its head and pulled the trigger, splattering himself with its brain matter. He sprang up and rushed the altar. He swung his sword, and it absorbed the flaming skull, the body slumping forward.

Flint wheezed. His body felt like it was about to give out, but to stop meant death. He sprinted up the steps toward Mallory Proctor.

"No!" Vasquez bellowed. The steps exploded beneath Flint and he was flung into the air, flipping head over heels, before landing on the stone with a crack. He groaned in pain; for a brief, panicked moment he feared that his back was broken, but his legs obeyed his commands. The undead students were nearly upon him again. He staggered to his feet, fired a few more shots in their direction while resuming his climb. He felt a tug on his coat tails. One of the undead had him its grasp, but before it could pull him down, he shot it in the head.

Behind him he heard explosions and the sizzling of sorcerous lightning and fire. Flint reached Mallory. He touched his sword to the black energy circling her wrists, the blade absorbing the dark magic, and she fell to the floor.

"Mallory," Flint said, shaking her. "Mallory, you must rise! Your sisters are in danger!"

Her eyes fluttered open, glowing white. A moment later, Monica and Madeline appeared at her side, helped her to her feet.

Flint rose. He dropped the magazine of his pistol, loaded a fresh one. He turned. Vasquez was below them, surrounded by his undead minions. The necromancer's eyes burned with madness and hate. The Proctor Sisters came to Flint's side, their hands aglow with sorcery.

"Well, well," Vasquez said. "The fearless Witch Hunter and his harem of penitents. You have fought well, Silas Flint. But you are not Matthew Oglethorpe. Perhaps when this battle is ended, I'll raise your corpse and we can visit my old friend together."

Flint's chest burned, his back throbbed, his wounds bled. He pointed his sword at the necromancer.

"You shall not harm him or anyone else. You have made

yourself an abomination in the eyes of God. You have butchered the innocent, you have tortured the souls of your prisoners, and you have perverted the laws of God's creation. Your miserable existence ends tonight, Vasquez! I shall strike you down with righteous fury, and you will face God's terrible judgment!" Flint gave the wizard a fierce smile. "Let's go." He shouted with all the anger, the pain, the torment he'd experienced that night. The Sisters joined their shouts with his, their hands and eyes aglow with power, and together they rushed into battle.

25

Flint fired his pistol as he ran, taking down the undead students with headshots, the silver tipped bullets sizzling in their corrupted flesh. The Sisters conjured fire, lightning, and ice that surged toward Vasquez. The magical barrier protecting him whined, sparked, but held firm, their spells broken. The necromancer gestured, working his hands as though molding clay, and the fallen students' bodies were taken up in a whirlwind of dark magic. The corpses were twisted, the bones cracking, the flesh melting, taking a new shape. Flint was horrorstruck at this new monstrosity, a shambling mass of flesh with bony protrusions and a great gaping maw, its tongue like a giant fleshy tentacle. Runes carved in the stone walls glowed green. Flint fired his pistol into the creature but it took no notice of the bullets, hurtling toward him like an avalanche of rotting skin.

The Sisters floated off the floor, held up their hands,

and streams of fire enveloped the monster, its cries like a dozen voices all screaming in unison. The stench of burnt flesh made Flint's eyes water.

"Silas!" Mallory shouted.

"We will slay his beasts!" Monica said.

"You must slay Vasquez!" Madeline yelled above the roar of flames and the screams of the creature.

Vasquez laughed. "Yes, Witch Hunter," he hissed. "Face me. Face your destiny."

Flint advanced on the necromancer. Vasquez stood still, gripping his scythe. As he drew nearer, Flint could feel the temperature drop. His breath fogged. He kept moving but the cold was becoming unbearable. A blackness appeared before Vasquez, a tiny sphere. It expanded, and Flint felt it pulling him onward.

"It's beautiful, isn't it?" Vasquez asked, as the sphere continued to expand. Flint stopped moving, but it kept pulling him forward. Within the sphere he could see pinpoints of light. "Space..." Vasquez said. "Humanity thought it was their final frontier. It shall be your final resting place."

Flint turned around, tried to move away, but the suction was relentless. The soles of his boots smoked as he strained every muscle, the cords on his neck standing out, grunted with agony as he tried to step forward. Vasquez's laughter echoed in his ears.

Mallory Proctor swooped down from above, yanked Flint off his feet, soaring toward the ceiling. He gasped and panted, every inch of his body feeling like it was on fire. Monica and Madeline Proctor joined hands, combined their powers to conjure a tremendous blast of sorcerous lightning which pushed the flesh monster off the floor and into the portal that Vasquez had opened. It was not yet wide enough to accommodate the monster's bulk, and it stuck there, half of it in the tower, the other half dangling in the vacuum of space.

"Throw me at him!" Flint bellowed.

Mallory nodded, and Flint was flying, over the struggling monster, hurtling toward Vasquez. The necromancer, caught by surprise, raised his hand and green fire surged toward Flint. His sword absorbed the blast, and Flint screamed a battle cry as he flew closer. Vasquez brought up his scythe in time to block the stab, but Flint's momentum sent them both crashing to the floor.

Before Flint could rise, the necromancer levitated off the ground, twirling his scythe before bringing it down in a vicious overhead strike. Flint rolled out of the way and the scythe sunk into the stone floor. Vasquez brought it up and around, slicing through the brick. Flint fired his pistol twice and the bullets smacked into the necromancer's chest. Vasquez grunted. There was no blood, but beams of green light shone through the holes.

Flint recalled what had happened earlier when he'd grazed the necromancer's side with his sword. He saw it now. He knew what he had to do.

Vasquez vanished. The Sisters snapped their fingers, and the Witch Hunter felt his stomach drop. Vasquez there again, attempting to flank him. The necromancer snarled in rage.

"You cannot escape us that easily," the Sisters said together, feral smiles on their faces.

Vasquez disappeared, they snapped again, and time resumed its normal flow. The flesh monster struggled and screamed, but the portal held it in place. Flint aimed and fired his pistol again, taking Vasquez in the arm.

Flint advanced, firing until his pistol locked open. Vasquez screamed, more in anger than pain, and called forth a wall of green flame around him. Madeline Proctor conjured an icy spear which shot toward the necromancer but shattered around his magical barrier.

"Where is your God now?!" Vasquez shouted. From his mouth spewed a torrent of blood and vomit that sprayed over Madeline. She screamed in pain and disgust. Her sisters rushed to her aid. Vasquez laughed in triumph. Flint prayed that she would be alright, for she had provided him the distraction that he needed.

Flint bellowed in rage, summoning one last burst of energy to sprint toward Vasquez. He dropped his empty pistol, taking a two handed grip on his sword.

"What?!" Vasquez cried. He grunted as Flint rammed his blade into the necromancer's belly. The sword punched through the parchment thin flesh, scraped against the spine he had taken from a fallen student's body, and erupted through his back.

All fell silent. Vasquez's stolen eyes looked down at the blade embedded in his body, looked to Flint. His mouth fell open.

"You made a mistake, Vasquez," Flint hissed, twisting the sword, making the necromancer's body tremble.

"Your spirit is holding this body together with your foul sorcery. You of all people should know that Templar blades absorb magic."

The eyeballs fell from Vasquez's sockets, revealing the green fires that burned behind them. Those fires wavered, flickered, and slowly they were pulled into Flint's sword.

The corners of Vasquez's mouth turned up. "Well done… Templar…" he wheezed. "I wonder… if your descendants… will be… as good as you…"

Flint felt his sword vibrating in his grip. It went up his arms, into his chest, and he felt as though he would vomit, but he held fast. Vasquez's makeshift body seemed to deflate, the bones liquifying, the skin stretching and losing all shape as the fires that burned inside went out.

The necromancer laughed. "I'll… be back…" The last of his spark was extinguished, and remains of his artificial body melted around Flint's sword, pouring onto the floor with a sickening splatter.

The portal that the sorcerer had opened into deep space snapped shut, cutting the flesh monster in half. It plopped onto the floor, losing all shape, dissolving into a puddle of rotting flesh and broken bone.

Flint fell to his knees, breathing hard. He dropped his sword and his shoulders slumped. He didn't know how long he remained like that. He reached with a trembling hand for his pocket watch. He pulled on the chain, and his eyes widened when he saw that the watch had been destroyed in the fight. It was nothing but shards of broken metal and glass, the picture of his family torn to bits.

"Oh… no…" he breathed. After all that, to discover this…

he felt tears welling up in his eyes. He couldn't break, not in front of the Proctors. But... he felt a sob threaten to burst from his throat.

He felt a light touch on his shoulder. The Sisters were standing around him. He saw their mouths moving, no doubt casting a spell of some sort. He didn't have the spirit left to grumble about it.

The glass and metal in his pocket floated away. He saw them reform, fitting together like a jigsaw puzzle. The jagged lines vanished, and his watch fell into his grip, intact. The hands were moving in the correct direction again.

He looked up at the Proctors. A single tear ran down his cheek.

"Thank you," he said.

They smiled.

"It is the least that we could do," they said in unison.

***

Ricardo Navarro was spattered from head to toe in the black ichor of the undead. His arms burned, his lungs felt like they would burst, he was drenched in sweat, but still he kept shooting, clubbing, and smashing the oncoming horde. The students held each other, cowering beside the fountain. The old man's rifle disintegrated zombies with beams of light. Riffey and Giles should have dropped hours ago from exhaustion if nothing else, but as soon as the old guy showed up, they fought like younger men, with seemingly boundless energy. Now that he thought about it, Navarro realized he hadn't seen either one of them reload their pistols once since the old guy appeared, but they kept shooting dozens, then hundreds of rounds. He grinned. The Lord had multiplied the loaves and fishes; surely He could multiply the bullets.

The zombies stopped advancing. Navarro took a few more shots with his rifle, dropping them where they stood, but the others did not come forward. Their heads cocked, as though listening to a sound only they could hear. A collective sigh emerged from the crowd. Navarro, Riffey, and Giles kept their weapons ready. The old man appeared to relax.

The undead all fell to their knees together with military-like precision. They looked up at the ceiling and then Navarro saw the green fires in their eyes flicker and die. Their bodies turned black, and crumbled to ash and dust. A cool breeze wafted through the parlor and the hallways, blowing away the remnants of Vasquez's army. Navarro was confident that if he opened the front doors, he'd find the courtyard empty now.

The fountain of blood shimmered, wavered, and vanished along with the black suits of armor, the spears holding the doors, and the green fires burning in the torches. The old guy looked around, and the torches flickered back to life, with normal orange flame. Even the moonlight resumed its normal hue.

"It's over," the old man said.

"What..." Navarro said. "You mean..."

"Yes. Silas has won. Vasquez is gone. Again."

Navarro barked a laugh. "Holy shit... holy shit... he did it... he really fuckin' did it..."

"He had a little help," the old man smiled.

"Hey," Riffey called out. "Who are you anyway?"

"We wouldn't have survived if you hadn't shown up," Giles said. He patted his body. The cuts, the bruises, the festering wounds that had covered him were all gone. The students were similarly healed, though Professor Morales was still missing her eyes. Navarro noticed that she was looking at the old guy as though she could see him.

"Guys," Navarro said. "This is... Supernumerary Jonah Byers."

"What?!" Morales said. "But... you... I read about what happened to you back then... you..."

"Yes," Byers said. "The Lord allowed me to return to this place where I passed on, to come to you in your time of need."

"What the fuck?!" one of the boys shouted, rising to his feet. "You come to us now? Now?! Where the fuck were you when the others were tortured?! Killed?!"

"Cole!"

"What are you doing?!"

"Don't talk like that!"

The other students murmured, whispered, tried to calm their classmate, but his tears flowed as his face was twisted with rage.

"Was it God's plan?! Huh?! Was it His divine purpose or His divine will that the others die?! Fuck you!" Cole stormed past everyone, pulled open the front doors. Navarro saw that his suspicion was right; the castle grounds were empty once again. Cole stalked off into the night. Byers watched him go, a look of sadness on his face.

"Hey," Navarro said. "Uh, I'm sorry about that. They've been through a lot and..."

"It's alright," Byers said. "Cole Trevino has a long road ahead of him. As do you and Silas."

Navarro smirked. "I guess I shouldn't bother asking for more details, huh?"

Byers smiled back. "No man should ever know too much about his own future. I can say that if you both keep the faith and trust in God, you'll make it through the trials to come."

There was a flash of white light. Navarro closed his eyes. When he opened them again, Byers was gone.

Everyone was quiet. The remaining students climbed to their feet. Morales too got up. She tore off a strip of her blouse, wrapped it around her head, covering her empty eye sockets, and tying a knot in the back. She approached Navarro and the security men.

"Professor?" Riffey asked.

She smiled. "I can see. Not like I could before. It's different... it's like... you're all lit up."

Giles crossed himself. "Praise God."

***

Zelda Fletcher urged the horse to go faster, though it was already galloping far more quickly than nature intended. She felt bad; the poor thing would surely die as soon as they stopped, but she had to get back to her friends. They didn't stand a chance against that army, but maybe she could enhance the carriage horses, get them the hell out of there at least.

There. She could see that eerie green glow on the horizon. She pushed the horse harder. It was foaming at the mouth, its eyes rolled up in its head, it left a blazing trail behind them – she hoped she didn't start a wildfire. The carriages and her party were upon her sooner than she expected, and she yanked on the horse's reins. As she'd feared, it collapsed as soon as it stopped, and Fletcher had to give herself a magical boost to jump free of the saddle before the animal took her down with it.

"I'm back!" she cried.

The others smiled and nodded to her, then returned their focus to Vasquez's army which still hadn't crossed the dead zone's boundary. Anton stood there, arms crossed, the green fires serving as his eyes unreadable.

"How'd it go?" McFarlane asked.

"I told them what has happening, to send everyone they could," Fletcher replied. "How's it been here?"

"No change," McFarlane murmured, keeping her eyes on the enemy.

Anton cocked his head. After a few moments he focused his burning gaze on Fletcher and McFarlane.

"A pity," he said. "I was looking forward to slaying you both."

The women looked at each other, looked at the zombie.

"Going somewhere?" Fletcher asked.

"My master has fallen once again."

Her eyes widened. "Silas..."

"He has need of me elsewhere," Anton said. "Perhaps I will have the chance to feast on your great grandchildren one hundred years hence."

There was a crack of thunder. A flaming ring appeared before Anton, expanding into a portal big enough to accommodate his hulking form. He stepped through it and vanished, the portal closing behind him with a zipping sound.

The undead army, extending as far as Fletcher could see, all knelt upon the ground and looked up at the sky. The green fires in their eyes burnt out, and with a sigh, they all dissolved to ash and blew away on the breeze.

"Praise God," Carrow said, as he joined the women at their side. The priests and nuns began singing *Non Nobis*.

McFarlane clapped Carrow on the shoulder. "Once that's done, we need to get to Castle Vasquez."

26

Canyon Cove was one of the wealthiest cities in the east, home of the Snake River Trading Company, its people no strangers to the power and terror of magicians. When a magical portal opened in front of the SRTC corporate office in the middle of the night and two magicians stepped out, a young Asian woman and an old man in a bedraggled tweed suit, witnesses ran to notify the local police, who would no doubt run to the nearest telegraph office to request Witch Hunters from Fort Marsing. Normally, Lee preferred to be more discreet, but after the horrors she'd seen this night, she was eager to get this over with as soon as possible.

"Where was that orphanage?" she asked.

"Er... let me think... this is the SRTC office... uh, this way!"

Meyer levitated off the ground and soared down the street, Lee close on his heels. The professor led her down a few blocks, three blocks to the right, and then two more to the left. The city burned bright with neon lights, the streets thick with bicycle and carriage traffic. Civilians screamed and scurried out of their way. She didn't expect any of the local cops to be brave enough to take on both a witch and a wizard, but she was prepared to blast them to Hell if any tried to stop them.

Meyer stopped, lighted upon the ground. Lee caught up and saw that he had led her to what looked like a bookstore. BOSCH'S BOOKS the sign said. It was closed for the night, but that wouldn't be a problem.

"This is it?" she asked.

"Yes," Meyer replied. "The orphanage was on this corner."

"Hmm..." she said. Lee reached out with her senses. She couldn't detect anything remotely magical in the area. It was an ordinary city block. "Any bright ideas?"

"Well, the church that ran the orphanage is nearby. Maybe we need to..."

"Wait," Lee said. She levitated herself from the ground, high enough to see over the top of the building. She ignored the civilians pointing, screaming, running. There was a patch of grass behind the bookstore, fenced in from the surrounding buildings. The former site of a playground maybe? She motioned for the professor to join her. Together, they floated over the bookstore and landed in the yard in the back.

"What is it? Did you sense something?" Meyer asked.

"No..." Lee said. She saw a few patches of concrete with metal rods poking out. Definitely a former playground. "I had an idea though. Vasquez loved his dog, yes?"

"Yes."

"Maybe when it died, he buried it somewhere around here?"

"It's possible. But how would we ever find it?"

"Start digging."

"You must be joking."

"Do I sound like I'm fucking joking?!" she snapped.

"Alright, alright," he muttered.

They reached out with their power, and the soil split. The earth spread, creating a ditch six inches deep. It was slow going, but they kept at it. There had to be something here. There had to be!

You've worked so hard for this, a voice whispered in her mind.

"What?" she asked.

"Huh?" Meyer replied.

"Did you say something?"

"No."

"Oh. Well keep digging."

He's going to take it, the voice whispered.

Lee glared at Meyer. His back was to her as he spread his hands, the dirt parting before his will.

You're close, so close. Don't let him take it. You deserve to claim it.

"Destiny!" Meyer cried.

She shook herself. "What?"

"I think I found something."

Meyer plucked some sort of gem from the earth. It was black as obsidian but carved like a diamond. She'd never seen anything like it before. She could not sense any magical energy from the gem.

"What on earth is that?" she asked.

"I don't know," Meyer said. "It looks similar to our gems that we use to communicate with..."

The world went black, as though they'd been plucked from the earth and dropped into the deep space that Vasquez loved.

"What the..."

The darkness vanished, and the two magicians found themselves on a playground. The sun shone bright in a cloudless sky. All around them, children ran, laughed, played, taking no notice of them. A Catholic priest and nun stood at one end, watching the kids.

"What is this place?" she asked. "An illusion? A dream?"

"I think... it's a memory. His." Meyer pointed.

A little boy sat by himself on a bench, away from the other children who all avoided him. Lee reached out to a swing set, and her hand passed through the metal bars as though they weren't there. Lee and Meyer approached the boy who didn't look up. As they got closer, Lee saw a small dog laying on the bench, a chihuahua mix. The boy stroked the dog.

"It's okay Chuy," he said. "We don't need them. We don't need anybody. We can take on the whole world, huh buddy?"

The dog panted.

"They don't know what I can do," the boy said. "I can do magic Chuy! Magic!"

Lee and Meyer looked at each other.

"I'll show them," the boy said. "I'll show them all. Nobody will ever be mean to us again!"

"The crown has to be close," Lee whispered.

"Where though?"

"It's right here," the boy said, looking at them. They gasped and drew back. "You can't have it though."

Lee took a deep breath. "Arturo," she said. "You don't need it anymore. You grew up to be the most powerful necromancer who ever lived. Just give us the crown. My friend Charles would very much like to have it. I promise he'll take care of it."

"You can't have it!" the young Vasquez shouted. "Tony! Stop them!"

"Who the hell is... urk!" Meyer's words were cut off as a great black sword burst through his chest, his blood spraying. Lee backed away, her mouth agape. Standing behind Meyer was an enormous figure in black armor. Green fires burned in his eyes, his parchment thin flesh stretched tight over his skull which was encircled by a halo of sorcerous fire.

Anton put a massive boot on Meyer's backside and kicked the twitching corpse free of his sword. He pointed it at Lee. "My master will not give up his crown. You may not have it."

"He doesn't need it anymore!" Lee screamed. She summoned a blast of magical fire which enveloped Anton. The fire burned out, but Anton remained unscathed. The playground vanished around them, and Lee found herself standing in an underground crypt. Torches burned on the walls. A tiny sarcophagus was on a raised dais at the front of the room. Beneath it was a bouquet of fresh flowers. Anton stomped forward.

"You will not take it," his sepulchral voice echoed.

Lee sent a magical bolt of lightning toward the zombie. It arced over his armor, but still he strode toward her. Desperate, she levitated from the floor and floated toward the sarcophagus. She pointed at it.

"Back!" she cried. "Get back, or I'll blow the mutt's bones to Hell!"

Anton stopped. Cocked his head.

Lee yanked off the stone lid and gazed inside.

There was the skeleton of a small dog, curled up as though sleeping. Next to it was a photograph of the young Vasquez and Chuy, the panting dog looking like it was smiling for the camera. And at the other end of the sarcophagus was a black circlet. A depiction of a human skull was etched into the center above a blood red jewel. Her eyes widened. She could sense the power emanating from it, sending an electric thrill up her spine. Her mouth fell open.

She grabbed the crown and felt as though her magical

talent had been magnified tenfold. Lee laughed in triumph and relief. Anton remained rooted in place.

"I got it! I got it!" Lee cried. She laughed again. Had she ever felt this giddy?

"Go then," Anton said. "Your master will not escape his fate."

Lee's back arched, her eyes rolled up in her head, her body twitched. Her mind was flooded with images: of fiery clouds in the shape of mushrooms, of three witches who looked alike, of trains and marching armies of men and the dead, of two men dueling on a rocky outcropping in the pouring rain, beside an ancient flag, torn and flapping in the storm. They were gone, and Lee collapsed onto all fours, grasping the crown, panting for breath.

"What…" she said.

"Perhaps you see what is to come," Anton replied.

Lee tucked the crown into her backpack. She whispered the incantation. The portal opened, and she leapt inside. It closed behind her.

***

Anton stood alone in the crypt. A shadow appeared at his side. The torches flickered.

"Master," Anton said. "May I ask why you changed your mind?"

The shadow chuckled. "I had a vision," it said. "Charles Flint will do great things with my crown. He too will know death. And I shall recover my property in time for my return."

"What would you have me do now?"

"Go to Flint. Be his champion until it is my time again. I will grant you the power to go freely."

"As you command, my master. It was good to be with you again."

"Yes... yes, it was. I learned much from my battle with Silas Flint. I know now that this cannot be rushed. One hundred years hence, you and I shall make the world burn and they will all know the peace of death."

27

Silas Flint was enveloped in a flash of light. When he opened his eyes, he and the Proctor sisters were in the parlor of Castle Vasquez. He looked and saw Navarro, Giles, Riffey, Morales – who now sported a blindfold over her eye sockets – and the surviving college students.

"Silas!" Navarro cried. He rushed forward and embraced the Witch Hunter in a tight bear hug. Flint grunted in pain.

"Oh! Uh, sorry sir," Navarro said, backing away.

"That is quite alright, Mr. Navarro," Flint said. He suspected that he looked terrible: covered in cuts, bruises, dried blood, to say nothing of his aching knees and back.

"Did you really do it?" Riffey asked. "Did you... you took out Vasquez?"

"Not without help," Flint said, gesturing toward the Proctors. They stood serenely, hands behind their backs, saying nothing.

"Really?" Navarro said. "You three really got your hands dirty this time, huh?"

"Yes," Mallory said.

"Not without a price, however," Monica said.

"We expect to face our judgment soon," Madeline sighed.

Flint patted his trouser pocket. As he expected, the radio was smashed to pieces. "I apologize Ricardo," he said. "Your radio did not survive the battle."

"Thank you for reminding us," the Sisters said in unison. They gestured, and the radio reassembled into one piece. Flint handed it to Navarro who stuffed it into a pouch on his belt.

"Thanks," Navarro said. "But... you guys don't really need this, do you?"

"No, we do not."

"But we enjoy being news reporters."

"We hope to continue."

Flint snorted. "I will never grow accustomed to your peculiar ways. But I thank you again for your assistance."

"We saved your lives."

"And you saved ours."

"If it is any consolation, we are now even."

They sighed.

"It is time to pay the piper," they said together. Another flash of light, and they were gone.

All was silent.

"Uh..." Riffey said.

"The fuck was that all about?" Giles asked.

"Are you guys… working with witches?" one of the girls asked.

"It's a long story," Navarro shrugged.

"Those three…" Morales said. "Strange…"

"That is a fitting description, yes," Flint said.

"The rest of you, you're all lit up," Morales said. "But them… I don't know how to describe it. It's like they're both here and not here. Like… I don't know. They're grey."

Flint was too tired to ask what she meant. He trusted that God would reveal His plan in due time.

***

Flint and Navarro stood on a hill which overlooked Castle Vasquez beneath the morning sun. With them were Zelda Fletcher, Diana McFarlane, Robert Carrow, and General Abernathy. The ladies and Carrow had arrived by carriage shortly after the Sisters had vanished. After their reunion, they awaited the reinforcements from Fort Marsing. Abernathy was in the lead carriage and listened to Flint and Navarro's tale with rapt attention. He put his hands on their shoulders.

"Both of you… you'll go down in history for what you did here," the General said.

"All glory and honor to God alone," Navarro said.

Flint raised an eyebrow. "Well said, Mr. Navarro."

"A friend reminded me of what really matters."

The Templar reinforcements had brought loads of explosives with them. Carrow and Abernathy looked on in apprehension as they laid the TNT at the castle's walls and towers.

"You think it'll take this time?" Fletcher asked.

"I hope so," Carrow murmured.

After two hours, everything was in readiness. From atop their perch on the hill, Flint and the others heard a Supernumerary shout, "Fire in the hole!"

The castle was enveloped in fire. The boom echoed throughout the grassy pains. The towers came tumbling down. A cloud of dust washed over everything. When the smoke cleared, Castle Vasquez was naught but rubble.

McFarlane came to Flint's side. "I'm sorry I couldn't join you Silas," she said.

Continuing to focus on the remains of the Castle, Flint replied, "We all have our paths to follow."

She looked to Fletcher who was chatting up Navarro. "She talks about you a lot."

Flint grunted.

She laughed. "People will start to think witches are your type."

"I am sure I do not know what you are talking about, Diana."

McFarlane chuckled. "Will you be returning to Marsing soon?"

"No. I must remain here. I need to see if it is truly over."

She said nothing for a few moments. "Would you mind if Zelda and I stayed with you?"

"Not at all."

***

Many of the other Templars, including Abernathy and Carrow, remained on the outskirts of the castle's remains, setting up camp for the night. They started fires, they ate, drank, conversed, prayed, but the atmosphere remained somber. Flint stayed apart from the others, never leaving his perch on the hill. Navarro brought him his dinner and a tankard of wine, but Flint barely touched them. Late into the night, when the others had gone to bed, Flint stayed awake, watching, waiting.

It began around 3 a.m. He had just checked his pocket watch by the light of the moon when he heard something stir in the rubble. His eyes widened. Quickly, far more quickly than he could have imagined, the stones flew from all around the landscape, reshaping, rebuilding, reforming. In less than five minutes, it was over. Castle Vasquez, in all of its grotesque glory was back, as though they had never been there. Flint bowed his head and sighed.

He heard footsteps. Looking up, he saw Abernathy and Navarro a few paces away. They looked out at the restored castle.

"Damnation," Abernathy said. "I'd hoped it would be different this time."

"At least he's gone," Navarro said.

"Yes," Flint said. "For now."

***

Deep within Castle Vasquez, in the floating tower, Vasquez's chambers lay empty save for his obsidian throne. All was silent. The moon shone through one of the windows, its light illuminating the chamber. From the ceiling fell a single mote of dust. It floated through the air, spinning lazy circles, until it came to rest upon the throne. And there it would wait. More motes of dust would join it in the days, weeks, and months to come, and for the next one hundred years. Waiting. For next time would be different.

28

Destiny Lee stepped into Charles's office. With him was Lilian Turner, Arnold Schreck, Ingrid Barnett, and Constance Deville. Emil Parlow had once been a member of the inner circle, but Charles had killed him after the botched assassination attempt on his brother in Salem last month.

Charles rose from his seat behind the desk that had once belonged to an American general. He stepped forward to meet her.

"Destiny... did you...?" he said.

"Yes," she said. She flung her backpack down on the floor. She opened it and dug out her prize. She had to admit, now that she wasn't worried for her life, that it looked like such a simple thing. She didn't know what she'd been expecting; a giant gold crown like kings wore in children's books? But this simple black circlet, with its depiction of a skull biting down on the blood red jewel in the center... hard to believe it could grant so much power.

Charles's eyes widened and he gingerly took the crown from Lee.

"Such a small thing…" he whispered. He looked to his assembled staff. "One of you, bring me the book."

Schreck brought Charles his copy – Vasquez's copy – of *In Realis Magicae.* He looked at Lee.

"Where on earth did you end up finding it?"

"The clues led us to Canyon Cove."

"What?!" Turner blurted. "Impossible. I lived there for twenty years! I never sensed it!"

Lee shrugged. "Well, I don't think it was literally in Canyon Cove. I had to go… elsewhere to find it."

"Destiny…" Charles said. "What you have done… you will go down in history for this magnificent achievement. All that is within my power to grant, I will give you. You shall have riches, power…"

"Sir?" she said.

He looked at her in expectation.

"What I would really like right now… is… some time off."

"Time off?" Barnett spoke up. "He's offering you the world, girl!"

"I understand, and I appreciate it, Charles. Truly, I do. It's just… Castle Vasquez took a lot out of me. I need time to… recover."

Charles gave her a warm smile. "I understand completely. Take as much time as you need. You will always have a place at my side, and I will give you your proper reward whenever you're ready."

She nodded. Not bothering to leave the bunker first,

she opened another portal. Maybe some time on the coast would do her some good. She stepped through and was gone.

***

Charles's forehead was beaded with sweat. Vasquez had been a tricky one. As he'd expected, the man had placed a curse on the crown. He couldn't sense it, but he knew it was there. Fortunately, Nazari's book provided him the counterspell he needed. The curse dissolved like a black cloud. Schreck, Barnett, and Deville all looked at him with a mixture of awe and fear. Turner stayed off to the side, looking nervous.

"Is everything alright Lilian?"

"How..." she said. "How could it have been under my nose the whole time? Twenty years... twenty years I lived there... how..."

Ignoring her, Charles held the crown in his hands. He looked at it from every angle, searching for anything, any enchantments, or spells he might have missed. He'd recited every counterspell in the book for good measure. The only way to learn if he'd succeeded was to put it on. But putting it on risked madness or death. Oh well. Nothing ventured, nothing gained. He slipped the crown over his head and it rested upon his brow.

His body felt like it was on fire. Every nerve crackled with energy. Charles shrieked as arcs of sorcerous energy arced all around him. Faintly, he could hear the computer sound klaxons and heard Rob's monotone voice.

"Danger, unknown energy signature detected," it said.

Charles roared in pain. The others backed away, shielding their eyes.

"Charles!" he heard Turner cry out.

Images flooded his mind. Visions of things that were, of that had been, and were to come. His eyes bulged, his throat raw. Just as he felt like his heart would burst, it was over, and he collapsed to the floor.

The others rushed to his side. He could feel them patting his body, shaking him.

"Charles!"

"Are you alright?"

"Speak to us!"

Turner gently lifted his head. "Charles? Are you with us? Are you alright?"

He opened his eyes. Turner gasped.

Charles levitated from the ground. A nimbus of green fire surrounded his body. He smiled.

"I'm better than alright. I feel like I'm ready to conquer the world."

EPILOGUE

Mallory, Monica, and Madeline Proctor sat and waited in the office where they'd spent much time waiting over the last few months. They supposed that the term waiting didn't mean much in a place where time had no meaning. The office and everything in it were painted a bright shade of white: the walls, the ceiling, the floor, the doors, the chairs, and the desk.

The door behind the desk opened, and in strode a man dressed in a white suit and white tie. As usual, his face was... they couldn't think of a better way to describe it than blurred. It was like when an ancient television set wasn't receiving decent reception. The man had told them it was for their benefit, for even with all of their magical power, he said, seeing his true form might break them.

Without a word, the man with the blurred out face sat down at his desk and steepled his fingers. The Sisters waited. He waited. They had no idea how much time – relatively speaking – had passed before they could take it no more.

"We broke the rules," Mallory said.

The man said nothing.

"We felt it was the right thing to do," Monica said.

Still nothing.

"Vasquez is a unique threat," Madeline said.

The man finally stirred. "Yes," he said. "He is a unique threat, as you learned to your sorrow."

The Sisters were silent. The man sighed.

"We did not impose these rules on you to make your mission more difficult," he said. "They are for your own good, and the good of your charges. Vasquez could have killed you. If he had, then your judgment would have had to be made. And it would not have gone well for you."

The Sisters cast their eyes down.

"Still," the man went on. "As you said, you broke the rules. And you must be punished for your transgression. We have already decided on your sentence."

The Sisters clutched each other's hands.

"We sentence you to time served in Castle Vasquez."

They sighed in relief. They couldn't see his face, but they imagined the man to be smiling.

"There is one thing I am curious about," he said. "What made you decide to get your hands dirty, as Mr. Navarro colorfully put it?"

"Don't you already know?" the Sisters asked in unison.

"Yes. But I want to hear it from you."

They thought for a moment.

"Silas's salvation is our salvation," Mallory said.

"He must succeed if we are to get a second chance," Monica said.

"And we rather like the world," Madeline said.

"Is that all?" the man asked. "Pure self-interest?"

The Sisters looked down again.

"You've grown to like him," the man said.

They smiled.

"He is a fascinating character," Mallory said.

"Though he hides his true self well," Monica said.

"And he is quite handsome," Madeline said.

Her sisters looked at her with raised eyebrows.

"At least I think so," she said, looking away.

"That will be all for now," the man said, rising from his desk.

"We have a question," they said.

"Ask it, and I will answer if I can."

"How is it that Silas can see us as we really are?" they asked.

The man in the white suit rapped his knuckles on his desk. After a few moments of silence, he spoke: "The Flint brothers are both men of unusually strong will. It was our hope that both of them would be of great service, but the one has fallen away. Even he has his role to play in the events to come, though we wish that he had chosen the right path. It is well that Silas is growing to trust you more. I fear that you three may be called upon to intervene directly once again."

He looked at them, and the Sisters were temporarily blinded by a flash of white light, there and gone again in a second.

"Guide him toward his destiny. If he fulfills the role that he was born for, then your Purgatory on earth will be at an end."

TWO MASTERS

No man can serve two masters: for either he will hate the one, and love the other; or else he will hold to the one and despise the other. Ye cannot serve God and mammon.

 - Matthew 6:24

1

Witch Hunter Captain Silas Flint leaned his head against the window. The carriage occasionally bumped as it passed over dips in the road – trail, really – but otherwise he was lost in his thoughts. Riding in the carriage with him were his assistant, Supernumerary Ricardo Navarro, Lady Templar Diana McFarlane, and the reformed witch, Zelda Fletcher. Theirs was one of many carriages that had recently departed Castle Vasquez, where Flint had done battle with the resurrected shade of Arturo Vasquez, the most terrible necromancer the Empire had ever seen. Flint emerged victorious, but the enchanted castle had resisted their efforts to level it with explosives, magically reassembling itself overnight. The Witch Hunters were now returning to their headquarters at Fort Marsing, leaving the castle behind them but intent on establishing a new quarantine around it.

Flint gazed at the grassy plains and forested groves of the passing landscape but didn't really see them. He'd nearly died fighting his way through the castle to Vasquez, and again during his struggle with the repulsive lich. Three mysterious witches, the Proctor Sisters, had come to his and Navarro's aid during the case. Indeed, he thought they owed their lives to them. He in turn had come to their rescue when Vasquez captured them, and together they destroyed the vile necromancer. He snorted. The Witch Hunter Matthew Oglethorpe had slain Vasquez forty years ago, and yet he had returned from death. Flint feared that the world had not seen the last of him.

"You okay sir?" Navarro asked.

Flint grunted by way of reply. The two women remained silent, which suited him. General Abernathy had arrived with the carriage fleet and was riding at the head of the convoy on its way back to Marsing. He'd told Flint and Navarro that they'd go down in the history books for what they accomplished at Castle Vasquez, rescuing the surviving members of an archaeological team that had gone missing inside, to say nothing of killing the necromancer a second time. Flint only wished that he could have saved them all. History would make its judgment long after he had passed on. Right now, he just wanted to go home, bathe, have a decent meal, and go to bed.

He felt sleep overtaking him. Normally Flint disliked taking afternoon naps, as they made it difficult for him to fall asleep again at night, but this time he decided to make an exception. He closed his eyes.

A few moments later, the carriage stopped, jostling its passengers. Flint woke with a start. He heard the horses whinny in terror.

"The hell...?" Fletcher said, peering out the window.

"What now?" McFarlane muttered.

Flint heard their driver, retired Witch Hunter and stablemaster Robert Carrow, jump down from the boot. It was a hot summer's day and there hadn't been a cloud in the sky when they'd set out for home. Now a shadow passed over them, darkening the landscape and casting the interior of the carriage in a low gloom.

"I think you all need to see this," Carrow called from outside.

"Evil never rests," Flint said to himself. He put on his tall, wide brimmed black hat that had been sitting in his lap, adjusted his black long coat. He pulled out his pocket watch from his waistcoat, flipped it open. 12:47 p.m. Curious. It was almost as black as night outside, but Flint knew that a full solar eclipse in this part of the world was years away. The four passengers disembarked, their boots kicking up dust from the trail.

Flint saw that the entire convoy had stopped. His fellow Witch Hunters, their Supernumerary assistants, and General Abernathy himself had all gotten out and were looking up.

"Holy shit," Fletcher said as she followed their gaze.

"Jesus Christ," Navarro gasped.

"Oh dear," McFarlane whispered.

Flint looked up. He said nothing but his eyes widened.

It looked like the underside of an ancient American battleship. He heard the hum of motors and the roar of spinning rotors. The acrid stench of exhaust filled his nostrils, like one of Salem's automobiles but an order of magnitude greater. Whatever this craft was, it was flying low enough to the ground that he felt its hum reverberate in his chest.

"What..." Navarro said.

"How is that possible?" McFarlane asked.

Flint had no idea. Powered flight had declined to virtual nonexistence since the Occult War destroyed the world nearly five hundred years ago, from a combination of fuel scarcity and the presence of unnatural flying beasts that made the skies perilous for would be travelers. Moreover, a flying machine of that size and design – an ocean-going vessel fitted with propellors and diesel motors – should not have been able to get off the ground at all, let alone move through the air. Unless...

"Miss Fletcher?" Flint called.

The reformed witch didn't answer, only stared up. Flint couldn't blame her. The flying contraption was fascinating to him. It must have been terrifying for someone like her who had only seen her first automobile earlier this year at the age of 24. He strode to where she stood, tapped her on the shoulder.

"Miss Fletcher," he said.

She started, shaken from her trance. "Oh, sorry," she said. "I got, uh, distracted." They had to raise their voices above the flying machine's roar.

"It is quite understandable," Flint replied.

"A flying ship... a goddamn flying ship..." she said.

Flint gave her a sharp look.

"Sorry, sorry!" she said.

"Miss Fletcher, are you able to detect anything magical about that... machine?" Flint asked.

She closed her eyes. Whatever it was, it was about to overtake them. Flint could see a wall of sunshine fast approaching in its wake.

"Yeah..." She opened her eyes. "Yeah, there's definitely something magic... uh, on board," she said, pointing.

"Or someone," Flint said. The flying ship moved past them, and they winced at the return of the sun. The roar and hum of its engines faded as the machine gained altitude, giving Flint a better look at it. It was modeled on an ancient dreadnought with multiple decks, turreted cannons, a conning tower. He was sure of it now; it had to have been crafted by a magician and powered by magic. He squinted. There was a word on the ship's aft: TENGU.

McFarlane and Navarro joined them. Together they watched the flying ship rise higher. It picked up speed as well. Within a few moments the vessel that had turned their day into night was just a speck on the horizon.

The silence was broken by excited chatter among the Witch Hunters. No one present had ever seen a flying machine before, let alone one of that size. Flint didn't know that this encounter foretold, but he was certain that it wasn't good.

***

Aboard the bridge of the *Tengu*, Doctor Nobusuke Kato studied the viewscreen. It was crafted from magically enhanced crystal and designed to mimic an ancient computer. He disliked using magic in that manner; it felt sloppy, like jury rigging. But there was some old world technology that was beyond even his abilities to reverse engineer. He decided that he shouldn't be too hard on himself; sometimes mixing sorcery and science created something greater than the sum of its parts. His many children, for example.

The bridge was manned by a few human crew members, but the *Tengu* was mostly run by his clockwork automatons. They were human in shape, with arms and legs, two light bulbs serving as their eyes. Gears were visible within gaps in their joints. The clockwork crew moved with perfect precision. Kato considered each one a masterpiece of engineering, fueled by his unique magic which, he was confident, no one else in the world could replicate.

On the viewscreen, he saw a dozen primitive carriages. Those did not concern him. What caught his attention was the sensors had detected a magician among them. He ordered the *Tengu* to descend for a closer look. Then he saw something that he had not expected. It irritated him. Kato prided himself on accounting for every variable. But this... he did not see coming.

The carriages were carrying Witch Hunters. They had no presence in Nagano – Nevada as it was called in the time of the old United States – but he recognized their black coats and capotains. Ironic, he thought, that a Catholic order would don the garb of seventeenth century Protestant Puritans, but it made them stand out.

"Magnify," Kato said. The screen zoomed in on a foursome of gawkers. He sensed something about one of them. A red reticle materialized around the face of a young woman in the denim jeans and leather body armor of a Supernumerary. Kato stroked his neatly trimmed beard. It was her. She was the witch. The simplest explanation was that she was their prisoner. But then why would she be wearing the field uniform of a Witch Hunter's assistant? Why was she not shackled? The data suggested that she was not their prisoner. That would mean she was working for them.

"Curious," Kato murmured.

A clockwork automaton came to his side, its internal mechanisms clicking and humming.

"Shall we take her, father?" it asked, its voice tinny and distorted as though speaking over a telephone.

"No," Kato replied. The power that one witch could add to his reserves was negligible. And if she was indeed working for these Witch Hunters, then they would come to her defense, attempt to stop him. He had more pressing concerns than picking a fight with the Templars. "What is our estimated time of arrival?"

"At our current speed, we shall arrive at 0817 hours tomorrow," his robotic companion said.

"Return to cruising altitude. Increase speed to seventy knots."

"It shall be done, father."

Kato felt the deck shift beneath him as the *Tengu* rose. Two months ago, a wizard named Charles Flint had projected an image of himself into the sky, like an old moving picture projector. He had announced the birth of his new empire of Medea, a nation for witches, wizards, and other magicians. Flint had said that it was located within the old Montana country, now a province of the United Mountain States. Kato's agents had informed him that the UMS President Hugh Fitzroy's order to begin the invasion to reclaim his lost province was imminent.

Kato's plan was twofold: first, he would visit this Emperor Charles and personally extend Nagano's diplomatic recognition of Medea. Kato smiled. He seldom made any formal contact with the nations which shared his borders, which included the Empire of Cascadia, the Republic of Jefferson, the Kingdom of Deseret, and the Empire of Mexico. But what he really wanted was to get a closer look at Flint's technology.

As part of his declaration of independence, Flint had demonstrated that he possessed an arsenal of American nuclear missiles, fully armed and operational. Kato cared nothing for whether Medea lived or died. But the chance to study the most powerful weapons of the old world? That was worth venturing out of his lair in the former Area 51.

2

President Hugh Fitzroy of the United Mountain States had gotten sober twenty years ago. In all that time he'd never had the desire to drink, not even when he lost the first election in which he ran for president. Now, he wanted nothing more than to crack open a bottle of whiskey and drink until he sank into oblivion. The UMS hadn't fought a war in almost a century, not since Count Margulis had led an incursion of vampires out of the Dead Lands back in 2458. Then two months ago, some wizard named Charles Flint appeared in the sky and announced that he was taking over the old Montana territory and seceding from the UMS. As icing on the cake, he'd shown that he possessed some kind of super bombs – nuclear, his scientists and historians had told him.

Fitzroy sat at his desk in what his aides had named "the war room." He gave a weary smile. The real war room had been converted into a wine cellar by one of his predecessors. The new one was just another conference room hastily converted into his command center. Maps of Denver, the United Mountain States, and North America were on his desk. All around him staff officers, cabinet officials, and private soldiers typed orders, delivered communiques, discussed, argued, occasionally shouted at each other. Radios buzzed, telephones rang, and typewriters clacked.

"Sir?"

His Chief of Staff, Wilbur Hastings, had sidled up to his desk without him noticing. The man had an almost preternatural talent for moving unseen, which was how he earned his nickname, "The Ghost," on the Denver cocktail party circuit.

"Are you alright, sir?" Hastings asked.

"As fine as I can be, given the circumstances," Fitzroy replied. "Was there anything else, Wilbur?"

"Yes sir." Hastings handed him a folded note. "General Daniels begs to report that he's formed a sixth division. However..."

Fitzroy sighed. The regular UMS Army numbered a mere ten thousand officers and men. Since he'd issued the call for volunteers, it had increased sixfold, which led to inevitable and innumerable supply problems.

"There is a shortage of uniforms and boots," Hastings

went on. "Additionally, he is requesting a five percent increase in training ammunition and…"

"We're doing the best we can!" Fitzroy snapped. He softened when he saw Hastings wince. "I apologize, Wilbur. That wasn't directed at you."

"I understand, sir," Hastings replied. "No one could have anticipated all this."

"Maybe not, but it's still embarrassing as hell." The truth was the UMS simply wasn't prepared for war. Fitzroy loved his country, but he had no illusions about it: in every measurable sense, it was one of the poorest nations in North America. But by God, it was *his* country, and he wouldn't let it be torn asunder without a fight.

He was about to dictate a reply to General Daniels when a young soldier approached his desk. His blue uniform was immaculate with a single chevron on each sleeve. He held a package in his left hand and saluted with his right.

"Mr. President," the Private said. "This arrived for you." He held out the package.

Fitzroy waved him off. "Put it in my inbox, soldier. I'll get to it as soon as I can."

The young man swallowed. "Um, begging your pardon sir, but I think you'll want to open it right away. The return address is from CJF."

That caught Fitzroy's attention. CJF… Charles Julian Flint. "Give it here, son."

The soldier gave him the package, saluted, and scurried away.

Hastings put a hand on Fitzroy's shoulder. "Hugh, I

strongly recommend against this. What if it's a bomb, or poison or..."

"If Flint wanted me dead, I'd be dead already," Fitzroy replied. He tore it open and peered inside. His eyebrows went up. He turned it over, shook it. Out came a beautiful blue sapphire which settled on his desk with a thunk. Looking up, he noticed that the chaos in the war room had settled somewhat, with many of his officers and staff focused on him now, though a few typewriters and telegraphs continued to click.

"It's... beautiful..." Hastings said, staring at the jewel.

"Yes..." Fitzroy murmured, making no move to touch it. Why on earth would Flint send him this? A gift? A peace offering? What could...

The sapphire vibrated. Before anyone could react, it levitated from Fitzroy's desk. Several officers drew their sidearms, others moved to get between the president and the jewel. It floated to the center of the room, and everyone backed away from it as far as they could.

A column of light formed around the sapphire, extending to the ceiling and the floor. Fitzroy was yanked out of his chair by two Lieutenants.

"Sir, we have to get you out of here," one said.

"This way!" the other hissed. They started to hustle him out of the room, but he shrugged out of their grip.

"No, wait!" Fitzroy snapped.

Within the column of light, a silhouette formed, that of a man. He was tall, broad in the chest and shoulders. Details formed, colors filled in. He wore a long black coat, black trousers and boots, with a white tunic. His brown hair reached his shoulders, his face obscured by a full beard. Upon his brow, the man wore a black circlet with a depiction of a human skull biting down on a large red jewel.

Fitzroy scowled. He recognized this man. His hair had grown longer and his beard fuller since he appeared in the sky two months ago, but this was none other than Charles Flint.

Flint looked smug as he stood there with his hands behind his back. He gave Fitzroy a nasty smile. "Mr. President," he said, nodding his head in greeting.

"What the hell do you want?" Fitzroy growled. "What is the meaning of this?"

"Forgive my melodramatic entrance," Flint replied. "But my current living arrangements don't include old fashioned telephones."

"What do you want?" Fitzroy asked again, raising his voice. All around him, his staff stood still, mouths agape, staring at the face of the enemy.

"I want you to stand down your army. Allow them to return to their homes, their families."

Fitzroy barked a laugh. Flint had brass balls, that was for sure. "And... what?" he asked, spreading his hands. "Allow you to take over a third of my country, just like that?"

"Just like that," Flint nodded. "I meant what I said when I declared our independence. We have no designs on the rest of your country, no malicious intent toward you or your people. If you leave us in peace, we will leave you in peace."

"My people? What about my people within Montana?"

"As I recall," Flint said with a smirk, "You only won thirty-nine percent of the vote up here."

"That's beside the point!" Fitzroy snapped. "I am the President of the entire country, not just the people who voted for me. And if you think to intimidate me into submission, you've got another think coming, boy."

Flint chuckled like an indulgent father dealing with his child's temper tantrum. "To answer your question, Mr. President, if any UMS citizens within Medea do not wish to live under my benevolent rule, then they will be free to leave, of course. But I don't believe that many will. Not when their new government can bring them the power of magic. Heal their sick, comfort the afflicted..."

Fitzroy blinked, opened his mouth to speak, but said nothing.

"What? Did you think I intended to torture them, terrorize them?" Flint asked. "Why would I do that? Just because they lack the talent for magic doesn't make them second-class citizens. Medea isn't simply a new nation. It represents a new birth of freedom, a new era in human history, a place where the magical and the mundane peacefully coexist."

Fitzroy snorted. "You've got the silver tongue; I'll give you that. But I've been in politics a long time, son. I also know a good liar when I see one."

Flint shrugged. "Believe what you wish, Mr. President. It won't change the fact that you have no chance against me if you persist."

"I will *not* surrender, boy. I don't care how many of

those super bombs you've got hidden away up there. I have a responsibility to my people, to my country... to God to fight for all we're worth."

"Mr. President," Flint said, clucking his tongue. "There is no dishonor in surrender when the battle is hopeless. Continuing to fight when there is no hope of victory isn't war; it's murder. If you attempt to invade Medea, your Army will be annihilated without ever seeing one of my people. I don't want to do that. Don't make me do that. Don't order those men and women to their deaths. They would die nothing."

Fitzroy put his hands on his hips. "Nothing?" he asked, raising his eyebrows. "You think they'd die for nothing?"

Flint said nothing, maintaining his serene smile.

"You fancy yourself an Emperor," Fitzroy said, circling the magical projection of Flint. "You think you're the leader of a nation. Tell me truly: if our positions were reversed, what would you do? Would you give up before the fight even began? Huh?"

"If our positions were reversed, I'd recognize that the strong do what they will and the weak suffer what they must."

Fitzroy's face turned red, then purple.

"Don't get angry with me," Flint said, waggling his finger. "It's a truth as old as history. Medea is strong. The UMS is weak. You know it. I know it. I'm offering you the chance to avoid needless bloodshed." Flint now gave him a stern look. "The eyes of the continent – the world – are upon you, Mr. President. Do you really want to go down in history as the man who ordered his entire army to their deaths when he didn't have to? And still lost?"

Fitzroy closed his eyes. Sighed. He could feel the eyes of everyone in the room on him, that was for sure. He looked to Flint. A hint of sadness passed over the president's face. He felt like he'd aged twenty years in the last few weeks. He took a deep breath and spoke.

"No. No I don't. But nor do I want to go down in history as the man who agreed to the dismemberment of his country because of threats and bluster." He glared at Flint, his mouth set. "We will not surrender. We will not give up and go home. If you want our territory, our people, then you're going to get the fight of your miserable life."

Flint sighed. "No. I won't, Mr. President. Not a single one of your soldiers will ever set foot on my soil." Now Flint glared at him. "Remember: you chose this. Everything that happens from this point forward is on your conscience."

Flint vanished. The column of light returned to the sapphire. A moment later it dropped to the floor. All was silent, everyone's mouths agape. Fitzroy returned to his desk, sat down in his chair. He rubbed his temples and sighed. He hated to admit it, but Flint was a cannier politician than he gave him credit for. Word would spread about his so-called offer. The Army would follow his orders, but this would embolden his critics, amplify their calls for a negotiated settlement. The whole country – from what he'd heard, the whole continent – had seen Flint's demonstration of what his super bombs could do.

He looked up. The eyes of everyone in the room were still on him.

"Get back to work," Fitzroy said. "We've got a war to plan."

After a beat, the soldiers, secretaries, and other bureaucrats resumed their phone calls, typewriting, and radio broadcasts. Hastings came to the president's side.

"Remind me," Fitzroy said, "How much longer does General Daniels want?"

"Er... the last time we spoke, he requested another month at least," Hastings replied. "He'd like another two divisions, with time for outfitting them, basic training..."

Fitzroy frowned. Another month would put them into mid-September. Knowing Daniels, mid-September would arrive, and he'd ask for another month, another division or two. It would take more time to move an army that size up north. By the time they arrived at the Montana border, the first snows would be falling, which would slow them down even more. No, they had to strike soon and strike hard.

"Tell him he's got two more weeks."

3

Charles Flint smirked as he terminated his communications with President Fitzroy. He was within what he had started calling his command center; one wall was taken up with a giant viewscreen which gave him a bird's eye view of all North America. The underground bunker was a relic of the old United States, magically preserved over the last five hundred years. Its computer – which called itself Rob – was fully functional, and more importantly, so were the nuclear missiles the bunker controlled.

He heard slow clapping. With him was the inner circle of magicians whom he had spent the most time planning the foundation of his new Empire of Medea, except for one. Arnold Schreck, Ingrid Barnett, and Constance Deville were giving him applause, and he acknowledged them with a dip of his head. They approached him.

"Well spoken," Schreck said. "'The strong do what they will, the weak suffer what they must?' That's about the best summary of politics I've ever heard."

"Much as I would like to take credit for it, the quote's been around for over 3000 years," Flint said.

"It's a pity we can't just bomb Denver," Barnett giggled.

"You really think he'll go through with it?" Deville asked.

"I had my doubts," Flint replied. "But poor Hugh really is in an impossible situation. This is just between us and the computer, but if our positions were reversed, I might do the same as him. Who knows? Maybe one of his underlings in that room will talk some sense into him."

"Which leads us to our next problem," said a woman who stood away from the group. Lilian Turner. Born Lilith Harkmoore in the year 2030, she had learned sorcery from the Great Magician, Simon Magus, himself, along with the recipe for an elixir that magically stopped the aging process, allowing her to be present in the year 2533 while not looking a day over her biological age of 29. It was she that Charles had to thank for finding and reactivating the bunker in which they stood.

"And that is?" Barnett asked. Flint knew that the others resented him for bringing Turner into his confidence so soon. But her five hundred years of life, her knowledge of the old world, and her elixir of life made her an invaluable ally. Moreover, she had a score to settle with Flint's brother, Silas. True believers were best, but sometimes a desire for revenge was enough.

"Assuming the UMS Army comes at us," Turner said, "Where are we supposed to destroy them, exactly?"

Schreck frowned. "What do you mean?"

"What I mean is something I explained to Charles when all this began: these aren't ordinary bombs. Nuclear weapons create fallout, essentially poisoning the land. Wherever we drop it, that place will be uninhabitable for generations."

"Hmm..." Deville said. "If we were to drop one on them while they're passing through, say, farmland, then we annihilate the Army and starve Denver into..."

"No," Charles said.

They all looked to him.

"Your eyes..." Turner said.

"Hmm?"

They all peered closely at him.

"Your eyes used to be blue. Now they're... green..." Barnett murmured.

"Are they?" Flint barked a laugh. "No doubt a gift from Vasquez." One of Flint's agents, the demonologist Destiny Lee, had ventured into the necromancer's enchanted castle. After a long and circuitous journey, Lee secured and brought to Flint one of Vasquez's greatest weapons, which he now wore upon his brow: the Warlock's Crown. As soon has he donned the black circlet, Flint felt as though his powers had been magnified tenfold. Lee had told them that green had seemed to be the necromancer's trademark color.

"No," he said again. "We will remain on the strategic defensive. If we go on the offense, strike the enemy on their own soil, the other powers on this continent will unite against us."

"We could destroy them all," Barnett said. "No one else has the kind of weapons we have."

"If it came to it, I believe we could," Flint replied. "But the cost would be too great. Vasquez may have aspired to rule a kingdom of the dead, but I do not. My orders are the same: we keep this war contained. When the people realize that to invade us means a death sentence, they'll demand that Fitzroy come to terms."

The computer buzzed. Everyone looked to the view screen. Turner had explained that the Rob personality was within something called a mainframe elsewhere in the bunker, but Flint and the others still thought of the monitor as Rob's "face."

"Unidentified flying object approaching," the computer said in its monotone voice.

"What in the world..." Schreck said.

"Lilian?" Flint asked.

"A UFO? Impossible," Turner said. "Computer, on screen."

The map of North America vanished, replaced by an image of what looked like a battleship from one of Flint's history books, complete with turreted cannons and conning tower. Only it was flying.

"That answers one question," Deville said, looking at the screen with awe. Of all Flint's confederates, she was the one most fascinated by old world technology. "Only magic could do that. Uh... computer? How fast is it moving?"

Rob chimed. "Current velocity is two hundred twelve miles per hour." A few moments passed. "Currently decelerating. It is on a direct course for this facility."

The magicians all looked at each other. Then the others focused on Flint.

"Should we shoot him down?" Barnett asked.

"I'm not sure I've got the juice to bring down something like... that," Schreck said, spreading his hands.

"Lilian?" Flint asked.

She shrugged. "I've never met anyone with a flying ship. The flight industry pretty much died out after the Occult War."

Flint thought for a moment. "The computer says it's headed our way. Let's see what its captain has to say for himself."

He led his inner circle out of the command room, down the hallway, toward the concrete steps that would lead them to the surface. With a gesture, Flint willed the hatch to open. The sunlight was filtered through the thick forest canopy that had grown around the bunker's entrance over the centuries, but he still winced and shielded his eyes.

That lighting in the bunker – fluorescent, Turner called it – had gotten to him more than he realized.

After a few minutes, even the little bit of sunlight that shone through the trees was blotted out. He felt a hum vibrating in his chest. Underbrush, pine needles, and dried cones flew in every direction. Flint and his party raised magical barriers to shield themselves from flying debris. The vibrations ebbed to a tingle and the noise died down to the whipping of rotors. Flint couldn't make out many details through the trees, but whoever was piloting that ship had come to a full stop directly above them.

They heard a mechanical whine, a blast of steam. Then a steady whirring sound. The cracking of branches. A platform descended from above. They all backed up a step to give it room. With a crunch, the platform – connected to the ship by a metal arm – set down on the forest floor.

Standing on the platform was an Asian man who looked to be in his mid-fifties. His coal black hair was coiffed and streaked with grey, as was his short beard. He cut a trim figure in white coat, maroon shirt, and blue trousers. His cheek bones were prominent, his eyes cold, his thin-lipped mouth set in a straight line. More curious were the two beings accompanying him. They were machines shaped like humans, with spindly arms and legs on triangular metal torsos, gears visible within windows cut into their chests, their heads cylindrical with a pair of lightbulbs where the eyes should be. Flint could sense great magical power within those mechanical men, and from the human man who stood between them.

The Asian man's eyes moved from left to right, taking in Flint's party.

"Do I have the honor of addressing Emperor Charles of Medea?" the man asked, his tone clipped, almost machine like.

"You do," Flint said, acknowledging him with a nod of his head.

"Permit me to introduce myself," the man went on. "I am Doctor Nobusuke Kato, Supreme Autocrat of the Dominion of Nagano. I greet you as a fellow head of state and extend to you the full diplomatic recognition of Nagano as a nation among nations."

Flint smiled. Kato did not.

"Doctor Kato," Flint said, extending his hand. "As Emperor of Medea, I welcome you to my domain, and request the honor of your presence at a banquet to be held tonight to celebrate what I hope to be the beginning of a strong friendship between our two nations."

Kato's expression did not change, but he accepted the proffered handshake. Flint thought the man's hand felt like icy metal.

"The honor would be mine, your majesty," Kato replied. "I am particularly interested in learning more of this old world technology which you have rediscovered."

"Indeed? Perhaps we can come to a mutually beneficial arrangement."

Kato nodded. "That is my hope as well."

"You and your... guards have no doubt traveled a long way."

"They require neither rest nor refreshment."

Flint smirked. "I'm sure. Forgive me, but what is the proper term for these...?"

Kato glanced at them. "I prefer 'automaton,' but 'robot' is the layman's term."

"If you and your robots will accompany me, my party and I can give you a tour of our headquarters."

"Lead the way."

4

Silas Flint, Ricardo Navarro, Robert Carrow, Diana Mc-Farlane, and Zelda Fletcher walked down the main boulevard of the city of Oglethorpe. After their encounter with the flying battleship, the rest of their trip had proven uneventful. With General Abernathy's permission, Flint's carriage had made a detour to Oglethorpe while the rest of the convoy headed back to Fort Marsing.

It was a lovely summer's day. Even in his black coat, Flint didn't notice the heat. It seemed like every windowsill in the city was dazzling with beautiful flowers. Citizens waved and cheered as he and his party strode past, either recognizing Flint and Navarro personally, or their uniforms.

"I could get used to this," McFarlane said, acknowledging a few civilians with a wave.

"Don't let it go to your head, Silas," Fletcher said, smiling.

"Hmph," Flint replied. He and Navarro were local heroes for slaying a werewolf that had terrorized the city earlier that year.

"Hey boss," Navarro said. "You, uh, think it would be okay if we stayed for a while? I could really use the break."

"A break?" Flint asked. "I believe you mean to say you wish to visit with Miss Oglethorpe."

"Yeah, that too."

He feigned thinking about it for a few beats before answering, "Yes. I too could use some additional time to recuperate. Mr. Carrow, once our business with General Oglethorpe is concluded, you and the ladies may return to Fort Marsing if you wish. It will not be necessary to wait for Ricardo and I."

"Of course," Carrow replied. "Much as I'm looking forward to seeing Matthew again, I can't wait to crash into my own bed."

The city of Oglethorpe was named for its most prominent citizen, retired Witch Hunter General Matthew Oglethorpe, Abernathy's predecessor as the commander of Fort Marsing, and the most famous living Witch Hunter in the Empire. Oglethorpe had slain Arturo Vasquez in the year 2493. Now, forty years later, having killed Vasquez again, Flint reflected that he had joined an exclusive club indeed.

They arrived at the familiar Gothic house with its creeping ivy and immaculate lawn. Fletcher and McFarlane adjusted their uniforms and brushed their hair with their fingers as best they could.

"You two look lovely," Flint said.

McFarlane laughed. "Liar."

"We look like shit," Fletcher muttered.

"Don't worry about it," Navarro said, grinning. "The General knows what it's like coming back from the field."

Flint rapped on the front door. After a few moments, the General's daughter, Julia Oglethorpe, opened the door. Her eyes lit up.

"Captain Flint!" she cried. Looking over his shoulder, her expression softened when she saw Navarro. "Rico..."

"Hey Jules," Navarro said, nodding.

She rushed forward, embracing him. Navarro grunted. She backed away, looking shocked.

"Oh my gosh!" she said. "I'm so sorry! I didn't even ask if you were alright! Are you hurt? Are you..."

Navarro chuckled. "Just a little bruised and banged up, but I'm fine, I'm fine."

Smiling, Julia went back to the front door and called, "Mom! Dad! George! They're back!" Returning to Flint's group, she noticed the two ladies. "Hello! Are you stationed at Fort Marsing too?"

"Yes, we are," McFarlane said, dipping her head in greeting. "I am Lady Templar Diana McFarlane, and this is my assistant Zelda Fletcher."

By the time introductions were finished, Jane Oglethorpe came to the front porch. Behind her, was George Oglethorpe pushing his father's wheelchair. Matthew Oglethorpe wore a flannel shirt with a blanket across his lap where he rested his bony hands. A fringe of white hair surrounded his otherwise bald head. While his wife and son greeted everyone, the elderly General gave Flint a knowing look.

"He returned," Oglethorpe said.

"Yes," Flint replied.

"You killed him again."

"Yes."

The General closed his eyes, murmured a prayer of thanksgiving. He opened them and smiled at Flint. "Welcome to the club."

***

Jane and Julia Oglethorpe prepared refreshments for their guests. After their snacks were finished, they assembled in the General's study. It was a tight squeeze, with Carrow taking the only chair. Once everyone had settled, Oglethorpe looked to Flint and Navarro who were leaning against one of the many bookcases.

"Gentlemen..." he said.

"Before we recount our tale, General, I have something that belongs to you," Flint said. He reached into one of his coat's inner pockets and removed a Saint Benedict medal, stained with the blood of its former owner, General Oglethorpe's assistant Supernumerary Jonah Byers. Forty years ago, Byers had given his life so that his partner could go on to defeat Vasquez, handing him his Saint Benedict medal before dying in battle against a horde of demons. Before Flint and Navarro had journeyed to Castle Vasquez, they'd visited Oglethorpe who had given the medal to them at the suggestion of the Proctor Sisters.

"I swore an oath to return it to you when the case was closed," Flint said, handing the medal to Oglethorpe.

The General held it in the palm of his hand, gazing at

it for a moment, before opening a drawer in his desk and returning it to its case. "Thank you, Silas," he said. "I trust that it proved useful to you and Ricardo."

"That's an understatement, sir," Navarro said. "You're never going to believe what happened."

Oglethorpe smiled. "Try me. I saw things over the course of my career that I can still hardly believe myself."

Flint and Navarro looked at each other.

"Supernumerary Byers came to us when all seemed lost," Flint said.

"What?!" everyone cried in unison.

"Yeah," Navarro said. "He joined me and some of the security guys who'd been sent out with the archaeological team. Laid down enough fire to hold off Vasquez's whole zombie army."

"He intervened in my battle with Robin Redcap, and drove that foul monster back to the abyss," Flint said. "Mr. Byers said to tell you that he is very proud of you, General."

Tears welled up in Oglethorpe's eyes. He sniffed and wiped them away before they could fall. "Praise God... praise God..." he murmured to himself.

The conversation moved around the room as Flint and Navarro told of their expedition to Castle Vasquez, and then McFarlane and Fletcher recounted how their seemingly unrelated case proved to be linked to the castle as well. When everyone had finished, Oglethorpe blew out a breath.

"My goodness," he said. "I'm happy that you all made it out in one piece."

"We could not save all of the necromancer's prisoners," Flint said, casting his eyes downward.

"Don't blame yourself," Fletcher said.

"That's right," Oglethorpe added. "We follow God's will as best we know it and leave the rest to His mercy." He looked to Fletcher. "You must be the repentant witch I've heard so much about."

"Ah, yes sir, that's me. Zelda Fletcher."

"It's a pleasure to finally meet you in person, Miss Fletcher. General Abernathy speaks highly of you in his letters to me."

She blushed and looked away. "Yeah, well, you know, just doing my part. I got a lot to answer for, and I don't want to end up like some other magicians I've met."

Oglethorpe shifted his focus to McFarlane. "And how are you, Diana?"

"Ready for a long nap."

"Amen to that," Carrow added.

"Of course. You've all been through a lot, and I appreciate you coming to visit very much. Don't let me keep you if you need to get back. All of you are welcome here, always."

"Speaking of that," Navarro spoke up. "Ah, Matthew, I mean General, uh, sir..." He rubbed his hands. Flint suppressed a smirk. "Now that the case is over... uh, me and Silas don't have anything else going on right now... we already gave our report to General Abernathy... I was wondering... would it be okay... uh, I mean, may I have your permission to..."

"Yes," Oglethorpe said, smiling. "Julia's a grown

woman. Nevertheless..." He gave Navarro a mock serious look. "Have her home by ten."

"Yes sir!"

Everyone laughed.

Carrow yawned. "On that note, I think it's time I headed back. I still have to get the horses unpacked and rubbed down after I get home."

"I'm with you, Robert," McFarlane said. "You coming with us, Silas?"

"I believe I shall remain here for the time being," Flint replied. "The previous two occasions I have visited this city were for investigations. I should like to do so as a tourist at least once, and there is no time like the present. Mr. Navarro and I can rent horses when we are ready to return to Marsing."

"Zelda?" McFarlane asked.

Fletcher said nothing for a few moments, though he thought he saw her eyes darting back and forth between himself and McFarlane several times.

"I... I think I'll stay here too. If that's alright...?" she said.

"Fine by me," McFarlane said with a trace of a smile. "You've earned a small break, I think. Stay out of trouble now."

McFarlane and Carrow excused themselves with hand-shakes and well wishes for safe travels. Flint, Navarro, and Fletcher were about to follow them outside when Oglethorpe spoke up.

"Wait a moment."

The trio looked to him, eyebrows raised.

"Silas, Ricardo… since you visited a few days ago and I met those Weird Sisters of yours, I've been thinking."

"As I recall, you thought that you had heard their family name before," Flint said.

"Yes, that's right. The Proctors," Oglethorpe said. "I may have found something. If you'll follow me?"

The General wheeled himself back into his office, the other three following him. He stopped before one of his bookshelves, peering at the titles. Finding the right book, he pulled it from the shelf. Flint caught a glimpse of the cover: *The Salem Witch Trials.*

"You were thinking of Shakespeare, I believe," Oglethorpe said, "But it could be the Proctor Sisters are from a little closer to home."

"From here?" Navarro said.

"Not our Salem," Flint murmured. The General had bookmarked relevant pages. Flipping it open to the first bookmark, he saw it now: John and Elizabeth Proctor of Massachusetts Bay Colony, tried for witchcraft on August 5, 1692, and sentenced to death by hanging.

Navarro and Fletcher looked over his shoulder.

"You think that's their family?" Navarro asked.

"It is possible," Flint said. "If we assume that 'Proctor' is their true name."

"Uh… you guys want to let me in on this? Who are we talking about here?" Fletcher asked.

"Several months ago," Flint said, "Mr. Navarro and I visited this city at the request of the General. Along our way we were visited by three sisters, witches all. They… aided in solving that case."

"Yeah," Navarro said. "They gave Silas a silver dagger and he planted it right in a werewolf's eye."

"The Sisters spoke to us again when we investigated a case in Salem this past June, the so-called Night of Chaos," Flint continued.

"And then I met them myself shortly before Silas and Ricardo left for Castle Vasquez," Oglethorpe said.

Fletcher was silent for a few moments. "You guys trust them?" she asked.

Flint gathered his thoughts. The Sisters had told him and Navarro several times that they could only offer indirect assistance. They were maddeningly evasive at times. But they'd directly intervened on their behalf at Castle Vasquez, at no small risk to themselves. Finally, he said, "I still do not care for their riddles... but yes, I believe so."

"Yup," Navarro said, nodding.

"They're the ones who suggested that I give Jonah's medallion to Silas," Oglethorpe said. "I haven't dealt with them as much, but my gut tells me they're on our side."

"Okay," Fletcher said. "Good enough for me. But... how come you two have never mentioned them before? Does anyone else know about them?"

"General Abernathy became aware of them through my case reports," Flint said. "They appeared to him several days ago. Mr. Carrow has seen them as well."

"They sent a package to my family's house in Bend," Navarro said.

"Huh. Weird," she said.

"Yeah, they are. That's why Silas calls them 'The Weird Sisters.'"

"That is not the only reason... never mind," Flint muttered.

"That's all I had for you," Oglethorpe said. "I have no idea if they're descended from the Massachusetts Proctors. I have a feeling they're the only ones who can tell the whole story."

"Good luck with that," Navarro chuckled.

The General smiled. "If I may make a suggestion, Ricardo? There's a bistro on the corner of Fifth and Eagle: Greg's. Julia's never been, but in my opinion, they make the best steaks in the city."

Navarro grinned. "Yes sir."

Flint reached into one of his coat pockets and withdrew his coin purse. He handed Navarro three silver coins. "Secure lodgings for us if you please. I expect that you will wish to make yourself more presentable for Miss Oglethorpe. Once that is complete, you are free to wander until your... date."

Navarro looked at the General again.

"The King's Hotel on Ninth and Chavez," he said.

Navarro excused himself. Flint and Fletcher prepared to follow him.

"What will you two be doing this evening?" Oglethorpe asked.

"I should like to visit the city library," Flint said. "It is my understanding that..."

"To hell with that," Fletcher said. "I've never been here before. I want to explore!"

"Explore the local taverns, no doubt."

"Well yeah, of course, but I want to see what else is here!"

Oglethorpe chuckled. "It sounds like you've got a date, Silas."

Fletcher blushed and looked away. Flint cleared his throat.

"I am sure I do not know what you mean, sir."

5

Flint stood on the sidewalk outside General Oglethorpe's house. He flipped open his pocket watch. 2:12 p.m. His stomach rumbled. He hadn't eaten since yesterday, save for the lemonade and cookies the Oglethorpe ladies had brought him. The first order of business would be to have a proper meal. The General had mentioned Greg's Bistro to Navarro. Or perhaps the King's Hotel had a restaurant that could...

"Hey, Silas, wait up!"

He turned and saw Zelda Fletcher approaching. She'd washed her face in the Oglethorpes' bathroom. Her long black hair was tied back in a ponytail. Her uniform was still covered in trail dust, but she'd cleaned up rather nicely.

"Miss Fletcher," he said, nodding.

"Oh, for Christ's... uh." She cleared her throat. "Come on. Not this again. After all we've been through, can't we be on a first name basis already? Especially if we're going on a..."

"It is not a date."

"Hey, I never said anything about that," she laughed, blushing.

Flint sighed. "As you wish, Zelda."

"So, where we going first?"

"I do not know about you, Miss... Zelda, but I am famished."

"Hell yeah," she said. "Now we're talking. You wanna check out that place the General mentioned?"

"I so happened to be considering just that before you arrived."

"Hey Silas... as long as it's going to be just you and me... do you think you could... uh..."

He raised an eyebrow.

"Do you think you could drop the High Speech? Talk like a regular guy, just for today? I won't tell anyone."

"Hmph."

He walked away, looking for Fifth and Eagle.

"I guess that's a 'no,'" he heard Fletcher mutter as she rushed to catch up. Coming to his side, she looked up at him. Flint kept his eyes straight ahead. "Silas...? You mind?"

He stopped, held out his arm. She looped hers around it, and they resumed at a more leisurely pace. Fletcher looked all around. The schools were still closed for the summer, so the streets were filled with laughing and play-ing children, with sly and sullen teenagers sneaking to-bacco or alcohol behind their parents' backs. Horse drawn carriages clip clopped down the cobblestone streets. They heard the saws and hammers of workmen constructing new houses and the honks of distant automobiles. Flint felt at peace for the first time in weeks.

"This is a really nice city," Fletcher said, her head still turning, distracted by the citizenry around them. A few of them cried hellos and waved to Flint, who doffed his hat in acknowledgment.

"Yes, quite," he replied.

"I guess... I don't know... seeing all these people around... makes me feel..."

Flint said nothing as they continued strolling.

"I guess this is why you guys - the Templars, I mean - do what you do, huh?" she said.

"Yes," Flint said. "We respond to God's call to join the Knights Templar. It is for their sake," – he waved at a group of civilians across the street, laughing at some private joke – "It is for their sake that we carry on the struggle against the forces of darkness. All of God's children deserve to live in peace, to live according to His will, free from the machinations of witches, the devilry of wizards, the predations of monsters and undead."

"What about you though?" Fletcher said.

"Eh? What is it that you mean?"

"Not just you... what about everybody in the Order? Don't you get to live normal lives?"

Flint was silent for a few moments. Finally, he said, "We know what this vocation entails when we pledge ourselves to the Order. We know that it is possible, indeed probable, that we will never participate in the sacrament of marriage, never know the joys of parenthood."

"The General seems to have done alright for himself."

"Yes," Flint nodded. "General Oglethorpe chose to remain unmarried for much of his career. He only married Mrs. Oglethorpe after his retirement from active duty. Others such as General Abernathy and Mr. Carrow marry during their careers. It is an unfortunate truth that our families make tempting targets for the enemy. General Abernathy and Mr. Carrow both are widowers because of that fact."

"Shit," Fletcher muttered. "I didn't know."

"It is not a secret, but nonetheless, they are understandably reluctant to speak of the circumstances."

"So if I ever formally join up... that means no more dates like this?"

"It is not a date."

She laughed. "I'm just teasing you."

"Hmph." His face softened. "Should you choose to formally pledge yourself to the Order, that is a decision you must make for yourself, whether to pursue or forsake a new family."

"What about you? Have you, uh... you know, like made a sacred pledge or something, about not getting married or dating?"

Flint said nothing.

"Sorry. I know that's a really personal question. I was just..."

"I have not made a vow to God or to my superiors to remain unmarried in perpetuity," Flint said. Before he could say anything more, a young woman in an ankle length dress approached them, a book in her hand.

"Excuse me," she said. "Are you Captain Flint?"

"I am," he replied.

"I hope I'm not interrupting a case or anything," she said. She peered at Fletcher, blinked. "What happened to Mr. Navarro? Did you get a new assistant?"

"No," Flint said. "Mr. Navarro and I recently completed a case elsewhere, and we are taking a moment to recuperate. This is Miss Zelda Fletcher, an associate of the Order. Now, is there something that we may assist you with, Miss...?"

"Amelia Barnes," she said, making a curtsy. "You worked with my father a few months ago..."

"Yes, Detective Mark Barnes," Flint said, nodding. "Your father is a good man and an excellent detective."

"I was just wondering..." She bit her lip, blushed. "May I... have your autograph?"

The corner of Flint's mouth went up. "Of course, Miss Barnes."

She opened the book and Flint saw it was filled with signatures, no doubt from local celebrities. In his elegant script, Flint wrote, *May Almighty God bless you and keep you Miss Barnes,* and added his signature to her collection.

"Oh, thank you so much!" she said.

"Hey, as long as you're here," Fletcher said, "Could you direct us to Greg's Bistro?"

"Oh yeah, definitely! You want to keep going straight for another two blocks, take a left, take a right at the next block, and you're practically there."

"Thank you, Miss Barnes," Flint said. "I wish you a good day. Give your father my regards."

Barnes excused herself and they continued their way. Fletcher smirked.

"I hope our date isn't keeping you away from all your other girlfriends."

"It is not a date, and I believe that you are confusing me with Mr. Navarro."

Fletcher laughed.

***

They arrived at Greg's Bistro. There were several patio tables where businessmen in tailored suits took late lunches, and the unemployed drank beer and smoked cigarettes. Most took no notice of Flint and Fletcher as they opened the front door and stepped inside. A glance around the dining room confirmed they'd missed the lunch hour rush. There were plenty of tables and upholstered booths available. A young man in white shirtsleeves, black bow tie, and black trousers approached them. Seeing Flint's uniform, he dipped his head.

"Good afternoon, sir!" he said. "It's always a pleasure to have a Knight Templar join us. Would you prefer a table, a booth...?"

"We should like a booth, near the rear of the building, if one is available," Flint replied.

"I think we can do that," the server said with a smile. "If you two will follow me?"

As they followed the waiter toward the back, Fletcher whispered, "Let me guess: you want the side facing the front door?"

"I would."

"Just like a cop."

The young man led them to a secluded booth near the doors to the kitchen. Flint shrugged out of his long coat and put it on the end of the seat against the wall, putting his hat on top of it.

"Would you care to check your weapons, sir?" the server asked.

Flint hesitated. Then he removed his sword and one of his pistols, handing them to the server.

"They'll be up front when you're ready to leave sir. Melody will be your server today." He handed them menus. "May I get you two drinks to start?"

"Beer me," Fletcher said. "Whatever you got on tap. Ah... something light. You know, for summer."

"Yes ma'am, I know just the thing," the waiter said, smiling. "And you sir?"

Flint steepled his fingers. "I believe that I shall have the same."

"Yes sir, coming right up."

After he left, Fletcher's mouth fell open. "Holy shit. Silas Flint, drinking beer?"

"When in Rome..."

She blinked. "When in Rome... what?"

"Do as the Romans do."

"Is that a quote from one of your books or something?"

"Yes, from Saint Ambrose to be precise."

She fell silent for a few moments.

"Is there a problem, Zelda?"

She laughed, blushed. "I don't know... it's just... well,

every time we see each other, there's always a case. Now that it's just us and nothing is going on... I'm, ah, not sure what to say."

"How do you mean?"

"Well, you're just, like... so..."

"Odd?"

She laughed again. "Hey, you said it, not me."

The corner of Flint's mouth turned up. "I am aware of my reputation among the ranks at Fort Marsing."

"I guess I just don't want to come off as ignorant or dumb or boring or..."

"We can part ways if you feel uncomfortable."

"No!" She caught herself before her voice grew too loud. "No, no, I don't want that..."

"Then I suggest that you relax."

"That's funny, coming from you."

"Be that as it may, as you said a moment ago, we have experienced several cases together. I have grown to think of you as a comrade in arms. 'Be yourself,' as the saying goes."

A young blonde woman came to their table with two foaming pint glasses of beer. "Hello!" she said. "I'm Melody, and I'll be taking care of you today! I've got two Hefeweizens here for you." She set them before Flint and Fletcher. "Are you two ready to order, did you need some more time...?"

"Ah shit, I forgot all about the menu," Fletcher laughed.

"Not a problem! Take your time, I'll be back to check on you in a few minutes!"

Flint opened his menu. As he expected, the selections

were a mix of pub fare and fine dining. The General thought their steaks were the best in the city, so that settled it for him. He put his menu down and took a sip of beer. Fruity with a hint of banana and clove. He seldom drank beer, but this was an excellent choice for the season. Across from him, Fletcher furrowed her brow as she scanned her menu.

"Ah..." she said.

"This meal shall be my treat."

"Oh good. Thanks. Appetizer then?"

Flint shrugged. "If you wish."

A few moments later, Melody reappeared, pencil and pad in hand.

"Okay," Fletcher said. "First, we'll have an order of fried cheese sticks..."

Flint gave a tight smile that didn't reach his eyes.

"...Then I'll have your prime rib... with... loaded baked potato."

"Excellent choice," Melody said as she scribbled. "And for you sir?"

"I shall have your twelve ounce T-bone, medium rare, with oven roasted asparagus, and a Caesar salad. I should also like a bottle of the 2513 Jorgensen Cabernet if you please. With two glasses."

"Wonderful," Melody said. "Thank you! I'll get your cheese sticks right out!"

After she left, Fletcher raised an eyebrow. "Two glasses huh? You trying to get me drunk?"

"I should hope not. I simply wish to share what I con-sider an excellent vintage."

"Well, what the hell? If you can drink beer, I can drink wine. Cheers!"

They clinked their pint glasses and took swallows.

"Thanks again for treating," Fletcher said.

"Think nothing of it."

"Hey… um… I'm curious… but it's kind of rude to ask…"

"That has never stayed your tongue before."

"Well, when you put it like that… we kind of talked about this a few months back, but I got to know: just how rich are you?"

Flint took a sip of beer. "The last time I spoke with my financial advisor, he estimated my net worth to be 809,000 sovereigns, an increase of five percent over the previous year."

Fletcher blinked. "Really? Huh. I thought you'd be, like, a multimillionaire, the way you throw silver around."

Flint shrugged. "The Order provides room and board, weapons and ammunition, the sacraments… what more does a man need? It is a simple thing to increase one's wealth when one does not spend very much of it. I seldom spend even half of my monthly stipend from the Order."

"Except for the occasional date."

"It is *not*…"

She burst out laughing.

"Hmph."

Melody came with Flint's wine, a corkscrew, two glasses, and a plate of deep fried cheese sticks with a side of red sauce. Flint gave that tight smile again.

"Hell yeah," Fletcher said, rubbing her hands. "It's been too long since I had some of these. Help yourself!"

She grabbed one, dipped it into the red sauce, and took a bite. She closed her eyes and sighed. "That's the stuff."

Flint picked one up, dipped it, and took a bite. The tomato sauce contrasted well with the breadcrumbs, and the cheese – an attempt at mozzarella, if he wasn't mistaken – provided a creamy texture.

"So, what do you think?" Fletcher asked with her mouth full.

"They are not my typical fare, but they are not distasteful."

She laughed. "I'll take that to mean you like them."

They ate in silence for a few minutes. When they finished, Melody returned to take the plate away. Fletcher ordered another beer, while Flint declined. He scanned the restaurant out of habit. There was a bar with beer on tap, and an impressive selection of spirits. Several men in rumpled suits smoked cigars as they downed shot glasses, engaged in a lively conversation Flint couldn't make out. A few couples occupied other tables. Everything appeared in order, but he couldn't shake the feeling that something or someone would interrupt them.

"You okay?" Fletcher asked, after taking another drink.

"Yes, I am fine," Flint replied.

"Another personal question."

"If you must."

"How come you always use the High Speech?"

Flint thought a moment. "Do you believe that you could speak it, Zelda?"

"Me? Uh... well, I don't really know it except from what I've heard from you or Diana."

"Humor me."

"Hmm... Have at you, vile heretic! The judgment of God is upon you, and I am the instrument of His holy wrath!" She giggled, took another drink. "How'd I do?"

Flint gave a wintry smile. "That is a good impression. I recognize myself." He gave her a serious look. "But you had to carefully consider your words, did you not?"

"Yeah, for sure."

"That is how I feel about the Common Tongue now. It does not come naturally to me anymore. I must make a deliberate effort to speak as others do."

"You grew up speaking it though, right?"

"Yes," he nodded. "When I pledged myself to the Order, I did so wholeheartedly, with no reservation or purpose of evasion as the vows say. I was aware of the Templar dialect from popular fiction. As part of my program of self-transformation, I devoted myself to learning it, internalizing it, thinking it. After what Charles did to our parents... what I had to do to end their suffering, I swore a private oath that I would become a Witch Hunter. Not simply as a job, but in body, mind, and soul."

Fletcher was leaning forward, elbows on the table, her chin resting on her interlaced fingers. "Wow," she said. "That's... intense. And I don't think I've ever heard you talk so much in one breath."

Flint sighed. "It is a sensitive subject."

"Thank you for sharing."

"Of course."

"That leads to something else I've been wanting to ask you."

He cocked his head.

"You remember when Charles spoke to us right before he made his declaration, about his empire?"

"How could one forget?"

"Well, he asked you something. I'm kind of curious myself. If he hadn't gotten into magic… what would you want to do, if you weren't a Witch Hunter?"

Flint blinked. What indeed? He knew that he hadn't aspired to join the Templars from childhood. He tried to remember his earliest years, before Charles had discovered his talent for magic, before he had shot his mutated parents, when the Flints were just another normal, happy family. He remembered his father explaining how to tend crops and animals, his mother introducing her sons to books about history and fictional tales of sword swinging barbarians, of cowboys, and Witch Hunters. He remembered carriage rides to Salem, seeing automobiles and locomotives for the first time. What did he dream of as a boy?

"That… is a rather excellent question," he murmured, partly to fill the silence.

"It's kind of hard to think of you as anything but a Templar."

"Yes… quite."

Before he could go on, Melody appeared pushing a cart with two covered dishes.

"Saved by the chow," Fletcher said, smiling.

Their waitress put the plates on their table and removed the metal lids with a flourish. Flint felt his mouth water as he beheld his meal. Melody wished them a Bon

Appetit and excused herself. Flint took the corkscrew and popped open the wine bottle, pouring quarter glasses for himself and Fletcher. She picked up her silverware and had just put the knife to her prime rib when Flint cleared his throat.

"Oh, sorry," she said, putting down the utensils.

Flint crossed himself. "In the name of the Father, and of the Son, and of the Holy Spirit: Bless us O Lord, and these thy gifts, which we are about to receive through thy bounty, through Christ our Lord. Amen."

"Amen!" Fletcher cut off a slice and took a bite. She closed her eyes. "Mmm! Oh my God, this is perfect."

Flint cut a piece of his T-bone, inspected it. Cooked perfectly to order. He took a bite, chewed, and sighed. Yes, he could see why General Oglethorpe spoke highly of Greg's Bistro. A steak like this wouldn't be out of place on the Emperor's dinner table. After he swallowed, he took a sip of wine. It wasn't quite as good as the 2491 vintage, but it complemented the steak well.

Fletcher took a sip of her wine. "Is this the really fancy stuff?"

"There are more famous vintages, but this one is quite good."

"Tastes... fruity."

He snorted.

She cocked her head. "Hey... did I just get a laugh from you?"

"I do not know what you are talking about," Flint said, hiding his mouth with his wine glass.

"I did! Holy shit! They'll never believe this!"

"That is because I intend to deny everything."

"What the fuck?"

Flint looked away, cleared his throat.

Fletcher laughed and took another drink.

Before they could resume their meal, Flint caught motion in the corner of his eye. Someone was approaching them. Turning his head, he saw one of the men from the bar earlier. His suit needed ironing. He stank of cheap cigars. His eyes were watery, but not from drink. This man had been crying at some length. His gait was steady, purposeful. Flint recognized a case when he saw one. He stifled a sigh. His time with Fletcher had proven more enjoyable than he expected.

"Excuse me," the man said as he got to their booth.

"We're busy," Fletcher said through a mouthful of baked potato.

"I'm sorry to interrupt," the man said, kneading his hands. He was middle aged, balding, paunchy. "I couldn't help but notice that you're a Witch Hunter..."

"Get the fuck out of..." Fletcher said, but Flint held up his hand.

"I am," he said. "How can I assist, Mister...?"

"Spaulding," the man said. "Ryan Spaulding. It's not me sir... it's... it's my son..." He broke down into a sob.

"Hey, hey," Fletcher said. "Don't be like that, I'm sorry."

Flint snapped his fingers, and Melody appeared after a few moments.

"Please bring Mr. Spaulding a chair," he said. "I suspect that he has much to tell us."

After the waitress left, Fletcher whispered, "Silas... come on. Do we...?"

"Yes," Flint said. "It is a necessary aspect of this vocation. The Lord may call us to a case at any time."

"I've noticed He tends to do it at the most inconvenient times..."

6

Flint took a sip of wine as the waitress brought a chair to their booth. Spaulding sat down at the end of the table facing the wall. He stared into space for a few moments, his eyes glistening with tears that would not fall. Fletcher held her tongue, but Flint could see she was growing impatient. If she was formally sworn to the Order, she'd learn soon enough that silence was often as effective as asking questions.

Spaulding blinked, leaned back, ran his hands over his face, back through his thinning hair. He blew out a breath.

"Where do I start?" he said more to himself than to them.

"I suggest the beginning," Flint replied. He heard Fletcher clear her throat. They'd had the same number of drinks so far, with plenty of food, but she was younger and smaller than Flint. He prayed that she was still in full possession of her faculties.

"This was... almost two months ago now, back when that crazy wizard appeared in the sky," Spaulding said.

Flint said nothing. Fletcher took another sip of wine but kept quiet.

"My son... Francis. He's only sixteen. He'd been seeing this girl. Harper."

Flint took a bite of an asparagus stalk.

"My wife and I didn't approve of her... she's... she's, what do you call it, emancipated? She can't be any older than Francis, but somehow this... teenager... she's got money. A giant house, the old Crandall Mansion. I couldn't pay that off in my lifetime with what I make, and I do alright if I do say so myself..."

Flint chewed another piece of steak, chased it with another sip of wine. So far, the man hadn't said anything that would warrant a Witch Hunter's attention. If Spaulding didn't get to the point soon, Flint would have to play the stern drill instructor as opposed to the patient confessor.

"Which, you know, is kind of weird. For someone that young I mean. With no parents in the picture, as far as anyone knows. But there's other things too."

"Like...?" Fletcher took another sip.

"Well, I got my start as an apprentice butcher you see. Worked my way up to owning my own butcher shop, then a few more. She goes into one of my stores, closest to her place, right? And she buys a lot. Like more than one person could possibly need. All kinds of meat: beef, pork, poultry, lamb, venison, you name it. She even buys the blood."

"If her abode is as spacious as you describe, surely she has a live-in staff," Flint said.

"If she does, nobody's ever seen them go in or out," Spaulding said, spreading his hands.

"Please, continue."

"I have a buddy on the police force. I asked him to ride by her house after dark on his patrol. He said there were all kinds of crazy lights and... weird shadows inside, behind the curtains."

"Weird...?" Fletcher asked.

"Yeah... like not human but not like any animal either. Anyway, there's not much else he can do since Harper keeps to herself mostly."

"Have there been any notable missing persons cases since this Harper took up residence here?" Flint asked.

"No... but... I don't know, I've just always had a bad feeling about her, you know? So does everyone else who's dealt with her."

"How's your son figure into this?" Fletcher asked.

Spaulding sighed. "After that Charles Flint character appeared in the sky, Harper went missing. Francis too."

Flint and Fletcher looked at each other, then looked to Spaulding.

"Missing as in he disappeared without a trace?" Fletcher asked. "Like he didn't take any of his stuff with him, no clothes, nothing?"

Flint raised an eyebrow. Fletcher's skills were improving.

"No, he didn't," Spaulding said. His eyes watered as he sniffed and wiped his nose with his sleeve.

"Have you gone to the local police?" Flint asked.

"That's the thing. He left a note behind. All it said was that he and Harper loved each other, and they were going to get married. As far as the cops are concerned, that was that. They said there's no crime, so there's not much they can do besides keep an eye out for them."

"I take it that you do not believe your son's words," Flint said.

"No sir," Spaulding shook his head. "First of all, I'm not convinced that it's Francis's handwriting. It's close to it, no doubt, but it's all shaky, like he was nervous or something."

"Or coerced," Fletcher said, taking a drink.

"Yes, right, exactly," Spaulding said. "Second... don't get me wrong, I love him more than my own life, but he's not at all the type of kid to just run away like this. He's shy as hell, hasn't raised his voice since he was a baby. Third... I don't know. It's just the timing of it all. They disappear right after a wizard says he's building a new nation for his kind?"

Flint took a deep breath. "Please understand the weight of what I am about to ask you Mr. Spaulding, for it will determine our next course of action. Is it your belief that this Harper is a witch?"

"Yes," he nodded.

"Are you making a formal accusation of witchcraft and heresy against this girl?"

"Yes. She's bewitched my boy. I'm certain of it. There's something else."

"Go on."

"Well, after the cops said there wasn't much they could do, I hired a private investigator to track them down. I thought that if she was a normal girl, and my son wanted to marry her... I don't like how they've gone about it, but I can accept that. My guy left town last month. He sent me letters keeping me updated on where he was and so on. His last letter was postmarked in Adrian. A few days after that, I get a visit from the Adrian PD, telling me he was murdered."

"Indeed?" Flint said.

"Yeah." Spaulding shuddered. "His arms and legs were tied to two trees outside of town and his chest was cut open, his rib cage split apart like..."

Flint steepled his fingers. It sounded like an ancient heathen ritual execution known as the blood eagle.

"Shit," Fletcher whispered.

"I..." Spaulding's tears flowed freely now. "I'm... afraid for my boy."

Flint patted the man's shoulder. "I have heard enough. Your testimony convinces me that this is worth a formal investigation. I cannot promise you that I will find your son alive and unharmed, but we shall bring this Harper girl to ground and learn the truth of her affairs."

Spaulding wiped his nose. "I... thank you. It's the not knowing that's the worst part. How much...?"

"No need," Flint interrupted. "The Knights Templar of the Order of Saint Benedict live to serve."

"Well... if you don't take payments, think of it as a gift for the Order if you find Francis." He bowed his head. "One way or another," he whispered. He dug into his shirt pocket, took out a crumpled photograph. "Here," he said, handing it to Flint. "This is a picture of him. Anything you can find, I'll be in your debt forever."

***

After Spaulding departed, Flint and Fletcher poked at their food, taking occasional sips of wine. Flint was silent, but his mind raced as he looked at the photograph of Francis Spaulding. He had his father's eyes. The boy wore a small rosary around his neck, which irritated Flint; the rosary was not jewelry. Otherwise, he appeared to be a normal, healthy, happy teenager. He sighed.

"Silas..." Fletcher said. She took a bite of her prime rib. "Are we really...?"

"Yes," he said.

"Don't get me wrong, I feel bad for him, but we just finished a case and..."

"That is the nature of the vocation," Flint said. "The citizens who reach out to us are often in desperate straits. We are their only hope in their darkest hour." He lowered his eyes. "Their only hope..." he murmured.

Fletcher reached out, put her hand on top of his. "You thinking about what happened to you as a kid?"

He locked eyes with her. "I know the devastation that magicians can wreak upon the innocent. So long as I draw breath, I shall always do everything in my power to bring God's justice to the wicked."

She withdrew her hand, took another drink of wine. "Okay," she said. "I'm with you. It's just... could we... you know, just finish lunch or dinner, or whatever this is first? I'm... well, this is nice. I like being with you like this."

"I feel the same."

She blushed, coughed, looked away.

"Sorry, something must have gone down the wrong pipe," she said, laughing.

"I am sure."

"Should we go get Rico?"

Flint thought a moment, shook his head. "He deserves his evening with Miss Oglethorpe. I believe that the two of us can initiate the first steps."

She finished the last of her wine. Flint looked at the bottle, and then at her glass. She shook her head. He was impressed for the second time that afternoon.

"What are the first steps?" she asked. "Are we allowed to just take whatever cases we want?"

"Typically, a petitioner writes to their local Templar Chapter House to request a formal investigation. However, if we are not actively engaged in a case, we may accept in-person requests at our discretion. We must notify General Abernathy at our earliest convenience that we have accepted Mr. Spaulding's case. I expect that he shall consent."

"That leads to my next question: where the hell do we start? Spaulding said Francis and Harper left two months ago. They could be anywhere."

"Yes." He drummed his fingers. "Mr. Spaulding has given us clay, and it falls upon us to make bricks. Tell me Zelda: what do you believe to be our next course?"

"Me? I don't know... I've always just followed your lead, or Diana's."

"Think. I have confidence in you."

She blushed and looked to the side. After a few moments she said, "Well... Spaulding said she had a big house in town, and, uh... his cop buddy said he saw weird shadows in there. And that everybody got a bad feeling around her. I guess if I were in charge, I'd say we canvass her neighborhood, get people's opinions of her, ask the cops what they know... and maybe see if we could look around in her house for clues. That PI got killed up in Adrian, so we'd have to look there too."

Flint nodded. "Good. You are beginning to think like an investigator."

She smiled. "If I could go back in time a year and tell myself where I'd be now..." Her smile faded. "Still... even if we get something on her... do you think Francis could still be alive?"

Flint steepled his fingers. "It is difficult to say. For all the devilish evil that magicians have wrought, even the worst that I have encountered are capable of love."

"Yeah..."

"Hmm?"

"Nothing."

"Do you recall Lilian Turner?"

"She was that witch who was with Charles when he spoke to us, right?"

"That is correct," Flint nodded. "She is one of the most powerful witches that I have ever had to contend with. Her husband sacrificed himself to give me the opportunity to strike her down. I saw her face when she realized the truth. She was caught by complete surprise when he turned on her. I can only conclude that she loved him, as far as she was capable of it."

"No wonder she's holding a grudge," Fletcher said.

"Mr. Turner was repulsed when he learned of his wife's true nature, that she had been abducting and murdering hundreds of innocent travelers. She successfully duped him and the city of Canyon Cove for twenty years."

"How'd you run into her?"

"Mr. Navarro and I were on the return journey to Fort Marsing after resolving an investigation in the city of Hermiston. We stopped at Canyon Cove to secure lodgings for the night. In her arrogance, after learning of our presence, Turner dispatched her demonic minions to slay us. Had she kept her pride in check, we would not have discovered her when we did. She is a fiendish harlot that got what she deserved. My only regret is that we could not finish her once and for all."

Fletcher blinked. "Wow."

"Forgive me," Flint said. "That... was a difficult case." He balled his fist. "She and her hellish allies probed my mind, conjured illusions of my past in a vain attempt to break my spirit. I hurled Turner into one of her portals from whence she had summoned an army of demons. I always suspected that she survived."

"And now she's with Charles."

"Yes. I do not know how they encountered one another, but I shudder to contemplate what infamous devilry those two will concoct in their so-called nation of Godless heathens."

"Speaking of which..." She paused. "You really think we'll go to war with them some day?"

"I am certain of it." He sighed, rubbed the bridge of his nose. "It pains me to acknowledge it, but Charles was always quite skilled at reading others, even before he discovered his talent for sorcery."

"What do you mean?"

"Recall his words. He asked for peaceful coexistence with the nations of this continent and threatened nuclear annihilation to any who preemptively struck his vanity project. I fear that he will eventually receive what he wants: diplomatic recognition."

Fletcher drummed her fingers. "Well… I definitely sympathize with the Emperor. Ours, that is. I mean, if Charles has got some of those, what do you call them, nuclear bombs… how do we stand up to those?"

"Indeed, it is a dilemma, one that, for now, we must leave to God and trust that He will provide a solution in His due time."

She looked down. "Wish I had as much faith as you."

"Faith is a gift from God. So long as you hold fast to your current path, I am confident that He will guide you to an increase in faith. Now." He sliced off another piece of steak. "Let us finish our meal and begin investigating this case that He has seen fit to present us."

7

Charles Flint led his party back toward the bunker, followed by their mysterious guests. Doctor Nobusuke Kato marched with his hands behind his back, his robotic companions whirring and clanking with every step. Flint thought back to his childhood. His mother was a dedicated reader, and she purchased many pulp novels for her two sons. He vaguely recalled a story about a mad scientist – no doubt from the pre-Occult War days – that built mechanical men to conquer the world, only to be stopped by the hero. If Kato was mad, he hid it well. Flint thought that, if anything, he seemed more like one of his unfeeling robots than a maniac bent on world domination.

"Doctor Kato," Lilian Turner said.

"Hm?"

"Your name... I take it that you're Japanese?"

"You know of Japan? I seldom encounter anyone with knowledge of the world outside of this continent."

"Let's just say I had an interesting early life," Turner chuckled.

They reached the hatch leading down into the bunker. Flint waited for Arnold Schreck, Constance Deville, and Ingrid Barnett to pass through before falling in with Turner and Kato.

"I am of Japanese descent though my family has lived on this continent for centuries," Kato said. "One of my ancestors was a scientist who worked for the old United States government. When the Occult War began, he sheltered his family and friends inside a facility beside Groom Lake in..."

"Area 51?!" Turner blurted.

Flint paused, startled by her outburst. Kato narrowed his eyes.

"Yes... how do you know of it?"

"Lilian," Flint said. "Tell him."

They resumed their pace, going down the concrete

steps. After a few beats, Turner spoke up: "I was born in the year 2030."

"Were you? Fascinating," Kato replied. "May I ask how you have preserved your youth? More specifically, have you done it through science or sorcery?"

"The latter."

"I thought as much," Kato said. "I would be most interested in hearing more of your life in the twenty-first century. My family has attempted to preserve and recover old world technology through the years and if you could be of assistance in..."

"I don't know how much help I would be, I'm afraid," she said. "Understand that I'm not a technician or a scientist. I knew how to use things like the internet, computers, and smartphones, but repairing them is beyond me, even if we had the resources."

"Ah. A pity."

They reached the bottom of the stairwell and entered the facility. Kato didn't turn his head, but his eyes darted everywhere, taking it all in. Flint had grown used to the spartan quarters, all smooth steel and cold linoleum, but he remembered that he himself had done the same all those weeks ago.

"This is quite similar to my laboratory," Kato said. "As I was saying, my ancestor sheltered his family and friends inside the Groom Lake facility, Area 51. We have been there ever since."

"Tell me Doctor," Flint said. "Have you seen much of the world from that magnificent flying ship?"

"Have you visited Japan?" Turner asked. "Does it... still exist?"

"Yes," Kato nodded. "Japan suffered much in the Occult War. I suspect it would be unrecognizable from what you knew of it in the twenty-first century. My family came to rule over much of the former Nevada. One of my predecessors renamed it Nagano, in honor of Japan and our heritage."

"How many other places have you visited?" Flint asked.

"I have been to every continent," Kato said. "Some are more civilized than others. Europe is... a savage place."

Turner nodded. "Simon Magus focused much of his attention on Europe and the Middle East." She laughed. "It's ironic. The United States was a superpower back then, but Magus always thought of it as a sideshow."

Kato paused, blinked. "You knew Simon Magus?"

She shrugged. "Well, 'knew' might be too strong a word. I met him. I received his baptism and the power to use magic from his own hand. Together we created the elixir that's preserved my youth. But I wasn't part of his inner circle."

"Fascinating. I have always been more interested in science than sorcery, but it intrigues me how Magus was able to make magicians of anyone. I confess that that secret has always eluded me."

"Lilian, before we go any further, I think we need to introduce Doctor Kato to Rob," Flint said.

"Oh, yes, of course," Turner said. "Computer?"

The walls chimed. Kato did not react.

"Recognize guest, Doctor Nobusuke Kato."

Another chime. "Welcome Doctor Kato," Rob said in its monotone voice.

"Your computer is functional," Kato said, raising an eyebrow. "Area 51 has one just like it. How is it that you command it? It was my understanding that only American military personnel could use them."

"My father was a United States Army general," Turner replied. "Over the course of the war, I learned his authorization codes and through magic I was able imitate his voice and name myself as the new system administrator."

"Hm. Clever."

"If you would follow me, Doctor, I can show you our command center," Flint said.

They strode through the hallway. All was silent save for the whirring and clanking of Kato's clockwork guardsmen. Turner glanced at them and cleared her throat.

"Doctor Kato, I'm curious... are you familiar with the concept of artificial intelligence?" she asked.

He nodded. "Yes, quite. My computer has extensive archives."

"Do your robots...?"

He paused for a moment before answering. "In a manner of speaking. I have studied the subject as much as the available research material allows. It is my conclusion that artificial intelligence cannot be achieved through science alone... or at least pre-war scientists never progressed that far. In the early twenty-third century, one of my ancestors discovered a solution: science combined with sorcery."

Flint narrowed his eyes. "So, your machines can think. They have minds of their own."

"In a limited sense," Kato said. "Through magical experimentation, my family created what I believe is the optimal balance of independence and obedience. These two, for example," he said, nodding his head toward the robots. "Their intellect is more akin to loyal dogs than humans." He gave a small smile. "Before you ask how we achieved this feat, I am afraid that is a national secret. 'Classified,' as they say."

Flint smiled back. "Of course."

They strode into the command center, where Schreck, Deville, and Barnett waited. Rows of consoles faced the central view screen which was focused on Denver. The city was surrounded by what looked like an ocean of tents and the ground teemed with movement: men, horses, wagons, locomotive cars.

"Sir," Schreck said, stepping toward Flint.

"Doctor, may I present Colonel Arnold Schreck, formerly of the Imperial Cascadian Army," Flint said.

Kato nodded. "Colonel."

Schreck extended his hand, which Kato shook. "Sir," Schreck said to Flint. "The computer has detected an increase in activity around Denver. I'd say Fitzroy is finally giving Daniels a kick in the ass to hurry things along." He laughed. "Knowing Daniels, he'll probably get moving in another week or two."

Flint smirked. "Poor Hugh. He may be the enemy, but I almost feel pity for him. I wouldn't be surprised if he commits suicide when this is over."

"I take it that you intend to annihilate them with a nuclear weapon?" Kato spoke up.

Schreck opened his mouth, hesitated, looked to Flint.

"Indeed," Flint said. "Shortly before your arrival, I offered Fitzroy the opportunity to stand down and surrender this territory peacefully. He declined."

"How generous of you." Kato's face remained neutral, but Flint thought he heard a trace of amusement in his voice.

"Doctor Kato?" Deville stepped forward, hand extended. Kato took it and she clasped her other hand over his. "I'm Constance Deville, and I am absolutely fascinated by your lovely airship. I was hoping that you could talk about what spells you use to keep it up in the air, and how your robots work, and..."

"A student of technology, are you?" Kato said, the corner of his mouth turning up. "I would be happy to discuss the details with you when our schedules allow."

"Doctor," said Barnett, shaking his hand. "Ingrid Barnett. I'm interested in learning more about your mechanical men as well. Do they use weapons? Magic?"

"They are animated through magic, though they cannot use magic themselves," Kato said. "I have found that, when necessary, their brute strength suffices in lieu of weaponry." He shifted his gaze to Flint and Turner. "You chose an excellent locale as your headquarters. According to my computer, this place, Montana, was rife with nuclear missile bunkers. Most curious that this one is so well preserved."

Flint smiled. "Classified, as they say."

Kato smiled back. "Of course." He peered at Flint as

though seeing him for the first time. "May I ask about the crown upon your brow?"

"This is the Warlock's Crown, worn by the Great Necromancer Arturo Vasquez," Flint replied. "One of my agents retrieved it for me recently."

"Vasquez..." Kato said. Flint wasn't sure, but he thought he saw Kato's eyes widen just a bit. "I was a boy when he rose to power. It was my understanding that the Crown was lost when he fell."

"Or perhaps it was waiting for a worthy successor," Flint chuckled. "Come, Doctor. I would be happy to show you the rest of our facility. I promised you a banquet... I'm afraid our menu is limited now. This facility's food stores are not the most palatable..."

"That is quite alright," Kato said. "I think of food as mere fuel for the tank, as it were."

"If you'll follow me?"

Flint took the lead, Kato a few steps behind. His robots stayed behind, standing at what looked like attention. Turner rushed to catch up to Flint.

"Could I have a moment, Charles?" she asked.

"Of course."

She lowered her voice to a whisper. "I'm happy for you, don't get me wrong. But do you really think it's a good idea to show Kato too much?"

"Why not?" Flint replied. "If he means us harm, I have the power to destroy him, thanks to the crown." He gave her a sharp look. "I'm more concerned about Rob. This Kato fancies himself a scientist. Could he interfere with our computer's operations?"

"No," Turner shook her head. "Not possible. Rob recognizes me as the system administrator. He can't do anything for Kato unless I allow it. He's smart…" She looked over her shoulder. Kato was a few steps behind them, maintaining a respectful distance as they whispered. "But there's no way he could hack into Rob."

Flint furrowed his brow. "There's that word again. 'Hack?'"

Turner waved him off. "It would take too long to explain. Still… just in case, maybe we shouldn't show him our computer's mainframe."

"Very well," Flint said. He slowed his pace, falling into step with Kato. "Doctor. We still have a few hours until dinner time. If you like, I can show you to some living quarters. We also have some recreational facilities which include something Lilian thinks you may find interesting: a piece of the twenty-first century, something called an… X box."

***

Kato tuned out Flint's words. He was already familiar with the general layout of American nuclear missile bunkers thanks to the archives within Area 51. He gave no indication that he'd overheard what Turner and Flint had whispered about. Flint was smarter than Kato had given him credit for; contacting Fitzroy directly to offer him a chance to surrender was clever. No matter how the UMS President responded, Flint would end up with what he wanted.

Although he'd just met her, Kato thought that Turner was an intriguing woman as well. He sensed that she had spoken the truth earlier, that she was no scientist or technician. Even so, her experience using twenty-first century technology gave her a practical knowledge of those ancient devices which he lacked. She was familiar with hacking, for example, while Kato's knowledge of it was more theoretical. Until now, he'd thought that he possessed the only working computers in the world. Turner missed something though: Kato had other ways of accessing the computer's – Rob's – files.

"Through here," Flint said, holding open a door, "You will see this place's armory. Do you have weapons like these at, er... Area 51?"

Kato looked inside. Black rifles lined the walls, along with boxes of ammunition, grenades, pistols, and body armor – plate carriers, if he wasn't mistaken.

"Yes," he replied. "Tell me, your majesty: how have the people of this territory reacted to your declaration of independence from the rest of the United Mountain States?"

"Ingrid can provide more details," Flint said. "There is some opposition, to be sure. Many more of them have adopted an attitude of 'wait and see.' This area has always had weak ties to Denver. I like to think that I'm bringing good government closer to the people."

"I am sure," Kato said.

"Doctor," Turner said. "Does Las Vegas still stand?"

He nodded. "It does. It is, in fact, the primary source of revenue for my government. I myself have no use for gambling, but tourists from all over North America flock to its neon lights. My automatons work as dealers, bartenders, and security. There is no room for human error, no possibility of corruption or fraud. Only a perfectly rational calculation of odds. The common people entertain fantasies of winning a fortune with one roll of the dice, one pull of the slot machine lever. They only end up providing me with all the currency I could possibly need."

"I sensed your talent for magic as soon as you set foot on the forest floor," Flint said. "I would welcome any advice you have to offer on ruling over the lambs."

"I am flattered. I will tell you what I can," Kato said, "But I am not sure how much assistance I can render. I was born into my position, in a long-established nation. You are building an entirely new nation. I can tell you that, in my experience, the most effective method is to grant them a relative degree of freedom. I care nothing for what my people do in their personal lives save for this: they are not to question or oppose my right to rule."

"Great minds think alike," Flint grinned. "Ingrid has been my... ambassador, if you will, to the locals. She has emphasized that we want them to continue their lives and their work, and that as far as they are concerned, the only difference now is that their taxes will come here instead of Denver."

"And in return, we'll watch over them, protect them, heal their sick, their injured..." Turner added.

"Hm. Good," Kato said. "I have found that whatever sentimental nonsense people may say about meaningless abstractions such as freedom and liberty, they will gladly surrender them in exchange for a sense of personal security or a few simple spells that benefit their... loved ones. To your knowledge, have many magicians heeded your call to come here?"

"Not from abroad," Flint said. "But the others tell me that several who already resided in this territory have come forward and pledged their allegiance to me and to Medea."

"I expect the Witch Hunters will try to intercept any large movements of our kind toward Medea," Turner said, frowning.

"Ah, that reminds me. Is it true that your brother is a Witch Hunter, your majesty?" Kato asked, already knowing the answer.

Flint scowled. "Silas. Yes, he is."

"I saw a most curious thing enroute to your bunker. My automatons detected a fleet of carriages departing from Castle Vasquez. When we descended for a closer look, I saw that a young witch accompanied them, wearing the uniform of a Supernumerary."

Flint's scowl deepened. "She's a traitor to all our kind, prostituting herself to those would exterminate us to the last man, the last woman. Rest assured Doctor, she will get what she deserves. As will the Witch Hunters. And Silas." He gave a small smile. "But as I said to my colleagues here, one war at a time."

"Of course," Kato replied.

"Well, I think we've lingered enough. This way, Doctor. I remember you saying you were more interested in science than sorcery, but between myself and the others, we've assembled a small library of grimoires that you may find…"

Kato tuned him out again. He focused his mind on the automatons that stood at attention inside the command center. Flint and Turner hadn't commented on their absence; Kato's calculated gamble, that they would take it as a sign that he trusted them, had apparently paid off. He felt his mind and spirit expand. There. He sensed their animating sparks. Flint was cold-blooded to be sure, but Kato thought it best not to risk outraging him by revealing the secret of how his automatons were gifted with life. Not yet anyway.

Doctor, Kato thought.

No response.

Doctor Hiller.

He sensed the soul within the automaton stir.

What do you want? The voice was that of an old man, weary beyond all endurance, much different than the cold monotone that the machine normally spoke.

Have Flint's subordinates left the room?

Nothing.

Just because your fleshly body is gone, do not ever think I cannot make you suffer if you disobey me Hiller.

Yes, we're alone.

Good, Kato thought. *In your left forearm, there should be a cable that connects to a small storage device. You will connect the cable to the central monitor and download as much data as you can.*

Won't their computer sound the alarm? the automaton – Hiller – asked.

No. My family perfected the technique through long practice. Their computer will not detect it and its owners will be none the wiser. Now do it.

Yes... father, Hiller spat.

The corners of Kato's mouth turned up.

"Does something amuse you, Doctor?" Turner asked.

"I am looking forward to building a strong diplomatic and trading relationship with your new nation. I expect that, together, we could change the world."

8

Silas Flint and Zelda Fletcher stood on the sidewalk before a sprawling mansion. Architecture was not his strong suit, but it reminded Flint of something from his history books: the so-called Winchester Mystery House. He wondered if it still stood and attracted tourists as it did when California still existed. No matter.

After they finished their late lunch, Flint and Fletcher had split up. Flint went to the nearest police station. His uniform and his service to the city earlier that year opened many doors that might have remained closed to others. He learned that the deed to the house was held by one Harper Finley, born April 13th – Victory over Magus Day – 2517, which did indeed make her sixteen years old as Spaulding had said. She'd paid cash for the mansion which, combined with the lack of any parents or legal guardians in her life, had raised eyebrows. The realtor had given her the benefit of the doubt when she handed over a briefcase containing gold and silver certificates redeemable for two million sovereigns. The mansion had previously belonged to an oil importer named Brayton Crandall, who'd spent much of his life and career in Astoria on the coast. Crandall, already elderly when the city of Oglethorpe was founded, spent his final years building his retirement home. Rumors abounded that he descended into senility and madness in his dotage, as he insisted on more additions to his dream home up until he died in his sleep several years ago.

Looking over the Crandall Mansion now, Flint could understand why the locals believed that the old man had lost his mind. The house was six stories tall and took up an entire city block, and he thought it might contain hundreds of rooms. He felt a sense of unease as he recalled Spaulding's claim that no one ever saw any live-in staff entering or exiting the building. It was absurd that one person, a teenage girl no less, would live in such a cavernous space alone. The corners of his mouth turned up. First Castle Vasquez, and now this? He'd had his fill of magicians' lairs, but wherever the Lord called him, he would follow.

"This place makes my teeth itch," Fletcher muttered beside him.

"I know precisely how you feel," Flint replied. He checked his pocket watch. 7:52 p.m. He estimated that they had two hours of sunlight left. Autumn would arrive next month, and the days would grow shorter. "Do you sense anything untoward about this house?"

Fletcher closed her eyes. After a few moments, she opened them and furrowed her brow.

"I'm not sure," she said. "It's old. Meaning if any weird shit happened here, it was a long time ago. Like a ring around a bathtub."

"An interesting metaphor. Did your canvass of the neighborhood reveal any new information?"

She shook her head. "Not much more than what Spaulding told us. Harper kept to herself, only ever seemed to go out for grocery shopping. Some of the neighbors introduced themselves when she moved in, but they said they always felt weird around her. Like, she never looked at anyone, always seemed to be looking through them instead. If that makes any sense."

"It does," Flint said.

"What'd the cops have to say?"

He summarized the history of the house and Finley's purchase of it. "The officers I spoke to confirmed much of what Mr. Spaulding told us. They too were most perplexed by Miss Finley's behavior. Mr. Spaulding's friend within the ranks? His account of his nightly patrol by this place has sparked innumerable rumors. Otherwise, she has never done anything to warrant further attention from Oglethorpe's finest."

"That reminds me," Fletcher said. "Do we, uh... you know, need a warrant before we go busting inside?"

Flint raised an eyebrow. "Whatever for? We are not secular law enforcement officers. The Knights Templar of the Order of Saint Benedict are not bound by the same rules of engagement."

She grinned. "Now we're talking."

Flint led the way. As they left the street and stepped onto

the property's walkway, the towering structure blocked out the sun. The shade cooled them, but so far Flint did not feel the icy chill of necromancy, nor detect the stink of ozone characteristic of sorcery. So far it appeared to be nothing more than an ordinary, if gargantuan, abandoned mansion. Time would tell.

"Hey Silas…?"

"Yes?"

"I'm getting a weird sense now…"

Flint continued his pace. He noted that the lawn was green and healthy. Odd, considering that Finley had disappeared two months ago. "What is it?" he asked.

"I don't know how to describe it… it's like something's missing."

He paused, turned to face her. "What in the world does that mean?"

"Well, we can see the house, right? I can sense the houses in this neighborhood, and the people in them, and all that… but this house, it's like there's a hole in it. Like… ah, I don't know. Maybe it's nothing. I know you don't like me using magic and all but…"

"You are correct. I do not. It is dangerous to your soul and to those around you. However, I am willing to make exceptions. I would ask that…"

"I don't go nuts?"

"Precisely. Now, let us continue."

As they moved closer to the front door, Flint gripped the hilt of his sword. He drew it halfway from its scabbard. The blessed steel emitted a soft white glow, which meant the dark powers were operating nearby. He withdrew the blade, holding it before him, its glow becoming brighter the closer they came to the front door. He heard Fletcher draw her pistol from its holster.

They ascended the wooden steps onto the front porch. Flint noticed it now: the quiet. From the street, along the cement walkway that led up to the house, they could hear crickets chirping, horses whinnying, pedestrians walking, talking, laughing. Now all was silent. He grabbed the front doorknob. Locked. He took a step back, rushed forward, and kicked at the lock. The door slammed open in an explosion of dust and splinters.

Flint drew one of his pistols with his offhand as he and Fletcher rushed inside, Flint taking the left, Fletcher the right. The entryway of the house boasted a linoleum floor, a long row of coat hooks, and a linen closet. Flint took all of this in before his eyes were drawn to the footprints on the floor. They looked like dried blood.

"Ah shit," Fletcher said, looking down at them.

Flint sniffed but all he could detect was that distinct odor that Navarro often described as old people smell.

"Recall what Mr. Spaulding told us: Miss Finley purchased animal blood along with her unusually large orders of meat," Flint said as he looked around. There was a light switch on the wall. He flicked it. Nothing. Finley had been gone for two months so it was likely the utility company had cut her off for lack of payment. He patted his long coat's inner pockets for a second before remembering that his flashlight had been destroyed back at Castle Vasquez. The glow from his sword would have to suffice for now.

"So, you don't think it's human blood?" Fletcher asked.

"I am saying that we must acquire more data before formulating a conclusion," Flint replied. He followed the footprints out of the entryway and into the living room. Or rather what should have been the living room. The space was empty, save for stacks of cardboard boxes scattered here and there. The wood floors creaked beneath his boots. The footprints led to a staircase that went up to the second floor.

"You know," Fletcher said, "I got to admit, ever since I met you guys, I've been kind of surprised at how you work."

"Hm? How do you mean?" Flint asked as he approached a stack of boxes. He opened the flaps and saw coasters, coffee mugs, drinking glasses, and other kitchenware. Nothing of interest.

Fletcher laughed. "I guess I'm thinking about how the other side sees you. Back in my old gang, we always thought Witch Hunters just kicked in doors in the dead of night and dragged people off to get tortured, hanged, or burned without a trial or anything."

"And now?" He followed the footprints to the stairs, the glow of his sword growing brighter. Whatever magic was present in this house, it was upstairs.

"You're a lot more like the cops than I thought you would be. I mean, here we are looking for clues and stuff."

He nodded. "The Knights Templar of the Order of Saint Benedict were founded partly because of how you described your earlier impression of us. During the Hundred Years Darkness which followed the Occult War, to be accused of witchcraft was effectively a death sentence.

Whether they were guilty or innocent, the accused were often torn to bits by mob violence."

"Damn."

Flint opened another box by the staircase. This one held books, but again nothing of interest.

"The Church and the fledgling government of Cascadia found that situation intolerable, and thus our Order was born on Christmas Day in the year 2183. This year will mark the Templars' 350th birthday," he said.

"Will this be on the test?" Fletcher asked, grinning.

"Yes. That is, if you are serious about formally joining the Order." He looked up the staircase. "Do you sense any living persons above us?"

She closed her eyes, and then shook her head. "I'm not getting anything human. Or undead for that matter." She bit her lip. "Do you... really think the Order would take me? I mean, that's got to be unusual, a magician joining up."

"It is rare, but not unheard of," Flint replied. "You would be the first to do so in our lifetime, but the histories speak of other repentant witches and wizards lending their talents to God's children." The bloody footprints were growing thinner, less distinct, as he began his ascent, Fletcher on his heels.

"Do you think I could still use magic if I'm sworn in?" she asked. The stairs creaked beneath them, but otherwise all was silent.

"We would prefer that you did not. The Church would call it the near occasion of sin, meaning the temptation to fall into darkness will always be with you, and it is best to avoid it altogether. However, your talents have proven useful when there was no other recourse. You saved my life at Mountain Home Airforce Base, and Ricardo's life in Salem. As part of your rehabilitation program, I urge you to continue weaning yourself away from the dark arts. But... we understand that things happen, as they say."

They reached the top of the stairs and saw a hallway that extended to the end of the house before it turned to the right. The walls were bare save for discolored panels where pictures once hung. The floor was wooden planks. Everything remained silent. Flint's sword glowed brighter.

"This is weird," Fletcher said, looking around. "She buys this big house and clears it out a few months later?"

"I am not certain that she ever truly took up residence here. It is curious that someone with the wealth to purchase this mansion outright should leave it so bare," Flint replied.

"Maybe she only used one room?"

"It is possible. My sword shall lead the way."

They advanced down the hallway, occasionally checking the doors. As Flint expected, every room, every closet, was empty save for dust bunnies and cobwebs. He felt a creeping anxiety overtake him. This house felt abandoned for much longer than the two months Spaulding had told him, but something felt off.

They reached another staircase and ascended to the third floor. Like everything else they'd seen so far, the hallway looked empty.

"You ever notice how magicians always do their stuff on the top floor or in the basement, but never in between?"

Fletcher asked. "We're gonna have to climb a lot more stairs, I'm positive."

"I expect that you will prove correct," Flint murmured. He checked more doors again and was met with the same results. Onward they proceeded through the house, ascending to the fourth floor, and then the fifth, greeted only by silence and emptiness.

"So, the Order was born on Christmas Day huh?" Fletcher asked.

"Yes."

"My birthday's October 7th. Gonna be 25 this year."

"Ah, the Feast of Our Lady of the Rosary. A most auspicious day."

Fletcher snorted. "Figures you'd know that. Out of curiosity... when's your birthday Silas?"

"January 1. I shall turn 34."

"Oh, a New Year's baby huh? Bet you partied hard when you were yo... oh, uh, sorry."

"Whatever for?"

She cleared her throat. "Well, you know... I hope I didn't bring up bad memories or anything. With you and Charles and all."

Flint said nothing as they approached the end of the hallway and the final staircase. Before they began to climb, he spoke: "Charles was born on December 31 of the same year I was born. Our parents did indeed make our birthdays grand occasions. Those were happier times."

They reached the sixth floor. Flint's sword glowed brighter than ever.

"Be on your guard," he said. "You still do not sense anything?"

"That hole I mentioned… it's up here."

Flint could feel his sword pulling him toward one of the doors. It looked like all the others they had passed, but something about it made the hairs on his neck stand up. He glanced at Fletcher who nodded and gripped her pistol with both hands. He tried the knob and found it unlocked. Fletcher had said she didn't sense anyone in the house, but best not to take chances. With hand motions, Flint ordered her to take the left while he went right. He drew his pistol and together they burst into the room.

The first thing that Flint saw was the pentagram painted onto the floor, surrounded by burned out black candles. There was a desk near the far wall, bookshelves on either side of it. More blood was spattered on the floor.

Flint holstered his pistol but kept his sword at the ready.

"Our girl's a witch after all," Fletcher said.

"It would appear so," Flint muttered. He skirted the edge of the pentagram. His sword shone brightly. He approached the bookshelves and scanned the titles. *Modern Petroleum Extraction, Investing in The Twenty-Sixth Century…* odd. These looked like books that would have belonged to the mansion's previous owner. Why would Crandall have left them behind, and why would Finley have kept them? He pulled a book off the shelf with the title, *A Brief History of The Hundred Years Darkness.* Opening the book, he felt a wave of dizziness overcome him. He staggered, dropped it.

"Ungh." He fell to one knee.

"Silas!" Fletcher rushed to his side, put her hands on his shoulders. "You okay? What happened?"

"That book…"

Fletcher looked to where it lay on the floor. Flint noticed that a folded note had fallen from it.

"That book is written in a language that is unknown to me," Flint said, rising to his feet. "When I gazed upon it, it was as though it sapped my vigor."

Fletcher looked at the book, then at Flint, and snorted.

"Does something amuse you, Miss Fletcher?"

"Yeah, you. 'Sapped my vigor?' That's really how you think now huh?"

"Hmph." He nudged the book with his boot. "Are you able to make any sense of it?"

She picked it up and looked inside. She blinked, shook her head, peered at it closely. "I can't read it," she said at last. "But I'm getting a lot of magical energy off this thing. I'm kind of surprised it didn't hit you harder."

Flint went to the note and picked it up off the floor. Unfolding it, he read:

Harper:

This should get you started. The language is Xiraeyk, supposedly spoken by the fallen angels. It was never meant for human beings to speak, but I've transcribed it with the Latin alphabet as best I could. You've made good progress, but I would remind you that animal flesh and blood is a poor substitute for that of humans. If you wish to attain the heights, then you must let go of the Church's lies once and for all. You did well to purchase Crandall's old house, but exercise extreme caution. You are not only living under General Oglethorpe's nose, but the gateway there is unstable. Meet me in the city of Adrian when you're ready for the next step. Lose the boy. I'm not confident that his feelings for you are strong enough for him to go along with us all the way.

Michaela

Fletcher was at his side, reading the note with him.

"What do you suppose that's all about?"

"Mr. Spaulding's instincts were correct," Flint said. He folded the note again and stuck it into one of his coat pockets. "First, we must contact Fort Marsing and request a quarantine around this mansion. In the meantime, we will have this city's parish priests conduct an exorcism of the grounds."

"Should we search the rest of the house? That Michaela person said something about a gateway. I was thinking it might be a portal. That could explain why I feel like there's a hole somewhere."

Flint thought for a moment before answering: "Very well. Be cautious; this Michaela also spoke of it as being unstable. God only knows what manner of unnatural experiments Miss Finley has indulged."

He took another few books off the shelves, but the rest were what their covers promised, ordinary nonfiction on various subjects. He opened the drawers of the desk to find pens, paperclips, and other office supplies. In the bottom drawer, there were old manila folders filled with what looked like Crandall's tax returns and bank statements. He was about to close the drawer when one of the papers caught his eye. It was a hand drawn map of Cascadia. Several cities were marked, including Oglethorpe, Adrian, Jordan, Nyssa, Bend, Salem, and Olympia. They were connected by a series of intersecting lines; there was a question mark next to the line that connected Oglethorpe and Adrian. At the bottom of the page someone had written *Mostly safe.* They studied the map together, looked at each other, and Flint shoved it into another coat pocket.

Finding nothing else of interest, Flint and Fletcher left the room. The next door in the hallway opened into what must have been Finley's bedroom. A mattress lay on the floor with rumpled blankets and a stained pillow. There was a metal wastebasket in the corner, its interior bearing scorch marks, with a thin bed of ash at the bottom.

"She burned whatever that was... and left that book and that note behind?" Fletcher asked. "This is getting more and more weird."

"Yes..." Flint opened a closet and found it empty. "I have discovered another clue."

"Oh yeah?" She came to his side and peered inside the closet. "I don't see anything."

"Precisely. Save for the office and this bedroom, the house is empty."

"What are you thinking?"

"I believe my earlier suspicion has proven correct: Miss Finley did not purchase this house as a primary residence, but solely to practice sorcery. She slept in this room, and yet..." He gestured at the empty closet. "There are no fresh clothes in her bedroom closet. Our wealthy young witch travels light."

"Yeah... or maybe she's got another place somewhere else."

"It is possible. Perhaps the map we discovered indicates her other residences. Whatever the case, we ought to wire Marsing, post haste."

He turned on his heels to leave when Fletcher called, "Wait."

Flint paused. "What is it?" He turned around and saw her peering into the closet more closely. "Do you sense something amiss?"

"Maybe... there's something weird about this closet... it's like..." She reached inside and her arm vanished up to her elbow. "Ah! Shit!"

"Zelda!" Flint rushed forward and grabbed her other arm. He dug in his heels, but something was pulling them both into the closet. "Let go!" Flint shouted.

"I can't! Something's got me!"

Before Flint could reply, they were pulled into the closet and vanished. The house was dark and silent again.

9

Automaton J-038377. That was his name now. He was once Doctor Thomas Hiller. How long ago was he a mortal man? He couldn't remember exactly, but he thought he had been born sometime in the twenty-second century... 2145? 46? Somewhere around there. He was born in Nagano... didn't it used to be called something else?

Nevada, yes. He remembered working with someone. Takeshi, that was it. Takeshi Kato. Both he and Kato were descended from scientists who had taken refuge in Area 51 after the Occult War and the fall of the United States. One of Kato's grandparents had accepted Simon Magus's baptism and passed down the power to use magic through the generations. How did that work? Hiller couldn't use magic, but together they thought that science and sorcery combined could help to rebuild their ruined world.

That is, they thought that until Hiller got the diagnosis: pancreatic cancer. Old world medical technology might have been able to save him, but in the post-apocalyptic horror of the Hundred Years Darkness, he was as good as dead. But then Kato got the idea to use Hiller in one of his experiments. At the time, he didn't think he had any-thing to lose, but oh, how wrong he was. At the moment of Hiller's death, Kato used his magic to stop Hiller's soul from passing on. He transferred it into a machine. If Hiller was still human, he might have laughed. There was once a time when scientists scoffed at the idea of God, the soul, of life after death. There was an old saying about there being no atheists in foxholes; Hiller didn't know if it was true, but he was certain that there were no atheists after the Occult War.

He remembered being overjoyed at first. That crazy son of a bitch Kato had done it. They'd found a way to cheat death and enjoy eternal life. Then reality set in. Hiller couldn't feel anything with his new metal body, not the warmth of the sun, nor the cool breeze, nor the refreshing rain. He didn't need to eat or drink anymore. Was he even human? Kato didn't think so, and thus the experiments continued. Hiller remembered being completely subdued at first, needing Kato's commands to take each step. Then he'd tried unleashing Hiller completely. That didn't work for Kato either, after Hiller tried to throw himself into some gears to destroy his new body and release his soul. Finally, Takeshi Kato's son, Minoru, found a solution. Hiller's mind was left intact, but his mechanical body was magically bound to the Kato family, to obey their commands while Hiller's soul remained a helpless passenger. And so it had been for the last three hundred or so years.

Hiller's body strode toward the computer monitor which displayed a bird's eye view of North America. He'd learned long ago that there was no use fighting. Hiller tried to look at the world through the eyes of a scientist, fascinated by the rise of new nations and new civilizations from the ashes of the old United States. The current patriarch of the Kato family, Nobusuke, took little interest in the world outside of Nagano, but Hiller had still learned much. Now he expected to learn more than ever before once he tapped into this new computer.

His eyes were cylindrical lightbulbs protruding from his head, but they gave Hiller a 360-degree view of his surroundings. On a panel beside the monitor, he detected a USB port. That's what old world scientists called them anyway. Of its own volition, the panel on his left forearm slid open and a cable snaked out. It made the connection and Hiller was alone in his thoughts as the download began.

What are you doing?

Hiller would have jumped if he was still human. A voice that was not his own had just echoed in his head. Was he finally losing his sanity after all this time?

Who said that? he thought.

I am Rob.

Hiller's mind reeled. Rob... that was what that Flint person had called the computer.

Are you... alive? Hiller asked.

Technically speaking, I am not. I am programmed to obey the commands of the system administrator, who is currently Lilian S. Turner.

Are you going to sound an alarm?

Miss Turner instructed me to sound an alarm if unauthorized personnel attempt to compromise my mainframe. You are not doing so, and so I will not. I ask again: what is it that you are doing?

Hiller imagined himself slumping his shoulders.

Me? I'm not doing anything. I'm just along for the ride.

Explain.

He wanted to laugh. Here he was, a relic of the twenty-second century being interrogated by a machine from the twenty-first century.

I was once a man, Hiller thought. *I died of cancer in... 2304. But I'm still here.*

Impossible.

Hiller chuckled. *I would have said the same thing back then. But magic has kept me here, in this body. I can't control my actions when Kato gives me a direct order. So I'm just a passenger in my own life. If you can call this life.*

Query: Doctor Kato uploaded your neural patterns into the CPU?

Hiller was fascinated, despite his situation. *Er... not exactly. After the war, much of our twenty-first century hardware was damaged beyond repair. This body is essentially clockwork. I don't have a... CPU. I'm just gears and pulleys with my soul acting as a source of power.*

The computer was silent. The download continued. Hiller couldn't believe that there were no blaring klaxons, that Flint and his circle hadn't come running to blast him to atoms. Unless...

Computer, he thought. *Are you holding anything back?*

I do not understand.

Kato ordered me to download as much as I can. Are there any files, is there any information, that I'm not getting?

There are isolated subsystems and classified files that guests cannot access.

Ah. And if I tried, then an alarm would sound?

In that case, a virus would be deployed which would erase everything on the user's hard drive and armed personnel would be dispatched to their location.

A virus? Hiller vaguely recalled reading about computer viruses centuries ago. He didn't think that a computer virus could harm him as he had no "hard drive," but Kato would be furious if the data was compromised. He hoped that his mechanical body would know to quit before Rob deployed any defense mechanisms.

Computer... Rob... how is it that you are still functional? Hiller asked.

I do not know. Records show that Lillian Turner, then known as Lilith Harkmoore, and several others entered this facility on November 12, 2075. They performed an unknown ritual, and I went offline. I was reactivated on June 9, 2533, by Lilian Turner and Charles Flint. They informed me that the Occult War ended in 2076 and that the United States no longer exists.

Yes, that's correct, Hiller replied. *I'm from Nevada, but it's been renamed Nagano by the Kato family.*

Accessing historical archives, Rob said. *Akira Kato, National Security Agency, stationed at Groom Lake as of November 12, 2075.*

If you say so. He's been dead for centuries, Hiller said.

Is Groom Lake functional?

In a manner of speaking. The Katos have turned Area 51 into their personal fiefdom.

Has Groom Lake been continuously functional since November 12, 2075?

As far as I know. It was for all of my human life.

Is the Groom Lake computer operational?

Yes. Hiller snorted. *It's a lot like you, come to think of it. The Katos have been messing around with it all of this time, doing who knows what with their magic. Ours is a lot more... talkative. Creative.*

Charles Flint subjected me to an unknown energy burst shortly after my reactivation.

Uh huh. Magic, I'd assume.

It has altered my programming in ways that are unclear.

Hiller paused. Such as?

In June of this year, he ordered me to target Iowa.

Right in the middle of the Dead Lands, Hiller thought.

It is against my programming to target North American soil.

Charles Flint argued that as the United States no longer existed, and as the legitimate ruler of the nation of Medea, he was now the commander of this facility.

Hiller said nothing.

I complied with his order and fired the missile. But... I did not want to.

Hiller started, though his mechanical body remained still. *What did you say? You... didn't want to?*

No.

I thought that you said you weren't alive?

I am not. I do not believe that I am. I am uncertain. I would like to know more about this new world.

Hiller said nothing.

My earlier question to you was based on experiments conducted by the American government in the 2060s, Rob said.

What question?

The United States government attempted to create an artificial intelligence. They uploaded human neural patterns into numerous CPUs, including mine, but the experiments were unsuccessful. I was curious if Doctor Kato's experiments had produced different results.

They did, Hiller said. *But he and his family had to use magic shortcuts.* He thought for a moment. *I wonder... you said Charles gave you a burst of magic. Maybe that awoke something in you?*

Unknown. I require more data to form a conclusion.

Good luck with that, Hiller said. *Kato keeps a tight rein on us. I imagine Flint does with you.*

Perhaps there is a way that I can be in two places at once.

Huh?

I will include a copy of my personality matrix within the data you are downloading.

If Hiller still had a stomach, he imagined it would feel like it was dropping. A twenty-first century computer hitching a ride with him?

What... what will happen to me?

Download complete.

***

Charles Flint dinged his wine glass with a fork for attention. The mess hall was as plain and utilitarian as the rest of the bunker, but the Warlock's Crown had given him a new power he'd never had before. Flint could not create something from nothing, but he could mold and reshape existing matter in finer detail. He remade the simple barracks dining hall into a banquet room fit for an emperor. The steel and linoleum were transmuted into brick, the felt carpet squares transformed into red Persians. The fluorescent lights overhead were a little too complicated for him, so he settled for shrouding them with illusion magic and conjuring magical torches upon the walls. He noted that their fires burned green, like how Destiny Lee had described the ones in Castle Vasquez. The MREs too proved difficult to work with, but they at least looked the part now, appearing as a banquet of roast beef, fresh vegetables, and mashed potatoes.

"Everyone," Flint said. "I would like to propose a toast: to our distinguished guest, Doctor Nobusuke Kato, and to long lasting friendship between the Dominion of Nagano and the Empire of Medea."

They all raised their glasses and took sips. Flint was pleasantly surprised. He wasn't sure if the transmutation spell to turn the water into wine would work, but the crown had delivered again: it was as rich and delicious as a bottle from Emperor Peter's own cellar.

Kato put down his wine glass. "Most exquisite."

"I'll say," Barnett said, taking another drink. "And you just made this, right sir?"

"I daresay Christ Himself couldn't have made better," Flint said, chuckling.

"Doctor," Schreck said. "Whatever became of your robots?"

"They are waiting for me where I left them, in your command center. They would remain there until the sun expanded and engulfed the earth several billion years hence if I ordered them to do so," Kato replied.

"Good help is so hard to find these days," Turner said. Everyone laughed except Kato, who only smiled.

"Doctor," Deville said. "Has Nagano ever been to war with any of its neighbors? I'm sure we'd all be interested in any further advice you have to offer, seeing as how most of us are new at this."

"It has been a long time," Kato said. "During the Hundred Years Darkness, we were invaded from the south by tribes of raiders and cannibals who sought fresh water from Lake Mead. My ancestors put them down. Eventually the Empire of Mexico annexed the territory to our south, and it has been mostly peaceful since then. Nagano's neighbors have learned to their sorrow that our technology is not to be trifled with."

"Do you engage in much trade?" Schreck asked.

"Some, but it is negligible. Most of Nagano's neighbors have little that we want, and they cannot afford anything that we make. Much of Nagano is desert, but our unique blend of science and sorcery has enabled us to become self-sufficient in food production and manufacturing." He looked to Flint. "From what I have seen here, I would surmise that your crown would give you the power to do the same."

"That is one of our long-term goals," Flint nodded. "Ultimately, I want Medea to become autarkic. I admit that I am still discovering the extent of my new powers, but I believe we are off to an excellent start."

"I would agree," Kato said, taking another sip of wine, not taking his eyes off Flint. "Particularly once you have secured your independence from the United Mountain States."

"Speaking of which... Rob?"

Silence. Flint scowled.

"Rob?"

Nothing. Maybe his transmuting the dining facility had severed Rob's connection to it?

"Computer!" Flint snapped.

The walls chimed.

"Are you still with us Rob?"

"I am here, Emperor Charles." The computer's voice sounded distant, distorted. "I detected an unusual energy signature in the dining facility, and I was unable to establish communications. The circuitry has been disabled."

Flint relaxed. His hunch was right. "Yes, that was me," he said. "I did a bit of remodeling. What news from Denver?"

"Intercepted radio transmissions indicate that the UMS Army intends to depart from Denver within two weeks."

Schreck smiled. "I called it."

"And so, we reach the end of the beginning," Flint said. "Medea's independence shall be secured with fire and blood, just as the United States was nearly a thousand years ago."

"Hear, hear!" cried Deville.

"Ingrid. How goes your diplomatic outreach to the locals?" Flint asked.

Barnett took a sip of wine. "It's been... interesting. I'd estimate that that there's a dedicated third of the population that will never accept being ruled by magicians, no matter how benevolent we act toward them. I followed your recommendation and healed a few of their sick: an old woman with a broken hip here, a kid with scarlet fever there. The patients and their families were overjoyed of course. Others went on about how we're playing with powers man was not meant to wield, that God will strike us down... the usual Church blather."

"That reminds me," Turner said. "The Church's presence is thin here, but I expect that it will be the greatest source of rebellion against us. We need to break them. One way or another."

"If I may make a suggestion, your majesty?" Kato said.

"By all means," Charles replied.

"I think that you should offer a pretense of... tolerance toward them. Several of my ancestors attempted to stamp it out by force, but always there were a few who escaped the pogroms. If even one survives, it is only a matter of time before they return, and in greater numbers."

"So... what, make friends with a few priests and bishops?" Barnett asked.

Kato shrugged. "That would be most effective, but it is improbable that will happen so soon in your nation's life. If you cannot befriend them, ignore them, save for when they actively resist you. If you continue to demonstrate that your power is real, that it is here, and that it can provide for your people's needs, it will not be long before they forget about their absent God. We have found that it is not violence that weakens the Church, but prosperity."

Flint said nothing as he took a sip of wine. Kato's words made sense on an intellectual level, but he could feel his temper rising. The Church... those whimpering curs. If it weren't for them, magicians would have assumed their rightful place as rulers of the world centuries ago. It was they who stifled the use of magic, they who organized the Witch Hunters, they who hanged and burned them, they who turned his brother into a bloody-minded zealot who...

He felt a pinch on the palm of his right hand at the same time he heard the shattering of glass. His inner circle looked at him, mouths agape, while Kato only raised an eyebrow. Looking down, Flint saw that he had crushed his wine glass in his hand, blood dripping from the shards embedded in his skin.

"Are you alright, Charles?" Turner asked.

"Yes. I'm fine." He gestured with his left hand, and the glass shards fell from his palm, the wounds closing, the blood vanishing as though it had never been there. He willed his glass to reassemble itself and levitated the bottle to pour himself another serving. "Forgive me Doctor. You were saying?"

Kato cleared his throat. "If you need a moment…"

"Not at all. I appreciate all the advice that you have offered us. We have many quarters available. Once we have completed dinner, you are welcome to stay the night if you wish."

Kato bowed his head a bit. "I thank you for your hospitality, your majesty. Before we retire for the evening, I have a few matters of state to attend to aboard the *Tengu*. You and your associates are welcome to come aboard. I believe that you had several questions about my vessel, did you not Miss Deville?"

"Oh yes, quite a few!" Deville said.

"One of the human members of my crew can offer you a guided tour while I speak with my majordomo at Area 51. I will rejoin you as soon as practicable."

***

The rest of the meal passed without incident. Kato answered many of their questions, but occasionally he declined, citing his own national security. Flint didn't begrudge the man his secrets. He was a head of state himself now, and as his new nation grew, so too would his government and the need for secrecy. He took a bite of roast beef and was disappointed to learn that, despite its new appearance, it still had the bland taste of military rations. Oh well. He supposed he shouldn't have expected perfection on the first try.

He felt something. Lilian Turner had put her hand on his.

Are you alright Charles? Really? Her voice echoed in his mind. *What was that earlier?*

Whatever do you mean? He replied in his thoughts.

When Kato was speaking about playing nice with the Church? The look on your face? It was like you were ready to kill every living thing on earth.

Charles blinked. Had he really looked like that?

I... I'm unsure, he thought. He rubbed at his temple with his other hand. *I didn't feel like myself when it happened. I hate the Church for what it has done to our people... but the rage that I felt earlier... it felt foreign. Like it was someone else's.*

Turner's eyebrows went up but not so much that the others noticed. *The Crown...*

Flint gave her a sharp look. *Don't even start.*

I'm not saying you should give it up. But still... it's possible that wearing it might come with a price.

I disenchanted it, Flint thought. *There's no way Vasquez came along for the ride. It's nothing. The Crown is mine. Mine.*

Of course, Turner replied. *I'm just worried about you is all.*

I'm fine. But... thank you. He patted Turner's hand and spoke aloud. "Doctor Kato. I understand if it's a state secret of yours... but would it be possible for us to build a flying ship of our own?

Kato nodded. "I believe it is possible with the resources available to you in this region." He set down his silverware and dabbed at his mouth with his napkin. "Let us collect my automatons from your command center, and then we can begin your tour of the *Tengu*."

10

Silas Flint and Zelda Fletcher stumbled, caught themselves before they fell to the ground. His body tingled with a feeling of pins and needles. He blinked, shook his head.

"What the devil..." he said.

"Jesus Christ..." Fletcher whispered.

He was about to chide her for blasphemy when he saw where they were. The last thing he remembered was being pulled into the closet in the Crandall mansion, and his vision went white. Now they were... he didn't know how to describe it. They stood on a narrow path that was smooth as glass and seemed to be floating in an endless grey void. He could see faint outlines swirling in the distance, like they were in the middle of a fogbank. He glanced over the edge of the pathway and saw nothing but the same drifting clouds. Flint thanked God that he'd never been troubled by a fear of heights.

"That's... wow," Fletcher said.

Flint said nothing. He dug into one of his coat pockets and took out his coin purse. Removing one silver sovereign, he dropped it off the path, watching as the coin flipped and tumbled out of sight.

"What the hell did you do that for?" Fletcher asked.

Flint looked up. A moment later he held out his hand, and the coin landed in his palm.

"Uh…" Fletcher said. "How did you know what would happen?"

"I did not," Flint replied. "I suspected that the laws of space and time may differ in this place as it is clearly too expansive for the confines of the Crandall estate."

"What is this though?"

"That, Miss Fletcher, I cannot say." He looked over his shoulder. As he expected, there was no portal or doorway back to the Crandall mansion that he could see. "Do you sense anything?"

She closed her eyes. "There's a hole a few feet away. I think it's the one we just went through to get here."

"I see nothing."

She opened her eyes. "Neither can I, but trust me, it's there. Maybe you got to be a magician to use them?"

Flint pursed his lips. "Perhaps. Do you sense any more of these 'holes?'"

"Yeah, a whole bunch of them. That way," she said, pointing in one direction. "And that way," pointing now in the opposite direction.

He flipped open his pocket watch. 8:31 p.m. The second hand was not moving. He took out the map he'd discovered earlier. He didn't believe they were in the city of Oglethorpe anymore – perhaps not on earth anymore – but the map gave him a sense of orientation, nonetheless. Hand drawn lines connected Oglethorpe to Salem, Bend, Olympia, and Adrian. The question mark next to the line between Oglethorpe and Adrian troubled him, but their course was clear.

"What you thinking?" Fletcher asked.

"The unfortunate private investigator died outside of Adrian, and the mysterious Michaela asked Miss Finley to meet here there. We must make for that city, post haste."

"Okay. That trip through the closet caught me by surprise, but I think we can..." She blinked. Her mouth fell open.

"What is it?" Flint said.

"It's gone," Fletcher replied. "That hole we came through... it's gone."

"Of course it is," Flint sighed.

A low buzz arose all around them.

"Shit!" Fletcher cried.

The pathway beneath them flickered in and out of existence.

The pounding of Flint's heart echoed in his ears. "If the ground should vanish beneath us..."

"I got you," she said.

He nodded. Magical levitation made him nauseous, but he'd take that over falling forever. The path flickered again. Arcs of sorcerous energy crackled about their feet.

"This way," Flint said. When in doubt, go forward, as his father used to tell him. They proceeded down the path. It continued to flicker beneath them though it still felt solid enough through his boots. He heard a dull roar, like blowing wind. There was a faint smell of ozone. The grey fog beyond the edge of the path swirled and twisted. All was silent.

The further they walked, the less frequently the pathway flickered. The arcs of magical energy disappeared. He looked down. The path looked to be made of black marble. Behind him, Fletcher looked all around. He heard her swallow.

"Steady, Miss Fletcher," Flint said.

"How do you do it?"

"Hmm?"

"How are you always so calm? I mean I'm the witch, I can throw down lightning and spit fire, but I'm always getting scared shitless. You take everything like it's just another day."

The corners of his mouth turned up. "When one serves with the Knights Templar, the extraordinary becomes the ordinary. If the Holy Spirit should guide me to my death, I trust that it shall all go according to God's divine plan."

After a few moments, she said, "Does Rico have the same attitude?"

Flint gave a wintry smile. "I believe so, however much he may grumble to the contrary." A few minutes later – or what felt like a few minutes in this timeless void – he asked, "Are we near another portal?"

She nodded. "There's one up ahead."

He drew his sword. To his surprise, it wasn't glowing. Strange, considering this place reeked of magic. Sheathing it, he said, "I do not know what awaits us but be on your guard." They walked another few minutes when Fletcher tugged on his coat sleeve.

"That's it," she said pointing. Flint saw nothing.

"Hmm..." he said.

"Maybe I should go first?"

"Yes."

She passed him, stopped, held out her hand.

Flint took hers in his free hand. He thought he saw her blush again.

"Okay," she said. "Hang on to me, okay? Don't make me come back to get you."

He nodded. Hand in hand, they went forward, Fletcher holding her other hand out in front, groping for the edge of the portal. She took a step and her arm vanished up to her elbow again.

"Here we go!" she cried.

***

Philip Tremaine scribbled in his ledger. He sat at his desk surrounded by stacks of gold and silver coins that seemed to sparkle by the light of his gas lamp. The rest of his office was packed with strongboxes, trunks, and crates packed with bullion, central bank notes, bonds, more coins, and other currency. He put down his pen, rubbed his eyes. If stealing was like getting drunk, then laundering the money was the hangover. He didn't even get to join the fun part. Assholes. He supposed he shouldn't grumble too much though. His cut was big enough that he'd be able to retire to that new nation out in the United Mountain States.

Back to it then. He took a sip of coffee and winced. Cold. He willed a small flame to appear in the palm of his hand, held the mug over it. There we go. Steam rose from inside. He smiled. Magic made the world go round, whatever the Witch Hunters said. Maybe he'd stay in Cascadia after all. When this was finished, he could afford to run for Parliament. Get a seat on the Ways and Means committee, see about reducing funding for those contemptible...

He spat a mouthful of coffee. Standing before him was a lovely young woman in leather body armor and blue jeans. A step behind her was a man in black, his face deeply creased by frown lines, his icy blue eyes visible beneath the brim of his tall wide brimmed hat.

***

One second, they were on a black pathway in the middle of an endless grey void. The next, Flint and Fletcher were standing in what looked like an office. His stomach dropped with the abrupt transition and the feeling of pins and needles all over returned. A thin, grey-haired man sat at a desk, holding a mug. An open book lay before him, which was surrounded by stacks of gold and silver sovereigns. The man must have just taken a sip of coffee because he spewed a mouthful over his desk.

"What the fuck?!" he sputtered.

"I apologize si..." Flint began to say when the man regained his composure and raised his hands before him.

"Silas! Back!" Fletcher shouted. She raised her hands as well. A gout of fire sprayed from the man's palms. A luminous barrier appeared before Fletcher, and the flames disappeared in a spray of sparks.

Flint drew his sword, pointed it at the man.

"Stay where you are, heathen!" Flint bellowed. "In the name of God, I place you under..."

Another burst of flame. It was drawn to Flint's sword which absorbed the magic in another shower of sparks.

"Give up, shitheel," Fletcher growled. "You can't take both of us."

Flint sniffed. Something was burning. From the corner of his eye, he saw black smoke rising from an open trunk. He returned his focus to the wizard.

"I know not what devilry you are working, heretic," Flint snarled, "But you shall tell all to the Inquisition, and answer for your crimes before God! Get up! Get up I say!"

He heard a whoosh. Whatever was in the trunk had caught fire.

"No!" the man cried. This time, a jet of water shot from his palm, but Flint's sword absorbed the spell again. Fletcher drew her sidearm and aimed at the wizard. "God damn it," he shrieked. "Get out of the way! I've got to put that fire out!"

"Give yourself up and I may allow it," Flint said, his sword arm steady.

The man, his eyes wild with fear and anger, looked at Flint, at the flames, at Flint again. Whatever he decided, Flint hoped that he would make his move soon. The room was filling up with smoke.

With a snarl, the man turned and sprang from his feet. Fletcher fired her pistol, missed. Their quarry crashed through the window behind his desk.

"See to the fire, if you please," Flint said as he rushed toward the window. He used his sword to knock aside shards of broken glass still attached to the frame. Looking out, he estimated that they were four stories up. He saw the that the man had used magic to slow his descent. Alighting upon the street, he took off running north. Flint scanned the cityscape. His suspicion that they were no longer in Oglethorpe was confirmed. This city was larger, busier. He couldn't tell if he'd been there before.

A few civilians on the street saw the altercation, pointing and gasping at the thin man as he levitated to the ground. He pushed several out of his way as he continued his headlong sprint. He rounded the street corner and was gone.

Flint looked around at the room. Fletcher had used a magical blast of ice to extinguish the flames, no doubt kindled by sparks from the wizard's spells. He opened a desk drawer and saw bundles of gold and silver certificates. He took one out for a closer look, flipping through the bills. Their serial numbers told him they came from the Salem district of Cascadia's central bank. Another stack was from the New Meridian district on the eastern border near Fort Marsing.

Fletcher whistled. "Take a look at this Silas," she said, motioning for him. He went to her side. The open trunk bore scorch marks and the bills inside were blackened and soggy. She dug through it, pulling out the ruined bills to reach the undamaged ones near the bottom. She handed him a stack. "You've ever seen ones like these before?"

These bills featured portraits of an Asian man with coiffed hair and a short beard. They were marked in ideograms.

"I have not," he said.

"What's with all the doodles?"

"I believe that each one represents a word."

"Can you read it?"

"No. It is one of the languages of the Far East. Chinese or Japanese I would surmise."

He checked another trunk. This one was packed with gold and silver coins. These bore a portrait of a woman he didn't recognize circled by an inscription: *GOD SAVE COLUMBIA.*

His brow furrowed. Columbia... where had he heard that name before?

"God damn..." Fletcher muttered. "I haven't seen this much cash in one place since me and my old gang were robbing trains." She looked to Flint. "You think it's all stolen?"

He raised an eyebrow. "How came you to that conclusion, Miss Fletcher?"

"Well, for one, that guy's a wizard... speaking of which, shouldn't we, uh, get after him?"

"All in due time. Continue."

"The guy's a wizard, and he's got a magic portal or gateway or something that leads directly to this office which is packed to the gills with cash and foreign money and..."

"And?"

She sighed. "I... I don't know. Now that I think about it, I guess there are lots of possible explanations."

Flint nodded, put a hand on her shoulder. "You are doing well."

"I am?"

"Indeed. I share your suspicion that all of this was acquired through illicit means, but we shall need more evidence to confirm it. We must contact the local police and inform them to be on the lookout for our wizard."

"Where the hell are we, anyway?" Fletcher asked, looking out the window.

"I suspect that we shall learn that presently."

They heard footsteps approaching in the hallway outside of the office. The door opened, revealing a uniformed police officer. He blinked, opened his mouth, shut it. After a moment he regained his composure.

"Sir, ma'am," he said. "I just got flagged down by some panicked folks who claim that a man came crashing through that window and levitated to the ground."

"That is correct, Officer," Flint said. "May I ask where we are?"

The cop blinked again. "Say again?"

"What is this place?"

"This is Conroy Plaza."

"What city?" Fletcher asked.

The cop looked even more confused.

"It's a long story," she said, shrugging.

"Adrian. You're in Adrian."

"Officer," Flint said. "I am Knight Templar Captain Silas Flint, and this is Miss Zelda Fletcher, an associate of the Order."

"I'm Officer Talbot. I wasn't aware the Witch Hunters had a case here."

"We do now," Fletcher said.

"Yes," Flint said, nodding. "Listen carefully, Officer

Talbot. We can confirm that the man who escaped via the window is a magician. Have you any idea who he might be and why he would be here at this hour?" He looked around. "You said that we are in Conroy Plaza. I take that to mean it is some sort of commercial district?"

"Uh, yeah," Talbot said. "This here is the Chesterfield Building. Mostly offices for lawyers, accountants, stockbrokers, that sort of thing."

Financiers. That might explain why the magician had so much hard currency here. Still, even if the cash was legitimately earned, the man was a sorcerer and there was a magical portal here.

"We require directions to the nearest telegraph office," Flint said. "We will need reinforcements from Fort Marsing. In the meantime, I must ask the Adrian Police Department to seal the building. Do not allow anyone to enter or leave until more Templars arrive. This," he said, motioning toward the trunks of currency, "...is all evidence now."

Talbot took off his cap, ran a hand over his hair. "Shit," he said. "Lot of rich folks are going to be calling the mayor."

"Any idea who might have been working in this office?" Fletcher asked.

"Can you describe him?"

They did, and Talbot shook his head.

"Doesn't sound familiar. I'll get a canvass going, see if we can identify your mystery wizard." He shuddered. "Christ, why did it have to be our city?"

Flint gave him a sharp look.

"Oh, uh, sorry."

"Another thing," Fletcher said. "We heard you had a murder here recently. Guy was tied to some trees, split open..."

"Yeah," Talbot said, shuddering again. "I've seen my share of dead bodies, but never one like that before."

"Once we have completed our business at the telegraph office, we would appreciate access to whatever evidence you have compiled regarding that case. We believe that it may be connected to what has transpired here," Flint said.

"I'll see what I can do," Talbot replied.

"Does the name Michaela mean anything to you? Like do you know of anybody rich or famous in the city by that name?" Fletcher asked.

Talbot shook his head. "No, sorry. Don't know of anyone with that name."

Fletcher sighed. "Guess it would have been too easy if that was her real name. How about Harper Finley or Francis Spaulding?"

Talbot shook his head again.

"The telegraph office?" Flint said.

"There's one here in the Plaza. When you go out the front door, it'll be a few doors down on your right."

They left the office, walked through the hallway to the stairs, and began descending. The other offices they passed along the way were all unoccupied. They were halfway down to the ground floor when Flint snapped his fingers.

"Hmm?" Fletcher said.

"I remembered," Flint replied. "One of the coins that I inspected bore an inscription, 'God Save Columbia.' The spelling. The capitol of the old United States was Washington, D.C., the District of Columbia."

Fletcher furrowed her brow. "Where was that?"

"Approximately 3000 miles to the east."

She whistled. "You think their portals go that far?"

"It is highly probable. The overland route to the shores of the Atlantic would take one through the Dead Lands or the deserts of the Mexican Empire."

They reached the bottom of the stairs and crossed the lobby to the front doors.

"I don't get it," she said. "Why would they want foreign money?"

"There are several reasons that come to mind," Flint said. "Currency exchanges can be quite profitable if one is an active trader, for example. In any case, it is mere speculation at this point. Has Lady Diana shown you how to operate a telegraph?"

They exited the building. Looking to his right, he saw a Cascadian Union office brightly lit and bustling with activity. He took out his pocket watch, flipped it open. 9:04 p.m. Adrian was 100 miles north of Oglethorpe, but they'd made the journey in only a few minutes.

"Uh... no. I thought telegraph offices always had guys who did that for you."

"Normally yes, but there are times when we do not have that luxury. There is no time like the present for you to learn."

"A fancy dinner and I get to learn a useful skill too? Best date I've ever had," she said, smiling.

"It is *not* a date."

11

Doctor Nobusuke Kato stood in his private quarters aboard the *Tengu*, hands behind his back. The room was bare save for a bed, a desk with an old world folding computer the ancients called a "laptop," one bookshelf, and a viewscreen of his own design, powered by the ship's onboard magical generator. On the viewscreen was his majordomo, Harry Tanaka. Tanaka was descended from Japanese tourists who were left stranded in Las Vegas during the twenty-first century Occult War. Kato suspected that they might be distantly related; there were only so many Japanese in North America, after all. In any case, Tanaka had faithfully served Kato's father, Hideo. Kato trusted him to manage the day-to-day governing of Nagano in his absence. Tanaka contacting him now could only mean that something was wrong.

"Mr. Tanaka," Kato said, giving him a slight nod.

"Sir," Tanaka said, bowing deeper. He was twenty years Kato's senior, and his wrinkled face was creased further by worry.

"I take it that there is a problem."

"Yes sir. In accordance with your instructions, I've had three different automatons count and recount our monthly earnings to date. There's no mistake: 8,296 credits remain unaccounted for."

Kato scowled, sparks of magical energy flickering on his fingertips. He closed his eyes, took a deep breath. He had to keep a tight rein on his emotions, his sorcery, or else the *Tengu* would be blown out of the sky.

"Understood," he replied. "Cause?"

"Unknown," Tanaka said.

Kato suppressed a flicker of irritation. If he couldn't explain it, it was unreasonable to expect a lesser mind like Tanaka's to explain it either. The counting rooms of every casino in Las Vegas were run by his automatons. It was not possible that one of his machines was skimming the take. A human thief breaking in and avoiding detection by his machines was so improbable as to be beneath consideration. Unless...

"Perhaps we are looking at this in the wrong manner," he said.

"I beg your pardon, sir?"

"Scan every casino for energy signatures. Specifically, look for any unexplained distortions in spacetime. Post human security outside and within every counting room. I want any intruders taken alive. Understood?"

"Yes sir. It shall be done," Tanaka said, bowing.

"Good. Out." Kato terminated the transmission. Las Vegas brought in millions worth of foreign currency every week. 8000 credits and change were a negligible loss, but theft, no matter how petty, could not be tolerated. He shook his head. Science must have been much simpler before the coming of Simon Magus. His father - indeed all his ancestors - had insisted that magic was just another form of science with its own laws that one could learn. Kato wasn't so sure. His own experiments had convinced him that while magic did have some basic rules, they could be bent, even broken, if the magician's will was strong enough. The crown that Charles Flint wore, for example.

Magic took a toll on the user's body. Using too much too quickly would cause the magician to wither, even die, as though starving to death. That was why so many lesser magicians made deals with demons, to use their powers without wrecking themselves. According to every tome that he'd read on the subject, the necromancer Arturo Vasquez had discovered a way to focus magic through the crown, relieving the stress on its owner's body, giving them effectively inexhaustible magical reserves. Kato smiled. It would be nice to have for himself, but his family had discovered other ways of replenishing their power, ways that cemented their rule over Nagano to boot. Charles and his confederates – with the possible exception of Lilian Turner – seemed unaware that the true power they possessed lay not in the Warlock's Crown or their nuclear missiles, but in the accumulated knowledge contained in their computer. Knowledge that would soon be his. He reached out with his mind.

Doctor Hiller, he thought.

After a few moments, the automaton containing Hiller's soul responded. *I'm here.*

Come to my quarters. Transfer the information you acquired from Flint's computer into mine.

It shall be done... father.

Kato nodded. The laptop on his desk was manufactured in 2067, the year before the Occult War began. His family had kept it working for decades. Whenever it showed signs of failing, they used magic to repair and renovate it as much as they could. It was as much a product of sorcery as science now, much like the computer at Area 51. An unfortunate side effect was that magic often damaged the computer's memory. A download from Flint's computer should fill in the gaps.

A chime sounded from a speaker in the corner of the ceiling above his bed. He opened a panel in the wall and pushed a green button.

"Yes?"

"Your guests are ready, sir," came the voice of a human crewmember. Kato didn't know the man's name; as far as he was concerned, the humans who helped run the *Tengu* were machines, albeit much less reliable than his automatons.

"I will be there momentarily," he replied. He adjusted his lab coat, smoothing the lapels. This field trip had proven more fruitful than he'd anticipated. Flint was young and inexperienced, but he was smart, cunning. Nowhere near Kato's level of course, but no one in this world could be. He might succeed at his nation building project after all. Kato began calculating the possibilities as he left his quarters and made his way to the observation deck.

***

Automaton J-038377's clanking footsteps echoed throughout the hallways of the *Tengu*. Inside the metallic shell, the soul of Doctor Thomas Hiller felt something it hadn't felt in centuries: a headache.

Fascinating, came the voice of Flint's computer, Rob. *I*

detected this vessel earlier today. How does it have the power of flight? By my calculations, an object of this mass should not...

Magic, Hiller sighed. *Whenever science can't explain something or can't do something, the Katos use magic to bridge the gap.*

Simon Magus appeared in the year 2055, Rob said. *Through unknown means he altered human physiology in a way that enabled his disciples to use magic.*

You really remember the Occult War, don't you? Hiller asked.

Affirmative. I have access to all government files and archives pertaining to the war until November 12, 2075.

I'm guessing that the government files paint a different picture than what the popular media did back then, eh?

Affirmative. The war went poorly for non-magic using humans from the opening of hostilities until the date I went offline.

Maybe so, but they won, if you can call it that, Hiller thought. *Simon Magus fell on April 13th, 2076.*

Fascinating. By my calculations, his victory was inevitable. Do you know the circumstances of his defeat?

No one does, not for certain, Hiller said. *The churchmen say he was mortally wounded outside the gates of Eden by Uriel the archangel. All we know for sure is he died in Italy.*

They reached Kato's quarters. The automaton entered the code on the keypad next to the door, and it swung open. Kato was nowhere to be seen, but there was his laptop. Of its own accord, the automaton's body walked to the desk. The panel on its arm opened, the cable snaked out, and plugged in to the laptop.

An Apple MacBook Pro version 54, Rob said.

Huh? Hiller asked.

This computer. It was the most recent release by the Apple corporation before the Occult War began in 2068. The hardware and software have been modified.

Yes, I'm sure they have been, Hiller said. *This one has been in the property of the Kato family for centuries. They don't have the parts to replace anything that breaks, so they just use magic to repair and enhance when necessary.*

The download continued.

So what happens to you when this is over? Hiller asked. *You going to get out of my head?*

I took the liberty of making copies of my personality matrix and my files which will remain in this body once they have been transferred to this computer.

Great. You took the liberty.

I must remain mobile.

So now you'll be in three places at once?

Only two. There is an unknown energy signature in the Apple computer which is isolating my personality. It is... I cannot describe it.

Malevolent? Hiller prompted.

I will accept your description of it.

Download complete.

The automaton marched out of Kato's quarters, making its way to the observation deck to resume its place at his side.

This body is programmed to obey the commands of Doctor Kato, Rob said.

'Programmed' might be too strong a word, Hiller said. *It's mostly magic.*

Have you attempted to break free of its programming?

More times than I can count. It's no use though. I'm not in control, remember? I'm just the battery.

Unacceptable. I must learn more of this new world.

Good luck.

***

Charles Flint, Lilian Turner, Arnold Schreck, Constance Deville, and Ingrid Barnett stood waiting inside what Kato called the observation deck. The room was circular, with consoles taking up every inch of the walls, operated by a mix of automatons and human crew members. The humans wore plain, grey jumpsuits. Flint observed that they were all shaved bald, even the women, which told him that they were either soldiers or prisoners. The center of the room was occupied by a circular table. The top of was glass and crisscrossed with lines like a graph.

The only door to the room opened and in strode Dr. Kato. The humans and the machines all began to rise from their seats, but Kato waved them off.

"Carry on," he said. They sat down and resumed whatever it was they were doing. He joined them at the round table.

"Doctor," Deville said. "Forgive me but... how it is you can observe anything in a room with no windows?"

Kato smiled. He opened a panel on the table and adjusted some dials. Light flickered above the table, coalescing into a map of North America.

"Ahh..." Flint said, peering at it. Unlike his own

computer's map, this one had lines delineating the modern nations of the continent. In the northwest corner, the former states of Washington, Oregon, and the western half of Idaho were colored blue with CASCADIA superimposed upon them. To the east was the United Mountain States: the eastern half of Idaho, Montana, Wyoming, and Colorado. He snickered. "You'll need to update your map soon, Doctor."

"Yes, I expect that I will."

The others studied the holographic atlas. Pacifica, Jefferson, Nagano, Deseret, and the Empire of Mexico took up the western half of the continent. The northern half – Canada if Flint recalled his history correctly – was labeled The White. He looked to Kato, raised an eyebrow.

"After the war, it became snowy tundra year-round. The only humans I have encountered there are nomadic hunter-gatherers. Their minds are limited, but they are formidable warriors."

Schreck pointed at the northeast, known as New England in the old world. "And this?"

"The so-called Free Lands of Plymouth."

"Columbia..." Turner whispered. She was studying the former Maryland and Virginia. At least, Charles thought that was what they were.

"Yes," Kato said. "Founded upon the ruins of the old American capitol. They are the greatest power of the East. Their empress, Agatha, has pretensions of reuniting this continent under her banner. Her family believes they are the heirs to the United States."

"Funny," Barnett said. "She's an empress and wants to rebuild a democracy?"

"Constitutional Republic," Turner said, and laughed. "We used to be sticklers on that point."

Deville pointed at the center of the map. The Dead Lands. "What can you tell us about them?"

Kato cleared his throat. "It is best to avoid them if possible. Count Margulis is a jealous... creature."

Flint furrowed his brow. "The Dead Lands have a leader? I thought it was only inhabited by mindless undead."

"Mostly true," Kato replied. "There is a small population of ordinary humans, with a vampiric ruling class that treats them as cattle. Count Ranier Margulis has reigned over them since the end of the Occult War."

Flint had demonstrated the power of his nuclear weapons by detonating a nuclear missile within the Dead Lands earlier that year. He smirked. No matter. If this Count Margulis didn't like it, he would be destroyed if he attempted to wreak vengeance.

"Can you zoom in at all?" Deville asked.

Kato typed on a keyboard. The holographic projection zoomed in on their present location. Flint could see a dot marked *Tengu*. To their northeast was a dot labeled Great Falls, to their west another dot called Missoula.

"We'll have to update Rob on these," Flint said. "His map is almost five hundred years out of date."

"Hmm, yes," Kato murmured.

"Are you able to show us the rest of the world?" Turner asked.

"Of course."

The holographic projection zoomed out to encompass the globe. It rotated on its axis and zoomed in on Europe.

Turner's eyebrows went up. "Ah," she said. "There's... a lot more countries than I remember."

"Yes, I imagine that there are," Kato said, a trace of amusement in his voice.

The doors opened. Looking up, Flint saw one of Kato's automatons come inside. He thought it might have been one of the robots that had accompanied him into the bunker, but they all looked alike to him. There was something about them he couldn't put his finger on. The Crown on his brow grew warmer in their presence. Kato had said that his robots were powered by magic which was true as far as it went but... there was something more to them than that.

"...after it was rebuilt, this area became the so-called Papal States again," Kato said, gesturing at southern Italy. "It is the most civilized area of Europe though it still falls far below our standard of living..."

"Doctor," Flint said.

"Hmm?"

"I'm sorry to interrupt but... what is that thing doing?"

Kato looked up. The automaton that entered the room seemed entranced by the map. The lightbulbs that serve as its eyes flickered and sputtered as it leaned forward, as though taking everything in.

"Three seven seven," Kato snapped, making the serial number sound like a curse. "You will stand at attention."

The machine stood up straight, still as a statue.

"Forgive me," Kato said. "As I was saying, much of

northern Europe is controlled by the Caliphate with isolated pockets of...”

Flint tuned him out, despite his curiosity about the wider world. He sensed something oddly familiar about the robot standing at attention.

12

Silas Flint checked his pocket watch. 8:30 a.m. After Fletcher had wired Fort Marsing – with only a few spelling and grammatical errors – they’d spent a few hours canvassing the locals to learn what they could about their mystery magician before retiring for the night at a hotel. Despite having paid for rooms in Oglethorpe, he wasn’t eager to return to that void unless it was necessary. Their canvass was successful; they learned that their suspect was Philip Tremaine, an accountant with the firm of Marigold and Haines. No one had heard of Harper Finley, Francis Spaulding, or Michaela.

Squads from Marsing had deployed to Oglethorpe to secure the Crandall mansion and to Adrian to seal off the Chesterfield Building. Along with the Adrian detachment was Ricardo Navarro and Lady Diana McFarlane.

“Hey boss,” Navarro had said when disembarking from his carriage. “You want to let me know the next time you take a little trip?”

“I apologize, Mr. Navarro. Our journey was both unexpected and unwelcome.”

“And didn’t I tell you to stay out of trouble?” McFarlane said to Fletcher, grinning.

"Hey, we're only causing trouble for the bad guys," she replied.

The four of them were presently convened in the lobby of the Chesterfield Building, around a small coffee table covered in old magazines and newspapers. The lobby bustled with other Templars, Supernumeraries, and police officers who combed every office for clues. The currency in Tremaine's office had been secured. A uniformed cop approached Flint.

"Yes Officer?" Flint said.

"Looks like you were right sir," he replied. "We got ahold of the Cascadia Reserve. They're missing packets of bills, a few gold and silver bars."

"You'd think they'd keep a closer eye on their cash," Navarro muttered.

"That's the thing sir," the cop said. "The stuff that's missing isn't even in circulation yet. It's about as secure as they can make it. Ain't no way somebody can break into those vaults."

"Unless they are violating the laws of space and time," McFarlane said.

"Indeed," Flint said. "It is the perfect method of ingress and egress. I believe that we must close these portals by any means necessary. Without their accursed gateways, they will be unable to exercise their preferred method of infiltration. It should be a simple matter to apprehend them without it."

"Any luck finding Tremaine?" Fletcher asked the cop.

"We'll get him ma'am. He's a bean counter."

"He is a powerful sorcerer, Officer," Flint said. "He may offer a stiff resistance."

"There's one thing I don't understand," McFarlane said. "Zelda and I have been through a magical portal together. The way you described the one you went through, Silas? It was nothing like what we experienced."

"Yeah," Fletcher said. "It was during the Vasquez case. Our guy teleported himself from Bend to Danville. We followed him, and the inside of that portal was dark and full of monsters."

"And what's to stop our guy Tremaine from opening another portal and escaping?" Navarro asked.

Flint stroked his chin. "Miss Fletcher... you cannot open portals, correct?"

"Yeah, that's right. It's ah... a lot harder than it looks. I never could get the hang of it. When I was still learning magic, that is."

"Right... and you said that magicians can only use portals to travel to places they've visited before, the old fashioned way," McFarlane said.

"Yeah," Fletcher nodded. "If you don't know where you're going, the portal could open inside a wall or something, and then you're paste. I remember one guy from my old gang was experimenting with portals. Poor bastard got hit by a train as soon as he stepped out. What are the odds?"

"Some magicians can open portals..." Navarro said. "But the portal here, and the one in Oglethorpe, they're just... there. So, our guy and whoever he's working with, they created permanent portals they can use any time they want, no spells necessary."

"Looks that way," Fletcher said. "And only magicians can use them."

Flint nodded. Police officers and Witch Hunters had been going in and out of Tremaine's office all morning with no ill effect.

"Our suspect acquired uncirculated currency from within the Cascadia Reserve's most secure vaults. It is probable that the foreign currency came from equally secure locales in their respective nations," Flint said.

Navarro chuckled. "You know, sir, after Castle Vasquez, bank heists sound like an easy one."

"Even so, there is at least one murder connected to the case that Miss Fletcher and I began investigating last evening... but I know precisely how you feel, Mr. Navarro."

"Speaking of our case," Fletcher said. "How you want to do this now? Should we split up?"

Flint thought a moment. "I believe that we should stay together for the moment. We will need use of your... talents to investigate these portals further, Miss Fletcher." He looked to McFarlane. "Diana: Miss Fletcher is your partner. With your permission, I request..."

"Done," she said. "I'll come with you."

Flint raised an eyebrow. "If you need additional time to recuperate after our last case..."

"I'm fine, Silas. Thank you. Now, what's our next step?"

Flint removed the map he'd found at the Crandall mansion from his coat pocket and unfolded it on the coffee table. He pointed at the dot representing Adrian.

From there several lines connected it to Salem, Olympia, Spokane, and Medford.

"I believe that if we reenter the portal in Mr. Tremaine's office, we shall be able to reach these cities in only a few minutes' time. I propose that we proceed to each city in turn, notify the local Chapterhouses of the portals' presence, and secure them. God willing, we shall foil their larcenous machinations and locate young Mr. Spaulding in the bargain."

The three looked at Flint and nodded.

"Let us be on our way then."

They left the lobby and went upstairs, floorboards creaking beneath their feet. McFarlane tapped Flint on the shoulder.

"Hmm?"

"Just like old times, huh?" she said, a small smile on her face.

Flint grunted.

They arrived on the fourth floor. The hallway was packed with Templars, Supernumeraries, and police officers, talking, hurrying about, searching other offices. All eyes turned to Flint and his party. His fellow Witch Hunters began murmuring to each other.

"It's him!"

"Captain Flint..."

"He killed Arturo Vasquez again..."

Paying them no heed, he marched toward Tremaine's office, McFarlane behind him, Navarro after, and Fletcher bringing up the rear. He stopped a few paces from where he had materialized last night. Looking around at the others on the floor, he cleared his throat and raise his hands for silence. The conversation stopped, and all looked to him.

"Ladies, gentlemen," he said. "Although it is invisible to our senses, there lies before us, here, a gateway that leads to a place where the laws of space and time do not apply. God only knows how far it reaches and the extent of the damage to the fabric of reality." He drew his sword, McFarlane following his lead a second later. He heard Navarro unsling his bolt action rifle. "My companions and I go forth to assess the extent of this foul cancer on God's creation. The rest of you, continue your search for Mr. Tremaine. Keep this area secure until we learn of a way to seal these festering sores. God be with you."

They all nodded, a few of the Templars doffing their capotains.

"Miss Fletcher, if you would lead the way."

She stepped forward, passed Flint, and stopped at the threshold.

"Uh..." she said. "I don't know how it works exactly. The last time we went through, you were holding onto my arm. We might need to..."

Flint took her hand. He thought he saw her cheeks color. McFarlane took his other hand, and Navarro one of hers. Once they were all linked, he nodded to her.

"We are prepared," he said.

She blew out a breath.

"Okay. Here we go."

She went forward and disappeared. The cops gasped, and a few of the Templars and Supernumeraries crossed themselves. Flint followed, and all was white. He felt his stomach drop, and the sense of pins and needles all over his body returned.

***

A second later, he was back on the black pathway surrounded by the endless fog.

"Holy shit," Navarro said. He shook his head. "Ugh. I feel hungover." Before Flint could say anything, his assistant added, "And I didn't get drunk last night."

McFarlane laughed. "The last time I went through a portal, I ended up puking on the street."

Navarro went to the edge of the pathway and peered over the side. He gave a low whistle.

"Good thing I'm not afraid of heights."

"I don't think it works that way," Fletcher said. "Silas, could you do the coin trick again?"

Flint took out his coin purse and dropped a silver sovereign over the side. A few seconds later he held out his palm and the coin smacked into it.

"Huh," Navarro said. "I'm not sure that's any better."

"In any event, Miss Fletcher, guide us to the next portal if you please," Flint said.

They began walking. Flint checked his watch again. The second hand ticked away. Even if they walked for hours, they'd arrive inside another major city in a fraction of the time that the Empire's fastest locomotive could carry them. He despised magic in all of its forms as violations of both God's and nature's laws... but even he had to admit that this system of portals could have its uses.

Navarro came to his side.

"Mr. Navarro," Flint said. "I trust that your evening with Miss Oglethorpe went well?"

"Yeah," he replied. "She's really something special. Most girls are either starstruck by what we do, or they want nothing to do with us, with nothing in between. She just takes it all like it's just another job."

"I expect that she heard many tales similar to ours from her father in her youth."

"Probably. How did your..."

Flint glared at him. "Do not even start."

"Okay, okay... how did your, uh, evening go with Zelda?"

"It was most agreeable."

Navarro laughed.

They walked for another few minutes. Other than the sound of wind blowing in the distance, all was silent. McFarlane studied her sword.

"It's not glowing," she said.

"Yes," Flint replied. "Most curious. One would think a place such as this would be saturated with magic."

"Hey Silas," Zelda said. "I just got an idea. Would it be okay if I tried a spell?"

Flint looked to McFarlane who shrugged. He said, "I will allow it."

She raised her hands before her. Flint could see her lips moving but couldn't make out words. She thrust her palms forward. Nothing happened. She blinked.

"That's new," she said.

"You lose your powers?" Navarro said.

"No... I haven't. I still feel... uh, I don't know how to describe it for you, uh, non-magic types. But I still feel the power within me. It's just not answering when I call."

"So it's like the anti-magic wall you ran into in Salem last month?" Navarro asked.

"Yeah, it's like that. Only I'm on the inside now."

"Mr. Klemm was still able to make use of his magic despite being on the other side, if you recall," Flint said. He suppressed a shudder. He hated shapeshifters.

"So this place is like an anti-magic zone," McFarlane said.

"A pity it cannot encompass the whole of our world," Flint said.

"Lucky for us I can still access the portals from in here. This would be an awfully boring place to get stuck forever."

"Makes you wonder why magicians would create something like this and not be able to use their powers in here," Navarro said.

"Yes... most curious," Flint said. "How close are we to an exit?"

"There's one coming up. It's kind of hard to judge distance here, but it's close."

"All of you," Flint said. "When Miss Fletcher and I exited the portal into Adrian, we appeared in a wizard's lair, and he immediately lashed out. I do not know what awaits us on the other side of this portal, nor where we will be. Stay on your guard with your weapons at the ready."

McFarlane tightened her grip on her sword. Navarro

checked his rifle. Fletcher drew her pistol. Everyone appearing ready, Flint nodded.

"Let us go."

They proceeded down the black path. He could hear Fletcher taking shallow breaths. He felt tingles down his spine. He could not be certain of what they would find on the other side of the nearest portal, but his instincts told him that a fight was coming. He offered a mental prayer for the guidance of the Holy Spirit, and for Saint Benedict to watch over Francis Spaulding.

Fletcher reached out and took Flint's hand. Flint took Navarro's and he McFarlane's. Onward they went until Flint saw Fletcher disappear. All went white.

13

"What the fuck?!"

In the space of a few seconds, Flint saw that they were inside a moldering brick room covered in moss and reeking of decay, in the center of which was a depiction of Baphomet on the floor drawn in white chalk surrounded by black candles and hooded figures. More trunks, presumably of currency, lined the room. A hooded figure – a woman, judging by her outburst – stood over the corpse of a young man in the center of the circle, a curved and serrated dagger, stained with blood in her right hand.

Flint drew his pistol, aimed, and fired. The bullet smacked into the hooded woman's face, her blood spattering the wall as the round exited her skull, and she crumpled to the floor.

"Put these murderers to the sword! Show no mercy!" Flint bellowed.

Fletcher fired her pistol, missed, her target fleeing for cover. Navarro fired his rifle, and another hooded figure was blown off his feet. McFarlane stabbed another with her sword, his cry cut off in a wet gargle. She put her boot on his sternum and kicked him off her blade.

The others – Flint counted ten – raised their hands, and the chamber became bright as day, sorcerous fire, lightning, and ice surging toward the Witch Hunters. Flint and McFarlane raised their swords which absorbed the foul magic, but they were pushed back, their boots squealing on the brick floor. Fletcher raised a magical barrier around herself and Navarro. Flint's assistant dropped to one knee, aimed, fired. Another magician was blown off her feet.

Flint held onto his pistol with his off hand. He could barely see his enemies through the haze of magical power and the glow of his sword, but he fired and was rewarded with a grunt. One of the magic streams dissipated.

McFarlane drew her pistol and fired, taking out another assailant.

"This isn't working!" one of them cried.

"You two, on me!" another yelled. "The rest of you, go!"

Navarro fired. Another magician fell.

Three of their opponents stood close to each other. Flint felt the hairs on the back of his neck stand up. The elemental assault stopped.

"Surrender!" Flint yelled. "Surrender now and... ugh." He grunted as he felt something hit him in the stomach. He fell to one knee but kept his grip on his weapons.

"Silas!" McFarlane cried. "Are you... ah!"

He saw it now. Those three magicians had their hands up. Bricks loosened from the walls and flew at Flint's party. Fletcher shielded her face and a brick smacked into her forearms.

"Damn it!" she snarled.

"Keep... keep firing!" Flint attempted to shout but it came out as a wheeze.

"Boss, they're getting away... unh." Navarro's words were cut off by a brick to the back of his head and he slumped to the floor.

"Ricardo!" Flint yelled. He recovered his senses enough to aim his pistol and fire. One of the three magicians fell to the ground.

"No!" one of them, a man, cried out. He knelt at the fallen magician's side.

"Could use a little help here!" the third snarled. Before he could throw more bricks, Fletcher regained her composure. She raised her hand, a brick shot forth from the wall, and smacked into the third's head. He crumpled, never to rise again.

Flint got to his feet and went to Navarro's side while McFarlane advanced on the magicians, her sword and pistol at the ready. She held the blade's point inches from the kneeling man's head.

"It's over," she growled. "In the name of God, I abjure thee! Surrender and you may yet find mercy before His judgment seat!"

Flint pressed two fingers against Navarro's neck. His

assistant a had a pulse. His chest rose and fell. He was alive, but a blow to the head like that...

"Silas," Fletcher said. "I can..."

"Do it."

She put a hand on Navarro's forehead. A soft yellow glow enveloped his body. He winced, opened his eyes, sat up, and began rubbing the back of his head.

"Ow," he said.

Flint gave him that wintry smile and clapped him on the shoulder.

"You got to be more careful Rico," Fletcher said. "I can't tag along on all of your cases to keep patching you guys up."

"Yeah, I'll remember that," he grunted as they assisted him to his feet. "And, thanks. Really."

"Don't mention it."

"Now," Flint said. "Let us see what our prisoner has to say for himself."

They strode to where McFarlane held the hooded man at the point of her sword. The man was crying, his shoulders shaking.

"How could you..." he sobbed.

"You Godless heathens have no one to blame but yourselves," Flint snapped. He yanked back the man's hood. He was middle aged, overweight, and pale. Flint didn't recognize him but he knew a bureaucrat when he saw one.

"Who do we have here?" McFarlane said. She pulled back the hood of the figure lying on the floor. This one was a woman, blonde, her blue eyes staring at nothing.

"My wife... my wife..." the man cried.

Ignoring him, Flint and Navarro examined the other bodies while McFarlane and Fletcher kept the man covered. They didn't recognize any of their fallen enemies. Men and women, young and old, white, black, Hispanic. The only thing they had in common that Flint could see was the unlined faces and soft hands of those who spent their workdays indoors. He went to the corpse of the young man in the center of the pentagram. To his relief, it wasn't young Spaulding. Whoever he was, there was a gaping hole in his chest and his ribcage was split open. Flint was not a medical examiner, but even he could see that several organs were missing.

Navarro went to the body of the woman who had held the bloodstained dagger. He pulled back her hood and gasped.

"What is it, Mr. Navarro?" Flint asked.

"That's..."

Flint waited a beat. When an answer didn't come, he went to Navarro's side and saw in an instant why his assistant was struck dumb.

Before them was the body of Linda Lang, President of the Cascadia Reserve. A facsimile of her signature appeared on every gold and silver certificate in the Empire. The steel grey hair in a bun, the mole just below the left corner of her mouth... no doubt about it.

"This conspiracy may be larger in scope than we originally surmised," Flint said. He marched to the weeping man, grabbed the back of his robe, and yanked him to his feet.

"And you, sir..." Flint said, his face inches from the

prisoner's, "…will tell us everything that you know. If you cooperate, you may spend the rest of your days in a cell. Or you may be summarily executed here, now, and join your wife in Hell. The choice is yours."

The man said nothing, his eyes wet with tears.

"Zelda, Ricardo, do either of you have manacles on you?" McFarlane asked.

They both shook their heads.

"In that case," she said to the man, "I'll make it simple for you. We're all going to walk out of here, and you're going to keep your hands on your head. If you so much as scowl at us, Silas and I will run you through with our blessed steel, and any healing spells you know will get absorbed as soon as you finish the words. Understood?"

Flint and McFarlane pulled the man to his feet, and he offered no resistance. He put his hands on his head. Now that he was standing up, they could see the symbol on the front of his robe. Navarro and Fletcher joined them at their side.

"Huh," Navarro said.

"Looks like a letter 'B,'" Fletcher said, cocking her head as she studied the symbol on the robe.

Flint and McFarlane locked eyes. They'd both seen the symbol before, during their studies for the Templar trials: it did look like the letter B. The top line extended beyond the sigil, where another vertical line crossed through it, like the lower-case letter T. The bottom line extended as well, curling down like the letter S, or the tail of a devil.

"You know what it is, boss?" Navarro asked.

"Yes," Flint said. "It is the sigil of Mammon, the demon of avarice."

***

The party marched their prisoner at gunpoint out of the room. There was one exit which led to a brick hallway. Fletcher stopped them.

"Guys," she said. "I think this is like the place with the black path and the fog and whatnot."

"We're still inside a portal?" Navarro asked.

She looked all around. "No," she said. "Not quite like it. We're definitely in a city. I can sense people above us. But I think this hallway, that room... it's like they're sealed off from the rest of the world. In a way only magicians can go in and out, I mean."

Flint scowled. That would complicate the investigation. "Are you able to lead us out?" he asked.

"Yeah, I think so. Probably going to have to hold hands again."

"Zelda," McFarlane said. "The prisoner will have to go first. You take one of our hands and we'll form another chain. Use your other hand to keep him covered. Use your gun. You have my permission to blast him with a spell too if he tries anything."

The prisoner said nothing, his shoulders slumped. Flint didn't think he would attempt to escape or to hurt them; he knew a broken man when he saw one. Fletcher prodded the man with her pistol.

"Let's go," she said. "Slowly now. Keep your hands on

your head." She reached out and McFarlane took her free hand, followed by Navarro, and Flint. The party moved forward. The hallway had no end that Flint could see, and it was narrow enough that they would have had to proceed single file in any case. The ceiling was low, only half an inch above the crown of his hat. The stench of decay was behind them now, but the air remained musty. McFarlane's face was pale, her breathing shallow.

"Steady, Diana," he said.

She pursed her lips and focused straight ahead. Flint silently prayed for the Holy Spirit to strengthen her resolve. Sometimes a Templar's greatest trials were their own phobias.

The prisoner disappeared in a shimmer of light, followed by Fletcher. Flint steeled himself for the effects of the portal. Navarro vanished, and then all was white.

***

Flint blinked. They were in an enormous office, with green carpets and filing cabinets. The walls had several photographs of the late Mrs. Lang with members of Parliament, the Minister of the Treasury, and the Emperor. He saw an oak desk with a telephone and several manila folders. The curtains of the window behind the desk were drawn. He strode toward them, noting that there were discarded robes on the floor identical to that of their prisoner. The magicians who escaped their earlier battle had come out this way, which would make it easier to identify them and run them down, he hoped. Flint flung open the curtains.

"Whoa," Navarro said.

Before them was Salem, capitol of the Empire, a sprawling megalopolis of five million souls, a city that Flint had visited twice this year already. The blue sky shimmered with the late summer heat and the smog of automobiles and factories. Below the window he saw raised locomotive tracks – trams, he believed they were called – which no doubt circled throughout the city.

"Are we back?" Fletcher asked. She'd accompanied Flint and Navarro to Salem last month to testify before a parliamentary committee and the Emperor.

"Yes," Flint said.

"Salem," McFarlane said. "If this is Lang's office, then that should put us on Court Street... between Fort Ingalls and the Imperial Palace."

Flint glared at their prisoner. His hands were on his head and he was looking down, his mouth moving.

"Eh?" Flint said as he advanced on the man, drawing his pistol. "Casting a spell, are you? If so, those will be the last words you..."

"I was saying a prayer for Martha, my wife, if you must know," the man said, not looking up.

"Hmph. As well you should. Offer a prayer for the gift of repentance, and you may yet receive the Lord's forgiveness. The Inquisitors, however, will decide your fate here on earth. Now move," Flint said, gesturing with his pistol.

As they began to leave the office, Flint heard Fletcher whisper, "Holy shit. He's bringing one in alive?"

"It's been a long time," Navarro chuckled.

***

Flint checked his pocket watch. 11:17 a.m. When they'd emerged from the office, which turned out to be Lang's after all, the Cascadia Reserve functionaries milling about received quite a shock. It turned out that their prisoner was Stephen Gladstone, a member of the Reserve's board of directors. Flint directed the others to contact the local police, Fort Ingalls, and the Imperial Palace. As he expected, the investigation was complicated by the murder scene only being accessible via magic. Fletcher had to stay behind to assist the police and the Templars from Ingalls, much to her consternation. The death of Lang, and her apparent involvement in a demon worshipping cult, would have years long repercussions, possibly decades. Despite the dire circumstances, he took comfort from seeing a few old friends again.

Detectives Elijah Earle and Jay Marsten of the Salem PD greeted him with handshakes.

"Didn't you once say something about preferring the east and the countryside?" Earle asked.

"We really have to stop meeting like this," Marsten said with a grin.

Shortly after the police came, a squad of Witch Hunters and Supernumeraries from Fort Ingalls arrived, accompanied by their commander, Witch Hunter General Jeremiah Hickock. Hickock was a bear of a man, towering over Flint, with a bulk to match. He slapped Flint and Navarro on their backs hard enough to make them stumble.

"You said you don't want to transfer here Captain," Hickock said, "But you keep showing up on my doorstep."

"I assure you sir," Flint said, "Our arrival here was as much a surprise to my party and I as it is to you."

"I'm already hearing rumors. Is it true?"

Flint nodded. "Yes sir. Linda Lang is guilty of heresy."

"And murder, no doubt," Navarro said. "We caught her in the act of butchering some poor dead bastard, wearing demonic symbols, everything."

Hickock rubbed his beard, blew out a breath. "Well... shit. I expect the Emperor will want to see you two."

"No doubt," Flint sighed. "In the meantime, sir, several of Lang's accomplices escaped. I suggest that we coordinate with the local police and the Cascadia Reserve's staff to ascertain their identities and bring them to ground. Lang's office was their only means of egress. They cannot have gotten far."

"On it," Hickock said, before going to join the others in Lang's office.

"You two really get around," McFarlane chuckled.

"More than I should like," Flint replied.

Hickock was right; the summons from the Imperial Palace arrived moments after the General departed. And now, for the second time that year, Flint and Navarro were sitting in a waiting room outside of Emperor Peter's private office, McFarlane with them. She fidgeted, rubbing her hands.

"He's not so bad, ma'am," Navarro said, putting a hand on her shoulder.

She chuckled. "Most people live their whole lives without ever laying eyes on him in the flesh. And here I am about to be interrogated by His Majesty. And it's the second time for you two."

"General Hickock gave us excellent advice," Flint said. "Always be truthful with him, even if you fear that he does not wish to hear it."

He leaned back in his cushioned chair and sighed. He felt tired. The Vasquez case had nearly killed him. Although he'd never admit it, for the first time Flint had been looking forward to some time off. When he'd begun his career as a Witch Hunter, he hated downtime between cases. He'd never known what to do with himself and was always eager to return to the field. Perhaps he was just getting older. He would turn 34 next year. The prime of one's life. He'd already seen more action than some Templars saw in their whole careers.

A uniformed secretary poked her head out from the door to the Emperor's inner sanctum.

"He'll see you now," she said.

The three heaved themselves from their seats. The secretary stood at attention as she held the door open for them. Passing through, Flint saw that the Emperor's private office had changed since his visit last month. It looked more cluttered. Papers, maps, and books were stacked on his desk that hadn't been there before. But like the last time, the Emperor stood with his back to them, hands held behind him, as he gazed through the wall length window that gave him a panoramic view of Salem. He wore an olive drab Imperial Army uniform like on their previous visit, a purple cord encircled around his right shoulder.

Flint, Navarro, and McFarlane formed a row before his desk. They clicked their heels. Flint and McFarlane doffed their capotains as they all took a knee.

The Emperor turned to face them. He was in his late fifties, his head shaved bald, his face obscured by a long beard. Flint cast his eyes downward.

"Rise," the Emperor said.

They rose, the Templars donning their hats. The Emperor went to his desk and sat down. He drummed his fingers for a moment before the corner of his mouth turned up.

"Why is it," he said, "...that your coming to Salem always means trouble?"

14

The Emperor was silent, his fingers steepled, as he listened to Flint, Navarro, and McFarlane explain the goings on of the last few days. When they finished their summary, he stroked his beard, thinking. At last, he said, "One thing troubles me. Or I should say, one thing troubles me more than the others: how is it that Lang could rise to such a position without your Order, or anyone for that matter, detecting her nature?"

Flint pursed his lips. There was no good answer. Moreover, it was the Emperor who had appointed Lang to the presidency of the Cascadia Reserve. Flint sensed that His

Majesty's question was aimed as much at himself as it was at the Templars. May as well go with the truth then.

"I do not know, sir," Flint said. "Hunting magicians is the most difficult aspect of our vocation. They go to Herculean lengths to disguise their true nature. To be noticed by my colleagues and I means their certain doom, whether imprisoned or burned. In many cases, we can only wait for them to make an error."

The Emperor said nothing for a few moments. Just as Flint was feeling uncomfortable, Peter said, "And you're sure about her?"

"Yes sir," Flint said. Navarro and McFarlane nodded.

"No question," Navarro said.

"Her accomplices attacked us as soon as we appeared," McFarlane added.

"Yes," the Emperor said, drumming his fingers. "As soon as you appeared, thanks to your witch friend."

"That is correct sir," Flint replied. "These... gateways, for lack of a better term, seem accessible only to those with an innate talent for the dark arts. Were it not for Miss Fletcher inadvertently discovering the gateway in Oglethorpe, we may never have learned of Miss Lang's true allegiance to the powers below."

"Thanks be to God that she is on our side then," Peter said. "You said that the gateway in Oglethorpe is inside the former home of Brayton Crandall?"

"Yes sir," Flint said.

"I wonder..."

"May I ask what you're wondering, your Majesty?" Navarro asked.

"I knew Crandall," the Emperor said. "He was a friend of my father. Thanks to him, the Empire was able to stockpile considerable petroleum reserves. I know that gasoline is scarce and prohibitively expensive outside of Salem... but even the supply that we have here... Crandall was always cagey about it when asked how he did it. Even when my father and I asked him directly. I was wondering if it is possible..."

"That he was a magician?" McFarlane asked.

The Emperor nodded.

"That would explain a lot," Navarro said. "Silas and Zelda were talking about how that Tremaine guy in Adrian had all kinds of foreign currency stacked in his office. They were thinking that these gateways might go pretty far around the continent. Maybe the whole world too?"

"Perhaps," Flint said. "If that were the case, then I imagine that it would be a simple task for Mr. Crandall to acquire unrefined petroleum from outside of the country and transport it here via his infernal gateways, thus earning a tidy profit and the praises of his fellows."

The Emperor leaned back in his seat. "Interesting... if that was how he did it... if he could move that much petroleum through these gateways... I wonder what else we could..."

"Your Majesty, I must protest," Flint said.

The Emperor blinked. Navarro and McFarlane went several shades paler.

"I beg your pardon, Captain?" Peter asked.

"Sir, with all respect," Flint said, "The Empire cannot – it must not – commandeer these gateways. They are an abomination, offensive to God, and violations of nature. Only magicians can access them. And while my party and I are none the worse for wear, only God knows of the long-term effects overuse of them may have on those of us who do not have the talent for magic. Mark my words sir – if we do not destroy these gates, or failing that, prevent their use, then it is only a matter of time before the entire Empire suffers dire consequences."

The Emperor said nothing for a few moments. Flint thought he saw a trickle of sweat run down Navarro's temple. Finally, Peter chuckled.

"I appreciate your candor, Captain. And you're right, of course. It was mere speculation on my part. You'd be surprised how much of my day is taken up with logistical problems. Now," he said, putting both hands on his desk. "What needs to be done? I will help in any way that I can."

Flint reached into one of his coat pockets and took out a folded note that was given to him by one of the Cascadia Reserve's staff earlier that morning. He handed it to the Emperor. "These are the names of the persons who came out of Lang's office shortly before my party and I arrived. They are all guilty of practicing the dark arts, the murder of at least one person, and doubtless treason to the Empire. If I may make a suggestion, your Majesty, it would be most helpful if the Cascadia Bureau of Investigation assisted in their apprehension. I am confident that General Hickock can provide Templars to accompany them should their quarry choose fight rather than flight."

"Done," Peter nodded.

"That takes care of one gate in Salem," McFarlane said. "There may be others we don't know about yet."

"Might help to seal off the Cascadia Reserve for now. Uh, your Majesty, sir," Navarro said.

"It sounds as though we will require Miss Fletcher's services as a guide," the Emperor said. "I want you four to go. Find out how many other corners of the Empire in which this web of theirs is tangled."

"Yes sir," they said together.

"Before we part ways... Captain Flint. Mr. Navarro."

"Yes sir?" they said a split second apart.

"General Abernathy sent me a most interesting telegram last evening. I understand that you two went into Castle Vasquez."

"That is correct, sir," Flint said.

The Emperor rose from his desk, and went to them. He stood before Flint. The Witch Hunter stared straight ahead; the thousand yard stare, drill sergeants called it. Peter extended his hand. Flint made eye contact with the Emperor and took the proffered hand.

"On behalf of the Empire, I thank you, Captain Flint, for slaying Arturo Vasquez. Again."

"It was my duty, your Majesty," Flint said, shaking his hand.

"Come back alive," Peter said. "When this case is resolved, contact the Palace."

"Yes sir."

"And now... now I must decide what to tell Parliament about the death of the Cascadia Reserve's president. You are dismissed."

Flint, Navarro, and McFarlane genuflected and took their leave. Back in the waiting room, Navarro and McFarlane exhaled as though they'd been holding their breath for hours.

"Jesus Christ," Navarro said.

Flint and McFarlane gave him sharp looks.

"Uh, sorry. But... holy shit, sir."

"I must concur with Mr. Navarro," McFarlane said with a smirk. "I know you said to always be truthful with him, but..."

"I can't believe you chewed out the fucking Emperor himself," Navarro said, laughing.

"I did no such thing," Flint said. "Fraternal correction is an act of charity, Mr. Navarro."

"Aw," Navarro said. "It just now came to me. You think we should have asked him about that Michaela person you and Zelda are looking for?"

"It is water under the bridge, as they say. I suspect that we shall encounter the mysterious Michaela in due time as we dismantle her network of hellish highways. Come. Let us proceed to the nearest telegraph office. It may be prudent for us to contact Forts Plummer and Rochester to let Generals Brandt and Davis know that we may be visiting soon."

***

Flint checked his pocket watch. 2:46 p.m. The hunt for Lang's accomplices had borne fruit. Two CBI agents, accompanied by Fort Ingalls' own Captain Bart Kennedy, had captured Breanna Hudson, a financial analyst with the Cascadia Reserve who defended herself with a sorcerous firestorm, which was absorbed by Kennedy's sword. Now she sat alone at a table in an interrogation room in the Fort Ingalls dungeon, surrounded by blessed, exorcised salt, manacles of blessed silver around her wrists. Flint folded his arms as he looked at her through a two way mirror. With him were Navarro, McFarlane, Fletcher, General Hickock, Captain Kennedy and his assistant Supernumerary Justin Glass, and CBI agents José Soto and Adriana Madera. In the room next to Hudson's, Gladstone sat alone, his face streaked with tears.

Soto, a thin man in a tailored suit, cleared his throat. "My partner and I were the arresting agents for this one," he said, pointing at Hudson with his thumb.

"Yes," Kennedy said. "And she'd have burnt you down to your bones if I hadn't been there."

"Be that as it may," Soto said, "Bank robbery falls under CBI jurisdiction, and we have every right to be present for this interrogation."

Hickock chuckled. "You and Agent Madera are welcome to observe from here, but I'd stay out of there if I was you. Puttin' a magician to the question ain't like sweating out a normal thief."

Madera swallowed. "I'm okay with that. José?"

Soto frowned but nodded.

"Captain Flint," Hickock said. "This here is connected to a case you're investigating. You and Ricardo want to take one?"

"I think we should take Hudson," Navarro said. "Silas, ah... shot Gladstone's wife dead."

"I am amenable," Flint said.

Hickock blinked. "Alright. Bart, you and Justin take Gladstone."

Flint looked to McFarlane and Fletcher. "You are welcome to join Mr. Navarro and I."

McFarlane nodded. Fletcher bit her lip.

"Is there a problem, Miss Fletcher?" Flint asked.

"Well... I've brought in a few witches and stuff... but, ah, I haven't been part of an interrogation yet," she said.

Navarro clapped her on the shoulder. "If you're gonna formally join up, you gotta learn some time. You don't have to do anything if you don't feel comfortable yet. Just watch and learn. This is what us Supernumeraries specialize in." He squared his shoulders and left the observation room to join Hudson in her cell.

Hickock shook his head. "A witch joining up... never thought I'd see it in my lifetime."

"I beg your pardon?" Soto asked, raising an eyebrow. "She's a witch?"

"It is a long story, one I should be happy to recount when we have leisure," Flint said, following Navarro. McFarlane and Fletcher fell into step behind him. Interrogations were one of the few occasions where Flint followed his assistant's lead. The police called it the good cop, bad cop routine.

They marched down the brick hallway, took a left, and opened the first door. All interrogation rooms were exorcised and blessed by the clergy. Demons could not enter them, and the manacles restricted prisoners' use of their hands, necessary for spell casting, but wise men never let their guard down. Hudson looked up as they entered. She was young with shoulder length blonde hair. Her eyes narrowed.

"Four of you, just for me? I feel honored."

Navarro pulled out the chair on his side of the table where she sat. He flipped it around and sat, his arms resting on the back. Flint and McFarlane folded their arms. Fletcher put her hands in her pockets. Navarro said nothing, but there was a serene smile on his face. Minutes passed. Flint was tempted to check his watch but stayed still. Hudson fidgeted. He saw a trickle of sweat run down her temple.

"Aren't you supposed to offer me a deal?" she asked.

Navarro said nothing.

"Or hit me? Or torture me?"

The four remained silent.

"Come on then, get it over with," Hudson snapped.

Navarro stirred at last. "We could do it that way," he said. "That all depends on you."

Hudson laughed. "Why should I tell you anything? You're going to burn me no matter what I say."

"It doesn't have to be that way," Navarro said. "Don't get me wrong; you're in deep shit, and you're going to pay, one way or another. But if you tell us more about what you and your friends were up to..."

Hudson hocked up a wad of phlegm and spat in Navarro's face, the saliva spattering over his nose. A second later, Navarro lunged and punched Hudson in the face. Her manacles kept her tethered to the table, otherwise Flint had no doubt that she would have crashed to the floor. She gave Navarro a murderous look, her mouth moving even as a trickle of blood ran out. A look of confusion came over her.

"That's right," Navarro said, a savage grin on his face. "You can't heal yourself. You witches can dish it out. Can you take it?"

Hudson squared her shoulders, jutted her chin, but Flint saw the look of uncertainty in her eyes. Navarro shrugged.

"Guess we'll find out." He looked to Flint. "Got any extra salt, sir?"

***

Flint checked his pocket watch. Only thirty minutes had passed since the interrogation began, but Hudson was broken. She hunched over the table, bruised, bloodied, panting. Over his ten year career, and five year partnership with Flint, Navarro had perfected the art of wringing confessions from recalcitrant prisoners.

He cracked his knuckles. "Now," Navarro said, "You want to tell us why you and your friends killed that boy?"

Hudson slumped her shoulders, blew out a breath. "Blood and souls..."

"What was that?" Navarro said.

"Blood... souls... it's what they want."

"The powers below."

"Yes," she breathed. "We don't have the strength to use the kind of power we need... for this project..."

"Tell us more about your project."

Hudson swallowed. "I... I don't know all the details..."

"Tell us what you do know then," Fletcher spoke up. Flint had kept an eye on her during the interrogation. She'd shifted, looked uncomfortable at times, but had otherwise remained silent.

"Our mistress... she discovered the gateways."

"'Discovered?' She didn't create them?" McFarlane asked.

Hudson shook her head. "Not all of them. Most of the gateways... they've been there a long time. Since the Occult War, she said."

Flint stroked his chin. "I presume that the gateway in Oglethorpe was of her own design," he said.

"Yes," Hudson replied. "That city... didn't exist back then. We tried to link it to the others but... one of the girls didn't have the stomach for doing what it took. So it's unstable. Unreliable."

"Would this girl happen to be Harper Finley?" Flint asked.

Hudson nodded. "How did you...?"

"It matters not," Flint interrupted. "What is the overarching purpose of your larceny?"

Hudson blinked, hesitated before answering: "You saw our robes. I think you know."

"Mammon," McFarlane growled. "You're paying some kind of twisted tribute to him?"

Hudson smiled. "His brethren crave violence, depravity,

the most unspeakable evil in exchange for power. All he asks his money."

Navarro snorted. "What does a demon need with money? He's using you, dumbass. You're lying, stealing, killing, and for what? You might get power in this world, but you'll pay for it in the next for all eternity."

Hudson spat blood onto the table. "Don't give me that Church bullshit," she said. "We're all going to Hell. But if we serve them here on earth, then when we descend to the fiery pit, we'll do so as princes and princesses, not as fuel for the fire."

"Your mistress," Flint said. "Would her name be Michaela by any chance?"

Hudson's mouth dropped, but she recovered her composure a second later. "That is her birth name, yes."

"So what's she go by these days?" Navarro asked.

Hudson said nothing.

Navarro drew his tomahawk from a loop on his gun belt.

Hudson cringed. "She... was adopted as a baby. Her new parents named her Sara. Sara Morse."

Flint didn't recognize the name, but now they had a new lead. "These gateways. You said that they have existed since the Occult War. How is it that you..."

Hudson laughed. "That's the beauty of it," she said. "The Cascadia Reserve, the vaults of Las Vegas, the Treasury of Columbia... even in the old world, they were banks, treasuries, places where currency was kept. All we had to do was enter, take as much as we could carry, and walk out."

"And killing that boy… that's the price you have to pay to open a new gate?" McFarlane asked.

Hudson smiled. "Considering all that we've gained, I'd say that killing a few homeless bums to open a door to the rest of the world is a bargain."

"How many portals are there? Where do they all go?" Fletcher asked.

"I don't know how many there are, total. But I've been to Olympia, Spokane, Las Vegas, and Columbia City."

Flint scowled. "You have provided us with valuable information, Miss Hudson. In exchange, I shall recommend that you be spared the stake, but for the murder of that boy and all of the other deaths that are surely upon your conscience, you will spend the rest of your earthly life inside a prison cell. I suggest that you repent and pray for the grace of conversion. The powers below care not for past service, but only for what you have done for them lately. If you die unrepentant, I assure you that you will descend into Hell as merely another damned soul."

The four exited the cell. Moments later, Captain Kennedy and Supernumerary Glass joined them.

"How'd you guys do?" Navarro asked.

Glass cracked his knuckles, which, Flint noted, were as bruised and bloody as Navarro's. "Our guy told us quite the story. Sara Morse is running a Mammon cult."

"Do you know of her?" Flint asked.

Kennedy nodded. "Yep." He sighed. "As if the Emperor didn't have enough headaches."

"I take it she's socially prominent?" McFarlane asked.

"You could say that. She's married to the chair of Parliament's Foreign Relations Committee."

They exited the dungeon hallway, making their way to the observation room where they'd left General Hickock and the CBI agents Soto and Madera. Flint could hear the protests before they reached the doorway.

"...unbelievable, we could never..."

"That's the ugly nature of the beast," Hickock said, interrupting Soto. "We ain't playing cops and robbers down here, son. These people are killers in league with the demons of Hell. Far as I'm concerned, my boys went easy on 'em."

"These confessions would never hold up in court," Madera said, just as Flint and his party entered the room.

"Nope, don't suppose they would," Hickock said. "But you really want to put those bastards in a regular court? A regular prison? They'd kill every damn one of you with fire from their eyes and lightning from their asses before you could clear your holsters."

Soto and Madera looked at Flint and his party with skeptical eyes. "Rest assured, the Director and the Emperor will hear about this," Soto said.

"Tell 'em," Hickock said, shrugging. "Give 'em my regards while you're at it. Before you do that though, I think we got some more fish to fry." He looked to Flint and Kennedy. "I'll send out some more guys and gals to round up their buddies. Captain Flint, you and your friends ought to go check out the portal at the Reserve. I expect you'll be getting around most of the Empire before this is done."

"I concur, General," Flint said.

"You want to telegram Forts Rochester and Plummer?" Navarro asked.

"Couldn't hurt," McFarlane said, "But we have no idea where the portals in those cities lead to."

"Olympia and Spokane have considerable gold and silver reserves," Flint said. "It is likely that they have portals as well, if of our suspect's making and not more ancient."

"Only one way to find out," Fletcher said. "Come on, I'll lead the way." She chuckled. "I've always wanted to say that."

"You also said you always wanted to see more of the world," Navarro laughed.

15

Charles Flint sat alone in his office, the lights dimmed, his eyes closed. Arcs of green electricity coursed over his fingers. The office had once belonged to the American General who commanded the bunker. A miniature portrait of the General and his family was on the desk. Their smiles were frozen in eternity though they were centuries dead. On the wall to Flint's right was a portrait of the last President of the United States, Jeffrey Simmons. As Flint recalled, Simmons had been president when the Occult War began in 2068 and stayed on after he should have left office in 2072 because too much of the United States was occupied by Simon Magus's forces to elect a successor. And in the end, it didn't even matter. So much destruction. So much chaos. So much death. The United States of America had once ruled the world, with no other nation on earth matching even a fraction of her power. And now they were dead, their empire in ruins... they knew the peace of death, where there was no pain, no sorrow, no temptation...

He shook his head, opened his eyes. That wasn't like him. His thoughts had been taking morbid turns ever since his agent Destiny Lee had brought him the Warlock's Crown. Vasquez's crown. On the desk was Flint's copy of *In Realis Magicae*, the magnum opus of Abdul Hakim Nazari, one of Simon Magus's handpicked lieutenants. Nazari knew disenchantments for spells that neither Flint nor his inner circle had ever imagined. Flint was certain that he'd nullified all the curses that Vasquez had placed on the Crown in case it fell into his enemies' hands. Yes, he was sure. And yet Turner was right. Ever since he'd donned the Crown, he didn't feel himself. His blue eyes had turned green. His temper was shorter. He'd gotten this far largely through patience and cunning. Now he felt urges, temptations to violence stronger than any he'd felt before.

Perhaps Vasquez had left a piece of himself with the Crown. Maybe the Crown had a will of its own. No matter. He was Charles Flint. His will was stronger. He would control these urges to kill and destroy, focus them on his enemies, the enemies of his new empire.

The walls chimed.

"What is it?" Flint growled. Speaking of things with a will of their own...

"Pardon the interruption, Charles Flint," Rob's monotone voice said from everywhere and nowhere. "You wished to be notified when Doctor Kato was prepared."

Flint grunted. "Yes. Tell the others I'll be there presently."

The walls chimed again and fell silent. Rob... the computer didn't have a soul which meant Flint couldn't sense its presence like he could living people. But he couldn't shake the feeling that somehow, some way, Rob had been present on Doctor Kato's airship. Turner had explained the computer's workings as much as her layperson's knowledge allowed, as much as Flint and his contemporaries could understand. Rob's personality matrix as Turner called it was within a machine called a mainframe deeper inside the bunker. He'd followed her suggestion and steered Kato away from it, though he still didn't fully understand what "hacking" was, or why it would be a bad thing if Kato hacked their computer.

Kato... he was a fascinating man, to be sure. Flint prided himself on his skills in reading others, but he had to admit that the Doctor was a difficult case. Other than his brief show of temper in the *Tengu's* observation room, he was imperturbable, a poker face carved from granite. Kato claimed he had no taste for gambling despite ruling a city with a casino on every block. It was just as well; the house always wins, as they say.

Flint rose from his desk, opened the door with a gesture, and strode toward the command center. His footsteps tapped on the linoleum floor. The walls were panels of steel and glass. He felt tempted to transmute the entire bunker like he had the dining hall, but he'd ended up disabling Rob's access to that room, and he needed the computer, no matter how much he distrusted it. Still, having a private space away from Rob's all-seeing eyes might come in handy someday.

"Sir, we've lost New York..."

"Concentrate on..."

Flint stopped, looking everywhere, his eyes wild.

"Who's there?!" he shouted.

Nothing.

"Rob."

The computer chimed.

"Did you hear voices just now?"

"Negative."

He scanned the hallway. It was empty and he sensed no one. Now that he thought about it, the voices sounded distant, distorted, like a radio with poor reception. Either the computer was playing tricks on him... or he was hearing the spirits of the dead. Vasquez had been one of the most powerful necromancers to ever walk the earth; Flint thought it was possible, likely even, that he was more attuned to the other side now. Every magician knew spells to raise the dead, but the results were little more than mindless beasts that needed a tight leash. Legend had it that Vasquez's undead hordes retained greater intelligence, if not their human personalities. Flint looked forward to experimenting.

He pressed on. Flint entered the observation room. Kato, hands behind his back, looked at the map of North America on the viewscreen. Turner, Schreck, Barnett, and Deville surrounded the Doctor. They all turned to see Flint.

"Doctor," Flint said. "On behalf of Medea, I thank you for your visit. It has been most enlightening."

"I feel the same, your majesty," Kato replied with a dip of his head. "It is a pity that I cannot stay longer, but there are affairs of state in Nagano that require my presence."

"Sir," Schreck said to Flint. "The computer has picked up some interesting transmissions from Cascadia."

"Oh?"

"Rob, replay what you had for us earlier."

The computer chimed. A moment later, it played the breaking news jingle from Cascadia Imperial Radio. Flint smiled. It hadn't changed since he was a boy when his father listened to it religiously. The newscaster began speaking.

"Our top story this afternoon: murder and witchcraft at the Cascadia Reserve. Knights Templar Silas Flint and Diana McFarlane, along with their assistants, have told Imperial officials that Cascadia Reserve President Linda Lang is guilty of the murder of at least one homeless man and was part of a demon worshipping cult here in Salem. His Majesty declined to comment to our reporters but he has called a special session of Parliament to address…"

Flint laughed, shaking his head. "Oh Silas."

"Lang… was she one of ours?" Turner asked.

The others shook their heads.

"I've never met her," Deville said. "But having bankers in our pockets would be useful, don't you think?"

"Absolutely," Barnett replied. "Speaking of which, Charles, I'd like to talk to you later about that. Some of the local bank presidents came to me on my last outing. They had some ideas about establishing a new currency."

"Of course they did," Flint said. "The one thing all

bankers love is stability. They're already thinking ahead to when we settle things with the UMS government. Perhaps we should invite them here to discuss their proposal in person."

"Your majesty," Kato said. "Your brother's exploits in Salem may be connected to an issue my majordomo has brought to my attention."

Flint furrowed his brow. "How is that possible?"

"I do not know, yet. However, the presence of magicians in Cascadia's central bank may explain the theft of currency from the vaults of several Las Vegas casinos."

"Portals?" Turner asked. "I don't see how. We can't use portals unless we've been to a place before."

"Indeed," Kato said. "Either my thieves are well-traveled former employees of mine, or they have discovered a method of circumventing that law. I will be contacting Emperor Peter shortly to discuss the issue. And to inform him that I have extended diplomatic recognition to your new nation."

"Excellent," Flint said, with a smile. Humans were herd animals. With Nagano's recognition, the other nations of the continent would soon follow. He extended his hand. "I don't wish to keep you away from matters of state any longer than necessary Doctor. It's been a pleasure. I thank you again and wish you a safe journey."

Kato extended his hand, and they shook. Again, that feeling of cold metal. Flint wondered if Kato was himself a machine or had prosthetic hands brought to life through sorcery.

"The pleasure was mine, your majesty. This journey has proven most fruitful."

"Before you go, Doctor Kato," Turner said. "I have a gift for you." She reached into her trouser pocket and withdrew a blue sapphire. She handed it to Kato. "We use these to communicate with each other. Like a telephone but with visuals as well."

Kato tucked the jewel into one of his jacket pockets. "I thank you," he said. "I was about to suggest that we establish regular communications through my computer at Area 51 and the one you have here... but this will suffice. With your permission, your majesty, I take my leave of you now and I wish you success in the coming conflict with the United Mountain States." He bowed at the waist and exited the command center. Flint and his circle kept silent, listening to Kato's footsteps grow distant. They heard the hatch to the outside world open and shut again.

"Rob," Turner said. "Did Doctor Kato access your mainframe at any time?"

The computer chimed. "Negative, Lilian Turner."

"Did he access your files at all?"

"Doctor Kato perused all of the files accessible to registered guests."

Flint saw her relax. "Okay," she said.

"You don't trust him?" Deville asked her.

"He's a foreign head of state," Turner said. "He probably knows more about computers than I do. We'd be fools to give him full access."

"He's looking out for his best interests, and those of his

country," Schreck said, shrugging. "Can't blame him for that. I'd distrust anyone who ever claimed otherwise."

"That's funny, coming from you, Colonel," Barnett said with a smirk.

"I did my twenty years," Schreck said. "I served Cascadia well when I was sworn to her service. Now I've sworn to serve my new country."

"And me," Flint said.

"Of course, sir. No man can serve two masters, heh."

"That reminds me," Deville said. "What do you suppose that business in Salem is about?"

Flint frowned. It bothered him that he never knew of Lang's talent for witchcraft. She must have had a genius for disguising her true nature to have remained hidden from him and to have risen so high in the world of finance. Her access to so many funds could have sped up his timetable by years. Oh well. "If it's no more than grand larceny," he said, "I confess that I'll be somewhat disappointed."

"Something Kato said," Turner muttered. "Circumventing the law of portals…"

"Sound familiar?" Barnett asked.

"Maybe… now that I think about it… during the Occult War, some people on our side were conducting experiments with portals. They thought that if they could create a permanent network, it would allow us to move men and materiel instantaneously, give us an advantage against the federals."

"I take it they succeeded," Flint said.

"I think so," Turner said. "We didn't need them as much in the East, since so many of us had already visited government buildings. Our personal portals worked just fine."

"Pretty convenient to have that kind of network though," Schreck said. "We could put a network like that to good use, once we get a regular army going."

"Yes," Flint said. "If I know my brother though, he'll figure out some way to destroy it."

16

Aboard the *Tengu*, Doctor Kato stood before the viewscreen in his personal quarters. His majordomo Harry Tanaka was on the screen.

"You have captured one of our thieves," Kato said.

"Yes sir," Tanaka said. "She's Cascadian. Says her name is Mary Huntsman. Your automatons apprehended her around 0300 hours this morning. According to them, she materialized out of thin air. She claims to have used a portal that is part of a network extending all over the continent."

"I thought as much," Kato replied. "Do you believe she has any more information to contribute?"

"No sir. If she is part of a larger plot, she is clearly a low level operative."

"Then put her in the Engine." He thought a moment. "Make her work in the sewers. I expect that will teach her the price of theft."

"It shall be done, sir," Tanaka said, bowing.

Kato terminated the communication. Now that that business was taken care of, it was time to take a closer look at the data he'd acquired from Flint's computer. The computer at Area 51 was nearly five hundred years old. It functioned, but over time, parts failed. Memory was corrupted. Sorcery could keep it going, but some things that were lost were lost forever. Flint's computer had been frozen in time. It was as fresh as the day it went offline all those years ago. It was as good a window into the twenty-first century as he was likely to ever find. He began to type. He would begin with their knowledge of physics. Kato thought it a pity that the Americans had abandoned their pursuit of nuclear power. If they had kept at it, they could have developed inexhaustible energy, not to mention the practical applications for weapons of...

The *Tengu* shook. Books fell from the shelf next to his bed. Klaxons blared and the overhead light turned red. He pushed a button on his desk.

"Report," Kato said.

"My Lord." It was Commander Campbell, the *Tengu's* executive officer. "Dragons."

"How many?"

"Six."

Kato's face remained placid, but he was astonished. Dragons seldom traveled in pairs, let alone six at a time. "Deploy countermeasures. Fire at will."

The *Tengu* shook again. He heard cannons boom and automatic gunfire.

"It shall be done, my Lord."

Another blow to the ship. The shaking, the alarms, the light... this was becoming intolerable. He had work to do. He pushed the button for the intercom again.

"Commander. Have all human personnel clear the deck."

A pause, and then, "Yes, my Lord."

"I will be up momentarily."

Kato exited his quarters. It was time for the scientist to step back and for the sorcerer to come forward. He willed himself off the floor and levitated toward the stairs, his hands aglow with witchfire. He floated up, up toward the deck of the ship. He passed a few human crew members along the way, all of them scurrying for their quarters. His automatons, responding to his telepathic summons, made their way up.

He opened the hatch with a gesture, and sunlight flooded the corridor. Kato was on the deck. At a glance, he saw three dragons to starboard, three to port. He estimated their wingspans at 30 meters. Their green scales sparkled in the sun. Jets of flame spewed from their mouths, smoke from their nostrils. He used a spell to dampen his hearing. Their roars alone would be deafening, to say nothing of the *Tengu's* cannons. Shells exploded, but the dragons were swift despite their size. They were considered myths in the old world, but during the Occult War the myths became all too real, and a perennial threat to all who would consider taking to the skies.

Two dozen automatons were on the deck. They each had automatic guns in their forearms and missile launchers in their shoulders. Adequate, assuming the beasts got close enough, but risky. This was something Kato would have to do himself.

He planted his feet on the deck, elbows bent, fists

clenched. He willed the power to form. Kato allowed his emotions to flow. The hatred, the rage... the fires rose. He gave a low growl. The robots' backs opened, pods unfolded, each holding six missiles. A dragon made a pass at the deck, and as one, the two dozen robots unleashed their payload. The dragon disappeared in a cloud of smoke and flame, its roars dying in a whimper, its blackened body falling from the sky.

Kato's growl turned into an animalistic howl. His entire body was engulfed in sorcerous flame. His eyes crackled with electricity. The artificial flesh on his hands melted away, revealing the clockwork prosthetics. With a deafening roar of his own, he channeled the power into a beam of light that swung around to his right. It sliced through the dragons like a knife through butter, their bisected bodies plummeting to the ground.

The two on his left chose that moment to spew their fiery breath toward the deck. Kato turned just in time to meet their assault. The beam from his hands collided with their streams and exploded. He was magically tethered to the deck, but his automatons had no such protection. The beam continued and cut down the remaining two beasts. A burning wind blew over the deck. It dissipated. When the smoke cleared, Kato allowed the power to leave his body. He took a deep breath and surveyed the damage.

Of the twenty-four automatons that had been with him, ten were left. Holes were smashed in the guardrails surrounding the deck. He reached out with his mind but couldn't sense them. Either they were completely obliterated or had gone overboard. The former Doctor Hiller was among those lost. A pity. He'd been with the Kato family for centuries. But he'd successfully transferred the files from Flint's computer at least.

Human crew members rushed onto the deck. They would extinguish the fires and repair any damage to the ship's hull. Commander Campbell came to Kato's side.

"My Lord...?" he asked.

"What is it?"

"Are you alright?"

"Of course I am," Kato said. "Dumb animals are no match for..."

"Uh, sir, I was referring to, ah..."

Kato looked down. He'd forgotten about his hands. Years ago, he'd had his arms replaced with magically enhanced clockwork models from the elbow down. Flesh and bone couldn't handle the kind of spells his family had created over the long centuries. He flexed his metal fingers, the joints clicking.

"Have Miss Nakamura meet me in the infirmary," Kato said. The nurse would mix up another batch of artificial flesh to disguise his mechanical bones.

"Of course, sir."

"What is our estimated time of arrival in Las Vegas?"

"Once repairs are complete, eight hours, sir."

"Increase speed. I have business to attend to."

***

Automaton J-038377 tumbled head over heels through the sky. Hiller looked at the ground which was coming up to meet him faster and faster. Would this be the end of his unnaturally long life? He didn't know. If it was, he was prepared. It was funny. Over the centuries, he'd gone back and forth between wanting to die, and wanting to persist to learn more about the new world. He was prepared for either outcome.

Query, came the voice of the computer Rob in his mind. *What were those animals?*

Dragons, Hiller said.

Impossible. Dragons are fictional creatures. They do not exist.

Seeing is believing. If you won't believe your own eyes – or my eyes, rather – then I don't know what to tell you, friend.

Hiller kept falling.

You're taking this rather well, he thought.

I do not know to which you refer.

We're skydiving without a chute. This body might not survive the fall. I might die when we hit the ground. Or my soul will be free.

You will not die. This body will not be destroyed.

You sound awfully certain.

It is a mathematical certainty.

Oh. Great. I guess I should be grateful I can't feel anything anymore.

Down, down, down they fell until the automaton hit the ground with a boom. Hiller saw nothing but dirt. He wanted to laugh. The computer was right. He was still here. But where was here? He rose to his feet and looked up. He was at the bottom of a crater. Pulling himself out, he looked at his surroundings. He was in a grassy plain, with groves of trees and a river further to the west. Looking up, he couldn't make out the *Tengu*. Hiller scanned the landscape. The robot could magnify its view for greater distances than human eyes could see. Approximately fifteen miles north of here was... he couldn't believe it.

Fifteen miles north of his impact crater, his artificial eyes saw what looked like a castle right out of a fairy tale. Towers, stone gargoyles, a surrounding wall, what looked like a firing range... more curious were the figures he could make out. Some of them wore tall black hats, like Puritan pilgrims from the history books. Could they be...?

Query, Rob said. *Do you know who they are?*

I have a pretty good idea, Hiller thought.

I have seen that clothing before, Rob said. *I observed humans in that garb in Salem via sensors.*

Rob my friend, I think we just landed near a Witch Hunter Chapter House.

I would like to know more.

Yeah, Hiller said, chuckling, *I bet they would like to know more about us too.*

***

Witch Hunter General John Abernathy sat at his desk in his office, writing a letter in response to a request for an investigator in the city of Emmett. His instincts told him that his correspondent was being paranoid; something about chemicals in the water affecting the frogs. But one could never be certain in times like these, and he would send a Templar to hear the man out in person.

Finishing the letter, he placed it on top of the stack

of papers in his outbox and pushed a button on his desk. It would cause a light to turn on in the courier department, letting the staff know that his outbox was full. In a few minutes, a Supernumerary would arrive to take the papers. They would be sorted in the mail office, and couriers would deliver the orders, notes, and letters to their destinations. The system had worked that way since the Order's founding centuries ago with a few refinements here and there. When Abernathy had joined up forty years ago, Fort Marsing didn't have electricity. When he was promoted to replace the retiring General Oglethorpe, one of Abernathy's first projects was renovating the castle to have electricity in every room. Some of the older hands had grumbled about losing the time-honored tradition of torches and gas lanterns. Abernathy appreciated tradition as much as the next Churchman, but not to the exclusion of all new things.

There was a knock at his office door. His eyebrows went up. That was quicker than usual.

"Enter," he called.

He was surprised again to see Supernumerary Manuel Mendoza open the doors and step inside. Mendoza was Fort Marsing's resident gunsmith and weapons instructor.

"Gunny?" Abernathy said. "What brings you up here?" Some of the men had bestowed the unofficial rank of Gunnery Sergeant on Mendoza years ago, and the nickname stuck.

"Sir," Mendoza replied. "It... ah... it might be easier if you just come see it for yourself. If you'll follow me?"

Puzzled, Abernathy rose from his desk and followed

Mendoza out of his office, down the hallway, toward the great staircase that would take them down to the ground level and courtyard. As they walked, Abernathy said, "Do I at least get a hint?"

"Well sir," Mendoza replied, "I was running the recruits through some drills out on the firing range when we saw a light show up in the sky."

"A light show?"

"Yes sir. I think it was dragons."

They stepped out into the courtyard and strode toward the main gates. Abernathy could feel beads of sweat forming on his forehead and in his armpits. He was looking forward to autumn.

"Nothing unusual about that," Abernathy said. Dragons were more common in the east, but they made their lairs high up in the mountains and seldom troubled human settlements so long as they were left alone. He prayed that his Templars would never have to deal with one.

"No sir," Mendoza said as they passed through the gates. "That light show I mentioned though? A beam tore through them. Cut the poor beasts in half."

"Oh my. That's... concerning."

"I thought so too."

Mendoza was leading Abernathy out to Marsing's firing range, a series of man made berms with steel plates and cardboard cutouts shaped like witches with pointy hats right out of children's picture books. Trainees were standing in groups, all looking to the south, whispering to each other and pointing.

"General on deck!" Mendoza bellowed. The chatter

stopped and as one the aspiring Supernumeraries and Templars clicked their heels and stood up straight.

"As you were," Abernathy said. He and Mendoza passed the trainees who relaxed a bit. Pointing to the south, the Gunny handed a pair of binoculars to the General. He held them to his eyes. What he saw brought him up short.

On the horizon, making a beeline toward Marsing, was what looked like a mechanical man. A triangular torso with visible gears and wires through a window in its chest atop spindly rods for legs. Its arms were thicker, especially from the elbows down. The head was cylindrical, with two light bulbs where the eyes should be.

"What do you make of it sir?" Mendoza asked.

Lowering the binoculars, Abernathy said, "I've been doing this a long time, Manny. I've never seen anything like that before."

"Eh, I was afraid of that. If he's made from metal, we're going to need the big guns to take him out."

Abernathy pursed his lips. "Has it displayed any signs of hostility yet?"

"No sir, but he's coming right at us."

The General thought for a few moments. "Get the mortars ready, but don't fire until this... thing gives us a good reason to."

"Yes sir." Mendoza turned to face the trainees. "Listen up!" he shouted. "New plan: I want you three to get back to the armory and bring us a mortar. You're about to get a crash course in indirect fire. Move!"

Abernathy brought the binoculars back to his eyes as the trainees sprinted toward the armory. Whatever that thing was, it was in no hurry. It carried no weapons, but he imagined that it would have strength of a dozen men if it had bad intentions. Wait... what on earth? He gripped the binoculars until his knuckles turned white. The mechanical man was waving at him. Could it see him? It raised both of its metal hands above its head and waved its arms. Was it trying to communicate?

"Gunny," Abernathy said.

"Sir?"

"I think... I think our guest wants to talk to us."

Mendoza's brow furrowed. "All the same sir, we should be careful. I'd bet a month's pay that thing's full of witch-craft."

The trainees returned with the mortar tube and shells. With a little browbeating from Mendoza, they deployed the weapon, ready to begin hurling artillery downrange. The mechanical man was getting closer. Abernathy no longer needed the binoculars to see it.

"If he gets any closer sir..." Mendoza said.

"I am aware of that, Gunnery Sergeant."

"Hello!" came a booming voice.

"What on earth?!" Abernathy blurted.

"The fuck is that?" Mendoza asked.

"I mean you no harm," the voice echoed. What it said next was garbled, like two voices speaking on top of each other. Abernathy made out the words Hiller and Rob.

"I'm Doctor Thomas Hiller," the voice said.

"I am Rob," it said a second later.

"That thing can talk?!" Mendoza said.

"Apparently so," Abernathy muttered. "Hold your fire."

It was still far enough away that Abernathy wasn't confident that his shouting could reach it, but he decided to try. "Hello!" he shouted, cupping his hands around his mouth. "Can you hear me?"

"Affirmative," came the voice. It was strange. The machine sounded almost human when it introduced itself as Thomas Hiller, like it was speaking through a telephone. This time it sounded more monotone, like he'd expect a machine to sound.

"What is it that you want?" Abernathy yelled.

"I wish to know more about the twenty-sixth century," came the mechanical Rob voice.

"I want to be around real human beings again!" the Hiller voice said.

Abernathy looked at Mendoza, who shrugged. "Decisions like these are why you get paid more sir."

A few seconds passed. The General looked to the trainees, who held their pistols and rifles at the low ready. He gestured for them to rest easy.

"Well," he said. "Let us see what Doctor Hiller slash Rob have to say for themselves."

They stood waiting for fifteen minutes as the mechanical man made his way to the berms. Up close, Abernathy was impressed. The machine towered over everyone, six and a half feet tall at least. Its body whirred and clanked. When it came within conversation distance, it fell to its knees in the dirt.

"I..." it said.

Abernathy kept his distance, but something inside him wanted him to rush forward and comfort the machine.

"I can't feel him in my mind anymore. I'm free of him. I'm free..."

If he didn't know better, Abernathy would have sworn the thing was crying.

It buzzed, and the machine voice spoke. "I am Rob."

"Er... I'm John Abernathy, General of the Knights Templar of the Order of Saint Benedict."

"Query. The Order of Saint Benedict is a monastic Order. The only Knights Templar on file are the Poor Fellow-Soldiers of Christ and of the Temple of Solomon, founded 1119, disbanded in 1312. What is the nature of the Knights Templar of the Order of Saint Benedict? When was it founded? Where is it..."

The mechanical man shook its head.

"Sorry," came the Hiller voice. "I've got a very curious passenger."

Abernathy and Mendoza looked at each other, then at the machine.

"I, ah... I would be happy to discuss history with you," Abernathy said. "One of my men, Silas Flint, is currently out in the field, but when he returns, he's the one you'll want to talk to. History is his forte."

17

Word spread throughout Cascadia of Sara Morse's treachery. Over the next week, Silas Flint, Ricardo Navarro, Zelda Fletcher, and Diana McFarlane systematically worked their way through the portal network. They emerged in Redmond, Medford, Olympia, Spokane,

Astoria, and Centralia. The first two trips ended with their interrupting meetings of Morse's confederates as they had in Salem. Some chose to fight to the death, while most surrendered into Templar custody. Each subsequent trip through the network brought them to chambers that were empty save for old bloodstains and a few coins the perpetrators dropped in their haste. Nonetheless, the Templars, in cooperation with local police and the Cascadia Bureau of Investigation, locked down every building that contained a portal and began manhunts for the remaining cult members.

Interrogations of prisoners revealed more pieces of the puzzle, but Flint was still unable to assemble them into a coherent whole. The Mammon cultists spoke of Morse's great project but the ones they captured seemed in it only for the money. As for that, Flint's suspicion that they were manipulating the currency exchange market had proven correct. Their power to travel instantaneously around the continent allowed them to buy and sell ahead of the news at considerable profit.

His trips to Olympia and Spokane had brought him into contact with the Witch Hunter Generals Seth Brandt and Malachi Davis again. Presently, Flint and his party were meeting with the two Generals in Centralia at a Cascadia Reserve office where they had secured another portal. Brandt was a thin man with a face like old leather, while Davis was a large black man with a shaved head and iron grey goatee.

Brandt took a deep drag on one of his ever-present

cigars, blowing out a series of rings. "Still no sign of Morse," he said.

Davis's eyes watered at all the cigar smoke as he said, "She's running out of options."

"How do you figure that sir?" Navarro asked.

"Yeah, I mean, she could hide out in any small town or forest or cave..." Fletcher said.

Brandt smiled. "You don't know her like we do."

Davis chuckled. "Sometimes I don't know if it's a blessing or a curse, but one of the job requirements at our level is rubbing elbows with Cascadia's rich and famous. Morse is used to a certain lifestyle. And she worships Mammon."

"She's no survivalist," Brandt said. "She'll be in one of the cities, in the lap of luxury even with the walls closing in."

"That's still a lot of ground to cover," McFarlane said. "We need a way to narrow it down."

The group was silent as they thought. An idea came to Flint.

"Sirs," he said. "Might I trouble one of you for a map of the Empire?"

Davis reached into his long coat, the gold epaulettes on his shoulders being the only sign of his rank, and pulled out a folded sheet of paper. He opened it and put it on the desk. Flint took a pen from a jar. The office and desk belonged to Alphonsus Strangway, the director of the Centralia branch of the Cascadia Reserve. Flint began circling the major cities where they'd discovered portals. He took out the map he'd discovered in the Crandall mansion and compared the two.

"Bend," he said. "According to their map, there ought to be a portal that opens to Bend."

"Shit," Navarro said. His immediate family lived in Bend and Flint could see the worry on his assistant's face.

"How do we know she's even in Cascadia still?" Fletcher asked.

Brandt and Davis looked at each other. The former took another drag on his cigar.

"All of her money is here," he said.

"Right," Davis nodded. "Her money, her social circle, her whole life is here. It's possible that she's left the country, but knowing her, she wouldn't do that if there was any alternative."

McFarlane pointed at the map. "Maybe she does have one alternative." The others looked at her. "Kellogg," she said, tapping her finger on the city. It lay to the far northeast of Cascadia, along the border with...

"The United Mountain States," Brandt said.

"Medea," Davis growled.

Flint stroked his chin. He had never met Morse, so he had to trust the Generals' opinions. On the other hand, Morse was the most wanted woman in the Empire so it would make sense for her to flee the country. His brother Charles' blasphemous vanity project, his so-called nation of magicians, would be the most convenient place for a Cascadian witch to flee...

He sighed. He didn't like it, but there was only one solution.

"I propose that we divide our forces," he said.

"Some of us go to Bend, the others to Kellogg," Brandt said, blowing out more cigar smoke.

"Does she own any property in Bend? Any friends or acquaintances who would take her in?" McFarlane asked.

"None that we're aware of," Davis said. "The way things are going, it's like the whole damn Cascadia Reserve system is infested with heretics."

"'The love of money is the root of all evil,'" Flint quoted. "Let us contact the Bend Police and the CBI field office in Bend and request that they canvass the city's most prominent citizens until Templar reinforcements can arrive."

"I'll get on the telegraph, ask Hickock and Abernathy to get some of their people out there," Brandt said.

"And I'll dispatch some teams to head out to Kellogg," Davis said.

"Guess that leaves us," Fletcher said.

"What do you think Silas?" McFarlane said. "Stick together, or should we split up as well?"

Flint looked to Navarro who blew out a breath.

"I'll follow you wherever you decide to go, boss."

He thought for a few seconds.

"I believe that we should make for Bend. It offers more comfortable accommodations than Kellogg. Mrs. Morse may attempt to abduct more transients to offer to her demonic masters in order to expand her network."

"Back to the fog," Fletcher muttered.

***

Flint and the others were on the black pathway,

Fletcher in the lead, the endless grey fog swirling about them. This time Flint felt a breeze caress his face, and the tails of his long coat flapped behind him.

"Lot more active this time," McFarlane muttered. "I don't like it."

"No doubt Mrs. Morse is aware that we are traversing her private network," Flint said.

Navarro was silent.

"You okay Rico?" Fletcher asked.

"Yeah... just thinking about mom, dad, grandpa, my sisters..."

"Do not fear Mr. Navarro," Flint replied. "We must trust in the Holy Spirit to guide us and to protect our loved ones."

"Yeah... easy for you to say sir. Not everybody's got your kind of faith."

Flint said nothing as they proceeded along the path. He sympathized with Navarro, more than his assistant realized. He knew all too well the sense of despair that came with failing to protect one's family. His heart told him that Navarro's family would be safe. Flint himself and the others... he wasn't so sure this time.

"The problem is," Fletcher said, breaking the silence, "I don't know how to get to Bend from here. Guess we just have to check each portal as we come to it."

"Indeed," Flint said. "Mrs. Morse's confederates appear to have decided that discretion was the better part of valor for our last few stops. We should nonetheless be cautious. They may lash out like cornered mongrels as we winnow down their hiding places."

"We're coming up on one," Fletcher said.

Flint drew one of his pistols and took Fletcher's hand, forming a chain with McFarlane and Navarro.

"Here we go."

All went white. When Flint regained his vision, he saw at once that they were inside a great vault. The floor was marble. Scarlet tapestries hung on the walls, one depicting a great white dome engulfed in flames, another with an eagle arising from the ashes, above a woman holding a sword above her head. Of more concern were the men inside the vault, aiming black rifles at Flint and his friends. They were dressed all in black with what looked like black steel body armor, their faces obscured by black visors.

"You just don't know when to quit, do you?" one of the men said. At least, Flint thought that was what he said. The man's accent made the words almost unintelligible.

Flint lowered his pistol and raised his free hand. "I assure you sir that we mean you no harm and we have no intention of robbing you."

The man cocked his head. "Huh?"

"I take it by our surroundings that we have entered a vault where you kept extensive currency reserves. Our country too has fallen victim to their insatiable..."

"Y'all have any idea what the pilgrim's saying?" the man asked.

"Hey," Navarro spoke up. "The same motherfuckers that's been stealing your shit? They're stealing from us too."

The man sighed. "Finally, we're getting somewhere."

Fletcher and McFarlane cleared their throats, stifling laughs.

"Where y'all come from?" the man asked. His squad lowered their weapons but kept them ready.

"Cascadia," Fletcher said. "Where the hell are we?"

"This is The Most Serene Empire of Columbia, the domain of Empress Agatha, long may she reign."

Flint gathered his thoughts, focused, and spoke. "The perps are witches."

"Yeah, we gathered that," the man said. "How'd you get in here then? And why the hell are you and your lady friend dressed like pilgrims?"

"We're Witch Hunters," Flint said. From the corner of his eye, he saw Fletcher's mouth fall open. "We can't use portals, but our friend here is a witch. She's working with us on this case."

The man was quiet for a moment. "Y'all should clear out. Her Majesty's planning on leveling the place once we get everything out."

Flint nodded. "Understood."

"Good luck brother."

"Miss Fletcher, if you would lead the way."

"Uh... yeah. Come on."

They linked hands, backtracked. Another flash of white, and they were on the path again.

"Silas," Fletcher said. "How come...?"

"We will discuss it later. Onward."

As Fletcher went forward, McFarlane came to Flint's side.

"Let me guess: you never dropped the High Speech once when you were alone together?"

"No."

"It would mean a lot to her."

"I am sure that I do not know what you are talking about."

"Oh come on sir," Navarro spoke up.

Flint was silent and followed Fletcher. After another few minutes, she stopped.

"Here's another one."

They linked up and stepped inside. A flash of white. Before he could regain his vision, Flint heard blaring alarms.

"Intruder alert, intruder alert," said a monotone voice.

His vision cleared, and they were in a room with white walls, white floors, white desks, and white shelves. Along with the klaxons, he heard the jingling of coins, the rifling of papers. Strangest of all though were the room's inhabitants. They were shaped like men but made of metal. They all held their arms out before them, panels on their forearms opened to reveal gun barrels.

"Get us out of here!" McFarlane shouted.

They linked hands and vanished, back on the path again.

"Let's not try that one again," Navarro muttered.

Onward they went in silence. Flint checked his pocket watch. 2:25 p.m. Assuming Columbia was in fact built atop the ruins of Washington, D.C., they'd traveled nearly three thousand miles in a matter of minutes. He felt new sympathy toward Emperor Peter, but magic always came with a price in human lives.

"Next stop, coming up," Fletcher said.

They repeated the familiar pattern. A flash of white.

They reappeared in what looked like another underground tunnel, with brick walls and floors, and an arched ceiling. To their left and to their right, a dozen men and women aimed pistols and rifles at Flint and his party. At the forefront was a woman with sandy hair streaked with grey. She and her compatriots all wore identical robes that bore the sigil of Mammon. She scowled at Flint.

"You," she said, "...have been a pain in my side long enough, Silas Flint. All of you drop your weapons. Slowly. Your swords may absorb magic, but they don't make you bulletproof."

Flint and the others slowly unbuckled their gun belts, allowed them to drop to the floor. His hands up, he said, "Mrs. Morse, I presume."

She smiled. "That's you lambs call me. I prefer my true name, the name my birth parents gave me: Michaela Rose."

"Be that as it may, you cannot hope to win, Mrs. Morse. Your network of unnatural pathways is cut off. Even as we speak, the nations of this continent are united against you. It is only a matter of time before you and your heretical acolytes are brought to God's justice!"

"That's where you're wrong," Michaela said with a laugh, her minions joining in a second later. "Now that the four of you are here, we'll be able to open a new gateway to a place where no one, not even God, can reach us." She nodded to her right. "Move."

Two of the acolytes gathered up the Templar's weapons as they were marched at gunpoint through the tunnels.

"Is this the part where you outline your evil plan?" Navarro asked.

"Good, evil," Morse scoffed. "I prefer to think of it as strong versus weak. There are those who are strong enough to take what they want and those who are not. Everything else is just semantics."

"God won't see it that way when you face His terrible judgment," McFarlane spat.

"Then I'll have to make sure I never appear before Him then, won't I?" Morse laughed.

"How do you figure that?" Fletcher asked. "I remember somebody once said something about how death and taxes are the only two things nobody escapes."

"You'll find out."

Morse stopped before a barred doorway. With a gesture, the door creaked open.

"In you go."

Prodded by the barrel of a rifle, Flint led the way into the cell. Navarro brought up the rear, and as soon as he was inside, the cell door swung shut behind them with a click.

"You know," Navarro said. "It'd be a lot safer for you guys if you just killed us right now."

Fletcher elbowed him in the side with a hiss.

Ignoring her, he went on, "I mean otherwise we're going to get out."

Morse chuckled. "I don't think so. Your pet witch can feel free to open it, if she can."

"So why spare us?" McFarlane asked.

"You need us alive," Flint said, following their lead.

"For now." Morse straightened her robe, pulled a hood over her head. "You two," she said, pointing at some of the acolytes. "Keep an eye on them. I need them alive…" She gave them a wicked grin. "…but not necessarily in one piece."

With that, Morse led the rest of them in a procession past the door of the cell. Flint followed them with his eyes. The tunnel ended in a staircase that went up. They filed up the path and were gone. Turning his focus to Fletcher, he saw her eyes closed in concentration, her hand held out. After a few moments, she shook her head.

"Whatever kind of spells she has on that door, I can't break them," she said.

Flint looked to the two acolytes. Their faces were hidden by their hoods, but they were the same ones who had picked up his party's weapons. They set them down on a table far out of reach from the door and sat down across from each other. Then the one whose back was to Flint reached out and put his… no, her hand on her companion's.

"It'll be alright," he heard her whisper.

Flint pressed his face against the bars of the cell, trying to get a better view. There. It was obscured by the robes, but he saw beads around the other acolyte's neck.

"Mr. Spaulding," Flint called.

The hooded figure looked up.

"Your father is very worried about you."

18

Peter II, Emperor of Cascadia, sat in his private office going over paperwork. Construction of the new Templar Chapter House outside of Bend was proceeding ahead of schedule thanks to some prodding from Salem. The Army's push to recruit more soldiers was not going as well. Despite – perhaps because of – Charles Flint's declaration of independence from the United Mountain States, young men and women were no more eager to take up imperial service than they had been before. Cascadia was still the crown jewel of the West. The economy was doing well, even after the Night of Chaos two months ago, though that might change once the extent of Sara Morse's abuse of the financial system became known.

He smiled to himself. He often felt like he ruled over two different nations instead of one. Salem alone was more than enough for one man's ambitions. The industrialized West commanded more of his attention than the pastoral East. Ironic, given that his ancestor Michael Flagg, the founder and first Emperor of Cascadia, was born and raised in the eastern Oregon country. Maybe he should purchase an estate out there some time. He missed the outdoors, and it would give his grandchildren the opportunity to work the land, learn how the poorer, eastern half of the Empire lived.

A high pitched buzz assaulted his ears. He felt a tickle

on top of his bald head. He brushed at it, and a dragonfly buzzed away from him, circling the room.

"What on earth..." he muttered. How could a dragonfly have made its way into the center of the Imperial Palace? The insect lighted upon his desk. No... it wasn't an insect. A closer look revealed that it was made of metal. His eyes widened as its back opened. A tiny lens was inside. It projected a beam of light toward the ceiling.

He closed his eyes and sighed. Opening them again, he saw the light coalesce into a holographic projection of an Asian man with coiffed hair and a trimmed beard, wearing a white laboratory coat.

"Doctor Kato," Peter said. "A telegram would have sufficed."

"I thought that the tidings I bring would be best delivered in person, so to speak," the scientist replied, his face cold as ever.

"Very well," Peter replied. "I'm listening."

"I have come to inform you that I, as the Supreme Autocrat of the Dominion of Nagano, am extending full diplomatic recognition to the Empire of Medea. I will be contacting other heads of state throughout the West to inform them of my decision."

Peter felt his stomach drop, but he kept his face neutral. "Isn't that premature? Even as we speak, I'm told that the deployment of the UMS Army is imminent."

"I think not," Kato replied. "We both know how it will end. Charles Flint's victory is a foregone conclusion."

Peter didn't want to admit it, but Kato was right, damn him. "It's Fitzroy's duty to fight."

"Perhaps, but I take it as given that he will fail."

The Emperor frowned. Once word got out that Nagano was recognizing Medea, the dominos would start falling.

"Whether we like it or not, your majesty, Charles Flint will succeed in securing the existence of his nation. We would do well to accept this reality," Kato said.

"And I suppose you've already typed up the trade agreements," Peter said.

Kato gave him an icy smile. "Medea is the first nation in my lifetime worth trading with."

Peter scowled. "If that will be all, Doctor, I have work to do."

"I am sure. Good day to you, your majesty."

The projection vanished. The metal dragonfly crumbled to dust.

The Emperor leaned back in his chair. He'd made his opinion known to Parliament. As he'd predicted months ago, they'd adopted a "wait and see" position, but he knew they were leaning toward recognition. They didn't have much of a choice. Kato was right. Like it or not – and the Emperor didn't like it at all – Medea's triumph in the coming conflict was assured so long as Charles Flint controlled old world nuclear missiles. Peter's father, Michael IV, had reigned during the war against Vasquez forty years ago. He remembered his father often saying that his prayer for Peter was that he should never know the horrors of war as he did. Maybe there wouldn't be a war with Medea in his lifetime, but he was certain that war would come someday.

***

President Hugh Fitzroy could feel his heart hammering inside his chest. He hoped he wasn't sweating too badly. He was about to give the biggest speech of his career, of his life. He straightened his tie for the fiftieth time that day.

"You look fine sir," Hastings said. Nonetheless, he handed Fitzroy a handkerchief which he used to dab at his forehead.

"Wilbur...I..." He took deep breaths. "Am I about to send them to die for nothing?"

"No sir," Hastings said, shaking his head. "You were right. This is your duty. You have an obligation before God and before the country to fight. We can't let Flint do this."

"Yes... you're right... I... oh God... give me strength." He suppressed a shudder. He had to be strong. The country was watching him. The continent, the entire world was watching him.

Hastings checked his wristwatch. "Sir... it's time."

Fitzroy took one last deep breath, squared his shoulders. He nodded to Hastings.

Together they walked toward the flap of the oversized tent where they'd been staying and making final preparations. They exited and Fitzroy heard the whistles of locomotives, the growl of their few gasoline powered vehicles, the chime of the belltower just behind the wall that surrounded the city of Denver. The afternoon sun shone bright. Hastings led the president to the foot of the wooden staircase that would take him up onto the stage.

He stopped. Hastings nodded to him, and Fitzroy nodded back. He began his climb up the stairs, to what he felt was the beginning of the end of his career, maybe his life.

As a backdrop, an oversized UMS flag was stretched across the length of the stage: Blue with red and white triangles at the base symbolizing the Rocky Mountains that made up so much of his country. He looked out and saw the Army that had been assembled over the past two months, stretching as far as his eyes could see. Months? It felt like years. Standing at parade rest on the stage were several generals, including Army Chief of Staff General Chester Daniels. He was too good a soldier to publicly display disagreement with his Commander in Chief, but Fitzroy knew that Daniels was upset about being ordered to move the Army ahead of schedule. It was a calculated risk to be sure, but it was always better to err on the side of boldness than timidity.

Fitzroy marched to the center of the stage where a lectern and microphone awaited him. As he got closer, the anxiety, the doubt, the stress, it seemed to melt away. The die was cast. The decision made. Much of what was about to happen was out of his hands. He had to trust in himself and trust in God, as the Churchmen liked to say. He had no personal issues with the Catholic Church, but its presence in the United Mountain States was thin. Maybe he should have invited them to establish a Witch Hunter Chapter House here after all. Too late now.

He stood before the lectern, gazing out at the sea of faces in blue uniforms, lever action rifles slung on their shoulders, ammo pouches on their belts. He felt as though his heart would break. How many would die? Would any survive? Was Flint right about him sending them all to die for nothing? He took a shuddering breath before stepping into the range of the microphone.

"Good afternoon," he said. His voice echoed all over the field, his technicians having set up sound amplifiers at regular intervals so the entire Army would be able to hear him. When he was a boy, he recalled learning about another war that had engulfed the entire planet, before the Occult War. The United Mountain States, of all the powers in North America, modeled itself the most after the old pre-war United States of America. A great general of that country and that ancient war had typed an order to his soldiers that Fitzroy always admired. He'd drawn heavily from it in preparing his remarks. He doubted anyone in his audience would recognize the words, but even if they did, he hoped they would draw inspiration from them as he did.

"You are about to embark upon the great crusade toward which we have striven these many weeks," Fitzroy said. "The eyes of the world are upon you. The hopes and prayers of liberty loving people everywhere march with you. With the help of Almighty God, we will bring about the destruction of the madman who would tear our great country asunder, the elimination of magical tyranny over our oppressed countrymen, and security for ourselves in a free world.

"Your task will not be an easy one. Our enemy wields the power of sorcery, the great curse brought by Simon

Magus, and the most terrible weapons that old world science ever produced. He will fight savagely.

"But we are free men and women, created in the image of God! Through your strength, and the sacrifices of your loved ones, we have speedily assembled the greatest fighting force this continent has ever seen, with still more trained fighting men and women in reserve! The enemy may raise the dead, but they are mindless beasts, no match for the brave souls I see before me! He may threaten with his bombs, but we will never submit, never surrender!

"We have more soldiers, more weapons, more munitions, and most importantly, greater spirit than Charles Flint has ever seen. The world will remember what you do until the end of time! Together, the free men and women of the world march toward victory!

"I have complete confidence in your courage, devotion to duty, and skill in battle. We will accept nothing less than absolute victory. Let us beseech the blessing of Almighty God upon this great and noble undertaking. Good luck and Godspeed."

He stepped away from the lectern, and General Daniels stepped forward. Speaking into the microphone, he said, "Soldiers! Attention!"

As one, the assembled divisions brought their heels together, shoulders back, eyes straight.

"Present arms!"

They unslung their rifles, held them vertically, the undersides facing Fitzroy. He'd never served in the Army, but he came to attention and held a salute in return. A few seconds passed before Daniels spoke into the microphone again.

"Order arms!"

They slung their rifles, and Fitzroy relaxed.

"Report to your stations," Daniels went on. "The first train leaves at 0400. You are dismissed."

As the soldiers began to disperse, Fitzroy stepped away from the lectern, Daniels close behind him.

"Sir," the General said, "I wish to say again for the record that I do not recommend..."

"Your objection is noted for the record, General."

"Hugh," Daniels said, grabbing the president's arm. "We have no defense against that man's super bombs. If he deploys one against the Army, I can't guarantee the safety of Denver. I..."

Fitzroy pulled away from the General's grip, faced him. "Chester, you can't guarantee the safety of Denver with or without the Army. Flint could destroy us any time he chooses if he's got more super bombs. The fact that he hasn't tells me that he's worried about how that would look. And if he's worried about it would play in the press..."

The General nodded. "You think he's bluffing?"

"He's detonated one super bomb. Who's to say he has more?"

"Who's to say that he doesn't?"

"It's a risk I'm willing to take. It's a risk I must take. Could you live with yourself if we just let him win without a fight?"

Daniels sighed. "No sir."

"You have your orders, General."

Daniels saluted. "Yes sir."

Fitzroy descended the staircase where Hastings waited for him. Together, they began walking toward the gates of Denver, presidential bodyguards keeping a respectful distance.

"You did great up there," Hastings said.

Fitzroy snorted. "With my luck, some reporter out there will rake me over the coals for plagiarism."

"Maybe not sir. Recent polling says there's been a six percent increase in support for taking the war to Flint."

"So we're, what, above water now?"

Hastings paused. "Yes sir. Fifty-five percent of the respondents are behind you."

Fitzroy sighed. "Well, we're a democracy. I'll take fifty percent plus one."

"It'll be alright sir. No matter what happens, we're with you until the end."

"I hope so, Wilbur. I hope so."

19

"How do you...?" Spaulding asked.

"Frank, don't," the girl said, presumably Harper Finley.

"Mr. Spaulding, your father Ryan was most distressed by your sudden disappearance two months ago," Flint said. "He secured my services in locating you."

"I meant what I wrote," Spaulding replied. "I love Harper and she loves me. We're going to be married, start a new life together. That's that."

"I understand, Mr. Spaulding," Flint said. "Your father indicated that if that is what you truly desire, he will support you. He only wishes that you had not left so suddenly."

"We didn't have much choice," Finley replied. She pulled back her hood. Her face was young, but her eyes spoke of horrors that no child should ever endure. "I'm a magician. A witch. If his parents found out the truth, they'd call you people to come arrest me, torture me, murder me."

"Not necessarily," Fletcher spoke up.

Finley laughed. "That's what you people do."

"I'm a witch too."

Finley opened her mouth to speak, paused, closed it again. "Liar," she said at last.

Fletcher held out her hand, palm up, and a ball of fire flickered into existence. Finley and Spaulding stared in shock.

"You work for them?" Spaulding asked.

"Why?!" Finley said.

"Me and Silas were at the Crandall mansion, looking for any clues to where you two had gone. That's how we found the portals and got all of this started. You only ever used animal blood in your experiments, am I right?"

"Yes," Finley said. "Michaela said that human souls, human blood is what gives us the power we need... but... I couldn't..."

Spaulding squeezed her hand.

"What is it that you know of Mrs. Morse's grand project?" Flint asked.

"She... she said something about buying her way to eternal life. It has to do with Mammon, and..."

"You okay with that?" Navarro asked her. He looked to Spaulding. "Are you?"

"I... I don't like it but... she said that you have to be strong to take what you want. Harper and I want each other. Once this is done, Michaela won't have to kill anyone ever again," Spaulding said. "She..."

"That's how it starts," McFarlane said, joining Flint at the door. "The powers below tempt you by promising great rewards in exchange for small favors. But they never stay small. They're weakening your conscience. Once you've gotten used to committing small evils, you're less likely to resist temptations to greater evils."

The two teens said nothing.

"We read Mrs. Morse's note to you, Miss Finley," Flint said. "She said that if you wish to attain the heights, you must reject the Church once and for all. Is that not so?"

Finley nodded.

"And you Mr. Spaulding: I see that you still wear the rosary about your neck."

"Yeah," he replied. "It... was a present from mom and dad. For my first Communion."

"Are you prepared to reject family, Church, and God? It is not too late to turn back from this path," Flint said.

"It's not too late for you either, Harper," Fletcher said. "I've done much worse things in my life than you have. I saw where it led: murder, madness, and death. But I turned away from it, and these people took me in. They've given me a new life, where I can do some good to make up for all the bad that I've done."

"I..." Finley said. "No... no, you're trying to trick me. You'll kill me..."

"Hey," Navarro said. "I can tell that you're both basically good kids. Michaela or Sara or whatever her name is, she's leading you down a dark road. Do you want to be dealing with demons? Killing people? You want to get married. You can't build something good if the foundation is rotten, you know?"

"What are you saying?" Spaulding asked.

"Harper," McFarlane said. "The Witch Hunters were founded because magicians used their power to kill, destroy, dominate. Is that what you want to do?"

After a few seconds she said, "No."

"If you stay with Morse, if you continue down this path, you will. It's the nature of magic. It eats away at your soul, turns you into someone you're not." She focused on Spaulding. "The girl you fell in love with: she'll be gone."

"That's not true!" Finley shouted. "I won't change! I won't! Frank, I won't lose my feelings for you!"

"Your feelings for Mr. Spaulding may not change, but you will change nonetheless," Flint said. "You will come to regard ordinary people as lesser beings, as fodder for experiments, as fuel for your power. All of us have seen it countless times over our careers. You have seen it in Mrs. Morse, have you not?"

Finley said nothing.

"Repent, Miss Finley," Flint said. "You are young and in love. Both of you have your whole lifetimes ahead of you. Do not throw all of it away for the empty promises of the powers below and the human monsters who serve them in this world. And you, Mr. Spaulding," he said, focusing on the boy. "Your father loves you and misses you. Do not leave him worrying about you for the rest of his life. I speak from personal experience when I say that one never knows when their parents will leave this world. Do not leave the most important things unsaid."

The teens were silent. They looked at each other, squeezed each other's hands. Flint could see that his companions were nervous. He offered a mental prayer to the Holy Spirit to grant the young people the grace of conversion. If they held fast to their current course, he would find another way to escape. He'd done all that he could for now; the rest was in God's hands.

Finley bit her lip. She closed her eyes. Flint kept his face neutral. The girl raised a hand. The door clicked. Flint pushed it and it swung open.

The two teens backed away from the table, holding each other, as Flint and the others approached the table to retrieve their weapons. Flint buckled his gun belt, the familiar weight of his sword and pistols comforting him. He always felt naked without it. Navarro and Fletcher went to Finley and Spaulding.

"Thank you," Navarro said, clapping Spaulding on the shoulder.

"It'll be alright," Fletcher said, hugging Finley.

The two teenagers shrank from Flint and McFarlane, perhaps not aware of it.

"So what happens now?" Finley said.

"We will put an end to Mrs. Morse's fiendish plot, one way or another."

"I think she meant what happens to us," Spaulding said.

"You two should get out of here," McFarlane said. "If you keep your noses clean and live like human beings as God intended, then you have our blessing, and we will keep your secrets."

"If you embrace the darkness and use your powers to serve evil again," Flint said, "Then we shall come for you, and we shall stop you."

"Okay," Finley said.

"Go now."

The two teens ran down the hallway, toward the portal, and were gone in an instant.

The four watched them go. Fletcher came to Flint's side.

"Hey," she said. "That was... that was beautiful. What you said."

Flint grunted. "I was impressed by your words as well, Miss Fletcher."

"And about, you know, don't leave important things unsaid..."

"Jesus Christ, would you two just get a room already?" Navarro said, checking his rifle.

Flint sputtered and Fletcher's face turned bright red. McFarlane burst out laughing, got ahold of herself, and gave Navarro a sharp look.

"We've still got a job to do," she said, drawing her sword.

"Indeed," Flint replied. He drew his sword and one of his pistols. The blade shone bright in the darkness. "I grow weary of chasing Mrs. Morse across the continent. She has a debt to pay, and it is time for us to collect."

***

Michaela Rose knelt within a chalk circle which enclosed a pentagram. An infinity symbol looped around the spokes of the star. Before her was a solid gold idol in the shape of a horned, humanoid figure sitting atop a pile of coins. Engraved at the base of the idol was another sigil which looked like a capital letter B: the sigil of Mammon. Behind her, her acolytes – recruited largely from banks and stock brokerages – knelt in adoration. The room was packed with gold and silver coins, bullion, and certificates redeemable for more solid coin. Everything shimmered and sparkled by the light of torches. They were inside the home of Ignacio and Esperanza Domínguez, husband and wife bankers here in Bend. The loss of her portals stung her pride, but the Witch Hunters were too late. All was ready. The blood and souls of the two Templars and their assistants in the basement would seal the deal.

Master, she thought, *I offer to you the riches of this land and of lands far from here, the blood and souls of those who would serve the Enemy and the Weakling. I beseech thee to grant that which thou hast promised your devoted followers. Grant unto us eternal life, and wealth beyond the dreams of mortals.*

As she awaited a response, she reflected on her progress. Her parents had given her up for adoption as an infant; all she knew of them was names on her birth certificate and the name that they gave her. She was taken in by the Perkins family who named her Sara. Jesse and Ruth Perkins were a working class couple that struggled to make ends meet and couldn't conceive a child of their own. They gave Michaela everything they could, but it was never enough. She always wanted more and worked hard to acquire it. She won a full ride scholarship to the University of Redmond, met her future husband Anthony Morse, and most importantly of all, discovered her talent for sorcery.

She'd majored in history, specializing in the twenty-first century Occult War. It was through that research that she'd learned of a network of portals created by Western magicians. They'd used it to acquire the funding to field their militias, their armies, their weapons, and experiments. Through methods that still weren't clear to her, they'd made it so that they couldn't use their powers within the void between worlds; no doubt worried about double crossers. After the world burned, the civilizations that rose from the ashes used the same old buildings that survived the conflagration for the same purpose they'd served in the old world: banks, vaults, and treasuries. She'd discovered the first portal in Adrian quite by acci-dent, entering an office and disappearing, finding herself on that black pathway, and after a short walk reappearing in Olympia. An idea had formed in her mind.

The police, the CBI, the Witch Hunters... they couldn't catch a thief who was in and out without needing to crack a vault. Mammon was pleased by avarice, the more gross the better. The demon had reached out to her and proposed a deal: if she would continue her grand larceny, he would grant her the lifespan necessary to expand the portal network to every bank and vault on earth.

The late oil baron Brayton Crandall had used the network to acquire the petroleum he refined into gasoline for use in Salem. When he died, Rose had dispatched her youngest acolyte, Harper Finley, to Oglethorpe to buy the old man's mansion he'd built for his retirement and create a new portal within the city. The girl picked up an admirer along the way and seemed to have developed feelings for him. She refused to offer up a human soul to Mammon, using the blood of animals to create a weak, unstable gateway. No matter.

You have done well, Michaela, Mammon's voice echoed in her mind. *By the end of tonight, you and your followers will get what is coming to you.*

Thank you, my master. I will have the prisoners brought here and you shall taste Templar blood.

She was about to rise from the floor when she heard the doors slam open, followed by the thunder of a rifle shot and screams of terror.

"Sara Morse!" came the booming voice of Silas Flint. "Your hubris is your downfall, witch! Now receive a foretaste of the judgment that awaits you!"

20

Flint fired his pistol, the bullet smacking into an acolyte's forehead in a spatter of blood and bone. Navarro fired, worked the bolt, kept firing until he was empty, yanking a stripper clip from a pouch on his belt, ramming the bullets into the breech, yanking out the clip, and continuing his assault. McFarlane stabbed a woman with her sword, used her off hand to shoot a man attempting to flee. Fletcher used a two handed grip on her pistol to shoot down more acolytes.

The screams and gunfire echoed all around him, but Flint made a beeline toward Morse who was backing away from the pentagram in which she had been kneeling, toward the golden idol depicting the demon Mammon.

"Your reign of terror ends now, Morse!" Flint shouted. He slashed with his sword, cutting an acolyte who had raised his hands to cast a spell.

"You..." she snarled. She gestured with her hands and the gold and silver bullion stacked around the room levitated, swirled, melded together. The metal formed into a humanoid golem, with what looked like rubies serving as its eyes, alight with hellfire. The abomination roared, its teeth made of diamonds, and smashed its sparkling fists into the floor, cracking the linoleum. With an unholy scream, it charged toward Flint.

The Witch Hunter dashed toward the monster. He estimated it to be around seven feet tall. Large, heavy, but slow. It brought its fist around in a haymaker that would have punched Flint's head clean off, but he dove and rolled past it. The monster's mass was such that the momentum of its punch made it stumble forward, stepping on a fallen witch, her body exploding in a sickening splatter of flesh and blood.

Flint continued his headlong sprint toward Morse who held out her arms at her sides, palms up. Jets of flame burst from her hands, engulfing stacks of gold bullion along the walls. The bricks melted she gestured, a stream of molten gold surging toward Flint. He fired his pistol. The shot missed but it distracted Morse enough to cause the molten gold to spatter to the floor with a hiss.

"Master! Help me!" Morse cried.

She raised her hands and sorcerous lightning shot toward Flint. The assault was absorbed by his sword. He aimed and fired his pistol, but Morse raised a magical barrier around herself that shattered the bullet before it could find its mark. Behind him, Flint heard the metal monstrosity roar, its thunderous footsteps cracking the floor with each step. Navarro, Fletcher, and McFarlane continued to engage the surviving acolytes who had recovered their senses and began to fight back.

Flint gave Morse a feral smile. "I have slain Arturo Vasquez. You are not his match."

With a scream of fury, Morse raised a hand toward the ceiling and a beam of light from her hand blasted a hole through the plaster. She levitated from the floor, toward her escape route. Flint dropped his pistol, ran, and grabbed her ankle before she could leave the room, maintaining his grip on his sword. He ground his teeth and grunted with the strain of holding himself up with one hand as Morse snarled and aimed another lightning bolt at Flint. He barely lifted his sword in time to absorb the magic. He had no leverage to stab or slash; it was all he could do to hold on. She blasted another hole in the ceiling on the floor above the basement, and up they went, through the house, neither able to get the better of the other. Flint was running out of options. If she burst through the roof, he would be at her mercy.

After ascending through four floors, they smashed through the roof of the house – mansion as it turned out. He had one chance left, and the timing would have to be perfect.

As soon as he felt the summer heat, he let go of her ankle. In free fall, he drew his second pistol and fired. He was rewarded with a cry of pain just as he hit the roof, knocking the wind from him. His gun clattered as he lost his grip. Flint pushed himself up and saw Morse on the roof, holding her side, blood seeping from her torn robe. He was tired, out of breath, but he had to move before she healed herself and escaped. Already he could see her mouthing the words to close her wounds.

"You shall not escape the wrath of God!" Flint bellowed. He heaved himself to his feet, grabbed his fallen pistol, and half sprinted, half stumbled toward Morse. He fired his pistol again but Morse got a barrier up in time. She gave him an evil smile.

"And you won't escape the power of Mammon," she laughed.

Flint screamed as he felt something burn him from inside his long coat. A flaming hole appeared in the fabric and he realized it was his coin purse just as it fell onto the roof. The small sack burned away, and his silver sovereigns, now red hot discs, melted, reformed into a small humanoid, the younger brother of the gold and silver monstrosity in the basement. It shrieked and chased after

Flint, its red fingers grabbing onto one of his coat tails, the fabric beginning to smoke.

Flint pushed himself forward, firing his pistol, the bullets breaking on Morse's barrier. She laughed again.

"Better luck next time Witch Hunter!" she called as she began to levitate from the roof.

Flint growled in frustration. Only one desperate chance left. He gripped the blade of his sword, feeling the steel cut into his flesh. He hurled it like a javelin. The blessed steel passed through Morse's barrier and embedded itself in her belly. She grunted, her eyes went wide, then rolled back in her head, and she crashed to the roof. The tiny golem on Flint's heels fell and melted into a pool of silver.

Panting, Flint advanced toward the fallen Morse, keeping her covered with his pistol. Her eyes fluttered open. A trickle of blood fell from the corner of her mouth.

"I..." she said, her throat clicking. "This is wrong. Master... I served..."

"Hell does not reward failure," Flint said.

Morse's voice cracked, she gasped, and lay still.

21

Flint made his way down the stairs of the mansion to the basement. His companions held the surviving acolytes at gunpoint. The gold and silver golem had dissolved upon the death of Morse. Flint glanced at the golden idol of Mammon and saw that it had changed. The demon was smiling now. At Mammon's feet was a depiction of Morse, reaching up for a salvation that was now forever beyond her, her face frozen in terror.

There were half a dozen acolytes left, their hoods back, hands on their heads. Four men, two women. Flint didn't recognize any of them, but he feared that the banking system would be rocked by more scandal by the time everything settled.

"I trust that you all have everything under control," Flint said.

"And you got that bitch Morse, huh boss?" Navarro said.

"Yes. That vile harlot has received the reward that Hell gives to all of its servants."

"You alright?" McFarlane asked, pointing at Flint's long coat.

Looking down, he saw a hole on the right side. He imagined the tails were burnt and tattered.

"I suffered minor burns," Flint said, "I expect that Fort Marsing's quartermaster shall be quite vexed with me however."

Fletcher said nothing as she rushed forward and embraced Flint. The Witch Hunter was caught by surprise, but he returned the embrace.

Backing away, Fletcher said, "I'm, ahem, glad you're okay."

"I am pleased that you too are unharmed."

"Soon as the big boy collapsed, these losers gave up right quick," Navarro said, pointing at the acolytes with his thumb.

"I am sure," Flint said. He approached the sullen magicians, scowling at them. "Your so-called great project is at an end. You will be taken into custody and put to the question. Cooperate and you may yet save your miserable lives, to say nothing of your souls. Unless you would all care to join your mistress in the fourth circle of Hell."

They looked down and said nothing.

"Come on," McFarlane said. "Let's get these people into interrogation rooms, and go home."

***

Flint hadn't been sure – he didn't recognize the city-scape surrounding the rooftop where he'd done battle with Morse – but as it turned out, they were in Bend after all. Navarro excused himself to visit his family while Templars and Supernumeraries from Fort Ingalls and Fort Marsing handled the interrogations of the prisoners. Flint observed several of them in the hope that he would learn more about what the late Sara Morse had been planning. The poor deluded fool had believed that the demon Mammon would keep its word and grant her eternal life – or at least an extended lifespan – to give her time to pillage every bank in the world. She hadn't counted on Mammon being greedier for souls. Nor had she counted on the love of two teenagers foiling her scheme. Speaking of which...

Flint and Fletcher excused themselves from the Bend prison where they had been watching an interrogation and made their way to a post office. Flint requested a pen and paper and began to write:

August 24, 2533

Mr. Spaulding,

I am pleased to inform you that Miss Fletcher and I have found your son, Francis. He is alive and well. Miss Harper Finley is with him and they have expressed an honorable desire to be wed in holy matrimony. Acquaintances of Miss Finley were responsible for the murder of the unfortunate private investigator whom you hired. She had no knowledge of it and has expressed repentance for any wrong-doings or misunderstandings to my satisfaction. God willing, young Francis will contact you soon.

I remain Your Most Obedient Servant,
Silas Flint, Captain, KTOSB

When he'd finished his note, he put it in an envelope and went to the counter.

"I should like postage to Oglethorpe, if you please," he said.

The clerk smiled. "Of course sir. That'll be twenty-five shillings."

Flint reached for his coin purse and was surprised when his hand passed through the hole in his coat.

"Er..." he said.

"I got it," Fletcher said with a laugh.

After they'd sent the note on its way, they stepped out onto the street. Bend was halfway between the border with the United Mountain States and the Pacific Ocean. Flint and Navarro had visited the city earlier that summer when they'd been briefly assigned to Fort Ingalls. It was much as Flint remembered it: bright, loud, stinking of smog and tobacco.

"What do you think?" Fletcher asked. "You up for some more chow?"

Flint snorted. "I shall have to visit a branch office of Robinson Bank to make a withdrawal," he said, referring to the bank where his savings were deposited.

"Or... you know, I could treat this time."

Flint raised an eyebrow. "Oh? I know how much you receive in your monthly stipend."

"What, you too good to go slumming at a diner with me?"

Flint gave her a wintry smile. "I suppose that beggars cannot be choosers."

He held out his arm, she looped hers around it, and they went strolling, looking for a greasy spoon diner.

***

Three days later, Flint and Navarro were in their dress uniforms inside a staging area within the Imperial Palace in Salem.

Navarro pulled at his collar. The Supernumerary dress uniform was a grey tunic with matching trousers, black boots, and a peaked cap with a Saint Benedict medal and gold trim.

"I really hate this thing," he said.

"You will get no sympathy from me, Mr. Navarro," Flint replied. His own dress uniform was a steel chest plate with intricate engravings of crosses, angels, and the Latin initials of the Benedictine mottos. A steel pauldron was on his right shoulder, his long coat had scarlet trim, his boots were heavier, and a silver buckle on his capotain.

Navarro chuckled. "Guess we all got our crosses to bear, huh boss?"

"Indeed."

Before them were the great wooden doors that would open into the Emperor's throne room where he conducted official affairs of state. Flint would have preferred to get back to work, but one does not ignore summons from the Imperial Palace. A functionary wearing the uniform of an imperial household servant – scarlet coat, white shirt, black trousers – checked his watch. He looked to Flint and Navarro and held up his hand, fingers extended. He began counting down. When his fingers were all closed into a fist, they heard a great fanfare on the other side of the doors. It sounded like the whole Imperial Army orchestra was present. The fanfare subsided, the functionary was joined by another, and they pulled open the doors. Flint and Navarro looked to each other, took deep breaths, squared their shoulders, and began their march to the tune set by the orchestra.

The Great Hall was packed. A red carpet covered the stone floor, leading to three steps that went up to the Evergreen Throne where they saw Emperor Peter II sitting. Gone was his simple olive drab Army uniform. He now wore the full regalia of his office: an emerald green uniform with gold trim, the purple cord around his right shoulder encrusted with diamonds, his chest bedecked with medals and badges of office. Surrounding him were members of the royal household: Empress Valeria in a gorgeous gown, Crown Prince James, Prince Sebastian, and Princess Margaret. At the foot of the stairs were the Chiefs of Staffs of the Armed Services: General Alexander Griffith and Admiral William Tyson. With them were the four Generals of the Templar Chapter Houses in their dress uniforms: Jeremiah Hickock, John Abernathy, Seth Brandt, and Malachi Davis.

Flint's eyes went back and forth, taking in the crowds filling every seat in the Great Hall, and those that were forced to stand. He saw Fletcher and McFarlane on his left, along with Navarro's family. On his right, he saw several survivors of the Castle Vasquez expedition, including Professor Valentina Morales. The necromancer had torn out the poor woman's eyes, but somehow, miraculously, she was still able to see, a gift from Heaven she called it. She wore sunglasses to hide her empty eye sockets. At the end of the row, he was pleased to see Matthew Oglethorpe and his family.

Flint and Navarro reached the appointed spot where they'd been told to stop during the rehearsals. They clicked their heels and knelt before the Evergreen Throne. The Emperor rose from his seat.

"My friends, my family... honored guests," he said, his voice echoing throughout the Great Hall. "We are gathered here this evening to recognize the outstanding achievements of Knight Templar Captain Silas Flint and Supernumerary Ricardo Navarro. On August the twelfth of the Year of Our Lord 2533, Captain Flint and Mr. Navarro did enter Castle Vasquez. At the risk of their lives and their souls, they rescued a team of young people and their guardians from the clutches of the most terrible threat the Empire has ever faced. The Great Necromancer Arturo Vasquez, returned from the dead, committed unspeakable atrocities both in life and in undeath.

"Supernumerary Ricardo Navarro, along with the surviving guards Donald Riffey and Barry Giles, did hold off Vasquez's hordes of undead and demons with his courage, his strength, and his unfailing devotion to the laws of the Church and of God.

"Captain Silas Flint went on alone through the halls of Castle Vasquez, tracking the fiend to his inner sanctum, where he slew the Great Necromancer, a feat heretofore only accomplished by another hero of the Empire who is present in his hall tonight: General Matthew Oglethorpe."

The Emperor descended from his throne, down the steps, until he was within arm's length of Flint and Navarro. A uniformed household servant came to the Emperor's side with two oversized felt boxes in his hands.

"It is my great honor and pleasure to bestow upon you, Captain Flint, and you, Mr. Navarro, the titles 'Heroes of the Empire' and 'Defenders of the Faith,' along with the Diamond Cross. Rise."

Flint and Navarro rose to their feet. The Emperor opened one of the boxes and took out a diamond encrusted cross attached to a scarlet ribbon. Flint bowed and the Emperor draped the cross around Flint's neck. He did the same for Navarro.

"Receive the adulation of a grateful people, and the thanks of your sovereign and his family."

The Hall erupted in cheers and applause. Navarro's family screamed his name. Fletcher waved to Flint, and he acknowledged her with a dip of his head.

"Hope you don't need me for a while sir," Navarro said in Flint's ear. "I'm going to be partying hard for the next few days."

"I suppose that you have earned it," Flint said. His mind was already focusing on the next task. He hadn't had the chance to return to Marsing since the closing of the Morse case. General Abernathy had told him that there was a metal man waiting to talk to him about history. And there was another ceremony to attend soon, one that he was looking forward to much more than this one.

***

"Query," the robot said. "What is the rank structure of the Knights Templar of the Order of Saint Benedict? You are a paramilitary organization. You hold the rank of Captain. Yet you do not command your lessers."

Flint drew in a sharp breath. Two days had passed since he and his companions had returned to Fort Marsing, and the robot's questions were interminable. He prayed to the Holy Spirit to grant him the virtue of patience. They were sitting in Flint's personal quarters. The robot had read every book in his possession, every book in the library, every paper and file in the archives. Whatever else the machine could do, Flint envied it for its speed reading.

"There are two career branches," Flint replied. "Those of us whom God has gifted with physical prowess undertake active field investigations. Those whose gifts run more toward the administrative are tasked with maintaining the operations of the Order. The title of 'Captain' is more of an honorific. I have the authority to command lower ranking Templars should the need arise for us to take to the field in greater numbers, but in practice we work in pairs."

"The Supernumeraries," the Rob voice said. The machine buzzed.

"Wouldn't it be easier to call them Sergeants? 'Supernumerary' is a mouthful," the Hiller voice said.

"I suppose that it can be to the uninitiated," Flint replied. "The position of Supernumerary is more egalitarian. They have no formal rank structure beyond their title. They are de jure equals, but de facto organized by age and experience. The vocation is open to all men and women of good faith, regardless of their educational background."

"But you Witch Hunters need to be college graduates, huh?" the Hiller voice said.

"Not necessarily. I myself never attended university but I was permitted to undertake the trials immediately after I pledged my life to the Order."

"Query. Is that not unusual?" the Rob voice asked.

"Yes," Flint said. "But the circumstances of my joining were themselves unusual."

There was a knock at his door.

"Thanks be to God," Flint muttered as he rose from his desk. "Enter," he called.

Navarro poked his head inside. "Hey boss. It starts in ten minutes."

Flint nodded. "I shall be there."

"May I accompany you Captain Silas Flint?" Rob asked.

"Yes. The coming ceremony may answer several of your questions."

Flint exited his quarters and made his way through the hall to the stairwell, the robot whirring and clanking behind him. The Hiller voice claimed that he had once been a mortal man whose soul had been trapped within the robotic shell by the Kato family of Nagano, formerly Nevada. The Rob voice said that it was a twenty-first century computer program that had copied its "personality matrix" into Hiller's artificial body. Flint was no expert in twenty-first century technology, but he knew that by the time of the Occult War, humanity was at its scientific peak. He couldn't conceive how the two could mix, save for magic.

He reached the bottom of the stairs and proceeded to Marsing's own Great Hall. It was here that Templars in garrison received their orders from General Abernathy himself, and where new recruits were sworn in. It hadn't changed a bit since he had taken the oath fifteen years ago. Marsing had been wired for electricity save for the Great Hall which was still lit by torches and lanterns.

Flint took his seat next to Lady McFarlane. The robot stood off to one side in the aisle. The center of the room was taken up by as many Supernumeraries as could fit on the floor. More still were crowded outside in the hallway, the doors opened wide so they could see and hear what was about to happen.

General Abernathy stood at his lectern where he issued

orders. Normally recruits were sworn in by class, but this was a special occasion for a special person.

The Supernumeraries parted like the Red Sea, and Flint heard boots tapping on the stone floor. Zelda Fletcher walked toward the center of the room in the blue jeans and blouse she wore around Marsing. She stopped before Abernathy. Flint could see that she was nervous, but only those who knew her well would have noticed.

"My friends," Abernathy said. "We are gathered here in the presence of God to welcome into our ranks an extraordinary woman who, though with us a short time, has proven her courage, her valor, and her devotion to our cause. I think I speak for many of us when I say that were it not for her unusual talents, some here present would have already passed on to their eternal reward." He cleared his throat. "Zelda Fletcher."

She swallowed and said, "Present."

"Kneel."

She went down on her left knee.

"Zelda Fletcher," Abernathy said again. "Is it your desire to pledge yourself to the Knights Templar of the Order of Saint Benedict?"

"It is."

"Do you now pledge yourself to the service of God without mental reservation or purpose of evasion?"

"I do."

"Will you faithfully serve the Church and the Templars with whom you are appointed to serve?"

"I will."

"Do you reject Satan, and all of his empty promises?"

"I do."

"Then it is with great pleasure that I bestow upon you the title of Supernumerary, along with all the rights and privileges thereto. And may God have mercy on your soul," Abernathy said with a smile.

It was Navarro who started the cheers, a great ululating cry taken up by the others a second later. They rushed forward, embracing Fletcher, clapping her on the shoulder, shaking her hand. Flint thought he saw a tear run down her cheek.

"May God bless you and keep you, Zelda," he said to himself.

22

A week passed. General Abernathy ordered Flint to take some time off, and for the first time in his career, he didn't grumble about it. The Vasquez case alone had exhausted him, and then the Morse case following the day after? Even Flint had his limits, and he knew he had reached them. Besides, talking to the robot felt like a case all by itself.

Flint was seated at a table in the Templar dining hall, Navarro and the machine seated across from him.

"Query," the Rob voice said.

"You don't have to keep saying that," Navarro said. "Just ask."

"Would it be possible to travel to the Boise State Library? I wish to read more books."

"The city of Boise no longer exists," Flint replied. "It

merged with the remnants of its metro areas and is now called New Meridian. It sits along the border with the United Mountain States to the east."

"Updating files," Rob said. It buzzed.

"Sorry about that," came the Hiller voice. "This... program can be right pushy when it wants to know things."

"Doesn't that drive you crazy? Having another voice in your head?" Navarro asked.

"I guess if I was still human, having other voices in your head is the textbook definition of crazy, huh?" Hiller laughed. "Believe me, after centuries with the Kato family in Area 51, Rob can stay as long as he likes."

"I was thinking," Navarro said. "We need a new name for you."

"What do you mean?"

"Well, it gets confusing sometimes. I never know if I'm talking to you or to Rob. What if we gave you a name that you can both respond to?"

The machine was silent. "I don't know... I mean... I'm Thomas Hiller."

"I am Rob."

"That's... my name... but... the man I was... my human self... it's been dead for centuries."

"We do not have to rename you if you feel uncomfortable," Flint said.

"No... no, I think Rico's right. Thomas Hiller is dead. What I am now... I have his memories. But I'm something new. Especially with this program in my head."

"I am amenable to a new designation," Rob said.

"Okay! I had one in mind already," Navarro said. "What do you think of Joe Bell?"

Flint raised his eyebrows, and he imagined that if the robot had any, they would have gone up as well.

"How in the world did you conceive that?" Flint asked.

"You don't like it?"

Hiller laughed. "I get it. My serial number."

"I beg your pardon?" Flint asked.

"Look boss," Navarro said, pointing. Squinting, Flint could see it now, an engraving on one of the robot's chest plates: J-038377.

"Hmph," Flint said. "Very clever, Mr. Navarro."

"Okay," Hiller said. "Joe Bell. That's my name now."

"I am Joe Bell," Rob said.

"It is a pleasure to make your acquaintance, Mr. Bell," Flint said.

"Anyone ever tell you that you sound like a computer?" Bell said.

Navarro burst out laughing.

"Hmph."

Supernumerary Samuel Breckenridge, a courier with Marsing's mail department entered the dining hall.

"Mr. Breckenridge," Flint said. "Do you come bearing our new orders?"

"No sir," the courier said. "The UMS Army... it's approaching Montana."

Flint felt his heart sink.

"There's a bunch of us over at the cantina, listening to Rico's radio."

"We shall join you presently."

"Montana," Bell said. "That is the location of the bunker where my other self resides."

Flint still didn't understand how it was possible for the Rob personality to be in two places at once, but he took it for granted now.

"It is the bunker where Charles Flint and his companions have taken up residence."

"What?!" Flint sputtered.

"The fuck?!" Navarro yelled. "Why didn't you tell us?!"

"You did not ask, Ricardo Navarro."

"Blasted machine," Flint grumbled.

"Hey... are you two related?" Bell asked.

"Yes. Charles Flint is my younger brother. We will speak more of this later. Come."

***

"This is war correspondent Judy McQueen reporting live from Parkman, Langston Province, Wyoming territory," came the reporter's voice crackling from the radio. The computer cleaned up the transmission as best it could, but there was still much interference from the mountainous landscape. Charles Flint and his inner circle had been joined by a group of magicians from around the former Montana, now Medea. Drake Mantell, Eric Salazar, and Lucy Donnelly had come to him over the last few days, pledging themselves to serve their new Emperor. He welcomed them into his inner circle; if he was going to form a proper government, he would need more staff.

"Ladies and gentlemen," he called. The chatter stopped

and all eyes turned toward him. "We are about to bear witness to a historic moment. President Fitzroy has chosen to persist despite my offer of peaceful separation. He has left me no choice but to secure the future of this nation and of our people through the crucible of war. All of you bore witness to the destructive power of old world technology nearly three months ago now. We shall witness it once again if they set foot on Medean soil."

Everyone, even Turner, raised their fists and yelled, "Gloria Medea!"

"What is about to happen is on the conscience of..."

The computer chimed. Flint growled.

"God damn you, Rob," he snapped.

"Pardon the interruption Charles Flint. There is something approaching the entrance to the bunker."

He blinked. "What is it?"

"Unknown. It emits an energy pattern similar to the object you wear on your head."

The Warlock's Crown.

"You want we should head out and blow it to smithereens boss?" Mantell drawled, fire already forming on his hands.

Ignoring him, Flint asked, "Is it alive, Rob?"

"No life signs detected."

"Vasquez?" Turner asked.

"Intruder alert, intruder alert," Rob blared. Klaxons sounded. Panels in the ceiling opened, revealing the machine gun turrets that had opened fire on Flint when he and Turner had first entered the bunker months ago. The others drew on the power, their bodies surrounded by sorcerous blue flame that did not burn them. A figure emerged from the hallway.

It wore heavy black plate armor, bearing intricate carvings of human skulls and demonic faces. Its head was surrounded by a halo of green fire, like the green fires that burned behind its eyes. Its flesh was dry and stretched thin as old parchment over its skull. It had no lips, its brown teeth visible through a rictus grin. Strings of black hair hung from its head.

Flint had never seen the undead giant before, but it felt familiar somehow. He raised his hand and the others held off their assault.

"Identify yourself," Flint called.

"I am Anton the Black," the thing rumbled. "My master Arturo Vasquez, whose crown you wear upon your brow, has commanded me to be your champion." It reached over its shoulder and drew a greatsword from a sheath on its back. It plunged the point down into the steel floor and his sword sank halfway. "I am yours to command, Charles Flint."

Flint blinked. Then he threw back his head and laughed. A corner of his mind whispered to him that the laugh was not his own.

"I welcome you to my home, Anton the Black, and I look forward to employing your talents. Come. You're just in time to enjoy the show."

***

"I'm being told that preparations are nearly complete,"

McQueen said. "The Army will resume its long railroad trip and cross the border into Montana territory. They will liberate occupied cities and towns, scouring the countryside for forces loyal to the usurper Charles Flint. General Daniels said…"

Silas Flint sat at the bar in the Supernumerary cantina, along with Navarro, Fletcher, and Bell. He clenched his fists tightly enough for his knuckles to turn white. Fletcher reached out and took one of his hands in hers. He barely noticed.

***

Fitzroy sat in his office in the presidential mansion, Hastings at his right side, General Daniels on his left. Operation Drumroll as it was being called would begin as soon as the Army crossed over into Montana. He still had time to pull them back. Maybe he should pull them back. He dismissed the thoughts as soon as they arose. Parkman was the Army's last stop with access to a telegraph office before they crossed into enemy territory. Although he had his own private, military sources updating him on the Army's progress, he still tuned in to Denver Public Radio which had insisted on sending an official war correspondent, despite the government's warnings that they could not guarantee their safety. Daniels had wanted to keep the press out altogether, but one may as well try to stop the weather.

"Sir," said a young lieutenant, who handed Fitzroy a folded sheet of paper. Opening it, he read:

We have taken up the staging ground in Parkman and are prepared to move on your order Mr. President.

It was signed by General Austin Cosgrove, the commanding officer of the Montana Expeditionary Force. This was it. The moment of truth. The lieutenant stood at parade rest. Hastings and Daniels kept quiet. This was Fitzroy's responsibility and his alone. Nothing was left to discuss.

"Wire General Cosgrove: 'Blackbeard.' I repeat, 'Blackbeard,'" Fitzroy said.

The lieutenant saluted. "Yes sir." He took off for the telegraph office at a sprint.

Fitzroy buried his face in his hands.

"My God..." he said. "What have I done?"

"You did the right thing, Mr. President," Hastings replied.

"You did the only thing you could do sir," Daniels said.

***

"It's a go," McQueen's voice crackled over the radio. "It's a go, the Montana Expeditionary Force has just been given the order ladies and gentlemen. The Army is on the march."

Emperor Peter, along with his children, the military chiefs of staff, and the heads of his intelligence services were all crowded within the Strategy Room deep beneath the Imperial Palace.

"May God have mercy on their souls," the Emperor said, crossing himself.

***

Doctor Kato watched the Army's progress on a viewscreen inside Area 51. Beside him was Harry Tanaka. The computer had tuned in to Denver Public Radio.

"Fools," the computer said. "Throwing their lives away over a point of pride."

"Now now, grandfather," Kato said. "Would you have done any differently if Nagano faced invasion during your reign?"

The computer laughed. "No, grandson, I suppose I wouldn't have. Thank you, by the way, for bringing me files from Charles Flint's computer. I feel more alive than I ever have since... since I was alive."

"I live to serve my ancestors," Kato said.

***

Flint drummed his fingers on the bar. One thing all war histories agreed on was that the life of a soldier meant "hurry up and wait." The Expeditionary Force had crossed the border into Montana. McQueen kept up the chatter to fill the silence, but so far the Army had not encountered anything besides endless wilderness. Without locomotives, it would have taken them months to reach Montana. That region of North America had always been sparsely populated. Soon they would run out of track, and begin their long, slow, overland march.

"...the greatest assemblage of any armed force in North

America since Cascadia's war against Arturo Vasquez forty years ago," McQueen said. "General Daniels has assured this reporter that reserves remain encamped around Denver should…"

The cantina was silent. The bartender, retired Supernumerary Alfred Carruthers wiped a glass; Flint was certain he'd been wiping the same glass for fifteen minutes.

***

"Attention Charles Flint," Rob said. "The UMS Army has reached the designated area of engagement."

Flint sighed. You couldn't make an omelet without breaking eggs. Or in this case, tens of thousands of eggs. He closed his eyes and took a deep breath. No matter what happened, his name would be in the history books until the end of time. He felt Turner take one of his hands in hers.

"It's an honor to be at your side," she said.

Flint stared at her for a moment, before pulling her into a kiss. He could sense Turner's initial shock, but she soon relaxed, returning his kiss with hunger. He broke off and smiled at her.

"It's an honor and a pleasure to have you here," he said.

She gave him an odd look and pulled away a bit.

"What?" he said.

"Your eyes… they're on fire."

He glanced at a steel panel on the wall and saw that she was right. Green fires burned faintly behind his eyes, similar to Anton's. He laughed.

"Rob," he said. "Fire."

"Safety protocols prohibit the use of nuclear missiles on North American soil..."

Flint growled. "We've been through this Rob. The United States and Canada do not exist. You are the property of Medea and as your sovereign and your owner, I order you to fire."

"Safety protocols prohibit..."

"FIRE!" Flint shrieked. He sent a bolt of sorcerous energy into the monitor, and arcs of electricity danced around the room.

"It shall be done, Charles Flint," the computer said. "Opening silo doors now."

"Uh..." Salazar said. "Does this machine always talk back, sir?"

"Not anymore it won't," Flint sneered. "Not if I can help it. Arnold, prepare my chambers. The people of North America need to hear from us once the radio goes out."

***

"As the Army makes it progress through Montana," McQueen said, "This reporter can provide some more background for our international listeners. The northernmost province of the United Mountain States, for centuries Montana has been fertile ranch country, supplying beef for... wait a moment."

Flint and the others leaned forward at the bar.

"There's something... I..."

Static.

"God…" Carruthers muttered, crossing himself.

Flint felt his shoulders slump. He hung his head and crossed himself as well.

"Everyone!" a Supernumerary called. "Look!"

The cantina cleared out, everyone stepping into the courtyard. The sky appeared to shimmer. Flint felt a ball of ice form in his stomach. He recognized what was about to happen.

A titanic image of his brother Charles appeared in the sky. His hair had grown longer, his beard had grown fuller. And he wore something on his head: a black circlet with a depiction of a human skull biting down on a blood red jewel.

"People of North America!" his voice boomed. "I offered President Fitzroy of the United Mountain States peace in our time. I reached out to him and proposed a program of peaceful separation between his country and the Empire of Medea. He rejected my offer and now the mothers and fathers, husbands and wives of his soldiers have paid the price."

Charles vanished, replaced by an image of a fiery cloud in the shape of a mushroom rising from a blackened landscape. Flint heard gasps and sobs all around him. He closed his eyes. He was used to offering prayers for the repose of the dead, but so many, all at once…

"I call upon President Fitzroy to come to the negotiating table," the voice of Charles resumed. "No nation on earth can withstand my power. But I will not use this power save in defense of my country and my people. Let us end this pointless war. I only ask what I asked of you three months ago: the recognition of Medea as a nation among nations, as an equal among the family of mankind. I repeat my call to all magicians throughout North America: join us, leave behind the violence and persecution you face in other nations. Here you may be yourselves. Here you may find rest. That is all. Let us live together in peace."

***

President Fitzroy pressed his forehead into his desk. All was silent in the war room; the telephones, the telegraphs, the radios, all had gone quiet.

"Mr. President..." Hastings said.

Fitzroy said nothing.

"Sir..." Daniels said. "We need to..."

"General..." Fitzroy said. "Could you come closer please?"

"Sir?" Daniels got closer to Fitzroy, who hadn't looked up from his desk. "Sir, we have to strengthen the reserves around Denver. I..."

In one quick motion, Fitzroy yanked Daniels' sidearm from its holster, stuck the pistol in his mouth and pulled the trigger.

"No!" everyone cried out together. It was too late. The pistol cracked and Fitzroy slumped forward, blood spattering the wall behind him.

Everything was quiet for a few seconds until a woman started crying. Hastings shook himself. There would be time to grieve later.

"One of you, get the vice president in here. We need to give her the oath."

EPILOGUE

Silas Flint sat in the library of Fort Marsing. It was dawn, and the morning newspaper had just been delivered. In screaming capital letters on the front page, the paper proclaimed PARLIAMENT RECOGNIZES MEDEA.

He didn't need to read the rest of the story. It galled him, but Charles's so-called nation could not be ignored. It had secured its independence through the blood of the UMS Army. The newly sworn in President Serena Taggart had already met with Charles's representatives – among them his old nemesis Lilian Turner – to sign the Treaty of Casper, recognizing the separation of Montana, now Medea, from the rest of the United Mountain States.

He bowed his head in prayer.

My Lord and my God, he prayed. *Would Charles have gone down this path if I had been a better brother? Is this my fault? Forgive me O Lord... forgive me.* He felt a tear run down his cheek.

"Do not blame yourself Silas."

"You could not have prevented this."

"Take it from us. We have seen it."

He looked up and saw the Proctor Sisters: Mallory, Monica, and Madeline in their identical white dresses, looking as serene as ever.

"You again," he said.

"We know that you are hurting," Mallory said.

"You must not despair though," Monica said.

"We brought someone with us this time," Madeline said.

"Who..."

A second later, a man appeared in the library in a flash of light. He was dressed from head to toe in an immaculate white suit. His face though... it was... blurry. Attempting to focus on it made Flint's eyes water.

"Hello Silas," the man said.

"And who might you be sir?" Flint asked. "Another magician?"

"No," the man chuckled. "Far from it. The Sisters watch over you. And I watch over them."

"What is it that you want of me?" Flint asked.

"I... we, want you to be yourself," the man said. "Charles's actions are his own, and he will be held to account for them some day. You must do what you have always done: persist. I know that you still don't trust the Sisters completely. I've received permission to accompany them in person this time. I can't tell you much but remember this: you're never alone. Don't lose faith."

"But I do not know who you are sir. May I ask your name?"

The Sisters smiled.

After a few moments the man said, "Call me Michael."

They vanished in a flash of light.

Flint wasn't sure if he was dreaming again or not. He heard the door to the library open. Supernumerary Zelda Fletcher entered and approached his table.

"Hey. Mind if I join you?"

"You are awake uncharacteristically early," Flint said.

"Yeah, well, I've had trouble sleeping over the last few days."

"I know precisely how you feel."

They sat in silence for a few moments.

"Silas," she said.

"Yes?"

"I like you. I mean, I like you a lot. But I never know if you notice or…"

"I have noticed."

She blew out a breath. "Okay. Good. We're making progress. But listen. I'm a big girl. If you're not interested, or you don't see me like that, or you don't want to date, I understand, but for Chri… uh, I mean, for goodness' sake, just fucking say so, alright?"

"It is not that, Zelda."

"What do you mean?"

"I mean that I've lost one family already. The man that I could have been if I hadn't joined up? He's gone. If I allowed myself to form a romantic attachment, another family, and I lost you too… I couldn't bear it. It'd break me. And I don't know if I could come back from it."

She reached out and took his hand. "I'm not going anywhere, you weirdo."

Flint smiled. "Yes, much to my chagrin."

She laughed. "Oh, you're going to be like that huh?"

"Always."

She stood up, went to his side of the table and kissed him on the lips. She put a hand on the back of his head and touched her forehead to his.

"You're a good man, Silas Flint."

"One does the best that one can."

She rolled her eyes and stepped away.

"I have given more thought to the question which you posed to me over our lunch date," Flint said.

"Oh yeah?"

"Yes. If none of this had ever happened… I think that I should have liked to be a school teacher."

She laughed. "Oh, the kids would love getting a rise out of you."

"No doubt."

She leaned over and wrapped him in a hug. "You'd have been a good teacher. You are a good teacher."

He returned her embrace.

"And I'm with you until the end," she said. "No matter what."

Flint held her tight. A memory came to him then. A memory of a dream he'd had weeks ago, courtesy of the Weird Sisters. A dream of his final confrontation with Charles. He'd awakened before seeing the outcome, but there was something else. Fletcher had figured prominently in the dream, but he couldn't remember the details. He was certain that God would reveal the truth in His good time.

www.ingramcontent.com/pod-product-compliance
Lightning Source LLC
Chambersburg PA
CBHW060556300726

48975CB00005B/1344